The Dawn Stag

Also by Jules Watson

The White Mare

The Dawn Stag

Jules Watson

ORION

First published in Great Britain in 2005 by Orion,
an imprint of the Orion Publishing Group Ltd.

1 3 5 7 9 10 8 6 4 2

A CIP catalogue record for this book is
available from the British Library.

ISBN 0 75285 687 1 (hardback),   0 75286 870 5 (trade paperback)

Typeset by Deltatype Ltd,
Birkenhead, Merseyside

Printed in Great Britain by Clays Ltd, St Ives plc

The Orion Publishing Group Ltd
Orion House
5 Upper Saint Martin's Lane
London, WC2H 9EA

www.orionbooks.co.uk

For Claire, who held the vision,
and for Alistair, who lived it with me

Acknowledgements

For help in completing such a mammoth undertaking in such a short time, I want to thank everyone! – but especially the reams of people who offered wonderful and heartfelt feedback about the first book, and thereby bolstered the second.

I have some special thanks, too.

Thank you to the 'girls' – Claire Swinney, Amber Trewenack, Cassie Swinney and Lisa Holland-McNair – who read prologues and early chapters and gave me great constructive advice. To Mike and Trin McNulty, for stepping in with technological help after an incident with a cup of tea and a laptop keyboard. To Barbara Fletcher and Dennis Thair, for the most fundamental kind of support when I needed it most.

To Yvette, Rachel and everyone at Orion, and my agent Maggie Noach.

To Claire, who opened her heart in her usual unconditional way, offering love and understanding, tissues, ceramic angels, bonding over *Hornblower*, cups of tea and, on occasion, harder beverages. You know what you've done, even when it remains difficult to put into words.

My greatest gratitude goes to my husband Alistair, who over a few beers scrawled this massive, complicated plot out with me and then said: 'OK, go off and write that, then.' I did, Al, but I could never have done it without you. You walked beside me every step of the way – suggesting and re-reading and debating – and so we got there in the end, together. Your patience is eternal, your generosity infinite, your love all around me.

·ALBA· (SCOTLAND)

SHOWING THE FIRST CENTURY TRIBES

CORNAVII

SMERTAE

CAERENI

LUGI

ORCADES
(ORKNEY ISLANDS)

← SACRED ISLE
(ISLE OF LEWIS)

CARNONACAE

DECANTAE

DUN OF THE WAVES
(INVERNESS)

CREONES

THE GREAT GLEN

CALEDONII

VACOMAGI

TAEXALI

VENICONES

TAY INLET

FORTH INLET

EPIDII ▲ DUNADD

DAMNONII

X X X
X X X X X X X
X X X X X

VOTADINI

▲ DUN OF THE TREE
(TRAPRAIN LAW)

(FIRTH OF CLYDE) CLUTHA INLET

SELGOVAE

NOVANTAE

X ~ ROUGH LINE OF FORTS BUILT BY AGRICOLA 79~83 A.D.

Prologue
LINNET

My powers of seeing were strong in my youth, but I could never have foretold the path Rhiann's life would take in the years of the Romans in Alba.

For the Great Goddess is a weaver, and though to us in Thisworld the patterns of our lives seem chaotic, with threads twisting and breaking, colours stopping and starting, She sees the greater design on the loom. I feel like Her now, for though I am an old woman, my eyes dimmed, my fingers gnarled, I can see Rhiann's life unspooling before my eyes. I see it because I have memories and no longer need to rely on visions.

And they are light and dark, just like the threads in the cloth, which together make a complete whole. See how it works: my sister's life was taken as she birthed Rhiann – surely a great darkness. Yet I had recently lost my own child, and so Rhiann became that daughter to me, the great light of my heart, a brilliant child with a precocious will. I raised her from baby to girl, before she went to the Sacred Isle for her priestess training.

And then at the age of eighteen, just as she was initiated, Rhiann's fate turned suddenly, shockingly. For the Sacred Isle was raided, Rhiann's foster-family killed – those whom she had loved as blood kin – and Rhiann's body was violated by those raiders, and left for dead. It was not her body that died, however, but her soul.

She limped back to Dunadd, the seat of her tribe, the Epidii, feeling abandoned by her Goddess, blaming herself for her family's deaths, turning her back on the Sisters she so loved, with words of rage born of grief. Yet her destiny would not let her sink into numbness, the refuge of the broken-minded. Rhiann had more to fulfil than that.

A year later, as she had barely begun to heal, her uncle the king also died, leaving Rhiann as the only bearer of her mother's – his sister's –

royal blood. And at the very moment of his funeral, an exiled prince from the isle of Erin arrived on our shores: Eremon, son of Ferdiad.

After betrayal by his kin, the prince sought power and influence in Alba to win back his father's Hall – and our tribe needed a noble husband for their princess. So the chief druid Gelert offered Eremon the match with Rhiann. Yet though the old priest schemed for this union with evil in his heart, seeking to hurt Rhiann and further his own power, such dark motives only serve the Mother's great design.

Rhiann hated Eremon at first, because of the forced marriage. Yet respect did eventually dawn, and then friendship, and finally – so slowly! – some wary affection. And all the while things continued to evolve in the outer worlds as well as the inner. For the Mother had drawn these two together for a cause beyond themselves – to forge the warring tribes of Alba into a single people, to shield their land from the Romans who encroached from the south. Agricola, the Roman commander, had just received orders from his emperor to crush Alba under the empire's heel.

For two years Rhiann and Eremon travelled Alba side by side, in a partnership of minds if not bodies, and Eremon proved himself as the tribe's war leader. And though the other Alban kings and chiefs baulked at the idea of an alliance, Rhiann and Eremon did gain the favour of the great king of the Caledonii, Calgacus the Sword. It was a strong beginning.

And then . . . the dark threads surfaced once more, as an evil conspiracy created by Maelchon, king of the Orcades islands in the far north, sank Rhiann and Eremon's boat in a storm. For Rhiann had unwittingly earned this man's enmity long ago, when his suit for her hand was refused. He hated Eremon for possessing what he coveted.

Amidst even that chaos, though, the Great Mother's light still glimmered. She drew the sinking boat safely shorewards to a place Rhiann knew well, yet dreaded to return – the Sacred Isle, the place of her greatest joy and her greatest pain; where she had found her true self and lost it again. And though Rhiann quailed to face the Sisters, whom she felt she had wronged, the Sisterhood had kept their hearts and arms open, waiting until she was ready to come home.

And so that circle was at last joined and peace was made in Rhiann's heart. For in the sacred Stones, on the eve of the Beltaine rite, Eremon was sent by the priestesses as the Stag to Rhiann's Maiden. And though Rhiann was full of fear, for the first time they joined that night not just in body, but truly in soul.

With what fierce joy they and their friends left the Isle, after the uncertainty of their arrival! They had found each other, Rhiann had rejoined the priestesses, and Eremon had forged new alliances with the Caereni and Carnonacae tribes, who proclaimed him their Stag, their war leader, by giving him the sacred tattoos.

And yet. The weaving of Rhiann's fate was not complete, and the years of the Romans not over: greater dangers were still to be faced, greater evils to be overcome. This I wish I had known then, but one can only watch the spinning of the Mother's shuttle, the twisting of the wool, and wait for Her design to emerge.

And now the rest is clear, and no more marvellous pattern of intricate, subtle hues have I ever witnessed in all my years in Thisworld, and may so not again, until the Goddess calls me home.

BOOK ONE

LEAF-BUD, AD 81

Chapter 1

These days at sea were the most peaceful she had enjoyed in years, Rhiann realized, her cheek pillowed on the bow. It felt as if their little, open boat floated between the shining water and pale sky, its white sail a wing, suspending it in a void of blue.

As the journey unfolded, the drowsy sea rocked her into a trance, as it gathered itself every now and then for a listless roll against the hull, only to subside into a dark mirror all around, laced with drifting weed. The breeze had stayed westerly, a sea-wind to bring them home to Dunadd, but it barely roused the water to waves, or billowed the sail that rose from the centre of the hide *curragh*.

Rhiann loved this type of boat, for it sat close to the water, and yet skimmed like a gull over the swells, and when the side dipped, she could trail her hand in the cold sea, feeling its pull on her fingers. For now she lay, still aware of little beyond the tang of salt and tar, the creak of oars and the sun on her eyelids.

'Beast! I'll get you . . . *there*, hah! Cold, isn't it!' Caitlin's defiant words, floating over Rhiann's shoulder, were followed by an even louder screech, and Rhiann didn't have to turn to guess that Conaire, who had much bigger hands, had dashed another palmful of seawater over his wife. Either Rhiann's tansy brew had softened Caitlin's nausea or, true to character, she was gamely ignoring it. A rumble of laughter lifted from the others at the oar benches, those of Eremon's men who had come to the Sacred Isle with them, and the islanders who crewed the boat.

Rhiann's knees were numb, and she shifted on the willow ribs of the hull to ease them. As she did, she half-opened her eyes. Beyond the glitter of the sun on the water, the nearest island was sliding past in a fine weave of black cliffs thronged with sea-pinks, its green hills sprinkled with yellow gorse, the white surf edging bays of pale water. At the end of one spill of rocks a seal watched their passage, its head and tail curved into a bow, its eyes as dark and liquid as the sea itself.

'Hello.' Rhiann saluted to it with one finger.

Below the seal's perch the sea was being sucked between rocks in a turmoil of white foam. And as she stared at the roiling water, Rhiann made the connection, suddenly realizing what she had been sensing from afar for the past day: a deep thrumming on the edge of her hearing, resonating through the air. *The whirlpool.*

The whirlpool's spinning waters churned the narrow strait between the islands close to Dunadd, making a boundary between Thisworld and the Otherworld. And Rhiann knew, with the refinement of her priestess senses, that she was hearing it because it was a sign for her. So she did what any sensible person would do: bit her lip, and futilely clamped her eyes shut again.

The sun prickled her forearms where she'd pushed up the sleeves of her wool dress, yet inside Rhiann had gone cold. For the whirlpool was telling her she must wake from the sea dreams in which she'd been floating. It meant that her span of days must resume, that they were nearly home and must face all that lay there. And by the Goddess, Rhiann didn't want to.

Instead, she wanted to hold on to the deep thrill of joy, the thread of gold wound through her now that she had returned to the fold of the Sisters, and had been filled by the Goddess light once more, in the stone circle. Now that . . .

'Ah, my sea-sprite.' There was a creak of the hull, as a tentative hand brushed Rhiann's cheek. 'And have you returned to me at last from the faery deep?'

Now that Eremon was hers. Rhiann completed the thought and allowed herself a smile, for although everyone else had known somehow to leave her alone, Eremon hadn't, nor had she wanted him to. 'Just now,' she replied, although she couldn't stifle a sigh as she stretched, blinking her eyes fully open in the bright, leaf-bud light.

Rhiann's seat, a pile of leather packs and wrapped weapons, squeaked as Eremon flopped onto them. 'And were you pining for me from the depths of your watery abode?'

Rhiann squinted up at him from one eye, though in the glare she could only see a pale grin against a tanned face. 'Keep spouting such words, husband, and it won't be me in that watery abode, I can tell you.' Yet her hand crept out and laid itself on his warm, bare foot. Just to remind her he was really there, and laughing down at her.

'If I kept talking like *that*, I wouldn't blame you, wife.' Eremon grinned and hooked his arms around his knees, his green eyes catching the light off the waves. The narrow braids holding back his dark hair framed a face painted with sunburn across clear, brown skin. He had rolled his trousers up and cut the sleeves off his linen tunic, and even in this short time the sun had turned his bare arms as dark as oiled oak. 'Poetry makes my head ache, and it has only just cleared after all those Sacred Isle feasts!'

Rhiann rested her chin on Eremon's knees and toyed with one of his braids. 'I did wonder at the island chiefs . . .' She cocked one eyebrow at him. 'Going to all the trouble of proclaiming you their war leader, and then trying to kill you with ale . . .'

'Ah! As King Stag I must be able to do everything well, apparently – including drinking.'

'Well, I think your practice with Conaire stood you in good stead there.'

A shout drew both their heads around, and they saw their friends gesticulating wildly at each other in what passed for them as conversation. Fiery Fergus was daring to provoke the much larger Conaire by twisting the end of his oar, spraying all of them with water. With another squeal, Caitlin cupped a handful from the sea and this time flung it at Fergus, as Conaire folded his huge, sunburned arms over his oar and rocked with laughter. With a long-suffering grimace, Colum wiped his dripping grey hair, even as the web of lines around his eyes crinkled.

As they were thus occupied, Eremon slid his lean frame down the pile of packs until he was pressed against Rhiann's knees in the bow, his broad shoulders blocking them from the view of the others. The clean lines of his face were still as hard as when Rhiann had first seen him two years ago, his slanted eyes still sharp, and yet nevertheless some tense hunger in him had softened this last week, his defences lowering. And with their faces close together Eremon smiled now, his true smile that Rhiann had rarely seen, for before the Sacred Isle one side of it was always lifted with bitterness. Being on the receiving end of its full power was still a new experience for Rhiann, and she found her breath tripping in her throat again, which was most disconcerting.

'Rhiann,' Eremon breathed, as if tasting her name on his tongue. And, more confident now, he brushed back the tendrils of hair at her nape, his thumb moving in circles over her skin.

Somewhat shakily, Rhiann returned his smile. These last days, every time this look of secret wonder stole across Eremon's face – the look that said *I can't believe I touch you* – something fluttered at the base of Rhiann's belly, no, lower, like warm fingers, brushing between her legs. And with it, not surprisingly, came fear.

For ever since those raiders on the island, desire had always been mingled with fear in her. Every reach and expanse of her flesh had preserved the moment when those rough men threw her down and took her, with the blood of her family still on their hands, sparing her life, but not her soul.

In the stone circle on the Sacred Isle – the first time she and Eremon ever lay together – the Goddess energy and the flaming stars and the *saor* herbs had swept Rhiann to some place of surrender. What would happen now it was just she and he alone in their marriage bed? What if the old memories crippled her again? What if she couldn't help shrinking from him, despite her love, and he turned away?

No. Rhiann endeavoured to take her racing thoughts in hand. Surely everything had changed now. The Goddess had at last returned to her, the connection she had always felt before the raid. Rhiann's spirit had touched the Mother in the stone circle; she had filled with light in the old way. And Eremon was hers.

To banish all thought, Rhiann reached out to Eremon instead, tracing one high, sharp cheekbone and then brushing his lips, fuller than those of the other Erin men. This was because Eremon had British blood, too, in his veins, giving him darker skin, a leaner build and those sea-coloured eyes.

Eremon turned his head now to kiss her palm, and then held up the end of her braid so the sun lit it to flame, a flash of mischief crossing his features. 'Did you know your hair is the exact colour of amber, Rhiann? The darkest amber, not the light.'

Grateful for the distraction, Rhiann laughed. 'Yes, husband. And my eyes are like *violets*, I believe – the bards have got there before you, I'm afraid.'

Eremon ignored her, pressing her hair to his nose to inhale the scent of the honey soap in which she bathed. 'You should always wear amber near your hair, against your throat . . .'

Rhiann closed her eyes, as his fingers stroked the hollow below her ear. 'Then you may have to sail to the northern seas yourself, my prince,' she whispered, 'for it is far too rare for that. Even the amber for the royal jewels was traded long ago.'

'No.' His voice also dropped. 'Not the royal jewels. You shall have a necklace all of your own set with amber, so I can see it shine against your throat.' He paused. 'As a wedding gift.'

Her eyes leaped open. '*Wedding?*'

Eremon kissed her fingers. 'What a terrible memory you have, priestess! Our marriage was not to the highest grade, remember, and after a year and a day of the betrothal you were required to choose whether to permanently bind with me . . . or not.'

Rhiann's confusion dissolved in a hot flush across her cheeks. 'Oh, Goddess Mother! After all that has happened, I *did* forget!'

'I will try not to take that as an insult.'

Rhiann shook her head and laughed. 'Eremon, do you mean it, truly?'

'Certainly.' His brows knitted together in an exaggerated fashion. 'But will you have me? Now that you know I no longer command any people, beyond these few grumpy warriors . . .' He waved a vague hand over his shoulder. 'And I have no wealth, no home . . .'

'*Eremon!*' She thumped his chest, none too gently, and he caught her hand there at the neck of his tunic. When Rhiann felt the thud of his heart beneath her fingers she looked down, her cheeks flaming. 'Besides, my home is where you are, and yours mine. You were born a prince of Erin, but you are also of my people now.'

She glanced up to see him gazing at their entangled fingers, and the grim lines of old pain were back in his face. A few days of kisses could not erase these, even if she felt that everything inside *her* had shifted and settled into new curves and bends, like a river changing course.

'That is true, *a stór*,' Eremon murmured, 'and because of that I fear our wedding feast may need to be a trifle hasty.' A black-tipped gull passed over the mast, screeching as it spun. Eremon looked up and tracked it over the sky. 'Sunseason is getting closer, and I feel sure Agricola will not have rested his soldiers while we rested on the Sacred Isle.'

The day darkened for Rhiann as if a cloud had sailed across the sun. Without volition, her eyes drifted south, towards the distant whirlpool. There it was: the first mention in days of what waited for them at home. By unspoken agreement, each had sought to stretch out that interlude of peace on the island, knowing they weren't like other couples, free to revel in new feelings. They were pretenders, acting as if they had no cares beyond those of lovers. Rhiann's fingers pressed to the hollow of her throat, trying to loosen the sudden tightness. 'What will we do?'

Eremon was now staring east across the sea, where the Alban mainland was hidden by the long, blue islands, as if his gaze could penetrate the leagues that lay between the Epidii lands and those occupied by the Romans. 'This new alliance with the Caereni and Carnonacae, added to that with Calgacus, makes us a force to be reckoned with, at last. I think it is time to take advantage of that, to strike a blow before the Romans do.' His eyes came back and fixed on her face, dark with regret. 'Soon I will have to leave my bride and take to the field.'

'We knew that our partings would be frequent, *cariad*. Yet by the Goddess, if I'd wanted a quiet life, I would have married a cowherd, wouldn't I?'

Eremon snorted. 'Perhaps your council would have been better pleased with that! After all, they gained a war leader, but no gold or cattle in exchange for their princess.' A thought occurred to him, creasing his brow. 'Do you think they will refuse to make the marriage binding?'

'Eremon!' Rhiann raised herself up, pillowing her knees on her blue priestess cloak. 'You sail home with two major alliances, and you've trained our men so well we've already achieved one great victory against the invaders. How can you still doubt your position here?'

Eremon was chewing his lip, as he often did when thinking. 'Because it still isn't secure, and I can't make it so with a sword. Not when the enemies may be inside as well as out.'

'You mean Maelchon,' Rhiann whispered. They believed the king of the Orcades had engineered their shipwreck two weeks ago, but did not know his exact motives.

Eremon's mouth hardened into a straight line. 'Maelchon had left Calgacus's fort, so he couldn't be the only person behind the sinking of our boat. He would not have known we were leaving by sea, or when we sailed . . .' Suddenly he bit off his words, clamping his lips together with a hint of his old severity.

And although Rhiann had let the memory of the shipwreck subside, something cold now slithered up her spine. The plunge into the sea . . . the sucking of freezing water at her mouth and nose . . .

Eremon saw her shiver and curved his arm around her, lying back to press her cheek into his chest. His tunic was stiff with salt, and smelled of male sweat, although she found this oddly reassuring. 'I'm sorry I spoke of this now,' he whispered. 'Let me deal with it, a stór, my beloved.'

His voice vibrated in Rhiann's ear, yet she resisted closing her eyes and sinking into his strength. 'You said enemies inside. You mean within the Epidii, my own people?'

Eremon's hand stilled on her hair. 'Only the Epidii warriors knew we were setting sail from Calgacus's fort. No one else within the dun knew.'

Rhiann's mouth dropped open with instinctive denial, but just then all thoughts were banished by the sudden, startled shout of the boat's captain. He was a black-haired island man, and keen of eye.

'Lord!' he cried to Eremon, and when Rhiann raised her head she saw he was pointing at the mainland, his other arm clasping the mast, each tendon strung hard under the weathered skin.

Eremon leaped up so abruptly that Rhiann fell on her hands and knees across the packs, before scrabbling to her feet.

'Prince!' the sailor shouted again. 'Smoke! Thick smoke, in the air over Dunadd!'

Chapter 2

D riven hard by the now desperate oarsmen, the boat shot between the scattered rocks into the Bay of Isles like an arrow released from its string.

Yet once they rounded the great headland that sheltered the bay from the sea, Rhiann saw that the smoke staining the blue sky came not from Dunadd, but from the signal beacons, lining the high ground to north and south of the bay.

'They are burned out,' Eremon muttered to Rhiann, shading his eyes to look up at the ridges cloaked in bracken and sheep-bitten turf, with hazel and oak trees spilling down the slopes. There were no flames to be seen, only the trailing smoke of the bonfires.

Rhiann's breath was tight and high in her chest. She glanced at Eremon, wanting to speak, but was stopped by the hard glitter of his eyes. The man who had cradled her so gently moments before was gone.

Conaire, Eremon's foster-brother, had laid aside his oar to join Eremon in the bow, his lithe leaps from rib to rib belying his great height and build. 'Do you think it safe to land, brother?'

Eremon was still, his dark head thrust towards shore like a hound scenting the air. Ahead, the bay had opened up into full view: the broad sweep of marsh surrounding the mouth of the river Add; the river channels snaking over the tidal mudflats; and, further towards the eastern horizon, the blue hills that cupped the plain on which Dunadd sat. Close to the shore was the cluster of roundhouses and jetties that made up the port of Crinan. A pall of smoke hung over the village, yet the buildings themselves seemed whole.

Across from Crinan, on a headland that curved around the bay like a sheltering arm, the black skeleton of an abandoned dun crouched. That fort had been burned by the Romans less than a year before, and it was the reminder of this attack that had terrified them; the memory of coming over the hills to see smoke against the sky and bodies sprawled among the ruins. Rhiann's blood was now pounding so hard that her sight shook, and she wiped her sweating palms down the skirt of her dress, trying to calm her breathing.

Caitlin, Conaire's wife, flung herself across the oar benches to reach Rhiann, her haste making her uncharacteristically clumsy. Rhiann grasped her thin arm to steady her.

'Wh-what does it mean?' Caitlin cried, her tiny hand clutching at Rhiann's fingers. Rhiann looked down into the small, heart-shaped face beneath a cloud of fair hair, tugged from its braids by wind and damp. Caitlin was drawn and pale from the nausea of the voyage, which, though calm, had still affected her now she was expecting a child.

Rhiann forced a smile and stroked Caitlin's cold fingers, though she herself was fighting down a wave of panic. 'I am sure it is nothing,' she murmured. Just then the backwash from the rocks of the headland made the boat lurch, and Rhiann's hand had to steady both of them against the single mast.

'There is no outward sign of trouble,' Eremon at last pronounced, his gaze on the shore. 'The fishing boats are there on the sand, unharmed. Look! The nobles' boats are also tied up. There is smoke, but why?'

Rhiann peeled Caitlin's fingers from her arm and helped her to Conaire's side, moving closer to Eremon. 'Goddess, what of Dunadd?' Their fort sat in the middle of the marsh on a rock crag, and could not be seen from the sea.

Eremon chewed fiercely on his lip, then glanced at Conaire. 'What choice do we have but to land? We are only a few, yet I can see no people at Crinan.'

Conaire was nodding as he curved his broad arm protectively around his wife, his gold hair a fierce beacon in the sun. 'We can see nothing from here anyway, brother. If anything is amiss, we are few enough to land and approach Dunadd by stealth, in case there are scouts.'

Rhiann was feeling sicker by the moment, still trying to shake off the daze of the rocking sea and sunshine. It was still so early in leaf-bud, despite the fine weather. The marsh grass was new and green, yet the tops of the mountains that ringed the plain were still dusted with snow. How could the Romans have come so early in the season? How could they have been caught out again?

As soon as the boat grated on the mud beach beside the first pier, the warriors were splashing through the shallows, swords drawn. Above, on a spur of rock that guarded the river mouth, the scattering of roundhouses crouched silent beneath their pale thatch roofs. As Eremon had seen, the nobles' timber boats with their carved prows were bobbing unharmed on their weed-furred ropes. The little hide *curraghs* were drawn up in rows above the tideline, alongside dugout canoes. Yet there was no bustle of people coming and going, and no children crying. Only a lone dog, tied up against the first house, barked at them in a frenzy.

At Eremon's orders, Rhiann and Caitlin stayed in the boat with the Sacred Isle sailors, ready to push off at his sign. But no sooner had his warriors disappeared among the rocks, than Rhiann's eye was caught by a pale blur in the shadows of the houses. Her heart gave a great lurch as she recognized the shape – her mare Liath, led by a short, rotund man who stumbled past Eremon in agitated haste.

Drawing up her long robe with both hands, Rhiann put one foot on the railing and jumped down into the shallows, heedless of the freezing water that soaked her leather boots to the skin. 'Didius!' she cried, splashing free and breaking into a run.

In the middle of the sand they met, Didius stumbling and yanking on Liath's reins, making the mare throw up her head in protest. Rhiann halted, her initial smile of greeting faded. Didius's plump cheeks were quivering beneath his straggly, black beard, and his nose, the only large, straight thing about him, was red and streaming. 'Didius?'

Didius stuffed his fingers in his mouth to halt the sob that rushed out, his black, Roman eyes shining with tears. 'Lady, I am sorry,' he gulped at last, the musical Alban speech thickened by his native Latin.

As Rhiann soothed the mare, stroking her cheeks, Didius snorted and wiped his nose on his tunic sleeve. All of his Roman clothes were long gone, as were his clipped hair and shaven face. If it wasn't for his swarthy skin and oval eyes he could almost pass for one of the Epidii now, though, because of his girth, not a warrior.

'Didius, what is wrong? Where is everyone?'

Eremon stepped up now, sheathing his sword on his belt, and the Roman glanced up at the prince with some of his old fear. Yet his distress got the better of him, and he grasped Rhiann's hand and pressed it between his own. 'Lady, we thought you drowned! All of you, in the sea!'

Rhiann drew in a sharp breath.

'Dead?' That was Eremon. 'Who said such a thing?'

'The – the chief druid. Gelert.'

Eremon's eyes met Rhiann's, and she saw the same terrible question dawning there. *How did the druid know about the shipwreck?*

'Didius,' Rhiann strove to calm her voice, 'tell us how this happened.'

Didius's throat bobbed as he stumbled through an explanation: that after returning from Calgacus's fort by land, the chief druid went into seclusion, and then emerged to announce that he had been sent a vision from the gods. Rhiann, the tribe's Ban Cré, the sacred Land Mother, and her husband, the war leader, had drowned at sea.

As Didius reached the end his breath caught, and Rhiann closed her eyes for a moment, knowing exactly what this news had meant to him, a Roman prisoner, whose only protector among the Epidii had been Rhiann herself. She reached out to squeeze Didius's callused hand. 'Go on.'

'Well, that was three days ago, and the mourning has been terrible. People burned offerings in a big bonfire at the water – see, over there – and they lit all the beacons on the cliffs. Now many have gone to Dunadd, and the keening of the women has left no peace anywhere in the fort. The council of elders is at the King's Hall, and a mourning feast is being prepared. No one will speak to me, they are all so anguished!'

A chill crept over Rhiann's skin, for there was one other person who would be utterly devastated by this lie. 'And what of my aunt, the Lady Linnet? Have you seen her?'

Didius shook his head until his chins wobbled. 'No, lady, she has not come.'

'Goddess!' Rhiann whirled to Eremon. 'I must go to her *now*; she will be frantic!'

Eremon laid a reassuring hand on her arm. 'Soon, *a stór*.' He addressed himself sternly to Didius. 'If this was the news, son of Rome, then why are you here unaccompanied, with my wife's horse?'

'Eremon!' Rhiann exclaimed.

For a moment, the single, buried thread of iron in Didius rose to the surface, in a compression of his wet lips. Yet then it sank away, and embarrassment stole over his plump face. 'I wasn't escaping – where would I go? I wasn't. I just . . . didn't believe it.' He gazed pleadingly at Rhiann. 'I *knew* you would return, and I've been sleeping here with Liath ever since the druid emerged. Three days now, and watching the sea every day.'

Rhiann slowly nodded. 'Then you prove both your loyalty and your keen senses for, as you can see, we are alive and well.'

Above, faces were now appearing at doorways, and there was a growing murmur of surprised voices from the cluster of houses.

'Rhiann, we must go,' Eremon ordered, jerking his hand at Colum and Fergus.

Taking a deep breath, Rhiann glanced over her shoulder at the boat. Conaire had returned to sweep Caitlin into his arms, depositing her gently on the grey sands as Fergus and Colum now began tossing their belongings on to the beach.

Taking Liath's reins, Rhiann led the mare to Caitlin and explained what had happened. 'We must hurry to Dunadd,' Rhiann finished, 'and so I wish you to ride Liath, *cariad*.'

Caitlin swallowed hard and shook her head. 'Oh, no, Rhiann, I can't. You're the Ban Cré; the people need to see you entering at the gate with proper ceremony.' She tried to draw herself taller, with a bold toss of her fair hair. Yet though she was kin to Rhiann, she didn't share Rhiann's height, and the effect was less than defiant. 'I will walk.'

Conaire's blue eyes were shadowed with concern, and he bent his head close to his wife. 'Beloved, please ride. You got so sick on the boat . . .'

Conaire caught Rhiann's eye, as Caitlin set her lip and jutted her chin. Rhiann dropped her voice, wielding her best weapon. 'Do it for the babe, Caitlin. As your healer, I strongly advise you to rest yourself during these early moons.'

'I don't . . .' Suddenly, Caitlin clapped her hand to her mouth, her arm holding her belly. Her throat moved convulsively, as a fine sweat beaded her forehead, and Rhiann put her hand gently on the back of her neck. Choking down the spasm, Caitlin dropped her hand and breathed deeply. 'I suppose I must then,' she conceded at last, and in a rare show of submission allowed Conaire to lift her to the mare's back. The crew of the boat offered to accompany them, but Eremon refused, telling them to ask for food at the port and return home.

Desperate with haste, they could spare only moments for the few fisherfolk who emerged from their houses as they passed, touching Rhiann's hands. Throwing hurried answers to the questions coming from all directions, they took the trade path, which led along the river and across the marsh to Dunadd.

The banter of the sea journey had been replaced with silence. Colum's face had set into even grimmer lines than usual, his blue eyes hard beneath his stringy cap of thinning, grey hair. Fergus was watchful, scanning the shadows beneath the river trees. Didius's short legs made him the slowest, and though he must puff and pant with his head down to keep up, his black eyes kept darting to Rhiann's face, as if to assure himself she was truly there.

When Dunadd emerged into view above the banks of river alders and willows, Rhiann realized she had braced herself to see some sign of disaster on the walls. But from afar there seemed nothing amiss.

The single rock crag still reared proudly from the red marsh; the timber palisade of the village at its feet marching around it in stout oak stakes. The thatched roofs of the nobles' houses, high on the crag's crest, glowed like sun on ripe barley. And the scarlet and white banner of the White Mare, the emblem of Rhiann's royal clan, rippled from the apex of the King's Hall, set on the dun's highest point.

Something else was the same, too. The roofless circle of oak pillars that was the druid shrine still squatted beside the King's Hall, as threatening to Rhiann as ever. For the shrine was the chief druid's realm – Gelert must have announced their deaths there.

And how? Rhiann wondered again. *How could Gelert know?* Yet

Didius's words called forth a powerful memory that had been subsumed by the shipwreck and all that happened after; the druid standing on the shore above Calgacus's dun, watching their boat leave.

Glancing at her, Eremon immediately drew her close and raised her hand to his lips. *I know*, his look said. *I know, too.*

Even in his salt-stained tunic and trousers, with stubble shadowing his brown skin, Eremon looked every bit a prince, and Rhiann resolutely tried to take comfort from that. The more plainly he dressed, the straighter his back and shoulders seemed. And when his face was darkened with sun and dirt, the green of his eyes blazed all the brighter. He was a match for Gelert, she had to believe that.

And what about me? Rhiann thought, with a flare of fierce pride, remembering what lay within her own soul. In the stone circle she had felt the Goddess fill her with the light of the Source – the life force which ran through all things. In that sacred space and with her surrender to Eremon, the connection between her body and the spirit world had been mended.

And as she summoned it, the wordless joy Rhiann had floated in that night now surged again, strengthening her. Slowly, she opened her eyes, the afterglare of the sun dancing in spots before her nose. She could face Gelert and Maelchon and even Agricola. She could. She must.

They had not even fully crossed the causeway over the river when the first shouts rang out from people gathered on the meadow, digging the baking pits for the mourning feast. Then the cry of a horn soared up from the timber tower that spanned Dunadd's main gate.

They had been seen.

Chapter 3

They had barely emerged from the gatetower into the sun-filled yard inside the palisade when the shouts of recognition and surprise began, and the bellows of warriors from the walkway that ran along the walls.

Most people had been inside, sharing the quiet of mourning, their doors smeared with spirals of rowan-ash and mutton-fat, their house banners taken down and folded away. Yet now, drawn by the noise, people came running from their clustered houses and down the twisting paths between the workshops and granaries: men with skinning knives; women with flour spilling down their skirts. Dogs writhed and jumped about in a frenzy of barking, and crying children were dragged along by their mothers. Within moments Rhiann was surrounded by a crowd all talking at once, as Conaire lifted Caitlin down from Liath, and Eremon tried to field the clamour of questions.

Pale faces swam in the shadow of the gatetower, or were lit to blinding brightness in the sun. People touched Rhiann's cloak, grasped her hands, assuring themselves she was alive. Their distress and relief was palpable, catching Rhiann by surprise.

She was the Ban Cré, sacred vessel for the Goddess, servant for the people. Yet she hadn't understood, or allowed herself to believe, that they loved her. The realization rose warm in Rhiann's heart, overwhelming after what she had felt outside, and she had to swallow it down to smile her reassurance for them.

Caitlin, whose bravado had made her a favourite since her arrival the year before, had now all but disappeared beneath a mass of milling women, and Rhiann was just about to rescue her when a pair of sturdy arms were suddenly flung around her.

Stunned, at first Rhiann could not recognize the broken voice babbling in her ear, and it wasn't until the woman held her at arm's length that Rhiann recognized her friend, the blacksmith's wife Aldera, her round, ruddy face streaming with tears, her butter-coloured hair wet with them.

'Rhiann, we thought you dead! Yet Didius was right that you were alive . . . by all the gods!' Rhiann's face was pressed into a plump shoulder redolent with the scents of woodsmoke, swaddling cloths and sour milk.

'It . . . was a mistake . . .' Rhiann mumbled into the folds of Aldera's dress.

Then Aldera was holding her out again with one hand, wiping her tear-streaked face and blowing her nose into her sleeve, as three of her five children tugged on her skirts, the baby wailing at this unusual show of emotion. Aldera looked down at her eldest boy. 'Quickly now! Run to the King's Hall and tell the council there the war leader and Ban Cré have returned safely!'

The child nodded and rubbed his nose, his eyes huge, but as he turned to scamper away, a hand shot out and grabbed the back of his tunic, pulling him to a startled halt.

'No,' Eremon said, his eyes meeting Rhiann's over the boy's head. 'I will go myself, and deliver my own surprise.' He released the boy and clapped his shoulder in a more manly way. 'You stay here, lad, and look after the women.'

Eremon spared a glance for Conaire now and, as usual, the two brothers needed no words between them. Jerking his head at Fergus and Colum to follow, Conaire dropped a kiss on Caitlin's head and fell into step behind Eremon.

Those people flowing down towards the gate parted as the four warriors drove their way up the muddy path that snaked between the roundhouses, granaries and stables, up the steep, rock stairs of the crag and under the carved wooden arch of the Moon Gate, which guarded the crag's first tier.

Here, the nobles' houses were set above the village, but they were silent and grim now, their round walls in cold shadow. The bright banners of horse, stag and wolf that normally fluttered from every roof tree and carved door-post had been taken down as a mark of mourning.

Eremon spared no glance as faces appeared at every door, drawn by the shouts from below. Speed was of the essence, because on entering Dunadd he had been struck by an idea. If he took the council by surprise, their reactions might reveal what they would otherwise keep hidden.

With his men behind, Eremon leaped up the last set of rock stairs and through the carved arch of the Horse Gate, which led to the uppermost tier. The only buildings on the crest were the druid shrine and the King's Hall, the largest roundhouse in the village. Framing an ornate set of double oak doors, its conical thatch roof swept almost to the ground, rising to a point seven spear-lengths above.

There were no guards at the open door and, pushing past the few servants, Eremon burst into the hearth-space of the Hall, blinking to adjust his eyes to the dim, smoky haze. He ignored the confusion of spears and shields on the curved walls, the painted and carved roof-pillars, the flickering flames in the huge hearth-pit. All he sought for was the ring of council benches, and the faces of those who sat on them, staring up at him in utter shock. Unlike the men of Erin, Alban warriors all sported face tattoos, and the dark blue lines writhed fearsomely in the firelight.

Fixing on the palest robe, Eremon saw the chief druid Gelert first. Sure enough, within his tangled grey beard, the druid's thin mouth had fallen open in horror, and those yellow eyes gleamed with quickly veiled malice. Horror and hatred told their own story.

Yet beside Gelert was someone Eremon had not expected to see here at Dunadd: Urben, the chief of a secondary Epidii clan. A powerful noble who had wanted his son to be king and war leader when the old king died – hopes thwarted by Eremon's chance arrival – Urben's shock mirrored Gelert's, except that his grey eyes flashed with anger and clear dismay.

Urben's son Lorn, the object of his sire's ambitions, was different again. The immaculate young Epidii warrior had his ale cup halfway to his mouth. At Eremon's sudden appearance it paused in mid-air, but the glacial grey eyes above the gilded horn rim showed only surprise.

And that was all Eremon could see before the rest of the council reacted more forcefully. Talorc, the old king's cousin, leaped to his feet and threw his huge arms around Eremon, exclaiming his shock and delight. Lost for a moment in a bushy, red beard that reeked of ale and boar meat, Eremon had time to register a jolt of relief. Not Talorc, then. His loyalty had been real.

Belen, another royal cousin, backed up Talorc with a thump on Eremon's back, the fierceness of his tattoos melted by his grin. 'By the gods, lad!' he cried joyfully, quite forgetting Eremon's rank. 'We sit here drinking your funeral ale, yet here *you* are, alive!'

Extricating himself from Talorc's arms, Eremon quickly scanned the rest of the council, though they had by now guarded their expressions. It was a mixture, as he'd expected. Some were on their feet, some stayed seated. Some were pleased to see him, and some, like Tharan, always the greatest opponent of Eremon's schemes, had already carefully veiled their true thoughts.

But no matter. Eremon had seen what he needed to in one person. He turned now as the three Erin men he had left behind appeared at the edges of the fire, their faces pale with shock and relief. Old Finan,

Colum's sword-mate, was so overcome he also thumped Eremon on the back. The youngest warrior, Rori, stared and then ducked his face, his red hair swinging over flaming cheeks. Eremon's young bard Aedan was also speechless for once, clutching his harp to his chest as if he were drowning.

'Peace,' Eremon said to them, moved by their emotion, as Conaire, Colum and Fergus surrounded them, clapping shoulders and murmuring reassurance.

Not willing to lose the advantage of surprise, Eremon took a breath, and turned to plant himself before the muttering ranks of nobles, deliberately leaning on the ornate scabbard of his father's great sword, so the firelight glinted on its curling bronze and gold designs. 'Yes, I have returned,' he declared, his voice rising over the mutters, waiting for the men to fall silent.

And in that moment, Eremon struggled to gain some calm over the confused mix of anger, fear and hurt that suddenly bloomed in his chest, taking him by surprise. It had brought it all back to him, these faces of betrayal. His uncle and kin turning on him with jealousy and hatred in their eyes, exiling him from Erin and his dead father's Hall. The hurt that had lodged then in his heart like a ragged shard of iron, pierced even now. *You do your best for people, to serve them well, and they turn on you, like this . . .* Eremon fought for control, forcing the old feelings aside, holding up his hand. Not all had betrayed him here, not all. He had to remember that.

Gradually, the babble of voices died away, and it was only then that Eremon speared the chief druid with his hard gaze. 'It appears that the news of our death was somewhat premature. An easy mistake to make, no doubt.'

Many pairs of eyes slid towards Gelert, but the druid said nothing, his knuckles pushing white and bony through his dry skin, as he gripped his owl-head staff.

'These things happen sometimes, prince,' someone else put in hastily, and Eremon swung towards the speaker. It was Gelert's deputy, Declan, a reasonable man, and one not given to guile. 'The Source does not always reveal itself clearly,' Declan added, his eyes darting uncertainly from Eremon to his chief druid.

'No.' Gelert spoke at last, his voice as thin and cracked as the skin on his face. 'Not always clearly.'

Eremon shrugged. 'Certainly this time, not clearly. Still, no real harm is done.' He turned his attentions to the warrior-nobles, relaxing his face into a pleasant smile. He must re-establish himself right now, here, when they were disconcerted. He must take their attention from what they were no doubt beginning to discuss – the rule of the tribe – and bring them back into his vision, holding them there.

'I am glad you are all together,' he began, 'for I have a strange tale for you. I feel you may be even more pleased with it than my sudden reappearance.' He smiled wryly, and there was a ripple of uneasy laughter. Eremon then reached into the neck of his tunic and took hold of the boar stone, which hung against his skin on an ochre-dyed thong. 'Whatever you were discussing, I ask that you put it aside for the moment, for things are stirring in the matter of the Romans, beyond Epidii lands. And now I come to tell you that our tribe is no longer acting alone.'

Talorc was frowning. 'What are you talking about, prince?'

Slowly, Eremon withdrew the stone on its thong: a thin, polished disk of dark granite. 'One side is carved with the eagle, the totem of Calgacus the Sword. The other is the Boar.' He dropped the stone so it lay against his tunic. 'My own totem.'

'And what has this to do with us?' Urben interjected, his mouth hidden by his ale cup. 'Prince.'

Eremon met Urben's cold gaze. 'Calgacus of the Caledonii offered an alliance between his tribe and the Epidii, yet in your absence I could not speak for you. So he made this binding oath with my people, and any who wish to join me.' He straightened his shoulders, unable to hold back the pride that warmed his chest. 'We now have the strength of the most powerful tribe in Alba behind us, when the Romans come!'

Tharan was peering up at the boar stone, his sharp eyes unimpressed. 'And *if* they come, still it will not be enough. As rich as Calgacus is, of what use is an alliance with a tribe at the other end of Alba?'

Biting the inside of his lip for patience, Eremon transferred his attentions to the old warrior. 'Then listen to the other part of my news. By the will of the gods, on the Sacred Isle I was made the King Stag, the sacred war leader of the Caereni and Carnonacae – and given the sacred tattoos.' He paused, and with a dramatic flourish raised his tunic, showing them the flowing designs lately carved into his chest and the flat plane of his belly. 'Their warriors are now mine to command in defence of Alba, as I choose it. Their lands border your own . . . their people are many. Perhaps this interests you more, especially since you also border the Creones, and they are no friends of yours.'

As Eremon dropped his tunic he recognized expressions that were much more satisfying: greed, calculation and, above all, respect – grudging or otherwise. Yet he had not finished. In a sudden burst of inspiration he realized he had one more thing to announce, which would strengthen his power over these men even more. He glanced at Conaire behind his shoulder, but there was no time to gain his brother's leave.

'There is more news, closer to home but of great interest to you all,' Eremon added, holding his hand up again to stem the tide of rumbling voices. He beckoned Conaire forward, reaching up to rest his hand on his brother's shoulder. 'The Lady Caitlin is to bear a child to my brother, Conaire mac Lugaid.' Glancing at Conaire out of the corner of one eye, Eremon was pleased to see the pride which swelled his brother's chest, although the effect was diluted by Conaire's abashed grin.

Eremon had just opened his mouth to continue when there was the sudden, discordant twang of a harp string. Looking towards Aedan, he saw that his bard's sweet face was transfigured.

'My lord!' Aedan burst out, his shining eyes darting from Conaire to Eremon, forgetting in his joy just where he was. 'But the Lady Caitlin is the Lady Linnet's daughter, and so she too carries the old king's bloodline. Her son could be an Epidii king!'

Eremon closed his mouth to smother a smile. Though inappropriate, Aedan's outburst had clearly stated his message to these nobles. When Aedan realized what he'd done he'd be mortified, of course, but right now all Eremon wanted to do was embrace him.

There was another shocked silence as this news and its implications sank in. Eremon risked a glance at Urben, and now the old chieftain was truly glowering, the rage suffusing his heavy cheeks with blood. The darkness in his face made a glittering mockery of the profusion of gold rings and bracelets and brooches that covered his rich clothes. No doubt, Eremon thought grimly, Urben had been about to argue that his son Lorn was the obvious candidate both for the kingship, since there were no closer heirs, and for Eremon's rule of the war band, since there was no longer an Eremon.

Except that there is – and here I am. Eremon bit down a grim smile, but again it was Talorc who responded with the appropriate pleasure.

'*A royal heir!*' he cried, this time smothering Conaire in a bearded embrace. 'Well done, son of Lugaid! Well done!'

Grinning even more sheepishly, Conaire accepted the congratulations of the well-meaning nobles, while Gelert, Urben and Lorn sat frozen, as if part of the scene on the wall-hanging behind them.

At last Urben lumbered to his feet, the fringe of his bearskin cloak brushing the ground. He pushed past Eremon in a waft of sour sweat and ale, briefly dipping his blunt, grizzled head. 'My compliments to the lady, your man and to yourself, prince.' His eyes bored into Eremon's. 'We were discussing the appropriate form of mourning for one of your . . . position and talents . . . but happily these discussions can be put aside now.' Glancing sharply at his son, he barked, 'Come! We have spent enough time away from our own dun. We must ride now to be back before dark.'

Urben had barely disappeared out the door when Talorc gripped Eremon by the shoulder once more, his wide grin disappearing into his red beard. 'The funeral ale can easily be drunk in celebration, aye?' he cried heartily.

Eremon let his face relax into a more natural smile now, suddenly feeling exhausted. 'Well, it's not every day a man gets to attend his own mourning feast, after all.'

Talorc laughed, and beckoned to the servants hovering by the walls. 'Bring the pitchers!' he roared, waving his horn cup. 'And more food!'

As soon as Eremon disappeared, Rhiann had given in to her own sense of urgency.

On dismounting, Caitlin had turned so pale that Aldera, brooking no resistance, herded her into her own house by the gate, to let her rest. Rhiann waited only long enough to see Caitlin seated at the hearth among a pack of children, before she ducked back outside, nearly colliding with Didius.

Grasping him by the arms, Rhiann muttered, 'Stay and watch over her,' before she broke away and hurried up the village path in Eremon's wake. Her maid Eithne had also been left behind when they went north, and Rhiann must settle her distress first before she could seek out Linnet.

Though the day was warm, Rhiann was dismayed to see that her door-hide was down, not tied back for fine weather. She paused for a moment, apprehensive, then lifted it and bent under to enter the house.

The first thing that assailed her was the smell. Her rafters were clustered with drying herbs and roots, and many years of healing brews, beeswax, honey and sharp dyes had scented the wall hangings, rugs and cushions set on the floor around the hearth. But now a mustiness pricked at her nostrils, the sourness of unwashed linens and unclean cooking pots, and the dank that comes when no fire has been lit for many days.

Before the cold hearth-pit in the centre of the roundhouse sat a lone figure, curled into the rush chair that Didius had made for Rhiann. Around her the floor cushions were in disarray, as if they had been tossed around in a rage of grief. So sunk in misery was the girl, that she didn't even notice Rhiann's steps on the floor rushes.

'Eithne?' Rhiann whispered, sensing the sorrow hanging heavy in the air.

Eithne started and raised her face, eyes wide and unseeing with terror. 'Mother of All!' she whimpered. 'Don't hurt me, mistress, with your spirit breath!' She buried her head in her arms, quaking. 'Don't hurt me, please!'

'Eithne,' Rhiann said again, and reached out to touch the maid's thin, shaking shoulder. She could feel the delicate bones beneath her hand, pushing through the taut skin. 'I am alive, I am really here.'

Eithne curled herself into a tighter ball, though she did raise her dirty, tear-streaked face. 'Lady?' she whispered. 'Lady?'

Swallowing, Rhiann brushed Eithne's black hair from her flushed cheeks. 'See here,' she said, as if gentling a foal. 'I am here. Feel me.'

One tiny, work-roughened hand, the nails crusted with dirt, crept up to cover Rhiann's own. There was a moment of utter stillness, and then Eithne flung herself from the chair into Rhiann's arms, collapsing in a flood of choked sobs that rocked them both on their heels.

'Hush now,' Rhiann murmured, rubbing between the girl's shoulder-blades. Yet of course this outpouring drew the tears Rhiann had successfully squashed in her chest up to cloud her throat, and she swallowed even harder, her eyes stinging. She could feel the head-to-toe trembling of the small, seemingly fragile body in her arms, though she knew also of the wiry strength in Eithne that could grind grain for hours, and haul water from the well.

'Now,' Rhiann choked out, smiling through her tears, 'sit right there, and let me make this a place of the living once more.'

Shivering with shock, Eithne wiped her face on her sleeve and sank back into the chair, watching Rhiann light the fire and tie up the hanging. Then Rhiann sat on the oak hearth-bench and coaxed the same story from the maid that Didius had given.

'I thought of going back to my mother's,' Eithne whispered now. 'Even though Rori offered to look after me . . . but . . . but I wasn't ready to go anywhere, not with all your things here, lady, just as you left them.'

And indeed, the digging sticks against the wall still had earth clinging to them, and on a stool by the loom was a crumple of linen Rhiann had been embroidering on her last night here. Her healing bench was stacked with hastily sealed jars of macerating leaves, and covered trays of buds steeping in honey.

It was a wrenching thought, of Eithne sitting here alone amongst Rhiann and Caitlin's belongings. Just then Rhiann's eye fell on one side of the fire. Though Rhiann had taken her goddess figurines with her on her journey, the tiny, squat figure of the triple-faced Mother was still resting in her place on the hearth-stone, guarding the home. Yet her feet were nearly smothered in a congealing mess of dried milk and barley grains – Eithne's offerings, which looked like they had been flung there in desperate grief.

If this had been Eithne's reaction to the news, Rhiann did not know what might be waiting for her at her aunt's hut on the mountain.

After taking Eithne to be reunited with Caitlin, Rhiann quickly returned to the stables, feeding Liath some barley mash before saddling her again. She had put aside her long dress, and changed into her usual

26

riding outfit of buckskin trousers and tunic, her priestess herb-knife and pouch tied on her leather belt.

As she was strapping on her pack, Eremon came looking for her, ducking in from the bright sun to the shadows of the stall. Yet when Rhiann fumbled with the saddle straps he was at her side in three strides, and Rhiann briefly closed her eyes as his thumb brushed her cheek.

'You are tired,' Eremon murmured. 'Send a messenger instead, and go tomorrow.'

Rhiann shook her head. 'Rest can wait another day.' She tugged fiercely on one of the buckles. 'You know she will be desperate.'

Eremon sighed, and when Rhiann turned to face him, her hand on her knife sheath, the light spilling through the open door had deepened the lines of tension around his eyes.

Rhiann's heart jumped. 'What happened in the King's Hall?' she whispered, laying her hand over the tight skin as if her touch could smooth the lines away.

Eremon shrugged, staring at the stable wall behind her. 'Nothing that cannot wait for your return.'

Rhiann's impulse to discover what had disturbed him warred with her own haste. Yet her fear for Linnet was a keen, sharp edge under her breastbone, and she knew she must go. Her aunt loved her like a mother, and would grieve like a mother.

On a sudden impulse, Rhiann leaned up and pressed her lips to Eremon's mouth, and after a moment of surprise his hands came around her face to hold her there. The feathery touch gave another flutter low between her legs, as she pulled away, breathless, lowering her eyes.

And as Eremon helped Rhiann to mount, and she nudged Liath out into the sun, somewhere below the tension of this day Rhiann felt the strange, cold fear again stir with the desire, each entangled in the other.

Chapter 4

The Epidii territory between mountain and sea was burgeoning into the full, fertile life of leaf-bud, with a mist of green leaves on the trees and new bracken unfurling across the hills. Yet Rhiann, who loved riding alone through her land, now barely noted its beauty. Instead her eyes were fixed on the distinct peaks of Linnet's mountain ridge to the north-west, her weight forward in the saddle to urge Liath on with her knees.

The wind off the far, white-capped mountains still cut, yet as Rhiann left the open valleys around Dunadd and entered the wooded glens below the hills, she was warmed by the pools of sun in the hollows, and the still, sheltered air. Here, drifts of hyacinths and pale yellow primroses carpeted the slopes beneath the mostly bare trees.

For once, though, Rhiann didn't draw the smells in: sun-warmed damp soil; dew on wet leaves. She couldn't spare her heart for any of this. Caitlin, Linnet's only blood child, had been lost as a baby, before returning by chance a year ago. After her loss, Linnet had raised Rhiann as her own. So if Linnet thought both her daughters had been taken by the sea . . . Rhiann leaned forward again, her thigh muscles burning, desperately urging Liath to greater speed.

Dercca, Linnet's maid, was nowhere to be seen when Rhiann cantered into the yard surrounding her aunt's turf-roofed hut, which was nestled in a sheltered glen halfway up the mountain. Rhiann slid to the ground, looping Liath's reins over the brushwood pen that held the four brindled goats. Then she hastened for the path leading to the sacred spring that Linnet tended.

Rhiann hurried between the tangled hazels on the path, brushing away the catkins that caught at her hair. Yet when she came in view of the still pool surrounded by the circle of pale, silvery birches, she jerked to a halt. For a moment Rhiann didn't see her aunt in the dappled shadows cast by the thin cover of leaves. Then a figure uncurled itself from a pile of deer-hides on the stone-built lip of the spring. It was a tall woman, as slim and elegant as the birch trees around her, with Rhiann's auburn hair and fine bones, long nose, and tip-tilted eyes.

Although Rhiann was breathing so hard she gulped air, and her muscles were cramped from riding, all this fell away when her eyes met Linnet's. The impulse came over her to run like a child and fling herself into Linnet's arms, as she had so many times when she was younger.

But something arrested her feet. Rhiann's aunt had not slept for some days, that was clear, and her skin was translucent, her fine features drawn. Her hair was unbound – tangled by wind and the nap of the deer-hide – and her eyes far away, as if her spirit had not quite returned from its journeys. Yet Rhiann did not see the deep lines of grief that she had so dreaded. Linnet had known they were not dead.

Wordlessly, Rhiann and Linnet stepped forward at the same time, and then Rhiann found herself wrapped in the circle of her aunt's arms, as Linnet pressed Rhiann's face fiercely against her breast. And as they held each other, the sun at last sank below the crooked rim of the mountainside, and they were plunged into cold shadow.

'I tried to watch over you after you left Dunadd,' Linnet finally said. 'Every day I spent time at the pool, and sometimes I was rewarded with a seeing: you walking on the walls of a great dun; stepping on to a boat. Then . . . nothing . . .' She paused, and her collarbone moved against Rhiann's cheek. 'Until a messenger came with Gelert's vision.'

Rhiann stirred with renewed pain, but Linnet held her still. 'I would not leave the pool then, night or day, and begged the Mother to give me some news of you, any news. Yet most of the visions made little sense.'

Rhiann choked out, 'How did you know we lived?'

Linnet's breast rose and fell, with a smile or a sigh, Rhiann could not tell. 'There are other ways of seeing, daughter, between those who love each other.' She drew back to cup Rhiann's face with cold hands. 'I knew, as surely as my body lay here, that you and Caitlin were safe. Gelert's words came not from the Source; they were wrapped in the blackness that he himself carries. I would know, *I would know*, the moment you left Thisworld.' For a moment she gripped Rhiann's cheeks, her eyes burning fever-bright even in the shadows. The evening wind stirred the wisps of hair about her face as she gave Rhiann the Sisters' kiss on her spirit-eye, in the middle of her forehead, before releasing her.

Turning to the spring, Linnet swept up a handful of dried, crushed petals from beside the creased deer-hide, and scattered these over the dark water. 'All my thanks to you, Lady,' she said simply. Turning back to Rhiann, she took her hand, and they left the clearing together.

★

Rhiann sighed and placed her willow platter on Linnet's hearth-stone, crossing her legs on the floor cushion. Her belly was warmed with fragrant lamb stew and Linnet's goat's cheese, and she had washed and changed into a clean robe from her pack. Now she drew up her knees, wrapping Linnet's thick wool shawl around her so she was swaddled like a baby.

She wasn't sleepy, though. In between bites and swallows she had been telling her aunt all that had befallen them. The story was so long and involved that, by the end, the old maid Dercca was slumped against the loom by the wall, snoring softly, the grinding quern tilted between her knees.

At this point, however, Rhiann was grateful for Dercca's sleep, for the events on the Sacred Isle were for priestess ears only.

Glancing at Linnet now, Rhiann saw the glitter of tears on one firelit cheek, as her aunt listened with her head half-turned away, staring into the leaping flames from her place in her rush chair. Only Linnet could grasp how much the welcome of Nerida, the eldest priestess, had meant to Rhiann, ending an exile that had festered as a wound in Rhiann's soul for three long years.

'What I said to them,' Rhiann whispered, watching the birch logs snap and settle in the fire, 'I thought I could never go back. I blamed them . . .'

Linnet reached for the iron poker and nudged an errant branch back into the hearth. 'I knew they would understand, child. They were just waiting for you to return of your own accord.'

Rhiann nodded, unable to speak, and drew the fringe of the shawl through her fingers.

'And did you go to the village, daughter?' Linnet asked, in a carefully gentle voice. *To the beach. Where the raiders came.*

'Yes.' Rhiann cleared her throat, glanced up at her aunt. 'I had to. But Eremon was there, and that made it easier.'

Instantly, the shadow of Linnet's pain cleared, and her eyebrows arched. 'Eremon?'

His name hung there, all the unsaid questions behind it drawing a wan smile to Rhiann's face. However, what happened in the stone circle was too new to share with anyone, and instead she told Linnet about Eremon as the King Stag, and his sacred tattoos.

At that, the lines of strain remaining around Linnet's eyes smoothed out in the firelight. Rhiann's aunt was close to forty, but the fine bones of their family held the flesh well, and the life of a priestess – in Linnet's case, a life of quiet duty separate from the cares of others – lent her face an ageless tranquility. Rhiann, cradling her cheeks in her hands, severely doubted she would ever look so serene. She was the Ban Cré, the Mother of the Land. Her role was not to retreat into a solitary life on the mountain, but to embody the Goddess for her tribe and live among them.

And now I can serve them truly again. Suddenly Rhiann's eye fell on Linnet's doorway and the silver gleam of moonlight creeping under it, fading into the glow of the lamps. The joy that had infused her as she stood outside Dunadd's gates fountained up again, tinged with excitement. If her full connection to the Goddess had returned, then she should be able to see visions in the sacred pool again. She would no longer be blind!

'Aunt? Does the Goddess swim now in the sacred water?' At this time of year, the moon often passed directly over the spring.

Linnet sat up, the blanket in which she had wrapped herself falling from her shoulders. 'Yes, child – do you wish to speak with our Lady? I will give you what you need.' She rose, taking a rush lamp and making her way to the workbench that stood against the curved wall, between the two box beds. The rafters were so laden with dried herbs, roots and salted joints of meat that she had to duck to reach the shelves. 'I have the *saor* here.'

'No,' Rhiann said quickly, rising from her cushion, letting the shawl drop away. 'No *saor*.' She wanted to do this without the aid of the herbs that freed spirit from body. She used to be able to see unaided, when she was pure, before the raid. Now that she had returned to the fold of the Sisters, she should be able to do it again.

Her whole body ached with yearning at the memory of the light she used to sense, filling her body. Surely she would feel it again . . .

Out in the moist, silvered night, Rhiann tried to step softly and slowly. Yet as soon as the hazel trees closed around her she couldn't restrain herself – for the first time since the stone circle she was alone, and at one of the Mother's most sacred gateways. Rhiann's feet quickened, and she began to run.

Leaves trailed against her cheeks, and the cool air misted her breath, scented with loam and wet rock. Ahead, a soft light beckoned, and when she broke into the clearing, her chest heaving, it was as if she had fallen into a pool of molten silver, as moonlight spilled through the trees. The clearing held an unnatural stillness, too, as if the land was holding its breath, as if all the night sounds of wind and the stirring of the creatures had been suspended.

With fumbling fingers, Rhiann unrolled the deer-hide on the lip of the spring, setting out the flowers and bronze finger-ring Linnet had given her. Then she dug in her pack, her fingers closing on her goddess figurines, wrapped in their soft linen bag. One by one she reverently lined them up on the spring: Andraste, war goddess, with her spear and shield; Flidhais of the woods; Rhiannon the Great Mother on her white mare; and Ceridwen with her cauldron, bringer of life and death.

Finally, Rhiann knelt on the lip and opened the tiny vial of scented oil. With trembling hands she anointed her spirit-eye.

Calm down! she told herself, almost laughing aloud. Then she realized she ought to try to be serious, and so she folded her hands together. The most important part of freeing the sight was the priestess breathing, which centred mind and body into one flowing whole. It certainly would not be summoned by a pounding heart and heaving chest. So Rhiann closed her eyes and bit her lip in concentration, striving to subdue her pulse.

First, she took charge of her breath: one slow inhalation down to her feet, then up out of the crown of her head. Gradually, the breathing took up a rhythm of its own, and that in turn quietened the riot of her blood, until Rhiann began to feel the edges of herself merging more naturally with the steady glow of the moon on her skin.

When Rhiann was calm enough, she sprinkled the flowers on the water, murmuring her invocation to the spirit of the spring, and sent the ring spinning into the darkness of the pool. Then she sat for a moment longer, letting the slight undercurrent take the flowers out to the pool's edges, and using her breathing to expand the silver cord that ran through her body, anchoring spirit to flesh.

With each breath, so her spirit cord swelled and brightened, until it seemed behind her closed eyes that she was a fluid stream of moonlight, like a cup, overflowing . . . That was how she'd always felt, when the Goddess came to her as a child. As she remembered this, warm relief began to course through her veins alongside the silver light.

'Great Mother,' she murmured. 'Moon on the Water, Lady of the Three Faces, your daughter comes to you in love. If it be Your will, may Your light this night be revealed to me, illuminating what is darkness. By Your grace, so shall it be.'

Now Rhiann fixed in her mind what she most needed to see:

. . . *the sun glancing off bright Roman helmets; the swirl of red cloaks; the ranks of painted Roman shields* . . .

. . . and her breath stilled as she leaned out over the pool, her eyes closed, muttering the prayers under her breath . . .

. . . *the eagle standards held aloft in rows; the blast of foreign trumpets; the harsh cries of men* . . .

. . . and somewhere inside, with the softness of a sigh, she opened her soul and surrendered all will so that she could see at last; really see . . .

She hadn't even opened her eyes when it hit.

A bright flood of images erupted from inside her: *a man running at her with his sword raised, his black hair dripping seawater into dark, burning eyes. She felt herself rear back, stifling a cry, and turned desperately to run away. Yet she had just reached the hillside when a bruising hand grabbed her ankle and pulled her down . . . and then there were three of them, their eyes feverish with lust . . . and a greasy beard suffocating her, and a crushing weight across her chest, and callused hands closing around her neck, and the pain . . . the pain . . .*

She screamed, as she had not been able to do then, and screamed again, and suddenly something took hold of her shoulders and Rhiann arched and flung herself backwards. The impact of her body jarring the ground shocked her eyes open, and abruptly the harsh daylight of that awful day was gone.

It was night again, and Rhiann was sprawled in the middle of the birch clearing, wet grass soaking through her dress. Above her, Linnet hovered on her knees, trying desperately to take Rhiann in her arms.

'I am sorry, child . . . I am sorry but I heard you scream and I ran, and you wouldn't answer . . .' Linnet's face swam over Rhiann in a confused blur of silver and shadow stripes, as Rhiann, still fighting the terror, clawed her hands away. Something still felt tight around her neck; she gagged and coughed and fought for breath.

'I had to shake you to bring you back,' Linnet whispered. 'I had to. You were strangling yourself.'

Suddenly Rhiann became aware of the bruised ache around her throat, and she coughed again, blinking her eyes to clear her sight. Linnet's arms closed again, seeking to rock her. 'You were speaking what you saw . . . what you felt . . .' Linnet's voice broke, and hot tears fell on Rhiann's cheeks. 'Oh, Mother . . . my child . . .'

Dazed, Rhiann fought her way free of the enveloping folds of Linnet's priestess cloak. Blood roared in her ears, and she had to fight to draw in enough breath. Then her eye fell on the stones of the pool, the scent of the blooms sweet in her nose, and she suddenly realized what had happened — and what had not.

'*No.*' Rhiann staggered to her feet, glancing wildly around the clearing, which now echoed with the evil memories she had conjured, violating the sacred space. The moon's grinning face mocked her from above. 'No,' she whispered in anguish, and then she sank slowly to her knees. It had not worked. There had been no Goddess, only her own poisoned mind. *I cannot bear it.*

'Rhiann.' Linnet's hand was gripping her shoulder. 'It was a memory of the raid, that is all. It cannot hurt you now, my child. I will hold you through it as I did before—'

'It's not that,' Rhiann choked out. 'I thought in the circle that She had forgiven me, that I was Hers again.' Rhiann's shoulders shook, and she curled tighter around her heart. 'All this time . . . since those men . . . She has turned her back on me and I cannot feel Her any more!'

Linnet was grasping Rhiann as if she could press her within her own body. 'Child, you are a Goddess daughter, that can never change.'

'No!' Rhiann wrenched herself back and fell on her haunches, turning her face away with shame. 'I thought . . . in the Stones . . . it was *over.*'

She was barely conscious of Linnet's touch on her back. 'I don't understand.' Linnet's voice trembled. 'I have stood by you at the rites. You hold the Mother's energy and let it flow for the people. I felt it touch them.'

'For the people, *for the people,*' Rhiann whispered harshly. 'She comes to speak to *them*, to touch and love *them*, but not to me alone, when I call Her. Never *me.*'

Once, she could feel the Goddess like a light spilling into her from above. Once, she could hear Her like a real voice in her mind. Once she was sent visions of what was, and would be – the brightest, the best among the Sisters. But no more. The thread of light that joined her to earth and heavens was severed, and had not been mended at all. How could she have thought any different?

'It's not over,' Rhiann found herself murmuring brokenly. 'Because of what I did. It has not been repaid.'

'Did, daughter?' Linnet was breathing in her ear. 'Of what do you speak?'

Rhiann's whole body was trembling, her teeth chattering in shock as she bowed her head. 'I . . . I was so proud of my gifts, my powers . . . and . . . I should have seen the raiders coming, and found a way to stop it happening.' Her words were a whisper on the night air. 'But I did not . . . and they . . . they died . . . and because I failed them the Goddess turned Her face from me.'

Rhiann's words were swallowed by the silence that fell, yet she would not look up, for her breast burned with shame. Shame for how she had failed her foster-family; shame that she had never yet shared . . . least of all with Linnet, who thought her so bright, so strong.

But then Linnet's hands were cradling Rhiann's bent head, stroking her hair, her shoulders, firm and gentle at the same time. 'Child of my heart, their deaths could never be laid at your door; you never failed anyone.'

At those words, Rhiann gave a shudder in Linnet's arms. 'Then why am I exiled from Her grace? I am punished!'

'No.' Linnet struggled to raise Rhiann's face, to reach through her pain, brushing her cold tears away. 'It is the grief of the raid that blocks you, child, the pain of what those animals did. You will heal and regain what you have lost.'

Slowly, Rhiann shook her head, staring out at the dark, rustling trees over Linnet's shoulder. 'I must find Her again, and prove myself worthy. I thought . . . I thought surrendering to Eremon's love was the key, but it is not . . . my love is not enough.' Rhiann's mouth spasmed with despair, and Linnet pressed desperate lips to her forehead.

'The Goddess is love, not judgement,' Linnet whispered. 'It is pain that shrouds you, that is all.'

'That is not all, it cannot be all.' With aching muscles, Rhiann drew herself to her feet, swaying a little, wiping her wet cheeks with harsh fingers. 'There is more I must do. To atone.'

Linnet slowly rose. The chill of the night air was now creeping beneath the folds of Rhiann's wool dress, and the pool was wreathed in mist. She sensed Linnet's distress reaching out to her across the clearing, yet her aunt made no move forward.

After a long moment of silence Linnet's shoulders slumped, her head bowing, and the energy cradling Rhiann suddenly seemed to dim. In the cold space it left she shivered, wrapping her arms around herself. Her heart was cloven, and desperately she realized she must force the edges back together now. For if they spilled open, all the pain of all the years would bleed out, and there would be nothing left. She must gain control . . .

Her breath rattling in her chest, Rhiann turned and looked out at the dark woods, seeking to contain the despair, the disappointment, the *abandonment* in a shell of numbness. That had worked before, and enabled her to keep going. She had to cling to her mind, to protect her heart.

Abruptly, she was arrested by a thought from the deep recesses of her mind. *I must find a way to earn Her favour . . . but I have not gone far enough . . . loving Eremon was not enough . . .*

In desperation Rhiann grasped at the thought, and hung on. As the failure was great, so the task she had to fulfil must be greater still. And it had been given to her long ago; she'd known all along how important it was. She did not realize she had spoken aloud until Linnet took a step closer. 'A task, child? What task?'

Rhiann spun to face her, strength flowing back into her limbs. 'My vision, aunt, my dream! Over the years it has changed, but it has been there since I was a child, calling me.'

'You never told me of a dream.' Linnet's face was in shadow, the moonlight a sheen on her hair.

'I thought you would think me proud – that, or mad!' Rhiann's hand floated towards Linnet, then clenched by her side, the words rushing out like an undammed stream. 'I will tell you. I am in a valley of light, and all the people of Alba are around me. Eagles cry from the mountains above, bringing danger – they are the Romans, you see. Yet I stand in the valley, cupping the cauldron of the goddess Ceridwen, gathering the Source so that it will drive back the eagles, the shadows, protecting my land and people.'

Rhiann paused for a moment, savouring the feeling of the Source that resounded through her dream, the light that ran through all things and connected all worlds. In life she had to struggle to feel it, but in that dream it poured from her hands. 'By my side a man stands with a great sword; the protector to vanquish the eagles – I have seen his face now and know he is Eremon. And we have been charged by Her to bring the Source into balance and guard it for all the people – by ridding Alba of the Romans.'

Linnet stepped closer, taking hold of Rhiann's arms above the elbow. 'You should have told me.'

Rhiann swallowed. 'I would not allow myself to believe it for so long, but then Declan was sent a vision about Eremon, and it was the same, and that is why I gave Eremon my support for the alliance. Before . . . before I gave him my heart.'

Linnet's sigh clouded the chill air, and Rhiann clutched at her hand. 'This is what is drawing me, aunt, don't you see? *This* is the message: I must fulfil that task first, out of love and duty for the people and my land. And once I have proven myself worthy, then I know I will also find my true self once more. I *know* it is the path back to Her.'

The words swelled with a desperate longing. Disentangling her grip, Linnet gently stroked the side of Rhiann's face with her hand. The night wind soughed through the trees, blowing shadows across her features, making them unreadable. 'Much of your path is dark before me, as it has always been, yet this dream does hold some sense of truth.'

Rhiann breathed a harsh sigh of relief. 'You see?' She wiped her eyes and cheeks with both palms, raking back the hair that had blown free from its braids. 'It is the answer, aunt, it is what I must do. The pain came to remind me, to make my path even clearer . . . that's what it was.'

Now Linnet cupped both of Rhiann's cheeks, staring down at her, unmoving. Since the day Rhiann told Linnet the truth of the raid, they had often read each other's thoughts. Yet now it was as if Linnet's mind was shuttered. There was only the warmth of her hands, a steady glow on Rhiann's skin.

'Come.' Linnet's voice was tinged with a strange distance. 'The night grows late and chill, and you need your strength. Let me brew you a gentle sleeping draught, to keep your dark memories at bay.'

Long after moonset, Linnet remained awake, watching Rhiann in her bed by the faint glow of the coals.

Nothing moved in that darkened room but the shadows and her hand, softly stroking Rhiann's forehead to soothe her down into sleep. In the firelight, Rhiann's pale skin gleamed, her hair a dark spill over the linen pillow. Her eyes were closed, and one hand was tucked up under her chin, in the same way she had slept as a baby.

Dercca's snores floated from behind the other wicker screen, but

Linnet ignored them and listened closer to Rhiann's breathing. She would keep vigil for her daughter until Rhiann was truly asleep.

Outside, the wind had risen, scraping the branches of the young oak tree in the yard against the mud walls. But inside all was still and warm, and at last Rhiann's breathing changed, sliding into the slower cadence of deep, healing sleep. As it did, Linnet's hand stilled.

After a moment she rose, stirring up the coals to flame before sinking onto her hearth-bench. And only there, alone, did she allow her shoulders at last to bow, as she buried her face in her hands. A sob choked her throat, but she would not give in to it. For that was the crown of her burden. Rhiann could not know that Linnet carried it, or how heavy it had grown. So heavy, so painful that she felt it might tear her heart apart.

Linnet clutched at the moonstone pendant around her neck, fingering the smooth stone as she repeated the brutal words that after all these years her heart must accept: *I cannot give her the understanding; she must find it herself. The path must be walked alone or the knowledge has no value.*

So many times she had clung to these words, given to her by the Goddess on the day of Rhiann's birth, when Linnet glimpsed in vision the great deeds – and griefs – of Rhiann's life. She had understood then that her role was to prepare Rhiann and train her; to nurture her into a strong, accomplished woman who could face everything to come.

Yet the crushing part was that Linnet could not intervene in any significant way, because Rhiann would only then learn about Linnet's path and Linnet's choices, not her own, nor would she develop any strength of will. And so, although it had tried her hard, Linnet had for years bitten her tongue and held her counsel.

At first it had been simple. It was easy to let a three-year-old thrust her hand into a patch of nettles because she must feel how they stung, and respect them in future. It was not easy to behold a woman so despairing that she would cut herself off from her own heart, and say she must find her own way.

Linnet had felt the crushing loss of Caitlin, her own child, the guilt of that, and the grief of losing a sister. And when she saw Rhiann struggling with such pain, she burned with the need to soothe it all away. Yet Linnet had seen more than pain at Rhiann's birth; she had caught a glimpse, a bare glimpse, of Rhiann's fate.

A fate to change the destiny of a whole land.

And what did such a fate ask of someone? How could anyone counsel such a soul? What Linnet thought of as right in one moment may not be right in the greater pattern of Rhiann's life, which only the Mother could see.

A single tear squeezed out from one tightly closed eye, and Linnet let herself feel its long, slow slide down her cheek. Then she glanced over at the bed; at Rhiann's outflung hand, a pale flower against the dark fur cover. *All I can do is love her,* she thought, getting up, stiff-kneed. *If I tell her the Mother loves her, and that is all that matters, then that is all I must give, too.*

People had many illusions about priestesses, that embodying the Goddess must be simple and beautiful. And it was, sometimes. But not always. Linnet lived on this mountain, distant from the cares of the tribe, and made offerings at the gateway and kept the Source in balance as best she could. And sometimes it was lonely, and often difficult, for all the things she must see but not speak. Rhiann lived among the people, tending their daily hurts and giving her body as the Mother's vessel. Yet who could say which was easier?

Wiping her eyes, Linnet gently tucked Rhiann's errant hand beneath the cover, smoothing the fur up to her chin. For this brief time, at least, she wore only the face of the Mother, warding the hours of darkness for her child.

Chapter 5

Braced on the walkway atop Dunadd's upper palisade, Eremon waited only long enough to see Rhiann safely away to Linnet's before tackling his next challenge – the chief druid.

When Liath's coat was no more than a pale glimmer against the green hills, Eremon finally let his eyes drop. Below him, the bustling village sprawled around the crag's feet in the afternoon sunshine, cloaked in the thick haze of cookfires that curled lazily above the thatch roofs.

Sounds floated up in a murmuring cloud: children's cries and playful screams; the clink of smith's hammers; and the thunk of axes on wood. Eremon even fancied he could sense relief in the air, floating with the homely smells of smoke, animal dung and baking bread. The mourning feast would go ahead as a celebration when Rhiann returned tomorrow night.

Peering into the long afternoon shadows, he studied each layer of Dunadd's defences in turn. First, the main timber palisade encircling the village, guarded by the great gatetower. Then, the palisade on which he stood, on a natural rock tier of the crag.

The village gate was manned by a brace of warriors, the sun gleaming on their bristling spear-tips. Others strode the length of the palisades, their bright-painted shields hung for decoration on the pointed stakes. Eremon turned his face to the north. More spears glittered in a rain of iron above the river meadow, for already Finan had resumed the training of the warband. In the dusky light some warriors were wheeling on horseback, or practised with sword, while others hefted spear or bow for target practice.

A heavy thudding interrupted Eremon's thoughts, as Conaire's fair head appeared at the bottom of the palisade stairs. Taking them three at a time, Eremon's foster-brother sprang to his full height on the top planks. 'Caitlin is abed and feeling well again,' he announced, then stopped as his gaze took in Eremon's stance. 'You sport a face like thunder, brother. Is there a problem with the men? Have they grown soft while we were away?'

'Nothing a few days of our drilling won't fix.' Eremon gripped the edge of the palisade with white knuckles. 'It's not that. My guts are gnawing on something else, very unpleasant, and I'm just getting ready to fix the pain.'

At Conaire's raised eyebrow, Eremon flung out his hand angrily. 'Look! So many men, so many guards, so many gates. And it is us, from Erin, who have given the Epidii such strength; strength for more than a petty cattle raid, strength to resist the Romans! Gathering and training such a large warband was our idea. The tactics are our idea. The guards and the signal beacons – our idea.'

'*Your* idea,' Conaire interrupted quietly, folding his arms.

'My idea, then,' Eremon growled. '*And* the border patrols, *and* the scout network – and after all we've done, the attempt on our lives came not just from Maelchon, but from the Epidii!'

Conaire's brows rose higher. 'This you did not tell me.' Then the confusion on his face cleared into realization. 'You mean the druid.'

'Oh, yes,' Eremon answered bitterly, and both their heads turned in the direction of the druid shrine on the crag's crest. A wreath of smoke rose above it, merging with the high, white clouds drifting in from the sea. 'He watched us leave Calgacus's dun, he announced our deaths – he had a hand in it, I would swear it on my father's honour.'

At that, Conaire's mild, boyish features hardened, the scar at the edge of one eye flushing purple with blood. Caitlin and his unborn child had been on the boat that sank, after all. He flexed his broad shoulders, one hand coming to rest unconsciously on the sword at his waist. 'I will come with you.'

For a moment Eremon glanced back at his brother. In the low sun, the hair on Conaire's neck and arms was bristling with hostility, like a boar's crest. But this was something begun with the druid long ago, and it was Eremon's fight to pursue.

'No.' Eremon gripped Conaire's forearm to soften the word. 'Alone, he offered me this place in the tribe. And alone I will confront him.'

He didn't say that he wanted Gelert's wrath to fall on him alone. Better that he keep his men out of this. If there was one thing he had learned in Alba, it was to be wary of druids and their devious ways.

Eremon did not need to search for Gelert, for the old man was in the shrine conducting a sacrifice. Waiting for the attending druids to leave, Eremon edged around the outside of the pillars to where the shrine fell away directly from the western cliff to the plain below. Beyond the marsh and shining thread of river, the sea gleamed its last for the day.

When Eremon heard the murmur of voices and footfalls, he quickly ducked around to the side and entered between the pillars. Gelert was still standing before the bloody altar stone, the offering smoke curling to the sky.

The setting sun filtered through the wings of Gelert's unbleached robe, and ignited the expanse of marsh beyond to a glowing crimson. This spectacle, and the dark blood on the stone altar, the tainted smoke, and leering ring of oaken gods at the base of each pillar would have awed and intimidated anyone else. But Eremon was too angry to be awed, and he knew that of any druid he had met, Gelert was driven more by the lust for earthly power than doing the will of the gods.

'This was an offering of gratitude for our safe return, I presume?'

At the sound of Eremon's voice, Gelert swung around, his arms dropping to his sides. His face was in shadow behind a ragged curtain of pale hair, but his odd, golden eyes were unblinking and cold. 'Your manners leave something to be desired as usual, prince,' the druid replied, and with a flick of his fingers dismissed the last two novices. The white-clad youths dragged the calf's body to one side, took the sacred knife from Gelert for purification, then melted away.

Eremon and Gelert waited in silence as the boys' footsteps faded, facing each other across the roofless centre of the shrine. The sun gleamed on the torc set around each idol's neck, below oaken faces smeared with ochre and blood.

As soon as the novices were gone, Eremon's simmering anger could no longer be contained, and he strode forward. 'I know you planned our deaths.'

At Eremon's approach Gelert glided around the other side of the altar, folding his hands in his sleeves. The fading tattoos across his cheeks were drawn into grotesque lines by the deepening seams of age, and his lids drooped over those yellow and black pits of eyes. 'You rave, prince.' Gelert's white brows arched high with apparent surprise. 'I know nothing of what you speak.'

Breathing deeply, Eremon fingered the jewels on his sword hilt. 'Do not play innocent with me, druid. You had a hand in that shipwreck.' His voice was not steady, for he was finding it harder to keep his emotions in check than he'd expected. For the first time in weeks, snatches of memory kept darting through his mind: the fear in Rhiann's face when they knew the boat would sink, the moment that froze his blood more than the icy water – when he flailed in the pounding surf, and Rhiann's hand slipped from his grip.

Gelert was smiling thinly, as if he could read Eremon's thoughts, his face creasing like a scrap of old parchment. Then he raised one bony shoulder. 'I am of course innocent of this outrageous charge.' Abruptly the smile faded, the bloodless lips pursed. 'Need I warn you what a serious offence it is to accuse a druid falsely, prince? With so much on your mind, do you wish to risk the repercussions? A trial that will split the tribe, and lose you the whisper of support that you do enjoy?' He paused. 'You and your . . . *wife.*'

There it was, the special tone Gelert reserved for any mention of Rhiann, a mixture of fury and bitterness, but also, more alarmingly, a zeal that bordered on madness, a need to destroy. Rhiann had told Eremon how Gelert was scorned by her mother, and how his hatred of all women had been focused on her. But for the first time Eremon heard it clearly, in that one word.

Eremon didn't realize he'd stepped around the altar and drawn his sword until the tip reared between them, flashing brightly. 'Do not even *try* to play that game with me!' he found himself hissing. 'This is between you and me, as it always was.'

Gelert snorted, and the grey wisps of his beard stirred, stained brown around his mouth. 'You flatter yourself, prince. Why would I be concerned about a beast like yourself? You have your uses, of course—'

'Your concern with me is exactly the point.'

Faintly, Gelert's lip curled, yet his face drew back imperceptibly from the sword edge. 'I had more important concerns long before you came along – that was the only reason I supported you in the first place.'

Eremon barked a laugh. 'What you wanted, and thought you'd found, was a dim brute with war on his mind, a man you could prod and goad to do your bidding, a man through whom you could rule! You don't keep your concerns any more to the spirit world than I do. You want earthly power, want it so bad it twists in your gut and curdles your blood!'

The only movement in Gelert's face was the slow blink of his cold, yellow eyes, but his breath rattled suddenly in his chest, and his ribs fluttered. Too many times, Eremon had seen the moment when his own death leaped into someone's eyes, and he saw it now, recognized the wild fury that could strike out.

In answer, Eremon tilted the sword until it wavered only a breath from Gelert's sharp, red-veined nose. 'I know I cannot lay hands on you and live, that I will be thrice-cursed and put to death for a traitor, but I tell you now, *druid,*' he spat the word, 'if you harm my wife in any way, I will stab this sword through your rotten guts, and die gladly in your blood. Be careful what schemes you weave, for no afterlife punishment will ever stop me seeking revenge for her.'

Eremon sheathed the sword, and noted with satisfaction the slight flinch of Gelert's cheek at the grate of iron. Then he strode to the shrine's entrance, and turned. 'By the way, a majority of your council members have already agreed to make my marriage binding, to the highest grade.' Eremon smiled. 'So there is no way to unseat me now, druid, no way to take from me what you yourself delivered into my hands. Let that thought be your bedfellow at night.'

Gelert's voice stopped him at the edge of the pillars, each word dripping with suppressed fury. 'Know that you risk banishment for drawing your blade in this shrine. And the punishment for threatening a druid can be death.'

Eremon did not deign to turn. 'See how the people heed your words, old man, now that you have shown your much-vaunted powers of "sight" to be so fallible. It is the Romans your people truly fear, and it is I who hold the strength of the swords that defend them.'

There was only silence behind him as Eremon came out into the light, and when he broke from the dark circle and the sun hit him, his breath gusted from him with relief, and he brushed it all away with a shake of his shoulders.

The following day Linnet was silent at breakfast, but she gently touched Rhiann's cheek as she brought her nettle tea in bed, and Rhiann felt her steady compassion as a warmth reaching around her heart.

'I will be here for you,' Linnet said, as Rhiann mounted Liath. 'Come whenever you need to.'

A sheet of heavy drizzle blew in from the sea as Rhiann rode home, veiling the green of the trees and the bright flowers, turning the tracks to mud. Yet though her fleece hood was drawn up, Rhiann rode straight and tall in her saddle, with the water trickling down her cheeks. She almost welcomed the fresh coldness of the air, the brisk wind, for she had woken that day with the same fragile resolve that had taken her into sleep the night before.

The nettle tea had not masked the taste of bitter failure on Rhiann's tongue, but she had found something last night, a shaky sense of purpose, growing clearer all the time. And she had come to some new thought, too, as she rode along.

She would follow the dream and fulfil her duty, yet not allow herself to freeze into numbness, as she once had. She would not hide from the pain or deny the ache, because she had opened her heart now and would not close it down. Yet she would not let it conquer her, either. There was a path through all of this; she just had to find it, no matter how it twisted and turned.

She stopped only once on her way home, to make an offering of mead in the stone circle at the end of the ancestor valley, to Dunadd's north. There, a strong river of the Source ran close beneath the earth, and the Old Ones had marked it with a line of tomb mounds and standing stones.

Kneeling on the peat among the stones, Rhiann did not weep, but held the pain still in her chest as she would cradle a child. She prayed then to her ancestors, the Sisters who had channelled the Source for the Old Ones, for strength, wisdom and compassion, and that one day she would be accounted as an equal among them again.

She entered Dunadd more slowly than she had left it the day before, pausing to shake the rain from her cloak beneath the eaves of the King's Hall.

Inside, she raised her head in surprise when she saw Eremon on a stool by the long hearth, playing *fidchell* with Conaire, his wolfhound Cù stretched at their feet. The heavy drizzle was veiling the river and marsh, turning the training ground into a slippery mudpit, and the warriors on it into clay-cloaked wraiths. Yet only weighty matters would have kept Eremon and Conaire here alone, with no one but a few servants tending the fire.

Rhiann slipped off her muddy boots, laid them on the hearth-stone, and tip-toed over to Eremon. With a glance over his shoulder, she saw immediately by the dire position of his pieces that he hadn't been concentrating very hard.

Conaire glanced up. 'Rhiann, I will gladly concede the game if you'll only put him out of his misery. Such an easy win is, quite frankly, an insult to my honour.' Yet Conaire's light tone could not hide the concern in his eyes, and he swiftly excused himself to go to Caitlin, leaping up the stairs to the sleeping gallery that ran around the inside of the roof.

'*A stór*,' Eremon murmured, by way of greeting.

Rhiann did not move around to face him then, for she also heard the sigh under his breath. Despite her own exhaustion, she drew Eremon's head back to rest on her chest. 'How is Caitlin?' she began, digging her fingers into the hard muscles of Eremon's shoulders.

Eremon sighed again, then gasped as she burrowed into a tender spot. 'Well, I think, although she has not risen from her bed this morning. Eithne is with her.'

Rhiann stored that fact away with a stab of unease, knowing that Caitlin, when she questioned her, would no doubt make light of it. Looking at Eremon upside down, Rhiann could see that the tautness in his face had not relaxed; in fact, he looked even grimmer than usual. He wore buckskin trousers like her own, muddy to the knee, and a scarlet tunic that for once made him look pale.

'You found something out about the Romans?' she ventured, digging her thumbs deep into the base of his skull.

'Ah . . . What? No.' Eremon shook his head, yet his pupils were wide and dark, and fixed blankly on the roof as if his thoughts were turned inward. 'I've just sent the messengers to our border patrols. I am still waiting for answers.'

Then that was not it. Forcing a smile, Rhiann flicked the end of his

44

nose. 'If our entire marriage consists of waiting to extract information from each other, I fear it's going to be somewhat boring.'

Eremon didn't smile back. Instead his hand reached up to clamp on her wrist, and gently he drew her around and pressed her into Conaire's place on the other stool. 'Rhiann. There is something I must tell you.'

She sank back, surprised at the hard tension that gripped Eremon's forearm. And when she looked him full in the face, in the brighter flare of the great hearth-fire, she realized it was not mere preoccupation that silenced him, but fury, barely held in check.

And so Eremon proceeded to tell her about his confrontation with Gelert. As he spoke, every one of Rhiann's muscles became so still she felt as if she were carven from ice.

'Rhiann,' Eremon prodded at last, when she still had not broken her silence. 'You do understand? I saw with my own eyes that what we thought is truth. He tried to kill us.' His voice was harsh, but she only stared at the shower of sparks, as a servant offloaded an armful of hazel logs onto the fire.

'Yet he denied it,' she whispered at last.

'Of course he did! That changes nothing!'

When Rhiann next spoke, each word sounded thick, as if forced through honey. 'It is a serious thing, to accuse a druid of such a deed, with no proof, and no way of getting any.'

Eremon sucked in his breath, drawing back from her. 'What are you talking about?' he burst out, ignoring the faces that turned their way. 'None of this means anything to me. He tried to kill us, and I should have dealt with it then and there.'

'No!' At last Rhiann's hand shot out, groping for his fingers and pressing them. 'Lay no hand on him, I beg you, Eremon. If you harm him, the council will kill you.'

Eremon only stared at her, furrowing his brow. 'They would never do that.'

'They will, they will do it. Despite how far you've come, you are still an outsider. He is the chief druid. Only a trial of the Brotherhood itself can lay charges – they deal with their own.' Her nails dug into his palm. 'Please, please say you'll listen to me. Please, Eremon.'

Eremon's cheeks flamed as bright as his tunic. 'Then what do you suggest?' he forced out.

Rhiann was silent for a long while, before she lowered her face. 'We are home now; we are all here in our strength. We must watch him from afar, yet stay away from his sight.'

'Rhiann!' Eremon's anger roughened his voice, and Cù slunk close to his legs. 'The man tried to kill us, and you're giving up? Gods, woman, but you cannot seriously leave it at that. We can bring our own charges. I can challenge him.'

'No!' In her exhaustion Rhiann's anger flared. 'This is my tribe and I know its customs! Until we have proof, until we can accuse Gelert properly, it is too dangerous to confront him. He could weaken you, Eremon, split the warriors, undermine you.'

With a violent curse Eremon thrust her hand away and rose, placing both hands on the nearest roof-post. The servants discreetly melted away to the shadows of the storage alcoves that lined the walls. In the silence that fell, the only sound was the simmering cauldron of broth suspended on its chains above the hearth, and the crackling of the burning wood beneath.

Eremon stared into the licking flames, and then around at the swords and shields on the walls. 'Proof,' came his ragged voice. 'Aye, I'd get my proof, *when he kills you.*'

A bright warmth flooded Rhiann's veins, as she suddenly realized what Eremon's rage really was, and her own. They were the same thing – stark fear for each other. And when Eremon spun to face her, his eyes weren't hard now but wide, a pool of fear so deep she felt she could drown in it.

'Then,' she said quietly, anger draining away, 'let us not force Gelert to take that road. If we corner him, he will have more reason to do it.'

Eremon gazed down at her uncertainly. 'I thought you were as angry as me. I thought you wished revenge.'

'I do not wish revenge,' she said simply, 'if it means the sacrifice of you.'

She knew he understood, unwillingly, for fear, anger and confusion were at war in his eyes. But he wasn't going to say so. With a twist of his mouth Eremon swept up his sword from the *fidchell* table and made for the entrance, snapping his fingers for Cù.

In the daylight of the doorway he paused, his shoulders a blaze of scarlet. 'I will bow to your knowledge in this, Rhiann, yet I think you make a mistake. If we leave him, we leave him to do great harm.'

Rhiann drew a breath. 'Nevertheless, it is my wish.'

She knew they took a risk, yet last night had shown her that there was only one path for her to follow to make everything right again, and she must stay on that path, however many obstacles arose before her. A rift in the Epidii now would only weaken both of them, and she knew Eremon did not want that. They had to take the chance that they could deal with the druid later, once they were in a stronger position.

Wearily, Rhiann dropped her forehead in her hands and closed her eyes.

There was another reason for suppressing all thoughts of revenge, of course; a reason above all others. For Eremon was Rhiann's only light, since she'd been wrong about the other, and though she might risk herself she would never risk him.

Gelert hated her more than Eremon – and she wanted to keep it that way.

Chapter 6

The new commander's quarters in the centre of the Roman encampment reeked of lime-wash and raw timber, making Samana's eyes smart. Drawing her silk veil over her nose, she leaned on the door-post and gazed out at the ranks of Roman tents, workshops and armouries, crowding every foot of ground between the high, square ramparts.

Agricola said there were only 10,000 men here now – a portion of the full force he could draw from the province – yet there were still more soldiers than Samana had ever seen in one place. Her blood quickened as she scanned the perfectly straight rows of tents, with the racks of weapons, armour and standards staked outside.

The camp was on a gravel plain by a river that eventually ran into the Forth inlet, and then to the sea. The plain had been stripped of all trees, though, except the few alders that still clung to the stream banks, for this place had long been a marshalling site for the Roman army, and Roman armies ate up wood. The huge earth ramparts were surrounded by a deep ditch outside, and topped by a row of sharp stakes, and the ground within was churned and boggy, the paths rutted by wooden carts, artillery machines, hoof-prints from horse, ox and mule, and the endless streams of iron-studded soldiers' boots.

This was like all other Roman camps Samana had seen, and yet was growing differently. Between the rows of leather tents and lean-to workshops, timber barracks were also sprouting, with white walls of wattle-and-daub, and red tiles marching across gaping roof-spaces. The Romans were putting down roots in Alba.

The river was choppy and grey this clouded morning, and recent rains had made the going hard for the three ox-carts that lumbered up from the landing place by the stream. Every now and then a wheel got stuck in the mud, and the stacked jars of wine and oil lurched at crazy angles. The curses of the carters floated up then, accompanied by whip-cracks and bellows.

Samana drew a deep breath of the salt-tanged air, but she wasn't revelling in the view, or the fresh wind, or the smell of coming rain. Instead, her eyes were narrowed on the carts, and what they carried. A Roman trading vessel must have come up the estuary from the sea, filled with the goods that Agricola deemed necessary for his officers in this cold, god-forsaken place at the end of Empire.

God-forsaken. She had heard Agricola call it that so many times that she no longer took offence, even though it was her country. After all, she would give up the grim mountains, moaning wind and endless rain in a heartbeat if she could gain access to a land that was warmer, gentler, and richer.

She sighed, counting her meagre blessings. Despite Agricola's status as governor of the entire province of Britannia, and commander of its army, the two rooms behind her were equipped with the same sparse furniture of all his war camps: folding map tables; stools; camp bed. Agricola was a true soldier, and would never possess anything that was not useful or functional, including herself.

Of course, she could have spent more time this past year at her own fort, the Dun of the Tree, which lay to the east, in the centre of Votadini lands. Yet despite ruling her tribe, she couldn't afford to stay away from Agricola for too long. She had spent so much personal time and effort on him, but her hold was not secure, she could sense it. Without her constant presence, perhaps he would forget her, and she would lose her chance to become a real queen. *Or worse.*

'Madam.'

Her eyes came back into focus. One of Agricola's slaves stood outside the door. Behind him was a man in the garb of a government messenger, dismounting from a stubby little mule and shakily wiping his face with a fine linen napkin. Samana had seen a few such messengers in her time with Agricola and knew the insignia on his armband. Yet this man's clothes were damp, his face pale, and he smelled of sea-wind and sickness both. Obviously, he'd come from the trading ship docked on the Forth, and then by punt up the tributary.

Samana went to move aside from the doorway, but when her eyes fell on the messenger's face, she checked herself. In training on the Sacred Isle she had learned to wield the sight, and though she was never quite so gifted as her Epidii cousin Rhiann – the Goddess curse her memory – still Samana retained some useful powers.

So it was that suddenly she knew this man was not from Britannia, to their south. His body was fat and sleek, his dark skin sheened with oil, black hair trim, nails on his soft, pudgy hands clipped. The wool of his tunic was so fine it was nearly silk, the laced boots new-cut, the red cloak new-dyed. This messenger came direct from Rome itself.

Rome, the city of legend, with its gold and marble and perfumes, its cheering crowds, bustling markets and marching armies. All of it the ultimate prize, for her. And here was an imperial servant, straight off the boat from Rome. From the emperor himself, it must be.

Instantly Samana straightened, pushing her lush breasts out against the fine linen of her dress, brushing the green silk scarf to her shoulders to show off the shining black of her hair, the curve of her neck. She knew well how to make her dark eyes flash, and she did it now as she bowed to the messenger and moved gracefully back into the room, for all the world as if she were a Roman wife welcoming a Roman official into her husband's house. 'Welcome,' she murmured throatily.

The messenger, pale and sick though he was, started, and his greedy gaze swept her from head to foot, lingering over the out-thrust curves of breast and hip. 'Lady,' he responded, as he swept past.

Agricola showed no softness before his men, and his main audience chamber reflected this. Apart from the map tables and high stools, there was only one dining couch – its cover stained – one low dining table and two rush chairs covered in worn rugs. The three-legged braziers and numerous oil lamps were a necessity in this cold, dark land, but any other signs of ease had been banished to the bedroom. As she so often was, Samana thought wryly.

Agricola was going through tedious lists of supplies and requisitions with his quartermaster, but he immediately dismissed the soldier and swivelled on his camp stool. His face, always carefully devoid of emotion, for once registered surprise at the messenger's appearance, and Samana knew that she had been right about the man's importance. Or rather, the importance of his master.

The newcomer bowed his head, then straightened, drawing from his belt a package wrapped tightly in oiled linen and leather. 'Gnaeus Julius Agricola, Governor of Britannia and commander of Our army in the province,' he intoned, holding out the tube of leather. 'Greetings from Our Divine Emperor,' he paused dramatically, 'Caesar Domitian, son of the deified Vespasian.'

At the words, Agricola leaped to his feet, and Samana took one step forward, her hand to her mouth.

'What did you say?' Agricola demanded, snatching the message. '*Domitian?*'

The messenger smiled smugly, pleased to play his role in the little drama. 'My sorrow indeed to convey to you the sudden death of Titus, eldest son of our glorious Father Vespasian. My joy to announce the succession of Domitian, his brother, second son of our glorious Father—'

'Yes, yes, I know their bloodlines!' Agricola snapped, running his hand through his clipped, grey hair. Yet Samana, so attuned to him, saw the sorrow in his eyes masked with another swift thought as he turned his back, hastily unwrapping the protective coverings and breaking open the wax seals.

With his usual economy, Agricola unrolled the parchment sheet and tilted it to the lamplight, scanning it for the pertinent details. Then, abruptly, he threw it down on the table. 'Great Jupiter!'

His voice betrayed shock, and dare Samana believe . . . excitement? Then Agricola seemed to come to himself, turning back to order the slave to take the messenger to the bath-house and bring him wine and food.

Samana waited, quivering silently, until the man was led away, and then rushed to Agricola's side, tugging on his arm. 'My lord, what is it? What has happened?'

Alone with her, Agricola let the fire flare in his face, and instantly it stripped away the many careworn years of outdoor marches that had been carved into his weathered skin. 'The Emperor Titus, may the gods honour him, is dead.' He paused, breathing hard. 'He was a worthy man, like his father, yet my grief has already been assuaged by his successor, Domitian. The new emperor allows me – nay, *orders* me! – to undertake the subjugation of all Alba. At last!'

Samana's breath stopped. She swallowed. 'Subjugation?'

Agricola's dark eyes burned in the lamp-light, yet seared straight through her and fastened instead on thoughts of his real, and only, love: conquest. 'Lady,' he said hoarsely, 'our time of waiting is almost over. For two years have I stayed at heel, like a cur who knows no better than the master. My hands tied, my feet bound, stuck at a frontier of my own making, while the tribes in the north taunted me. The Emperor even took my men *away* to defend the eastern frontier! But no more. *No more!*' He slammed one fist into his palm as he paced the room, energy rippling along every lean muscle beneath his simple tunic and soldier's cloak. She had never seen him betray emotion like this. 'Now I have the god-given leave to advance, to win all Alba for the Empire!'

Samana was still, though a similar fire was surging along every fibre of her body. Only her chest moved, rising and falling so fast she panted. For when Agricola won Alba, then would she have her reward, her secret dream: riches and lands beyond measure, and the power and title that came with it, a title no one had ever held – *Ard-Ban-ri*, high queen of Alba.

And revenge, too, on those who had thwarted her. That scornful bitch Rhiann, of course. And Eremon of Erin, who had used and then rejected her body, as well as the allegiance she offered.

She repressed the fiery, confused swirl of rage and desire that still surged at Eremon's memory, and instead curled her arms around

Agricola's restless neck and pressed her body against his. There was some time until the messenger returned for his evening of political talk, and Samana knew she must take every chance she had to bind Agricola to her. And he was so alive at this moment, reeking with a raw excitement that belied his forty years. She rubbed, catlike, against his chest, and – yes! – Agricola's eyes did seem to come back into the room, to rake over her as a starving man would eye his food and, despite the hour, she knew he would take her right here and now, perhaps against the dark wall, where no one could see. She licked her lips, leaning up on her toes to him . . .

There was a cough outside, and a shadow fell over them from the open door. 'Commander?'

Abruptly, Agricola pushed Samana away and strode to the door, leaving her panting and furious. Another messenger, Goddess curse him, and this one a rider, who had come far and fast, by the muddy, sodden look of him.

This time the message was verbal and hastily given. The Novantae, a tribe of remote south-west Alba, had rebelled. Forts had been attacked, and a fleet of hide boats had crossed the straits to raid Roman-held lands in Britannia.

In the past, such news would have brought a grim anger to Agricola's brow, a fury reined in and only betrayed by white lines around his mouth and eyes. But now, he almost laughed in the messenger's face. 'Rebellion, is it?' he crowed. 'I'll show them with my own sword how far they'll get with that! Now there is nowhere within Alba that they can hide from my vengeance, nowhere that is not laid open to the might of our new Emperor's army!'

The weary messenger, his helmet under his arm, was unaccustomed to such outbursts from his commander. His face cleared in a relieved grin.

'Send for my legates!' Agricola cried to him. 'And my tribunes! I want them here in half an hour, for we must make the men ready to march soon. What say we go south for some sport, eh?'

At once forgotten in a flurry of barked orders and running slaves, Samana caught up her woollen cloak and slipped out of the door, unnoticed by Agricola, whose lust had vanished as quickly as it came.

Outside, in the biting wind that came off the bay, she flung her cloak around her shoulders and stabbed the brooch-pin home. But beneath the anger, it was fear that beat in her belly. For she was realizing that sexual favours, no matter how expert, how exquisitely targeted to one man's tastes, would always pall in time. She had become complacent, when in fact she must continue to seek ways of being useful to ensure that Agricola's favour continued.

And of course, she must also take heed of any other avenues to safety that presented themselves. Catching her breath, she tapped one fingernail on her teeth, looking down the path to where smoke rose from the beehive-shaped bath-house, the only brick building in the camp. Then a small smile lifted her mouth, and she glanced back. A few officers were already hurrying up the path to the headquarters, buckling on their swords, donning their crested helmets. Agricola was inside, and she forgotten.

Samana set off down the stony path between the rows of tents, the soldiers parting before her but never meeting her eyes. She didn't care what she was to *them*, or what they thought of her secret exploits. Like a spider in a web, she must cast threads out in all directions, and not rest too heavily on one.

Soon she was close enough to smell the wood burning in the furnace beneath the bath-house. Inside, the sleek messenger would be sitting in the steam, scraping the dirt from his oily skin with a strigil, unwinding from his travels, thinking, no doubt, of Rome. He was a slave, yet some slaves enjoyed a high rank, and this one looked as if he wielded influence. She could always scent such things.

After a casual look around, Samana ducked inside the bath-house, listening carefully. But there was no low murmur of male voices from the hot pool inside, or the changing alcoves. The soldiers were drilling hard now that leaf-bud had arrived, and would not be released for such pleasures as bathing until evening. All was silent, wreathed in thick, opaque steam.

Samana took a few more steps as she discarded her cloak and unwound her wrap, folding it carefully and stowing it in a niche in the wall. It would not do to spoil so fine a silk.

Chapter 7

'What are you doing, boy?' Colum cocked one eyebrow at Aedan, a glint in his eye. 'That's a song to send any man to sleep!'

Aedan, crouched on a stool at the edge of the fire-shadows, straightened, his pale cheeks flushing. But as Finan and Colum both let out a chuckle over their *fidchell* game, the bard raised his chin. 'I'm composing, as it happens.'

'What, a lullaby? Play a jig, man!'

Aedan opened his mouth for a retort, then thought better of it and, sweeping his curling, dark hair over his shoulders, removed himself and his harp to the farther reaches of the King's Hall. From the gloom near the storage alcoves, a soft strumming resumed.

'Good,' Eremon muttered to Conaire, on a hearth-bench by the fire. 'I've had my fill of noise tonight, no matter how pleasant.'

The feast had been rowdy, as would be expected for a mourning feast turned to celebration. Yet, after making stilted conversation with Tharan and his cronies, juggling cups of ale with platters of roast deer, pig meat and buttered salmon, Eremon was relieved when everyone finally retired, leaving only his men and the women in the Hall. Now the low chatter was broken only by the snapping logs in the great fire pit and the click of pieces on the *fidchell* board. Even Fergus, one of the most boisterous, had disappeared on some amorous exploit.

'We ride out to the eastern border tomorrow.' Eremon took a small swig of ale from his bronze-rimmed cup, pacing himself as he had done all night. 'We must know if the Romans have poked their noses out of their camps yet.'

'Finan has the training in hand.' Conaire stretched out his long legs to the fire with a sigh. 'I could do with some hard riding, brother – and some fighting too, aye?'

'That will come soon enough.'

'Although . . .' Conaire's eyes drifted to the other side of the fire, where Caitlin's golden head was bowed over sewing with Eithne.

Eremon followed his gaze, and clapped Conaire on the thigh. 'She will be in good hands,' he said. 'Remember that Rhiann cured you once, from an injury far worse than breeding!'

Conaire grunted in agreement, massaging the old scar in his groin, the product of a meeting with a boar's tusk.

As if Eremon's words had called her, Rhiann suddenly returned to the Hall from her house, a shallow bowl in hand, her cheeks pink from the night air outside. As she resumed her seat on the cushions beside Caitlin, Didius leaped to serve her more mead, but she waved him away with a gentle smile. It was that smile which arrested Eremon, for since their argument it had taken him a full day to stop being surly, and she, showing great wisdom, had left him alone. But now . . .

She had unbound her copper hair outside, and had donned a fine dress for the feast, a long-sleeved shift of purple linen and sleeveless robe of deep blue, embroidered in gold and pinned on each shoulder by mare-shaped brooches. The dress fell in loose folds to her feet, hinting at the curves beneath, subtle because of her height and fineness.

Rhiann laughed now at something Caitlin said, throwing back her head. Her laugh always surprised Eremon, too – so rich and throaty. And with that thought came a powerful surge of lust that burned his veins.

He drank again, his hand trembling slightly. Gods, but after all that time of wanting, he had finally joined with her on the Sacred Isle, and it had been magical. And since then . . . nothing, for they had had no chance to be alone. Yet the need Eremon had repressed for so long had broken free that night of the rite in an eruption of love and lust, and their two soul-flames had joined among the stars. There was no way, now, that he could contain all that again. And yet, what did she want?

Amidst all that had happened, Eremon had not forgotten what Rhiann had told him on the beach, about the raiders. Indeed, below everything else, it gnawed at him as an unreachable ache. *So she will be scared.* He knew that, must prepare for that. But how did he get past those memories? What if she felt those men when he touched her? There were things to consider when a woman was a virginal maid. But how could he banish ghosts? *She loves me, but may not want me.*

Gamely, he tried to swallow down the anxiety along with his ale. Yet it stuck in his throat, and would not be dislodged.

'Here.' Rhiann handed the horn cup of cooling brew to Caitlin, and shook out her damp hair, for the rain was still pattering down on the thatch outside.

Caitlin drank and grimaced, resting the cup beside her on the rushes. 'Urgh!'

'Urgh indeed.' Rhiann tucked loose hair behind her ears, sighing as the tension of her uncoiled braids eased. 'But it will strengthen your womb.'

'It was just the normal expecting sickness.' Caitlin flicked out her fingers as Rhiann peered into her patient's eyes. 'Honestly, do stop looking at me like that!'

'You should get to bed and rest,' Rhiann murmured.

Caitlin tried to toss her braids defiantly, but as they were wound about her head, her jerky nod did no more than make Eithne smile as she glanced up from her sewing. 'You're not really going to be like this for the whole five moons, are you?' Caitlin demanded of Rhiann. 'Once I'm back on my horse and in the fresh air I will feel fine!'

'Horse!' Rhiann's eyebrows rose. 'And just what do you expect to be doing? Riding the borders with Eremon's men again? Hunting for deer with your bow? Or perhaps raiding a Roman fort?'

Caitlin sucked in her lip as if considering. 'Yes, well, why not? Although not a Roman raid, of course, that might be too dangerous.'

Rhiann broke into a laugh that was echoed by Eithne. Even Didius gave in to a tentative smile, looking up from the stone loom-weight he was boring. In the days of Rhiann's absence he had taken refuge at Bran and Aldera's house, for he never spent time near Eremon and his men without Rhiann. He had combed his beard and braided his thatch of black hair in Epidii fashion, and the colour had returned to his round cheeks.

Rhiann smiled at him, but just then she sensed eyes on her, and she looked across the fire and met Eremon's gaze. The bones of his face were stark with a hunger her belly recognized, and as it lurched she realized that tonight they were going to their marriage bed, as if for the first time.

For the bed of furs in the alcove above had always been a cold place. Once Eremon was made war leader Rhiann had formally moved into the Hall with him, yet in reality she had often slept in her own house – and he in other beds if they were available. When they did share a sleeping place, they lay with their backs to each other, the gap between their bodies a symbol of the distance between their hearts.

Rhiann started now, realizing that her thoughts had made her blood beat faster at her temples. This husband was alive and real, and could no longer be kept at bay, far from the inner recesses of her heart, or her body. And she didn't want him far away, she didn't . . .

She forced herself to look at Eremon again. Conaire was talking animatedly to Rori on his other side, but Eremon's eyes rested on Rhiann, as warm as the touch of his hands. A knot of panic tightened in her, because she didn't want to fail him, and her eyes blurred as she turned her cheek away, cursing herself.

'*A stór.*' Suddenly Eremon was before her, holding out one hand, in his other a lit pine taper. Rhiann stared at the tiny, spitting flame and took Eremon's fingers, letting him draw her to the stairs, which led to the gallery above. The sound of Aedan's harp, the farewells of those well loved, all passed her by in a haze of woodsmoke and firelight.

As they climbed, the darkness took them, each bedplace along the gallery a pool of shadow, the fire-glow drifting up through the opening in the floor to dance on the sloping thatch. The bed boxes themselves, filled with heather and bracken, were surrounded by wicker screens and hangings on all sides, to afford some privacy. Yet sounds still carried, and there was always the sense of people close all around, breathing in the darkness.

When they reached their bedplace, Rhiann's limbs froze of their own accord, as Eremon touched the taper to the rush wick in the mutton-fat lamp. In the little pool of flickering light, he carefully took off his empty belt and laid it over his scabbard on the cherrywood chest at the bed's foot. He sat down on the fur covers to slip off his boots and unlace his trousers, and then he was before her in just his tunic, unpinning her dress with gentle fingers until it fell to the ground.

Fear was rising in Rhiann's throat, choking her, a fear that did not listen to her reason, that she loved him with all that was in her, that he was a man who would never hurt, never take what she would not give. The roof, sloping low over the bed, seemed to press down on her, and she realized she was clutching at the folds of her shift with rigid fingers.

With still no word, Eremon took her hands and eased them flat against his own breast, wrapping her in a warm circle of arms. When she at last slid her palms around his back, he sank to the bed, the bracken and feather mattress crackling beneath their weight. '*Mo chroí*, my heart,' he murmured, pressing her face into his chest. 'Do you think I've forgotten what you told me not one moon ago? Do you think I would take you, all unwilling and terrified, like those men did?'

His heart thudded against Rhiann's ear, strong against the uncertain tripping of her own. 'No,' she whispered. 'No, *cariad*. I . . . I just—'

'Shhh.' He held her tighter, and she breathed deeply of the smoke caught in the folds of his tunic. 'I told you I would be there as you faced those memories, and here I am. There is no rush, sweetheart, no rush at all.'

Her bitter laugh was half a sob. 'No *rush*? When you will be gone to war soon, and may not come back?' She curled around the sudden plunge of shame in her belly, but he only held her tighter.

'I knew it would be hard for you,' he continued evenly, 'lying here so close to those you know. But I have in mind a place, a way to make you feel safe, and there I will show you what it means to love, in a way that leaves no room for fear.'

'A place?' She raised her face, searching for his darkened eyes. 'What do you mean?'

He loosened his arms and pressed one finger against her lips, pupils wide in the flickering lamplight. 'You'll see. Just trust me.'

She stroked his cheek. He still hadn't paused to shave, and she wondered at the unfamiliar feel of stubble. 'I do trust you; you mustn't think I don't. Or that I don't . . . want you.' She glanced down to where his brown throat disappeared under the embroidered hem of his tunic, saw the lump there bob as he swallowed, his gaze following her own. She remembered when that wanting did flow through her, in the stone circle, the feel of that smooth skin under deer-hide. 'I won't disappoint you,' she whispered desperately. 'I won't—'

'Hush,' he only said again.

And though Eremon kept his tunic on as he always had, everything else was different this night. For the gulf of cold sheets between them was no more, filled now with the sweet, warm curve of bodies, as he held her, back tucked against his belly, legs tangled into one.

Over the years Rhiann's dream had evolved as she evolved, and this night it changed again, as she and Eremon held each other for the first true time in their own bed.

The valley was the same, just as she described it to Linnet, the cauldron warm and tingling in her hands, brimming with the light of the Source. Beside her, Eremon stood, his unsheathed sword in both hands. But now she could see his face fully, his dark hair spilling from beneath his Erin boar-crest war helmet, the line of shadow that edged his jaw as he raised his face. Up there, where the jagged peaks reared, the far clash of arms sounded, accompanied by the scream of eagles.

'Eremon.' She heard her own voice, a note of fear in it. 'They'll take it, Eremon. They'll take the Source and leave us nothing. I can't save our people then, don't you see? I can't save them without the Source.'

Yet Eremon gazed at her calmly, and the flame that licked up from the cauldron was reflected in his eyes. 'I won't let them take it, my wife.'

Suddenly an eagle's shriek pierced the air directly above, and they both looked up. For the first time in memory she saw it then: a shadow of great wings, a huge, outspread figure that blotted out the stars. And the cry broke free from Rhiann's throat. *'They come! The Romans come!'*

And Eremon's hands were on Rhiann's shoulders, shaking her gently awake. She blinked her eyes open into pure night, still tasting the echo of that cry on her tongue.

'It is me, love.' Eremon's voice was soft and sure in her ear. 'I am here. You are safe.' *His* hands, pulling her back to herself. *His* breath brushing her face, moth-wings in the dark.

Rhiann's chest heaved, and she pushed a hand under her breastbone to calm it. When at last she could speak, it was not to allay his fears. She groped for his cheek, cupped his chin. 'Eremon,' she hissed. 'The Romans are on the move – you must find out where they will strike, for they sit idle no longer.'

He was silent for a long moment. 'Are you sure?'

In answer her fingers found his mouth, and unthinking, desperate, she pulled his lips to hers as if to assure herself he was here, warm and alive. He tasted of ale and salty meat, he tasted of Eremon, and she broke away and buried her face in his shoulder.

When he felt her trembling, he rolled over to his back and pulled her into the curve of his body.

'I am sure,' she whispered, her eyes open in the darkness. 'They are moving.'

Though Eremon at last fell into an uneasy sleep, Rhiann could not. She lay until the grey dawn crept under the wide oak doors below and climbed the stairs.

Then she rose, sliding her cloak from the wicker screen, taking her shoes from beside the bed. Silently she crept past the other bedplaces and down the stairs.

By the banked fire, Cù raised his grey snout from among the old king's hounds. She paused to pat him as she stirred the coals up with a poker, feeding them with twigs and bark from the wood basket until the flames were bright and new, pushing back the last of the darkness. Against the walls, the dark humps of the other men did not stir, for they had sat up late drinking, judging by the scattering of empty alder cups on the hearth-benches, and the few pig-bones that even the dogs had left.

Rhiann set the tripod over the low flames, filled the iron kettle from the water pot by the door, and scattered in a handful of dried nettle-leaves. Then she went to the porch and scraped open the door, settling her cloak around her shoulders, deep in thought.

The eaves outside dripped with dew, and all was grey and cold, the thatched houses below hunched and silent, awaiting the sunrise. The women's waste pit was against the south-east wall of the crag, and she was returning through the Horse Gate, her head burrowed into her cloak, when she realized someone was blocking her path.

It was Gelert, on his way to the shrine for the sun greeting, his owl-head staff held high before him as if to cleave the mist.

The druids concerned themselves with things of the sky and stars; the science of marking time; when to sow and harvest and hold the festivals to honour the gods. The priestesses were of the earth, the slower rhythms of growth and birth. Each could respect the other, yet Gelert despised all things female. Rhiann knew that her mother had rejected him in his youth, but the hatred of women must come from somewhere deeper even than that. She didn't understand; she would never understand.

Such confusion always unnerved her, and now Rhiann drew her cloak closed and made to go past him, her chin down. As she did, she glimpsed the way Gelert's cold, yellow eyes slid over her body, suggestive not of lust, but of other dark things. Once, he'd waited to see that belly swell, as proof Eremon had taken her by force, making her life a misery. Now, she realized, he would want to see it flat, for his hopes of controlling them had come to nothing, and he would not want their heirs ruling Dunadd.

In a sudden burst of defiance Rhiann dropped her crossed arms and straightened. *Don't be afraid. It feeds him.*

At her scornful gaze, something in his own eyes lit and he smiled, the faint tattoos on his ageing cheeks stretching into jagged lines. 'I am pleased to see our Ban Cré so robust, so healthy. So unharmed by her recent travails.'

Rhiann's mouth twisted, the accusation hovering on her tongue. But she'd already decided she didn't want to invite his ire; she didn't want him to think of her and her loved ones at all. So she swallowed down the bitter words, brushing her hair back from her shoulders. 'Yes, I am well, as you can see, and I have you to thank for that.'

The wing of Gelert's eyebrow quivered among the straggling strands of his long, grey hair. 'Oh? Pray do tell me, that I may serve you the greater.'

'Why, choosing such a man for me, brother druid.' Rhiann smiled sweetly and, to her satisfaction, the muscle in Gelert's flaccid cheek jumped. 'You have given me more than I ever hoped for – how could any man win the hearts of the Epidii so quickly, so completely, as Eremon? Such a man has not been seen for generations.'

Gelert's thin mouth worked in what passed for a smile. 'He's won nothing so completely, girl.' His glance dropped again to her flat belly. 'Neither have you, I see.'

So insolent, as if he owned her. Hot anger rose in her throat. 'And yet a child of the Erin blood, of *my* blood, does indeed already quicken, as you well know. He will sit in this Hall when you are no more than ashes on the wind.'

Gelert blinked. 'Ah, yes, the other whelp breeds, does she not? Interesting.' He spoke of Caitlin as if she were a dog.

Rhiann's bold spurt of anger quickly died. She crossed her arms again. Under her fingers, bumps had risen on her skin. 'Conaire and Eremon, indeed all the men, have taken this child to their hearts, though he is not yet born.' She didn't know why she said it, for her voice was strained, and Gelert's gaze came back from the distant sky and sharpened on her face.

'Indeed? Then I hope that the child comes safely in these uncertain times.'

At those words the chill sank through Rhiann's skin. Then Gelert's eyes slid to one side, as a cough and shuffling of feet came from behind her.

Rhiann glanced back. It was Didius, standing there with a determined look on his face, his dark eyes wavering only slightly as he stared somewhere towards Gelert's knees. Rhiann nearly laughed aloud with relief. Didius had once vowed to be her personal guard, and he certainly had an uncanny knack of knowing when he was needed.

'Curious,' Gelert observed, 'how you and your man strive against our dreaded enemy and yet keep one of them here as your hound at heel. Anyone would think you had something different in mind than mere defence.'

'They *are* our enemies, and remain so,' Rhiann replied coolly, turning back to him. 'Didius is a prisoner, as you well know.' She was belatedly conscious that Didius was also best away from Gelert's attention.

Gelert eyed Didius's unbound wrists and legs with the same derision with which he'd studied her belly. 'A prisoner, or an envoy? It is remarkable how such things can be easily mistaken.' He glided away towards the shrine, his pale robe blending with the mist.

Rhiann held her tongue for a moment, breathing steadily through her nose. Then she smiled wanly down at Didius. 'I am sorry.'

Didius was looking after Gelert like a stiff-backed hound, his body trembling, and Rhiann laid her hand on his shoulder. 'Keep away from him,' she murmured. 'Do not let his eye fall on you for any reason. He bears me no love, and extends the same to those I care for.'

A flush of surprised pleasure warmed Didius's cheeks, and he dropped his eyes to his feet.

Rhiann smiled. 'You are part of my household now – I extend that care to you.'

The kettle was steaming when Rhiann and Didius went back inside the Hall. Rhiann poured tea for both of them and took hers back to bed. Eremon stirred when she eased under the covers, flinging an arm out over her thighs, but he did not fully awaken.

Rhiann held the cup to warm her fingers, gazing up at the hanging on the wall by the bed, seeing with her eyes only dark shapes against light, yet knowing every thread of it better than she knew her own face. Her mother had woven it before Rhiann was born, and it depicted the goddess Rhiannon on her White Mare. The mare's sides were so pure they shone almost silver, and Rhiannon's blue cloak trailed stars. The scene glowed with power, the power of woman and the Goddess, the Great Mother. And Rhiann had not only been named after this Goddess, but was also She incarnate, the Mother of the Land for her people.

So how can I let myself fear Gelert so? Rhiann grumbled to herself, burrowing deeper into the warm nest of furs. *I am my mother's daughter. She faced him and scorned him, and I can, too.*

But her mother was long dead now, taken to the Otherworld by Rhiann's birth. Safe from the reach of one such as he.

Chapter 8

On the hills east of Dunadd, looking out over the marshy plain, Eremon's black stallion, Dórn, snorted and pawed the muddy ground. In the two weeks since Rhiann and Eremon's return, leaf-bud had strengthened its hold, and the marsh and crag below were hazed by a pall of cooking smoke that hung low and still in the sun-warmed air.

'He's eager for home,' Conaire remarked, flexing the mailshirt stretched across his massive shoulders.

Eremon patted Dórn's arched neck. 'Eager for honey and mash, more like.'

'We all need to be home.' Lorn crossed his hands on his own reins. 'I must fly now to my father's dun, to deliver this news myself.'

Eremon glanced at the young Epidii lord, resplendent in a scarlet tunic and checked trousers, a hardened leather jerkin he had freshly greased, and over it a new-dyed green cloak. Lorn didn't look as if he'd just ridden hard over the mountains and slept for a week on the ground with the scouts, chewing dried venison and hard-baked bread. His silver-gilt hair was neatly tied back with a deer-hide thong; Eremon had watched him comb it from the corner of a half-opened eye that morning. Lorn had even shaved, so the rearing bear tattoo – Urben's totem – was clearly outlined on his cheek. Eremon, in contrast, probably looked as he felt, and he rubbed his temples now in an effort to soften his headache.

'There's no need to alarm your clan,' he replied, squinting in the bright sun that spilled over the heather slopes. 'I don't want any rumours spreading that the Romans are marching this way, because at present they are not.'

'Not yet,' Lorn corrected. 'But my father must know they have left their camps, for we command the southern defences, in case you have forgotten.'

Conaire, watching Lorn with veiled eyes, made a sound deep in his throat.

Eremon sat back in his saddle. 'No, I had not forgotten,' he answered dryly. They had seen nothing of Lorn or Urben, until Lorn turned up unexpectedly with a hundred of his own warriors, to continue their training as part of the warband. Nothing had been said, either of Eremon's return, or Urben's reaction to it. For the moment, Eremon had decided to let this lie, for he needed the men, and the cohesion of the tribe, and keeping an eye on Lorn was easier with him close by. And though Eremon wasn't thrilled to admit it, Lorn was a fine warrior.

'All we know is that there is a greater movement of Roman soldiers across their frontier,' Eremon added patiently, scratching his sweaty neck above his own mailshirt. 'In the absence of other information, this means little; I don't want to cause unnecessary panic.'

Lorn tossed his fair hair in a gesture Eremon had only seen Caitlin use. With her, it was amusing and endearing; with Lorn, strangely irritating. 'They are moving,' Lorn emphasized, 'and this means a change. If they come suddenly west, then by the Mare it will be my people who die first.'

'Eremon's chain of scouts works perfectly,' Conaire pointed out, yet Eremon sensed the effort of his even tone. 'We would know of their approach long before, leaving enough time to move your clan.'

Lorn turned glacial grey eyes on Conaire. 'As the Damnonii knew, son of Lugaid? As the Selgovae knew?'

Conaire flushed, and his head dipped bullishly between his shoulders. 'The Selgovae didn't have Eremon. The Damnonii didn't either, until we went to help them.'

Eremon shifted uncomfortably in his saddle, for this reminder of the Damnonii brought back the shame. He had helped them to destroy a Roman fort two years ago, but Agricola's retaliation had been more brutal than any expected, and now the Damnonii were a scattered people. It was not a success he wanted to repeat; if he hadn't offered his help, perhaps those warriors would still be alive. *And Roman slaves*, he reminded himself sharply.

'Son of Urben,' he said to Lorn, 'alert your father, but at this stage, not your other chieftains, and don't allow the rumours to start. Your defences are enough for now, until we know more. Agreed?'

Lorn raised his chin, nodded sharply and wheeled his horse, a bay larger than Dóm and with red-painted hooves. Sketching a wave, Lorn took off down the slope at a reckless speed into a thick bank of woods, his green cloak flying.

Conaire let out a strangled grunt, shaking his messy halo of gold hair, which could barely be tamed into braids. 'Why did he bother swearing to you as war leader if he argues about everything?'

Eremon rubbed his stubbled chin ruefully. 'He swore to support me against his better judgement, because he felt the gods were telling him so. But it makes him angry, all the same, and he must release that somehow.'

'I'd rather he release it on my fists,' Conaire grumbled. 'Or better yet, my sword.'

Eremon glanced at him, but he knew Conaire wasn't serious. A breach in the Epidii now would threaten everything they had worked for. As it was, they were fighting hard to bring all the tribes of Alba together; they had at least to hold their own as one. That was the reason for putting up with Lorn – the only reason.

Conaire saw the look and grinned. 'Don't worry, brother. I'll keep my head. Although,' he pursed his lips thoughtfully, 'next time I train beside him I *could* slip and thump him with my hilt. Accidentally, of course.'

Eremon laughed, and the heavy veil that had clouded his heart this last day lightened. 'If he thinks it accidental, too, then go ahead. He is a mighty test of my patience.' They nudged their horses on. 'Remember, brother, that he said his oath stands until the Roman threat is over, and I fear it has only really begun.' Eremon shrugged. 'I think we have little to fear from Lorn beyond hard words, for now. He is loyal to his people – frustrated, yet loyal.'

The gait of their mounts shifted as they edged down the slope and into the woods, yet as soon as they broke free of the undergrowth into sunlight they heard a high yip, and glimpsed another rider thundering towards them along the wide cart track that ran to Dunadd. The sun struck sparks from his red hair.

'My lord!' Rori cried, bringing his horse to a halt with an unnecessary flourish. Eremon saw Conaire hide his smile behind a sudden cough. 'My lord, we have some new arrivals!'

Eremon spurred Dórn towards his youngest warrior, brushing hazel catkins from his hair. 'Well, put us out of our misery, then! Who is it?'

Rori was agog, his red freckles blending into one great flush across his face. 'Warriors have just this day come from the Caereni. From a chief called . . . Nectan.' He swirled the unfamiliar name on his tongue. 'My lord, is this the man who helped you after the wreck? Who made the druids honour you on the Sacred Isle?'

Eremon's chest was suffused with a warm relief. 'Yes, indeed.' He and Conaire exchanged looks of surprise and pleasure. 'So who has he sent?'

Rori's grin was brighter than the sunlight. '*Archers!*' he breathed. 'The finest I have ever seen! They have yew bows and beaded quivers and they wear odd clothes and they are so dark and small and you can hardly see them until they move and they are dressed all in skins and everything is a colour that doesn't show up against rock or tree or grass . . .' He broke off suddenly, blushing furiously. 'Of course, you know all this. You were there.'

Eremon smiled, and leaned out to rest his hand on Rori's shoulder. 'You can hear any such good news more than once. They *are* fine archers, the finest. Nectan does me great honour to send them.' He looked again at Conaire, a question on his face. 'Yet the Caereni chiefs told me they would only send men in the event of battle. I was not expecting any aid now.'

Conaire drew a hunting spear from his saddle pack and hefted it idly, testing its weight. 'Rhiann was always saying that Nectan is far-seeing. Perhaps he knows we will need men soon.'

The dark spectre of the Romans flitted across Eremon's mind once more. Yet he could not deny the excitement that rose behind the cloud. 'Brother,' he said to Conaire, 'with the other kings set against the alliance for now, Calgacus and I don't have enough men to challenge Agricola openly. But we can ambush and stalk – and for that, a set of fine Caereni archers will be very useful!'

Rhiann paused in the sun at her own doorway to brush the dew from her skirts.

Just inside, Eithne was scouring the iron cookpots clean with fresh sand. Like all young things she had recovered from her shock quickly, and Rhiann saw that her black hair and eyes were gleaming again, and the bony angles of her body were already filling out. She was growing up so fast, and into a beauty, Rhiann suddenly realized, as Eithne jumped up to relieve her of the gathering basket and digging stick.

Once inside, Eithne set before Rhiann an alder bowl of water with soaproot, to wash the dirt from her hands, and a drying cloth, and knelt to unlace Rhiann's muddy boots.

Rhiann looked around her little house with a relief that it had been put to rights again. The pot by the door was full of water from the well. The basket by the hearth was overflowing with roasted barley grains from last year's harvest, ready for grinding, and there was a fresh joint of beef hanging among the herbs on the rafters. The goddess figures were lined up on their shelf, and the bright cushions and rugs had been beaten, aired and set neatly around the fire pit.

'The early sun has brought out the dog roses,' Rhiann told Eithne.

Eithne was now sorting through the basket, carefully brushing dirt off the roots, leaves and flowers, and laying them on the workbench under the herb shelves. Rhiann joined her there.

'I do not yet know this one.' Eithne held up one plant with spreading, pleated leaves.

'This is lady's-mantle; I went some way to find it. And you know feverfew.'

Eithne's brow creased as she repeated the names. 'But what are they for?'

'For pregnancy.' Rhiann busied herself pulling out the other bundles of leaves, so Eithne would not see the concern in her face. Caitlin was feeling worse, not better, and Rhiann was determined to try everything she could to ease her way. 'Did you sit with Caitlin, then?'

'Yes, lady. I helped her bathe, but then she wished to sleep, so I went to the well and came back here to boil water and wait for you.'

This pregnancy at least was timely, Rhiann thought, reaching up for a basket of the dried red haws. The festival of Beltaine was over, and the longest day still some weeks away, so there were no major rituals to organize. The sun's warmth was melting away the fevers and hacking coughs of the long dark. Offerings were required neither for planting nor harvest; the barley fields around the dun were blessed and sown, and sprouting strongly. The cattle from surrounding homesteads had been driven up to sunseason pasture in the hills, and the ripening of fruits, berries and nuts was still moons away. The heather was not yet blooming, for ale; the honey was not yet flowing, for mead; and it was too early to take the oak bark, wild onions and woad leaves for dyes.

Rhiann's floor rushes had needed changing after the long dark, but the cutting and hauling and strewing had only taken the women a few days, and then the only thing left to do was gather herbs. All the new leaves, buds and early blooms were strong in their first growth, reaching to the sun.

When the brew was ready, Rhiann and Eithne took a covered pot to Caitlin, who was up and squatting by the hearth in the King's Hall, kneading some barley dough on the warm stone.

Eithne took over the baking of the bannocks while Rhiann checked Caitlin's pulse, eyes, breath and tongue, as she did every day. And as she did every day, Caitlin rolled her eyes at Eithne when Rhiann was peering in her mouth.

Rhiann closed Caitlin's mouth with a tap on her chin. 'You can squirm and complain and protest all you like, but it won't make me leave you alone.' She reached for the cooling brew and horn cup, glancing sidewise at Caitlin with a smile. 'Anyone would think you ungrateful.'

She regretted that as soon as she said it, for the mischief in Caitlin's blue eyes fled instantly. Caitlin was acutely sensitive to anyone thinking her sudden turn of fortune, from orphaned foundling to noble lady, was unappreciated. She clasped Rhiann's hand. 'Oh no!' she cried. 'I thank you for all your concern, Rhiann, I just . . . hate being sick!'

Rhiann observed her thoughtfully. 'I don't think you're sick, Caitlin,' she corrected, ignoring the paleness of her pointed face with its upturned nose, the dark eye shadows that would not fade. Even Caitlin's fair hair was lank, falling unbound about her cheeks. 'Women's bodies cope with babies differently, that's all. You're adjusting, and I'm just making you stronger.'

Caitlin nodded trustingly, and Rhiann was shot through by a pang of pain.

She must not fear, Rhiann thought desperately. *It will weaken her more.* She knew that Caitlin's exhaustion wasn't right, but she didn't want everyone to be concerned, so she must keep it to herself. *And tell Linnet*, she amended, sometimes still needing to remind herself that Linnet was Caitlin's mother.

As for Caitlin's father . . . Rhiann, discreetly studying Caitlin's belly, stilled for a moment.

Now that the tribe knew of it, the child appeared to have indulged in an enormous growth spurt, and Caitlin's belly was already thrusting forwards proudly. Too proudly, Rhiann fretted. Too large, too soon. Conaire was a huge man, the largest she'd ever seen, and she had ascribed the child's size to him. Yet though Caitlin's frame was small, her own father had also been tall and broad, ruddy and strong; so perhaps there were twin reasons to be worried.

Inwardly, Rhiann sighed, her heart squeezing with a familiar guilt. She had reason to know the physical attributes of Caitlin's sire well – for he was Rhiann's own father. They were half-sisters, not cousins, as Caitlin still assumed. Only Linnet and Rhiann knew the truth of it, for Linnet had kept the secret out of the shame of being young and foolish and laying with the husband of her sister. And these taboos from long ago had also stopped Rhiann's tongue, for she had wished to give Caitlin the time to feel secure, without the taint of old guilt hanging over her. Yet soon Rhiann must tell her, even if Linnet still shied from it . . .

'Rhiann, come back.'

Rhiann blinked. Caitlin had been regaling Eithne with a tale of the wolves she used to track when she was a fur trader, and how the beasts did this and that just like Cù did. But now she was addressing Rhiann.

'I said, have you organized the wedding celebration yet?'

Flushing, Rhiann sat straighter. 'Yes, we have. But the details are secret; you'll see for yourself.'

Caitlin darted a conspiratorial glance at Eithne. 'You are not the only one with secrets, cousin.'

Rhiann glanced back and forth between them. 'What do you mean by that? What has Eremon told you?'

'Nothing!' Caitlin waved her hand airily.

'Conaire, then. What has he said?'

'Oh, nothing.'

Rhiann sat back on the bench, drumming her fingers on her knee.

'Caitlin, don't force me to dose you with something to loosen your tongue.'

Caitlin grinned weakly. 'I may not be myself, but I can keep a secret, Rhiann. Remember when you presented me with my dowry, as a surprise? How much you and Eithne and Linnet enjoyed it?'

Rhiann shrugged, spreading her hands. 'Fine, fine! I won't ask, then.'

Caitlin leaned forward, patting Rhiann's hand. 'I look forward to it so much. Since the Sacred Isle, Eremon is changed, as are you.'

And you, Rhiann thought with alarm, seeing so clearly now the startling thinness of Caitlin's skin across her temples, the blue veins pulsing.

After leaving Eithne to finish the baking, Rhiann's steps dragged as she made for her house, her mind still gnawing on the problem of Caitlin's pallor. Yet it was just as Rhiann reached to pull down another basket of herbs from her shelves that she felt the twinge low in her abdomen, an ache she knew well, because it meant her moon bleeding was beginning.

Suddenly breathless, Rhiann sank to her hearth-bench and, after a moment, drew her knees to her chest. So much had happened since the stone circle that she had forgotten she could have been with child herself. Obviously, though, she wasn't. Rhiann waited to feel sad or disappointed, but instead she realized her heart was pounding with relief.

For her mind was filled with a vision of herself like Caitlin: weak and tired, preoccupied with fighting some inner struggle. *And what good will I be to me or anyone else then?* she thought, her arms tightening around her knees. The night of the moonlit pool still burned in her heart; she knew that to fulfil that dream she must focus outwards, not inwards. Nothing was more important than that – she would die inside if she failed.

And fail she would, because Caitlin too had been robust, despite her slight build, always riding by Conaire's side with her bow at the ready. Yet this baby, though much wanted, had changed everything for her.

A memory now breathed up Rhiann's spine: Eremon's voice in the darkness of their bed. *I have a way to make you feel safe, and there I will show you what it means to love.*

Rhiann ached for that love between she and he, but with it would come a babe, and then another, and another, and soon she would be bound by the demands of a brood, all wound about her legs like tangled wool. How could she be anything more than a mother, then? She had vowed to put aside revenge against Gelert to focus on the task – so perhaps she needed to sacrifice something softer in herself, too.

Slowly, hardly daring to voice her impulse even to herself, Rhiann uncurled from the bench and reached for her cloak and then her digging stick, back in its place against the wall. There were herbs that grew nearby, which would stop a babe from starting in the womb.

By the time she was at the stables her thoughts were clamouring and colliding with each other, and though she ignored their persistent voices she couldn't avoid the shame that crept up her body in a hot flush. Only one thought emerged clearly from the rest: *Eremon must never know.*

After such a long time alone Rhiann had finally found this precious love, and she couldn't risk it now. She didn't know how a man of Erin might feel about such things, yet since noble blood there ran from father to son, not through the women as in Alba, she suspected that proof of a man's children might be more important there than here. In which case, her actions would fill Eremon with horror. He might look upon *her* with horror.

Rhiann just needed a little time, that was all: a time for this new, fragile bond between them to strengthen, for its roots to deepen. And a breathing space to discover exactly what it was she would be called upon to do.

BOOK TWO
SUNSEASON, AD 81

Chapter 9

During Linnet's solemn blessing, Eremon caught Rhiann's eye and flashed her a wicked grin. They stood outside the King's Hall for their marriage ceremony, with the people of Dunadd crowded between the houses on the lower tier. Though everyone could look up at them no one could see their expressions as they faced each other, holding hands. Rhiann stifled her own grin, her eyes darting to her aunt like a guilty child.

She doesn't look like a child though, Eremon thought, with a warm pulse between his legs. As the early days of sunseason continued to bloom, and they snatched sunlit moments together, so Rhiann's body was rounding into ever more pleasing curves. And, by the gods, Eremon's own body was not failing to recognize it.

It was a glorious clear day with no hint of cloud, but that was not all that made this day different from their betrothal nearly two years ago. It was also a more elaborate ritual, involving an intricate system of symbols carefully designed by Rhiann.

She had been led to the King's Hall on Liath, whose pale coat was brushed and gleaming, her mane and tail braided with white swan feathers. This invoked the Great Mother Rhiannon, beloved of birds, on her white mare, and reminded people that Eremon was wedding the land, through the Goddess's vessel Rhiann. It bonded him as defender of that land.

Eremon had been waiting at the Hall wrapped in a deer-hide cloak, but as Rhiann dismounted, she removed it to show him bare-chested, clad only in his trousers and every piece of jewellery he possessed. His torc neck-ring was thick braids of gold twisted together, terminating in twin boar heads, and there were also finger-rings and bronze bands set with red enamel on his forearms. Below his helmet was the gold circlet of his father's with its rare green jewel on the brow, and his boar tusk – another symbol of his own people – was tied around one upper arm.

The boar stone took pride of place on his chest, symbol of the backing of Calgacus, most powerful Alban king. And winding across the sharp muscles of chest and belly were the symbols of his other alliance, the curling blue tattoos making him King Stag of the western peoples.

All this was to remind the council, the druids and warriors that Eremon was a powerful man now, that he had earned his position as war leader and could not be challenged.

And has it worked? Eremon wondered, studying the crowd from the corner of one eye. *Yes.*

Rhiann had been clever, for the Albans, like his own people, loved spectacle, even when they did not understand all the symbols. Their eyes were greedily drinking in the glittering bronze and gold, the sword at his side, with its jewelled hilt, and the fierce bronze boar-crest on his helmet. In that gaze Eremon saw respect, yes, and awe.

After arriving here with nothing but his own wits, his men and his sword, he had won this — the light of their gaze. It made him feel warmer in his heart than the sun's heat on his bare skin, and he prayed his father could see him from the Otherworld. Perhaps then, at last, he would be proud of him.

The women's eyes were roving over Eremon's bare chest more than his finery, but their gaze also devoured Rhiann as his did now. The back of her shining, auburn hair fell to her waist, yet the front was braided and coiled high around her elegant head, held with gold pins. Her green and blue embroidered dress was pinned on each shoulder, and her priestess cloak clasped at her throat by the Epidii royal brooch: a mare's head set with garnets. She'd also put aside her own fine torc for the heavier royal torc, the terminals two rearing mares.

Eremon vaguely sensed the people murmuring and shifting on their heels below. Some would be genuinely pleased, some thinking only of the feast to come, and others, like Gelert, mercifully lurking in the shadows and therefore easy to ignore.

Eremon dragged his thoughts back now, bent his head as Linnet marked his forehead with the paste of sacred rowan ash and soil. He caught Rhiann's eye again and winked, and she bit down another smile, her fingers splaying out at him in the merest flick of admonition.

Yet when Linnet bound their hands with the red-dyed cloth, and held the jewelled cup of mead for them to sip, all the mischief in Eremon's heart died. For when they were bound like this at their betrothal, he hadn't known his bride, and Rhiann's eyes had frozen him with cold rejection.

Now, those same tilted eyes held him over the golden rim of the cup, gleaming with the reflected sun on jewels, and his breath was caught there in the shining net she made.

★

74

As the tingling mead slid down her throat, Rhiann's eyes dropped away from Eremon's piercing gaze. For he had suddenly become solemn, and she saw the heat there, and recognized it in her own body, surging up from her core, and as the wave of heat and desire rose, so the fear chased behind to douse it.

Now Rhiann forced herself to look at Eremon again, the sun so bright on his finery she could barely see. He stood there blazing and golden and alive, like a young god, burning the view of the Horse Gate and the thatch roofs and far blue hills into a background haze. How could Rhiann bear to see that light flicker and fade, if her body rejected him this night?

All she wanted was for love to be enough, and the wanting made her body vibrate with desperate need, like a plucked harp string.

As Linnet's words bound Eremon, the defender of the land, to Rhiann, the Goddess of the land incarnate, Rhiann at least strove to honour that in her heart. And as a cheer went up from all the people, and Linnet untied their hands, Rhiann caught her aunt's eye and saw there all the joy she knew her loved ones felt for her this day.

They trusted Eremon, and so must she.

Pushing through the cheering crowd, Eremon led Rhiann down the path on Liath, to parade her through the dun. Yet just as they got to the village gate, he suddenly turned off towards the stables on the southern side of the palisade.

'Eremon . . . what . . . ?' Rhiann's mouth dropped open, as Conaire and Caitlin suddenly appeared at the stable door, their faces flushed from running ahead.

'Eremon . . .' Rhiann tried again, leaning forward to catch his shoulder, but he spun around and, with a lift from Conaire, vaulted on to Liath's back behind her. Before Rhiann could get out more than a startled gasp, something soft and thick came down around her eyes and was tied behind her head.

'Fear not, fair maiden,' Eremon breathed, laughter catching in his voice. 'We are bound for more private surrounds.'

'Eremon!' Rhiann squeaked. 'Caitlin!' But her voice was lost in the hurried tightening and clanking of buckles, a low murmur from Conaire, and Caitlin's giggle. A small, female hand squeezed her knee.

Rhiann felt Eremon's thighs contract then as he dismounted, and Liath snickered a greeting to another horse being led forward on heavy hooves. Dórn; it had to be.

'What are you doing?' she hissed, as Liath was gently tugged forwards beneath her. 'We have a feast to go to.'

Eremon's disembodied laugh echoed back to her as they passed under the gatetower. 'The feast can go on without us. I'm stealing you away instead, as they did in the old days, and you're going to stay nice and quiet like all shy maids. Just hold on.'

From somewhere behind, Rhiann heard the murmur of laughter, and the sound of pipes and drums breaking into a ragged tune, and as Eremon pulled Liath into a trot, Rhiann's thoughts began to clatter as fast as the hooves below. *Goddess, I hope everyone is at the King's Hall because this is undignified and undoes everything I planned . . .*

Yet the ground soon grew uneven as they crossed the gravel causeway, jolting even those scrambled ideas from Rhiann's head, and she had to lean forward and clutch the reins. Then Liath began racing, and the air flew past cool and salty off the marsh.

Eremon didn't remove Rhiann's blindfold for the entire ride. By the splashing, she knew when Liath crossed a shallow stream, and then the mare's stance shifted, and Rhiann felt them climbing through shade, as tree branches caught at her hair.

At last the trees ended, the sounds opening out again, and finally they lurched over another rise and down into a hollow, where Eremon drew rein and dismounted. Rhiann sat quietly, the thumping of her heart very loud to her in the sudden stillness. Then Eremon's hands were on her waist, setting her down, and his fingers at last untied the blindfold.

Rhiann opened her mouth to speak, but when she saw where they were, the words died in her throat.

The afternoon was softening into the long sunseason dusk, and all the warmth and scents of the day had been gathered here in this hollow of grass, bound by slopes on all sides. At the lowest dip of the bowl was a tiny, turf hut, one of those used by the herders. Its walls were newly white-washed and a gnarled rowan splashed scarlet flowers over the roof.

Garlands of blooms hung about its doorway, and when Rhiann went to look inside she caught her breath. The single room had nothing more than a hearth and a bed on the floor, but the beams were hung with pink dog roses and creamy meadowsweet, and their scents were heady in the still air. The hearth was set with birch logs and hazel twigs, and there was a covered pot of beef porridge ready for warming, and beside that, several gleaming jars of mead and one cup of chased bronze. With one hand to her mouth, Rhiann peeled back the seal-fur bedcover, striped with silver and brown, and the fleece beneath, and pushed on the springy mattress that crackled with heather.

Eremon's shadow fell over her, and she turned as he dropped the saddle bags by the door and tossed his hide cape to one side. 'They all helped you,' she managed. 'Even Caitlin, that's why she was being so secretive. And why Eithne kept taking so long at everything, and why Conaire disappeared . . .'

Eremon smiled and came into the room, taking her hand. 'I told you I would find a place to make you feel safe. And we never had a honey moon before, when we should have.'

Rhiann eyed the jars of honey mead. 'We have enough for more than one moon; did you plan on keeping me here for ever?'

Eremon's teeth gleamed in the dusk. 'That was Colum's job; I think he got carried away.'

Rhiann shook her head, so torn with confusion she could not speak. Eremon was looking at her with a strange timidity – he was unsure how she felt. And so was she. At the sight of the bed, her fear rose; at the sight of his bare muscles, the desire. But Eremon was so right about one thing. Here, away from Dunadd, she could already sense her tension loosening. The blindfolded ride was like a journey in a bard's tale, when the heroine must travel through the darkness of the cave to emerge into the bright Otherworld. This would be their Otherworld, then.

Now Eremon busied himself lighting a pine taper from an earthern pot of coals, touching it to the stone lamps that stood by the bed and on the single shelf carved into the wall. Soon the room was glowing with golden light. Rhiann spied a woven basket sitting on the hearth-stone, and opened the lid. Inside, she sifted fine, barley flour between her fingers, smiling to herself. This was Eithne's doing; Caitlin would not have known the Epidii custom.

'We must light the fire,' she said to Eremon.

'But it is warm . . . I thought—'

She smiled softly. 'I need it for cooking, *cariad*, not for warmth.'

So while Eremon sat on the bed with mead in hand she knelt by the fire, mixed the barley meal, honey and water together in a clay bowl, and shaped the little moon cakes, setting them to cook on the hot hearth-stone. Soon the tiny room filled with the wholesome brown smell of bread baking, and when the cakes were done, Rhiann gathered them in her dress, and brought them to Eremon.

She held one out, hot in her palm. 'We must break new bread together, made by my own hand. So this binds us, ensuring we always have plenty, ensuring our bodies draw from the same strength.'

Solemn now, Eremon took one cake and broke it in two, and they fed half to each other. Yet as his lips touched her fingers, a jolt ran up Rhiann's spine, and she could hardly swallow, the dry crumbs sticking in her throat. Eremon smiled and held the mead cup for her, and when the fire of it was running down into her belly, he laid it down.

'I have something for you,' Rhiann suddenly blurted, opening the leather pouch she carried at her waist. Then she was holding her wedding gift across her palms: a sacred amulet of carved antler, stag-shaped, on an ochre-dyed thong. 'I have sung chants over it for nine days and blessed it in a sacred pool,' she murmured shyly. 'It will protect you in battle.'

Reverently, Eremon took it from her, and she helped him to bind it around his upper arm as a match for the boar tusk.

'I have something also.' He kissed her fingers and rose to his saddle-pack, dropping a bundle on the bedcover. 'I always keep my promises,' he said, stretching out on the bed.

Rhiann pulled away flax twine and bark, and gasped.

Eremon smiled. 'There wasn't much time, but I had your wedding gift made. It is from the last of the amber, just as I said.'

Rhiann held up the delicate necklace to the firelight, and it trembled within her fingers. Smoothed orbs of amber were linked by bronze beads cast into graceful swirls and spirals. The whole thing glittered and moved with the flames, the light picking out threads of gold weaving through the amber.

Rhiann's eyes filled. 'Goddess . . . it is beautiful.'

Eremon rose to his haunches, and moved behind so he could fasten the necklace. His strong thighs were against her back, as he pressed his lips to the nape of her neck.

'Rhiann,' his voice was hoarse, 'do you trust me?'

She didn't have to think about that. 'Yes, *cariad*, I trust you.'

'Then trust I will do nothing that you don't want me to. Do not be guarded.' He brushed tendrils of hair gently back over one ear, and then the other, drawing the long strands through his fingers, over and over, until she half-closed her eyes with drowsy, relaxed pleasure.

'Trust me,' came the whisper.

The dusk was long gone now, the dark of night driven back by the flames of the lamps.

Rhiann's dress had slipped down one shoulder, and Eremon's touch on the bare skin seemed part of the glowing trail of mead inside her, a natural step beyond their deep kisses.

The rhythmic stroking of Eremon's thumb echoed the ebb and surge of the blood beating in Rhiann's throat, and when his butterfly kisses moved up her neck, a fluttering awoke between her legs that came not from his touch, but from her own desire.

A part of her hovered anxiously, waiting for the unconscious jerk away, the freezing that she could not control. But his touch was gentle and languid, smoothing her skin and her soul into surrender, with no harsh breathing, no weight across her, crushing her, nothing urgent or painful. He didn't take, he gave, and the fire that flowed from his hands and those soft, unexpected lips was brighter than the flames against the wall.

Rhiann wanted to feel that slow touch all over, and her dress fell away from her own fingers as she stretched out like a cat, her skin sheened with the light. Eremon murmured then, matching the length of her with his naked body, touch gliding over the Goddess tattoos on her own belly, tracing them with unbearable slowness, then moving higher, over the mound of one breast, circling the nipple with his sword-callused fingers.

Then she did tense, but it was not with fear . . . *Goddess . . . it was with yearning* . . . as her back arched of its own accord towards him, aching for him to cup her, to claim her body with his palm. And the relief of not being afraid suddenly flooded her, sweeping away the hovering watcher with sensation. She did not return.

The tracing continued, around the base of one breast and then the other, Eremon's nails, then his fingertips, softly, softly, feather-light, exquisite, burning . . . and Rhiann's eyes flew open, seeking his, a moan trembling in her throat.

She had thought Eremon's gaze would echo the languor, the liquid warmth that was her blood. Yet it did not. Eremon's eyes were almost pained, quivering with a tension absent from his trailing fingers. He wanted something from her, and was feared he would not see it. She glimpsed the depth of the fear: raw, naked.

She raised a hand to his lips now, the yearning pushing up from within her . . . *claim me . . . make me yours* . . . But she couldn't say it, didn't know how to speak the words, and then came the whistle of his breath released . . . *beg for me, Rhiann . . . want me as I need you* . . .

So the realization came to her of what he desired, more than her body: the certainty she needed him as much as he her, that it was not his force that drove this.

Instantly, she wanted to give everything. The last whisper of the scared girl faded, and Rhiann placed his brown hand over one white breast, and drew his mouth to the other, and she dug her fingers into his hair and arched against him in triumph, the yearning free at last to flood every part of her being.

Here, she whispered, drawing his lips as he followed her fingers, sucking them, to every place she wanted his kiss, *and here*, ribs and wrist and ankle and throat, *here* . . .

Then suddenly he was no force to be guided but a power of his own, sliding down to place his lips on her thighs. And Rhiann gasped, confused, when his kisses nudged higher against the tender skin between her legs, his dark hair trailing across her belly, the tip of his tongue parting her, warm and wet. Oh, Goddess, she did not know that such a thing could happen.

And all that she was, all she existed for, was the keen, sharp pleasure that centred there, the molten fire that began to flare. And when at last he covered her, it was this burning core that he drew to him; neither thrusting nor grinding, but clasping her buttocks and raising her to him as if she were an offering, as if she were sacred.

Before Rhiann's blurred eyes the tattooed animals on Eremon's chest leaped and danced, slick with sweat, their fierce muscles given life by his own. He called her then, drawing her upwards with the power of her own need, and she opened with all that was in her, the outlines of skin and body fusing together.

And when her gasps turned to cries, the burning overflowed, and Eremon took her face and stared into her eyes, his soul-flame holding her close as the ecstasy crashed around them.

Chapter 10

For two days Rhiann and Eremon did not leave the furs unless they had to. Outside, the season bloomed, the sun shimmering and pooling in the little hollow, spilling through the chinks in the willow door. The air inside thickened as the garlands wilted, releasing scent from falling petals. All sense of day and night dissolved in a haze of deep, wet kisses, and salt and sweat, and Eremon's tongue stinging Rhiann's raw flesh.

Late on the second day, exhaustion claimed them long enough for a deeper sleep. At dusk, a cooler, rain-scented breeze blew in, brushing their hot skin, and Eremon rose again to see to the horses, while Rhiann stirred up the warm coals and set water to boil. When Eremon came back, she was sipping her tea, cross-legged in her linen shift on the edge of the bed. She had kept the womb herbs in the waist pouch under her wedding dress, where no one would see them.

Eremon wrinkled his nose. 'What are you drinking? It smells vile.'

Rhiann reached out her hand for him. 'A woman's tea,' she said, yet she flushed at the lie in her heart, and it was as if something dark at last crept into the sheltered cradle of the hut. *I have no choice*, a small, inner voice whispered. *For now.*

She kissed his outstretched fingers, and pointed to another cup on the hearth. 'Eithne packed something for you, too, *cariad*. It is mint and honey; tastes much better, I promise.'

He threw himself down over the rumpled sheets, naked but for a long undertunic. The movement rucked up the pale linen, and she was treated to a clear sight of his buttocks, the muscles sweeping firmly down the backs of his legs. When he saw the direction of her gaze, he grinned. 'And does this tea strengthen my man's parts, too?' He kissed the bare sole of her foot.

She squirmed away, smiling. 'No! You don't need any more strength in *those*!'

He lay his head across her lap and tickled her, and she jerked her hand, spilling hot tea over the bed. 'Eremon, look what you've done!' she scolded, laughing.

He pulled her shift from her shoulder, the neck opening across one breast. 'Yes, look what I've done,' he drawled softly, reaching up to kiss the pale skin. Then one hand moved lower, and she half-shut her eyes as he peeled back the hem from her legs, exposing the red, tender flesh between her thighs, raw with loving. 'And here, look what I've done here.'

'Eremon . . .'

A piercing whistle shattered the heavy, scented air, and was followed by a dull thud of hoofbeats. In one smooth movement Eremon rolled to his feet, his sword in his hand before Rhiann could even draw her shift to her knees.

'My lord!' came Rori's high, excited voice.

Eremon's shoulders lowered. Pulling his tunic straight, he went to the doorway and disappeared. Rhiann rose to her knees, craning to hear, apprehension stirring in her gut.

'My lord,' Rori said again, breathless from what sounded like a fast gallop. 'I am sorry to disturb you.'

'What is it, lad?' There was no trace of anger in Eremon's tone. He had left orders that no one should come here unless it really was a matter of urgency, and if it was, there was nothing to be done about it.

'A messenger has come from a people called the Novantae,' Rori declared. Rhiann could imagine him drawing his shoulders back with youthful self-importance. 'They have rebelled against the Romans, and they want our help. Their lands are south of the Damnonii, and they heard from those people how you rose up in arms to aid them before.'

Rhiann's belly gripped with the first coldness she had felt in days.

'Did they?' Eremon muttered, half to himself. 'I wonder if they heard also that, after my intervention, the Romans responded by razing the Damnonii villages?'

Eremon's men were used to answering questions not addressed to them. 'Yes, sir,' Rori piped up. 'I heard the lord Conaire speak of it with the man. Yet although they have always kept out of the struggles against the invaders, the Novantae king and three chiefs were recently killed in some dispute over taxes. The messenger says laying low didn't serve them, and so they have risen up instead. They want men, lots of men, to strike at the Romans with force.'

'They are in the south of Alba, you say?' Eremon mused. There was a pause. 'Digging away at the south could weaken Agricola in the north. Indeed it could.'

Rhiann looked down at her hands, swollen and soft from loving him, and wrapped them around her chest, her eyes stinging.

'Rori, go back now,' Eremon instructed. 'I will return tomorrow. And ready a messenger to ride to Calgacus for aid in this expedition.'

After a moment the hoof thuds gradually faded again, and Eremon waited a few moments, before coming back in. There he squatted before Rhiann, his eyes shadowed with apology and regret.

'Hush,' she said, pressing her lips to her favourite curve, where his neck met his shoulder. There the skin moved from rough to soft, holding his scent, so she closed her eyes now and breathed him right down into her.

She would not weep over him, for it would only spoil what they had. But when he took her again with an exquisite tenderness, drawing out her ecstasy until she clung to him, he would never know that tears and not sweat dampened her hair, that it was grief and not joy she buried in his shoulder.

When night had long fallen, and Eremon slept, Rhiann watched him. Her eyes roamed over him hungrily, seeking to capture in memory what she would not see for moons.

Lamp-flame gilding long lashes.

The down on his cheeks.

The plane of muscle under his breast.

His unbraided hair spilled over his arms, and Rhiann reached out a thumb now and stroked his lips, and he murmured and pressed them together before they fell slack once more, like a baby sucking in dreams. Only in sleep did Eremon look as young as his twenty-three years, for the world saw only the hardness in his eyes and the sardonic tilt of his smile, devoid of the tenderness which somehow still lay in his heart.

Rhiann rested her head on her arm, her hand against his cheek. For two days this bed had cradled her, and she had been astonished that when Eremon showed her gentleness and trust, her fears subsided enough for pleasure to have its time in the flame-light. Yet it was dark again now. Rhiann smoothed fingers over Eremon's chest, and when they drifted lower to the nubbed scar on one arm, a chill overtook her. That wound he had received in a duel with Lorn, yet Eremon's skin was webbed with many other fine, faded scars from other battles.

And because their flesh had joined now, the pit of Rhiann's belly suddenly understood what her mind had not: that this flesh she now loved could be pierced by blade and point as easily as her fears pierced her. Struggling for breath, she turned over on her back. In the stone circle she had given the power of her heart to Eremon, yet she hadn't thought beyond that, to a life spent watching him ride to war; followed by the moons of loneliness, expecting all the time to hear of his death.

With stinging eyes Rhiann stared at the roof beam over her head, looped with chains of fading roses. *I will not wait here, helpless to fear,* she thought fiercely. *The dream is my path, yet we walk it together, Eremon and I.*

She gained only a night of fitful sleep, but when she woke to a grey sky, a cold fire and Eremon's arm flung across her breasts, Rhiann knew already what she would do.

To Eremon's delight, his messenger to Calgacus had not gone far north when he met a warband of the Caledonii king coming the other way – a gift for Eremon of five hundred warriors.

Eremon inspected them at once on the river meadow before Dunadd's gates. It was a cloudy, wind-whipped day that was nevertheless heavy with unseasonal heat. The few horses among the Caledonii warriors tossed their manes, skittish in the dry wind.

'What news from your king?' Eremon asked the warband's commander, whom he had met at Calgacus's dun.

The man, a tall, powerful fighter with greying hair, slowly shook his head, his arm looped under his horse's neck. 'News that was bought at great cost, lord – the lives of ten spies and scouts.'

'By the Boar!' Eremon blinked windborn grit from his eyes. 'What news was worth such a price?'

'The Roman emperor has died; a new one has come.' The Caledonii warrior held Eremon's gaze, his mouth a grim line. 'And this one has renewed the excitement of the soldiers. The southern tribes say the Romans are restless, boasting of a coming fight. They are demanding more taxes of charcoal and wood for their smithies, more grain and meat for soldiers. The news is that they are preparing to march south to the Novantae rebellion.'

Eremon went very still. In a hollow voice he dismissed the men, and instructed Conaire to see them housed and fed. Then he strode away from the river towards the dun, his eyes blank and unseeing, his feet careless of their steps.

Some time later Conaire found him with Bran at his furnace, watching intently as the big, ruddy smith pushed air into the mud dome over his fire with a huge pair of leather bellows.

'I let Rhiann know about the extra men,' Conaire said, glancing from Eremon's still face to Bran's great, soot-rimed arms, the hardened muscles bunching with each push. Eremon grunted and nodded at Bran, then rose stiffly to his feet and laid down the hammer he had been hefting between his fingers.

With a jerk of his head, Eremon drew Conaire away from the roar of the furnace and the stifling heat of the small shed, into the dark coolness of the adjoining storehouse. The grey daylight filtering through the open door picked out the piles of new shield-bosses and spear-points on the long oak bench.

Conaire selected a spear from a bundle against the wall and eyed down its shaft. 'I've split the new arrivals into groups to train with our own men . . . some on spears, some on swords.'

'Archers,' Eremon said absently, picking out a point and testing it on his fingertip. 'We will need many archers; get all who show ability in this area to train with Nectan's men. We only have a few days; there is no time to lose.'

Conaire was watching him carefully. 'Why are you so disturbed, brother? It's not just the Novantae – you knew Agricola was bound to retaliate once they rebelled. It's something about the new emperor; I saw your face.'

Eremon snorted wryly, for there was little he could keep from Conaire. He took a deep breath of the tang of iron and raw wood. 'During those few nights I spent with Samana in the Roman camp, she told me that Agricola only stopped his initial advance at the Forth two years ago because the emperor then, Titus, had not given him leave to go further. Indeed, Titus had even taken some of Agricola's men to fight on another frontier, far to the east.' He blew out his breath, and dug the point into the bench. 'If this new emperor has a different mind, then perhaps the game begins in earnest. After dealing with the Novantae, they will come north, at last.'

Conaire rested the spear-butt on the earth floor and leaned on it. 'As we have been expecting they would eventually,' he reminded Eremon. 'We are ready.'

Eremon's bitter laugh took Conaire by surprise. 'These men are ready,' Eremon agreed, flinging his hand towards the open door. 'Ready for a tribal raid; ready to face a warband. But not an army, brother! Not the thousands of men Agricola commands! Without all the tribes of Alba, we can hold them back only a little while.'

'Then that's what we'll do,' Conaire replied, flipping the spear across his broad shoulders. 'These Romans haven't yet seen that there are more ways to fight than with numbers alone.'

Eremon sighed, and threw the point down. 'When we go south, we must find a way to slow them. Or, the gods save us, the storm will break over us and, soon after, those we call our own.'

A burst of laughter sounded from the second bonfire, carrying clearly across the river meadow on the damp, night air. So far, Calgacus's men and the Epidii warriors were feasting together quite happily. So far. Yet Lorn's head jerked towards the sound as he drank of his ale.

'I think it best,' Eremon continued carefully, 'that you take charge of the defence of Dunadd.'

He braced himself for one of Lorn's explosions, the indignant demands that he lead his own men on the southern adventure. But

Eremon didn't want Lorn along this time, however good a fighter he was. The warband would have to move far and fast, and Eremon couldn't spend his time knee-deep in the marshes and bogs of the Novantae territory arguing with Lorn.

Lorn gave no sign he had heard, however, as he slowly swallowed his ale. It was only after he wiped the liquid from his pale moustache that he spoke. 'I agree,' he said evenly.

'You do?' The words fell from Eremon's lips before he could stop them. He peered at Lorn, but the Epidii prince's eyes were in shadow, the outline of his nose sharp against the flames of the nearer fire.

'Of course. Your man Finan is a fine commander, but he is of Erin.' Lorn paused, as the far laughter slid into jeers, and one or two indignant shouts. 'An Epidii warrior in command here would be best. We don't know yet what Agricola will do – I can field a northern force to defend Dunadd, and stop him outflanking you. And the extra border guards and signal stations must be ordered as well as when you are here.'

Eremon frowned at Lorn's agreeable tone – he would have felt happier with some degree of protest. And yet there was an unease in the swift way that Lorn tossed back another gulp of ale.

Still . . . Eremon shrugged to himself, his eye caught by Conaire, tunic sleeves pushed back, wading into the middle of the scuffle which had broken out now between some newcomers and Dunadd men.

'Boar's balls!' Eremon rested his cup on the log and sprang to his feet. 'They'll kill themselves before we get anywhere near the Romans.'

As he made to go, Lorn stopped him by gripping his forearm, wrist to wrist. 'Prince.' He was looking up at Eremon now, but the glint of pale eyes in the firelight showed nothing. 'May the gods bring you success.' Lorn's breath pushed out through his teeth. 'Go safely.'

By the time Eremon reached the fighters, Conaire's great fists had downed enough to bring them into line, and Eremon had little to do but give orders: the Dunadd men back to their own fire, and another keg of ale to be opened. Soon, they would all be singing together under the stars, and no one would care then what tribe their drinking partner came from. *If only disagreements between princes were as easily resolved*, Eremon thought, glancing back at Lorn, who was moving off.

Conaire had argued about leaving Lorn in charge, his reasoning only voicing Eremon's misgivings. Yet Lorn had given his oath to follow Eremon as war leader, and though Urben's dismay that first day had been real, Eremon could, grudgingly, understand it. The old chieftain hadn't made an appearance since returning to his dun, anyway, and even Tharan and the other dissenters on the council had not argued against Eremon's southern expedition. Perhaps the act of giving Lorn a prominent role in the warband was finding wide favour.

Another drunken shout came, and more black shapes were suddenly flailing their fists before the fire. With a sigh, Eremon turned back, seeking once more for his brother.

Rhiann kept her plan secret for as long as she could.

This was made easier by being so busy with provisions for the warband, instructing the women to bake the men's trail cakes of beef and venison pounded with pig fat, barley and dried berries. She and Eithne also kept up their collection of leaves, roots and flowers, preserving and storing late in the long twilights. Rhiann's greatest concern was Caitlin, but her sister was so enthused by Rhiann's plan that she agreed to move in with Linnet for the few weeks Rhiann would be away.

Which only left one thing – informing Eremon.

It was hard to catch him alone, for at any time he could be on the training ground, with his own men, or at Bran's smithy. She trailed from one place to another, Didius trotting along at her heels, until at last she ran Eremon to ground at the port, Crinan.

He was standing on the end of the longest pier with Finan, to whom he'd given charge of the transport arrangements for the thousand-man warband. The old Erin warrior had commandeered every boat he could find along the coast, from hide *curraghs* to larger trading ships.

As Rhiann approached, she shaded her eyes against the afternoon sun, noting Eremon's easy stance, his hands on hips, his head down, listening to Finan. Cù saw her first, bounding over to jump up on his hind legs, and she was still brushing down her skirts when Eremon followed his hound, his eyes dismissing Didius with a cursory glance. Cù had now turned his attentions to the Roman, and was snuffling his crotch while Didius stood frozen, his plump jowls quivering. Romans did not live with hounds the way Albans did, and Cù seemed to have sniffed out the little man's fear along with his scent.

'Eithne's father is a fisherman,' Rhiann offered to Eremon. 'He says it will only take six days to land in the south of the Novantae lands.'

Eremon winced. 'Only six days!'

Rhiann grinned and patted his cheek. 'This time I will brew enough tansy to settle your belly ten times over.'

'I think I'll need some prayers, too.'

Rhiann bit her lip, glancing down at the hide boats which bobbed against their pier on their weed-furred ropes. 'Prayers I can give you, and not just my own.' She drew a deep breath, and then expelled the words in a rush. 'I have it in mind to return to the Sacred Isle while you are gone.' She braced herself for an argument, but Eremon only frowned.

'Why?'

'I wish to ask the Sisters for aid, and call the Source to strengthen you and your men.'

The crease in Eremon's brows deepened, and the sun shimmered from the water into his eyes, showing his fear clearly. 'I cannot deny we need it . . . but we just returned from the Sacred Isle. I don't like the idea of you roving the seas alone, not with Maelchon still at large.'

'It only takes three days in a good wind, Eremon,' she wheedled. 'No one will notice a little fishing boat.'

His jaw was setting in that familiar way. 'You can't go alone.'

'I won't be alone.' She waved behind her. 'I will take Didius; you know I could not have a more devoted guard.'

Eremon snorted, his eyes narrowing on Didius. 'More devoted, perhaps not,' he muttered, 'but more *effective* would be better.'

The breeze coming off the bay was keen, and Rhiann crossed her arms over her breast, shivering. 'I don't want to take any warriors away from you or the defence of Dunadd. Besides – not that you care – but it would be wise to remove Didius from Gelert's sight and—'

At those words, Eremon's expression transformed, his eyes jerking back to rest on her face with sudden intensity. And that's when she realized what she'd accidentally invoked: the attractive idea of placing *her* away from the chief druid's sight. 'Gelert,' Eremon repeated, absently rubbing her arms to warm them. At last he kissed the top of her head. 'Give my own regards to the Sisters, then, and take three of my armbands as an offering to your Stones.'

Rhiann smiled with relief. 'So I will, *cariad.*'

Three days later, from a lookout on top of the sea-facing headland, Rhiann managed to remain dry-eyed as the flotilla of boats passed out of sight beyond the wood-cloaked Isle of Deer. Caitlin, tucked under her arm, fared less well, and Rhiann felt the violent trembling in her sister's thin shoulders. It was a threatening, dark day, and spatters of rain began to fall, driven by growing gusts of wind that tugged fiercely at their sheepskin cloaks.

'I *won't* say I wish you were staying, Rhiann.' Caitlin swiped at the mingled tears and rain on her cheeks with impatient fingers. 'I *won't*. Anything you do that protects Conaire is right, it must be.'

Rhiann smiled, wrapping Caitlin's cloak tighter about her neck and repinning it with nimble fingers. 'I know this is hard. But though Dercca will coddle you, Linnet's mountain is beautiful – more like your old home. And Eithne will be with you.'

Caitlin nodded, staring out at the iron-grey sea, her hands absently rubbing her belly. 'He will come back, though, won't he?' she whispered. 'He'll see the baby?'

'Of course he will.' Rhiann brushed Caitlin's braids free of her fleece ruff and kissed her, trying not to notice how her belly jutted, and how it was already putting a noticeable sway in her narrow back. *Only five moons*, Rhiann counted, with a stab of unease. *It will be well for me not to stay away too long.*

As they waited out the rain among the damp hazel woods below, watching the drops denting the bay, Rhiann relived again the moment when Eremon left.

He had held her cold face in his hands, as his standard of braided boat-tails and horse-mane streamed above them on the pier. They had both remained silent in front of all those men swarming over the boats, yet Rhiann's fingers dug into Eremon's mailshirt as she searched his eyes, and there, at last, she had seen the farewell he would not speak.

Chapter 11

Though she had left the Sacred Isle on a day of sun, glowing with triumph, Rhiann's return echoed the cold knot of dread that had gradually come to rest in her belly, the further north they sailed. For two days rain lashed the little hide shelter in the timber boat, pattering ceaselessly on the worn leather, spraying her with every gust of wind. Its sail down, the boat was driven north along the edge of the restless swells, making an easier and shorter journey for the escort of six oarsmen Rhiann had taken from among the fishermen, and Didius.

When Rhiann at last ducked out of the shelter as they entered the sea-loch of the Sisters' settlement, she was stiff and cold, and her skin, hair and cloak were coated with drying salt.

The low, tumbled cliffs of the Sacred Isle's west coast were a featureless bank in the drizzle and mist, slowly emerging into jagged profile as the loch waters nudged the boat shorewards. Yet Rhiann would not need to see with her eyes in order to know the Stones were near. She raised her face as the boat passed under their headland, heedless of the rain being driven under her hood. Instead she closed her eyes, drawing into memory the Stones as she had last seen them: a cross and an inner ring of aged sentinels, tall and grey, watching the sea. On that day of her leaving, the sun had glittered on their pale surfaces, shifting and moving as if with joy that she had found Eremon, and been reunited with the Goddess.

And now . . .

Rhiann's eyes flickered open. This day the Stones seemed to huddle into the grey rain, and the rocks lining the shore as they drew close were slick with cold spray, darkly clothed with weed. Rhiann shivered and gripped the hood under her chin, shamed by the Stones' stern gaze. Did they know of the sacred pool, and how she had failed? Did they know what she had come to ask, despite this?

For the Stones not only marked a major convergence of the rivers of earth power – pathways for the Source – that ran beneath the land. They also cradled the spirit of each priestess, turning child to novice and novice to initiate. Rhiann had gained her own power here, power she had now lost, and she was unsure if she deserved to count herself among the Stones' children any more.

Yet I also gained love, she found herself thinking, and her fingers crept up to the amber necklace where it lay against her neck.

The Epidii rowers brought the small boat skimming over the dark water to the pier, which crossed the kelp-wound rocks on spindly legs. It was only then, peering into the drizzle, that Rhiann saw she was not the only visitor.

A larger plank ship was also tied up, its sail of oiled hide unfurled to display the painted emblem of a raven. It was of the Lugi tribe then, on the northern coast. Yet Rhiann's mouth had gone dry, for the Lugi lands also faced the strait to the Orcades islands – Maelchon's realm. Just as Rhiann's boat edged its stern side-on to the pier, a man in a rich, striped cloak stepped into the hull of the Lugi ship, guarded by warriors whose spear-tips gleamed dully through the rain.

And beyond the Lugi ship and pier, on the rocks below the cluster of priestess houses, stood a cloaked figure that Rhiann knew as well as the outline of the Stones. Her heart gave a peculiar lurch, and she waited only long enough for the boat to be secured by ropes before clambering out onto the slick timber planking.

The Lugi ship had now cast off, and the figure on the shore raised a pale hand that was answered by the call of a war trumpet, booming faintly across the water. And suddenly Rhiann realized she was running along the pier, hopping over the last few rocks and all but flinging herself into Setana's wiry arms.

'Child!' the old seer exclaimed, rocking on her heels. Her voice was muffled by Rhiann's cloak for, bowed with age, she only reached the younger woman's shoulder. 'Dear child, you have returned so soon?'

Her breath squeezed out by the fierceness of her own embrace, Rhiann remembered herself at last and pulled back. 'I am so sorry, Sister,' she said, with a half-sob she disguised as a laugh. 'It . . .' She trailed off, hands pressed to her breast, breathing deeply. 'It has been a stormy journey.'

Setana peered out from her own hood at Rhiann, her shrewd blue eyes a keen contrast to the rest of her face, which was round and almost childish. 'Ach, as it often is, my chick.' She waved her hand at the departing Lugi ship, beating under fast oar back down the sea-loch. 'Though the weather keeps few from our door, at such times.'

Rhiann put back her hood to her shoulders so she could breathe properly. 'Was that the Lugi king himself? Why was he here?'

Setana clamped Rhiann's forearm as the damp wind gusted, plucking at the deer-head brooch on her cloak. 'Why they all come – to expunge their guilt, child! Will they get this alliance, deserved or not? Will they be blessed with children? Is the fever sweeping the tribe a curse, and if so how can they regain the Mother's blessing?' She sighed and shook her head, and wisps of grey hair escaped her hood. 'They wish to control the world, dear souls, yet it is not like that. The Mother has her hand on the loom, more than they will ever know.'

'And why did this king come?' Rhiann asked evenly.

'He would not say. He begged Nerida to ask the Stones, and tell him if what he planned would be favoured by the Goddess or not, if it would keep his people safe.'

'And she did not know of what he spoke?'

Setana shook her head again, mouth pursed. 'He is not the first. Even before you came at Beltaine the visits and offerings from chiefs and kings had grown more frequent – and urgent. They sense the disquiet of the land, you see, as we do. Yet we are sending them away with little but the love of the Mother, and this is not enough for them.' She sighed again, and it was Rhiann's turn to pierce her with her gaze.

'The Stones are not speaking?'

Setana cocked her head to one side her full cheeks shiny and red with the cold, like crab apples. 'Oh, they speak to *us*, for the earth is restless, and Her power heaves and swells like a fractious sea. But no clear seeings have come, not for any of us here – there is only mist and confusion. Perhaps this is a time when men are to be guided by their hearts alone – and for this, I fear.' With one of her abrupt mood changes, Setana suddenly smiled up at Rhiann, clasping her hand. 'But enough! Nerida can tell you more; she will be so pleased to see you again, and so soon!' Setana's bright eyes came to rest on the pier behind. 'Goddess be! What have you brought us?'

Rhiann turned to see Didius swaying green-faced on the end of the pier, clutching his new sword and Rhiann's pack. The blade, made for tall Alban warriors, nearly dragged on the ground, while his too-large helmet had been pushed back above his high forehead.

'That,' Rhiann said, beckoning Didius forward, 'is our Roman captive, Didius. Yet he is my own personal guard now.'

'Welcome.' Setana studied him, and Didius couldn't help but shift uncomfortably from foot to foot. Then he thought better of that and sketched an awkward little bow, scraping his scabbard chape on the rocks. At that Setana laughed, though not unkindly, the lines around her eyes crinkling into folds. 'You look a trifle pale, Roman. Ask for our healer Tirena; she will have you feeling fit again before nightfall.'

Rhiann smiled at Didius, taking her pack from him. 'The boatmen know where to go, Didius. There are some huts for men. Take our things there and I will find you.'

Many of the blue-cloaked Sisters nodded at Rhiann as she and Setana made their way through the settlement. They appeared to be returning from the seeing rite in the Stones, for some clutched drums and elderwood flutes for the sacred music, and some pots of scented oil. All of them were soaked by the rain, and most hurried along with their hoods drawn up.

The cluster of roundhouses and worksheds crouched on the landward side of the Stones headland, sheltered from sea storms by a screen of stunted rowans and hazel trees. The mud walls were yellowed with salt, the thatch roofs dark with damp, and the garish decoration of noble houses was nowhere to be seen. There were no cries or shouts, beyond the faint, high piping of the novices chanting somewhere; no babies or dogs; no clanging smiths' hammers or male laughter or wood saws or rumbling carts. Everything the Sisters did not make was given to them in payment for their gifts of seeing, their blessings, their special dyes and herbs, and their stewardship of the Stones.

For a moment, Rhiann allowed herself to be soothed by this softer world, by the muted colours and low, murmuring sounds, and the dank mist that blurred all the shapes into paleness. Yet they were already at Nerida's modest house, and it was with trembling hands that Rhiann lifted the door-hide and entered.

Nerida glanced up from the fire and, with a cry of surprise, put aside the spindle she'd been winding and groped for her ash staff. 'Daughter, this is unexpected!' She was of the same height as Setana, but her face was a finer oval, and where Setana's hair was grey and frizzy, nearly untameable, Nerida's had turned to the pure whiteness of snow, held in two long braids. In her youth her beauty would have been severe, with arched brows and prominent bones, yet deep wrinkles and sagging flesh had softened that remoteness.

'I greet you, Eldest Sister,' Rhiann murmured, as Nerida stepped over the scattered tufts of unspun wool to embrace her fiercely.

'Come, come, warm your hands!' Nerida sank back into her rush chair, as Setana shook the rain from their cloaks.

'I have some gifts for you first.' Rhiann dug through her pack and, with bowed head, presented Nerida with pots of Linnet's best goat cheese, Eremon's three armbands and a large assortment of bronze brooches, since the Sisters had no smith. The other iron goods – cauldrons, pots, fire dogs and chains – were in the boat.

As the Eldest Sister gave thanks, Rhiann slid to the hearth-bench, at last able to study Nerida's face more closely. And what she saw there alarmed her. For Nerida's shoulders were distinctly more bowed, and her blue eyes had retreated further behind their folds of flesh, the skin stretched more thinly over her bones.

Something is weighing on her . . . With a shock, Rhiann suddenly realized that Nerida was regarding her with the same scrutiny, and no doubt coming to the same conclusion. Swallowing, Rhiann spread her hands to the fire, then tucked them under her skirts. 'Setana told me of the Lugi king, Sister, and I confess I am driven back to these shores by the same winds that drove him.'

'No doubt, daughter,' Nerida said softly, and for a moment sorrow gleamed in her eyes. 'The far, faint clamour of coming war, we will call it.'

The words hung there, as stark as the room around them, with its bare walls, earth floor, box bed and swept hearth. Taking a cup of honeysuckle tea from Setana, Rhiann fixed her eyes on her own fingers, stiff with cold. 'Yes, war. Yet as you had no answer for him, perhaps you have none for me.'

Silence fell, as the hazel boughs in the fire cracked and settled, and Setana moved behind the chair to put her hand on Nerida's shoulder. 'First you must ask,' Setana prodded Rhiann gently, and Rhiann drew a shaking breath, suddenly swept with the terror of so many things.

What would happen to Eremon if they would not help her?

What would happen if they agreed, but she failed them and him in the Stones, cut off from the Goddess as she was?

What would happen if they could draw no Source, and Eremon was left helpless, as the Roman wave broke over him?

With an effort, Rhiann steadied her mind and voice, and told her elders all the things that had so lately occurred. Then her eyes swept up to fix on Nerida. 'I know the Sisterhood has always remained outside the squabbles of the tribes, but this is different.' Her desperation was creeping into her words, and she forced herself to sit back, her palms slick with nervous sweat around the rowan cup.

'Daughter,' came Setana's seer voice, lower and slower than her usual tone, her eyes unblinking as she stared into the fire, 'do you think we do not know this is different? The Romans threaten all Alba; the Romans threaten our Mother, our Lady. They may be Her children, too, but they will throw down the Stones, and reshape the very land, and enslave our people.' Her voice faltered, and then her eyes closed. 'We know. Oh, we know, for though we can see nothing clearly, we hear the sound of battle, and the cries of children, and the mist is red with blood . . .'

Setana was the greatest of seers, and her voice had the power to draw the listener into trance. Rhiann carefully set down the cup, her skin pebbling. Setana's message was the same as her own dream.

'The kings and chiefs come,' Nerida continued heavily, 'and we look in the pool and the seeing bowl and the fire, and we tell them what we just told you. And they are troubled, give their gold to the loch, and their grain and meat to the Sisters, and leave. But we do not know what lies in their hearts, or where it will lead.'

'Eremon wants all the kings to join him and Calgacus in the alliance,' Rhiann murmured. 'Yet many will not, for they fear the shifts of power, and having their lands taken by the Caledonii or Epidii. They do not see it is the Romans they must fear!'

Nerida was thoughtful, her fingers twirling the empty ash spindle. 'We cannot lie to convince them, child; we can only tell them what we see and don't see. Their souls are darkened by their own greed and deceit and treachery, and that is what guides them. Yet . . . it is in my own mind that we must do more to protect the Mother, if indeed Her own warriors hesitate.'

'Eremon does not hesitate!' Rhiann burst out. 'He has taken a force to defend the Novantae homes! If he can strike a blow there, perhaps he will weaken this northern advance, and save us.'

Setana's gaze sharpened, returning to the room. 'Her man was made the King Stag in the Stones, Sister,' she murmured to Nerida, her grip tightening on her shoulder. 'Perhaps they will still be alive to his call. For the power we draw here is not for female alone, but for male too – God *and* Goddess. For those who draw swords for truth, as well as those who draw forth life. Perhaps we can forge a blade of it and send it homing, to him. It has been done, long ago.'

Rhiann's eyes darted from one to the other, hope daring to rise in her heart.

'When?' was all Nerida said, turning her face up to Setana, the line of her sagging throat blurred by firelight.

Setana paused, her head cocked to one side as if listening. 'The eve of the longest day is in two weeks. Let us do it then, for we offer to the sun, and the sun is the face of the God.' Suddenly she looked directly at Rhiann, the light in her eyes seeming to pierce all the veils Rhiann had drawn around her heart. 'Yet Rhiann must be the centre around which we circle, for it is her bond to her man that will direct what we call forth.'

Nerida paused, then bowed her head. 'So shall it be.'

The warm rush of relief in Rhiann was doused with sharp, cold terror. The centre, all of them relying on her to be the pillar for the power they would call. Did she have the skill and strength to be that any more?

Slowly, Rhiann rose to thank them both, exchanging the priestess kiss on their spirit-eyes. The Goddess still came through Rhiann for the people; She had even come for Eremon once before, called by Rhiann's love. Surely She would do so again, when the need was so great.

It was after Setana left, as Rhiann paused at the door on her way to her lodgings, that Nerida suddenly spoke once more. 'You were right to seek us out, daughter.' Looking back, Rhiann could see nothing in the fire shadows but two white ropes of hair across her breast. 'Yet while you are in retreat here, I ask you to consider the other reasons you have come.'

Rhiann's blood was suddenly beating hard against her throat. 'I don't understand, Sister. Why else would I come?'

With a sigh, Nerida took up the iron poker against the chair's arm and swiped at a crumbling piece of burning wood. 'Perhaps you are running from something also, child. Think on that.'

Rhiann stared at the back of Nerida's head, and suddenly she remembered another time they had both been caught in these same poses: Rhiann flinging up the door-hide to stalk out, trembling with rage and grief; Nerida silent, her eyes sorrowed, letting Rhiann's anguish about her dead family wash over her. For Nerida had understood then, as Rhiann did not, that her anger was not for the Sisters or even for the Goddess, but for Rhiann herself.

On impulse, Rhiann crossed the floor and knelt by Nerida's side, afraid to see in her eyes any hint of that rift still remaining, wanting to tell Nerida what happened by Linnct's pool, but constrained by the deep shame of it.

Yet Nerida turned and smiled at Rhiann with the old sweetness, and laid her hand in blessing on Rhiann's bowed head. 'You are welcome home again, child, as you always were, as you always will be. *Sa!* Do not let an old woman scold you.'

Her palm curved around Rhiann's head and rested there, stroking her hair.

In a hut buffeted by storm winds, Eremon squinted at a rough map scrawled on the earth floor, the lines of it wavering with the fire shadows. His Novantae hosts did not use or need maps, for they knew every expanse of sedge, stretch of bog and wind-blasted ridge-top as though it were their own dun. Yet things were changing, and if they asked for his help, they needed to accept his ways as well.

With his dagger-tip, Eremon had just drawn the line of Agricola's forts across the narrow neck of land between the Forth and Clutha inlets. The Novantae lands were well south of this, but Eremon could see now why Agricola had left them alone. The great bulge of Novantae territory was cut off from the rest of Alba by broken ranges of high, lonely hills, and wide stretches of boggy wastes. Behind this natural barrier, the coastal lands afforded good grazing and harbours, but one could only get to them by sea. So these strange, isolated people had remained behind their hills and defensive bogs, quiet and complacent, until the Roman fort across the southern strait sent troops to collect taxes and supplies.

At first the Novantae gave in, too scared by what had happened to the Damnonii and Selgovae duns to their north and east, battered into submission by iron bolts from Roman war machines. But as the year dragged into another year, and they were afflicted with sunseason floods that ruined crops and rotted the grazing, so the Roman demands began to bite more deeply.

The Novantae king, accompanied by his chieftains, went to the nearest Roman fort to explain the situation, and to offer up, in desperation, their weapons and the skills of their best fighters. But they were laughed at. In anger the king did the only thing he could do to retain his honour: he called out the commander of the Roman fort for single combat.

In reply, the king was speared where he stood.

Afterwards, the king's surviving son – the youth who now sat opposite Eremon – gathered more men and razed that fort to the ground, as well as raiding the civilian camp that had grown up around the larger fort over the strait. That was nearly two moons ago, and though the bulk of the people retreated to their fishing villages, the Novantae scouts had travelled far to glean that a large force of Romans on the Forth had been assembled and thoroughly provisioned, and was now on its way.

'So what is it that you want to do?' Eremon asked, swilling the murky brown ale in his cup, eyeing the king's son over the fire.

The prince, a heavy youth with a florid, blunt face and bulbous nose, held out one arm, the fringe of his cloak frayed against his tattered tunic. 'What you did for the Damnonii, prince of Erin! We need a great victory!'

Eremon pursed his lips, rubbing the stubble on his chin. 'A great victory it was, at first, but the Romans came down upon the Damnonii in fire and fury.' He shook his head. 'Most of them were killed.'

The young man's deep-set blue eyes raked over the men crouched around Eremon on the floor: Conaire silent by his shoulder; Rori and Fergus polishing their spear-tips; and Colum sharpening his meat-knife on a whetstone.

'What?' the Novantae youth cried. 'Do you come here flashing your gold torcs of Erin, only to turn coward on us?'

Conaire hissed, and Rori and Fergus both straightened with alacrity. Calmly, Eremon stretched his legs to the fire. His trousers, bound with laces up to the knee, were damp from spray and rain, and his shoulders ached from rowing. 'No,' he replied, his voice cool. 'But I won't let hot blood cloud my mind. If you think that we can take these Romans now in some pitched battle, you are mistaken.'

The youth's brows narrowed, and he struck the ground with his spear-butt. 'Then why did you come?'

Eremon picked up a burnt twig from the edge of the hearth. 'You have high ground, bogs and moors, thick forest. We must use them to our advantage.' He pointed at the map with the blackened stick. 'You tell us that an army comes from Agricola's northern base, perhaps three thousand strong. We cannot meet it head on, but we *can* do something else – bite its hide, harry and weaken it.'

The young man's mouth had by now dropped open. 'You speak of dishonour, grubbing about in the woods like badgers! We must storm them as one, in a glorious charge—'

'That glorious charge will get you all killed,' Eremon interrupted dryly. He crossed his legs and leaned forward. 'You asked for my help, and this is how it must be. Right now, we do not have the numbers to face the Romans on a battlefield. But we have other strengths, other ways to teach them a lesson. And if we drive these invaders out of your lands, we are also buying the rest of Alba another season.'

The prince's frown deepened. 'Another season for what?'

'To convince more kings to join together – only an Alban alliance gives us any hope of real victory.' Suddenly, Eremon grinned, brushing charcoal from his hands. 'Of course, in the meantime we may frustrate these Romans so greatly that they think twice about the whole matter of Alba!'

Eremon's grin was disarming when he wanted it to be, and he was pleased to see the frown melting from the Novantae prince's face, to be replaced by a wary hope. 'If what you say is true you have picked the right territory for that, prince. From our hill-tops we can see them coming from leagues away, for they must keep to the river valleys if they want to stay together.'

Eremon drained his ale cup and wiped his mouth. 'What of your women and children?'

'They will be safe in our coastal duns.'

Eremon tented his fingers and rested his chin on them, thinking, as the wind threw itself against the walls of the hut, screeching like some Otherworld spirit. 'No,' he said at last, straightening. 'Remember the fate of the Damnonii? I have another suggestion.'

Chapter 12

'What do you mean, you cannot find them?'

Agricola stared along the churning line of white surf, whipped into froth by a strong wind. Higher up the beach behind grassy dunes squatted a collection of thatched roundhouses, but there was no trace of smoke in the air above them, and no sound beyond the shouts of his own men as they searched the buildings.

The centurion, holding his helmet, nervously ran one hand through his sweat-soaked hair. 'They are gone, sir. Just like the last village. And the one before.'

Agricola bit down a curse and walked his horse a few steps along the beach, gazing out at the choppy, grey waves. Behind him his officers trailed closer, as silent as he.

Agricola was bone tired. The vigour that had flowed through his ageing limbs at the news of Domitian's orders had been seeping away for weeks now, the further south they marched. The Novantae lands they crossed were part of it – exceedingly bleak, cold and damp. And somehow, deserted.

The information he had from his southern forts was that the Novantae scratched a living along the sandy fringes of their territory, so naturally Agricola had targeted this area. After coming down the river valleys from the north-east, he split his detachment of 3,000 men into two columns, sending one north around the hilly, difficult core of the terrain, and taking the other column south. The plan was for both to reach the coast, then work their way around, subduing the Novantae villages until the two columns met. This plan fitted well with what he knew and yet, something had changed. The people had abandoned their villages, taken everything of worth, little though that was.

Agricola exhaled through his teeth with frustration, and the horse, feeling the tension in his legs, snorted and stamped.

One of his tribunes at last broke the silence. 'Where are they, then?'

'They must have retreated into the mountains.' Agricola folded the reins in his palm, restlessly turning them over and over.

'This is a change of tactics for them,' the *primus pilus* said, the senior centurion of the Ninth Legion, from which Agricola had drawn his detachment. His breastplate, greaves and crested helmet were always the most carefully polished, reflecting the glare even on such a cloudy day. 'They stick close to the coasts; they always have.'

Agricola nodded to himself, his apparent calm belied by his restless fingers on the reins. 'Yet it only continues the pattern we've seen with these savages elsewhere. They were quiet and subdued, and then they rebelled.' He paused. 'Some of them have begun to think differently, but it is nothing we have not dealt with before. They appear to mount a resistance, but at the first sign of real discipline and determination it all crumbles and collapses into ruin. Then we pick them off, one by one.' He turned his head, straightening his shoulders and spearing them all with his eyes.

Never let them see him doubting.

'They can run, but we know they are not many, and cutting them off from their villages will weaken them.' Agricola began to draw in the air. 'We will catch them – so! – between our two columns, and crush them.' He dropped his hands. 'Remember that whoever is directing them has shown neither inventiveness nor courage by raiding in the dark, then disappearing. This is the behaviour of a disorganized rabble, not a formidable enemy, gentlemen, and we will treat them with the contempt they deserve.' He eyed his officers, one by one, pleased to see the same firm resolve settling over their faces.

And so it lasted, at least until the greasy platters had been cleared away in the command tent that very night. For a muddy, wearied rider arrived then, gasping out the news that the northern column had been attacked by a significant force of barbarians, and could not win through to the coast. It could not even move beyond the valley in which it was penned, like a fish behind a weir.

It was waiting to be rescued.

In the silence that followed this announcement, the bravest – or most foolhardy – of the young tribunes once again ventured his opinion.

'So,' he said, carefully placing his cup on Agricola's map table, 'that's where their men have gone.'

'Goddess Mother of All!' Rhiann squawked, dropping the pot of boiling water and steeping seaweed, jumping back so the scalding liquid splashed the floor of the dyeing shed and not her feet.

'Rhiann!' Scattering shavings of alder bark everywhere, her friend Fola was at Rhiann's side at once, pulling her hand out from under her arm as Rhiann hopped on one foot. 'Let me see, Sister, let me see!'

'Ah . . .' Shaking her hand in pain, Rhiann let Fola uncurl her fingers to peer at the rapidly reddening skin on her palm.

'You poor thing! Come,' Fola tugged at Rhiann's elbow, 'into cold water, *now*!' Leaving the trays of steeping bark and empty basin, she dragged Rhiann to the water pot on the bench and plunged her hand into it.

Rhiann squeaked again as tears stung her eyes, drawn not only by pain but also by a fresh waft of the stale urine with which they set the dyes. 'It hurts more now,' she whispered.

Fola's broad, solid face only set more implacably, and she shook her head, fanning her black fringe over her eyes. 'I know, but keep it there for a moment longer. It helps, as you well know.'

When she saw that Rhiann would comply, Fola settled her green-stained hands on her generous hips. They both wore work tunics of brown wool, smeared with fading streaks of dyes. 'And how did you ever pour boiling water on your own hand?' she demanded now. '*You* are never clumsy!'

Rhiann blew wisps of hair from her mouth. 'I don't know how I did it – but scolding me is hardly going to make me feel better!'

The edge of Fola's mouth twitched, and her eyes, dark and round as blackberries, sported a distinct twinkle. More gently, she retrieved Rhiann's hand and peered at it once more. 'Your cursing made me jump, that's all. Few of us here use the Lady's name in such a way.'

Rhiann bit her lip. 'I think I picked it up from Caitlin,' she muttered, shamefaced.

Fola said nothing as she looked closely at Rhiann's palm. 'It is burnt,' she announced, somewhat needlessly, for the stinging was setting Rhiann's teeth on edge. 'Let us find a burdock salve for that; Tirena will have some.'

The sweet, high voices of the novices drifted out from the doorway of the meeting hall as they passed. The longest day was fast approaching, and there were wreaths of hazel branches and sacred herbs to be woven for decorating the Stones. Ducking through the drizzle, they skirted the back of the healing house, stepping between the little herb plots that Tirena guarded so carefully with stone walls and straw and lean-tos of willow.

The house itself was empty, and Fola made Rhiann sit quietly on a stool while she searched the benches laid with drying herbs, shelves full of jars and vials, and baskets that lined the walls. Carefully peeling back the linen cap on a small pot, Fola sniffed deeply and, having found what she wanted, drew a bench close to Rhiann. Laying the injured hand in her lap, Fola began dabbing the salve on Rhiann's palm.

'Why did you stumble, really?' Fola asked then, her dark head bent over Rhiann's arm. Black eyes darted up to Rhiann's face and then down. 'You have been strangely distracted this past week.'

Rhiann gasped a little at the pressure on her palm. 'I told you why I am troubled.'

When she was finished, Fola sat back and looked at her. 'I do understand, about Eremon and his men,' she said slowly.

And Fola did understand in her head, even though, like many of the priestesses trained here, she had decided to stay on the island to serve the elders and the Stones, not return to her tribe like Rhiann. As a Ban Cré, a noblewoman who was also priestess, Rhiann had always known she would have to face the tangled loyalties and threats of the outside world. Yet her friendship with Fola had always been a haven for her because of its simplicity, because Fola was not exposed to these things, and when they were together Rhiann forgot so much else.

Except before, when the wind changed course for a moment, and brought to Rhiann a vivid snatch of low priestess chanting. It was the elders this time, not the novices, drawing the Source up from deep within the earth for the longest day. Rhiann's sharp anxiety had suddenly flared, and she had jerked as she poured the boiling water on to the pulped seaweed.

She sighed now, rubbing her brow with her other hand. 'I am well enough.'

Fola's dark eyes, however, were veiled. 'You left here so happy . . . and yet now, you are as much troubled as you were joyous.'

As Rhiann's lips compressed with denial, Fola set her chin up. 'I hear you at night, in the hut. You do not sleep, and when you do, you whimper and mutter. Look at your face, how drawn it is; your eyes, so shadowed.'

'I fear for Eremon,' Rhiann murmured, and that was true, but the rest of it was weighing so heavily on her that she thought she could hardly draw breath. And it was only getting worse, as the longest day approached. Yet how could she tell anyone here of her shame? It ran too deep, and if she spoke of it she would have to feel it in all its clarity. She didn't even know if any priestess had lost her gifts before.

'If you won't unburden yourself with me,' Fola said, with her usual directness, 'then do it somehow.' She gathered up the salve pot and returned with a fresh comfrey leaf, which she bruised and bound to Rhiann's wrist. 'I must finish this batch of dyes now, for they are to be traded next week. You, though, should rest.'

Rhiann shook her head. 'I must do some collecting of my own.' She gingerly pressed the bandage into her palm. The herbs for her womb tea were running low.

'Does Tirena not have what you seek?'

'No.' Rhiann smiled tightly up at Fola, her good hand resting for a moment on her friend's fingers. 'In any case, my moon bleeding has begun, and we can always do with more moss to dry.'

'Moss we have,' Fola murmured, then said no more.

A man is at the top of the world here, Eremon thought, standing so high on a bare hill-top that if he reached one hand up he could touch the blue bowl of the sky, up-ended over his head. He could see for leagues in all directions through the thin, cold air: to ridges and banks of hills, green with sunseason growth; shadowed peat bogs; glens filled with bracken; and the dark teeth of rocks thrusting upwards. The wind was so harsh it nearly sliced the stubble from his chin, sharper than any razor, stinging his eyes until they wept. Beside him the Novantae prince also stood, one hand on his sword hilt.

From this height, they could not see any detail of the river valleys, and indeed there was no reason for them to be up here, except that Eremon wished it, for he loved to be scoured clean of camp smoke and the man-stink of war. Their scouts had certainly been tracking the Romans, however, and it was fitting to discuss their latest information up here, in the abode of eagles.

'You called, and the Romans followed,' the Novantae prince marvelled. He was eyeing Eremon with new respect, sunburn painting a swathe across his squashed nose and heavy cheeks.

'They followed because we gave them no choice,' Eremon amended. 'They have but one way to rejoin their northern column, and that is straight through these hills. If they go around the coast, their comrades will be dead before they get there. This is obvious to them, and so they have taken the road we wished ... but only because it is the lesser of two evils.' He turned his gaze on the other man, squinting up from under his helmet into the bright sun. 'Do not ever make the mistake of thinking these Romans foolish. They are not the kind to come after us out of fury.'

'How do you know this?'

Eremon shrugged one shoulder. 'I have met their chief commander Agricola face to face, and spent ... some time ... studying what he does.'

'Indeed?' The prince jiggled on his heels with the cold. 'Then around our fire this night you must tell me of these meetings.' He grinned. 'It appears that my trust of you was not misplaced – despite what you said about the Damnonii.'

Eremon's mouth tightened grimly. 'We learned from the Damnonii. It was well to hide your people in the hills. Now you don't need to be concerned for them – the wrath of the Romans can only fall on the warriors, where it belongs.'

The Novantae prince fingered his sword hilt again, the bronze piece cast into the head of an owl. 'I see now that the Romans and my own tribe do have something in common.'

'What is that?'

The young man's eyes were pained, thinking, perhaps, of his father. 'You say they have no choice but to take this way between the mountains. We had no choice, either, when we rebelled.' His mouth quirked at Eremon; wry, accepting. 'For it is better to die, after all, than to live under the heel of others.'

Eremon smiled and rested his hand on the prince's shoulder. 'If only I could convince the rest of the kings so, sword brother. If only.'

With a start, Rhiann was woken from her trance by the beat of a drum at the door, and a soft hand tracing patterns above her brow. With an effort, she blinked heavy lids and struggled to focus, and realized she was sitting cross-legged on the floor of Fola's hut before the fire.

She had begun the chants staring into the flickering flames with the other young Sisters, yet as their voices gradually wove a soothing cradle of sound around her, she did not remember to where she had flown. After two days of fasting, a night of chanting and the *saor*, she had entered a state where time and place had no meaning.

'It is time,' Setana said now, tracing the last spiral on Rhiann's forehead. The fire had burned to coals, yet behind Setana Rhiann could still glimpse the Sisters swaying on their knees. 'We have drawn the Source to the Stones; we have sung to Mother Earth and Father Sun. Now the Caller must come.'

Rhiann drew a deep, shaky breath, as consciousness plucked at her mind. 'He fights now?' she whispered.

Setana's hand cupped her cheek in the half-dark. 'This is the longest day, and here we open the gates of time. What has happened, will happen, or is happening, does not concern us. With you there, the power we call will find him when he most needs it. Come.' There was a swish of skirts and a draft of cool air, as Setana lifted the door-hide and slipped back outside.

Rhiann was roused by Fola and attended by the maidens around her, for she could barely move. Her body was heavy and warm, the edges of her limbs blurred. She could not feel where her physical self finished and the air around her began, and her thoughts turned slowly in her mind. Even the fear, which had so consumed her, was now only a dull ache.

By lamplight Rhiann's hands and feet were bathed, and she was clothed in an undyed linen dress, pinned with slivers of deerbone. Over that came a heavy deer-hide robe, tanned with smoke. *A robe for the Caller.*

Two young priestesses Rhiann did not know entered the room, their clay-painted faces a blur of white, black and brown. With gentle fingers and chanting, they painted the faces of Rhiann and the others, then all the Sisters donned their priestess cloaks, drew up their hoods and led Rhiann into the moonlight.

The night was cold for sunseason, the stars dimmed by the grey half-light. As she took the path up to the Stones, Rhiann could already hear the sacred drums booming, and sense something else through her feet: a pulse in the earth, a heartbeat. For a moment, sharp relief penetrated the veil of the *saor*. *She could feel the Source.*

Perhaps it was because she was not alone, that must be it; because she had the strength of all the Sisters. Raising her face, her cheeks stiff with the clay, Rhiann stepped strongly down the avenue to the inner circle, towards the fires burning in a ring.

The leaping flames illuminated a crowd of priestesses, painted and hooded, circling slowly in a spiral dance. They had been calling the Source for hours, gathering and focusing it here between the Stones, and as Rhiann crossed the boundary of the inner circle, the power hit her in a cresting wave. And through the eyes of the *saor*, Rhiann found she could see the Source as threads of light emanating from each priestess and the ground and streaming out from each Stone. The threads rose, glittered and rippled, twining together and parting, then crashing back again in bursts of light like sea-foam on a rock.

And Rhiann could see it, because they all held her.

Step by step she advanced to the centre of the circle, allowing the wave to sweep over and through her.

Then she was before Nerida, and all Rhiann could see was the firelight glittering in those aged eyes, deepening their power. 'Is the Caller ready?' Nerida's voice echoed around the circle.

Ready? Rhiann wondered. Yes, she was ready to try, for there behind Nerida rose the greatest Stone, and at its hallowed base Eremon had joined with Rhiann, and they had drawn the stars to earth. A pang of love arose in her, making her catch her breath, and she knew it was him she must feel, him she must call. As if in response to this thought, the threads of the Source swept around her, enveloping her in a whirl of light.

'I am ready,' she answered breathlessly.

At her words, the chanting of the priestesses abruptly changed. Now came the song Rhiann remembered from that rite with Eremon: a low, sibilant chant, panting and throbbing, a primal beat that surged up from Rhiann's soul. And there it began to awaken old memories, of when people ran with the deer in the endless forests.

Nerida rested one hand on Rhiann's forehead, and Rhiann breathed in the scent of the clay on her palm. 'Reach down into yourself, Sister. Reach back through the years, through the lives. Tonight, with our song, we have opened the door of time, and now you must step through it! *Become* the Caller! *Become* the Mother of the Tribe, who calls the deer for sacrifice, so that people may live. *Become* She who calls the Stags, so that they make Her fruitful!'

Rhiann closed her eyes, swaying on the spot.

The beat of the skin drums, the priestess chanting and the *saor* all swept her somewhere away from this night, with its grey light and faint stars, away from this hilltop. *She tasted the sharp damp of the forest on her tongue, she chased flashes of torchlight with her eyes, dancing with lithe limbs, she heard the whoops and cries in a forgotten tongue . . .*

She let herself remember . . .

She was the Caller, and They would come.

Chapter 13

Too restless to stay by the tiny, shielded fire in the hollow, Eremon crept instead in the darkness to the ridge-top. Now he crouched with both hands on the ground between his legs, and listened to the haunting calls of wolves as they rose and fell far away under the moonlight.

A cracked stick betrayed a man's step, and Eremon's head went up, his nose scenting the air.

'It's me,' Conaire said, his bulk blocking out the faint stars above, scattered over Eremon's head like campfires on a battle plain. His foster-brother squatted beside him, and handed over a skewer of what smelled like mountain hare. 'Get it out of your mind, and perhaps you'll sleep.'

Eremon hooked hands over his knees, his mailshirt clanking. 'There will be no sleep for me.' He cocked his head up to the night sky. 'Don't you feel it? Don't you feel them close?'

'They are close,' Conaire replied practically. 'We know exactly where the Romans are. And I bet their commander isn't sleeping either – he'll be pissing his little skirt at the prospect of traversing these valleys.'

Eremon sighed and dropped his shoulders, sniffing the meat. 'I still wish we could face them in battle; throw all we have at them . . .' He took a bite. 'Listen to me. I am restless, that is all. I feel as though my bones are pushing through my skin!' He snorted, scratching one leg. 'I do not know what is infecting me.'

'I do.' Conaire gulped down the meat. 'You're as keen to shed Roman blood as I am.'

Eremon raked a greasy hand through his hair. 'That is for certain, brother, although why it's burning in my bones the way it is—'

'Let it burn. It will be soon; this night, the next night. They are merely sheep for us to herd in those glens down there.' Conaire paused, talking through his mouthful. 'Perfect prey.'

The scouts had been keeping pace with the Roman advance up the long, river valleys for days, as the southern column drew closer to the warband's hiding place. In the north, the Novantae had pinned the other column of Romans on the shores of a wide loch. Unless they swam for it, they were not moving, apparently, until their commander joined them with reinforcements – *rescued them*, Eremon amended, with a stab of satisfaction.

'If we're lucky, Agricola has sent a commander with no stomach for being stalked,' Conaire added. 'We might be home before Lugnasa.'

Eremon heard the faint note of anxiety, and reached up to Conaire's shoulder. 'This mission may take weeks or even moons, for we must harry these Romans from the high ground, the bogs and hills, until we drive them north once more. But brother, once we are closer, you and I can circle to Dunadd, if only briefly. You will see Caitlin long before the babe is due.'

'That is what I need to do.' Conaire let out his breath.

'Don't forget that she is in Linnet's hands,' Eremon offered. 'And Rhiann will be home soon; she will never let anything happen to Caitlin.'

'I know.' Conaire rose, massaging the old scar in his groin, which bothered him when the ground was damp. 'You should give yourself some sleep.'

Eremon stared over the edge of the ridge, to the valleys falling away to north and south in long seams of black. 'I will.' When Conaire's crunching steps had faded, Eremon tilted back his head to look up at the stars, kneading the earth with his hands once more.

Rhiann. What was she feeling at this moment? Did she know that he rocked here, as restless as if his bones were on fire, alert to the very air? The wolves howled again, the eerie sound swelling and fading, and Eremon turned his head towards it. Did Rhiann know why his senses tugged at him, plucking at his heart until he couldn't sleep? For some primal sense told him that nearby was one he must face.

Perhaps sooner than anyone thought.

With her back to the greatest Stone, Rhiann breathed, sinking deeper into the space between worlds, her arms outstretched.
Cold night. Bright stars. Dark trees.
Come.
High moon. Pale mist. Stream on stone.
Come.
Skittering hooves. Pawing ground. Shuffling breath.
Come.
Scent of lust. White of eye. Red of flank.
Come!

Clash of hearts! Crash of heads! Scream of rage!
Come!
At last, they heeded her Call.

When she felt the breach of the pulsing ring of power, Rhiann opened her eyes, her sight unfurling within Thisworld and the Otherworld at the same time. Her spirit-eye burned on her forehead, the *saor* blurring the edges of the swaying Sisters around her, the cold stone, the damp sea air.

On the fringes of the firelight, among the looming Stones, two pairs of glowing eyes bobbed. And from Rhiann's outstretched fingers, threads of Source streamed, two rippling ropes. One reached away to the thick darkness on her left; the other to the shadows on her right.

Come! she cried in her heart, and they stepped out of the shadows.

The starlight glimmered on their antlers, dipping as they sniffed the air and the ground. The flames gleamed on wet noses, and the green points of their eyes. Dimly, Rhiann was aware of the drumming around her, through her, in time with the rhythm of her heart. And then her senses swelled, and she felt the great, pulsing hearts of the two stags, beating as one, beating with her.

Around her, the priestesses hummed and swayed, tossed their painted heads and blew out warm breath. And the stags dipped their necks again and pawed the ground.

In the dark tent, Agricola's eyes flickered open.

He had not slipped into deep sleep for days, for he couldn't stop gnawing on this decision to cross the mountains, wary of being trapped in such narrow valleys. But the men of his northern column needed him, and the sooner he merged their forces once more, the better.

For these Novantae were not just mindless, leaderless raiders after all. There was a force – a significant force – loose in this bleak moorland. Agricola turned over on his side, the flimsy blanket in his camp bed rucking up around his hips. *We are here now. We must just get through these mountains, and quickly.*

He had said that to his men. Yet when he was alone, the sick dread in his gut would not let him sleep; the fear that even though he led his army the most direct way, getting tangled up among these valleys and brooding hills was a mistake. The coastal route would have been safer, with the sea at their back, but his northern force would have been all but decimated by the time he got there, leaving his army vulnerable and far from its bases.

Agricola turned over again. Curse it! There never was an easy answer, not in war. It was the best decision, he must trust in that and the Fates – and rush through these mountains as quickly as possible. He wriggled a hand up to scratch his side. The skin felt hot, and it itched, yet it was not the skin . . . he somehow itched from deeper inside, in his bones. And he felt unnaturally awake, his limbs thrumming with some tension that made them quiver. Damn it, had he eaten some strange plant that didn't agree with him? Yet he didn't feel sick.

Suddenly, he sat bolt upright. His muscles burned, as if flames were licking along each limb. The lamp next to his bed was sputtering, but still gave off a feeble light. Agricola swung his legs to the floor and groped for a robe. There were those letters from his eastern forts that he'd not opened yet . . . he'd read them, and keep his mind busy.

In another two days they'd be free of these hills and emerge onto the plain to the north. Two days. He would not give in to fear and superstition in the meantime.

Drawn by the shining ropes streaming from her hands, the stags danced closer to Rhiann, snorting and pawing the earth, lunging forward, then leaping back. Their breath was a merged cloud of mist glittering above their tossing antlers. She could feel the heat in their blood, sense the blind rage building in her own heart and gut. Yes . . . it was the irresistible, single-minded focus on the rival, which blotted out all else.

Now one stag reared up on his hind legs, bellowing; now the other.

I must choose, Rhiann realized, with sudden clarity. *I must choose the King Stag.* Her consort. The one who would triumph.

She chose.

Eremon had given in at last to the twitching of his muscles, the impulse that tore at his mind as strongly as his heart. He could not deny this instinct that seemed to have arisen from the deepest corners of his being – and he had learned to listen to that along with his brain.

Now he crept among the hollows of wet bracken, rousing all the sword and spearmen. He had already sent Nectan's archers to dispose of the Roman sentries, for they were masters of coming upon an enemy unawares.

'Now, it is now,' he murmured as he moved among the sleeping men, his face burning despite the cold air on his cheeks.

The Novantae prince's hand was instantly on his sword, as he came fully awake. 'In the dark?'

'In the dark,' came Eremon's answer. 'They had no room in their valley to build a camp ditch. They will not be expecting a night attack.'

'Yet they have scouts,' the man said.

'No longer; the Caereni have done their work.' Eremon was struggling to rein in a surge of uncharacteristic impatience. 'It must be now.'

Agricola threw down the thin, wooden tablets and, wetting his finger, nipped out the sputtering lamp flame. Then he went to the tent flap, rubbing his eyes, straining his night vision to adjust to the faint grey sky. The mountain air bit at his fingers and nose. Around him, he could just discern the dark humps of the soldiers' bed rolls, stretching far out into the darkness. The valley was so narrow that 1,500 men could only be wedged in along a considerable, yet thin, line.

He had allowed no fires, even though for days these had been no sign of any men in these barren, wind-swept hills, and chosen a defensible position among the half-rotted stone dykes of an old farmstead.

But something still wasn't right.

The tugging and twitching in his bones was only growing greater, until at last he cursed, giving up on sleep altogether, and reached for his cloak and sword belt, squatting to lace his boots. Outside, Agricola strained cold air through his teeth, checking first on the handful of officers' horses at the centre of the camp, patting the snuffling nose of his own mount.

Then he made his way to the edge of the men, where a scree slope reared steeply from the valley to a ridge above. On the way he cocked his head as, far away, a wolf howled and was answered by another.

The guard posted on inner watch had come smartly to attention, and now he turned his back as Agricola passed his water against the scree slope, noting, in the starlight, the thin layer of frost on the tumbled stones. He raised his eyes higher, to the looming heights that seemed to frown down at them all like a dark fortress. 'Frost,' he muttered to it defiantly. 'In summer!'

Then he shook himself dry, dropped his tunic and stepped back, his boots crunching on a stray patch of frozen grass.

It was then that his head went up, sensing the air.

Rhiann let one hand fall, and that twisting, shining rope of light was instantly extinguished.

The other hand pointed now at the chosen stag, larger and more fiery than the other, his chest deep and proud, his eyes rolling at her. From the fingers of that one hand the Source surged even brighter, all of it focused now, no longer split. It entwined with his antlers, and rimed them with silver, like starlight on frost. It danced between the tines, glittering on his brow. It clothed his bunching flanks in pale light. It was power and rage and strength, glorious at its peak, but then a warm tide of love swept through Rhiann from her heart, and tinged the silver with red-gold.

My beloved, she found herself whispering, and the Source spilled out even stronger, pulsing in waves. *My dearest beloved, come back safe to me . . .*

The Chosen One reared, and his hooves struck the earth as he bellowed with rage and charged. The other stag also reared as the first rushed on, and their antlers met with a resounding crack.

Gripping his unsheathed sword, Eremon cast a glance back over his shoulder. The spearmen and archers had done well, creeping like ground fog to the dark places beneath boulders and in the shadows of the gnarled trees that clung to the hillside. Now he looked down the steep ridge to the broken walls outlined in silver, and the dark humps of men in between.

The flock at rest, he thought grimly, and sank deeper on his haunches, for the restlessness had now become rage, sweeping away his caution in a flood of heat, rising up from his loins.

In the shadow of a great rock beside him, Conaire was still, but his teeth flashed once in a grin. Eremon tried to grin back, yet what came was a baring of teeth, and then he knew it was time . . . it was time . . . it was time . . .

He stood and stepped into the light, raising his sword, heedless of anyone below seeing him now, for it was too late for them . . .

Eremon dropped his hand, and the silent air exploded in a hail of spears and arrows, before shrieking Alban men swept down the slopes from both sides of the valley in a flood-tide.

At the first screech Agricola instinctively unsheathed his sword, racing for the tumbling walls, heart pumping in sudden panic. But before he broke free of the cover of the scree slope, he heard the deadly hiss of arrows and higher whine of spears, and then all around the thuds and clashes and cries of pain.

A screaming savage landed right in front of him, leaping from a great height, and Agricola could only stab and slash at this daemon who danced around him, his face striped with starlight and shadow, his eyes those of a rabid beast.

Then the man fell under Agricola's blade, and the Roman governor of Britannia stumbled over the body, shouting to rouse his men.

The other stag screamed, its brow running with blood, as the hooves of the Chosen One raked down his sides. Fierce antlers stabbed at flanks again and again, and the hooves now stamped and shredded flesh into rags, as the chanting of the priestesses grew louder, resounding through Rhiann's mind and heart and out through her hand . . .

. . . Eremon slashed with his father's sword and leaped, lightning-quick, among the Roman soldiers rolling to their feet, slicing across white throats and unprotected heads until blood ran hot in his mouth and eyes.

And all the while his head swung from side to side as he sought the one he sensed, the one he had come for.

He cleaved the knots of fighting men with his blade, until before him the rotting, wind-scoured wall fell down into a tumble of stone steps, and Eremon raced up them until he stood on top of the wall, searching the fighters with desperate eyes.

Directly below him, a Roman soldier ran an Alban through with a javelin, and Eremon heard the bellow escape his own throat in answer. At the sound, the man looked up . . . and they were Agricola's eyes, filled with hatred. Eremon felt the breath leave his chest, replaced with instant rage.

That ruthless face had haunted his dreams, taunting him with its sneering mouth and cold contempt. And here was his own sword, and there the face.

With another yell, Eremon lowered his weapon and tensed to jump, but a knot of Roman soldiers swept around their commander just as a blade grazed Eremon's calf. In the darkness, screams and confusion that followed, Eremon was caught in the milling knots of fighters, until the men around him, Alban and Roman both, were dead or wounded, or had fled. It was then he heard the panicked whinnies, and far on the other side of the throng he glimpsed men in cloaks whipping their horses into a gallop, fleeing north.

Shuddering as the rage abruptly left him, Eremon's sword dropped to the ground and he sank back against the cold stone. And somehow, in all the darkness and blood he felt Rhiann, as if her breath brushed his cheek . . .

. . . and the Chosen One stood over its vanquished enemy, splashed in blood, its sides heaving, its head lowered until the torn velvet on its antlers brushed the ground.

Chapter 14

Rhiann barely remembered the first moments after the rite: the blood-soaked grass under her palms, the scent of damp soil, the pain in her head. She was carried by chanting Sisters, bathed by Fola's tender hands, and then she slept.

She awoke in darkness on a pallet by Fola's own bed, sensing a presence looming over her. Yet as she started, she recognized Didius in the shielded glow of a single lamp.

'Didius, why are you here?' she whispered, groggy from the *saor*. 'Were you not in the men's house?'

Didius leaned forward with a cup of water, pressing it to her parched lips. 'They let me come, lady,' he answered, glancing up at the dark hump of Fola in her bed. 'I . . . I needed to see you.'

Rhiann stared up at him as she drank. 'You saw, didn't you? You were there at the rite.'

Avoiding her gaze, Didius took back the cup and then hung his head, his jowls catching on his collar. 'No one knew; no one saw me.' His eyes swept up, the pupils huge and fearful. 'I am sorry if it was wrong, lady! I wanted to know you were safe – and then I could not look away – and the Sisters, I didn't recognize them . . . and the singing . . .'

'Peace.' Rhiann groped for his hand and held it, sinking back on the pillow as a wave of dizziness took her. 'There is no harm done. And perhaps it was right for you to be there. Perhaps the Mother called you, too.'

To anchor us to his people, Rhiann thought hazily, and a strange sadness swept her. Then her half-open eyes were caught by the flare of lamplight on the sword still strapped to Didius's side. It was the first weapon he had been allowed to bear, yet it was made for Alban men, to defend Alban land. With a jolt, Rhiann remembered Eremon.

Eremon! Oh, Goddess, what if it were *her* people who had been defeated?

The plunge of dread took her breath away, and she struggled to rise on her elbows, trembling violently. It hadn't worked; the Calling wasn't strong enough. Eremon might be lying somewhere even now, wounded or dead . . .

Murmuring, Didius eased her down with curiously gentle, though callused hands, pulling the wool blanket up to her chin. And it was that solid warmth and pressure that brought Rhiann back from the edge of panic, as she remembered what Linnet had once said to her: *I would know, the moment you left Thisworld.*

And Rhiann would know, too, if the bond of soul-flames had been severed, if Eremon walked this land no more. She repeated it to herself over and over, her eyes squeezed shut. *I would know. I would know.*

Gradually, as Rhiann sucked air in and blew it out, the thudding of her heart softened, and implacable exhaustion took hold once more. Though she struggled to open her eyelids, it was as if a hand was pressing them closed, and she was dragged back down into sleep.

Yet there, dreams still came, jumbled and tortured, frightening in their intensity. Rhiann sensed rather than saw anything: pressure and constriction; cramping pain and wounded cries; cold wind and the silence of desolation.

Early dawn found her fully awake, kneeling by Fola's side, shaking her friend's arm. Didius, giving into his own exhaustion, was a mound curled in a blanket at the end of her pallet.

'Something is wrong,' Rhiann whispered, when Fola rolled over with a sleepy exclamation. She'd re-lit the lamp from the coals, and now set it on a stool by Fola's bed. 'I can feel it in my belly. I must return home – now.'

Instantly, Fola was sitting upright in her bed shift, blankets tumbling around her waist. 'But it is not yet light.'

'I can't wait.' Feverishly, Rhiann tied her single braid with flax and pushed it over her shoulder, pulling her pack onto the pallet. There, she began flinging in her scattered belongings: her antler comb; sleep shift; medicine pouch; and figurines.

Now Fola was beside her, wrapped in a blanket, her dark pupils shrinking in the flickering light. 'Sister, the rite was powerful, it will have disturbed you. Come, I will make you tea and then you can rest—'

'No!' Rhiann strove for calm, for the impulse that had driven her from bed was growing stronger now she had spoken it – a summons in her bones, her belly. 'Fola.' She took her friend by the arms and stared into her face. 'Look at me. I am in my right mind. My sense is that I must get home, as soon as I can. Something . . .' She swallowed, the strength leaving her once more. 'Something is wrong.'

Fola bit her lip, her eyes straying to Didius as he began to stir. 'I will rouse Nerida. She will want to see you before you go.'

The sky over the inland hills was streaked with rose when they emerged onto the muddy path between the dark, crouching houses. Rhiann sent Didius to alert the boatmen and ready the craft with water and food, while she and Fola crossed to Nerida's door. When Rhiann entered the warmth and light of the Eldest Sister's home, her calm deserted her. Suddenly she was on her knees by Nerida's chair, grasping the old woman's hand.

'Do not say I am sick, or fevered,' she whispered. 'My dreams were so vivid, and spoke of harm and pain and disturbance. Do you . . .' The words hovered on her tongue. 'Do you think that Eremon has come to grief? *Was the rite not a success?*'

Nerida's grip on her wrist was forceful, and Rhiann met her eyes, which were unfilmed by sleep or age. Her white hair was unbound, and she had drawn a faded blue blanket around her shift. 'Daughter, the rite was strong and true. You anchored us to him; you sent him the Source with your hands, your heart. It will be well.' She squeezed Rhiann's arm, and at last her calm authority began to penetrate the frozen shell around Rhiann's mind.

He is alive, he must be alive. But what, then, calls me home? She didn't know, but she couldn't ignore it.

'I must go,' she said, stumbling to her feet. With Nerida's blessing warm on her forehead Rhiann was out then in the starry dawn, the chill on her skin drawn from within this time, and not from the wind off the sea.

Against a strong swell, the sailing to Dunadd took four days, during which Rhiann could hardly contain her impatience, sitting in the bow almost straining out over the waves. On disembarking, she hurried along the Trade Path, so quickly that Didius had to trot to keep up.

The land about did not share her unease. Calm weather had returned, and the field strips across the river were a rippling sea of green barley heads. The few homesteads they passed were deserted and peaceful, for the young people were in the high pastures with the cattle, and the men were clearing next year's fields in the Add valley. Even the trading punts on their way from their ships at Crinan glided lazily up the river.

When Dunadd swept into view Rhiann stopped so abruptly Didius nearly ran into her. Yet as she gazed up at the imposing crag and high palisade, the tension wound about her heart began to loosen. The dun still stood: strong, unassailable. Perhaps her fears had just been dark fancies after all. Perhaps if she was wrong about this, she was also wrong to fear for Eremon. Pausing in the hot sun, she unpinned her cloak, stiff from salt, and folded it over her arm. Then, with her head high, she endeavoured to continue more calmly.

There was not enough wind to stir the royal banner that crowned the

King's Hall, but the village gate stood wide open, and from afar Rhiann could see people moving in and out of it as normal. She barely glanced up at the gate guards or noted who was about, so intent was she on reaching her own house. It wasn't until she entered the Moon Gate on the crag that she realized something was indeed wrong.

It was the thick, heavy silence that alerted her, unnatural and tense.

Among the houses of the nobles – her royal clan – no one moved. *Has someone died?* she wondered, with a resurgence of panic, and found herself turning for the Horse Gate and King's Hall. Yet she had not got far before she was met by a sight that arrested her. Three men were advancing towards her under the oak arch of the carved stallion's legs.

The first was Gelert, his face carefully blank even as his raised brows registered surprise. The jet eyes on his owl staff, clasped in one bony hand, flashed in the sun.

Then came Lorn, his chin rearing up when he caught sight of Rhiann.

And finally Urben, commanding the space around him with his bear shoulders, his garish clothes and excess of rings, chains and brooches. His hair, the fair mingled equally with silver, was bound back with a gold circlet, and his moustache framed a profoundly satisfied mouth.

It was Urben who broke Rhiann's shocked silence. 'Ah!' he boomed. 'Our Ban Cré has returned to her people at last. Splendid!' Belying these hearty words, his grey eyes assessed Rhiann with a coolness that turned her belly.

'What has happened?' Rhiann struggled to keep her voice even, staring hard at Lorn, willing him to answer. But he would not meet her eyes.

That was when she knew.

'Alas, it appears that our war leader will not be returning from his southern adventure.' Urben spread his glittering hands in a parody of helplessness. 'At such an unstable time, I thought it prudent to lend my protection to the royal dun.'

The blood roared in Rhiann's ears. Struggling for breath, she spun around, only to notice belatedly that unfamiliar guards – Urben's warriors – were now flanking the Moon Gate. And the high timber gates themselves, which had never been closed in a generation, were now scraping shut behind her.

Cutting her off from the village below.

Chapter 15

R hiann rounded on Urben. 'Traitor!' she hissed, her face ablaze
with sudden rage.

Lorn turned his head away, but Urben merely smiled and
folded his hands on his jewelled belt. 'Traitor, lady?'

At his raised voice, a few pale faces appeared in the darkness of their
doorways – the nobles of the ruling clan. Rhiann could only wonder
how they'd subdued Talorc, who would never stand for such a betrayal.

'By traitor,' Urben boomed, 'think rather of a foreigner, a *gael*, who,
in pursuit of his own glory, puts our men at risk for other tribes' lands:
Caledonii lands, Damnonii lands, *Novantae* lands!'

Rhiann's mouth dropped open, her anger a bright flood in her veins
that burned away all fear. 'Eremon is putting his life at risk to save us all!'
she cried furiously, her hands clenched by her sides. 'And you repay him
with *this*? You take Dunadd by force?'

Urben's smile remained in place. 'No, Ban Cré, not by force. There
were many in the council who welcomed us. Your prince is the outsider
here, after all, not me. Since after a year you seem . . . unable . . . to bear
our next king, we must look elsewhere – and my son is the next best
candidate. How can I be a traitor when I am just doing what is best for
the people?'

'You have had that year to lay your claim,' Rhiann spat. 'And now
you act when Eremon's back is turned, like a sneaking, filthy coward!'
Her mind spun, the words on the tip of her tongue, that Caitlin also
bore the old king's blood; that this very moment she perhaps carried a
boy child in her belly. Yet something stopped those words in her throat.

'I will not allow you to insult me a third time, Ban Cré.' Urben's
voice held a dangerous edge. 'We have taken action *now* because the
war leader has obviously come to some grief in the south.'

The ground lurched beneath Rhiann; her heart flung itself against her ribs. Yet her mind grasped wildly for control. Eremon was well. Somehow she knew he was well.

'What has it been now?' Urben mused, spreading his fingers as if counting. 'A moon, nearly two? More than a moon and no word? He left us here, poorly defended and leaderless, and now someone must take up the reins.' His hand curled towards Lorn. Yet the young Epidii lord still would not meet Rhiann's eyes.

Rhiann's shock was beginning to recede, as the first flare of rage burned out. And with it, her mind suddenly cleared. *Caitlin, oh Goddess, where is she? Linnet? Eithne?*

She took one shaking step towards her house, but at a snap of Urben's fingers two warriors came from the Horse Gate and stood on either side of her, hands placed carefully on their sword-hilts. Urben's smile pulled down with feigned sorrow. 'My lady, in troubled times, I cannot have such a valued prize wandering around unaccompanied. My men will keep you safe.'

Rhiann fought to draw dignity around her, unwilling to give them the further satisfaction of her rage. Without another word she turned, her contemptuous gaze sweeping first the silent Lorn, then Gelert.

The druid's expression had remained unmoved, yet Rhiann saw the slight working of his thin mouth as he stared towards the banner lying limp on its post above the King's Hall. Her eyes involuntarily following his, Rhiann saw now that the banner was no longer the scarlet of the White Mare, but the pale blue bear of Urben's clan. She bit down on her fury. Gelert may stand there as if he had nothing to do with this. But she knew better.

Didius, meanwhile, was being stripped of his sword by Urben's men, his face stricken with shame and fear, and only then were they free to continue, the two guards trailing them to Rhiann's house.

All the way Rhiann sensed their presence like menacing hounds behind her, and when they attempted to follow her inside, she whirled, palm raised and trembling. 'This is my home – you cannot come here!'

One of the warriors fixed his eyes on the sun-warmed wall outside, his bear tattoo curling fiercely over one cheek. 'We have orders to watch you at all times, lady,' he murmured. 'For your own protection.'

Enraged words leaped to Rhiann's lips, but before she could speak there came a soft, anguished cry from inside, and instantly she dropped her anger and rushed to the sickbed against the wall. 'Caitlin!' She sank to her knees by the bed and grasped Caitlin's hand. Beside her, Eithne crouched on a stool, her small face pinched and fearful. 'But I left you with Linnet!' Rhiann burst out.

Caitlin's face was streaked with tears, her other hand spread protectively over her swollen belly. In the weeks Rhiann had been away she had grown much bigger, her face a blotch of paleness in the dark recess of the bedplace. 'Urben's guards came for us a week ago,' she whispered, her voice husky from weeping. 'They tore us from Linnet and brought us back here.'

At the mention of Linnet, Rhiann's fingers dug in to the fur cover. 'And what of her?'

'She is safe, alive and unhurt.' Caitlin's lips trembled, and she pressed them together to steady herself. 'That is all I could beg from Lorn.'

Rhiann leaped up, unable to stay still. 'Curse them all for lying dogs!' She pressed both hands to the bridge of her nose, her breathing swift and fierce. 'How *dare* they lay a hand on us, take our home! Wait until Eremon gets back—'

'Rhiann,' Caitlin's agonized whisper broke through Rhiann's anger, 'they called all the people together and said that Eremon and Conaire must have been defeated, since we have heard nothing. Urben said he had no choice but to put the people first, and give them a new king and war leader.'

'Did he now?' Rhiann snapped, staring down at her cold hearth, her hands curling into fists. 'Wily words from a cowardly traitor.' She sank to the bed and took Caitlin's hands, chafing her cold fingers, disturbed at the unhealthy translucence of her skin, and her haunted eyes. 'Come, cariad, you know they are alive, as do I.'

Caitlin buried her face in Rhiann's shoulder. 'Since the baby, my heart is so weak!' she sobbed. 'I can't think straight and when Urben said it, my heart just froze, Rhiann. I've been so frightened—'

Over her sister's shoulder Rhiann held Eithne's dark eyes, yet the maid's composure was also threatening to dissolve under an onslaught of fright and relief. Rhiann reached out and pried Eithne's fingers from the twisted knots of her skirt, willing strength into her. She had chosen Eithne as her maid for many reasons, not least her sharp mind and her spirit, and it was these she must draw forth now.

When Caitlin was quiet, Rhiann gathered Eithne and Didius by the hearth. There she drew a deep breath, dredging up a semblance of control with sheer will. 'We are all in shock,' she said to them. 'Yet it is Caitlin we must look to now. She is not well.' Rhiann took Eithne's trembling fingers. 'Can you be strong for her, and for me? I'll need you to help care for her, give her the draughts she needs, keep her spirits raised. Can you do this?'

Eithne straightened her thin shoulders, forcing a smile that did not reach her eyes. 'Yes, lady. I'll make you proud, you'll see. And do not forget that Eremon left us Aedan. He must still be in the King's Hall. Perhaps he can play for her.'

'Goddess help us!' Poor Aedan would be out of his mind with worry; she must go and retrieve him if she could. Yet first she addressed Didius.

'A bard I may have, son of Rome, but I need a strong male presence in this house, too.'

Didius nodded sombrely, his hand going to his sword-belt, before he realized with obvious dismay that it was empty. Swiftly he composed himself, hooking his fingers into the rope belt around his belly. 'You do not need to ask, lady.'

Yet when his eyes strayed to Caitlin in the bed, Rhiann went completely still.

We may be safe for the moment, came her sudden knowing, *but not the babe, for he is a king born.*

Her so-called guards did not stop Rhiann striding past them to the King's Hall, and to her relief the paths were empty once more. Aedan was crouching on a stool at one end of the great hearth, plucking dolefully at his harp, Cù at his feet. Yet at the sight of Rhiann he set his instrument aside with a startled yelp of relief that pierced the hound's excited barking. Aedan was never so undignified; this, more than the slump of his shoulders, told Rhiann of his state of mind.

'Urben and Lorn and their men moved in here,' he whispered to her, his grey eyes round and fearful, glancing over her shoulder. The cream and rose complexion that made him the target of so many warrior jests was now just pale, his dark curls for once uncombed. 'They make me play for them every night, but Lady, I am so frightened for my lord. They say he is not coming back, that he is dead!' Aedan's head drooped, shame creeping up his neck. 'They held a dagger at my throat, made me play a dirge to send his soul to the Otherworld,' he confessed.

Rhiann swallowed her disgust at Urben, and patted Aedan's knee. 'You and I both know he is not dead. And, though you are unquestionably talented, I don't think even your dirge could send a man to the Otherworld before his time.'

Aedan shook his head, his mouth lifting ruefully at one corner.

Rhiann rubbed Cù's head to calm herself, pushing the dog's flank into her leg. 'I will ask Lorn to release you to my household, Aedan, for I need you to keep Caitlin's spirits raised. Her pregnancy does not go as well as I'd hoped—'

Aedan straightened and groped for her hand, pressing his forehead to it. 'Lady, I will gladly discharge my duty to you and my lord thus. I will not let you down!'

His fervency brought a tired smile to Rhiann's lips. 'What happened to the nobles? And where is Finan?'

Aedan's face fell, and he sighed and drew his fingers over his harp. 'I am sorry to report, lady, that when Urben's warriors came, only one of the nobles put up a real resistance.' His throat moved as he swallowed.

'We were all here in the hall, eating. Talorc swept up his sword and ran at Urben . . . and was cut down by his men.'

Rhiann's heart plunged. 'Dead? Not Talorc?' The old warrior had been Eremon's staunchest supporter, his booming voice always one of the loudest raised in dissension, but also in laughter, in jests. 'How . . . long ago did this happen?'

'One week.' Aedan's eyes were deep with shadows. 'I think the death rites have been completed, lady, but it was a hurried affair, and involved only his own kin.'

Rhiann nodded, grief rising thick in her throat. 'And Finan?'

There Aedan was relieved. 'They removed him to the village, to be lodged with Bran. They did not harm him, though he drew his sword, too. I think . . . I think they did not wish to invite my lord's wrath.'

Rhiann glanced at Aedan keenly. 'Then they know Eremon is alive, too.' She nodded to herself, and smiled grimly into the fire. 'And they are afraid of him.'

Rhiann had another visit to make that day, a sad one, to Talorc's house. No priestess had been present to sing the death song for him, and though his body had already been consigned to the pyre, she knelt with his weeping wife by the hearth and made an offering of meadowsweet and scented oil, milk and barley meal to the statue of Ceridwen that rested in its wall niche.

Gently, she endeavoured to ask Talorc's wife about Gelert, but the woman writhed herself into fresh hysterics, giving full vent to her grief. It was left to Belen to provide the information that the chief druid had carefully avoided all suspicion of involvement in the plot.

'He said to the people that it was not up to the druids to choose the war leader and king, but the warriors.' Belen spoke in a hollow voice, sitting by the hearth, slack-shouldered and empty-eyed, his hands limp by his sides. 'He said he would give his support to a new candidate as loyally as to your prince, who had only been set in place as your consort and war leader until you birthed the next king. But . . . since you have not . . .' Belen's voice trailed off. 'Urben has stepped in with Lorn. He says he speaks for the other clans.'

Rhiann swallowed down her angry response, for before her sat a broken man, and she did not wish to hurt him further. But Eremon would not have let the dun go without a fight! She breathed through her frustration and gave Belen a blessing as he took her leave. It would clearly be left to others to be strong. Perhaps it would be left to her.

Rhiann walked unseeing under the Horse Gate again, ignoring the guards behind, searching inside herself for the echo of the power she had called in the stag rite. It was still there, faintly thrumming along her veins. Perhaps she could use that power, and keep it close to her.

'Lady,' Didius hissed, bringing her to a halt. Rhiann followed his eyes, and saw a man standing on the cliffs beside the druid shrine, outlined against the dusk sky. It was Lorn, and he was gazing out to the southern road.

Rhiann paused, with a challenging glance at her guards. 'Go on, Didius,' she said evenly. 'I will only be a moment.'

'You cannot see him alone,' Didius muttered, raising his chin, though his cheeks wobbled with effort.

Rhiann was warmed by this spark of defiance; she would need that in her household. 'Come, then, but don't invite his anger in any way.' She held his black eyes warningly. 'You are a foreigner, nothing to him. He could easily kill you.'

Back through the Horse Gate they went, past the deserted druid shrine, and then Rhiann approached Lorn with her face blank, veiling her emotions. For Caitlin, she would humble herself.

Lorn whirled before she spoke, and the light from the fading sky showed what her earlier fury had blinded her to. Lorn, always resplendent and perfectly groomed, looked almost haggard. His clothes and hair were as immaculate as ever, yet his eyes were red-rimmed and pouched from too much ale.

Abruptly, Rhiann dropped her gaze, not wanting to acknowledge the strange pity that flared in her, seeing only the blood being squeezed from Lorn's hands as he balled them. 'Caitlin is in a delicate condition,' she murmured, summoning priestess calm. 'Music and tales would ease her time. I have come to request that you allow Aedan to join my household.'

For a moment Lorn did not answer, and Rhiann raised her head and gazed out beyond him to the marsh, her face devoid of all emotion.

'I will grant this,' Lorn grated at last, 'only if you give your oath to plan no escape, no trickery, with your little group of . . . of . . .'

'Eremon's friends?' she countered. She couldn't help it.

His breath exploded outwards. 'The prince is dead!'

'Then any plan would lead to naught!' she retorted.

Lorn flushed, looked at his spread hands and tucked them under his armpits in a boyish gesture that did nothing to soften Rhiann's heart. 'Nevertheless, I wish your oath.'

Rhiann considered him. 'Then I give you my oath; that I, and those friends and family currently under my protection will effect no escape. May this oath be as strong and binding as your own.'

Lorn's jaw clenched, the muscles twitching. 'Aye, lady.' He turned back to his vigil. 'We wish no harm to the Lady Caitlin. If it will ease her, then have your bard.'

'Thank you,' Rhiann forced out. She stared at the tension tightening Lorn's broad shoulders; he seemed unnerved by her. 'There is one more thing,' she continued, 'news of the Lady Linnet.' Since he seemed to have some concern for Caitlin's safety, she added, 'Caitlin greatly fears for her mother.'

Lorn's shoulders lowered in a sigh. 'She is well. My father . . . we . . . keep her under guard just as you yourself. She and her maid can go about their business as before.'

'Except that she is a prisoner and cannot ease her mind over those she loves! She'll be mad with worry.'

Lorn paused. 'I will send word that you have returned and that all of you are safe.'

Safe. It was not the word that Rhiann would have chosen, but she swallowed all the bitterness in her heart, and thanked him formally – though it choked her – and left him to his watch.

Only that night, when the others were asleep, did Rhiann at last sink onto the side of her bed with her head in her hands, all the emotion of that day bearing down on her in a wave of utter exhaustion. She could not allow the others to see her rising fear. She would not show it! She would be strong, and keep the others strong, until . . . until . . .

Behind her eyes she summoned a vision of Eremon, riding proudly at the head of his warriors across a windy, heather slope. Alive. Unhurt.

I will keep strong for you, she thought, and wiped sweat from her face with nervous hands, straightening and staring into the dark.

Chapter 16

This could almost be a good time for him, Didius thought, as he carefully worked the chisel along the piece of rowan wood. A pale curl rolled up ahead of the iron point, and Didius did not take his eyes off the chisel's long glide, though his mind wandered. *He* had been a prisoner for more than a year anyway, so being trapped here wasn't that different for *him*. And he was still near the Lady, all he'd had to cling to since his capture.

Didius now glanced over the half-finished cradle to Aedan, Eithne and Caitlin, lined up in the sun on the outside bench against the house wall. True, it was hard for them all to stay busy, because the food came from Aldera and the other women in the village, and the Lady Rhiann was not allowed to leave the dun to search for her herbs. But they managed.

The bed linens had never been so clean, or the pots so shiny, scoured with sand by Eithne. And there was much weaving and spinning going on, though Didius did not understand these women things. Now he gazed down eagerly at the sun gleaming on the different woods and tools scattered on the ground between his crossed legs. He had embarked on the cradle to keep his own hands moving, for making, shaping and perfecting were all that ever called to him.

He wondered with a rueful smile what his fellow engineers in the army would say if they could see him now, spending days – weeks! – fashioning an intricate bed for a barbarian child. It wasn't exactly the same challenge as building camp defences, or long, straight roads that crossed mountains and rivers.

'The headboard should feature a hound,' Aedan said dreamily, his fingers keeping up their faint, soothing plucking on the strings.

'A hound?' Didius squinted up at him through the sunshine, spilling from high overhead.

'For Cúchulainn.' Aedan frowned, as if it were obvious.

Cúchulainn. Ah, one of Aedan's tales, Didius remembered. The tale of the most famous of the Erin heroes. How he loved the songs and stories, so strange and mysterious to his Roman ears. Well, this forced arrangement at least meant that he got to hear Aedan play every night, and he didn't have to put up with hordes of huge, terrifying, tattooed warriors making fun of him.

'Oh, yes,' the Lady Caitlin agreed now, her sweet face flushed from the heat. 'The bravest and most skilled of all warriors – Conaire told me! Cúchulainn will be perfect for my son!' She smiled softly, her hand over her jutting belly, the sweat standing out on her brow. She was wearing only a thin dress, but she seemed to be suffering the most from the unusual, sticky weather, and Didius saw how closely Eithne and the Lady Rhiann watched her. She was always so kind to him, and so he watched and worried, too.

'I will model it on Cù then,' Didius said, waving his chisel at the dog, and Caitlin and Eithne both laughed. In fact, Didius realized, applying himself to the wood again, this *could* have been the happiest time for him since the prince took him captive. He was treated by the others like a *person*, as though they were family, and he was being useful to the Lady, peeling rushes for lamps, hauling water, boring loom weights, and carving pots, ladles and chairs.

Then Didius sighed and laid the chisel in his lap. It wasn't happy, though, it couldn't be, because of the Lady. She had been sad and preoccupied ever since they returned after the shipwreck. And he had seen her being strong and clever before – hadn't she nursed him through so many illnesses; didn't she command the stags . . . ? He shuddered a little at that memory.

Now, however, the Lady seemed both at her saddest and yet strongest, and Didius was worried for her and in awe of her at the very same time. The way she faced down that Lorn, his hard-eyed father and the slimy druid had made Didius swell with pride. And he marvelled at the fierce will with which she held her friends, keeping their spirits up, caring for the Lady Caitlin, watching over their food and sleep. It was a wonder, seeing such strength in a woman, coupled with tenderness.

Yet Didius, always following the Lady with his eyes, also saw the way she took herself off every day and walked alone on the walls of the crag, looking south. They could all draw soft smiles from her, yet she never joined in their laughter, no matter how Aedan forced it from them with his funny stories. And every night, when Aedan sang his sad songs, the ones which took Didius's spirit away to the stars, the Lady lay on her bed alone and stared at the firelit roof.

Didius could only try to anticipate her needs and help her where he could, as well as pray to his own gods that her strength would not falter. And if it stayed like this, where they were left alone all through the long, sunny days, they could ignore the two guards that hovered outside playing dice, and perhaps convince themselves that all was normal. And soon the prince would come back, and then the Lady would smile again – her real smile.

It had been a moon of monotony that Rhiann thought would drive her mad. Yet when the request for her healing services suddenly came from Urben, she baulked at leaving Caitlin, even though she longed to escape the house.

Urben's kinswoman at another dun was suffering from a difficult birth, his messenger said, and reluctantly, Rhiann knew she must go to her. Despite her feelings for Urben she could not turn her back on someone in need.

Carefully, she packed herbs, needle and thread into her seal-fur medicine pouch, and set out. Yet as Rhiann rode south-west, though she threw off the stifling confinement of the dun, she couldn't drink in the scents of the sunseason air or the freedom of the wide blue sky. For her chest was soon burning with frustration to see the profusion of life burgeoning all around her as sunseason peaked: the heather blooming in a riot of purple all over the hillsides, ready for ale, for dyeing; the stands of golden rod and winding trails of honeysuckle; berries ripening; and bees buzzing over the spills of flowers, producing honey for salves and mead.

To make matters more frustrating and confusing, by the time Rhiann arrived at the dun, the birth was already over. Despite the reported urgency, the chieftain's baby had been safely delivered, and though it was small, it seemed healthy, already sucking lustily at the mother's breast. Rhiann left instructions to the attendants to brew the feverfew and woodruff she had brought, and dispense milkwort for nursing.

Waiting for her outside, the grateful chieftain offered her his best bed for the night and a hot meal, but Rhiann's unease was starting to grow as the light died in the sky. The birth had not been life-threatening, so why had she been sent?

Suddenly she spun on her heel. 'I must return to Dunadd now,' she barked at the two guards, who were lounging with ale and dice beside the chief's hall.

The one who always spoke glanced up at the sky. It had deepened to rose over the western hills, and even now shadows were gathering below the spur of rock on which the dun sat. 'It's too late to ride,' he announced, shrugging.

Rhiann stared hard at him, though she trembled inside. 'We can take torches, and there is always some light in the sky this time of year.'

His jaw working tightly, the guard looked at his companion, and then at the chieftain and the other nobles of the dun, all gathering nearby for the evening meal. Rhiann wondered how much support Urben really enjoyed, and how the other chiefs would take to seeing his own warriors lay violent hands on the Ban Cré.

So she strode straight for the stables, where their horses were waiting to be bedded down. In a moment Rhiann was in her saddle, nudging Liath back across the yard towards the chieftain. 'My blessings on your lady,' she said a little breathlessly, fear beginning to pound out a beat on her temples. 'I will return home now, for she is in excellent health, and I have left her some preparations that will make her strong. So my lord, if you could provide us with pitch torches . . . ?'

Stammering his gratitude, the chieftain moved to do Rhiann's bidding, ordering servants about until the darkening yard was milling with people. In the midst of all this Rhiann sat unmoving in her saddle, holding the eyes of Urben's leading guard until at last he sighed and shook his head, and both men untied their horses.

Although she tried to counsel herself to calmness, Rhiann's anxiety nevertheless grew on the path home. Her nerves leaped every time the wind set the torches flickering, casting eerie shadows on the rocks of the narrow valleys and the trees lining the paths. One guard went in front, one behind, and after a while all Rhiann could see was a confusion of wavering flame, slices of dark sky above, and firelit rocks and tree trunks.

By the time Dunadd's gates loomed over them, the moon was above the horizon, hanging in the sky like a silver shield. Rhiann dismounted and led Liath to the stable, then hurried up the path from the houses, her heart in her throat. She waited in an agony of frustration until her guards caught up and ordered the watch to open the Moon Gate, then she darted inside and outran them. The paths on the upper tier were dark, lit only by a few torches. The door of the King's Hall above was open, spilling firelight over the crest of the crag, yet little sound came from within. At last Rhiann reached her own house, and lunged under the door-hide, her hands stifling the cry that rose in her throat.

Aedan and Didius were gathered around a figure lying on the floor. Shaking herself into action, Rhiann threw herself to her knees, desperately scanning Eithne's dark hair and tightly closed eyes, as she lay moaning in Caitlin's arms.

Caitlin looked up, her fear as bright and wild as the moonlight, and Rhiann forced herself to suck in air then, as the maid's face spasmed again, and a trickle of her sweat ran from her cheek to Caitlin's lap. 'She wouldn't wait,' Caitlin said despairingly. 'She wouldn't wait for you.'

Rhiann forced away the rush of panic that welled up, and took Eithne gently from Caitlin. 'What happened?' she demanded, laying Eithne back so she could check her pulse and her eyes.

'The food came,' Caitlin whispered. 'But it was beef stew again and I couldn't face it just now, without you forcing it down me, and with the others so hungry . . .' She glanced up at Didius and Aedan, both frozen and watching the scene with wide, helpless eyes. 'So Eithne tasted it herself this time, just like you do . . .' Caitlin's eyes filled with tears, and she stroked Eithne's hand.

'How long ago did she eat?' Rhiann croaked. *I should have been here. I let them get past me, Eremon . . .*

'Hours and hours, lady,' Aedan offered, with a gulp. 'At dusk. But she only got sick just now and . . . we didn't know what to do . . .'

'We tried to give her water,' Didius said, his hands spread helplessly.

Then Eithne moaned again, clutching at her abdomen, and Rhiann leaned in close to smell her breath. Faintly, just faintly, there was the slightest taint of something bitter. But no vomit. 'Has she been sick?'

Caitlin shook her head, unable to speak. Her whole body was trembling violently, but Rhiann had no time to spare her.

'Then it is not inside her gut,' Rhiann murmured to herself, and as she ran her hands over Eithne's stomach, pressing and smoothing lightly, she was suddenly pulled up sharp by the smear of blood on the girl's thighs, below the edge of her dress. She caught her breath, and then glanced up at Didius and Aedan.

'But you men ate it!' she cried. 'Didn't you?'

As they both nodded, Rhiann's eyes slid instead to Caitlin, and came to rest on the swollen belly pressing against the fine shift, stuck to her by Eithne's sweat. Then she raised her gaze to Caitlin's face.

Caitlin gasped, her hand spreading across her belly.

Rhiann and Eithne had their moon bleeding at the same time, and it was not due for another week. 'It's her womb; cramping in her womb.' Rhiann gathered Eithne's head tenderly in her arms, stroking her brow. 'Aedan, Didius, help me to get her into the sickbed, and bring more water!'

All through the night the blood trickled from Eithne with the waves of the cramps, soaking the bed beneath her tiny body.

Rhiann used everything at her disposal to stem it; tonics and suppositories of the red herb, feverfew, knapweed, cranesbill. As Eithne muttered and tossed in the poppy delirium, given for her pain, Rhiann held tight to the thought that whatever Eithne had ingested, it was not meant to kill, for Aedan and Didius stood there unharmed. It was the womb that was the target, the aim a miscarriage.

As the hours of night slipped by, Rhiann went about her business, grateful for Caitlin's aid, but missing Eithne's efficient hands and ability to sense what Rhiann needed.

Once the first guilt passed, rage had again constricted Rhiann's chest and yet, as she put all her energy into Eithne, so the fury eventually cooled to defeat. She knew what would happen if she asked who delivered that particular broth, for the Sisters were not the only practitioners of herb lore. Rhiann had no doubt that the truth had already been lost among the shadows of the druid shrine.

With doses of strengthening brews, and bloody meat twice a day, Rhiann gradually nursed Eithne back to health, and though she had no clear recollection of the night, the maid remained weak and fearful for many days thereafter.

From then on, Rhiann would only accept grain or joints of meat from Aldera's own hand, passed through Aedan, for Rhiann was forbidden from approaching the Moon Gate. They survived on their own baked bannocks and meat broth, though it wasn't enough fresh food, and they all lost weight and grew pale.

Only once did Rhiann meet Gelert by accident, both of them alone, yet she would not deign to speak to him. She did no more than spit deliberately at his feet and turn away, ears closed to his hissed response.

They would all have gone mad but for Aedan's tales, and the freedom he gave them in their minds and dreams: of far lands and cool forests and fresh sea winds. And every night, in vision, Rhiann willed Eremon's steps to turn back towards Dunadd, and she pictured him coming closer, his boar-crest helm glittering in the sun.

Chapter 17

The harvest moon of Lugnasa grew and swelled in the sky.

Every night, Rhiann stood outside her door, watching the fires flaring in the fields to the south, as each was cleared of grain. Sometimes if the wind was right she would hear snatches of singing, and the scent of roasting meat drifted up from the river meadow. She tried not to be hurt by the sounds of revelry. Lugnasa was when the Mother's bounty was collected, and She must be honoured with mead, feasts and dancing, to secure Her blessings for the next year.

Yet on the second last night before the moon ended, Lorn made a surprise visit to Rhiann's house. After the usual stiff courtesies, in which Rhiann did not bother to get up from the hearth-stone, Lorn drew a deep, nervous breath.

'We wish . . .' His voice faltered, as Rhiann levered a bannock off the hot stone. Silently, she raised one eyebrow at him in query. He looked no better than when she had first seen him.

Lorn ploughed on. 'The people wish for Caitlin to be harvest queen this year. We will escort her and you . . . Ban Cré . . . to the procession and the blessing.' He seemed to want to say more, then compressed his lips, and fell silent.

Rhiann was swept with a tide of conflicting emotion. She glanced at Caitlin in the rush chair, her belly as swollen now as the grains on the stalks. Of course the people would wish her to be harvest queen – she would draw the Source to the fields with her very presence.

And yet . . . Rhiann could not abide Urben ordering them about as if they were his vassals. It was Rhiann's duty to take part in the festivities, though she had given up on that hope this year – and Urben was using them to make it seem there was nothing wrong. A proud refusal sprang to Rhiann's lips, but then she saw the desperate hope lighting in Caitlin's eyes, and realized how much she suffered at this imprisonment.

She had grown so uncomfortable in this sticky heat, her face pale and sheened with sweat, her slim ankles swollen. She moved slowly, where she never had before, pausing often to catch her breath, her hand on her back. Rhiann was in constant anxiety over her, yet after all her potions and brews, fresh air and movement was the one thing Rhiann could not give and which she perhaps needed most.

Rhiann gazed up at Lorn. 'We will attend the rite.'

The next night, the stubbled fields upriver to the south, in the Add valley, were golden in the torchlight, the still air thick with dust and chaff. Around the bonfire in the centre, the black shapes of dancers waited for Rhiann to conclude her blessing. The sky was the colour of heather, the perfume of the blooms gathered in the bowl of the dark hills.

The birds had fallen silent and there was no wind, just the crackling of the fire, the solemn beat of a drum and a single flute whose notes rose and fell, echoing from the valley slopes.

There was a stone in this field, half-buried in turf now, carved by the same Old Ones who built the tombs in the ancestor valley. The sacred spirals drawn on it told the story of the cycle of the soul, from Mother's womb to the world and back again. Yet tonight, the spirals that Rhiann traced with ash and filled with the first mead were for the grain, which was also born in darkness and then burst into sun, before dying back into earth — the same endless pattern.

Rhiann's best dress was stiff and heavy around her knees as she came to her feet and turned, reverently pouring the rest of the mead to the moist dirt beneath her, the last words of the sacred song on her lips. As she straightened, a great cheer burst out, and other musicians joined the flute and drum, for it was a night for celebration, not solemnity, as the black dancers around the fire came to life.

To keep her full wits Rhiann had taken no *saor*, and beneath the weight of Urben and Gelert's stern gazes her spirit was clouded with anxiety, so the touch of the Mother was merely a brush of moth wings in her heart. The druids were a dominating presence this night, anyway, since they read the stars with the aid of the standing stones, and proclaimed when the harvest could begin.

As Rhiann stepped down from the rock and deliberately made her way towards the crowd, she noticed that even though her two guards remained at a discreet distance, people seemed afraid to come near her. She felt their fear and uncertainty running beneath the wild music. Rhiann yearned to join with them, to know what they thought, yet Urben's warriors were scattered liberally through the crowd, and stopped their tongues.

Now Rhiann heard an even greater shout, as the people parted for the harvest cart, led by two mares with red-braided manes. In the cart stood Caitlin as harvest queen, holding a corn doll woven from the field's last sheaf of barley. At the sight of her pale face beneath its crown of hawthorn berries, Rhiann's frustration peaked and she pushed through the cheering crowd to walk close by the cart's wheel.

Her eyes fixed anxiously on Caitlin's face as she grimaced at the jolts of the wagon, Rhiann did not hear the whispered entreaty at first.

'Lady.' The whisper became a hiss, and Rhiann immediately recognized Aldera's voice, yet she did not turn. Among the jostling bodies, no one noticed Aldera touch Rhiann's hand. 'Lady, we have all been so worried . . . I have only seen you from afar . . . Urben has spread the word he had no choice, that your prince is not coming back, that the council thinks Lorn should be king.'

Rhiann risked a glance over her shoulder. On a slight rise to one side, Gelert watched the dancers, his aloofness a thin veneer over his disdain. He had kept a careful distance from Urben, arriving with his druids in his horse-head mask to sacrifice a yearling calf to the gods. On the other side of the ancestor stone, Urben surveyed the crowd with a wolfish smile, and Lorn with a set to his jaw.

Rhiann ducked her head, as if missing her footing. 'It is all lies,' she murmured to Aldera. 'We are safe, for the moment, yet I would know how Urben explains our imprisonment.'

Aldera nudged closer, clapping her hands above her head in time with the drum. 'It has been spread around that the war leader and his foster-brother are dead, and that you and Caitlin have been struck ill with grief and mourning, and must rest in isolation. He said that now the prince is gone Dunadd is vulnerable, and he has taken it upon himself to protect you.'

Rhiann let out a strangled grunt, and sensed Aldera's eyes flick towards her.

'Finan is with us,' Aldera hurried to continue. 'He and Bran have tried to stir up the warriors who are left, but your prince took the most loyal with him, and the Epidii men are . . . confused . . . their loyalty torn between their own people and their oaths to your man. Finan was all for launching an attack on Urben's guards, but not enough men would join him, and they feared harming the women and children. This is what has kept the people silent – it is the indecision, you see, the confusion.'

'Yet Lorn has not been made king,' Rhiann murmured. 'How does Urben explain this?'

'The chief druid announced that the day for the king-making is not yet – that they must wait for an auspicious day.'

Rhiann snorted with contempt. 'Auspicious!' she hissed. 'Urben is waiting because he knows Eremon is alive; that he will return and fight!

He wants that settled before he proclaims this new king. He is afraid, even now!'

'I pray that is true, lady, I pray.'

Rhiann shook her head, the fierce frustration she had felt at Belen's passivity burning in her gut. There were hundreds of people in the village, more than the warriors Urben brought with him. If they could only work together . . . Words, fighting words, sprang to her lips, then an image blotted out all else in her mind: Talorc's wife rocking herself before her hearth.

The words died in Rhiann's throat, and tears pricked at her eyes. She half-turned her head to meet Aldera's gaze beneath the confusion of waving arms and banging of a drum in her ear. That calm face could quiet five children with one look, and now it gave Rhiann strength.

'Tell the men to do nothing,' Rhiann said heavily.

Aldera blinked in surprise, opening her mouth to argue.

'Nothing!' Rhiann whispered urgently. 'I wish no harm to come to anyone on our behalf. We live, we are holding strong, and we will wait.' She glanced up at Caitlin, who forced a shaky grin as the cart came to a halt for her to receive the people's acclaim.

Rhiann saw the understanding dawn in Aldera's eyes.

'We will wait for Eremon,' Rhiann added firmly. 'He is the one who will find a way out of this.'

The next day, perhaps because of the long night, the tension of the rite and the jolting of the cart, Caitlin was fractious, aching and nauseous. Rhiann sorted through her herb stores, frowning, racking her brains for anything that would ease her ailments, and which were safe for the baby. Once every bark packet was unwrapped and every jar unstoppered, and the workbench was an untidy mess of unpacked baskets and earthen pots, she realized that her stocks of some herbs were low, because she had not been replenishing them.

The reordering, repacking, and pausing to explain the main properties of certain herbs to Eithne, took a satisfying amount of time. By late afternoon, they were both still at the workbench, and the air was scented with a heady mixture of pungent herbs, beeswax, lanolin and honey.

Caitlin was squatting by the hearth, leaning forward on one hand to stretch her back, stirring the pot of barley porridge set in the coals. Suddenly, she let out a strangled gasp.

Rhiann glanced over sharply, yet Caitlin did not move or speak, the spoon paused now in the air, dripping sticky globs of porridge.

'Caitlin?' She walked over and touched Caitlin's arm, and Caitlin looked mutely up, guilt flaming in her face. 'What . . . ?' Rhiann began, and then her eyes travelled lower, to Caitlin's bare feet against the floor rushes, splashed with bloody fluid.

As the shock hit Rhiann, Caitlin swallowed another gasp, and a further gush of blood-streaked water seeped a scarlet trail down her shin to her ankle.

Caitlin's frightened eyes dropped to her feet and, forcing down her own shock, Rhiann put a steady hand on her shoulder. 'It has begun,' she said calmly.

But early, at least a moon early. And the blood . . . She struggled for control, for the healer within her.

'Eithne,' Rhiann said, her voice sounding as if it came from someone else. 'Come and finish the porridge for Caitlin. I think we will all need it before this day is through.'

Caitlin drooped under Rhiann's arm, as they both shuffled to the end of the room and back, keeping up the steady pacing that had worn flat paths in the rushes. With every pain that came they stopped, and Caitlin panted, her nails digging into Rhiann's forearm.

It was night now, and twice Eithne had sponged Caitlin's sweating, swollen body with cool water from the well, dampening the thin shift she wore. Rhiann prepared every tonic she could think of to calm the womb and halt that trickle of blood.

Aedan sat on a stool by the hearth, keeping up a steady flow of songs and poems, retelling all the tales that had kept them sane these last two moons. Yet concern shadowed his grey eyes. Didius stayed silent, cross-legged on the rushes, whittling a child's wooden toy. At length Aedan paused for breath, wiping his brow and drinking deep of his ale, and Caitlin's pacing feet came to rest before Didius.

'What have you there, Didius?' Caitlin's voice cracked with dryness, though Rhiann had kept her sipping water.

Didius held up the alder-wood toy, a beast with pegged wheels for legs, so it would roll across the floor. 'It is called a lion,' he explained quietly, his dark eyes intent on Caitlin's face. 'It is like a huge cat, with a horse's mane.'

Caitlin laughed and took the toy in her hands, turning it over. 'How cunning! A cat! My son will be the only child in all Alba to have a . . . lion . . . as a playmate.'

'Lions are from a place called Africa,' Didius volunteered, with a shy smile. 'They are called the king of beasts.' Abruptly, he realized what he'd said, and blushed furiously.

Caitlin handed it back. 'Thank you,' she whispered. 'Then worthy indeed of this son.'

Then another pain took her, and this time she nearly bent double with it. Rhiann panted the breaths with her, gripping her hand, and gradually she straightened.

'Sit on the bench now,' Rhiann ordered, her fear a sharp kick under her breastbone. 'I have some willow bark brew cooling, for the pain. Here, I will fetch it.'

It was late in the night. An agonized cry rent the close air, and Aedan's voice faltered in its tale, though for a moment his fingers kept up their playing. Then the music, too, faded.

'Caitlin,' Rhiann begged, as her sister sagged in her arms. 'Come to the bed now, and rest. There I can rub you, help the pain.'

Caitlin held her belly, sweat running down her brow, her shift clinging to the bulge in damp folds. She allowed Rhiann to seat her on the sickbed, as Eithne scurried around to prop her up with cushions. Caitlin's pale face was blotched, and the shadows were now smears under her eyes. 'Keep going,' she whispered to Aedan, on the other side of the bedscreen. 'Take me away from this.'

Aedan's throat bobbed as he swallowed a sip of ale, his wide eyes searching for Rhiann on the end of the bed. Silently, Rhiann nodded and bent to rub Caitlin's feet, concentrating hard to blink her own tears away.

Yet Aedan had not got far into his next tale when he was cut off by the greatest of Caitlin's cries yet, and Rhiann was instantly on her feet, soothing her, struggling to smooth the fear from her own face. 'The tales will have to wait,' she said, around her dry tongue. 'It is time for you men to leave us; go to Talorc's house and bide with Belen.' She turned to Eithne. 'Top up the water in the cauldron, and find Lorn – tell him I need Aldera and the old women.'

'Yes, lady,' Eithne whispered.

Alone, Rhiann gave Caitlin a rowan stick to bite down on while she examined her, pressing on her belly, then carefully sliding a few fingers inside to feel for the womb. As she sponged her hands clean with soapwort, she turned away from Caitlin's pained gaze.

For though the waters had broken too early, the night was now far advanced, and the rest was happening nowhere near swiftly enough. Despite the pains, the baby would not come.

Chapter 18

The rest of the night was a dark tunnel that seemed endless. And yet somehow, the daylight did eventually return, creeping up from the east to spill, damp and cool, through the open doorway.

In the shadows of the bedplace Caitlin's eyes were squeezed shut, and she did not seem to see or hear any of the women around her. It was as if the dregs of her energy had been forced inward, to rally her for the waves of crushing pain. Against her drained face, the circles under her eyes grew darker as the sun rose outside.

'The babe should have come by now,' Aldera ventured. All there knew it, but it must be said.

Rhiann sat on a stool, her hands lying useless among the blood-stained folds of her dress. Sometime in the night her hair had worked its way free; now she smoothed it back over her ears with shaking hands, as if it mattered.

Aldera wiped sweat from her brow and upper lip with a clean rag. 'It must be turned the wrong way.'

Caitlin let out another whimper, and all the old women looked down at the bed. Those sounds were becoming softer, hour by sweat-soaked hour, as Rhiann's fear clutched at her ever more desperately.

'She is so small,' Rhiann whispered. 'She is small, and he is not.' Her face twisted; she bit her lip. 'And now she is losing strength. I cannot risk turning the babe when she is so weak, for she will tear, and bleed.'

Aldera placed a solid hand on Rhiann's aching shoulder, the pity clear in her eyes. 'Then we can do little but pray to the Mother for deliverance. For her, for the babe.'

Rhiann's eye fell on Eithne kneeling before the hearth, sprinkling more grain at Ceridwen's stone feet as she muttered her prayers. Ceridwen, goddess of life – and death. She wished Caitlin and the babe to be delivered from the agony. But to what? The Otherworld? *No!*

Yet it had been too long; a body could not last much longer.

With a deadened mind, Rhiann drew back the damp, rumpled sheets, and checked Caitlin once more. The skin of her poor, distended belly was pale, sweat-sheened, rippling with wrenching pains that brought only faint gasps. The child had dropped, but it must be twisted. The womb gateway had widened, yet still he would not come.

Rhiann covered Caitlin's naked body again. 'Leave us,' she ordered hoarsely, and with no arguments all the women did. Then Rhiann considered Eithne, hovering by the bed. She could send the girl on an errand, but they had shared too much for anything to be said that was not the utmost truth. 'I need to be alone with her,' Rhiann said simply. Eithne nodded, choking down a sob as she left.

When they were gone the house fell silent, and Rhiann drew the stool closer to the bed. Only Caitlin's laboured breathing disturbed the close air, scented with the cleansing herbs thrown on the fire. Every few moments Caitlin's breathing caught, and the hand that Rhiann held went rigid and clawed into a ball. At those times, Rhiann murmured, 'Breathe, *cariad*, breathe with me. Like this: one . . . in . . . two . . . out . . . there . . . there.'

And Caitlin's thin chest would sink back down under the covers, and the laboured rasping of the breath-between-pain would begin again, rasping until it rang in Rhiann's ears and she could barely stand it.

The day slowly brightened, yet only the fire, set for boiling water, gave the bedplace any light – a lurid glow that painted Caitlin's cheeks with false colour. Rhiann sat without moving now, her forehead resting on Caitlin's fevered hand. Now, when that hand clenched, Rhiann no longer raised her face to give any encouragement, for she was sure that Caitlin was beyond hearing. Instead, she found some part of her listening to that breathing and hoping – for one moment – that it would end, so that at least her sister would be free of the pain and struggle.

Rhiann had attended many births like this, first with Linnet and then on her own, and so much could go awry in bearing. Sometimes the babe would not come, and the massaging of the belly, the concoctions, the chants and prayers would be to no avail. The woman's strength would ebb, the cries turning to moans, and the moans to gasps, just like Caitlin now. The rippling of the belly would slow and stop, and more blood would leak from between the mother's legs, and when she died, sometimes the babe would be released from the body alive, and sometimes blue and still.

Conaire will not want the babe, Rhiann found herself thinking. *Conaire will not want the babe without her.* And as she said the words to herself, pain lanced her own belly.

Her mother, her father, her foster-family – all had died. Yet her love for Caitlin was an adult love, not that of a child, the love of soul-friendship found in the most unexpected place, shared and given back in abundance. And so its loss would be all the more unbearable for that. Only Caitlin had Rhiann been able to love freely, without fear or reservation.

The house was completely silent now, holding its breath, as once before it had waited, on a night when Eremon took Rhiann's hand for the first time. No wind crept through the door; no dogs barked. Nothing came but the occasional crack and spit of the fire, and that was all. Rhiann knew that the silence was creeping in from the edges of the house until, at the last, Caitlin's breathing would also stop, and then there would be nothing.

We need her, she found herself whispering. *Goddess, we need her.* She, the smallest of them, was their anchor. Someone moaned, and Rhiann raised her head, thinking it Caitlin coming back to herself. But it was not; the sound had escaped from Rhiann's own throat. *My sister . . .*

Suddenly, Rhiann sprang to her feet, surprised by the bolt of rage that struck her, a wild fury as bright and hot as the pain had been. 'No!' she cried, leaning over Caitlin, grasping her thin shoulders and raising her up. 'No, Caitlin, you will not! You will not go! *You are my sister*, my heart's kin. Come back to me!'

Caitlin's head lolled back, and now she did groan, her eyelids fluttering, her lips dropping open with a sigh. In the grip of the rage Rhiann shook her, as she would shake life into a baby who would not breathe. 'Caitlin!' she cried. 'Listen to me, Caitlin! This babe is a boy. He is a warrior, strong and handsome and fine! One day, he will bear a spear and shield and sword in great hands, just like his father, and strike down his enemies with fire and blade! He will be proud and fearless, Caitlin, and so you must be! Come now and fight for him! Come!'

She shook Caitlin again, her sister's head snapped back and, miraculously, Rhiann saw her struggling to open her eyes. It was then that Rhiann knew she had heard. With a relieved sob, she rested Caitlin back on the bed and grasped her hands, chafing them between her own, willing life back into her eyes.

And so it came, slowly.

'Fight, Caitlin!' Rhiann begged then. 'Scream and fight and never give in! *Fight!*' Her fingers dug in to Caitlin's arms and, with sheer will Rhiann forced her own strength down into Caitlin's body.

And at last Caitlin's eyes focused, as she took the first deep and true breath of the day.

'Caitlin,' said Rhiann, her voice shaking as she dashed her hands in the bronze basin of warm water, 'I am going to reach inside and turn the child. It will hurt and tear, but you must be strong. Will you let me do this?'

A pained sigh escaped Caitlin's dry lips, but with an effort she nodded. 'Do anything, Rhiann,' she whispered. 'Anything to save him. Let me go if you need to . . .'

'No.' Rhiann wiped her hands and set the rowan stick between Caitlin's lips, pausing to stroke her damp hair. 'I won't let either of you go.'

A shriek sounded, the first for many hours, and another, and another. And when Eithne and Aldera and the other women rushed in, prepared for the worst, they found Rhiann kneeling behind a squatting Caitlin on the bed, holding her up, their hands interlaced.

Aldera rushed to the bed, pushing aside the tangle of bloodied sheets around Caitlin's ankles. 'Good girl! Keep at it, not much more now! Push! Push!'

All the women leaned into the bearing. Yet with Caitlin's back wedged between her legs, Rhiann felt as if she was squeezing every grain of strength she possessed into that straining body, as if they both bore the child.

'I see the head!' Aldera cried. 'It's coming, Goddess be thanked, it's coming!'

Caitlin let loose one great, hoarse scream, her thighs rigid against Rhiann's own, and sagged back so violently that Rhiann could only collapse under her, bracing her fall on the bed, tears streaming down her face until everything was a blur.

Yet Rhiann didn't need to see, for over the exclamations of the women and Caitlin's wrenching gasps, the high, thin wail of a baby pierced the air.

Chapter 19

Rhiann jerked awake and, in the confusion of her returning senses, heard only the silence around her.

She half-started from her rush chair, struck with terror, desperately blinking sleep from her eyes. Yet something stopped her; an unexpected, languid weight across her breasts, a faint tug in her hair. It was a tiny hand, caught in the sweat tangles at the nape of Rhiann's neck. And in her ear was the strangest breath of all, rapid and shallow, like that of a bird. Nodding asleep in Didius's chair, Rhiann had held the babe across her chest, his head over her shoulder, her hand spread protectively across his skull.

For a long moment she didn't move, absorbing every detail of the warm weight on arms and chest and shoulder, the scent of new skin and tiny, wheezing breath. *The first day with my nephew.* The surge in Rhiann's chest then was a feeling that had no name. It stopped her heart and took her own breath completely away, so she could hear only his.

At last the beat of her blood returned, and she shifted in the chair, rising to stretch her aching back and stiff legs. From the open door came a waft of air, heavy with the last of the day's salted, briny heat. Rhiann tiptoed past Eithne on her pallet, and in the doorway carefully tipped the baby off her shoulder until he lay back in her arms, his fists falling out to each side from the linen wrap. The dusk glowed on his new skin.

At the disturbance the child squirmed and whimpered, but then his eyelids fluttered open and he stopped moving, looking straight up at Rhiann, his eyes dark and bottomless. As she'd expected, he was heavy as well as long and, though six weeks early, was nearly as rounded as a full-term babe.

'What will you be then, *cariad?*' Rhiann crooned to him, echoing the question all new mothers asked the priestess who attended their birth. *What do you see, lady? What will he be?*

And as his eyes caught and held hers, and she lifted him closer to her face, the colourless light seemed to waver before her sight, and for a moment out of time Rhiann glimpsed something that made her gasp. For the tiny, wizened face before her shimmered into the features of a man. The whisper of fuzz on his head flowed into braids of barley-gold, and the blue eyes now shone with such a commanding power, such fierce determination, that Rhiann did not need to see the circlet of gold that sat on his brow.

Her hands tightened with shock, and the child squawked and became a wriggling, squirming babe again. She clasped him to her chest, her eyes blurring, and then she heard a stir from the bed behind her. 'Rhiann?'

Rhiann smiled shakily as she returned the child to Caitlin's arms, helping her to sit up against the pillows. The flushed lamp-light hid the worst of the exhaustion and pain scored into Caitlin's face, and only pride and joy gleamed in her eyes as she gazed down at her son, stroking his cheek with one finger. Then at last she broke the long silence with a voice that breathed tiredness, yet great solemnity. 'What will he be, lady?'

Rhiann laid her hand on the child's head, still trembling with the wonder. 'He will be a king.'

Caitlin seemed to absorb that with no visible reaction beyond the ghost of a nod. 'I knew. I always knew.' She raised her face to Rhiann. 'You saved me, and him. I owe you our lives.'

Rhiann stared at the babe's mouth moving against his fist, until Caitlin grasped Rhiann's fingers in a firm grip. 'I heard you, Rhiann, when you called me. I floated far away, but I heard you.'

Rhiann's throat ached, and she swallowed to ease it, meeting Caitlin's eyes.

'In my heart I always knew, anyway.' Caitlin smiled through her tears. 'I always knew you were my sister.'

This time it was Caitlin who enfolded Rhiann in her embrace, her arms strong enough to hold. Squashed between them the baby woke and squalled, and as they both fussed him, Rhiann at last unburdened herself about the truth of Caitlin's own birth. And in the end it didn't matter, because of what Caitlin held in her arms.

Yet it wasn't until Rhiann had bathed Caitlin's stitches and changed the moss pads between her legs that her sister asked what pressed on her most strongly.

'Rhiann.' Caitlin cupped the babe's head to her breast and rested her own back on the pillow. Her eyes were steady. 'I won't be able to carry another child, will I?'

Rhiann paused in wrapping the bloody pads in a linen towel. 'No, I don't think so,' she whispered. 'I am sorry.'

Caitlin was silent, looking down and tracing the curve of the baby's cheek. 'It is well,' she said slowly, almost to herself. 'A king needs much care to guide him to his Hall. Now, he will have all of me.'

There was no chance of keeping the birth a secret, and the sun was barely one hand-span above the horizon the next day when Urben and Lorn appeared at Rhiann's door.

'Show me the child,' Urben demanded, shouldering his way into the room, glancing at Rhiann's herb stores, drying roots and goddess figures with such disdain that she burned to refuse him.

Yet Lorn rocked on his heels, for once catching her eyes, and in his gaze Rhiann saw pleading. She glanced at the two guards that hovered at Urben's shoulder, and went behind the screen to Caitlin's bed.

'No,' Caitlin whispered, clutching the babe to her breast, her knuckles white.

'We must,' Rhiann murmured. 'But I will not let them touch him, I swear.'

Reluctantly, Caitlin gave the child over, groping Eithne's hand for support. Holding him to her chest, Rhiann placed herself before Urben.

The old chieftain peered into the child's face. 'A boy?' he asked gruffly.

Rhiann nodded, her chin high. 'Indeed.'

Urben's cool eyes slid to the wicker bedscreen. 'And the Lady Caitlin? When will she be recovered?'

Rhiann frowned in some confusion, for Urben had never shown any interest in Caitlin's well-being. Yet her sharp eyes noticed the betraying flush creeping up Lorn's neck – the heat of guilt and shame. And the truth of their position came crashing down around her. Of course! All this time she had puzzled over what Urben wanted of her and Caitlin. Now she understood.

Lorn's claim to the kingship was through a kinlink several generations old, but if he wed either Caitlin or herself his claim would be much stronger. Sons gotten on them would be heirs of the last king, her uncle Brude. She and Caitlin would be Lorn's links between the old line and the new. No wonder Urben had not harmed them! Though this consideration, she realized with sudden terror, did not apply to the babe.

Her arms closed tight on his body, and he squirmed and mewed. 'My . . . my lord.' Rhiann's mouth had gone dry; she was too scared to be angry. 'Caitlin is not well; she had a hard birth. And as her healer I advise that she lay abed for some considerable time yet.'

Urben's grey brows rose, yet Rhiann ploughed on. 'And . . . it is vital that she be left to feed the babe herself, for the drawing of the milk will likewise draw strength back into her heart and limbs.'

Urben stared hard at Rhiann, blinking once. 'Then take good care of her, lady.' He paused as he turned to go. 'And yourself.' The smile that he hid in his moustache was not returned, and Lorn did not glance Rhiann's way again as he trailed out behind his father.

That night, Rhiann watched over Caitlin as she slept, the baby tucked into the crook of his mother's arm. In repose Caitlin's face was as childlike as her son's, both of them so small and vulnerable, and Rhiann was swept with a fierce urgency to protect them both.

Yet how? Gingerly, Rhiann lay down beside them on the furs, her face pillowed in one hand. *I must get the child out of Dunadd*, she thought desperately. It wouldn't be long before Urben – or Gelert – moved against him, for Gelert's scrupulous appearance of neutrality did not fool her.

The people would never accept a king who murdered a child, but they were alone in this house, hidden, and what was to stop Urben spreading the rumour that the baby had died? The women of the dun knew that Caitlin's son had come early.

Slowly, Rhiann rose. The night was still and warm, and her bare arms beneath the thin bedshift were damp with sweat as she stirred up the coals and steeped some dried cowslip flowers for a sedative tea. Didius and Aedan had not yet returned, and only Eithne's sleeping breaths disturbed the silent hearth-place. Staring into the glowing coals, her hands around her cup, Rhiann set her mind free to wander, to find the solution that danced there on the edge of her consciousness, elusive.

And at last it came. She had been so taken with the concerns here at Dunadd that her focus had narrowed to what went on within these walls. Only two things lured her mind away. One was thoughts of Eremon – and she certainly could not reach him. The other was Linnet, a fellow priestess.

Though Rhiann's own true powers had dimmed, as a priestess she had other means at her disposal for communication – and had used them before. It had crossed her mind, many times, to make the effort to reach out to Linnet, but besides assuring her that they were all well, there seemed little point. Such an undertaking left Rhiann weak and vulnerable, and she could not afford to undermine her own defences when so many were relying on her. Yet now, the need had become more urgent than the risk.

Only once had she used the sacred spores of the rye fungus to free her spirit from her body, and that had also been a period of dire need. It was time to try again, whatever the cost.

When Caitlin woke the next morning, Rhiann was sitting on her bed, rubbing the sleeping babe's back with scented oil.

As Caitlin yawned and carefully stretched her aching body, Rhiann's hand closed over her own. 'Sister, I must speak to you of the babe, and Urben.'

Caitlin stilled and, for a fleeting moment, Rhiann debated how honest to be. She feared hurting Caitlin, but she must communicate the urgency, and in the end she decided to be blunt. 'Your son is not safe here,' she began, tightening her hold on Caitlin's fingers when they jerked. 'But I have thought of a way to make him so.'

Swiftly, she outlined what she proposed to do, as Caitlin wrapped the sleeping child and drew him to her chest.

'He can live on goat's milk, Caitlin, for a while. And your milk will come back if it is only a few weeks. Conaire and Eremon will be back then, I am sure of it.'

Caitlin shrank into the pillow, shock and fear stiffening her features. Then she swallowed hard and gazed down at her son, silent for a long moment. 'It's the only way, isn't it?' she whispered.

'Yes. But do you trust me?'

'With all I have.' Caitlin's eyes rose to meet Rhiann's, shining with tears. 'But, oh, it is dangerous for you – you said it yourself!'

Rhiann shook her head. 'None of that matters, for sake of him. But I will need everyone's help to keep me safe, as well.'

Caitlin nodded, and wiped her eyes with determination. 'When?'

'Tonight,' Rhiann replied. 'Eithne must speak with Aldera when she brings the food this morning.'

Chapter 20

Linnet watched the rush lamp-wick sizzle out, plunging her hut into darkness.

She sighed and rolled on to her back, kicking the clinging sheets off her damp, hot skin. Better that the light was gone, for then she did not have to see these dreadful men – Urben's warriors – sprawled all over her floor, their feet on her chairs, their faces smeared with her food, their swords and spears sharp, bright flares in the light of her hearth. Oh, they treated her with the greatest of courtesies, and laid no finger upon her, but only Dercca was allowed the freedom of the sacred pool, the woods and goat-pen. Week after week, Linnet had sensed the path of the sun above, and she knew the moons of light and warmth were passing. Her anger and frustration grew.

At first she'd treated Urben's men with icy disdain, for only by holding on to her anger could she keep despair at bay. Even so, every night under the cover of darkness, the fear gnawed at her. How did Caitlin and Rhiann fare? And what about Caitlin's pregnancy? Ah, Gelert had been so clever, even though the men had come in Urben's name.

That first day, she had listened to her new guards' rhetoric with dawning amazement. Eremon must have been defeated, they said, in which case the threat of Roman reprisals or sudden raids by their neighbours was high, and it was with grave concerns for the Lady Linnet that Urben had given her four warriors for protection. Linnet had argued, of course, but it was so easy to hold her with the threat of those swords, for had she not, by her own choice, exiled herself on this mountain? No one would even know she was a prisoner.

The greater frustration was that she could have escaped, for she knew some means of dealing with such obstacles. Yet the only useful place for her to go was Dunadd, and if caught there she had no doubt that Gelert would devise a far more secure prison for her — or worse. Then she would be unable to lend her daughters any aid at all.

And Linnet knew that sometime, somehow, they would need that aid.

That was why she began to hide her desperation and rage, dropped the disdain and began to serve the men mead at night with gracious hands, and smile at them when they gave thanks for the food. She treated the minor aches and ailments of warriors with sweet salves and wax rubs, and strengthening brews. The guards responded swiftly to this kindness, their natural awe of her transmuting into an eagerness to treat her well.

She ensured that Dercca always came back from her chores exactly when she said she would, and only went a certain distance from the hut. After the first few weeks the warriors relaxed, stopped shadowing Dercca's every step, and hardly gave any notice to the old maid. And Linnet noted this, as she sat weaving baby clothes on her loom.

On the first day of Lugnasa, Linnet asked leave to make an offering in the sun-bright yard and, turning to the south, Rhiann came into her mind. She knew in that moment that the daughter of her heart was giving the same offering at Dunadd. And on the last day, heavy with restless heat, Linnet pricked her finger with the bone needle and threw down her sewing in frustration, knowing that something was very wrong. Yet because Gelert had forbidden Linnet access to the sacred pool or ingestion of any herbs, she might pace and wring her hands and send tearful prayers to her Goddess, but in all she remained blind and deaf.

Just as on this night, when the lamp burned out and the restlessness returned with force. Linnet desperately needed to rise and do something, but she must never alert the men that there was anything amiss. Eventually, she turned to her priestess breath training to calm herself. In this way, she managed to make herself sink into an uneasy sleep.

In her dreams, she often saw Caitlin and Rhiann, and would hurry after them on desperate feet. Yet always they were far away, riding on horses too fast to catch, or disappearing into the maze of paths between Dunadd's houses.

Which was why her sleeping mind shuddered with a kind of shock when, walking by the sacred pool as she often did in dreams, she saw on the path a figure robed as a priestess.

A woman who was not running away. A woman, she realized with a jolt of joy, who was seeking her.

Joined by a thin, silver cord, Rhiann's spirit-self struggled to ignore the urgent feeling of sickness coming from her body far away, and stay within Linnet's dreaming mind. Dimly, she sensed the presence of

Caitlin, Aedan, Eithne and Didius around her, anchoring the root of the soul-cord in the body that writhed in agony on the floor at Dunadd.

The rye fungus that released a spirit was the most dangerous of druid preparations, used only for the rarest trances with other trained people present. Yet those with Rhiann loved her, and she had discovered that love had a power and a will of its own.

Of course, this knowledge did not completely still her fear that the cord would be cut, and she would lose her way, but each time the fear surged she returned to her priestess breathing. With each breath the silver light of the cord glowed brighter, anchoring her more strongly. And in the centre she focused on her heart, and what she had nestled there as a beacon to guide her – the exact texture of the baby's cheeks beneath her fingers.

Walking in her dream by the night-dark spring, Linnet had now seen Rhiann. She stood there, arrested in all her spirit glory, her blurred features communicating a yearning that required no words. Rhiann could not speak either, for the boundaries of her strength were close to their limits, but she could show Linnet the images that were in her own mind, and hope that she understood.

For a long time they stood in the shadows among the sighing birches, hands clasped. Then Rhiann felt the tug of the cord grow insistent, and she reached out to caress Linnet's face. By the light of joy that transfigured it, she knew that Linnet did indeed feel something, and it was only that glow that remained when all else in the scene faded.

Suddenly, Rhiann was back in the swirling tunnel of light that she had first entered, spinning faster and faster. Whereas on the way from her body her spirit had contracted to a pinprick, now, as it re-entered, her soul seemed to swell. It expanded the faster she flew down the tunnel, growing denser and more solid and then spilling out to fill every vein and limb and pocket of flesh and muscle that was her body.

This time, she found it easier to ignore the wild calls of the Otherworld beings and spirit shadows that reached out with glittering fingers and haunting voices to entrap unwary travellers.

For waiting in a bubble of light before her, solid and strong, were those who called her back even more fiercely.

Behind, in the darkness, the guard sprawled before Linnet's door barely stopped his snoring as the old maid nudged him with her foot. He peered up at her in the faint starlight and rolled away as he did every night, when she went outside to pass her water. Old women!

And at Dunadd, in the firelight, Caitlin held Rhiann with great tenderness as she retched over and over into an earthen basin. Eithne's soft hands were there too, mopping her lip and brow, pushing a whining Cù away as Didius built up the fire.

And Aedan sang softly by the door, a slumbering song for the guards outside, who perhaps had never heard such singing in their dreams before.

Rhiann had used a great amount of the ground spores and, after the constant stress of the past moons, the reaction of her body was ferocious, and frightening for all those with her.

By the time dawn came, her watchers were hollow-eyed with fear and lack of sleep, and Rhiann still lay curled by the crackling fire, her back against Didius's solid knees, her robe soaked with sweat even as her shoulders shook with chills.

Eithne had been dosing her with mint and tansy, but she could not keep anything down, and when she said, 'It is time,' through gritted teeth, Eithne laid a timid hand on her forehead. 'Lady,' she whispered, 'You must rest now. Let me—'

'No!' Rhiann struggled to sit up, reaching for the child in Caitlin's arms. She held her sister's eyes. 'I did not go so far, at such great cost, to risk his life now!'

Caitlin's cheeks were streaked with dirt and tears, but at last she handed the baby over, carefully resting him across Rhiann's knees.

'Bring me the poppy tincture,' Rhiann instructed, her voice hoarse and cracked.

While they all gathered close, Rhiann rewrapped the baby's linen swaddling clothes, binding his arms and legs to his body. Then, wiping her sweating face on one shoulder, she trickled the merest drop of the poppy into his soft, sucking mouth, as Caitlin's hand cupped his head. His eyes, deep and colourless in the firelight, tried to focus on Rhiann, and she stared back, cradling his soul with some wordless reassurance.

Then Rhiann heard the rhythm of Caitlin's breathing falter, and she glanced up. 'It will be well, love, I swear. It's just enough to keep him sleeping; just enough for a little while, to keep him quiet.'

'The milk has come,' Caitlin murmured under her breath, her anguish plain. 'What will he eat?'

'Linnet can find goat milk,' Rhiann soothed her. 'It can be done. He is strong, remember?'

In answer, Caitlin pressed her lips to the crest of hair sticking up at the crown of the baby's head.

As the day lightened outside, Rhiann murmured a blessing over the child, her eyes on the figure of the mother goddess Rhiannon on the darkened shelf above the hearth.

The warrior sleeping outside Rhiann's door squinted one eye up at Eithne as she stepped over him, the food basket balanced on her hip. She was a pretty little filly, he thought, with her dark hair and flashing black eyes, though she had been looking peaky recently.

The girl blushed at his direct regard and glanced down at the covered basket. 'I need to get the food from Aldera now, for she will be leaving the dun early to get herbs for my lady.'

It was barely light – the sky still grey, the air chill – and the guard sighed, before throwing back his damp blanket. Then he heaved himself from his bed roll and followed the girl, stretching his arms as he buckled on his sword.

At the Moon Gate, another two of Urben's spearmen, unaccustomed to such an early awakening, grumbled at Eithne and spoke idly with the first guard about meeting for dice after breakfast. As they did, they caught the pretty maid's eye and completely failed to see that when the smith's plump, little wife gave the food over and walked back down into the village, she still had a basket balanced on her hip.

The warriors at the village gate were even more disgruntled, but at the scolding they got from the smith's wife, who had been charged by the Ban Cré to gain some rare dawn plant, they fell over themselves to open the oak crossbars. After all, the warriors depended on Bran the smith to repair their weapons, and it wouldn't do to attract the ire of his formidable wife, or suffer the lash of her sharp tongue any longer than they needed to.

High on Linnet's mountain, the guard across her door had to rise in the dawn light to pass his own water, and it wasn't until he walked back inside the hut, yawning and cricking his back, that he noticed there was only one dark shape lying in the bed against the far wall. He cursed in fright and sudden anger, leaping over the other men sprawled on the floor to wrench the bedcovers back.

The dark shape rolled over, and Dercca the old maid smiled up at him, the gaps in her teeth clear in the sun's first rays.

And in the shadows of a secret glen, where a stream formed a tiny pool known only to the women of the dun, Aldera uncovered the basket and the sleeping baby.

'Lady,' she whispered, bowing her head and holding out the basket.

A sliver of sun broke over the far hills, reaching through the shadows of the whispering birches to light the face of the priestess, who waited, hooded and silent.

Linnet smiled, and held out her hands. 'Welcome, grandson.'

Chapter 21

The news of Linnet's escape, Rhiann judged, would reach Dunadd by the middle of the day. She kept Caitlin to her bed, behind the wicker screen, and again sent Didius and Aedan to Belen. Didius refused to leave her unprotected, was so distraught that tears nearly came to his eyes, but she was implacable. When Urben's wrath fell, she wanted it to be on her and her alone.

Only Eithne remained, grinding barley in the light of the doorway. Rhiann was proud to note that, tired as the girl was, she did not falter in her rhythm when Lorn appeared. Rhiann was setting out the goddess figurines on the hearth-stone, the offering of milk in a bronze bowl by her knees.

Lorn waited for her to raise her face, and when she did not, he strode to the hearth. 'I am here to enquire after the child.'

Cù growled and edged towards Lorn on his belly, but Rhiann merely clasped her fingers in her lap and bowed her head to the goddesses, murmuring under her breath. With a muttered oath Lorn took a step towards the bedplace.

'No!' Suddenly Rhiann was on her feet before him, calming Cù's frenzied barking with her hand. 'Caitlin is not well.'

Lorn glared at Rhiann, the high colour of his cheeks stark against the pale gilt of his unbound hair. 'My men say they have heard no cries this day.'

Rhiann said nothing and, to her surprise Lorn crossed to her and gripped one arm. 'I have also just been informed that the Lady Linnet has escaped our protection as you will be pleased to know. Now, by the Mare, you will tell me about the child!'

Rhiann raised her chin, meeting his pale eyes. 'He is dead.'

'*Dead?*' Lorn's face blanched, which only ignited Rhiann's anger.

'Yes, last night. The lack of food and air made Caitlin's milk weak.'

Lorn clenched his fists, and before Rhiann could stop him he tore back the screen hiding the bed. Caitlin cried out and curled up under the covers. With a sharp word Rhiann ordered Eithne to control the hound, then pushed past Lorn to stand with her hand on her sister's shoulder.

Silently, Lorn gazed down at Caitlin, at the tear-swollen eyes and anguished, drawn face that she did not need to feign. Then he stared at Rhiann, and he was breathing hard. 'I don't believe you.'

Rhiann passed a weary hand over her eyes; her head ached so much she could hardly focus. 'Can you not leave us alone, out of pity if nothing else? Only yesterday we gave him to Aldera to bury outside the dun.'

At this, Caitlin gave in to a muffled sob, burying her face in the checked wool blanket. Yet Lorn's eyes never left Rhiann. 'I don't believe you. He lives, doesn't he? You got him away.'

Rhiann stayed completely still, though the fingers tangled in Caitlin's loose hair trembled. She was surprised, though, to see something flash deep in Lorn's eyes that was not the anger she was expecting. At last the tense, feline spring in his muscles slackened, and he turned on his heel for the door, sweeping past Eithne, who was crouching with her arms around Cù.

'Ladies,' he said over his shoulder, his arms braced against the doorpost, 'I sorrow for your loss, and will convey the news to my father.'

To Rhiann's relief, there were no reprisals from Urben or Gelert. Whatever plans Urben had for Rhiann and Caitlin, the child was not part of it, and no reaction was forthcoming from him. However, on her circuit of the walls late that afternoon, Rhiann saw a considerable detachment of warriors ride out from the dun, the golden light glittering on their spears as they broke into parties heading north, south, east, and west towards the sea. Urben might be willing to bide his time for the child, but not for Linnet.

Rhiann stood there while the sun slid lower, spilling fire into the far glimpse of sea, the marsh darkened by the shadow of the headland. And she prayed that Linnet's horse was swift, that the land itself, the Mother, would hide her. For Rhiann had done all she could – they would know no more until Eremon came home.

Eremon . . . As the whisper of his name touched her lips, all the tension and pain Rhiann had been keeping at bay caved in on her heart with a thundering rush. She'd had no choice – she'd *had* to stay strong for Caitlin, for them all.

Yet now the babe was safe, and Caitlin healing, Rhiann would at last allow herself to hear the cries in her own heart.

Every day for the next week, Lorn appeared at Rhiann's door, and every day all inside ignored him. Soon even Cù stopped growling when he came. The Epidii lord sat on a hearth-bench and watched Rhiann pound herbs, strain honey and steep heather flowers for ale and dyes, and all the while he said nothing.

As day followed day, Rhiann's tension began to grow to an unbearable pitch, although neither she nor Lorn would break the silence. It was a game of wills, after all. A game she intended to win.

Early one morning she'd managed to coax Caitlin, who was suffering her son's loss greatly, to sit in the sun outside with Eithne. The lack of a sucking babe had brought the milk fever to Caitlin's poor, swollen breasts, and she lay in bed most of the day with compresses of wood sage strapped to her chest. Yet Rhiann wanted her to get some air, and Aedan soothed her when he made up ditties about the great deeds Caitlin's son would do when he came to manhood.

This day Rhiann noted with a grim smile that Aedan did not soften the sound of his current song; about the king Caitlin had birthed, and what a warrior he would be, and how he would smite his enemies with a great sword. Lorn knew the baby was not dead, after all, though neither he nor Rhiann had mentioned it again.

It was a warm morning. Rhiann, pulping more sage flowers and leaves at her workbench, kept wiping her sweating face on her shoulder, conscious of Lorn's gaze on her. As usual she was ignoring it, when Lorn abruptly broke his long silence.

'Why do you continue to invite my displeasure this way?' His chin was shoved broodingly into his hand.

Rhiann scraped mashed leaves from her fingers and wiped them on the rag on her belt. 'Why do you invite mine?' Today she wore only a rough, stained robe, and she was barefoot, her hair carelessly bound up. The very way she dressed was a deliberate signal to him, that he meant nothing to her.

'You hate me.' Lorn's voice was flat, expressionless.

Rhiann snorted. 'Oh, and you expect me to flutter around you, do you? Ask if you would like an ale, my lord, a mead? Or one of these bannocks here, my lord, *my king!*'

Lorn's spirit had always been fiery, and even in his dark mood he could not resist such jibes. He sprang to his feet. 'I do not expect you to welcome me, but by the Mare you will give me some respect – and listen to what I have to say!'

Rhiann laughed bitterly. 'Listen to you *now*, after all these moons? You certainly took your time.' Suddenly her laughter died in her throat. 'And why now, then?' She caught the betraying quiver in Lorn's cheek, and her mind and heart leaped at the knowing. 'You've heard something, haven't you? About Eremon!'

When Lorn didn't answer, Rhiann flung the rag to the workbench and strode around it to grasp his arm. 'Is he alive? Is he coming? *Tell me!*' Lorn didn't have to speak for her to see the truth in his eyes, and she nearly cried out with relief. 'So that's what this is! You're afraid, aren't you, *my lord*!'

He shook off her arm. 'Stop calling me that!'

'And what would you rather I call you, son of Urben!' Rhiann thrust her face closer. 'Traitor, perhaps? And now the wolf returns to his den, and you are afraid!'

Lorn flinched. 'My first loyalty is to my father.'

'Your loyalty is to your people! And you gave your allegiance to Eremon because you knew that he was their best hope. So you do not only break faith with him, but with them!'

Lorn backed up until his calves collided with the bench. 'And what would you have me do?' he hissed, trying to lower his voice. 'By the Mare, he is my father! For the last two years my clan has expected me to take the kingship. They are my kin!'

'And their blood will flow the same colour as yours when the Romans overwhelm us.'

Lorn's head reared up at that. 'Do you think your lord is the only man who can save us? Can I, too, not command our people?'

'Your impulses put men in danger!' Rhiann cried. 'Yes, you are a fine warrior, and that is why you are able to make good your mistakes of judgement. But lead us to safety? Join all the men of Alba under one banner? That you cannot do!'

Abruptly, Lorn grabbed her wrist and pulled her close in his rage. 'And why not? Why can't the son of Urben lead us to glory?'

Deliberately, Rhiann curled her lip. 'Why indeed?'

Lorn's pale eyes blazed a handspan from her own, before he flung her away. Rhiann clasped her workbench for support, pulling herself upright, breathless with triumph. Lorn was a man of impulse, acting first, thinking later. But not now. She'd goaded him to rage, plucking at his pride, and he'd wanted to strike her, she saw it. Yet he didn't. He mastered the rage, fought for control and won. He must feel something for Eremon, then, and for her, for them all.

She dropped her voice, panting. 'You can answer your own question, Lorn, though it might have been better for you to seek my insights long ago. So listen now: if you try to lead our army, the other Epidii clans won't join you. You've shown that you can take the kingship by force, so do you think the other clans won't try the same? And while Epidii warrior fights Epidii warrior, weakening everything that Eremon has built, the Romans will be getting closer, day by day. And when they get here you will be too busy arguing over that Hall up there to notice when they burn it around you!' Rhiann reached out to touch Lorn's arm, but he averted his face, and she could only see the pulsing of blood at his throat. 'You are a fine warrior, one of our finest. But Eremon has shown he can bring all the clans together. He has made an ally of Calgacus, the most powerful of kings! The Caereni and Carnonacae have sworn to him as their Stag, their war leader in spirit as well as in blood. Can you say the same? Can you draw on such allegiances to protect us?'

For a moment the muscles along both sides of Lorn's jaw worked in anger, and his eyes blazed their defiance. Yet in the end the breath went out of him in one rush. 'No.' Lorn's shoulders slumped. 'No, the gods save me, I cannot.'

'Then you would prove yourself a king by putting your people first.'

At the anguished twist of his mouth, Rhiann was swept by a surprising surge of pity. And with that abrupt fading of anger came exhaustion, and she groped for the nearest stool and sank on to it. 'So,' she said at last, 'we are both trapped, are we not?'

Lorn stared down at her warily.

'My bonds, however, are not of my own making,' Rhiann added. 'And unlike you, I do not have the power to break them.'

Their gazes locked: his groping for understanding; hers holding a question. Yet there was no time to continue, for one of Lorn's guards appeared at the open door, blocking the sunlight. 'My lord,' he said, his tone rising with the barest note of urgency, 'you must come to the gate.'

It was when the man's eyes strayed to Rhiann that it came to her in a rush of blood to her face. And without making a sound she was out of the door before any could stop her, flying past the surprised faces of Didius, Caitlin, Eithne, Aedan and the guards, who reached for her, shouting.

As she raced for the high walls of the crag, her heart sang over and over. *He lives!*

Chapter 22

E remon stood so still in the fluttering shadows of the hazel copse that he could have been one of the trunks himself. Conaire had moved to stand two paces behind, but otherwise made no sound.

From the slopes of the hill, Eremon gazed west to Dunadd, separated from him by the track, the river and the water meadows. At first he'd thought it looked little different from when he left, except for the trading punts clogging the pier, and the thick green of the trees, which had been in bud yet now were in full leaf. Then one of his Epidii warriors had pointed out Urben's bear emblem flying above the King's Hall, and it was on this that his eyes were now fixed, as well as the blur of Urben's warriors lining Dunadd's walls.

He knew I would come, Eremon thought. *Yet he has kept all his men within Dunadd, the coward. He didn't try to head us off.*

The reason was obvious. Eremon would never attack Dunadd with the women inside, and therefore inside Dunadd was the safest place for Urben's warriors to be. The old chief must have already stretched his men thin between his own dun and this. All these cool thoughts slid one by one through Eremon's mind, but they only skittered over the turmoil of emotions battling within him, freezing his muscles rigid.

The extent of his immediate, towering rage around the campfire last night had been enough to scare Urben's scout back into the saddle, and from there back to Dunadd, the answer to his message Eremon's dagger stuck through his shield. Yet with the dawn, and his first sight of Dunadd, the hue of Eremon's fury had deepened, fuelled by a gnawing fear that he had never felt before. After so long as warriors, he and Conaire had forgotten to fear for themselves. Now he did fear for someone else, someone he loved, and it terrified him just how much more intense it made his rage. For that kind of rage could make him foolhardy, and prod him into mistakes.

I can afford no mistakes. Not for her.

With trembling hands, Eremon rubbed his eyes and massaged his aching jaw. After chasing Agricola most of the way to the Forth these past moons, his exhaustion ran bone deep, and he could ill afford more stress. Yet more had come.

After leaving the rest of his warband on guard in the mountains, he, Conaire and an escort of fifty Epidii had hastened here on foot. With little rest, they had all been dropping in their tracks, longing for hot baths and proper food, when Urben's scouts came upon them in one of the long glens that crossed the hills around Dunadd.

The scouts had been alerted to his movements, he now knew, by intercepting all the messages that he had sent since the first great victory in the Novantae lands, where they killed perhaps 700 Romans for the loss of 200 Albans. So he expected that Rhiann may not have received a single one of his messages – perhaps she did not even know if he lived. And last night, as Urben's words spilled from his scout's mouth into Eremon's disbelieving ears, the rage had consumed the last dregs of his strength.

Now Conaire's voice came from over his shoulder, roughened with exhaustion and strain. 'Does Urben honestly believe that we would leave our women, and sully our honour, by handing over the dun to him and riding away?'

'No,' Eremon forced through gritted teeth, scanning Dunadd's crag. 'Urben is marginally smarter than that. He wants something else.'

'Well, what? Our forces are evenly matched now that we come with so few. Perhaps he wants us to challenge his clansmen to battle.'

'Perhaps,' Eremon replied. 'But we don't want that.'

'Eremon.' Conaire propelled himself forward, his arm gripping one of the hazel trunks. 'My wife is in there, my unborn child. I care nothing for the safety of this tribe! I will storm their dun myself if I have to . . .' He bit off his words, and Eremon glanced at him, pained at the gauntness of Conaire's cheeks, ragged with dirty, blond stubble against grimy skin. Rhiann and Caitlin would hardly recognize them when they saw them again.

'Peace, brother.' Eremon struggled to draw air into his lungs, as his own turmoil threatened to break free. For her, he needed to keep his cool head. 'We will circle around to the southern ridge where the druid huts are, but cautiously in case Urben attacks.'

Conaire's shoulders fell in a sigh, and he took off his helmet and rubbed his forehead. When he looked at Eremon he seemed to have gained some control; his blue eyes harder, bright with thought rather than rage. 'We could use that Roman formation we've been teaching the men, to defend on the move.'

Eremon nodded, returning a weary smile. 'Good idea. They might suddenly release archers or spearmen on horseback, and we can't afford to get caught in the open and surrounded. With the shield wall we could hold them off and run for it, and that ridge is more easily defended.'

'Then what?'

'Then, we wait.'

The grunts and shouts of Rhiann's guards had soon faded in her joyous scramble to the rock outcrop that rose just outside the Horse Gate. It could not be built upon, and therefore gave a fine platform for viewing the river and plain to the north and east. Rhiann didn't even notice her panting captors catch up with her, for she was already squinting into the low morning sun, her eyes fixed on Eremon's warband.

It had appeared on the edge of the eastern hills, and now began to circle around Dunadd on the other side of the river, moving south. Stretching up on her toes, Rhiann struggled to make sense of what she saw, for the men were still in the shadow of the hills.

'What are they doing?' one of Urben's guards ventured to ask.

Rhiann didn't know, but she watched the warriors splash across the waist-high river where it swung around to the south of Dunadd in a curving arm, and then the sun wasn't in her eyes any more. 'They are using their shields as a wall!' she exclaimed.

At the initial shouts from the gatetower, Urben's warriors had come running from every corner of the dun, buckling on swords, catching up spears. The gates had been barred, and men lined all the walls, but no defence party rode out to beat Eremon back from the river.

'So they are,' the other guard muttered. 'By Mannanán's breath, they are.'

Rhiann couldn't tell which of the men was Eremon until they cleared the cluster of druid huts and climbed the ridge that lay only half a league from Dunadd. There she could discern Conaire because of his size, stabbing the standard with its tanned boar-crest into the ground, as another man strode to the edge of the rise to gaze across at Dunadd.

Even from afar Rhiann could sense the quivering fury that cloaked Eremon like a heat shimmer over the marsh. She couldn't make out any other details, and she was sure Eremon couldn't see her, but she waved anyway, with both arms, her heart breaking free of the dark chains that had bound it these past moons. He didn't return the wave, but he stayed there without moving for a long time, until his shadow grew shorter as the sun rose.

Rhiann would have remained there all day, holding her joy to her chest like a precious jewel, but she must tell the others. So at last she slid down off the rocks and ran back to Caitlin. And it was this news that brought the first real colour to her sister's cheeks, as Caitlin's face softened and bloomed like a flower unfurling.

Over the next two days the atmosphere of the dun thickened, the tension rising like a heavy fog over the village, the shrine and the King's Hall. The traders from foreign tribes hastily retreated to their boats downriver in the bay, and the village gates remained barred, the people within as securely imprisoned by Urben's men as Eremon and his warband were excluded.

From her outlook, Rhiann saw the villagers huddled in groups, talking, as messengers went from the walls to Eremon's camp and back again. Yet no one would tell Rhiann what was happening, and she could not discern the mood of the people beyond profound confusion. Those nobles on the upper crag, like Belen and Talorc's wife, had been roused by Eremon's appearance, for they had more reason than anyone to hate Urben.

But as for the others . . . Rhiann only hoped that the loyalty Eremon had gained was solid enough, the manner of Urben's takeover distasteful enough, that Eremon only had to face Urben's own men. Hopefully the other Epidii would wait until the two parties decided things for themselves.

After the initial joy, the tension also began to affect Rhiann's house. Aedan broke a string the first evening, as he nervously played a song out of tune. Didius immersed himself in endless tasks, fashioning loom weights, bone needles and more toys for the child. Caitlin's tension was at least productive, for it suddenly quickened her healing. She threw off the weakness along with her bedclothes, pacing the hearth to strengthen her legs.

Of them all, Rhiann was the most still, taking herself up to her rock outcrop every afternoon when she could clearly see Eremon's camp by the outline of the setting sun.

Eremon was often visible at the same time, for he left his distinctive helmet on – she liked to think it was so that she could know him. As she stared at the pale oval of his face above his shining mailshirt, she would imagine his gaze reaching for her own, telling her it would be well.

And then she would have to lower her face, and hold everything still inside her.

It was late night in the druid shrine, and a cluster of rush lamps on the altar gave off a flickering light, gleaming on the torcs of the wooden idols, masking their leers. The breeze was cold and fitful, gusting about the oak pillars, tugging at Lorn's cloak.

He gazed at the pinprick campfires on the ridge to the south, then turned his back firmly on them. 'You didn't really think he would just ride away and leave the women, Father? It was a gamble at best.'

The lamps only lit up one of Urben's eyes and half his mouth, but the shrug of his heavy, fur-clad shoulders was eloquent. 'I knew he would not.'

In the shadows behind the altar, the chief druid stood silent and hooded. At news of the Erin prince's approach Gelert had left the cluster of druid huts on the southern ridge and slithered inside the dun, with his brethren trailing behind him. Yet he still baulked at being seen too often with Urben – he preferred to work his schemes through others, as Lorn knew well.

Lorn sighed wearily now. 'You could always let them go, Father. All of them. Then it would be over.'

Urben's head whipped around. 'Over?' he roared. 'It will be over for us, yes!' He strode forward and thrust his face close to his son's. 'So the prince and his little band will just trot away, in possession of the royal bloodline, *and* his alliance with Calgacus, *and* the loyalty of most of the Epidii warriors! And you think that's the last we'll see of him, do you? Stupid boy!'

Lorn flinched, but checked his rage. The only thing he was afraid of was his father. He lowered his voice, along with his eyes. 'If we fight him here, many will die. You don't know how good he is on the field, Father, you haven't seen—'

'Yes, yes, I've heard every damn song about him from every damn bard. I know!' Urben's eyes glittered in the lamplight. 'But you, my son, are also fine, as fine as we could make you. You came close to defeating him once; you could do it again.'

As the meaning of his father's words sank in, Lorn's blood ran cold. 'Single combat? By the Mare, you cannot be serious!'

Urben raised one eyebrow.

Lorn's mind whirled, and he gripped his sword hilt to steady himself. 'Father, I am not afraid of an honourable fight. But it is risky, for we are evenly matched, the prince and I. How could you gamble all our clan has planned for, on the outcome of one duel? There must be another way!'

'My lords,' Gelert broke in silkily, 'the Erin prince, for all his faults, is known for his sword skills. While his defeat would solve all our problems, the risk to your son is too high.'

Lorn spun to face Gelert, surprised. But then he remembered those moons last year, when the druid fed him hatred for Eremon, whispering how the old man would bring Lorn to power, how they would rule together . . . Gelert wanted to strengthen the obligations between them then. He wanted Lorn to be king, for the time he had invested in trying to make Lorn's soul his own. Lorn wondered briefly, if the druid was so clever, why he didn't know he'd already lost that battle.

'It is a risk,' Urben agreed, striding to the altar and placing a hand upon it. 'Yet the prize is too tempting. Killing the prince would do away with all opposition in one stroke. I deem it worth the risk.'

I deem it worth the risk.

Lorn was speechless with disbelief. Urben had said nothing of the risk to his own son. Shocked, he stared at his father as if for the first time, and just then the moon swam free of the heavy clouds above, illuminating in his sire's face what he was not meant to see. His father's eyes were unguarded, dark pools of shadow, but Lorn could easily read there the brutal truth. He didn't care.

And the reason why came to Lorn as a stab under his breastbone. For all that Urben had supported Lorn, he had other sons, three others to be exact, and all of them fostered out to outlying clans. Lorn was expendable, then. He had a good chance of killing the prince, and that was worth the risk of Eremon killing him. If Lorn died, Urben could take another son and form a new plan. And then another – if he chose.

Swept by a plunging nausea, Lorn turned away, ignoring both the mocking, empty gaze of the shrine's wooden idols and his father's barked order to come back.

Rhiann was embroidering a tunic for the baby when Lorn raised her door-hide and entered along with a gust of wind. All within the house fell silent, their gazes hostile, but Rhiann took in the dazed expression on Lorn's face, and her priestess senses prickled at the nape of her neck.

She flicked her fingers at Caitlin, who beckoned to Eithne. Both retreated behind one of the bedscreens with their sewing. Didius only glared, but Aedan swiftly dragged his stool to the far reaches of the lamplight, hunching over to mend his broken string.

Rhiann eyed Lorn, as he flung himself to the hearth-bench and, in stumbling words, told Rhiann of the offer Urben had made to Eremon: that if he left now empty-handed, there would be no bloodshed. Rhiann dropped her embroidery in her lap. 'Your father knows little of Eremon's determination if he thought that would be accepted.'

Lorn continued to stare into the lamps set on the shelf of figurines.

'Yet he did know, didn't he?' Rhiann continued softly. 'He knew Eremon would never leave us.'

Lorn's mouth turned down. 'It was worth a try, that is all. It would have made this easier for everyone.'

Rhiann snorted, twirling the bone needle in her fingers. 'For you perhaps, but hardly for Caitlin and I. Or do you and your father believe that women's hearts will capitulate as quickly as defeated warriors?'

Lorn raised his hand as if warding her away, his cheeks turning a mottled shade of crimson. Silence fell, and one of the lamps hissed as the rush wick burned out. Yet although Rhiann took up her embroidery again, she recognized the bleakness in Lorn's face. And that brought the glimmering of an idea to her mind.

Something was amiss with Lorn; she could smell it. He did not have the air of confidence that might be expected in one who held such valuable hostages against his enemy. Watching him sidewise as she stabbed the needle into the cloth, Rhiann wondered if she might be able to goad Lorn into betraying something. She shot a warning glance at Didius, mouthing *stay*, and received a nod in return.

'All this scheming seems beyond even your father,' she suddenly remarked to Lorn, biting off her thread. 'In truth, it has Gelert's stink all over it. Tell me . . .' She pierced Lorn with her gaze. 'Do you dance for him when he orders you to?'

Lorn straightened as if he had been stung. 'I have kept a civil tongue for you, lady. You will do the same for me.' He reminded Rhiann of a cornered stallion, and she knew she must walk a careful line. Yet even if he struck her in rage, it would be worth it, for all of them.

'I will do nothing for you, Lorn,' she ploughed on. 'Because you are not just a traitor: Eremon sits there before your gate, and you are too much of a coward to go out and face him!'

It wasn't shock or outrage that flooded Lorn's eyes, but shame, and Rhiann pressed her advantage.

'If you care for the people at all, you will avoid the shedding of kin blood! Go and face him like the warrior you purport to be!' She flung her hand towards the door.

Lorn had now gone deathly white, and his grey eyes glittered with something unexpected, despite Rhiann's goading. *He does fear facing Eremon!* she realized with a jolt. Yet it couldn't be death he feared, for Lorn possessed all the courage of his class. She took her racing thoughts in hand, and raised one eyebrow. 'So? Will you go, or are you the coward *I* think you to be?'

Lorn gasped, then he stumbled to his feet, nearly wrenching the door-hide from its pegs as he left.

Rhiann stared at the empty doorway, breathless, her heart pounding with elation. For if she could just get Lorn and Eremon together, she knew that somehow Eremon would find a way out of this.

The whispers began at dawn the next day, which brought a sudden rainstorm to veil the sun.

The conflict between Urben's clan and the royal clan for the leadership of the Epidii, the right to the King's Hall, would be decided by single combat between champions. Lorn, of the Dun of the Sun, had already stepped forward as his father's champion.

And before the sun had burned off the clouds, Eremon of Erin sent word back that he accepted the challenge, on the royal clan's behalf.

Chapter 23

L orn did not speak to Rhiann again, but late in the afternoon she climbed the upper palisade to watch him ride out in his chariot, and her trained senses noted the slight difference in his stance. His shoulders seemed too carefully braced, his shield held too rigid as he swayed on the chariot platform behind his driver. She could almost taste the despair around him, and rejoiced in it, for it would make him weak.

Lorn's chariot left the causeway outside the gates and rode straight over the level turf towards the ridge, his driver's spear trailing plumes of woven horse-hair. The earlier rain had cleared the haze from the sky, and now the grass and the paths glittered with puddles, and the house posts, palisade and gate shone in the low sun. Behind Lorn, Urben rode in his own bright chariot, the bear banner streaming over his head, and then came five mounted warriors, three of them Lorn's own sword-mates who had fought beside Eremon.

Up on the low ridge to the south, the boar standard was held in Conaire's hand. Rhiann had to strain to discern Eremon, further back among his men. He would never agree to fight within bowshot of the walls, and so the people of Dunadd had to content themselves with what they could see, the far-sighted among them speaking for those less favoured.

'Calum has speared Lorn's banner into the ground, and Conaire has come forward with the Boar!' one of Talorc's daughters whispered nearby.

'The chief druid and the seer are between the two lines now, reciting the laws,' someone else ventured.

'Look! Now they're drawing back!'

Rhiann jumped down from the palisade next to the Moon Gate and, leaving Caitlin with Eithne, hurried along to the natural walls below the druid shrine. There she clambered up the slick rocks and perched with the young boys of the dun, enjoying a far better view. Her two guards climbed up too, making no move to take her down.

After listening to the druids and bowing to the gods, the combatants had withdrawn. Even at this distance, Rhiann could make out Eremon's dark head next to Conaire's blond one, as Conaire spoke to him, his hand in its accustomed position on Eremon's shoulder. Lorn's warriors were speaking, too, but in their midst Lorn stood remote, staring into the distance.

Watching one of the Epidii warriors with Eremon hand him a shield, Rhiann felt utterly impotent. Those men by Eremon's side knew his thoughts and what he had planned – for she knew he would have planned something. But what?

Once the druids had made their own bows, the two fighters strode forward into a clear space at the same time, shields and swords flashing sun from their wet surfaces. Still the men had not exchanged any words. Yet at least Rhiann could see how straight and tall Eremon stood, how proud his head. Love bloomed in her heart. He was confident, and so must she be.

Then all thoughts fled from Rhiann's mind as she squeezed her eyes shut, waiting for the clash of swords. Her pulse was hammering in her throat, and she found herself muttering prayers to Andraste, war goddess, under her breath, pleading with the fierce lady to bless Eremon's sword arm.

The clash she was expecting never came.

Rhiann opened her eyes to see that Eremon had gone down on one knee before Lorn, his sword laid across his hands. And as the murmurs of disbelief grew to cries around her, and shock turned her knees liquid, Rhiann could grasp at only one prayer now – that she might fly across the space between them, and hear what in Thisworld Eremon was saying.

The disbelief of all those in Dunadd shone from Lorn's eyes.

'What . . . ?' His voice failed him, and he cleared his throat as he looked down at Eremon. The horse-tail crest on his iron helmet shook slightly, betraying what his face would not show. 'By the Mare, what are you doing?'

Eremon gazed up steadily from under his own helmet guard, his damp hair sticking to his cheeks. 'I am pledging my allegiance to you, as the rightful king of the Epidii. My sword is in your service.'

Lorn glanced to the side, where his father and the druids had started forward with mutters of alarm.

'What do you mean?' The whisper was a hiss now, and confusion and hurt pride flared in Lorn's face. 'Do you mock me? Get up!'

Eremon did not move. 'I do not mock you. Hear what I have to say.'

As the other men came close, Lorn flung up his sword to hold them at bay. 'Come no closer! Under the laws of combat we speak alone!'

Urben halted, his red mouth working with anger.

Eremon spoke low and rapidly. 'If you want it so much, I cede the King's Hall to you gladly. Only give me Rhiann and Caitlin, and we will leave you in peace.' Eremon held his breath, for though he and Conaire had talked this through, they had no way of knowing how Lorn would react.

Lorn fell back. 'You would give up all you've fought for, just like that? Like *this*?' He gestured at Eremon's kneeling stance.

Eremon held his eyes. 'The women mean more to me than leading a tribe. And the people of Dunadd, and their peace, mean more to me than the walls that enclose them.'

Shame seeped into Lorn's features, as his sword gradually lowered. 'Then you are more king than I.'

Ah! This admission snagged on the edge of Eremon's sharp mind. 'But I never wanted to be your king, Lorn.' Eremon glanced at Urben, and back up at Lorn, suddenly changing tack. 'I was glad it was you who challenged me, and no other. I once told you we were brothers-in-arms.'

The grim line of Lorn's mouth twisted. 'And once I gave you my allegiance! So I am twice-cursed – a traitor, according to your wife, and now an oath-breaker!'

It was the first mention Eremon had gained of Rhiann, and though he yearned to ask more, now was not the time. He must press his advantage. 'And what oath have you broken?' he murmured. 'You vowed to me as your war leader – I am still the war leader, if you wish it.'

Lorn's brows drew together, yet a faint hope began to light far back in his pale eyes.

Eremon's knee was beginning to ache horribly, for he'd rested it on a stone. But he must hold strong now. 'I am a foreigner, and do not have the blood to be a king here,' he continued. 'You do. Yet I have the allegiances of the Caledonii, the Caereni and the Carnonacae. I believe there is room for both of us in the King's Hall of Dunadd.'

Lorn had always been impulsive, yet never witless, and it only took a moment for him to grasp the rope Eremon had thrown to him. The furrow on his forehead smoothed away, and his sword tip came to rest on the ground. 'You are sure?' He folded his hands over the hilt, a bear's head worked in bronze and horn.

'Quite sure. Now, let us put aside the jealousies of these old men, and wield our swords together, as it should be.'

For a moment Lorn did not move, then a great, shuddering breath escaped him and he laid his hand across Eremon's jewelled blade. 'Then

I accept your oath, prince. Rise now, war leader of my people.'
Gingerly, Eremon got to his feet, stretching his knee, and Lorn's hand
moved to his shoulder with a wry smile. 'You keep surprising me,
prince. I should be used to it by now.'

Urben had finally taken all of this in, and now he strode forward in
spluttering wrath, Gelert hesitating at his heel. 'What is the meaning of
this?' Urben thundered.

Instantly, Lorn dropped his hand and turned, and Eremon could see
that all the shame and pain had fled from his face. 'The meaning, Father,
is that the prince acknowledges me as king. And I also acknowledge him
as war leader, since he is doing such an able job of it.'

As Urben's jaw fell slack, Eremon's attention shifted to Gelert, and he
was satisfied by the stifled rage that crossed the druid's face. He could
almost see the thoughts scrambling behind his eyes.

Lorn's gaze, meanwhile, was sweeping from Declan to his own men.
'As you can see,' he continued, his voice spreading and growing,
proclaiming its authority, 'it is the best solution for us all. It is time to
end this siege and return our attention to the Romans, where it belongs.
Fighting among ourselves,' he held his father's eyes, 'weakens us when
we need to be strong.'

As Urben's brows knit together, his mouth opening, Lorn pressed his
point. 'You've gained what you wished, Father,' he said evenly. 'Your
son will be king. So now you can leave off your sword, and stand at my
kingship ceremony in gladness, and drink to my health in the King's
Hall.' The warning was clear in his voice.

And after a visible struggle, Eremon saw surrender descend over
Urben's ruddy, belligerent face. Despite his size, he was an ageing man,
after all, and now he shrugged his massive shoulders, his gaudy brooches
glittering in the clear dusk. 'As you will it.' With a sharp jerk of his head,
he and his two older warriors returned to their chariots.

With raised eyebrows, Eremon turned to Gelert, pleased at the dry
swallowing of fury even a druid couldn't hide. The old goat had been
outmanoeuvred, for there was no doubt in Eremon's mind that Gelert
had been in league with Urben, pushing Lorn as king. If Gelert
protested now, he would only reveal his true desire – to gain personal
revenge on Eremon.

'Thwarted three times, druid,' Eremon muttered, watching Gelert
toss his straggling hair and stalk away. 'When will you concede defeat?'

Now his gaze met Declan's hesitant smile. 'The people will praise
your wisdom, prince,' the seer promised. 'You have brought a peaceful
end to this . . . distressing . . . situation.' Yet his smile faded as he turned
to go, and he frowned as his eye fell on his chief druid's back.

As soon as the druids were out of earshot, the young warriors of both
sides sprang to life. The first thing Conaire did was grasp Lorn's

shoulders, heedless of the Epidii warrior's new rank. 'My wife,' he begged desperately, 'what of my babe?'

A shadow seemed to flit across Lorn's face. 'The Lady Caitlin was safely delivered of a babe nearly two weeks ago.' He drew breath. 'A son.'

'*A son!*' Without glancing at Eremon or pausing to take a horse, Conaire bounded away for the gates of Dunadd.

'Calum!' Lorn barked at his driver, pointing with his spear. 'Go and ensure no harm comes to him – or anyone he meets – for our fighters will not yet know of our peace.'

Calum did as he was bid, and Eremon found himself considering the new confidence of Lorn's movements. Then something occurred to him. If Caitlin had borne a son, he could be seen as Lorn's eventual rival for the kingship. Yet only Lorn could have kept the babe safe from his father and Gelert.

Eremon swept off his helmet and raked his sweaty hair. 'There is great honour in you over the matter of the child. I thank you.'

Lorn's eyes were sombre as he regarded Eremon for a long moment. Then, 'Come!' he said at last. 'Let you and I confirm our pledges over ale. My throat is as dry as an old woman's teat!'

His men and Eremon's men laughed, all of them suddenly foolish with relief, and it was together that they made for Dunadd's gates.

Rhiann jumped down from the rocks and, gathering her breath, paused before her two guards. 'Well?' she cried, suddenly too elated for bitterness. 'Did you not see? My husband has made peace with Urben's son.'

The warriors looked at each other, unsure what to do, but Rhiann gave them no chance to think. 'I no longer require your services,' she added sweetly, pushing past their burly shoulders. 'Be sure I will tell my husband of your kindness.'

She hurried away, bracing herself for the sound of heavy footsteps following. Yet they never came. The Moon Gate was standing open, unguarded, and as she flew through it her tread grew faster and lighter. She was free! *Free!*

The whole village was in a confused yet relieved uproar, as those who had watched the encounter streamed along the muddy paths towards the unbarred main gate. Rhiann slowed down to catch her breath, but as she passed the stables the gleam of sun on fair hair caught her attention. She glanced over and came to a sudden halt, before running for the stable door. 'What are you *doing?*'

Caitlin paused as she tightened a saddle strap, her hand on her mare's flank. For the first time in many moons she was dressed in her riding buckskins, a travel cloak pinned on her shoulders. 'Now that the gates are open,' she answered evenly, 'I'm going to Linnet's house to find my son.'

Behind her, Eithne hovered with a pack and bundled furs, her eyes mutely begging Rhiann's forgiveness.

'*What?*' Rhiann strode to the horse and took its bridle, her voice sharpening as the sun revealed the stark paleness of Caitlin's face. 'Conaire will be here at any moment!'

'I know.' Caitlin raised her pointed chin with some of her old vigour. Her hair was roughly bound, and still matted from the bed-furs. 'I do not wish to see him until I have our son in my arms.'

The horse tossed its head, wrenching the bridle from Rhiann's nerveless hands. 'What are you talking about? You are still regaining your strength, you nearly died! As your healer, I order you back to bed!' Her voice was rising with all the suppressed strain of weeks.

Caitlin bit her lip, but straightened her shoulders. 'And as your blood sister,' she said clearly, 'I tell you I am going.'

They glared at each other, but it was Caitlin who gave in first, guilt softening her trembling mouth. 'I knew you would object, Rhiann, out of love, and I thank you. But you cannot argue with me on this.'

Rhiann's resistance was undone by the small hand that grasped her own. 'But why?'

Caitlin took a deep breath, smoothing the loose hair at her temples. 'I asked Aedan about the birth rites of Erin. There, a man's bloodline runs from father to son. A new mother must leave her birthing bed and go to the father and hold the baby out to him, and only when he takes it and claims it is the babe acknowledged.'

Understanding began to flood through Rhiann's mind. 'But Caitlin, Conaire could never doubt he is the father. And what do the rites of Erin matter, anyway? This babe is of Alba.'

Caitlin nodded. 'I know. And so Erin will never claim this son, and Conaire will never pass him his own father's Hall. That is why I want to give him this.' She wrapped her arms around her belly, and Rhiann glimpsed what she would not speak: the deep shame she felt for surrendering her child. 'I *must* give him this, Rhiann – it is right and proper. Now, he will be here any moment, and I must slip away before he comes and stops me! *Let me go!*'

Rhiann pulled Caitlin close, breathing in the smoky scent of the tanned buckskins, and then released her. 'Eithne, at least take it slowly. And keep her warm, and keep to the paths – do not let her hurry! Do you have yarrow, and comfrey?'

'Yes, lady.' The maid smiled, proud of her responsibility.

A shout went up, louder than all that had gone before, and a crowd of people spilled into view, milling around the open yard inside the gate.

In its midst, one golden-haired man towered over the others, trying to pull away from those who threw questions at him and hung on his arms.

Caitlin stifled a soft cry, flattening herself into the darkness of the stable wall, as Conaire finally broke free and ran up the path to the crag. Her eyes lingered on his long back for one moment, before she turned to Eithne. 'Quickly now!'

With a brief, fragrant kiss on Rhiann's cheek, Caitlin pulled the hood of her cloak up, and together she and Eithne led their horses past the crowd and through the open gate, until they disappeared among the mass of jostling heads and spears.

Rhiann watched them go, and then lingered, indecisive, on the path before the stables. She knew that her duty lay in delivering this news to Conaire. And yet . . . her eyes strayed to the village gate. Eremon must be there. Torn, she gazed back up the path. No, Conaire needed her; he must be nearly mad with worry. Let Eremon enjoy the welcome of the people first.

She straightened her shoulders and turned to follow Conaire up to the crest of the crag, but just as she reached the Moon Gate she was halted by a striking sense of warmth between her shoulder blades, as if a ray of sun had pierced the shadows between the houses. And alongside it, she imagined she heard a sharp cry – her name. Her steps faltered.

No, Eremon would never cry aloud; he was the war leader, and must be strong and sure before his people. It must have been in her heart she heard it. And there was no power in her to ignore his call. For one moment she forgot Conaire and turned.

He stood halfway up the village path. Behind him, Lorn was smiling wearily, fielding questions from warriors and villagers alike. Yet Eremon stood separate, and her gaze took in his matted hair, his scruffy beard and the tunic stained with battle-blood weeks old. He was dirty and sweaty and unkempt, yet his eyes blazed bright, almost fevered. It was as if the sun shone on him alone.

Their eyes locked, and she began to walk towards him, stepping gracefully as befitted their rank and public dignity. But her feet quickened, and his slow smile broke out radiantly over his face. Then he opened his arms wide and she was running, heedless of the faces surrounding him, of everything except the moment when she flung herself into the circle of his arms.

It was as they closed about her, solid and warm, that all the fear and pain she had held at bay for moons crashed down upon her. And as he breathed in her ear, 'A stór!' she laid her face in his shoulder, and at last wept.

Chapter 24

'The valley attack turned the tide,' Eremon was saying to the warriors around him. 'Many of the red invaders died, and many fled, but by the gods we poured after them – nipping their heels all the way to the Forth!'

A murmur of laughter swelled. Seated on a hide by the riverbank, Rhiann could only see Eremon's back outlined against one of the bonfires, yet despite the wild music of the pipes and drums she could hear him clear enough.

Though it was late, few people had left the feast, and torchlight still bloomed all along the palisade. Many revellers still crowded around the baking pits, picking at the carcasses of the deer and pigs among the hot stones, and groups of men lounged by the ale kegs, watching people dancing at the fires. Even the children were still awake, screeching and dodging between the dancers' legs. A haze of rich, sweet smoke hovered over the riverbank.

'Lady.' Didius's shadow detached itself from the people as he squatted beside Rhiann, handing her a basket of hazelnuts, hot from the coals. Placing it between them, Rhiann crossed her legs and drew the wool wrap tighter around her neck. The first hint of crisp cold had come this night, as if in recognition that Eremon and his men were now safe at home. She crunched a nut and smiled at Didius, touching her mead cup to his as he settled beside her.

Rhiann was happy to stay on the edges here, listening to Eremon, savouring the relief that was seeping into her tight muscles along with the mead. Urben had left the dun, and Gelert had made himself scarce, and only Lorn remained with his retinue and some of his father's warriors. Rhiann caught snatches of conversation from the huddled groups of older fighters and cattle lords, and the talk seemed to be that the forced rift in the Epidii had not been a popular decision after all, even if Lorn did have a valid claim to the kingship. It was the underhand manner in which it had been done, the old men grumbled, with the warriors of the royal clan all off fighting with Eremon. Of course, Rhiann thought wryly into her mead cup, they were happy to make such pronouncements now, once the situation had been resolved.

The council members had addressed Eremon and Lorn in manners that ranged from relieved to reserved. No one would own to supporting Urben, protesting that they were afraid to resist. Even Tharan had paid Eremon his grudging respects. Despite his truculence, he was a member of the old royal clan, after all.

Another burst of laughter rose from those crowding around Eremon, as he described the disintegrating confusion of the Romans when faced with organized attacks, and their haste to rush back to the safety of their lowland bases. This was Eremon's first test of his ambush tactics, and he was making quite a point about their success.

The success of the stags, Rhiann thought, with a swell of pride that warmed her. *The stags did give him the strength, after all.*

Eremon turned to grip old Finan by the shoulder now, speaking quietly, and Rhiann gazed up at the side of his face. Though he had bathed and shaved, the exhaustion and aftermath of fear were still engraved around his eyes, and she could sense the effort to appear strong and bright and alive, to reassure the people.

Rhiann picked another roast hazelnut and gnawed it nervously. Surely he would leave for bed soon, he was dropping from exhaustion. Abruptly, she swallowed, as her lips suddenly remembered the taste of Eremon's skin, when she pressed them to that curve between neck and shoulder. As if he felt a touch, Eremon glanced over, his smile fading as his eyes ignited with a naked need. She fixed her eyes on her lap.

'The Erin lord misses his lady,' Didius said softly in her ear, crunching a nut, and Rhiann's cheeks flamed. Confused, she opened her mouth for some suitable reply, but then she saw Didius was not looking at her or Eremon, but up at the village palisade. Twisting to follow his gaze, Rhiann glimpsed a tall, broad figure pacing the walls. Conaire.

With a sigh, Rhiann handed her cup to Didius and rose, tucking her shawl under her elbows. With a small smile at Eremon she slipped away inside the gatetower, and climbed the torch-lit stairs. 'She will come back soon,' she said softly, pacing the walkway behind Conaire. 'Two warriors have been sent to Linnet's home, so Dercca will be a prisoner no longer. Yet Linnet also will know when to emerge – she sees these things.'

At the mention of Otherworld powers, Conaire's head sank down further into his neck. 'I should have been here, with her.'

'And the Romans should never have come.' Hesitating, Rhiann laid her palm on his back, between his shoulder blades. The iron-hard muscles trembled beneath her fingers, and she sought to send reassurance into his heart. 'It was women's business – her fight to win. And fight she did; you would have been proud of her.'

There was a muffled exclamation of pain, and Conaire's hand reached up and covered her fingers. 'I thank you, Rhiann, for looking after her so well, and for getting my son away. Neither of them would have been safe if it wasn't for you.'

Rhiann thought of the peace Eremon wanted so badly. 'Lorn protected us, too. I have no doubt that the babe would have come to harm if it wasn't for him. Do not hate him. He was trapped, I think, as we were.' When there was no answer, she squeezed his shoulder. 'Eremon needs us to be one people.'

And what about you? she asked herself, remembering the burning of her own rage. *Can you forgive?* She didn't know yet, but Conaire's peace was more important than hers, for he must fight by Lorn's side.

Deep in dreams of Urben's mocking face, and Gelert's thin smile, Rhiann blinked awake, disorientated. Something had touched her neck.

Then a much-loved voice whispered, 'Rhiann,' and instantly she came fully awake with the scent of Eremon's bare skin against her own. She groped for awareness of where she was. The air behind the bedscreen felt different, wafting up from the floor below, and the snores all around her spoke of the presence of men. She was back in their bed in the King's Hall, because Eremon had asked her to sleep there. He wished to make it plain to the warriors he still held power here, along with Lorn, and had lost none of his influence.

Under her fingers Eremon's arms felt wiry and lean from moons of travel and rough eating, and all the pain of missing him suddenly choked her.

'I am home now,' he murmured, cradling her. 'I am yours again.'

Rhiann tried to speak, but the words wouldn't come, and so instead she repeated his words in her mind, over and over, as his softly stroking hands drew her back into her body. And as the tension of the dream fled, her skin came alive, burning at every place that their bodies touched. He went to caress her again, his hand moving up from thigh to waist, but she said, 'Wait,' and struggled out from under him, pushing him back on the bed.

In the faint glow of firelight her fingers found the curve of his neck, just as she had seen it at the bonfire, and she pressed her lips there as she had longed to do. He gasped, but held still as she kissed her way along his collarbone and shoulder, reminding herself of every dip and rise in his form. To the soft place under his arm she moved, and across his chest, her hair brushing his neck and flanks. Then her lips found one nipple, and she sucked and kissed it tentatively at first, and then with greater force when he moaned and clasped her head.

Yet she never got to the other side, for as she moved over him he grasped her hips and pulled her down on top of him, and they joined easily. Then in the darkness she did not know where her skin and his ended, only that the exquisite burst of fire took them both by surprise, and melted away all the cold tears in her throat with its heat.

At the Dun of the Tree on the other side of Alba, Samana was enjoying no such soft reunion.

She watched Agricola eating by the blazing light of five oil lamps, which pushed the shadows to the far corners of her Roman-style dining room. She had thrown a blue wool robe carelessly around her nakedness, and her black hair fell down over the honeyed skin of one breast.

She knew she looked ravishing. And yet, after riding into her own dun in the middle of the night, wet and muddy, Agricola had paused neither to change nor bathe, but taken her almost brutally, with a single-minded fury.

Even before this southern expedition, he had been taking her this way with increasing frequency. The long nights of moans and gasping surprise were growing fewer, and instead he rode her mechanically, only interested in his own quick release.

Watching him eat now, Samana's priestess mind mused that perhaps he saw her body as all Alba, and attacked her as a way to conquer what he did not yet possess.

This was a most uncomfortable idea, and abruptly she rose from the couch to pour more spiced wine into his green-glass beaker, allowing the robe to fall completely open, hoping that the old desire would ignite in his face now his immediate urgency was assuaged. Yet Agricola only continued to shovel the beef broth down in between gulps of wine, his eyes fixed on the wall painting behind her.

Samana sighed and rested the ornate silver ewer on a three-legged table, folding her robe closed. 'Are you going to tell me anything?' she asked gently.

At last Agricola looked at her, and then threw his spoon into the half-empty bowl, splashing broth all over her new dining couch. His breastplate and tunic were smeared with fresh mud and old blood, his grey hair ragged, stuck to his forehead by rain and mist.

'The rebels were in far greater numbers than I could have foreseen,' he admitted, his voice shredded with exhaustion. 'And they were organized – they attacked us from the hills as we travelled up the valleys.' Here Samana detected a dark flicker of memory in his eyes. It was fear, which she had never seen in him. 'They killed half my men before I sounded the retreat.'

'But why did you not get more soldiers from your southern forts?'

Samana ventured in a low voice, taking the empty bowl and placing it beside the ewer. The fine red tableware he had given her was rare and valuable.

The lines of age and weariness on Agricola's face were deepened by the shadows of the lamps. 'The barbarians gave us no chance, but hounded us from valley to mountain and back again. They did not seem to sleep, leaping from hill to hill like mountain goats, killing at night, their archers flying ahead to attack when we least expected it.' He sighed heavily. 'The prince of Erin's skills have grown.'

Samana's sip of wine stopped in her throat, and she had to force herself to swallow. 'Prince of Erin?' Her blood roared in her ears, but she schooled herself to stillness. Agricola could never know of her long-standing struggle over Eremon mac Ferdiad. He knew only that they had shared the bed furs, as she endeavoured to make Eremon join the Romans, when he first arrived in Alba. But Agricola knew nothing about the spell Samana had woven to lure the Erin prince to her bed, or how it had turned on its maker and ensnared her as well. Eremon might have escaped its clutches – she must assume that, since he had then scorned her! – but the potent mix of rage and desire would not leave her at peace.

'Yes,' Agricola bit out. 'I saw him . . . I think. Someone was directing them, at any rate, or we would have crushed the rabble of fishermen I expected to find. They had a leader, and a good one.' He wiped his hands on the grimy edge of his knee-length tunic, rubbing intently at the ingrained dirt. 'It has taken me two months to get back, and altogether I lost three-quarters of my men – two thousand soldiers! Domitian has not returned my Ninth Legion units, and he may well not do so at all when he hears of this!'

Samana was dry-mouthed with shock, and a deeper fear. She had never seen Agricola defeated. She knelt by his side. 'My lord, you still have many, many more men than the prince of Erin. And he is no match for you in battle; you must know that!'

Agricola's gaze came back from far away, and he gained some hold of himself. 'I do know that,' he agreed, scratching the grey stubble on his neck. 'But I cannot let them band together like this. I must pick the tribes off, one by one.'

'Starting with the Epidii?' Samana was suddenly breathless. Perhaps Eremon's enslavement of her could be over soon.

Agricola frowned down at her. 'You do not start with the strongest; you start with the weakest. Divide and conquer has been the Roman strategy for two centuries now. It should not be difficult to shatter his support – after all, what is he but an exile, an upstart?'

'He is close to the Caledonii king,' Samana whispered.

Agricola shrugged, suddenly sure of himself after his moment of weakness. 'Our intelligence hinted that the outcome of the war council last year was not good for the rebels. We must assume that although the Erin cub has wriggled his way into the Caledonii king's graces, he enjoys little other support. He is a foreigner – with a talent for war, I grant you – but no Alban, nor will he ever be.' He wiped his mouth on his sleeve and rose. 'I must see to my men and horses.'

Samana placed a hand on his iron breastplate, over his heart. 'Won't you stay? We have only just begun to know each other again.'

Yet Agricola only snorted, tucking his war helmet under his arm and picking up the greaves he had discarded when he took her. 'My men and I have shared much these past months. I must be with them, not lounging in luxury with you.' His tired mouth quirked. 'Or have you learned nothing of leadership from me, my dark witch?'

Hiding her fury behind a bland smile, Samana waited until he left and then flung herself on to the couch. She tapped the silver spoon on the edge of the empty bowl, her thoughts churning.

Since the death last year of Calgacus's son, Samana had no more informants of her own to call on. The tide of battle had swept far beyond her and her own allies. All she'd been relying on these past moons were her abilities to please Agricola in bed, but even these were growing less powerful. A primal panic writhed inside her.

If bedding him no longer bound Agricola to her, and she had no information to sell, what good was she to him? If she wasn't useful, he could easily cast her aside, and she'd lose her chance of becoming queen of Alba. She gazed around at all the fine things in the room, so different from the dark, smelly roundhouses of her own people. There were wall paintings, clean floor tiles, dining couches covered in linen, three-legged braziers instead of smoky fires, silver and red tableware, and jewelled goblets and platters. All this, she could lose.

Samana rested her forehead in her hands, rubbing her temples with frustration. *Think!*

Then something scratched against her eyebrow, and she pulled her hands away and spread them out. On the third finger of her left hand was a gold band, her priestess ring, the mark of her initiation into the Sisterhood, engraved with the three moon faces of the Goddess.

Samana grew utterly still as she stared at it. Perhaps it was time to find other sources of information with which to please Agricola.

Suddenly energized, she called for a servant to boil water for a scented bath. Though it was still before dawn, she wanted to scour the stink of Agricola's sweat and streaks of filth from her body before he came to her again.

Stretched on the ground, Rhiann nestled her cheek into Eremon's thigh as he sat on the flat-topped outcrop beside the Horse Gate. His shield had been shattered in the Novantae rebellion, and he'd just had Bran make him a new one of alder and oak, with a tanned hide stretched across the frame. Now he was painting over the yellow background with his own red boar emblem.

Eyes closed to the cool sunshine, Rhiann heard him sigh as he tapped the bristle brush on his knee. 'I hope that is a contented sigh,' she remarked.

'I'm as content as I can be,' Eremon answered. 'Gelert has left us, after all.' The dun had woken to the news that the chief druid had disappeared, leaving no word of his destination.

Rhiann's jaw tightened. 'Don't invoke his name,' she begged.

For a moment, Eremon's hand rested on her forehead. 'He is gone, *a stór*, to the gods know where. Perhaps using Urben like that was his last attempt to gain a greater hold over this tribe and, like the others, it failed. Perhaps he wishes to try his luck elsewhere.'

A shiver ran from Rhiann's legs, pressed into the damp turf, up her torso. 'If he did have something to do with the shipwreck,' she ventured in a low voice, 'then he must have some connection with Maelchon.'

Eremon's stroking fingers stilled. 'I sometimes wish your mind ran less quickly, Rhiann.' He sighed again. 'I too have thought this, yet if that is the nest to which Gelert has flown, there is nothing we can do. After all, that is as far from us as he can go, so let us be happy with that.'

Rhiann opened her eyes and blinked in the sun. Pressed against Eremon's crossed leg, all she could see was a patch of sky between his arms, the blue deepening as leaf-fall took hold of the land, and beyond that, the top of the palisade. And there stood Conaire, who had barely moved for three days, waiting for Caitlin.

Eremon rubbed at a stray speck of paint on the boss in the centre of the shield. The bronze disk had been skilfully cast into a flattened boar's face, with large eyes, snout and curving tusks. 'Eremon?' Rhiann tilted her head. 'Will the baby be safe here with Lorn?'

Eremon tapped the brush handle on his knee again. 'The boy is a babe, and cannot claim his hall until he reaches manhood. By then Lorn's time will have passed; and as under your strange kin laws his own sons cannot be king, I think he will leave it be. He got what he wanted, in the end.'

Rhiann pursed her lips. 'Perhaps Lorn thought you would use Conaire's son to keep him away from the kingship, but you have proven you will not.' She kissed his wrist, looking at him upside down. 'For all my fears, you have an answer.'

Eremon's eyes glinted back, and with one swift movement he pulled out from under her and pinned her on the grass, the dripping brush poised in one fist. 'And what answer do you have for me?' he murmured, pressing his lips against hers. When their tongues met, she wound her fingers in his thick hair and crushed him closer, until they were both breathless.

Laughing, she whispered at last, 'What was the question?'

His green eyes danced as he looked down at her. 'How much do you love me?'

A shout at the gate forbade Rhiann from answering that, and she saw immediately that Conaire had disappeared. Struggling upright, she pulled her cloak out from under Eremon's leg, sending him sprawling and narrowly missing the scattered pots of yellow and red paint.

'It's Caitlin!' she cried. 'Come on!' She threw her bundled cloak over her shoulder and, leaving Eremon to disentangle his limbs, scrambled down the rock cleft to the path.

At the gatetower, she nearly ran into Conaire's back, for he had come to a sudden halt. Peering under his arm, Rhiann saw that the few people outside the gates had drawn back, and the raucous ball-and stick game taking place on the river meadow had been suddenly arrested, as the boys crowded together, muddy and curious. Then, across the open space of stamped down earth, Rhiann saw Caitlin approaching, the swaddled child tucked into her arms. Behind her came Eithne, holding the two horses. Conaire's shoulders quivered once, and then again.

To Rhiann's immense relief, Caitlin's face was no longer pale, but touched with the healthy flush of the sun. She had come in one of Linnet's finest dresses, of pale blue wool edged with white mink, fastened on the shoulders with gilded brooches. Her hair was washed and combed, unbound and flowing, and her neck was clasped with a deer-headed torc.

She was beautiful, but by far the greatest beauty was in her eyes, because of the love there. Rhiann swallowed the lump in her throat, as Eremon stepped up beside her. She risked a glance at him, and felt his fingers close on her own. When she looked back, Caitlin was standing before Conaire, and had shifted her son into her hands. Now she raised her arms, until the child was balanced precariously before his father.

The guards on the tower had fallen silent, looking down, and those inside the gates were respectfully still, even if they couldn't resist whispering behind their hands. Everyone was straining to see what Caitlin would do. The only movement came from the babe, who squirmed in his linen swaddling clothes, kicking one foot free.

'My lord,' Caitlin said distinctly, gazing up at Conaire, 'your son.'

Rhiann could not see Conaire's face, yet his arms slowly came out, and at the moment he took his son in his huge hands, a sigh rippled over the onlookers. Then Conaire raised the babe awkwardly. 'I name him Gabran, after my grandsire,' he declared, his voice cracking with emotion. Suddenly the baby wobbled and let out a loud squawk, before bursting into cries. People laughed, and the tension was gone.

Instinctively, Conaire drew his son against his broad chest, Caitlin ran to him, and the three of them were one in the circle of his arms. Rhiann sniffled and rubbed her nose, and Eremon pulled her into his side and smiled down, his own eyes suspiciously bright. 'It was all worth it, *mo chroí*,' he whispered. 'For that little scene, I'd risk Conaire's wrath myself!'

She smiled, and together they pushed through a chattering crowd of well-wishers to stroke Gabran's fuzzy head as he lay on Conaire's chest, his blue eyes staring up at his father with faint puzzlement. Then Eremon had to hold the babe, just as awkwardly, and proclaim him the finest son ever born, and the grip of his little fist on Eremon's tunic the sure sign of a good sword hand, until even Caitlin rolled her eyes and took her son back.

Yet when Rhiann recognized the eager spark in Eremon's eye as he gazed down at Conaire's son, her smile suddenly felt tight on her cheeks. The guilt of her secret brews returned with force, sharpening from an ache into a sliver of pain that pierced her heart.

'And here,' Caitlin was saying, beckoning Didius and Aedan forward, where they lurked beneath the gatetower. 'You helped to bring him, and guard him, and for that you have my everlasting thanks.' And she drew a surprised Didius into the centre of the group and deposited the babe in his arms. Struck dumb, Didius stared down at the wobbling bundle, his plump face flushing a mottled shade of crimson. But Aedan saved him, bending over the child to proclaim his beauty and fineness in the most extravagant bardic terms.

Summoning a smile along with everyone's laughter, Rhiann glanced up then to see Linnet standing silently on the edge of the crowd. Wordlessly, she hurried into her aunt's embrace.

At length, Linnet drew back and held Rhiann by both arms, searching her face. 'I had a strange dream,' she whispered, her eyes ringed with tiredness. Her auburn hair was bound back from her forehead, accentuating the strain in her face. 'A dream of you.'

Rhiann smiled softly. 'I'm glad you heeded this dream.'

Slowly Linnet shook her head. 'I am unsure about wanting to know how you did it, daughter, for it would have cost you much.'

Rhiann glanced over at Caitlin and Gabran. 'It was worth it, or you never would have risked yourself, either. But how did you leave?'

Linnet's smile was tinged with bitterness. 'I could only hold the glamour long enough to be free of my hut, and then hid in the secret places, protected by loyal ones. My guards were most vexed when Dercca made their morning tea the next day.' The anger was still bright in Linnet's eyes, but after a moment she took Rhiann's arm and turned her back towards the happy scene. 'No matter – today is a day for joy. The babe thrived in my care, and Caitlin's own milk is already showing signs of returning.'

As they all entered at the gate, Eremon noticed Rhiann's aunt hesitate, glancing up at the Epidii warriors who stood on the tower with their shining spears and armour. Leaving Rhiann with Aldera, he turned back to her. In the time since he arrived at Dunadd, Eremon had in fact spoken few words with Linnet, for she saw much and appeared as forbidding to him as Rhiann had once seemed.

'Lady.' He bowed to Linnet and turned his back on the gate to survey the river meadow. The rowdy ball game had by now resumed, making the most of a halt in training, for Eremon had judged it too soon for the different factions of warriors to be let loose against each other with weapons.

Linnet nodded gracefully, and from the corner of his eye Eremon saw her watching him. 'I was grieved at the news of your confinement,' he began, noticing the slight stiffening of her shoulders.

'As was I,' she answered bluntly, and he realized just how angry she was. Who would not be?

'I understand if you want to seek restitution from Urben's clan at this outrage—'

She half-turned to him, and now one elegant eyebrow was raised. 'Do you, prince? Though I sense a "but" lurking behind your speech.'

Eremon felt himself flush. A shout came from the meadow then, as half the game sticks triumphantly waved in the air, and Eremon smiled. '*But*, I ask that you do not take that course of action. I am not underestimating the damage done to your honour,' he added hastily, folding his arms, 'but you see far, and know that we must be united to resist the Romans. If you bring this matter to druid trial, I fear the tribe will be riven as surely as if I'd attacked Dunadd myself. You will be giving Urben what he wanted – bad blood between myself and his son.'

Eremon held his breath, for Linnet was a formidable woman. Yet the flare of heat in her eyes – so like Rhiann's eyes! – soon faded.

'We have had little speech, you and I,' Linnet said instead, watching the ball game begin again. 'Yet Rhiann has told me much of your gilded tongue.' As Eremon wondered whether to smile, she added tartly, 'And I am glad to see that she did not exaggerate.' She glanced at him sidewise. 'You will have your wish, prince, though not today. I cannot face that young buck Lorn yet, and my home calls me – I must scour the stink of men from it! Tell Rhiann I could face no crowd today, but will ride to see her soon.'

'As you wish, lady.' Eremon bowed again, then hesitated. 'And I thank you for your part in saving my brother's child.'

Linnet tilted her head to one side, and the sun lit her hair to the same auburn as Rhiann's. 'He is my grandson, too, Goddess bless him.' A mysterious smile caught the edge of her mouth. 'So the first connection of blood is made across the sea between Alba and Erin. Yet there will be others.'

As if in royal acclaim, the trees along the river hung out their own banners of gold and russet and umber for the day of Lorn's king-making.

At the carved rock beside the Horse Gate, Rhiann stood to one side as Declan painted Lorn's face with the blood of a yearling foal, and sprinkled him with sacred water. Rhiann had little to do for this most male of rites, as Declan now raised his white arms to the sky gods and sword gods, and sang to the sun sinking over the sea. Nor did the effect of the copper and gold circlet on Lorn's brow, the roan stallion hide around his naked shoulders, and the thick bronze arm-rings particularly impress Rhiann, for she knew at what cost the fine scene had been bought.

Instead, she gazed over Lorn's shoulder to the patchwork of hills and valleys with their rusted hues of bracken and turning leaves, holding this focus even when called upon to raise the mead cup to Lorn's thin lips. Just as on her wedding day, she had to bestow the sovereignty of the land upon Lorn with her own hand, by binding him to the protection of its Goddess.

Yet this time Rhiann resisted meeting the male eyes regarding her over the cup's rim. Lorn's manner to them all had remained confident, with a hint of apology and regret, and though Rhiann understood he could show no weakness, she was still angry with him, and he knew it. She had begged Eremon to return to their bed in her own house, now that Lorn would be officially residing in the King's Hall, and to her relief, Eremon had agreed. She did not think she could stand a whole season shut up in the dark with Lorn.

As Rhiann stepped back now, Lorn turned to face the sacred mountain Cruachan to the north, placing his right foot in the hollow carved in the ancient rock. Grudgingly, Rhiann had to admit he looked the part: his chin high, his silver hair spilling over the copper hide, his jaw outlined against the sky. Though the days were still sunny, the nights were growing frosty and, as the light now faded into the long, purple shadows, Lorn's breath misted before his face.

Lorn was trapped by his loyalty to his father, Eremon had been saying to Rhiann. *I understand.* All Rhiann understood, however, was Eremon's need for peace, and for sake of that she would keep the peace in their own Hall and among their kin.

Yet as the cheering of the people broke out, from the crag and the village and the walls, Rhiann found herself begging the Goddess to make Lorn prove his loyalty to Eremon once more – and this time beyond all doubt.

Chapter 25

The Orcades Islands at the northern tip of Alba were already in the grip of the first seasonal storms. On the rare occasions the sun struggled free from the wind-whipped cloud, it seemed to cast only pale, cold light, and soon sank once more into darkness.

Despite the weather, which bent the few hardy rowans almost double, the Orcadian king Maelchon wished nothing more at night than to prowl the village around his new broch tower. He had found few things to assuage the restless energy that plagued him, and one was pacing alone, mindlessly in the dark. His white-bear cloak was warm, and his huge girth, thick, black beard and mane of hair made him almost immune to wind and rain. Yet he would not pace this night.

This night he sat in his new tower, the roof timbers still smelling of sap and fresh wood, because here by the fire he could think clearly and calmly about the news he had just received. The peat coals in the hearth glowed brightly, but the wall hangings stirred when drafts from outside reached in cold fingers, defying the wealth Maelchon had expended to make this tower impregnable. The king, his female companion and two guards were silent, and only the hoarse snores of his hounds, stretched out by the hearth, gave any life to the vast, round room.

The Epidii druid who had borne this interesting news was used to travail, but he was old, and had crawled to his guest bed long ago. Though Maelchon was grateful for his insights, he had no wish to look upon those unearthly yellow eyes for any longer than necessary.

The king's thoughts turned to his gods now, and what they might be asking of him by sending this man. For just when he thought the sea had delivered him his victory over that red-haired bitch and her Erin cur, so they returned to haunt him. The gods didn't want him to forget them.

Staring into the fire, Maelchon tapped one finger on his lips, still greasy from the meal of buttered salmon. He must be careful about what this information awoke in him, for he knew that when something burned in the soul with such a single, white-hot flame, it could consume bodily strength. And as a king, he could not afford to lose strength in the face of what was coming.

Maelchon's eye fell now on the wench with red hair from across the bay, gnawing on dark bread at the end of the table with tiny, pointed teeth. He had moved her into his new hall, and was pleased with what this brought out in her. Most of the island women feared him, and though this involved its own delights, even that had palled on his return from Calgacus's war council. However, this copper-haired slut, though common-born, shared a spark with her king – a lust for power. So she delighted in his carven cups, soaring roof and soft furs, the sweet wine, roast boar and bright rings for fingers and toes. And to keep them, she was not going to allow herself to be scared of him.

He watched her now as she rose and swung around the table, her skirt hitched up so her long, bare legs caught the firelight. She enjoyed trying to provoke his guards with her scanty clothes, flashing her eyes and curving her rump when she walked. All this only amused Maelchon, of course, for they both knew that if she touched another man he would kill her with his own hands.

At least the game was a fine diversion on these long nights, and better than the quick, brutal couplings with which he used to amuse himself. Just as the careful nursing of bitterness was a sweeter brew than gulping rage down all at once, as he had been wont to do. And didn't he have many more slights to add to the brew now?

That Epidii bitch priestess scorning him with her fine eyes, first as a maiden and now as a woman. The Erin cub snatching her as his prize – a prize Maelchon had desired for years. The Caledonii king, Calgacus, exulting in his jewels, cattle, lands and men. And most bitter of all, the sea death to rid him of these first two thorns had, according to the druid, been thwarted.

Maelchon grunted and took a gulp of wine. Well, he had tried to lay the distant past at rest, and the gods had chosen otherwise. They wanted something more from him, then.

He surfaced from his thoughts to see that the red-haired slut was drunkenly writhing before him, in what passed for a seductive dance. Though sodden with ale, she must have sensed that his attention had drifted. Stumbling, she came to a stop before him, her blue eyes glazed, pulling her dress higher until the moist, dark triangle between her legs was exposed, beckoning him. Without waiting for a word, she straddled his lap, winding her fingers in his black mane.

He shifted to let her settle, and she grabbed his wine cup and drank, letting the liquid spill down her chin like blood. Her shift had been pulled off one shoulder by her dancing, and the wine stuck the thin linen to her skin. She wiped her mouth and trailed a wet finger over one breast. 'Oh, am I not clumsy, my lord?'

Maelchon regarded her silently from half-lidded eyes, yet when he said nothing she groped between his legs, fingers furrowing under the heavy belly that rested on his thighs and down into his trousers. He did harden at her clumsy touch then – not for her dance, or her spilled wine, but for all the other things that turned in his mind. And there was her hair to inflame him, too, bringing to mind the Epidii bitch. He grabbed a hank of it, as she eased him free and wriggled on top, taking him inside her. Then he yanked the hair down, thrusting deeply until the slut gasped with pain and bit her lip.

All the while, Maelchon kept his gaze on the two guards at the door, as they kept theirs on the wall hanging behind him.

Yet the firelight flared along the bladed tips of their spears and the swords at their sides. And when Maelchon felt the fire-burst in his loins, all he saw were thousands of those spear-tips under an Alban sun, marching south across a green plain.

Chapter 26
LEAF-FALL, AD 81

amhain. Womb-time. The great fire festival that heralded the start of the new year, and the start of new life. When growth turned inward and the unseen seed gestated in the darkness, building strength until it burst forth into sun.

The sacred meanings sang in Rhiann's blood along with the *saor* herbs. Yet for her they were edged with guilt as sharp as the icy night air, and the frost on the stones of the tomb mound, slippery beneath her feet.

Below the first cairn at the head of the ancestor valley, the druids had spilled the bull's blood for their sky gods. Yet as Rhiann stood aside for the king-making, so Declan and his brethren stood aside now. Druids studied the stars and marked the time, so knew when Samhain fell. But they did not grow life in the dark of their wombs – it was a woman's task to bless the long sleep of living things.

At the tomb mound's base, the feast for the dead had been set out – platters of honey cakes and pitchers of milk. The tiny need-fire had been kindled at Rhiann's feet, and all the hundreds of people spread on the plain now waited for her to light the hazel brand and throw it in the firepit of sacred woods below her. Their breath was a mist that rose above them, their eyes lit only by moon and starlight, for at Samhain all hearth-fires were extinguished. This long moment of utter darkness beneath the sky represented the void of Her inner world, where She created new life from nothing.

And here Rhiann stood, warding away that life with the bitter brew she still tasted on her tongue beneath the *saor*. Was it any wonder she felt the surge of the Goddess as only a faint trembling in her limbs? For since Eremon's return, and the gathering inside for the season, the guilt over the matter of the babe had risen to claim all of Rhiann's attention.

I called the Stags, Rhiann whispered inside now, with a stab of desperation. Yet in this other thing she was trapped. For if she gave in to creating that life, she feared she would be turning her back on the dream – and that she could not do, not even for love of Eremon. Not after the despair she had tasted that night by Linnet's pool.

So the struggle between the desperation and the guilt held Rhiann rigid this night, her undyed robe falling from her outstretched arms like a frozen waterfall under moonlight. And the sacred words were carried from her to the people on a surge of fierce shame, leaving only ashes on her tongue.

Rhiann only came down from the mound once she'd thrown the brand into the sacred bonfire, and riders were streaming back to Dunadd with their new-lit torches. The points of flame bobbed and wove down the dark valley.

'*A stór.*' As the flutes and drums broke out into music all around, Eremon tucked Rhiann under his arm beneath his new wolfskin cloak. Like her he wore a crown of scarlet rowanberries, tilted rakishly on his dark hair, for after bringing the warband home from the borders the druids had taken him at sunset to offer the spoils of Roman armour and weapons to the sea-gods. And when they killed the calf, it was his brow they had marked with blood.

Still flushed with this honour, Eremon seemed now to glow as bright as a brand himself, kissing Rhiann's cold nose and enveloping her in warmth and the scent of ripe blackberries on his breath. Yet over his shoulder Rhiann glimpsed Caitlin smiling, and the tender clasp of the fur-wrapped bundle against her breast.

Rhiann closed her eyes, her heart leaden.

Samhain. Womb-time.

'By the Mare! By the Mare!'

Liath snorted and threw up her head, as the bare, snowy wood suddenly exploded around Rhiann. Two packs of screaming warriors in a patchwork of hides and furs dodged back and forth through the black, leafless trees, shooting blunted arrows at each other.

'The Boar—!' Rori stifled his own war cry as he slid to a halt in the snow slurry before Rhiann, making Liath rear back.

'Rori!'

'Forgive us, lady!' Rori called over his shoulder, leading his men into a screen of feathery dwarf birches, their red branches rimed with frost. From behind, another volley of arrow shafts flew over Rhiann's head, and she glimpsed Lorn pounding over the floor of the snow-filled hollow, screeching the Epidii war cry once more.

Liath was still snorting indignantly when she and Rhiann crossed the bridge to the village. Below, the Add flowed sluggishly, its banks lined with clumps of frozen sedge, and on the snowy meadow scores of other warriors practised with spear and bow. Conaire Rhiann easily recognized, whirling his arms to urge the men on, his frame bulked up by layers of wool and a bearskin cloak. The palisade stakes were tipped with white; the wooden gate and thatch roofs dark with melted sleet.

Rhiann stabled Liath and discovered Eremon on top of the gatetower, studying his men from above. Unlike Conaire he was clad only in a thin wool tunic and trousers, and his breath merged with the steam coming from his skin.

'You should be in a cloak,' Rhiann scolded, touching the sweaty hair at the nape of his neck.

Eremon smiled distractedly, pulling her into his arms. 'I've been running back and forth from plain to walls so much I'm hot,' he replied. 'Feel me!'

'If you insist.' Rhiann squeezed his waist and kissed his neck, tasting the snow on his skin. 'You are training again already?'

He shrugged, his attention on the field. 'The Romans may have retreated south for the long dark, yet I imagine Agricola keeps them in training.'

'Well, your men in the woods set a fine ambush – they managed to scare the life out of me and Liath just now.'

Eremon grinned down at her, his eyes crinkling. 'I gave Rori his first command. How was he doing?'

'I think he was winning.' Rhiann pulled off her sheepskin mittens and tucked them under her arm, cupping her wind-blown cheeks. 'Lorn seemed to think so, too – he looked furious.'

'Good.' Eremon's grin widened. 'Our new king may be suitably chastened, but he still hates me drilling the men Roman-style. I thought he'd be happier raiding in the woods. And anyway,' he stretched his arms up and cricked his back, 'the strike and run worked so well last year. There's no time to lose if we want to be in peak condition come leaf-bud.'

Come leaf-bud.

Those words rang in Rhiann's mind as she carefully made her way to the ground on the wet, slippery stairs. The long dark was a testing time for them all – to be almost constantly inside, the air stifling with the scent of unwashed bodies, damp fleece and wet boots. For Rhiann, though, this long dark had been worse than all the others, for every day she lavished care on Gabran, with sweet oil rubs for his griping belly, and beeswax salves for his rashes. And every night, she forced the bitter tea down in the shadows of the bedplace, but held Eremon's warm shoulder to her mouth in the dark.

Yet she was still grateful for the snow and storms. For with the thaw the sun would return and, like armoured insects drawn from the ground by its warmth, so would the Romans.

Chapter 27
LONG DARK, AD 81

'Ah!' Rhiann threw down the strip of raw beef and swiped at her eye with the back of her hand.

'What's wrong?' Caitlin asked, cross-legged on a bench against the wall of the curing shed. She was wrapped well against the cold seeping up from the earth floor, in sheepskin breeches, tunic and wool cloak, her fair hair spilling from under a fleece-cap. Nestled in his hide sling, Gabran had all but disappeared into his otter fur wrappings, but his loud suckling announced his presence.

'I rubbed salt in it.' Suddenly, Rhiann stamped her foot in a rare show of frustration, and the women at the other workbenches glanced up from their salt pans in surprise. With a glance at them, Rhiann pulled the cloth hanging on her belt free and dabbed her streaming eye.

The last of the bulls had been slaughtered for the long dark, and the final cuts of beef were being cured or pickled or hung for smoking. Despite lavish applications of beeswax salve, Rhiann's hands were raw from gritty salt and cold flesh. Yet she preferred to be busy rather than sit by a fire gnawing on secrets.

'Here.' Caitlin offered the rest of her berry bannock, and Rhiann joined her on the bench, wrapping herself in her sheepskin cloak. The rows of women bent back to their conversations and their pans, pressing the strips of flesh into the mounds of sea salt.

'Sister,' Caitlin ventured, her brows drawing together, 'what is wrong? Don't think I haven't noticed you've not been yourself.'

The words reminded Rhiann suddenly and sadly of Fola, but Gabran saved her from replying by losing the nipple, and with it, his temper, and it took some moments for Caitlin to soothe him and help him latch back on.

Outside the grey daylight was harsh on the snowy path, glittering on the ridges of frozen mud. 'I am just afraid of Eremon leaving again come leaf-bud,' Rhiann said, gazing at the curve of Gabran's baby cheek.

Caitlin was silent, her breath clouding the air. 'It is more than that,' she whispered, and when Rhiann's head swung up she added, 'Is it . . . is it something about Gabran? When you hold him and bathe him, sometimes there is a look on your face . . .'

She broke off as Rhiann started, and clamped her small hand on Rhiann's arm. 'You are longing for a babe of your own, aren't you? And you're afraid it won't happen. But Rhiann, you know that some women take longer to bear than others.' Her face flaming, Rhiann dropped her eyes to their linked hands, as Caitlin ploughed on. 'That's why you take that special brew of yours, isn't it? Does it help women to conceive?' Rhiann tried to stifle her gasp of pain and Caitlin glanced at the chattering women and back at Rhiann. 'Come,' she suddenly said, pulling her to her feet. They bundled themselves up against the cold, and only when they were through the Moon Gate did Caitlin stop. 'If you tell me,' she said. 'I can help you.'

She held Rhiann's eyes with her worried gaze, and standing there shivering with fear and shame Rhiann suddenly found herself blurting it out. 'The tea, sister, is to stop a baby taking root in me.'

Caitlin's mouth dropped open in surprise. '*Stop* a baby? Why, Rhiann?'

Rhiann's head sank among the folds of her cloak, and she fixed her eyes on the slushy ground, dented with muddy footprints. 'I cannot become a mother,' she whispered. 'I must be able to follow Eremon if he needs me; lead the rites to help him. We have never faced such a threat as the Romans before . . .' She lifted her face, her cheeks set and cold. 'There is no room in me for a baby, not now, not until we are safe.'

'But, sister,' Caitlin hitched Gabran higher in his sling, 'you love my son as if he were your own, as does Eremon. I may not be a seer like you, but you and he are meant to raise children.'

'I wonder if I am fit to be a mother at all,' Rhiann murmured, tucking her mittened hands under her arms. 'A priestess, a healer, yes . . .' Her eyes blurred. 'I am afraid I cannot give enough to be a mother.'

Caitlin was frowning with immense bafflement, and suddenly Rhiann knew that the difference in their hearts meant Caitlin would never understand. Caitlin had no walls inside herself, she had given her heart to Conaire and her son completely. Yet neither had she been charged with the task of caring for a whole people.

'That is not true,' Caitlin whispered, brushing stray drips of sleet from Gabran's hair. 'Yet I will not argue with you – I know how set are your thoughts.' She paused. 'I must respect your decisions, Rhiann.'

The heat of Rhiann's shame swept her body, and she found her fingers fastening on Caitlin's arms with urgency. 'Sister, Eremon does not know, and you cannot tell him.'

Caitlin's cheeks coloured. 'But Rhiann—'

'You must swear to me!' Rhiann cried in sudden terror. 'Please! The Erin rites are different; you said so yourself. I don't want him to look at me like that.'

At last Caitlin's chin dropped, and she nodded. 'Whatever you wish, sister. Though it grieves me greatly.' Her trembling breath stirred the white hare fur edging her cloak.

'I know you find it hard to understand,' Rhiann added desperately, for Caitlin's sadness was worse than any judgement. 'But . . . but this is how it must be, for now.'

Caitlin nodded and forced a smile, pressing her lips to Gabran's head. 'Well, my prince could have no more devoted aunt. Isn't he the luckiest boy?' In answer Gabran writhed and gurgled, and Caitlin held him close as she turned to go.

Rhiann trailed after them along the muddy path towards her house, forcing the pain back into the shadows around her heart.

Caitlin and Conaire decided to combine Gabran's naming ceremony with the feast for the longest night.

Every feast of that season was a sweaty, noisy affair, as people endeavoured to dance and sing and drink away all the nervous energy they were not expending outside.

Now Rhiann rested her head on the ivy-covered post beside her bench, her temples pounding from mead and the heat of the Hall's two hearth-fires, a feast cake of ground acorn and hazelnut half-eaten in her hand. Caitlin was on her other side, deep in a discussion about teething with Aldera.

One of Gabran's naming gifts caught Rhiann's eye, as the baby waved his fists in Conaire's broad lap. It was a tiny armband of rowan wood, into which Rhiann had sung protection and safety, and on which Didius had carved a string of fierce animals. The other gifts were also on prominent display, piled at Conaire's feet. And Eremon sat beside Conaire, brandishing the wooden toy sword he had caused Bran to make, along with a tiny shield painted with the Boar. He was chuckling as his brother reminded him of their own early exploits in Erin, and when he leaned over to tickle Gabran under the chin, the softness in his eyes was clear.

'When your son is born, brother, we will train them together!' Conaire proclaimed, placing his hand over the width of his son's belly, the joy on his face incandescent.

Eremon smiled and placed the sword in Gabran's grip, wrapping his tiny fingers around the hilt. 'Aye, and imagine the terror they will cause for ever after.'

They laughed, and suddenly Rhiann was struggling for breath among the hot press of bodies in the close, ale-fumed air. Lurching to her feet, she tried to nod calmly at Caitlin's soft enquiry and, picking up her cloak, hurried for the door.

Outside the night was frozen and still, moonless. Rhiann hastened beneath the torch-lit Horse Gate and down the path to the village, drawing in great lungfuls of icy air to steady herself, before her senses picked up the soft pad of feet behind her. She tensed instinctively, as warm arms came gently around her, pulling her close, with a wash of that familiar, sweet male scent.

'Eremon!' A flood of guilt sharpened her voice, and she tried to laugh. 'You scared me half to death!' She nudged him with her elbow, but he suddenly pulled her to one side, into a dark, doorway. The air within tickled her nose, thick with chaff and the scent of old hay. It was one of the small granaries, used only for horse fodder.

'I wanted to see you alone,' Eremon murmured, mouth buried in the nape of her neck.

'Well, there were other ways to do that.'

'True, but none as much fun.'

Then all playfulness died as his lips claimed her own, his soft tongue reaching through her guilty pain and plucking a string that vibrated deep in her belly. As his warm hand slid under her cloak and dress and up the back of her thigh, she wrenched her lips free. '*Cariad*, it's freezing in here!'

'Don't worry,' he murmured, edging her back until her shoulders came up against the mud wall, 'you won't be going anywhere near the ground.'

'Eremon . . .'

His palms were stroking her buttocks now, and then he dropped to his knees on the tumbled hay and lifted her dress, drawing her to his eager mouth, cupping her like a goblet in both hands. His tongue swirled and savoured, circling until her breath came fast and high, and she buried her fingers in his hair.

Just as the opening began inside her, the overflowing of the flame, he came to his feet and lifted her onto him, burying himself up to the hilt. Then all of her protests dissolved in the animal fierceness that swept her, born of guilt and desperation. And she clawed him deeper, faster, her back scraping against the rough wall.

Later, in their own bed, Eremon soothed her raw, swollen skin with a more languid tongue, and the second peak was slow and sweet, the fierceness a strange memory.

'*A stór*,' Eremon whispered into her hair, as their breath slowly calmed. 'Never have I felt that you wanted me more, in the granary.' He paused, touching his nose to her forehead almost shyly. 'Perhaps it was a babe we called this night. In such fire, we say, a king is made.'

The warmth and sweetness in Rhiann was instantly drenched; she felt as if he'd thrown her into an icy stream. When he sensed her stiffen, Eremon cupped her head and pressed it into his shoulder. 'Oh, love, I did not mean to hurt you.' He hesitated. 'It hasn't been long. The babies will come soon, I know it. We must be patient.'

When Eremon felt a tear on his hand, he exclaimed and soothed Rhiann with gentle words. Yet each soft murmur was a blade sunk into her heart, twisted there on its hilt.

BOOK THREE
LEAF-BUD, AD 82

Chapter 28

At the festival of Imbolc, Rhiann poured the streams of ewe's milk into the river to thank the Mother Goddess for the return of the sun, despite the still-bare branches and continuing sleet. In defiance of the fertility blessing, a knife-edge wind caught the liquid and spattered it over Rhiann's sheepskin cloak, and she needed two cups of hot mead around Aldera's fire to unclench her frozen fingers.

And it was there, as the women passed the afternoon sewing, that Rhiann discovered it was not only she who had found the long dark so difficult, letting fears take root.

'The warmth won't come,' one of the old women croaked, biting her thread off between two yellow teeth. 'It is the doing of the ice spirits – we are unlucky.'

Glances came Rhiann's way, but she kept her eyes on her sewing. She and Caitlin were making Eremon and Conaire a new battle standard, with blessings sung into every corner of it to keep them safe. Caitlin was hemming the white woollen background with neat stitches, and Rhiann was working on the boar figure, in crimson-dyed linen.

'Aye,' another woman said into the silence. 'And just yesterday my man saw a flock of nine crows in the dead oak by the seal's bay. Nine, and all lined up on one branch!'

'War crows,' one of Aldera's grown daughters whispered, peeling a pile of rushes to make into lamps.

Aldera snorted loudly, plunging the glowing fire poker into more cups of mead on the hearth. When the steam cleared, she fixed her daughter with a sharp eye. 'We all know the men will be going to war again – it doesn't take any crows to tell us that! Isn't your da up to his elbows in hot iron all day and all night?'

There were murmurs of agreement as she handed around the cups, but the bronze-smith's wife, always in competition with Aldera, sniffed and wiped her long, dripping nose on her sleeve. 'There are more signs than that. A redshank was heard calling eighteen times, exactly. A dead horse washed up below the Dun of the Cliffs.' Her voice dropped dramatically. 'And a grey man has been seen on the marshes.'

Rhiann stabbed her finger as her head jerked up. 'Grey man?'

The bronze-smith's wife smiled, her pointed teeth gleaming. 'Yes, lady, with his pale robe flowing out behind him. Ebra saw him in the fog last week, flying over a marsh pool like a swan.'

Rhiann laid down her sewing and fixed a calm eye on her. Eremon wouldn't want needless fears to flourish, for a warrior's strength could easily be eroded by his woman's talk. Yet the bronze-smith's wife flushed at Rhiann's regard. 'That's what Ebra said. But others have seen him, too, all cloaked and hooded.'

Another woman timidly cleared her throat. 'My man swears he saw him gliding among the trees on the maiden's hill.' She spoke in a whisper, and many of the women darted fearful glances at each other and over their shoulder to the door.

'What does it mean, lady?' Aldera's daughter asked Rhiann, nervously twirling one of the peeled rushes. 'A grey man bodes ill . . . perhaps he has come to claim our men!' She was just fifteen, and new-married. 'Will the Romans kill them all, and us, too?'

Rhiann slowly let her breath out and smiled, looking around at them. 'Your men are in the hands of the war leader, and a better war leader has not been seen in Alba since the Goddess herself walked these mountains; we all know that. So grey man or no, Eremon will guide our men with a clear head, as we must keep our own heads clear. Do not let your fears make you quaver, for the fire you hold steady in your hearts will reach out to your men and give them strength in battle.' Suddenly an idea slipped into Rhiann's mind as surely and rightly as a sword to its sheath. 'I myself,' she found herself announcing, 'will be returning to the Sacred Isle when the sea lanes open.' A surge of excitement and relief rose in her. 'The Sisterhood gave us great aid before, and can do so again. So you see, there are many with the power of sight, working to keep your loved ones safe. Do not let your fears weaken your hearts.'

When Rhiann and Caitlin emerged, the wind had given way to a dank evening fog, dripping from the eaves of the houses, cloaking the dun in near darkness. The stones on the upper path were slippery, and Rhiann took Caitlin's elbow protectively as they walked.

'You're going back to the Sacred Isle?' Caitlin adjusted the hide wrap to cover Gabran's bare head.

Rhiann nodded, the excitement still vibrating along her veins. 'It came to me so clearly! After all, the men will leave when the weather breaks, and I cannot stay here while they risk themselves. I *know* there is more I can do, and the Sisters will see what that is.'

Caitlin glanced down at Gabran, as he began to fuss and wail. His cheeks were red and swollen from teething, and he had been fractious all day. 'And I have to stay here,' she said softly.

Rhiann halted, breathing hard as she felt herself fill with a new strength. Goddess, it was better than the guilt. She turned to Caitlin, slipping an arm around her shoulder. 'Which is why I do what I do,' she pointed out gently. 'You have the important job of caring for our future king; I have another calling.'

At Rhiann's house, Eithne knelt by the hearth, grinding roast barley in the quern, her sleeves rolled up to the elbows. Caitlin and Rhiann shook the damp from their cloaks and hung them by the door, and Caitlin stretched Gabran out on his sheepskin rug. Immediately, he wriggled on his belly towards Cù, and began tugging at the hound's ragged grey ears.

'Eithne.' Rhiann distracted Gabran with a rowan peg to chew for his teeth. 'Have you heard talk of a marsh spirit around Dunadd? A grey man, they are calling him.'

'Yes, lady.' Eithne sat back on her heels and brushed sweat from her brow, leaving a smear of flour. 'All the servants are speaking of it.'

Rhiann reached for the cooling brew of willow bark on the hearth, drawing Gabran into her lap as he began to fuss and suck on his fists. 'Well, I'd like you to spread a new rumour at the well. Tell people I have said it is nothing to be afraid of, and we will drive him forth with the songs at Beltaine, if he has not returned to his Otherworld home by then.'

She measured the brew into water and held the cup to the baby's lips as he cried. When it was down she kissed and rocked him, her chin pressed thoughtfully into his hair.

Over the past few weeks, Rhiann had noticed Eremon and Conaire huddled in conversation, glimpsing them in the smithy and the stables, and corners of the dun away from the other men.

Yet when a day dawned suddenly bright and still, with a warm sun glittering on the last frosts, Conaire took Caitlin and their son out walking alone, and Eremon appeared in the middle of the day outside the house. In his arms was his fighting saddle, and a pot of mutton-fat.

Scooping up two honey cakes, Rhiann joined him in the cool sun, pressing her lips to his forehead before settling down beside him on the bench. She drew up her knees and gestured at the four-horned saddle, which had been stored away through the long dark. 'I take this to mean your plans with Conaire have been laid?'

Eremon paused at rubbing fat into the leather of one saddle horn, cocking an eye at her. 'I didn't want to burden you, *a stór*, until I had thrashed it out with him, until I was sure it was right.'

'And now you are sure?' Rhiann took one of the cakes, looking at

Eremon expectantly. Despite the sun the breeze was still cold off the sea, and she drew her sleeves to the ends of her fingers before biting into the cake.

Eremon smiled, though his eyes were solemn. Then he seemed to brace himself. 'Rhiann, after our success in the south, we think we should strike first this year. Agricola won't be expecting it, which gives us an advantage, and we've shown our raiding tactics can work against the Roman army.' He rubbed the cracked side of the saddle horn vigorously, rushing on. 'If we lure them northwards, we can take them by surprise, and draw them up into the mountains. On their own ground, I have seen then what the tribes can do.'

Despite the plunge in her belly, Rhiann recognized the light in Eremon's eyes: the warrior's excitement. She herself knew that zeal, after all, for her heart was also grasping for its strength. She cleared her throat. 'Where will you go?'

Eremon glanced at her as if he had expected an argument. Yet Rhiann had something to tell him as well, and she certainly didn't want an argument about that, either. 'North, to Calgacus,' he said. 'To start a rebellion of our own. We need all the men he has pledged to us.'

Rhiann nodded and swallowed, slowly brushing crumbs from her skirt. 'Then I must tell you that it is in my mind also to return to the Sacred Isle, for Beltaine. The strength of the Sisters helped you once, and this time I intend to call more priestesses to attend – all the Ban Crés and healers of our allies, and those of tribes who have so far refused an alliance. Through this, I may be able to convince them to pressure their kings to join you.'

Apprehensively, Rhiann glanced up to meet Eremon's eyes. Over the long dark they had spoken many times of the stag rite, and so Eremon knew of its power, and what it had given him. With the other Sisters she had drawn the Source once, and knew she could do it again. *This* was her true path, her only path, and she hoped that the compulsion to follow it would assuage the guilt of betraying Eremon. She would give herself to their cause, and therefore to him, in the best way she could for now.

And though concern was there at the edges of Eremon's mouth, something else passed between them with that one look, beyond the fear for each other: a simple, wordless acceptance of what must be.

Chapter 29

Samana edged gingerly down the gangplank of the Alban ship, for the thick fog had coated the timbers with a dangerous slick of moisture. Underneath her feet, the Abus river was black and oily, and the sounds of the men tying up on Eboracum's pier were strangely muffled.

It was too early in the season for trading ships to come inland from the sea to the headquarters of the Ninth Legion, and hers was the only vessel she could see, although the mist had turned its outline ghostly as it rocked on the slow river.

Before her in the near darkness loomed the legionary fortress, less than ten years old, with its huge square ditch encircling a high earth bank, topped by pointed timber palisades and gatetowers at each corner, looking out over the plain. Within the fortress was the town, a place for soldiers, made of straight streets, storehouses, long barrack blocks and workshops. Yet Samana had no intention of going into *that*. Her arrival here would be most unexpected, and probably unwelcome.

She shrugged deeper into her lynx-fur wrap, shivering, as two men shuffled past her with a large oak chest, pushing her back against a line of barrels waiting to be loaded. Hazy pools of torchlight spilled down from the fortress walls, illuminating a ragged collection of civilian buildings that had sprung up along the riverbank like mushrooms: houses for traders in hides, salt, meat and grain, she remembered Agricola telling her; craftsmen's workshops; and rooms for whores.

Samana could see little beyond dark, humped walls, oddly angled roofs and glimpses of lamplight spilling under shutters. Dogs barked and people cursed, the sound faint in the mist, and from within the fort itself came clearer sounds of trumpets and shouted orders. Perhaps on a day like this, most people stayed inside.

Samana gripped the edge of the barrel behind her, struggling to calm her pulse, sucking in freezing, clammy fog with each breath. She was the queen of the Votadini, she reminded herself. Yet she didn't feel her exalted rank here. Eboracum was a daunting place; the headquarters of Agricola when he retreated south from Alba in the long dark, and home to one of his legions. The thought of all those soldiers only a few steps away discomfited her in a way that living among them never did.

Suddenly she heard a slip and curse, as a sailor stumbled off the end of the gangplank from her ship, an amphora in his arms. This, and the thought of how angry Agricola would be, were enough to rouse her. 'You!' she barked, straightening. 'I did not pay more money for that wine than you will ever see in your life, only for you to spill it into the river!'

The man gaped at her, open-mouthed.

'Put it safe in the cart,' she ordered, through gritted teeth, 'and find me someone to take a message inside the fort.'

The man bowed. 'Yes, lady.'

Because of her bribes, he at least knew she was important, even though she had kept her hood up for the entire journey down the coast from Alba. It would not do to embarrass Agricola openly, after all. She had not seen him for more than five moons, for when he was not subduing the wild northern tribes, he must govern the province itself. Every long dark he came south with his men, the four legions he commanded dispersing to their fortresses in other towns. Then he attended to all the business that had been delayed while he was in the field – correspondence with the emperor and visits from leading citizens and officials of the southern cities to discuss taxes and complaints and building programmes. There were, as Agricola explained to her, always minor rebellions to quell, outlaws terrorizing citizens in country estates, tribes defaulting on payments, and native princes pleading for aid against their enemies.

Samana knew all this would have been dominating Agricola's thoughts and energy. Yet she was gambling that her body, expensive gift and new idea would all help to quell his fury when he found her on his doorstep.

A native boy skidded down the muddy bank out of the dark fog, and once she had given him her message, and a coin for his troubles, she asked him where travellers stayed when they came to town.

The boy sniffed. 'Officials and messengers all stay in the fort,' he offered unhelpfully.

Samana shook her head. 'Not inside. Is there anywhere in the village?'

The boy's white teeth flashed in the gloom. 'My aunt has the only inn, lady. It's cheap.'

Samana clinked her other coins in her hand. 'Clean is better than cheap; I do not wish to be assaulted or robbed.'

The boy shrugged. 'Sometimes traders come, who want a good bed and meal. It is clean.'

'Then take me there. And remember: when you deliver your message to the commander, say *only* that a gift awaits him at the river, and his benefactor awaits him at this inn of yours. You will not say it is a lady, you will say it is . . . one who bears the mark of the panther.' She smiled to herself. Agricola once said she reminded him of a black panther he saw in a theatre in Africa, although she did not know what such a creature was. She stared down at the boy severely. 'You will only get the other half of your money if he comes alone, and if you deliver this message to him exactly as I have said it.'

The boy nodded and pocketed the coin she dangled before him, then darted off so quickly she had to shout at one of the sailors to guard the stores, before hurrying after him.

The child led her into the maze of buildings by the river, most of them stinking of fish, tanned hides and damp, and she was so busy dodging the puddles that she failed to notice where they were going. Those few people about were huddled in cloaks, their boots barely crunching on the gravel paths, yet from far above, on the fort walls, came the thud of marching feet and the muffled clank of weapons.

Suddenly the boy stopped before one of the only properly constructed buildings, a long, low house of wattle-and-daub, with a dripping thatch roof. He left her then, and a show of her precious coins to the woman innkeeper got her ushered through a smoky den of men and bright-painted women, already gabbering drunkenly, and along a corridor to a tiny room, which fronted the path. The woman who led the way paused at the door to light an oil lamp with a pine taper, and as the room filled with soft, wavering light, Samana saw that there was a narrow, straw-filled bed, a three-legged brazier, a bedside table and a bench set before the window.

As the woman bustled around, lighting the coals in the brazier bowl and muttering about the chill fog, Samana pulled back the blanket on the bed, and from the smell she could tell it was reasonably clean, the sheets laundered, the ticking fresh. It would do.

When the innkeeper left, Samana opened the shutters on the single window and looked out over the foggy river, wrapping her cloak about herself with mingled terror and elation. She had done it! Agricola wouldn't turn her away, not now. He had been away from her body for more than five moons, and though she knew he would have sought relief elsewhere, surely no whey-faced southern whore could be any match for her beauty or sexual prowess.

Over the next few hours, the afternoon gloom deepened. Samana riffled her damp hair over the brazier to dry it, hung her cloak over the door, and sat on the bench and dozed, jerking awake at every noise on the path outside. Irritable and aching, she roused herself long enough to order some hard cheese and cold fowl from the innkeeper, then picked at the clay platter without enthusiasm. Finally, she realized that it would not do to be so ill of temper when Agricola came, so she ordered a basin of hot water and sponged herself, combed her hair and dressed in his favourite red robe.

The fog outside was darkening into night when at last he arrived.

There was no knock at the door; he just burst straight in and stood staring at her, until the innkeeper had puffed her way back down the corridor. Then he kicked the door shut and unwound the long cloak from his head and shoulders and tossed it on the bed. Underneath, he was dressed in his plainest tunic and boots, with no armour or insignia of rank. He had taken a chance coming here; she knew it. Samana adopted a meek expression and waited for the explosion.

'What the . . . ?' In a familiar gesture, Agricola ran his fingers through his damp, grey hair, the harsh lines beside his mouth deepening. 'What are you doing here? Is there trouble on the frontier? Why didn't you send a messenger?'

Samana forced a smile and swayed closer to him, wetting her lips with a pink tongue. 'There is no trouble. I needed to see you . . . to speak to you in private.'

Agricola's eyes widened. 'You mean, you had no reason for coming?'

'I needed to speak with you about military matters,' she replied evenly.

'Gods!' he barked, his nostrils flaring. 'There are high-ranking officials here. My wife is here . . . my life is here! How dare you come when I gave you no permission to do so!'

Bitterness rose in Samana's throat, but she kept the smile in place. She never glimpsed such scruples when he was buried between her thighs! 'Well, I am here now.' She raised her chin, wondering how best to handle him. He admired boldness, that he did, so she put her hands on her hips. 'And I came to deliver my gift in person. Does a shipment of the best Falernian vintage not sweeten my arrival? We can drink some of it here.' She glanced towards the bed.

'*Wine?*' Agricola stared at her for a long moment, and then at the table, where she had set out her implements: the enamelled pan to heat the wine, the spices, and the strainer, as well as two red samian-ware cups. The hard line of Agricola's mouth softened, and abruptly he threw back his head and laughed. 'I might have known the panther would not remain caged in the north for long.'

Encouraged, Samana swayed forward and curled her arms around his neck. After five moons, his growing boredom with *her* would surely have been replaced with boredom for his own enforced captivity – the tedious feasts, the tedious wife. Now Agricola ran his hands up her body, roughly cupping her breasts, and sure enough, the fire flared in his dark eyes.

'Go on,' she purred, 'admit you've missed me. Admit you are bored with your slack-eyed whores and your endless dinners and your fat, sleek administrators and your talks and letters and orders and—'

'Enough,' he growled, and his mouth came down on hers, wrenching, violent, sliding to her neck as she threw her head back, and down into the cleft between her breasts. Then the bed was beneath her, and he was above, and soon his back was a leaping shadow against the wall, as all his frustration poured into her in a frenzy of thrusts.

Samana pretended her moans and cries, too wrapped up in the glow of renewed triumph to focus on the sensations in her body. *I'm not beaten yet*, she thought fiercely, as he lay on her afterwards, the sweat slick between their bodies, his breath rasping in her ear. *Nowhere near beaten yet.*

In the north of Alba, Calgacus, king of the Caledonii tribe, paced the timber battlements of his fort, the Dun of the Waves. He was a tall man, lean and muscled despite his advancing years, beak-nosed and sharp-eyed. He barely felt the biting sea-wind on his face, for the Epidii messenger just arrived from Eremon had delivered news to light a fire in any old warrior.

'So,' Calgacus muttered to himself, gripping the edge of the palisade with sword-hardened hands, staring out at the sea as it darkened with the dusk. Below him, the belt of trees by the river was already deep in shadow, and torches were being lit on the battlements. 'My young Erin friend wants to bring the Romans to me.' Calgacus grinned, surprised at the spark of excitement that flared up in his soul at the thought of Eremon's plans.

He had considered himself past such fiery exploits – a grave, ageing king whose only role was to extend advice to bold young princes like his Epidii ally. But then, he'd discovered early on that Eremon had a way about him, a gift for oratory that could stoke the fading coals in a man, and prod him out of complacency. And Calgacus had also been brooding on the Romans for the entire long dark, as the sea storms howled around his firelit hall. They would come north eventually, there seemed little doubt of that, and the rich Caledonii lands were probably their first target.

Better to go down fighting than hiding in my hall, Calgacus thought now, stroking his jutting jaw, staring up at his royal banner rippling on its gold-tipped mast. He wasn't so old that the idea of glorifying his name had lost its allure either.

Calgacus grinned again, and turned his eagle face to the wind, letting his cloak fly behind him.

Far in the west, the dusk was still and golden over the sea, as Nerida stood watching the messenger striding away to the guest lodge.

'So Rhiann will return to us, and soon,' Setana remarked from the bench against Nerida's house.

Nerida nodded. 'She asks us to send riders to the priestesses in the northern tribes, asking them to come for Beltaine. She has already dispatched those to the southern tribes.'

'Then the great change we have sensed is drawing near now, Sister.'

Nerida sighed, her shoulders bowing with the weight. 'I know.'

Suddenly Setana stood by her side, and they clasped hands, as they had many years ago when their skin was white and unlined. 'The dreams, the visions, they hint at an ending,' Setana murmured. 'Though how it will come to us, I do not know. It rises like a distant wave, growing ever closer: now I can hear the far roar; now I sense the wind driven before it. Yet we must not fear.' Her soft voice cracked. 'Our Mother wants us not to fear.'

Nerida tightened her fingers. 'You will help me, then.'

Setana shook her head, and the shells woven into her grey braids sounded faintly. 'Our fates are tied together, dearest friend, and so we will help each other.'

Chapter 30

The first sip of Falernian wine slipped down Samana's throat, though she was too excited to note its taste.

Agricola had left the bed now and, after shrugging on his tunic, he dragged the bench to the brazier. The coals in the iron bowl glowed brightly, but it was their only light, and the rest of the room was entirely in shadow.

Samana reached across and put her wine cup on the table. As she slid forward, she held the sheets up around her breasts with one hand, covering her nakedness. There was a time and a place for such things, and that time had passed for the moment – now she needed him to listen to her.

Swiftly, she finished relating the details of the visit she had recently made, to an old Damnonii priestess who had managed to remain in her isolated hut despite the ravages that the Romans had unleashed on her tribe. Yet despite Samana's urgent tone, Agricola's eyes never left the curve of her breasts, visible through the damp linen that clung to her body. Samana wrapped an arm over them, biting down frustration. He was not excited about what she had to say. Not yet.

When she paused, Agricola tossed back a careless gulp of her expensive wine, stretching his bare legs along the floor and yawning. 'Your women priests – these Sisters – are healers, you told me, muttering chants over birthing women. What care I for them?'

Inside, Samana allowed herself the slightest curl of contempt. Warriors would never understand the power of the spirit. Weak arms did not make a weak mind. 'No, my lord. The Sisters can do more than that, especially when they act together, with one will. But they have not wielded that power in a military manner for generations.'

He frowned, scratching lazily behind his ear. 'And they have now, you say.'

Unconsciously, Samana had been leaning forward, her arms tightening about her knees. Now she realized what she was doing, and forced herself to play with one of her blue-glass bangles, breathing deeply. *Never be desperate before him.*

'I have . . . inserted myself back into the web of the Sisters, my lord, just on the edges. And some interesting rumours have come drifting over the high mountains. Last sunseason there was a powerful rite on the Sacred Isle. The old priestess I spoke to knew little more than that; she herself lives alone and receives her news only sporadically.' Samana paused, noting the bored cast of Agricola's hard mouth as his gaze wandered over the window shutters and shadowed walls. She waited for it all to change at her next words. '*My lord*, what she heard was this: the rite was to give strength to the Novantae . . . and the Epidii war leader who came to their aid. The rite delivered a great victory over Roman soldiers at the time of the longest day.'

The transformation was instant. In one movement Agricola sat straight on the bench, the cup gripped so hard it tilted, spilling that fine wine over his tunic. '*What?*'

'She knows no more,' Samana added, gratified to see the anger etched around Agricola's eyes as he slowly placed his cup down. She abandoned her calmness, and moved on her knees to his side. 'They understand their own power, now. They will try again this season, I know it. When you are in the field.'

Agricola's breath came quickly now. 'Can it be?' he muttered, staring up into the shadows, his eyes glazing over with some memory. Then his head swivelled towards her. 'Where is this Sacred Isle?'

Samana raised her finger to gesture towards the west, but when she opened her mouth, no sound came out. Then she watched with horror as her finger trembled before her . . . *and in slipped a memory of laughter around a dawn fire, warm barley bread on her tongue, her legs cold and tired from standing all night in the Stones* . . . With a strangled gasp Samana buried the offending finger in her fist. Curse the Sisters! Always trying to subdue her will, worming their way into her . . . Abruptly, she cleared her throat. 'The Sacred Isle is in the sea to the west of Alba – not on any of your maps.'

'No matter.' Agricola was again staring at the walls, but he was no longer at ease, no longer yawning. Instead, he leaned forward, rubbing the dark, wet patch on his tunic with rhythmic rolls of his knuckles. 'There is more than one way to hunt down a pack of she-wolves. Hound, horse, or man?' He paused, and at last she caught a glimpse of a tight smile. 'Hound, I think. Definitely hound.'

A cold surge rippled through Samana's belly, for Agricola seemed to have forgotten her now, and that was not the reason she had come so far, at such great cost.

Her hand crept to his muscled thigh, and she wiped the wine from the hair and skin beneath, touching it to her lips, seeking for his eyes. Then his gaze did fix on her, and the hot anger and tension there wavered, drawn back into something more indulgent. 'You did well to bring this to my attention, my dark witch.'

Samana licked the last taste of wine from her lips, hiding the rush of relief. And she resolutely replaced the image of the Stones and the dawn fire with a more satisfying one: Samana in the marble hall of a Roman palace, dressed in cloth-of-gold, rubies and lapis dripping from fingers and ears, black hair arrayed around her. Yes, she would be the very image, from what she'd heard, of the great Egyptian queen Cleopatra. A woman who had captured the heart of an emperor.

Samana kneeled between Agricola's legs and edged the hem of his tunic up his thighs, a smile playing about her lips. Tilting his head, Agricola opened his legs wider and drew her close, one callused hand grasping her chin while he explored her mouth with his tongue. From the hardness pressing into her belly, she knew she had won again.

Eremon's public farewell was no easier for Rhiann than the private one.

Huddled in her fleece cloak, she stood outside the village gate beneath a leaden sky, as Eremon mounted Dórn at the head of his warband. Yet in front of all these people she could not repeat the words that she had whispered as a litany over his sleeping body in the night: *I love you. Come back to me. I'm sorry.*

So many times Rhiann had seen him ride out with sunshine glittering on his armour and weapons, and that glorious spectacle was always a reassurance of triumph and invincibility. Yet today the silent, drifting rain dulled his boar helmet and bright sword and mailshirt. Rori was sitting straight in his saddle, proudly bearing aloft the new scarlet and white standard, but it hung wet and limp, the fierce Boar obscured in its folds.

All around Rhiann, the fleece and fur trimming the warriors' cloaks and hoods was sodden with water. Hair was plastered to foreheads, moustaches dripped, and rain pattered on leather capes and saddle packs. It was a thoroughly miserable day to be outside, and though it hadn't stopped the women from farewelling their men, the cheering crowds were absent.

Eremon was taking only 400 warriors himself, which didn't seem nearly enough to Rhiann, yet as he had pointed out to her, he must leave sufficient forces behind to guard Dunadd's land and sea approaches. And Calgacus had many warriors: that was the reason the alliance with him had been so valued, after all.

Her throat aching, Rhiann now gazed up at Eremon, and the mist that rose from the river to merge with the drizzle seemed suddenly to wreath about him, like the cold breath of the Otherworld. Her fingers tightened on Dórn's bridle.

Conaire huddled in the shelter of the gatetower, his bulk shielding Caitlin and the baby from the rain. Eremon's eyes strayed to them now, and beneath the dripping browguard of his helmet Rhiann saw a glint of regret. Yet this was what men like Eremon and Conaire did; this was what they gave their lives to.

'You will be with Calgacus in two weeks,' she repeated, more for herself than for him.

Eremon nodded, wiping rain from his cheek with the back of his hand. 'With so many men, it will take much longer than our last trip. But at least we don't have to look over our shoulders for Romans.' The Great Glen along which they would travel was separated from the Roman frontier by the highest, most impassable mountains of Alba.

'But where will you go then?' She needed to be able to picture him somewhere, even though all roads they were likely to take led him towards the Roman lines.

Eremon shrugged, and rivulets of rain ran down his wolf cloak, clumping the surface of the fur. 'I won't know any details until I speak to Calgacus. It doesn't matter how we do it, anyway, so long as we launch an uprising that draws the Romans from their bases.' He grinned suddenly in private amusement. 'Imagine: Ferdiad's son, a common rebel!'

'Hardly common.' Rhiann blinked away drifting drizzle, desperately trying to commit every curve of his cheeks and jaw to memory, as if it would keep him nearer over the coming moons. He was freshly bathed and shaved, and after a season of good food, as strong in body as he could ever be. Yet as she gazed up at him, another image was suddenly overlaid on this one, just as she had once seen Gabran's features shift from babe to king. Eremon's same dear-loved face looked back at her, but for a moment it was pale and blood-streaked, sheened with sweat, and so hollow-cheeked he looked like a death-wraith.

Rhiann started, stifling a cry, and Eremon's hand closed over her own on the bridle. 'It will be well, *a stór*,' he murmured. 'I will see you again.'

She bit her lip, not meeting his eyes. 'Yes,' she forced out, cupping her elbows with her hands. 'I will see you again.'

He smiled with relief, but there was a tightness around his mouth that had not been there before. 'Well, priestess wife, I am glad you think so.'

Yet she couldn't smile back, and despite the men murmuring among themselves, the clanking of armour and impatient stamping of horses, Eremon leaned down to stroke her cheek. '*Cariad*,' he murmured, his voice thick with concern. And so Rhiann raised her face, straightening her shoulders, forcing strength and boldness into her eyes. The dream called them both: he had his role to fulfil, and she had hers. That's all there was.

'The Goddess bless your sword arm, husband.' She smiled. 'I will be watching over you, and sending you all my strength.'

A war horn suddenly blew from the gate above, answered by another at the head of the warband, and only the warmth of Eremon's fingers stayed with Rhiann then as the horsemen and foot warriors marched over the causeway, to be swallowed by the curtain of drizzle and mist, their shouts echoing faintly back along the palisade.

Rhiann remained still, her fingers pressed to her mouth. She was the Ban Cré, and as she'd told the women that there was no need to fear, so then she must show no fear. A tiny fist batted her arm, breaking into her thoughts, and she caught Gabran's hand in her own. Holding him, Caitlin pressed her cheek into the back of her son's head and met Rhiann's eyes.

'Come.' Rhiann drew a determined breath. 'It is time to plan my own leave-taking.'

Chapter 31

A sudden rash of leaf-bud fevers kept Rhiann and Eithne busy, and Rhiann's sailing was delayed further when Linnet herself took a chill that settled in her chest, and proved difficult to shift. 'I tell you I do not wish you to go to the Sacred Isle without me! There is danger around . . . and a dread in me, daughter, a sickness . . .' Linnet's head tossed restlessly on her pillow, her unbound hair lank and damp from sweat.

'The poppy brings such dreams, aunt, and the sickness in the belly.' Holding a bowl of bruised coltsfoot leaves and cup of linseed tea, Rhiann drew a stool to the bed with her foot. 'And you cannot go; it is too risky for your chest.'

Linnet swallowed with difficulty, her breathing shallow, as Rhiann peeled back her shift and began smearing the coltsfoot poultice over her breast bone. 'If I can't go,' Linnet whispered, 'then you must not. I feel a . . . a *wrongness* . . .'

Just then the door-hide was flung up as Eithne entered with another armful of floor rushes from the saddles of the pack ponies. The morning sun spilled over the bare floor, laying a bright slice across the fading blue blanket on Linnet's bed.

Rhiann lowered her voice, wondering how to impart what she herself felt in her belly; that Eremon was riding into true danger, and for Rhiann that outweighed all else, even Linnet's fevered dreams. 'The danger you sense is all around us,' she murmured, binding linen over the poultice, 'and I will not sit here and do nothing while it draws closer. The rites with the Sisters will strengthen our men, and thereby keep us *all* safer, and they need my connection to Eremon to direct the Source. As a priestess, you must understand.'

Linnet's breathing rattled in her chest, and she coughed impatiently into both hands before resuming her agitated grip on the blanket.

Behind Eithne, Dercca now appeared with a pile of washed linens she had been drying in the sunshine.

Rhiann used Linnet's distraction to push her advantage. 'Besides, Nerida herself sent a message back to my own, saying that she would look for me at Beltaine. Setana already knew that I was coming.'

Linnet frowned. 'Did she?'

'Most certainly.' Rhiann moved to the edge of the bed and took Linnet's hand. 'I do not wish to grieve you, aunt, but I am going, and you must stay and get well, so you can care for Caitlin and Gabran.'

Linnet's mouth pursed, then crumpled. Rhiann stroked her hot cheek, red and lined from the pillow. 'Anyway, no one even knows the path I sail. I am nothing more than another priestess on her way to the Sacred Isle for Beltaine.'

Linnet's fevered eyes were dark with pain, yet at last she managed to summon a blessing to her cracked lips. However though she returned Rhiann's embrace, she left warm tears on her niece's neck.

A week later, Rhiann and Didius set sail from Crinan. Caitlin eventually sought shelter from the cold wind that blew in over the Bay of Isles, ducking into a nearby house to warm Gabran by the fire. But from far out on the choppy waves Rhiann kept her eyes on Linnet's tall, straight figure standing alone on the edge of the rocks.

And she saw that Linnet did not move at all, until the distance and sea-mists took her from Rhiann's sight.

The lamp-flame rose steadily against the cold walls of the vast underground tomb, sheening the moist stone.

Outside, a moaning storm swept across the flat Orcades lands, straight from the sea, heavily laden with salt rain. Yet the stone was so perfectly worked that not a single gust penetrated the heavy, silent air inside. At the farther reaches of the central chamber the light fell away into dark shadows that moved and whispered of their own accord, restless, and sometimes there came a glimpse of gleaming, aged bone.

The old man lay naked, spread-eagled on the earth floor, his white hair trailing around his head. The burning cold seeped up from under him, and with every breath he drew it in deeper, sensing the power like an underground stream, black with secrets. It pulsed in waves of oily darkness, curling into each of the symbols daubed on his wrinkled skin in black mud and ash, joining him to Arawn, lord of the underworld.

With every surge of the druid herbs he sensed his spirit contract, and the aches of his body dissolve into a cold, sinewy strength that turned within him. *Come, lord,* the Otherworld spirits were already calling. *Come and let us bow down to you! Speak, and let us serve!*

You have no choice, Gelert thought, and his spirit flexed and slithered free of the body, and down into the streams of power that ran beneath the land.

Free now, he writhed and spun among the tangled threads of dark and light that joined all times and all places into one web, unseen by the eyes of man. Some threads glowed silver, but he arched away from their harsh light and followed the others deeper into the dark. For they had the strength of that which bides its time, hoarding energy and warmth, coiled in darkness, wet and cold. And as he had so many times, he fixed Dunadd once more in his mind.

Spiralling through the deepest chambers, his spirit drew closer to its crag, to the bright glow of its inhabitants, the memories it held for him flaring with points of rage and pain. Up from the depths he swam, towards the surface – for he had found his rage could hold a part of himself there long enough to haunt the marsh pools and dark woods gliding silently, cloaked as a grey man. There, he would stalk and trap the stray thoughts of men, using the ways of the spirit to give him vision, where he had no eyes.

Chapter 32

'Rhiann! Rhiann!'

Fola's shout floated over the calm loch to the Epidii boat, wending its way among the clutter of sea-craft in the bay below the Sisters' settlement. Dragging her eyes away from her friend, Rhiann clasped the neck of the swan prow, staring around at the *curraghs* littering the weedy rocks, and the larger vessels tied up at the pier. Her call to all the priestesses of Alba had been answered.

'So many of the Ban Crés have come,' Fola gasped out, when Rhiann disembarked to be swept up in her friend's arms. 'Eight at least. And many elder priestesses from the mountains and the islands.'

Disconcerted, Rhiann broke free and massaged her temples, which were pounding from squinting into the sunlight over the sea. 'I . . . I did not expect . . .'

'Did you not?' Fola panted, one hand pressed to her side, for she had scrambled at a mad pace down from the Stones. 'Young you are, Sister, but known to them all the same.' She straightened and grinned, her sloe eyes twinkling with pleasure. 'Their kings may not have joined your man, but they certainly have been talking about him the length and breadth of Alba.'

Rhiann glanced up at the Stones as something trembled in her despite the sun on her arms, bared by the sleeveless shift. The Ban Crés were, like her, noble women trained as priestesses, and, like her, they walked the line between the demands of their tribe and the demands of the Sisters. They were no maidens, but shrewd women versed in the politics of their kings. And she was the youngest of them all – so why would they listen to her?

Because of the longest day rite she reminded herself. Trying to release her nerves along with her breath, she smiled at Fola, and turned to gesture Didius to bring their packs along behind. As the guestlodges were bursting with visitors, the sailors who had escorted the priestesses had thrown up a temporary camp against the rocks in the little bay, surrounded by fishing nets spread to dry, bundled ropes, and kegs of ale and food. Yet Didius could not be abandoned to their mercy, for despite strutting along the pier in his over-sized Alban sword and helmet, his Latin skin had grown swarthy in the sun once more, and his straight hair, round eyes and stockiness would soon proclaim him a foreigner.

'I am so glad you are here,' Fola whispered more fiercely, squeezing Rhiann's arm to draw her close. Her eyes had now lost their twinkle, and as they plunged into the shadows of the houses, she hunched one shoulder. 'Nerida and Setana have had faces like thunderclouds for weeks now, though they try to hide it by huddling together around Nerida's fire.' She shook her head, drawing a crease between her brows. 'Can you sense the weight over the Stones, Rhiann? Over us all?'

Rhiann glanced up at the headland again. From here she could only see a pale glitter of sun on grey rock, yet this time a nameless fear seemed to emanate from the air itself, not her own heart, brushing over her skin with a cold breath. 'It is a dangerous time for Alba,' she replied slowly. 'We are all feeling it.' For a moment, she drew into her mind the warmth of the glowing cauldron in her dream. There *was* danger, yet also light, somewhere, somehow.

'Perhaps.' Fola shrugged unhappily. 'Well, we will soon be able to share what is really going on, for we have all been called to farewell the sun in the Stones.'

Thoughtfully, Rhiann followed Fola to her little house, and spread her belongings on the pallet beside Fola's bed, absently greeting the other young women who had been moved from their beds to make way for their elders.

Didius had gone to make his own bed in an old stable nearby, and Rhiann now dug out her mother's bronze mirror and peered at herself by the light of the stone lamp on Fola's stool, noting the smears of sunburn across her high cheekbones, her reddened eyes, and the doleful tangle that was her hair. Hastily she unbraided and combed it. Fola stood before her, jiggling with impatience, before pushing Rhiann's hands away and binding it herself.

Rhiann couldn't do anything about her skin, but she changed her salt-stiff dress and grabbed two bronze arm-rings to add to the torc around her neck. Then she let Fola hurry her out of the door among the chattering girls.

On the path to the Stones Rhiann pulled on her priestess cloak and pinned it with the Epidii royal brooch, and only then did she concentrate on taking proper breaths and calming herself. She knew she would be scrutinized by the other Ban Crés, and was glad she had paused to adorn herself with some signs of rank.

Though the path was shrouded in shadow, when Rhiann and Fola reached the top of the headland the flame of the setting sun was still warming the ring of Stones. At the end of the avenue that led to the inner circle, Nerida waited to greet the Sisters, and Rhiann grasped both her arms after the kiss of greeting, registering a great stab of shock at Nerida's appearance.

Nerida's white braids hung heavy around her, casting her wrinkled cheeks into shadow. Her eyes seemed too large for her face, and her shoulder bones were sharper beneath Rhiann's fingers. 'They heeded you, and came,' Nerida murmured, yet there was no joy or triumph in her voice.

'I only hope they listen,' Rhiann managed, studying her.

Nerida met her gaze directly, though her eyes remained veiled. 'Your message told us of the siege, and the baby, and the manner of his survival. It was well done indeed.' Nerida's hands closed over Rhiann's, squeezing them tight, and for the first time she smiled. 'We sent you our blessings, Setana and I, for we were so proud of our daughter, and the courage and love you showed.' Her eyes searched Rhiann's face as if she looked into her heart. 'You are indeed the bright light we always thought you – a light to pierce the darkness.'

A strange, confused sadness took Rhiann's breath, the knowledge of how she had really failed to find that light. Yet Nerida was already turning away, beckoning Rhiann into step behind her.

The sun-bathed hill was crowded with all the priestesses from the island, and all those who had come from elsewhere – four-score altogether. The white-robed novices formed an outer ring around the Stones, their sweet voices chanting a farewell to the reddening sun, and the young initiates with their blue cloaks clustered around Fola, eyeing Rhiann with excitement, whispering behind their hands.

The forty or so elders, by contrast, held a place of calmness in the very air around them, each standing as still and centred as if they were tall trees rooted in the Source that ran beneath the Stones. The lives of those who lived in retreat, like Linnet, were written in the seams on their faces, and in their willowy frames, which spoke of sparse food and long days spent in prayer. Nor could the Ban Crés be mistaken, for though they all wore the same cloaks, the dresses underneath were of a finer weave and torcs gleamed at their necks. Their hair was dressed in a variety of elaborate styles, despite the fact that most were greying, and they held their heads with pride, their eyes glittering with a shrewdness that was not unkind. After all, even if their kings had as yet not joined Eremon, the Sisterhood warded the land itself, and in the end that loyalty would outweigh all others. Or so Rhiann fervently hoped, her hands clasped behind her to stop their shaking.

Nerida did no more than explain who Rhiann was and why she had called them here, and that they would hear from her in detail before the

Beltaine rite, a week hence. It was then that they would call on the Source to give them guidance, and decide what could be best done to serve Alba.

Rhiann stood silent beneath the Sisters' intense scrutiny, her cheeks warmed by the sinking sun, her eyes half-shuttered to its flaming heart. Yet inside the trembling ran in waves up and down her spine. It did not come from nerves, though, she realized with a shock, nor from fear that the Sisters would not listen, for among them she sensed a deep undercurrent of openness, wary as it was.

What plucked at Rhiann's awareness instead, with a sharp urgency, was the look Setana and Nerida exchanged when Nerida stopped speaking. In that look, something had been shared. Yet Rhiann missed the swift flash of it, and felt only the echo of its pang.

The great oaken gates of the Dun of the Waves were a stirring sight.

They were the height of three men, wide enough for four chariots abreast, and flanked by two sturdy gatetowers. The stakes along the top were capped with gold, and the rivets were of gilded iron. Above the gate soared twin masts that bore the blue and gold eagle banners streaming out in the sea-wind.

Yet as he stood on the walkway above the gates, Eremon remained insensible to the intricacies of the twisting ditch and bank defences, and the grandeur of the dun's position on a spur of land between river and sea. He didn't even take in the first warm sun that had graced his face for the entire damp, cold, muddy journey up the Great Glen. Instead, his eyes were fixed on the wide meadow that spread out below the dun, and before he could stifle it, a loud whistle shot through his clamped teeth.

Calgacus was not a king to stand on ceremony unless it was necessary for show, and now he grinned, his web of wrinkles melting for a moment into the expression of any excited young warrior. 'I take it then, prince, that you are impressed at our numbers.'

Eremon could only nod, his eyes devouring the rank upon rank of fighters arrayed below for his inspection. There were 500 of Calgacus's best warriors, 200 from the young Taexali King Garnat and 200 from the Vacomagi. In addition, another 100 clustered untidily beneath a banner he didn't recognize, though he felt sure he'd seen it at Calgacus's last council. Besides the ranks of spear and swordsmen, there were the 200 Caereni archers attached to Eremon's warband of 400, their hide clothes and braids and quivers all beaded with shell and horn, and another 100 Epidii bowmen that the Caereni had trained.

'So many,' was all Eremon could force out. And yet behind the surge of excitement came the sobering thought that it was still only a fraction of the Roman forces.

Beside him, Lorn gripped the edge of the battlements. 'By the Mare, it is the biggest warband I have ever seen.'

Calgacus glanced at the Epidii king. 'An army, I think the Romans call it. But using it as such isn't what the Erin prince has in mind, I believe.'

Eremon shook sense into himself, tipping his helmet back on his forehead. He had ridden with it on all the way, for the men responded well to it as a badge of his office. Yet he had barely dismounted at the gate before Calgacus, shouting at his captains to get the men into some order, had dragged him up the stairs to see what had been assembled. Now he fought to clear his throat. 'No,' he said, his voice lowering to normal levels. 'Agricola can draw men from all Britannia, assembling an army perhaps twenty thousand strong. We will never face him in open battle with any less than that number.'

'Then we must keep pushing for that alliance, prince.' Calgacus spread his hands. 'I have not been idle, though. Over the long dark, as you see, I convinced the Decantae to send us some men. It is a start.' He indicated the men under the unfamiliar banner.

Conaire spoke up now, his fair brows drawn together. 'But where in Hawen's name will we get an army of twenty thousand warriors?'

Calgacus smiled. 'Our land may seem impenetrable to you, my Erin friend, with hidden glens and narrow coves and high ridges a plenty. But those glens and coves all contain men. If something could bring them together, Alba could rouse at least twenty thousand, perhaps thirty thousand.'

Conaire grunted, but seemed content with that.

'This may not be an army like Agricola's,' Eremon said slowly, 'but it is seventeen hundred men nevertheless – more than we have ever gathered. Enough men to attack the Roman frontier with some force.'

'So what will it be then, prince?' Calgacus's smile was grimmer now, and his eyes were those of a king again, measuring. 'Roman forts? Watchtowers? Supply lines? Camps? These are all the terms I have had to learn from you, since first we met.'

Eremon shook his head, still reeling. Then he turned and clapped the Caledonii king on his broad shoulder. 'I am sorry such knowledge comes along with my counsel. But if you wet my throat with some of that heather ale of yours, between the information of my scouts and yours, we can pick our targets this very night.'

The first two days of Rhiann's visit were taken up with a council of elders, exchanging news from the tribes. When Rhiann was not sharing her own she listened carefully, but most of what was spoken she already knew.

The kings were too wary of Calgacus's power to join his alliance with

Eremon, for they viewed it as a move of his to subdue them. The Alban tribes had never banded together – their enemies had always been each other – and they felt secure behind their grim mountains and in their hidden glens.

For the first time, Rhiann tasted Eremon's exquisite frustration when faced with this ignorance. When she spoke of what she had experienced, she knew the Ban Crés believed her, but no one who had not faced Roman soldiers down, as Rhiann had done, or seen the aftermath of their destruction, could truly understand. It was too large a concept to grasp, that the Romans did not spare women and children, as Alban warriors did, that they did not adhere to careful codes of fighting conduct and honour.

Yet Rhiann forced herself to speak up around the evening fires, painting pictures with her words. And as she did she sensed the minds of those elders hovering around her own, seeking to absorb what she drew for them.

So they would listen and consider, and on Beltaine eve, decide what could be done, and if they would do it.

In between the councils, Rhiann helped prepare the dyes and herbs, spent time with Fola, and didn't for one moment think of returning to the beach below the village where her foster-family had been slain.

Yet after a week, the call came for a healer to attend the village chieftain, Brethan, and Rhiann decided to gain a respite from the heavy words and long silences of the priestess gatherings. She knew Brethan from her visit last Beltaine, and thought it might be wise to keep the young chief informed of Eremon's plans. And perhaps there was more to it; perhaps she needed to see if she could face that place again.

Brethan had lately fallen from his horse, and though the lower arm bone had set, the skin wound was still painful, and not healing well. Sitting in the sun outside the chieftain's stone tower, Rhiann had lanced the infection with a bone needle and packed it with honey and yarrow leaves. Didius perched on the low wall facing the sea, polishing his sword blade and whistling under his breath.

'You can tell your man that the sea lanes have been quiet,' Brethan muttered through gritted teeth, as Rhiann began to bind the arm.

Rhiann's face, however, remained averted as she finished her task, for the beach was out of sight down a tiny glen to the north. Her family had fallen there on a clear day just like this, when the gulls cried and wheeled overhead.

'And yet,' she murmured, clearing her throat, 'I assume you guard the sea approaches, nevertheless . . . ?' If she glanced over her shoulder and the low wall on which Didius sat, she would be able to glimpse the little bay that sliced into the hills further north, where the lapping waves had run red.

Brethan gasped at a shooting pain, his forehead sheened with sweat. 'The raiders who killed your family were from Erin: everyone knows that.' He tried to smile at her, the fingers of one hand clenched in his sealskin cape. 'We watch the south and west as well as we can, lady, but it was only bad chance the Erin ships were so far north, and it has never happened before or since.'

Rhiann opened her mouth to argue, and then wearily shut it again. It was true such a raid had never happened before, and this place was Brethan's to rule, not hers. Yet from Erin, truly? She did not know. A servant came outside with horn cups of heather ale, distracting Brethan, and as Rhiann politely refused hers she found her eyes roaming over the hill behind the broch, patched with bright green moss and dark heather, the protruding rocks still glistening from recent rains. She remembered that brown, peaty water, for it had stained her hands and face when the men threw her down. She swallowed hard and looked at her fingers, green now with herb residues, and suddenly nodded to herself, coming to a decision. Slowly she rose, packed her medicines and took her leave of Brethan.

Courageous, Nerida had called her. *Well*, she thought, slinging her pack over her shoulder and striding down the glen with brittle defiance, Didius following behind, *we will see*.

Soon the beach shingle was crunching beneath her boots, which she had laced high to keep her feet dry on the journey over the hills. At first she focused hard on that sound – the faint squeak of coarse sand at each step, the jingle of buried shells. Then she heard Didius pause halfway along the little crescent of tidal sand, sensing that she needed to be alone, and she ploughed on to the end of the strand, her head down.

When she stopped on the edge of the waves, Rhiann realized that she was trembling, despite the warmth on her hair, and the high, clean cries of the gulls. So she closed her eyes and raised her face to the sun, summoning instead the feel of Eremon's arms around her, for that was truly the last memory of this beach. Here, he said he would keep all dark things at bay, and she had replied that she must also deal with it herself.

'Lady.' The whisper was tentative, close behind, and she opened her eyes and turned to see Didius shuffling from one foot to the other, peering up from under his helmet as if feared she would be angry. 'Are you cold? You can have my cloak.'

A smile curved Rhiann's stiff cheeks. 'No, not cold. Just sad.' She turned back to the bay, its waves glittering in a ripple of wind. 'Is it not strange, Didius, that though we say our enemy is Rome, the truth is that we are our own greatest enemies – Alba, Erin, Britannia. Warlike, your people call us, and it is true.' She sighed.

There was a long silence. Then Didius said, 'Warlike you may be, lady, but that is not what I will remember.' She saw him gaze out to sea.

'For the Albans have many riches beyond their swords. Beauty and music and tales to break your heart . . . Many treasures, this land has birthed.' He broke off abruptly, a flush creeping up his neck. 'That is what I will tell my people, if I ever go home,' he finished.

And suddenly, the knowledge came to Rhiann, like the taint of smoke on the air, that Didius would not see his homeland again.

Her eyes blurring, she made a warding movement with her hand, pushing the spirit sense away. Many things might prevent Didius from leaving Alba – perhaps the great battle she had once glimpsed in his future, between her people and Rome. Or perhaps, Rhiann suddenly and resolutely decided to believe, that when this was all over Didius would choose to stay, for the sake of the tales he loved so much.

'Come, my friend,' she murmured, turning her back firmly on the glittering bay. Here, Eremon had clasped her to his heart, and from now on it would be his smile she summoned when the scent of the sea-pinks on the cliffs drifted to her in dreams. She would make it so.

It was as the strip of sand fell out of sight behind the headland, that Rhiann suddenly knew she need never come here again.

Chapter 33

Samana returned to the north on horseback, after a dreadful trip by sea from Eboracum and a frustrating moon lingering in her own dun, waiting for Agricola. Now he too had returned and, on the way back to the main camp, they were staying overnight in the small port on the Forth inlet.

Samana had taken Agricola's summons back to his side as a good omen – that he was pleased with her information – and the subsequent return of his desire had offered final proof of this. Or perhaps it was just that he had worked his anger at last year's defeat out on her body now, and was feeling flushed with renewed anticipation of a better season.

This morning was fine, though cool, and Samana yawned and stretched with pleasure, for her tiredness and the ache between her thighs, were both products of Agricola's renewed attentions. The tiny crescent of muddy bank on which she squatted was screened from the soldiers' tents by a fringe of alders and scrubby willows, their buds still unfurling, the hairy willow catkins providing some shelter from prying eyes. Now she bent to rinse the sodden undergarment in the shallow water on the edge of the estuary, steeling herself against the icy bite of the water.

She could no doubt have ordered a slave to clean her underclothes, or done it herself inside, but her moon courses had come unexpectedly, and she was wary of Agricola's anger at too much female intrusion into military life. Of course, she was still pleased that the herb brew and dried moss continued to prevent a baby.

Now she slapped the cloth on a stone, wrinkling her nose. The sheets were one hard job she *would* leave to that insolent body slave of his, though. Agricola had been up so early since they arrived, dictating a flood of letters to be carried by the ships at anchor in the bay, that she knew he hadn't noticed such trifling matters as sheets.

In fact, he'd been so excited by his plans that he had for once told her about them unguardedly. He was asking his son-in-law Tacitus to speak for him in Rome, to contain the damage to Agricola's reputation that the Novantae disaster had wrought, and to beseech the Emperor Domitian to return the men he had taken to fight on the German frontier.

Samana still marvelled that though Agricola was all-powerful in Britannia and Alba, ridiculously, he must also dance to the tune of another man far away in Rome; a man known to be capricious and lacking in the foresight of his dead elder brother and father, whom Agricola had loved well.

Agricola did not trust Domitian, and although the commander had always been a ruthless man of little emotion, Samana was beginning to glimpse the real toll of this constant worry over the emperor's motives, which gnawed at Agricola ceaselessly. And this is what they meant by the glories of Empire! Privately, Samana thought little of an empire where a local king could not do what he wanted to do. Where was the power in that?

She wrung out her shift and laid it next to the cloth strips for her moon bleeding. Then, rolling up the damp bundle, she set off back along the shore. As she rounded a wooded point, the cold sea breeze hit her, and she looked up and came to an abrupt halt, the balls of her feet sinking into the muddy shore. Samana narrowed her eyes, counting.

She was sure that two of the sleek-prowed Roman warships anchored in the estuary had disappeared since yesterday. She counted again, but there were only thirteen, lying there meekly as if asleep, their long oars shipped, their sails folded, their decks all but deserted. From the taut anchor ropes, streamers of dark weed flapped in the sea-wind, and the timbers creaked as they drifted a little in the current.

For a moment, Samana's heart pounded crazily. Agricola would not weaken his numbers for the new campaign season by sending men back south, and in any case, all the southern peoples had fallen quiet. Even the Novantae remained hidden, after the Romans, in what seemed to her a fit of pique, sealed them off behind their hills with forts and all but forgot them. So the missing ships must have sailed north.

And he didn't consult with me exactly where or when to go, she realized, her mouth drying.

Fear crawled up her spine, echoing the damp of the clothes pressed to her chest. Agricola had often hinted at his other sources of information, sources he would not reveal to her. Perhaps this was where the ships had gone.

Samana strode for the end of the path, ignoring the soldiers, carters and natives who leered at her. Whomever Agricola had won over in the north mattered little to her. That person didn't share Agricola's bed, and thereby a large part of his thoughts, or know the secret places of the body that made him cry out to all his gods.

No one else could do these things to him but her. And she would make sure it stayed that way.

The boar tusk held loosely in Eremon's hands gradually turned from moonlit white to dawn grey, along with the sky above the narrow glen.

Here in the centre of eastern Alba, another Roman frontier crossed the wide peninsula between the Tay and Forth rivers. The frontier consisted of a chain of forts on a low ridge overlooking the Earn plain, yet the links were not yet complete, the chain still weak at many points and the defences untested.

Hawen, my lord, Eremon prayed silently now. *Give me the strength of the boar this day.* Without opening his eyes, he drew in a breath. Dawn was his favourite time, and he was never so confident to forget it might be his last. The faint breeze carried the smells of damp moss, rich, turned earth and the metallic tang of rock from the hills above. There was no smoke, for the Roman fort sat at the end of the glen, and Eremon had allowed no fires. There was only the smell of the earth and its growth – the scent of life.

Crouched next to Eremon in the lee of a fern-covered rock, Conaire blew on his hands and flexed them. 'Do you think our friend Lorn can count the days?' he grumbled. 'He might have attacked yesterday, and got the Romans signalling up and down this entire ridge.'

Ignoring the steady rumble of nerves in his belly, Eremon tied the thong of the tusk around his neck, where it sat against the carved boar stone and Rhiann's stag amulet. Conaire wore the twin of the tusk around his own arm, won in the boar hunt that gave him his scar. Eremon normally wore the tusk and the amulet around his upper arms, but not today. Today those muscles would flex and bunch with every sword thrust, and he did not wish to break the thongs.

After knotting the leather, Eremon took up his sword from where it lay at his feet. 'Lorn has followed our plan without complaint,' he remarked mildly, and when Conaire snorted, Eremon smiled. '*Almost* without complaint.'

Conaire rose to his feet now, taking care to stay in the shadow of the rock. Eremon heard the faint jingle of his sword-chain as he belted on his blade, and then Eremon joined him, his back against the rough, cold surface as he inched his own belt around his waist.

Around them, the stealthy movements of their men came as a faint rustling in the carpet of thick bracken. The raiding party had sensed their rising, and all were watching for sunrise.

'Perhaps Lorn is quiet under your beady eye, brother,' Conaire continued, adjusting the straps of his mailshirt, 'but why you gave a third of our men over to him, and sent him off out of sight days ago, I'll never know!'

Eremon tightened the buckle holding his scabbard. 'Formation fighting is not his strength, but raids like this are close to Lorn's heart. And he's good – it surely isn't impossible for you to admit that.'

Yet Conaire only snorted again, settling his war helmet on his head. His relationship with Lorn was still strained, though both treated each other with a wary acceptance, for the sake of peace.

The end of the glen opened directly to the east, and the horizon was fast lighting up with flame now, the feathered clouds flinging great gouts of scarlet across the silver bowl of sky. Just to the south, high on a farther ridge, the angry glow drew in the outlines of the small Roman fort, crowning the low rise. The dark scar of its encircling ditch was topped by a tall row of timber stakes, and from behind this palisade a trumpet call floated high in the clear, chilled air. It didn't seem to have the urgency of an alarm, or so Eremon hoped.

His men had managed to crawl into position over five nights, lying low in the day and then creeping through the undergrowth in the dark, using the hidden paths that could bring them right to the Roman frontier undetected by scouting parties. Now the still air beneath the bracken was reeking with urine and sweat and churned mud, but it couldn't smell any sweeter to Eremon. *I have done this before*, he reminded his churning belly, bending to lace his boots more securely over his knees. One fort attack; one fort imprisonment. He should know better than anyone else what they faced.

Metal scraped across a rock high above them, and Eremon whirled to face the mouth of the sheep trail that wound down into the glen from the hill peaks. One hand reached for the cold, wet rock, to propel him forward, the other went to his sword hilt.

'My lord,' came a murmur in his own dialect.

Eremon forced himself to relax, though his heart was now thudding so loud he could hardly hear. 'Rori.'

Rori was breathless, his thin shoulders heaving as he swiped at his sweaty lip with his sleeve. 'I have seen the fire arrows, my lord, to the south, and to the north along this ridge. The other two forts are now alight.'

A jolt of excitement shot up Eremon's spine, and instantly every muscle was tense, poised for action. 'I suppose that Lorn and Calgacus can both count,' he remarked to Conaire, drawing his sword and, heedless now of the need to be silent, leaping up the few steps to the top of the outcrop.

There, his boar-crest helmet was outlined against the lightening sky, as a signal for his archers. In a moment a scattering of tiny flames sprang up further down the glen, and he raised his sword as the warriors near him shook themselves free of the leaves and the ferns, unsheathing blades, hefting spears. The rustling and murmuring grew louder, spreading up the glen as swiftly as fire up a heather slope. This was Eremon's power and his role – men waiting to kill at his signal.

He paused to summon Rhiann's image to his mind, his fingers pressing the stag amulet to the hollow of his throat. And as he slashed his sword down and the sky burst into a flaming rain of fire arrows, he sent another prayer to his gods: *Bring us soon to peace, so I am never sundered from her again.*

Leaf-bud was the time for herbs, so after another long day of collecting, sorting and drying, Rhiann should not have been surprised to find herself dreaming that night about plants.

In this dream she was holding up the tiny, clustered blooms of a plant whose name, in the usual dream-way, kept slipping from her mind. Arrayed around her were a crescent of girls, the novices and young initiates, their eyes fixed on her, as she described the plant's properties.

She hardly registered shock at first, when something appeared in the distance beyond the girls' heads, even though it made Rhiann's speech falter. Then, suddenly, she found she was trying to scream, but no sound was coming out. And she was tossing and writhing and trying to move, but she could not, and the white petals were crushed, and fell to the ground . . .

Peace. A calm voice flowed into Rhiann's dreaming mind, soothing and cradling, and abruptly the panic began to recede. After a moment, only a dark mist remained. *It is not now . . . not now . . .* Each word fell down through the darkness like notes on a harp, soothing her, and soft fingers brushed her hair back, trailing down her cheeks, melting the frightened tears. Her heart was still racing, but something was penetrating her mind; the knowledge it was only a dream. Rhiann began to struggle upwards to full consciousness. *Hush, daughter.*

Now there was a light, a soft sheen of moonlight seen through half-closed lashes. Yet still Rhiann could not open her eyes, and all her limbs felt heavy, the edges indistinct, as if she only barely held on to her body. A wisp of conscious thought floated past, that she had taken no *saor*, or indeed any draught of herbs, so what was wrong with her? The feeling was like *saor* and yet not like it, and now she tasted, with a faint awareness, a bitterness on her tongue.

Other voices were calling Rhiann now: fey, silver voices she knew from the times she had left her body before. It was the Otherworld spirits calling her to join them, stretching out their shining fingers to draw her away from her body for ever. The candle of her soul flickered, yearning to go. It stretched out its flame . . .

No, Rhiann. The musical voice forbade it, and the fingers on her brow pressed into both temples. *Do not listen to them, listen only to me, to us. Hold to your body, Rhiann.*

Her name. The word called her back, and she let it, gradually realizing that though she could not open her eyes or move her limbs, she could feel a definite sensation of ground under her buttocks, the pressure of one shin on another as she sat with crossed legs. Her arms were out, resting on her knees, her palms turned upwards. A cool drop of water fell into one hand now, and a warm stone was pressed into the other. And she sensed the faint shuffle of feet tracing a spiral dance around her.

Why am I here?

Two voices answered, one low, one high. *Because we called you.*

Why?

You must become One, when there is no longer Many. An empty ship on the waves you must be; a mare with her saddle; a cup to hold all. We must fill you.

Rhiann's brain rolled slowly over, grasping for sense, and finding nothing. She struggled to open her eyes again, but those trailing fingers came down on her eyelids, pressing them closed. *Feel. You do not need to see.*

The singing began then, one voice, rising and falling in a primal, wordless tune; an old woman's voice . . . no, an ancient voice . . . and though no music accompanied it, its deeper ranges suggested the boom of a drum.

Earth. The thought dropped into Rhiann's mind and, as if the word opened some doorway within her, in flooded a host of images: dark caves in the ground; walls carved with spirals; bones of rock rising from green turf. She saw her open hands, the crushed white blooms on her palm, and then all around her, stalks were suddenly bursting up through the soil, seedlings of every kind of plant and root and tree, their names and natures a whispering tide in her mind.

Rhiann gasped, and a great breath rushed in, filling her to overflowing as the plants all around her unfurled. She struggled not to drown in that tide, and when she could breathe through it, she realized that a second voice had taken over from the first. It rose and fell in cool ripples of sound, and Rhiann felt rain on her face, running over her tongue. *Water,* came the thought, and a wind brought her the salt of the sea, streams fell down from high mountains above, and a woman dropped an offering into a sacred pool, as tears fell from her eyes. The grief of this pierced Rhiann so sharply she cried out and, as she opened her mouth, the second great breath rushed in. She felt herself swell with ideas and thoughts and snatches of words that swirled by so quickly she could grasp none.

The first voice returned now, leaving the low drumming chant behind to soar in flares of sound that leaped and danced. *Fire.*

And Rhiann saw burning rock flowing over the ground like a river, and pools bubbling up as steam. Lightning struck a lone tree, and it burst into a crown of flame. And in the centre of a dark forest, people danced around a glowing firepit, which kept the wild things at bay. Rhiann's third breath pushed inwards of its own accord, searing her nostrils and lungs. It roared like a burning wind, and when at last it eased, the heat rose in a column in her body, bearing on its warm drafts a sparkling multitude of feelings and bright images.

Her attention was claimed then by the return of the second voice. It had changed again; no longer cool and rippling but hoarse and reedy, like wind in a sea-cave. *Air.* Rhiann saw clouds racing across a bright moon, and there were ice winds screaming over a high moor, before they sank down into the warm gusts that bring leaves to bare trees. Then Rhiann saw an image of a babe, its first breath flooding its tiny chest, and Rhiann breathed with it, and the entire tide of knowledge that had rushed in with earth and water and fire gathered itself and crashed over her as a wave, human faces and feelings and memories all tumbling by so fast that she could catch none of them, name none of them, own none of them.

Rhiann's body was drowning, and she was crushed backwards on the earth, clutching the warm stone to her as an anchor. Dizzy, she clung on and on, until at last the wave receded, leaving only wisps of sense and thought cast up on the shores of her mind.

So Rhiann lay, gasping with her own breath now, and the two voices came as one again. *It is well. The One Who Carries has been filled. The ship has its burden, the mare her rider, the cup its draught.*

She slept.

It was far into the day when Rhiann surfaced slowly from sleep, the scrape of Didius's knife on wood and his soft whistling the only sounds in the otherwise empty hut. Blinking to clear her eyes, Rhiann rolled slowly onto her side, noticing a strange tightness in her muscles.

She recalled little of the night before, beyond the strange dreams that had troubled her. A sudden yawn split her face, and she covered her mouth with one hand. Her spirit must have travelled far indeed in her dreams to mimic the fatigue and lethargy of *saor*. It happened sometimes, that the spirit flew such great distances it was slow to return to the confines of the body.

Abruptly, Rhiann blinked again, her gaze sliding down her outflung arm to her hand, which she suddenly realized was clutching something. Hardly daring to breathe, she slowly uncurled her fingers. Lying there was a small, white stone, warm from the heat of her palm.

Chapter 34

Conaire coughed as an acrid belch of smoke from the burning fort gate billowed over him. His sword out and balanced in his grip, he blinked his streaming eyes and peered through the swirls of ash and cinders.

He had just completed his circuit of the fort walls, fighting his way around the narrow walkway that ran inside the timber battlements. Now he was back on top of the gatetower, swiftly realizing that he must abandon it before the fire streaming away above his head claimed him, too. He kicked his way through a tangle of Roman soldiers, their bodies flaccid and heavy in death. Then, sheathing his sword, Conaire threw himself over the side of the gate platform, holding on by his hands for a moment before dropping to his feet before Eremon.

His foster-brother had tugged off his boar helmet and was wiping all the soot and blood from his face through his damp hair, in an effort to stop it running into his eyes.

'Fine cut there,' Conaire remarked breathlessly, squinting at the shallow slash under Eremon's right eye.

Eremon shrugged. 'Doesn't need binding.'

'Rhiann will have another scar to admire, then.'

Eremon's exhausted grin was lost in a cough. 'She is not a woman to admire scars.' He gestured sharply at Rori, Colum and Fergus, who were raiding the Roman bodies inside the gate for weapons, to be offered to the pools around Dunadd.

Conaire glanced at the bodies piled in the gateway, including those which had fallen from the battlements above, and others who had been cut down as they ran from the burning barracks. Swaying arrow-shafts sprouted from eyes, mouths, groins, and the soft places between the segmented armour plates. The long sword rents in guts and flanks were obscured by blood and trampled mud, but where throats were thrown back in death, the gaping wounds lay open to the sky. 'She may not love killing, but even she would admire the work of this day, brother.'

Eremon shrugged again, his mouth tight as he scanned their handiwork. 'How many dead?'

'Nearly two hundred – and eighty of our own.'

'And how many Roman survivors?'

'Twenty-three.'

Eremon leaned down to pull a spear free of one of the bodies, then turned it over in his bloodied hands. 'Call our men together, and line the prisoners up here. I want them kneeling.' His eyes blazed for a moment into Conaire's. 'We will execute them, one by one, except for he who will carry this tale to Agricola.'

'Execute them?' His chest heaving, Conaire swirled saliva and ash on his tongue before spitting it out.

'That's what I said,' Eremon muttered, gazing at the bodies.

Conaire looked down at his own huge hands: dirt-grimed, callused, the nails broken and crusted with drying blood. These hands had stroked his wife's back as she tried not to cry into his shoulder. These hands had cradled his babe, his son, as gently as an egg in a nest. They were honourable hands, and killing men in cold blood was not their purpose. His belly burned sick with it, as he had not felt sick at anything else on this gut-churning day. Conaire fixed his gaze on the scorched, splintered gate. 'We are not like them, brother. We must stay true.'

'And leave more of them to slaughter our women and babes?' Eremon snapped.

Glancing up, Conaire caught a flash of the same guilt in his brother's face. Slowly, he let his breath out, as all the tales of the invaders tumbled through his mind: stories of Roman pillage, rapine and slaughter that had been visited on the southern duns. And he'd seen with his own eyes what they had done to the people of Crinan when they burned it. These men would take his baby son and dash his brains out on the walls of Dunadd.

Conaire's hands clenched slowly into fists, as the churning sickness drained away. Raising his head, he met Eremon's eyes, and saw that his brother's guilt had been pierced now by a cold determination, a ruthlessness, that Conaire also must find in himself.

'Then we will do it, my brother,' he said.

Agricola strode up the timber pier beside the Forth, still glowing with satisfaction from his flying visit to the camps on the Tay estuary. His heart had swelled upon seeing for himself how well the rich territory – formerly Venicones land – had already been turned over so completely into a storehouse for Roman supplies.

In the valleys, the pines, elms and oaks were falling under Roman axes, the timber to be carried along the new frontier for the construction of watchtowers and fortlets. The grain was already shooting up in the fields, the cattle were being readied for summer pasture, and virtually all of this fine food would be going straight into Roman bellies. It was as if the whole peninsula between Tay and Forth was one great larder for his men. Surrounded by sea on three sides, the area was easy to defend and well protected by his line of forts on the fourth side. It was a fine foothold for his northern conquest, as he always knew it would be.

Agricola smiled to himself now as he left his ship behind, drawing in a great lungful of sea air. His swift, energetic steps soon outdistanced his tribunes, and he was alone when he reached his horse, held by a cavalry officer at the end of the pier.

Agricola's grin was a rare sight to his men, and the soldier holding the horse was still recovering from it even as his commander mounted the block and began to lever himself into the saddle. Yet Agricola only had one leg over his stallion's back when he saw another horseman come flying into the outskirts of the port camp. As the soldier on it galloped recklessly down the main path through the tents, heedless of the scattering men, Agricola's smile froze.

The approaching horse was as wet as if it had swum a river, but the lather around its jaws and flanks left Agricola in no doubt that it was sweat that streaked its coat. It had been ridden hard, and fast. He swung back to the ground and held his own bridle, murmuring to calm his shying mount as the other horse thundered up.

And Agricola knew then, looking up into the messenger's face, that he had left the Tay too soon. The snatch of sixth sense curdled in his belly before it became coherent in his mind.

'Sir . . . an uprising . . . on the northern frontier,' the soldier gasped out, his chest heaving, his face dripping with sweat. 'Three forts were destroyed; four watchtowers. They also crossed the Gask line and took one supply train. Everything is gone, sir: the cattle, the grain, the mules, the armour.' He gulped again, nearly gagging, for he was only young, and there was blood and ash on his face and streaking his armour. 'Some left only naked bodies, sir. Naked bodies without . . . who weren't men any more, sir.'

Agricola said nothing, and for three heartbeats did not move. 'Survivors?'

'Yes, sir, there are three, one from each fort. They are coming behind me, sir. Two days behind.'

'Three survivors,' Agricola repeated softly.

Three, from 600 men.

And Agricola realized, in the midst of the red rage that blossomed behind his eyes, that the savages had taken a third again of the number that the emperor had already recalled from him to Rome. The shreds of his dispassionate mind turned over the certainty that the chances of those soldiers being returned were diminishing by the day, in direct proportion to these numbers falling to Alban arrows.

He'd thought he was the only one with a surprise brewing, but it seemed he had been wrong.

Chapter 35

Rhiann wound each end of her vervain wreath together, and stood back to see if the hawthorn base would grip the surface of the Stone securely. The other Stones were already dressed with their wreaths, one from each Ban Cré, but it was the last evening before Beltaine, and Rhiann had waited until she could be alone to add hers. Tomorrow morning, the chanters would claim the circle, to begin drawing the Source up from the land with their singing.

Just as she had when a child, Rhiann now walked with her hands outstretched, first one and then the other catching on the glittering surface of the Stones as she wheeled and turned, her steps those of the spiral dance. Dusk was fast fading into twilight, and the sweep of gilded loch and dark rocks and glowing bracken hills spun as she turned, like a jewelled cloth of many colours. The air was sharp with salt and seaweed, softened by the peat smoke which drifted up from the houses below.

Sometimes, when Rhiann danced these steps as a child, images had come of lives she'd lived before. Once she found herself singing a song older even than those remembered by the Sisters, and glimpsed herself walking down the avenue of Stones with a collar of jet heavy across her breast. Then, the Stones had been new, and she had woven words of magic into their roots as the holes were dug, and ropes creaked over timber sleds. Sometimes she had even caught glimpses of the ages before the Stones were raised, when she crouched with a deerskin fringe about her feet, cracking open mussels still hot from the coals. And even further back, when all she could remember was wind that cut her lungs with shards of ice, and the crunch of boots on endless snow.

Spinning to a breathless halt, Rhiann gazed out across the sea-loch. It was the time of day when the water and sky merged into one pool of liquid gold, and though the rim of the sun had already gone, there seemed to be so much more light in the sky, light diffusing from all directions, reflecting back as if inside a shell. The wind had dropped and all was silent, even the gulls.

'It is very fine, is it not?'

Rhiann turned to see Nerida and Setana on the edge of the ridge, standing arm in arm. The dying light was in their faces, blurring their wrinkles so for a moment they appeared to her not old at all.

The dream of three nights ago had faded from Rhiann's mind, becoming only a vague snatch of memory. And though she wondered if Nerida and Setana would be able to shed any light on her sore muscles and that white stone, something stopped her tongue. She had learned here that some mysteries were best left alone. Perhaps they'd sought to bless her, and give her strength for the rite – or perhaps she really had dreamed it.

'You have grown this past year, daughter,' Setana said abruptly, her bright eyes turned to Rhiann. 'Did you listen to us after all?'

'Listen?'

Nerida seemed to be breathing harder than normal, and as she turned from regarding the view, the corners of her mouth twisted with something Rhiann could not name. 'We said to you,' she murmured, 'that we must show women how the Goddess lives in them, by sharing all their joys, their pains, their birth pangs.'

'And you have shared such things, have you not?' Setana asked softly.

Rhiann heard in her mind an echo of Caitlin's screams, and Gabran's triumphant wail. 'Yes,' she whispered.

Nerida's bony hand tightened on her staff. 'What else did we say, child?'

Rhiann fixed her eyes on the ripples of the loch's surface, yet her memory had been trained here along with her heart. 'That I had to surrender to love, that it would root me in the land.' Her fingers fluttered unconsciously across her flat belly, as she tasted the bitterness of her secret brew on her tongue.

'And have you surrendered, daughter?' Nerida's voice wavered.

Rhiann dropped her hand, turning to face them. 'No,' she admitted. 'Not with everything that is in me, Goddess forgive me.'

She held her breath, yet Nerida's blue eyes were only sorrowed. 'It is yourself you must forgive,' she sighed. 'Yet the question only becomes more urgent each time, until you heed it.'

'So it does,' Setana agreed, looking at Nerida.

Abruptly, cold fear washed over Rhiann, sweeping away all the strange, blurred sensations. And she was just herself, in her own time, and chill was beginning to creep up from the ground as the light faded. 'May I ask you, my sisters, what weighs so heavy on your hearts?'

Setana's gaze shifted to Rhiann. 'Yes, you can ask. But we cannot answer, child. We have our own path to walk.'

'A path . . . away from me?'

Nerida shook her white head. 'No, never away, never lost. Have you not trod the ice path with us? Have you not looked upon the Stones on their first day, as we stood beside you? Have you not run with the deer, as we ran with you?'

Rhiann's throat closed over, and she nodded.

'She was always stubborn,' Setana remarked to Nerida, her eyes warm. 'Though she usually listened in the end.'

'Stubborn I may be,' Rhiann said slowly, her voice hoarse with unshed tears. 'Yet it seems you were often pleased with demonstrations of my will, even as you scolded me.'

'Pleased!' Nerida's staff swept out, pointing. 'Remember that bramble bush just down there? You nearly broke an ankle scampering after that hare, and then tore your hands and new cloak to pieces rather than give up the chase!'

'Its leg was hurt; I wanted to save it,' Rhiann protested. Yet her smile was no longer so forced.

'Come!' The staff thumped once into the ground. 'There is enough light to go as far as the Golden Loch – perhaps the otters will be at play. We need such reminders of life, after the dark words shared this week.'

Troubled, Rhiann let herself be drawn down the slope in their wake, guarding their slow steps from behind, silent as they exclaimed over the view and the scent of the soft air. She did not wish to darken its beauty with her questions.

'Rhiann!' Fola was shaking her. 'Rhiann, wake up!'

Sleep lay as heavy as lead in Rhiann's limbs. She couldn't understand why she was slumbering so deeply, and finding it hard to wake. She propped herself up on one elbow, but could see from the grey light seeping in under the door-hide that it was still very early.

'I went to the waste pit,' Fola was saying, kneeling by Rhiann's pallet. 'And on the way back I passed Nerida's house. She told me that she wants you to take all the novices and young initiates out to gather may blossom today.'

'Today?' Rhiann covered a yawn with her hand.

'It's Beltaine, silly, or have you forgotten?'

That got Rhiann's attention. With a jolt she remembered just what would happen tonight, and how important it was for Eremon. And the nagging fear reawakened, that perhaps it wouldn't happen because of her. Rubbing her face, she struggled up. 'But we have not even spoken about the rite tonight. I cannot leave—'

'She said the rite will have greater power if you approach it with an open mind. And she also said she knew you would argue, but that the villagers have stripped the thorns nearby already, and the girls must go far into the hills for more, and she thought you could tell the ones who will be Ban Crés about politics and such, and the others about herbs.'

Rhiann frowned in the half-dark, then said, 'I must go to her.' She drew on the nearest dress, then, pulling on her cloak, tiptoed over the other girls wrapped in their blankets, and stepped out into the chill, wet dawn, ducking the dew drips coming off the eaves.

The sun was still below the horizon, but she could clearly hear the rumble of men's voices – the villagers from the broch were already hauling wood for the bonfires to be lit at dusk. They sang and called out to each other as they worked, trailing up and down between the horse-drawn sledges and the Stones.

As she hurried along, Rhiann sniffed the familiar salt and seaweed, turning her face to the lightening east, where the last stars speckled a sky as blue as a duck egg. Eremon was waking to the same sky, clear and unclouded. Perhaps he stared at it right now, thinking of her. A pang of longing almost burned her throat in its intensity, as did the fear he could have already been harmed. Rhiann had asked him to avoid battle until Beltaine, but she had no way of knowing if circumstances had allowed him to keep to his promise. Hopping over a puddle, she breathed through her nose, calming herself. Nothing would keep the knowledge of Eremon's death from her – the land would sense it, and bring the change to her on the wind, or through the soil. It hadn't come. The King Stag still lived.

And with the Mother's blessing he will be even stronger after this night, Rhiann told herself, forcing confidence down into her cold chest. The stags had come before, when all the priestesses held their energy together. And the same would happen tonight. It would not all rest on her abilities alone.

As she hurried past the glow of the bakeovens, Rhiann nodded at the priestesses stoking the fires and preparing the sacred moon cakes, and reached Nerida's door just as the sun broke over the hills. And there was Nerida herself watching it rise, wrapped in her cloak, her breath misting the air.

Swiftly, Rhiann gave her the priestess kiss. 'Surely you cannot mean me to leave here this day!' she burst out. 'If you do not wish to meet with me, I must understand, but at the least I should stay inside and fast and meditate—'

Nerida's tired smile stopped her, for in contrast to her own torrent of words, it spread over her face soft and slow. 'Daughter, do not make me order you. You are young, and there is still a girl in you, though you try to believe otherwise. Just for today, be a child in your heart. That will do more to prepare you for the rite than any meditation. There is more than one way to honour the Goddess, after all.'

Rhiann tried to argue with her, yet though the soft smile never wavered, Nerida's words were implacable. Rhiann must leave the other Ban Crés to decide on the rites, and take the girls to hunt for blossom.

'As you wish, Sister,' Rhiann said heavily at last, bowing her head. Unease burned in her chest, though she could not disobey the Eldest Sister. Yet as she turned to go, Nerida suddenly clasped her close in her fierce, bony arms.

'*Promise me*,' the old woman murmured, looking up into Rhiann's eyes, 'that one day you will judge yourself by what you do and say, and not by what you believe yourself to be.'

Rhiann gazed down at the old woman's lined face, still spare and elegant beneath the softening flesh. Despite Nerida's smile, something unsure had wavered there for a moment. 'I will try,' Rhiann answered, her hand clasping Nerida's, though the meaning of the words were obscured by the unreasoning fear that clutched at her. 'If soon you promise to take tea with me around your fire.'

Nerida's eyes flickered, and the mysterious world held there was again veiled. 'As we have done so many times, child, so will we do so again.'

Rhiann left the settlement behind a group of chattering young women and girls laden with empty willow baskets and food for the day. The initiates of Rhiann's own age were doing their best to be severe, led by Fola, whose own face could barely summon such gravity even when she tried.

Besides Rhiann strode Didius, fully armed despite the heat promised by the strengthening sun. His fine sword and dagger and helmet seemed to make him feel more secure in his self-appointed role of guard, but had no effect on the younger girls, who were now over their fright of him and had decorated his neck and wrists with a chain of sea-pinks.

As the girls streamed up the path into the nearest hills, Rhiann paused to glance back across the broad vale towards the Stones.

Among the chanters who sat within the circle, drawing the Source with their songs, other figures were now outlined against the sky: the elder priestesses, walking alone and in groups. Now the sun glowed bright on the white robes of one who detached herself from the rest and came to the edge of the ridge, looking across the vale at Rhiann. And as Rhiann raised her hand, so Setana raised hers. It was like the glimmer of a gull's wing against a storm cloud. *But there were no clouds.* The sky was clear, and that was why she was leaving them for the day.

'Rhiann,' Fola was at her elbow, '*please* tell us a story as we walk. These girls squawk incessantly, like ravenous chicks, and it will be a long day indeed if my headache begins before we even leave! Tell them about your adventures – they will love that.'

Rhiann turned her back on the Stones and raised her face to the sun, summoning a smile. 'Such stories may sound exciting, Sister, but I can assure you that in reality they are usually frightening, cold and uncomfortable.'

'Well, don't tell them that, or my head will never have peace!'

In the narrow glen along which they walked, all was in shadow, and a chill still rose from the boggy ground. But up ahead, the youngest girls had already clambered to the crest of the ridge, and the warm morning light spilled over their unbound hair and round, ruddy faces, fresh from scrubbing.

A day in the sun will cure me of my dark mood, Rhiann thought, quickening her step. *But later I will ask Nerida what ails her, and this time I will get my answer.*

Chapter 36

Though there was much to do after the sun salutations that day, Nerida indulged herself and remained with the elders in the circle, straightening her back against one of the outer Stones. She turned with closed eyes to face the north, and savoured the sensation of sun-warmth on her eyelids.

These Stones had witnessed many other mornings of her life: days of sun and wind and rain; visits by kings and princes asking for counsel; the rites of the Sisters. And it seemed to Nerida then that for one moment out of time she was given a glimpse of the spiral pattern of her life: coming from and returning to the Mother along the same path, a pattern too subtle and beautiful for a human body to fully grasp. Yet perhaps now, as her body grew ever more frail, the veil between Thisworld and the Otherworld was growing thinner to her spirit eyes.

The singing of the other women pulsed and surged through the air, and with her enhanced sight Nerida watched the rivers of the Source below ground grow brighter as they were called to the surface, welling up like many fountains of silver that flowed into one. And as the sun poured down, Nerida let those lights hold her – the gold from above; the silver from below – as the steady thud of her heart marked out the hours.

When at last they came, there were no sails, which surprised Nerida. For Setana had always dreamed of sails.

Instead, Nerida opened her eyes, dazzled by the glare, to see the blur of oars beating fast up the sea-loch, so fast that the twin Roman warships were like arrows loosed from a string, easily outdistancing the three smaller Alban ships that followed in their wake.

In the calm of the midday sun, Nerida watched them come in silence. *All Sisters vow the sacrifice, for the greater good*, she said to herself. *The Mother is just calling me closer to Her, that is all.* Yet her heart could not help but beat faster, for although the elders had sensed a calling, they had not known what its instrument would be.

The songs of the chanters grew stronger, and the air shimmered with waves of sound that echoed from the Stones until it was as if the monoliths themselves were ringing with song. The men who had built the fire-mounds had returned to their village, taking all the boatmen to ready the male part of the rite.

The Stones had been left to the women.

Setana's hand crept into Nerida's, and on her other side Nerida sought for and found the wrinkled palm of another Ban Cré. She didn't know which one, nor did it matter, for they were all daughters of the Goddess now.

'They knew to come this day,' she murmured to Setana, and could not help the echo of anger that stirred in her. *Betrayal.* Betrayal by one of their own. Then Nerida took a deep breath, and let it go. She would not spend herself in anger, not now.

'We knew it would be soon, however it came,' Setana replied, her voice as calm and steady as the sunshine. 'The dark wave has been rising for moons, and now it will break. It is a fitting day.' She turned sad, luminous eyes on Nerida, and all the lines seemed to smooth from her skin. 'Remember to surrender, my Sister, for that is what She told me above all other things. Find how not to be afraid, for all that She has taught us will come down to that one thing. Trust. Love.'

Nerida nodded, and as she did felt the heavy dizziness of the *saor* descend, the brew they had all shared that morning. It would help them to let go of their human attachments – fear, survival, anger, grief – and enable them to find something else, perhaps, something of the spirit.

'So they come,' Setana said, her arms out, the white robe falling back from her thin, pale wrists.

From the shore below, harsh shouts in a foreign tongue floated up on the warm air, along with the hollow thud of feet on timber, the grating of ropes. And despite all her years of training, despite the *saor*, despite her great belief and trust, one last flare of grief bloomed in Nerida's heart.

Grief for the light of dusk on the loch, for she had always loved that sight above all others.

Chapter 37

The sun was high now, and to escape its heat Fola and Rhiann had herded their charges into the shade of a birch grove by a shallow mire. The silver leaves had unfurled just enough to throw some faint shade over the Sisters' flushed faces, as Rhiann sat on a log before them, racking her mind for more tales. Didius, meanwhile, leaned against a pale tree-trunk, and began whittling a piece of hawthorn with his meat-dagger, sprigs of white flowers now tucked into his dark hair.

Rhiann smiled around at all the expectant faces, somewhat at a loss. Then, mindful that she was also supposed to be teaching the novices something, she fell back on herb-lore. The most basic of lessons suddenly came to her, but perhaps a good reminder on this Beltaine day. She took a bunch of creamy blossoms from the basket at her feet and held it up. 'We decorate at Beltaine with hawthorn because it is pretty and smells nice, and because it is one of the first flowers to bloom. Yet hawthorn is much more than that: the fruit and leaves make powerful medicines. Who can tell me what we use it for?'

A young hand raised in answer, but it wavered before Rhiann's eyes as a burning pain suddenly lanced her breast. She gasped, her hand falling to her lap, the edges of her sight closing in and growing dark.

'Sister?' a high voice piped. 'Are you well?'

'I . . .' Rhiann tried to speak, but only a croak came out. Then, as all those concerned faces turned up to her, her vaguely remembered dream suddenly came alive in her mind: these faces – so young, so trusting – and what she had seen rearing up behind them. It was unclear in the dream, but the vision that descended on her now was stark and brutal in its clarity.

No! Rhiann lurched to her feet, struggling to breathe.

'Rhiann!' That was Fola, rising from a crouch, white blossoms falling from her lap. They were the same blossoms that were crushed in Rhiann's hand, the same as in her dream.

Rhiann blinked to focus on her friend's worried face. 'I must go back.'

Fola pushed her way through the murmuring girls, taking Rhiann's arm. 'Why? What is wrong?'

'It is the elders!' Rhiann pulled her arms free and grasped Fola's shoulders. 'We have not come as far as they wished,' she whispered in anguish. 'Keep the girls here, Fola. Hide them, *please!*' Then she took off at a run, pelting back along the path that skirted the mire.

Fola's commands came faintly from behind, her voice sharpened with fear. 'Dera, take these girls higher into the hills. Didius, let us away after her, man! Hurry!'

Yet Rhiann soon lost their voices, focused solely as she was on the path that led back to the Stones. Over the hill pass she thudded, and then down a broad, shallow glen, leaping around scattered boulders and outcrops that thrust their way up to block her, and splashing through brown puddles. In the low places she ploughed through bogs, falling over in the cold mud, sobbing as she pulled herself up and stumbled on.

Faster! she screamed to herself, ignoring the burning in her lungs, the stabbing pains in her legs.

If she could have grown wings and flown she would, but there was only the maddening slowness of her heavy, earth-bound body, holding her back.

His short-sword sheathed at his waist, the young Roman soldier stood rigidly in the line his century had formed after disembarking. Yet inside, where no one could see, he was trembling with fear and excitement. He tipped back his head, looking from under his helmet guard to the crest of the ridge, where those barbaric stones reared from the headland he had seen from the ship's deck. *Witches*, his fears whispered to him. Black witches waited up there; sorceresses who would unman him with their spells and dark incantations; evil, savage women who sought to take the emperor and all his men down into their vile underworld, never to return; sacrificers of babies. Children's blood had run down these very stones in their black rites! For the Empire and all the gods, he had to rid the world of such savagery. So his commander had said; so the barbarian king had said.

What made it worse was that women were conducting these savage rites, and women were writhing in sexual union on this tainted earth, coupling with goats and stags and who knew what else, laying their thighs open to the men who came here in orgies of lust and depravation. The soldier's breath was coming faster now, and he gripped the butt of his javelin with a slick hand. The skin under his plate armour was prickling with heat, and his scalp itched with sweat that ran down into his eyes.

Suddenly he was startled by a strange noise behind – the bellow of a horn, blasted out by a blue savage in the ship coming behind. He risked a glance over his shoulder. The three barbarian vessels were close to shore now, the men within screaming curses and battering their spear-butts on the mast, the hull and their shields. Their faces seemed transfigured with fury and lust. Yet although they would land, they wouldn't come to interrupt the Roman work on the ridge-top. For some reason they still held these women in fear and awe, though it was hard to believe such warriors could look so terrifying and still be cowards.

It would be left to the Romans to be the cleansing fire in this place of darkness. He himself would bear a sword of truth and light!

A curt, clean command rang out from his centurion, and eagerly the soldier pressed forward, his heart hammering against the tight lacings of his armour. In perfect time, all the Romans began marching, and his own feet fell into line, digging into the soft sand as they scrambled up the hill slope in a tide of red shields and flashing metal.

For Jupiter and Mars I do this, he prayed fervently. *Praise be to the gods of light.*

Croaking for breath, Rhiann stumbled to a painful halt where the pass from the hills spilled out into the vale before the Stones. Spent and sick, she leaned over on her knees, her sight blurred and dizzy as she nearly fainted with pain and lack of air. Yet she forced her head up to see what was before her – a sight she had prayed never to see again.

The thatched roofs of all the huts were alight, and smoke billowed up and out, obscuring the buildings and the loch. But when the sea breeze gusted and parted the thick, choking cloud, Rhiann glimpsed two ships hard against the pier, barbed ships that were not of Alban make.

'*No!*' she screamed, the wind ripping the sound from her throat, the smoke slapping it back, choking her. '*No!*'

Just as Fola appeared at her side, Rhiann was taken by a burst of retching and coughing, and she vaguely heard Fola's breath become lost in an unearthly moan. And then Didius was there, supporting Rhiann by her heaving shoulders, silent with disbelief.

Above the pall of smoke the Stones reared free, glittering in the sun that had bathed them for years uncounted. Between them, the Sisters stood in a ring that echoed the rock circle, yet on the slopes below the peak the sun also glinted on armour and helmets and crimson shields. *Romans.* Here, in this most sacred of places.

'M-my lady,' Didius now urged her, out of breath from running, 'I must get you away from here, to somewhere safe.'

Fola gulped, tears marring her cheeks. 'Rhiann, that is why they sent us away. They knew.' A sob twisted her swollen, blotched face. '*They knew.*'

Rhiann's awareness was fast receding now, to a place of numb shock that was cold and muffled, where sounds barely penetrated. She was hardly conscious of Didius and Fola drawing her away from the burning and ruination, back up the path to the ridge-top, unprotesting and limp. At every step, though, something deeper in her began to stir, fighting to break free of the tempting numbness, the dark veil that was descending over her soul.

Then Didius was turning her, so that all she could see was sky, a blue sky unmarred by smoke, almost as if it were not happening . . .

The thing inside Rhiann struggled harder against the shock, biting and writhing, until at last, as the vale was disappearing from view, it clawed its way to the surface. And as it shattered the ice forming around Rhiann, sounds returned to her with a jolt.

Didius's breath, rasping unevenly in her ear.

Fola's sobs, harsh and keening, tearing at her heart with terrible claws.

The sobs of Rhiann's foster-mother, watching her son being gutted where he stood.

The sobs of her foster-sister as men tore her insides to pieces with their thrusts.

With a flood of enervating rage, Rhiann tore herself free of Didius and gripped Fola's arms instead, digging her nails in until her friend's eyes fixed on her with some agonized awareness. 'Get back to those girls and hide them until you know it is safe!' Rhiann cried. 'Do it for Nerida, for Setana! *Do it!*'

Fola gulped and shook her head, tears spraying from her eyes. 'Both . . . we both go.'

'No!' Rhiann held her gaze. 'I cannot leave them again. I failed once before, I didn't come in time, but I will now!' She swiped at her wet cheeks fiercely. 'Don't you see?' Her voice broke, and she turned Fola and gave her a great shove forward, so her friend fell down the other side of the slope towards the mire, rolling on the springy turf. 'Run!' Rhiann screamed at her and then, sparing no glance for Didius, she plunged down the path towards the Stones, into the smoke.

'Didius!' Fola cried, but then all sound and sight was lost in Rhiann's wheezing breath, and the acrid smoke that clawed at her throat and eyes. Blinded, stumbling, she started to circle north away from the pier and the soldiers, around the Stones hill to where a hidden path would lead her back up the ridge-top to the Sisters, a path where brambles had grown, long ago.

Didius sucked air into his lungs with great heaves, pumping his short legs as fast as he could. He kept his gaze fixed on the flame of Rhiann's hair that flickered in and out of the billows of smoke, giving no thought to his stubbed feet or aching sides, and certainly, never for one moment, about surrendering to his own people.

After all, he was bearded and ragged now after years spent with Rhiann's tribe. He wore their clothes and smelled like their food and skins and soap and ale. The soldiers would run him through before he could ever make them see he was one of them.

'Afterwards,' he found himself gasping, chasing Rhiann as she ran ahead. *Afterwards, when she is safe. Then I may go to them. I may.*

He skirted another shallow mire, the thin reeds bristling the surface of the pool, the reflection of the sky in it sick and yellowed from smoke. His ears strained for the sounds of battle nearby, and although he heard faint shouts, he didn't think they were coming this way. Not yet, anyway.

Abruptly, he yelped as a figure lunged out of the murk at him. It was an Alban savage, all blue tattoos and dripping hair and clothes, as if he'd swum to shore. For one frozen moment Didius read desperation in those rolling eyes, a lust to kill and rend, before Didius flung himself to one side, tumbling down into the mud that fringed the mire. The Alban let out a strangled yell, casting about in the gloom for him, but Didius was already up again, and the savage howls were lost in the ragged billows of smoke that immediately hid him from sight.

Coughing, Didius propelled himself along the rear of the worksheds and granaries, his mind racing to remember what he had seen that could give shelter. At last the ground began to rise, the soft, boggy turf growing drier with earth and gravel, and as Didius cleared the smoke he threw himself to his knees on the faint path that led to the Stones from the west.

Raking the scene with desperate eyes, Didius saw the looming Stones first, and soldiers approaching them, and towards the end of the headland, old women standing all in a row. Then Didius's gaze came to rest much closer, on Rhiann's back where she lay at the lip of the ridge, hidden from the soldiers by distance and tufts of sedge.

'My lady!' he whispered painfully, crawling closer. 'My lady, come back! Come back!'

The young soldier had burst into the circle of Stones at a trot, bracing himself for a bolt of lightning to hit him from above, for hordes of screaming, black-clad harpies to throw their lustful bodies and their curses and their charmed spittle at him, clawing his heart with yellow nails.

And there were women here, perhaps forty of them, blue-hooded, straight-backed. The standing ones were unnaturally still and silent, but a sibilant chanting emanated from others seated at the base of those barbaric stones, which reared over the soldier like the evil titans of old tales.

To his horror, his hands trembled with fear, and defiantly he raised his javelin to train it on the two women who stood forward from the rest, holding hands.

One of them, a slight, white-haired crone, said something in an old but strong voice, and the men near him instinctively recoiled. It was a spell perhaps, a curse. The young soldier hefted his spear again, feeling safer with its grip in his hand, and with his other hand he sought for his sheathed sword.

Rhiann buried her choking, furious sob in the sodden grass before her nose, her fingers digging into the damp earth.

'Come in peace,' Nerida had said to the soldiers, her voice ringing out as Rhiann had heard it reverberate so many times among these Stones. 'We are all beloved of the Mother. Put down your weapons and take what She gives you here this day.' Yet the tide of men clothed in hard, bright iron still advanced, step by step, as if terrified that the Sisters would suddenly strike them down where they stood.

'They have no blades!' Rhiann whispered in torment. 'They have no blades, so let them be!'

Setana and Nerida stood straight and calm before the inner circle, no longer hunched, no longer leaning on staffs, but on each other. And the glow that Rhiann had seen when she last walked with them was in their faces, though now it came from no earthly sun.

Suddenly, she felt a voice rather than heard it, as a touch, a thought, inside her. It was the silent mind-speech that she and Nerida had only once shared, a year ago. *Go now, child*, it said. *For if you are harmed, then we are truly lost.*

Rhiann gasped and raised her face, rubbing her eyes so she could see. Yet Nerida had not moved, was not looking at her, but at the soldiers that walked towards her.

I cannot! Rhiann wailed inside. *I let them die, but not you!*

A smile came to her as a caress. *It is our time, and we are ready. But heed me and go, for in you lies our hope.*

No! Every muscle in Rhiann's body went rigid, as she prepared to fly across the space between them, to throw herself on a Roman blade alongside Nerida.

The Otherworld lies close, daughter, as we will lie close to you. But you have more to do. Heed me now — your duty is to live!

Rhiann struggled to breathe through the agony of her chest, straining to keep her sight on Nerida and Setana as her line of vision was obscured by shining armour, helmets and a forest of spears.

Yet at the last, Setana looked somehow through the approaching soldiers, and her eyes found Rhiann. In that look was love, and a command.

To obey. To live. To remember.

A river of warmth ran up Nerida's arm from Setana's fingers, curling around her pained heart, soothing and rocking as she herself had soothed so many babes with her own hands.

Then Setana turned to her and, leaning forward, gave her the priestess kiss on her spirit-eye. 'Fear not,' she murmured.

On the edge of Nerida's vision, a young soldier drew his sword.

'I will not,' Nerida whispered and, dropping Setana's fingers, she stepped towards the soldier, her hands outstretched, the blade shining in the sun before her face. Despite the steady billows of smoke hanging over the houses below, the clouds had not reached the summit, and the Stones remained free under a blue sky. For that, Nerida was glad.

She smiled at the soldier's young, beardless face now, and surrendered all, as the Goddess had asked her to do. And love for him burst into her heart like a white flame, banishing all the fears and the grief to a darker place that would only be memory to her now.

'Come,' she said. 'I forgive you.'

His chest heaving, the young soldier hardly realized he had stepped out from his line, drawn to the old woman before him by her cursed powers, by the hands that reached for him, the spell she wove around him.

Now her eyes caught and held him, too, reaching deep into his heart and ensnaring it in the vilest of evils, for they were soft and blue and deep, those eyes, and in them he saw his own mother, and a promise and a gift he could not name.

'Sorceress!' The scream wrenched itself from his throat, and with it a fierce tide of rage swept over him, denying all that he saw there in those eyes. His sword was up before he could stop it, but even as he stabbed down, desperate tears came to him, and he knew not why he wept.

The sun flashing on the blade pierced Rhiann where she lay, and as an anguished cry flew free of the rent in her heart, something hard hit her across the back of her head.

She fell down into darkness, as the last crushed blossoms dropped from her fingers.

Chapter 38

'Forgive me,' Didius whispered, repeating it with every stumbling step he took among the half-buried rocks and reeds of the mire's edge. Rhiann was tall, but not heavy; he was short, but with strength in his stocky limbs. Once she was flung over his shoulder, it wasn't so bad.

Her head lolled against his waist. Didius had never struck a woman before, and didn't know if she would ever wake from the blow of the dagger hilt – or if she did, whether her mind would still be sound. But what choice did he have? He'd vowed to protect her, and protect her he would. He couldn't let her scream reach the ears of the soldiers, or allow her to run out before them, as she had tensed to do.

Even though his head was bent over, his eyes on his dragging feet, Didius could smell that the smoke was growing lighter. He stopped, turning slowly, peering up and around him, desperate for somewhere they could shelter and he could defend. Ahead, over the hills to the north, more smoke was trailing into the sky. That way lay the broch village; he and Rhiann had gone there only days ago. There would be no safety there, then.

Now he heard more shouts behind him, in the barbarian language, and he knew that the Alban men must have poured ashore at last, seeking their own prey. Didius racked his brains again, reliving all the walks he had taken with Rhiann here in these hills, sifting his memories for a place of shelter. And then he had it.

On the other side of the mire a shallow vale led into the hills, and on the far spur of one ridge a ruined tower stood – some old house or defensive building. The stones were sagging, the thatch roof long gone, but taking him there one day Rhiann had run up the narrow rock staircase within its walls. At the top of the staircase, half the timber of the upper floor still survived, and though Didius had stepped across the rotting beams gingerly, Rhiann had danced over to the gaping wall that once supported the roof and now provided a view to the sea.

Taking a deep breath, Didius grasped Rhiann's legs more firmly and skirted the mire by balancing precariously on the half-submerged stones, praying to all his gods that they still had enough smoke cover to avoid detection. His mind was so intent on his task that he barely registered the pulse of pain and regret in his heart, that the old women who had smiled at him had been cut down by his own people as if they were cattle. And perhaps something slipped then, a tiny shift that sundered him from Rome for ever, because all that came to him, as he blinked stinging tears away, was a yearning to be by the bonfire again, with Aedan's harp singing to the stars.

The path around the muddy pond had provided good cover, but now Didius reached the drier ground on the other side, and as he looked up to the tower he realized that the hill slope rose bare to its door. There was nothing for it but to cross that ground in the open, as quickly as he could.

Unfortunately, Rhiann's hair blazed in the sun that reached from the clearing edges of the smoke, and she wore her priestess cloak, a blue that was bright against green turf and grey stones. Gasping for air, Didius stumbled across the bare slope, but just as he slipped around the spur of the hill, two shouts came from behind, like the baying of hounds sighting game. Men were coming, and they were Albans, by the muffled inflections of their voices. He was not sure if that was better or worse than Romans.

Didius plunged through the door of the tower, and instantly the cold darkness of the staircase swallowed them. Desperately, he lurched halfway up and lay Rhiann's still body across the stone steps. Now he could clearly hear voices coming closer. He looked down at the small square of bright sun that was the doorway.

A narrow stair; one door. Rhiann had shown him a place that could be defended by one swordsman, for a time. Clever, his lady.

He drew his sword and kissed the barbarian blade, murmuring prayers to Jupiter and Mars and, remembering Aedan's tales, to Manannán of the waves. Last of all, he sent a plea to Rhiann's Mother Goddess, thinking, with a certain bleakness, that he might be meeting her soon enough to speak the words in person.

Didius took one step down, then another and, as the square of sunlight grew larger, so he was taken by a sudden flash of memory – the first time he met a barbarian warrior. It was when he sat in his saddle in a freezing dawn as the prince of Erin looked up and made ready to steal Didius's horse. Then, Didius's bowels had turned to liquid at the sight of those blazing green eyes and that sword. His heart had pounded and his legs had shaken so much that the horse almost bolted. Strange how weak he had been then, and how he didn't feel weak at all right now.

He glanced up the staircase. Now he had something to guard; perhaps that was it. He had to protect her.

Outside, heavy feet pounded on the path up to the door, and there was the ringing of drawn blades from their scabbards. Didius took a deep breath, and went down to meet them.

It was the cold that woke Rhiann, the burning cold of stone that had never felt the sun. She struggled to open her eyes, yet even that sent a shaft of pain through her head.

Her eyes clamped shut again, and she reached out with her hand instead, her nails scraping on the moss of a damp wall. She could feel steps beneath her – it was a staircase. Gingerly, she pulled herself to the wall, leaning her forehead on it, gathering her legs under her so that she was on all fours. Goddess, but the back of her head hurt, aching all the way through her skull.

Suddenly a lurch of nausea took her, and she sank back on her side, half-opening her eyes so she could look down the stairway, to where the brightness forced its way through her lashes. And that was when she heard the grunt nearby, and curses spat in her own language in the jeering tone she knew well – warriors at sport.

'Didius?' Rhiann's voice leaked out in a hoarse whisper, and when she got no answer she began to edge her way down the staircase, legs first, crabwise, step by painful step. The staircase curved, so it was some moments before she got low enough to see the doorway itself. By then, her brain was beating on the inside of her skull with steady, agonizing blows. Every now and then one came that nearly made her faint, but she clung to consciousness as she clung to the sharp edge of each step.

She squinted at the sudden brightness of the door, the light lancing her with new pain. Didius was outlined there in a protective crouch, his sword held before him. Just beyond, on a tiny patch of packed sand, she could see the still legs of an Alban body at length on the ground.

'Didius?' she whispered. The Roman's shoulders quivered, but he did not look around, or take his eyes off what awaited him outside. Just then there was a quick flurry of feet, a flash of blade and a dark shape that blocked the light for a moment. Didius grunted again and twisted as metal clashed, and Rhiann saw his assailant fall back. From outside, the jeers began again, along with the sound of dragging as the legs of the dead body disappeared.

'He nearly got you there, Kinoth – little fox nearly got you!'

Someone hawked and spat on the ground. 'Got him back, didn't I? If you think you can do better, you get in there.'

'No need. He's bleeding like a pig.'

Rhiann's breath tripped as another wave of pain and nausea broke over her. When it cleared, she was only five steps above Didius.

'Lady,' Didius's voice was faint, 'please stay there. They will not get past me.'

Looking down at him, Rhiann noticed through her haze the way he hunched over to one side, clutching his sword arm. 'You're hurt,' she whispered. 'Don't hurt yourself for me; tell them who you are. They came with the Romans – tell them.'

Didius's breathing was hoarse, and each halting word scraped against the cold stone. 'I . . . do not think . . . that you will be safe . . . if I do that.'

Rhiann's eyes clenched shut, as suddenly the full memory of what had happened swept over her.

The sword falling on Nerida.

The blood that sprayed across the Stones.

'I don't want to live,' she heard herself saying in a strained, high voice. 'I don't want to live anyway.'

Didius gasped and clutched at his belly as some spasm of pain took him. 'Your man . . . has been no friend of mine . . . but . . . you love him well. He waits for you.'

A sob rose in Rhiann's rigid throat. 'And you, dear friend,' she choked out, 'make sure you wait for me, too.'

Yet the men outside were not going to give them time for such words. Another shape blocked the light, and another behind him, and together they ran at the door. Didius half rose, clutching at the wall, and involuntarily Rhiann reared back, losing sight of him. Yet his grunt at the collision was unmistakable: pain so strong it was only shock; pain that could make no sound.

The first voice Rhiann heard then was one of the attackers, hissing the other man's name, and for some reason both retreated again. As sun flooded the stairway, Rhiann ignored the pounding ache in her head and scrabbled down to Didius, but when she took him in her arms his weight was more than she'd braced for, and she couldn't hold him. Clutching him close, they both slid down the last two steps, coming to rest across the doorway, Didius's legs splayed out on the blood-stained path.

'There is the woman,' someone muttered, but Rhiann hardly heard them. The sudden flood of sunshine blinded her, and she could see nothing of the men besides a crowd of feet that stood some way back. Squinting, she looked down at Didius in her arms and saw only then the great rent under his heart, laying open his tunic and the thick flesh underneath. Blood oozed between her fingers; blood that should have spurted, but now seeped only slowly, for Didius had lost so much already. Her heart clenched when she saw the score of slashes that ran across his arms, legs and face. How long had they been sporting with him?

'Lady.' Didius's hand reached up, catching in her hair, and she bent over so the unbound part swung forward, shielding him. 'Lady . . . they have . . . gone? I . . . cannot hear them. They have gone.'

Rhiann stared down into Didius's black eyes, her throat closing as she recognized the familiar glaze creeping over them. 'Yes,' she whispered, drawing him closer, 'they have gone.'

His breath stirred the fine hairs on her forehead. 'Then I did it . . .'

A muttering began somewhere above Rhiann's head, and the feet on the edge of her vision shifted restlessly. Yet Didius was beyond that now, beyond all sight and sound except that of her own voice.

'Yes, *cariad*,' she murmured, bending her head closer to shut out the other men. Her tears fell on to Didius's upturned face; one, and then another. 'Our bards will sing of you for ever, I swear.'

Didius smiled through the blood that bubbled on his lips, then did not move again.

Rhiann gazed down at his slack mouth, unable to absorb the truth of the stillness and glassy eyes, barely noticing the men around her drawing back, their ranks parting like a receding wave.

Yet the silence that fell then penetrated even her shock, and some force drew up her head. Among the rabble of black-haired men surrounding him, *he* was somehow blacker, though the darkness of his face was nothing to the void in his eyes.

Maelchon, king of the Orcades, had come to claim his prize.

Chapter 39

The Orcadian king said nothing at first, as those eyes seared their way from Rhiann's splayed legs, laid bare by her rucked-up skirt, to the rapid rise and fall of her breasts. Then he glanced at his men. 'Did I not say,' he growled, 'that all of the young sluts should be spared for my inspection? So the red crests heed me – but not my own men?'

The man named Kinoth gulped. 'Lord,' he whined, 'we only saw her clearly just now, once the man was drawn out.'

'You would do well to thank your gods for that,' Maelchon hissed. Then he barked so abruptly that all the men jumped. 'Join the others at the broch now, all of you, and raid what you will on the way!'

'I can stay as your guard, lord,' Kinoth ventured, sheathing his bloody sword.

Maelchon twisted only his head on its thick, corded neck. 'Did I not say all of you?' he roared. 'Now!'

Men who had jeered at poor Didius with contempt now scrambled away, like children before their enraged father. Only then, as their retreating backs faded from view, did fear for herself at last begin to penetrate Rhiann's shock. Her eyes darted to the side, where the lip of the path fell away to the mire. Without further thought, she slipped out from under Didius and flung herself as far as she could, hoping to tumble down the slope below. But something clamped on her ankle, bringing her down with such an impact that she nearly lost consciousness again.

'You've slipped my net before, but no more.' Maelchon yanked her leg towards him, her knees scraping painfully over the stones. Before she could even curse him, he grasped her scrabbling arms and swung her over his shoulder as easily as if she were a sack of grain.

Then all went dark and cold, and Rhiann realized with dizzy horror that they were climbing the inside stairs of the tower. 'No,' she moaned, her face pressed against Maelchon's cloak, which stank of fish and seal-oil. '*Eremon.*'

It was the wrong thing to say. Maelchon stiffened, then climbed faster, emerging on to the upper floor only to fling her sprawling along the mossy planks. 'Eremon,' he mocked, his chest heaving. 'That tit-fed, mewling puppy! He won't get his paws on you again – never again!'

Rage seared its way past the pain in Rhiann's head. 'It is his sword that will send *you* to the Goddess, and you will find no comfort there, I swear!'

'*Goddess!*' Maelchon squatted next to her; a wave of rotten fish-breath slapped her in the face. 'You're nothing more than a whore, torturing me with the promise of your wet hole and the white legs that surround it.'

Rhiann turned her face away from the vile words, her hands pushing her back on the slimy floor. Yet Maelchon hunched forward and took her face with one hand, twisting it to look up at him. The sun pouring over the broken stones flashed on his jet ring, blinding her. 'I've waited five years to see this face below me, crying out for me, and you won't turn it from me again! You will *never* scorn me again, you white bitch!' And suddenly his wet tongue was plunging crudely into her mouth like a squirming eel.

Rhiann raked her nails down his cheeks, and he caught both struggling hands in his own before flinging her away. She gagged, spitting saliva down her chin with deliberate, fierce disgust.

In answer Maelchon grunted, and drawing back, carefully struck her across the jaw with the back of his hand, so she skittered over the floor. She came to rest against the wall, but it was some time before her vision cleared of the sparks, which at first stabbed her with a wild agony. She tasted blood, and then the pain began to fade into a heavy haze that threatened to descend and sweep all away.

I don't want to live, she'd said to Didius. Rhiann tried to shake off the haze and make herself remember who waited for her. 'Eremon will never rest if you harm me.' Painfully, she hauled herself into a sitting position against the wall, fingers pressed to her bloody lip. 'You'll be hunted through Alba.'

Maelchon snorted with amusement as he loomed over her, his hands on his thighs. 'And what care I for that? Or did you not notice I have allies of my own? Soon your *prince* will be in no position to hunt me down, but skewered by a Roman spear, along with Calgacus and all the southerners who dared to scorn me!' His fingers rolled and clenched the cloth of his trousers.

Rhiann squinted up at him through the cramping pain in her temples. 'You . . . you raid the Sacred Isle because you feel . . . *scorned*?' The last word came out as a disbelieving whisper.

Maelchon smiled, something awakening in his eyes that was not rage, and not hate, but something far worse: a twisted, obsessive lust. 'Oh no,' he murmured, drawing his sword with a sibilant hiss. 'This was all for you; to take you as I've wanted to all these years. Didn't you know?'

Me. I brought it to them. Me.

The lurch of sickness darkened Rhiann's vision then, and bore her down to the damp wood floor, sourness flooding her tongue. As if from afar, she felt the nudge of a toe that tipped her onto her back, and then the cold blade at her throat, deftly slicing through her dress, laying her skin bare to the chill breeze off the sea.

Dimly, she sensed Maelchon kneeling over her, and felt a tugging at her waist. Her eyes drifted to one side to see her waist-pouch flung there, the herb-knife she had used only that morning falling free, tangled in stems and flowers. And all the time Maelchon's rasping breath echoed around and through her, and she was back under the men who attacked her on the beach – the harsh pants the same, the stink of fish, the same, the black, coarse beard, the same, the thumbs digging into her flesh, all the same . . .

Yet Maelchon wanted more from her than those men had. His hand shook as he struck her again. 'Look at me, you goddess whore!' he hissed furiously. 'You will want me with those cat-eyes! You will use that tongue on me the way you use it on *him*!' He wrenched Rhiann's jaw around, and she saw the sweat standing out on his brow, the spittle running down his beard as he worked himself into a frenzy. Something nudged between her legs, but it was soft and flaccid against her flesh. 'Witch!' Maelchon's weight fell across her, extinguishing her breath, and then his hand was fumbling, trying to rouse himself. 'Witch, you've cursed me!' he sobbed hoarsely, his shoulders shuddering.

Yet Rhiann had clawed her soul far away from this ugliness and terror now, far away from Didius's unseeing eyes and the sword slicing Nerida in two. *I don't want any of it. I don't want to feel any of it.* Instead, her eyes came to rest once more on her waist-pouch, lying at the end of her outflung arm. The leaves spilling from it were gathered only that morning, the green juice on the blade was fresh that morning . . .

Maelchon felt how limp she had gone, and grasped her by the arms, hauling her up. 'Fight me, you bitch! Fight me!'

Rhiann's head lolled sideways, and he let her go with another curse, working harder at himself with his hand, hissing, 'Five years since they denied me your body. Why does blood not cleanse me? Their blood, yours, why? *Why?*' He groaned. 'Is it because revenge could never be as sweet as what lies inside you? Is that it, *whore, is that what I need?*'

Their blood . . . revenge . . . The meaning of the words sliced through Rhiann's numbness, and every nerve-ending suddenly jerked awake as fire swept her muscles. Yet she kept herself perfectly still, for her helpless state was the only power she had left. Her dry lips moved, and toneless words emerged. 'You sent the men to kill my family. Before.'

The frenzied rubbing stopped, but she could not see Maelchon's face until he leaned in close to her. 'Yes,' he whispered. 'And does this anger you? *Do you hate me for it?*' Rhiann steeled herself as that thick tongue slid along her throat. 'Does it make you want to hurt me?'

Rhiann swallowed convulsively. 'Did you know, king, that your men found their way between my thighs long before you? On that day, as it happens.' It nearly killed her to speak the words, but she sensed Maelchon freeze and draw back.

'Did they indeed? You were foolish to come and join that fight then, for it was a gift for your family alone. For refusing me your hand, aye, but more for the slap in my face!'

Rhiann squeezed her eyes shut, desperate not to cry.

'As this fight,' Maelchon whispered, a finger tracing her cheek, 'was for you alone, because your stinking druid said the gods favoured me, because they wanted me here! Because *you* were here.' A rough hand closed over one of her bare breasts. 'A great many have laid here, no doubt, one after the other. But I will be the last, vixen. I will be the last.'

A strangled gasp of desperate rage escaped Rhiann's throat, and her eyes flickered open despite themselves. *Gelert and him. For this, they killed Nerida and Setana.*

Her head was still turned away from him; she saw only her own white fingers, outstretched, and the knife-blade, dark with plant sap. And when Maelchon suddenly wrenched her thighs wider, and she felt a prodding hardness there, the feeling, stink and sound of him coalesced into a ball of white-hot fury Rhiann could no longer contain. It forced its way up from her very guts, burning as it exploded free, and her fingers closed over the knife and she thrust it blindly in the direction of Maelchon's face, buried somewhere over her left shoulder. The blade sliced into her own fingers yet the tip sank home, for an unearthly scream split her eardrums as Maelchon rolled off her.

Borne up by rage, Rhiann stumbled to her feet. Her legs shook violently as Maelchon writhed on his back, hands over his eyes, his trousers around his ankles. Yet when he wrenched himself to his knees, his face was awash with so much blood Rhiann could not see how she'd injured him. She leapt back from his clawing fingers. *I should kill him. I must kill him!* Yet Maelchon's sword was trapped under his knees, and she could not risk going within range of those bloody, grasping hands.

Slowly, Rhiann backed towards the stairs, her feet slipping on the mossy timbers, the shreds of her dress falling and tangling around her knees. Maelchon scrabbled forwards on all fours, screaming curses at her, and she kicked the scraps of linen free of her ankles and threw his stinking, discarded cloak around her bare shoulders. Then she stumbled down the staircase, nearly tripping over Didius's body before plunging down the slope to the mire, insensible of where she was going.

The upright movement brought a renewed surge of agony and, with the shock fuelling it, Rhiann had no room left for sense. Her dizzy steps wove brokenly one way and then the other. She was aware only of the choking smoke and the eerie silence. Vague shapes loomed out of the murk, forcing her to avoid them: the corner of a wall; an abandoned cart; an empty, discarded keg. Terrible shudders overcame her, and she wrapped the reeking folds of Maelchon's cloak closer around her clammy, bare skin, warding away the waves of grief that reached through her shock.

Not now. Now, she must keep moving. Anywhere but back. Anywhere.

More smouldering houses surrounded her, the roofs falling in with great gushes of cinders and smoke. But no sounds came, no moans for help, nothing human at all, which was why the sudden hoarse shout behind her was so brutal to her ears. She glanced back over her shoulder, and through the rents in the smoke glimpsed the dark figures of men, running along the shore of the mire towards her from the direction of the burning broch.

Rhiann's dizziness and pain were pierced by a shaft of sheer terror then, and she found the strength to run, darting away like a maddened hare. Her feet bounded down sandy paths and over firm turf, dodging the crumbling huts, until finally the ground fell away to the dark rocks that lined the loch shore. Only one incoherent thought came to her – to fling herself beneath the waters and there escape it all.

Blinded by smoke and tears, at first she didn't understand what was falling all around her. Then she cried out and froze, her fist crushed to her mouth, as an arrow shrieked over her head. She braced herself for the impact, unable to take in what her eyes and ears were showing her – more whizzing arrows, yet none striking her.

It was only then that Rhiann realized the arrows were not being shot at her, but over her shoulder at Maelchon's men. Then a familiar face swam in her blurred vision, scampering over the patches of slippery weed to reach her, as the rest of his men raced past.

'Lady!' Nectan cried. 'I am here; I am coming!'

But Rhiann's legs went out from under her, and she sank on to her back on the hard rocks, her hands clinging to the streamers of cold, wet weed. And the sun was still shining, shining down on her.

Chapter 40

It was still too early in the season to venture into the central spine of Alba's mountains, but Eremon's lingering glow of triumph did much to ward away the icy chill of the snow-crust caught in the high passes.

He and Calgacus, Lorn and Conaire were this night sharing an unguarded fire with the other tribal commanders, crowded close beneath a rock overhang on the sheltered side of a ridge. A dead rowan at the edge of the path had been pulled over and set alight, and the line of flaming branches at the mouth of the shallow cave made it almost cosy, with the damp ground piled high with saddle hides and furs.

After weeks of enforced silence near the Roman frontier, guarding every noise, the relief of feeling safe in this high eyrie more than made up for the freezing winds. That relief, along with a newly struck keg of ale, accounted for the volume of the jests, growing louder and bolder by the moment. Only Calgacus was silent, sharpening his meat-dagger with a stone, his long back against the sloping wall of the cave. Glancing over at him, Eremon poured another ale and stretched himself on the hides at the Caledonii king's feet, one hand behind his head. After a while he ventured, 'A problem shared is a lighter burden, my lord,' and held out the cup.

Calgacus smiled and took it, resting his dagger on his knee. 'I am turning over the idea, prince, that I should move my people up into the hills until this is resolved one way or another.'

'Abandon your dun?' Slowly, Eremon wiped his chin dry of spilled ale.

Calgacus sipped and shrugged unhappily. 'We know Agricola has a war fleet, and he is well established on the Tay – I just saw that for myself. There are too many of them too close to me.' Eremon was silent with sympathy, yet Calgacus seemed to read it as disapproval. 'Not that we have not struck a great blow, prince,' he hastened to add, handing over the cup. 'But my heart beats with a great foreboding, and I haven't forgotten King Maelchon, either.'

At mention of that name, Eremon's fingers slid lower over the smooth bronze cup, tight with anger. 'Make no mistake, I too am uneasy that your dun is caught between the Orcadian king and the Romans. Do you think we should launch an attack on him ourselves?' Eremon held his breath for the answer, for his warrior self yearned desperately to confront Maelchon, even as his leader self knew it was presently out of the question.

Calgacus shook his head. 'The men required for such an attack would drain our resources here, and we will need all the warriors we have marshalled when the Romans seek their revenge.'

'As they will.'

'So we hope.'

A burst of good-natured arguing rang out from behind them. Lorn was making some loud, fiery point, stabbing the air with one finger, as Garnat, the Taexali king, protested with equal vigour. Conaire hid a smile as he poked at the stew boiling in a skin strung between sticks over the fire.

'We are hoping,' Calgacus murmured to Eremon, with a glance at them, 'that Agricola will be drawn into the hills, even though that was his mistake last year, and he will know it. I confess I fret at wondering if he will take the bait again.'

'He'll have to,' Eremon replied grimly, balancing the cup on his chest. 'If we keep attacking, he cannot just sit there. He will have to come after us, and if we don't meet him in battle he can only follow where we lead: into the mountains. Or better yet, see that this total conquest of his is unattainable, and leave Alba alone.' Even as he said it, Eremon's sinking heart told him he did not believe this would ever happen.

'But prince,' Calgacus pursed his lips, staring over Eremon's shoulder into the burning branches, 'this leads me back to my original thought. If Agricola has no army to attack, he will look further afield for targets to destroy. Targets like duns.'

Eremon raised his face. 'I am truly grieved that supporting me in this makes your tribe a target when it was perhaps not before.'

Calgacus merely smiled, turning his dagger in his hands. The flames flickered on the pockmarked wall behind him, glistening with moisture. 'We were already known to the Romans. And now I would rather ride out to meet a threat than cower in my Hall, as I'm sure you will feel when you reach my age.' His eyes glinted. 'Save your guilt, my noble prince. You have better things on which to spend your energy.'

Suddenly they were interrupted by the hail of an Epidii scout, hastening up the path that led from the valley below.

'My lord, a messenger has come for you, from the Caereni people.'

Eremon remained at length on the ground. 'The Caereni?' he repeated, puzzled.

'Yes, my lord. A man of Nectan, son of Gede. He has tracked us hard over many leagues, and his message is therefore two weeks old.' The man paused, pressing his lips together, his hand going unconsciously to his sword hilt. 'He . . . has news of your wife, the Lady Rhiann. Ill news.'

Eremon was on his feet in one abrupt movement, the cup spilling to the ground. 'Where is he?' he barked, the hoarse sound slicing through the men's laughter. They all fell silent, and Conaire slowly rose to stand by Eremon's side, where the frozen path fell away into darkness.

The Caereni messenger took shape from the night around him, a short man in the forest garb of Nectan's people, his black eyes showing nothing but the reflection of the flames. 'Lord.' He went down on one knee before Eremon, the fletching of his arrows in their quiver a pale ruff against his dark nape. 'At Beltaine, Maelchon of the Orcades and two Roman ships attacked the Sacred Isle.'

Eremon's breath hissed out through his teeth. In the utter silence, it was as if water had doused the fire.

'Your lady lives,' the man added hastily, after a quick glance up at Eremon's face. 'But the elder Sisters were slaughtered in the Stones, the Goddess keep them. My own lord has taken your wife and the others to Dunadd.'

Eremon's wide eyes met Calgacus's sorrowing gaze, yet Eremon saw nothing but Rhiann's face, her fine bones distorted with terror.

'I must go home,' he muttered, his voice faint, and he stumbled for the path, seeking his horse.

Conaire caught him before he had gone but five paces out into the darkness. 'I will come with you, brother.'

A shudder ran over Eremon's shoulders, and he hid it by wrapping his cloak around his neck. 'No. I do not know how long I will be.'

'You need me by your side.' Conaire grasped his elbows, his voice urgent.

'I need you here. You must act as me, in my stead, if there are any more attacks.' Eremon peeled Conaire's fingers from his arm. 'Only you fully know my mind. *Please.*' His control was beginning to break, as images of Rhiann's face thrust their way again and again into his mind. Yet he didn't want to order Conaire; he couldn't bear it right now.

At last Conaire sensed this and dropped his hand. 'Then may Hawen speed your way, brother, and . . . take pity on your lady's heart.'

For Conaire had always loved Rhiann well.

It was Linnet who met Eremon at Dunadd's stables, seven days of maddened riding later. Here on the sea plain the warm season had come, and sweat was running down Eremon's sunburned face, sticking his hair to his skull. Yet he hadn't noticed the green grass or the spreading trees or the birds, for he rode as one possessed, carrying the cold of the mountains in his heart.

'Let me go to her!' he demanded, as Rhiann's aunt stopped before him in the doorway of the stall.

'First you must hear what I have to tell you,' Linnet returned, implacability hardening her wavering voice. 'Please, for Rhiann's sake.'

Eremon stared at Linnet as if he did not know her, his chest rising and falling. Then, for the first time, he noticed the scores of grief on Linnet's face, the tightness of eyes that would not weep, and he remembered that Linnet, too, had grown up on the Sacred Isle.

'Forgive me,' he croaked, all his breath rushing out. 'Tell me what happened.'

So Linnet told him. And with every word, so the clear sky above Eremon seemed to darken, and the weight that had lifted from his shoulders with the successful raid settled around him again, like a collar of cold, biting iron.

'Maelchon . . . *abducted* her?' He forced a swallow past his dry tongue. 'What did he do to her?' His voice sounded foreign to his ears.

Unconsciously, Linnet's hand splayed out as if to ward away the idea. 'I don't know . . . she won't say. She demanded to burn the dead on the island, and since their return a week ago she has not woken again from the shock. Caitlin and I,' she drew a shaky breath, 'we cannot reach her. She only wants Fola near, and the other girls – all that remain of the Sisterhood.' The pain in her eyes hit Eremon in the belly.

'Where is she?'

'In her house. She has as many of the girls staying there as she can; the rest are living with the women of the village.'

His eyes strayed up the path towards the crag, and he made as if to go.

'Eremon.' Linnet's hand found his arm. She had never called him by his own name. 'You will find her changed. She may not wish to see you.'

Eremon stared at her, uncomprehending. 'Why wouldn't she? She needs me more than anyone else.' He said it defiantly, for a great fear had begun to hammer on his heart.

Linnet's eyes were swimming with tears. 'I know you love her. But . . . you are a man. She saw the Sisters murdered by men. Didius was killed defending her, by Maelchon's men. And Maelchon himself . . . she will not speak of him. But it has brought it all back, the first raid . . . what she suffered.'

Eremon's chest constricted with the memory of what had been in

Rhiann's eyes the day she revealed her pain to him. And what it would mean, if it was there when she looked at him now. 'Still, I must see her.'

Linnet wrapped her arms around her chest, just as Rhiann often did. The familiar gesture pierced him. 'As you will, prince,' she said, stepping back, and though Eremon would not run before the people, his feet had never carried him through Dunadd so swiftly.

At the door of Rhiann's house, the chanting stopped him cold and raised the hairs on the back of his neck. The door-hide was tied back, and there were girls lined up on the bench outside Rhiann's door, and more young women kneeling in a circle around her hearth-fire. They were the chanters, and though they glanced up at him with surprise, they did not falter in their singing.

Eremon caught a glimpse of Rhiann's goddess figurines all laid out on the hearth-stones, as well as flowers, shells and other talismans that he did not recognize.

Then a soft cry of surprise claimed his attention, and he saw Caitlin in Rhiann's rush-backed chair, Gabran nursing at her breast, her face blanched with strain. Behind her, Eithne paused from grinding something pungent in a bronze bowl at Rhiann's workbench, the pestle hovering in her hand. Eremon paused to clasp Caitlin's outstretched fingers, but his gaze had already swept to the bedscreen, partly folded back to the room. Someone was sitting by the bed, though it wasn't Rhiann, and he approached slowly, mindful of Linnet's warning.

It was then that the floor dropped out from under him.

For Rhiann lay against the pillow, her face white and mottled with green bruises along her jaw, slashed by the scarlet of her swollen, cut mouth. Her lustrous hair was limp from sweat, and tangled around her shoulders.

Fola stifled a noise when she saw Eremon, and went to rise, but Rhiann's hand shot out and clamped on her wrist, holding her there. The ends of her fingers were bandaged. 'No,' Rhiann whispered to Fola, staring at her friend with a dazed desperation that tore Eremon's heart. With an uncertain glance at him, Fola sank back on the stool.

Swallowing the lump in his throat, Eremon approached the bed. 'I have come, *a stór*,' he murmured and groped for her hand. Yet she jerked it away with a soft cry and buried her face in the bedsheets. 'Rhiann, speak to me,' Eremon begged. 'I am here with you; I have come—'

'No!' Rhiann's voice was muffled. Fola met Eremon's gaze, and there was great pity in her dark eyes, even as she shook her head with gentle warning.

Rhiann's shoulders had begun to tremble now, and she pressed her face deeper into the bed. 'No soft words for me, no more, never!'

Eremon stared down at her, burning with a sudden terror as great as his grief. 'Rhiann . . . did Maelchon hurt . . .' But there he broke off, for Rhiann's whole body clenched at Maelchon's name, and Eremon realized he had struck unthinkingly, and wished to yank the words back as they flew from his lips.

'Get him away from me!' Rhiann cried brokenly, whether about the man in her nightmare or her own husband, Eremon could not tell. Yet instinctively he fell back a step. *You are a man*, Linnet had said. And him being here was causing Rhiann pain.

Eremon had never faced such raw grief before, and he stood helplessly, as Rhiann's hand crept out to clasp Fola's fingers. Then he suddenly became aware again of the chanting women, as Linnet appeared silently by the bedscreen. He didn't belong here, that was clear.

'I will come back later, love.' Unconsciously, Eremon's hand reached out to stroke Rhiann's hair, but he let it fall before touching her.

As he slowly took the path from the house, Fola came behind, calling him to stop.

'Prince,' she said nervously, when he turned back, 'she is still in deep shock; she doesn't know what she says.'

Eremon stared at Fola, eyes tight with pain, at last biting out what frightened him most. 'Has she gone mad?'

Fola shook her head sadly. Eremon remembered her face as being plain, round and solid, yet alive with humour. He didn't recognize that memory in the drawn features of the young woman before him, sunken with grief. 'She is the strongest woman I know,' Fola whispered, 'yet what happened has broken even her. I think if it had not been for the first raid she would perhaps not have gone so far . . .'

'Gone?'

'You may know little of healing, prince.' Fola twisted her fingers in her blue robe, the edge of her wide mouth trembling. 'Sometimes when the soul has been badly hurt, it doesn't want to come back to the body. That's what shock is – the soul doesn't wish to stay in Thisworld; it wishes to flee. Usually it is only temporary, until the mind is strong enough to endure the knowledge of what has happened. The Lady Linnet has told me that she nursed Rhiann through such shock four years ago, when her family was killed. But the blow is that much greater now, for it is the loss of the Sisterhood . . .' Her voice faltered, and she covered her mouth with a shaking hand.

'Are you telling me she won't come back?' Eremon spoke more harshly than he intended, for he couldn't breathe properly.

Again Fola shook her head, before glancing down. 'I think she has more to come back for, now,' she murmured hoarsely. 'This is important for healing, so take heart.'

Yet Eremon could accept little comfort from that, as he took his leave of Fola and strode blindly towards the King's Hall. For the young priestess's words had summoned the fear that perhaps Rhiann's love for him was not enough to call her back from the shadowlands. After all, what could he offer her but more blood and slaughter?

Outside the Hall, he paced fiercely in the churned mud, trying to take his emotions in a stern hand. A few servants crept by, but he ignored them, until Cù himself came bounding out, tail thumping against Eremon's shins. It was only when Eremon gave him no more than a cursory pat, his eyes fixed unseeing on the great oak doors, that the hound sensed his distress and sat down with a single whine.

It was then that Eremon took a breath, and went inside to seek Nectan.

He and the little, dark Caereni chief had not seen each other in a year, and though there was much news to exchange, Eremon was interested in only one thing: the completion of the tale that Linnet had left unfinished in her haste.

Nectan had brought twenty men with him, sprawled about the hearth eating mutton porridge, but at Eremon's appearance Nectan gently steered him away to the quiet, dark reaches of the Hall, and there sat him on a stool.

After pressing a cup of ale into his hands, Nectan began to speak in a soft tone that somehow managed to reach around Eremon's heart. Nectan's eyes, as dark and fathomless as those of a seal, never wavered from Eremon's face, and without touching him his steady presence soothed Eremon enough to enable him to concentrate.

A week after Rhiann left for the Sacred Isle, Nectan said, Linnet's fears had grown to an unbearable pitch. She undertook another seeing in the sacred pool, this time with the help of *saor*, and what she saw there confirmed her worst forebodings: Rhiann was in real danger.

With Eremon far to the east, she despatched the swiftest trading ship she could find to Nectan's settlement, begging him to gather his men and make all speed for the Stones and the Sisters. His boats came upon the coast of the island when the smoke was already rising into the sky.

'We saw no trace of any Roman ship,' Nectan said, chewing on a birch twig with a deliberate pressure that spoke of his pain. 'The red invaders seemed to have only one target – the priestesses themselves. Yet Maelchon's boats were still at the broch, plundering the village.' He paused, furrowing his sun-browned forehead. 'My orders were to seek out the Sisters, though it was too late, even though we rowed with no break. Then, as we landed, some of Maelchon's band were returning from over the hills, and your lady was running to the shore. She would have been trapped there against the water.'

Eremon's eyes briefly closed. 'And then?'

'It was too dangerous to engage them all, though by the Goddess, I wished to. We took your lady and pushed off, but the Orcadians did not stay long once their work was done. When we judged it safe we found a new landing and sought the other Sisters the Lady Rhiann had left in the hills.'

Eremon raised his cup, let the ale run slowly down his throat. 'What of Maelchon?'

Nectan's head dropped. 'I glimpsed him among his men. There was much blood on his face, and he roared like a bear and pressed forwards. But our arrows drove him back.' His breath quickened, as anger deepened the web of lines around his eyes. 'There was blood on your lady's hands and face and arms, and her fingers were cut. Yet beyond that, I do not know what happened to her. The Roman died defending her, and she held him, so some of the blood was certainly his.'

Eremon nodded, then his hand came out slowly to clasp Nectan's wrist, and he met that dark gaze. 'I owe you my life, my friend, for if she had died, it would be as if my own heart ceased beating. This is what you have done for us.'

Nectan nodded gravely when Eremon released him, for his own people spoke with such words. 'I wish, by the Mother, we had come soon enough for them all.' Fury sparked in his eyes, and he fingered the broken point of the stick as if it was one of his arrows. 'They committed sacrilege, and for that, they will pay. The Mother will make them pay.'

Every morning for a week, Eremon went faithfully to Rhiann's house, only for Linnet to report that the shock still had not lifted, and that she feared his presence might unbalance Rhiann further. He agreed, for although he was desperate to see his wife, he did not think he could bear either that blank, distant stare or the way she flinched from him.

Just what had that black Orcadian bastard done to her? Eremon shied away from completing that thought, yet continued to pace outside Rhiann's house, scoring a furrow in the ground. Eventually Linnet came out, sensing with one look exactly what tormented him so thoroughly, and immediately dealt with it. There were bruises on Rhiann's upper arms, she told him brutally, but nowhere else. Fola had been the first to tend her, and she believed, as did Linnet, that no outrage had been committed on Rhiann's body beyond the blows on her face. It would be well to seek some rest, she added, for he was upsetting the other girls.

Chastened, Eremon transferred his pacing to the outcrop of rock outside the Horse Gate, yet the relief about what Rhiann had escaped was soon eclipsed by his knowledge of what she had not escaped. Rape or no, Maelchon had terrorized Rhiann to the point that she would flinch away from her own husband, who had only ever treated her with tenderness.

Maelchon had driven this wedge between them.

It was this realization that forced Eremon's outward rage to settle into a simmering in his gut that he knew would never leave him. One day he would take his revenge, and Maelchon's death would not be quick or painless.

The rage carried Eremon for many more days, and kept him from despair.

Chapter 41

The fog around Rhiann was beginning to thin, though she tried to draw its dank folds closer, hiding her away.

All she remembered was a dim glimpse of sun on sea, and the sound of voices, followed by a dark house and Fola's face looming over her while girls sang. Then came nothing but a soft, muffling haze, and the instinct that she did not ever want to face what lay beyond it.

Over time, though, the singing began to grow louder and more distinct, and the pressure of hands bathing her brow grew gradually more clear. Then came the time Rhiann knew she had eyelids, and they were pressed tight against her cheeks; and she had fingers, and they dug into what felt like sheets, trying to stop the spinning of the bed around her.

Smells slipped in then: herbs and roots; earth clinging to shoes and digging sticks; the mingled Rhiann-smell of wild mint, soap and honey; beeswax, onion dye and smoke-tanned skins.

She was in her house, and suddenly, terrifyingly, she was awake.

For one moment, she hung suspended in time long enough to sense the heat of damp sheets against her skin, and the dryness of her mouth. But then, in the act of swallowing, her tongue slid across the sweet-salt cut on her lip, and with that she was pinned to the bed, for she could hide no longer. The memories rushed at her, vague and formless, bathed in nameless terror. And behind them a black wave of emotion reared, attached to the memories and yet separate. Then she knew she had nowhere to run.

Snatches of vision and sound and smells swirled around her, glimpses of the Sisters, Maelchon and Didius, and the vileness stopped her tongue in her throat and her heart from beating, and she wished she need never breathe again. Yet the black wave was still behind, coming on, and though Rhiann closed her eyes and stilled her chest, it rushed on, and finally broke over her in a maelstrom of regret, shame and guilt that would outlast memory, always.

They died because of me, because I called them there, because I drew the dark king.

Endlessly, the wave wept from her eyes, pouring through her with such force that she was taken down into darkness again. *I am not worth the love they bore me.*

Eremon and Nectan were breaking their fast on a bench outside the King's Hall when the Caereni chief suddenly straightened, his eyes fixed on the arch of the Horse Gate. Eremon laid down his platter of cheese and bread, and pulled his aching legs under him to rise.

It was a young messenger that appeared, muddy from his riding boots all the way up his thighs, with red-rimmed eyes and stubbled cheeks that signalled hard travel and no rest. Eremon decided he must be Caledonii, since he did not recognize the youth, and Nectan made no move to claim him as his.

The boy looked as if he would drop in his tracks, so Eremon hastened to draw him to the bench and thrust a flask of ale in his hands. 'Drink,' he ordered, and the youth did as he was bid, staring up at Eremon with trepidation as he swallowed.

'My lord,' he gasped at last, wiping his thin moustache and leaving a wet streak across his dirty cheek. 'I come from my king, Calgacus the Sword.'

'So I assume. What then?'

The boy seemed uncomfortable delivering his message while he sat and Eremon stood, so he rose shakily to his feet, grasping at the wall above the bench. 'My lord bid me tell you the Romans have assembled an enormous force, bigger than any we have ever seen. We have information that it is making ready to leave the Forth, to go north. My king fears this army will seek for the Dun of the Waves, and any other duns in its way.'

Eremon's chest was gripped by the first coldness in days to penetrate his rage. 'How long did it take you to get here?'

'Four days and no sleep,' the boy announced, with a glimmer of exhausted pride. 'But my king is not planning to attack the Roman column. He will wait until they have committed themselves far enough to be beyond reinforcements; until they have stretched their supply lines. He is waiting for you, lord.'

Eremon rubbed his chin. 'So it begins in earnest then, friend,' he said to Nectan, even as his gaze slid in the direction of Rhiann's house.

'If a man's heart is full of rage,' Nectan murmured, 'he should take it to battle.' Thoughtfully, he fingered the shell collar across his breast. 'So he tames the beast within. So he sees then with a clearer mind – and a clearer heart.'

Eremon summoned a pained smile. 'You are right, as ever.' He glanced back at the messenger. 'You have done well, yet your ride is over now, as mine is about to begin. Stay here and rest: I will go on alone.'

The youth's mouth dropped open and then clamped shut, twisting indecisively, until Eremon's hand came down most firmly on his shoulder. 'There are scouts only two days away,' the boy offered at last in surrender. 'They can guide you to where my lord waits.'

Eremon forced the flask on him once more. 'Then drink your fill, lad. I will leave before dusk.'

Yet as he was turning back to Nectan, Eremon's attention was arrested by Linnet, standing under the Horse Gate.

'At last she weeps,' was all Linnet could say when Eremon hurried to her. Her hands were spread, eloquent in helplessness. 'She weeps, and will not stop.'

This time Eremon did not pause to consider whether his presence was appropriate or not; he ran and then flung himself under the door-hide of Rhiann's house, to be confronted by an empty room. Linnet had cleared it of all people, even Caitlin, and it was silent but for the sobs that echoed from the rafters; sobs of such a wrenching pitch that each one seemed to curl around Eremon's heart and squeeze it painfully.

Rhiann was crouched against the wall by her herb shelves, her head in her arms, and when he went down on his knees and gathered her close, this time she did not resist. Yet the relief that came with that was instantly quenched when Eremon felt the true depth of her weeping, which racked her body.

She clung to him, fingers digging into his arms, her words barely coherent between each wave of tears. 'I did it to them, Eremon, it was me . . . me he came for, only me . . . I brought him, *I brought him!*'

These last words were so anguished that Eremon could only rock her, his lips against her damp hair. 'No, love,' he whispered. 'This is not your fault.'

'Yes, yes, it is!' Rhiann choked a breath. 'I did not foresee them, but the Sisters did, they knew.' Suddenly she wrenched back her head so violently that Eremon was caught off-balance. 'It happened again, didn't it?' Rhiann cried, staring wildly up at Linnet. 'Why couldn't I see in time? Why? The Mother has truly forsaken me!'

Linnet shook her head, her hand at her mouth. 'You are not forsaken by Her, my darling. Never, not by any of us.'

Yet Rhiann was beyond hearing, head buried once more in her arms. 'It *is* that – I must be cursed! I cannot save them, and when they love me they *die!*' Eremon gathered Rhiann closer, mute with shared pain, but she pushed weakly on his chest. 'Leave me; you must leave me or the curse will claim you, too!'

'Hush,' Eremon murmured, pressing her face into his chest. 'I will not leave you, ever. I love you.'

Yet that seemed to bring no comfort. 'No, no, I don't deserve it . . .'

Eremon caught Linnet's eye, and the raw distress there stabbed him to the core. 'Do not speak such words. I love you and you love me, it is what we have—'

'*No!*' With surprising strength, Rhiann threw him from her, and he fell to his haunches, his fingers and palms spread in the rushes. 'No!' she cried again, her hands balled into her eyes. 'I am not wife to you, not wife enough, and I fail you as I failed them . . .' She stopped to struggle for breath, her shoulders heaving.

'You've never failed me—' Eremon began, confused.

But Rhiann gave a piercing cry and lowered her hands, her eyes wild with grief and fury. 'And what wife would keep a babe from her womb! What love is that, to make it a barren place where no child can take root, no child so wanted by the man who loves her! I am cursed, *cursed*!'

Eremon reared back, too shocked to do anything but stare at Rhiann as her words penetrated the haze in his mind. Beside him, Linnet gasped and clutched at one of the roof-posts, swaying.

'You . . .' Eremon had to clear his throat. 'You stopped . . . a babe? Those draughts of yours, that's what they were?' Yet the only answer he had was Rhiann's sobs as she turned her face away. And suddenly Eremon couldn't feel her pain any more, only his own, which split his chest like the bloody rent of a sword, snatching his breath away.

Betrayal.

The betrayal of his own kin in Erin turning on him, exiling him; the wound it had torn which had never healed but only festered, for it broke open again now as he stared at his wife. 'So you . . . never really gave yourself to me?'

'Eremon,' Linnet broke in sharply, 'control yourself. She is over-wrought; she speaks from grief. This is not about you.'

He ignored her and rose to his feet, the hurt taking away all reason and control. '*Did you?*' he demanded hoarsely, glaring down at Rhiann.

Rhiann's head jerked up, her swollen face unrecognizable. 'No, no I did not! Is that what you want to hear?' She knelt and shuffled towards him. 'Then hear it. I cannot love you, Eremon of Dalriada; I cannot love you true! So by the Goddess, leave me with my shadows and my cursed love, and go far from here!' She flung her hand at the door, and then buried her face in her palms, her sobs robbing the words of all meaning.

Eremon had been slowly backing away, and when his heels struck the hearth-stone he halted, panting and staring at Rhiann as if she were a stranger.

'Eremon, stop it now!' Linnet cried, her own voice cracking. 'She knows not what she says.'

But he heard no more, and stumbled from the house towards the marsh.

And all that afternoon he walked as if sightless among the reeds, for all he could see in his mind were Rhiann's eyes. Where once they had looked on him with soft love, now they lanced him with the greatest pain she could inflict. And deep inside something in him cried with a wordless anguish, something that had once been betrayed and abandoned and could not bear it again.

His babe, she didn't want his babe.

Then she doesn't want me, he thought, dazed. *She cannot want me.*

Chapter 42

As the day ended, Eremon could put off leaving no longer: they needed him in the north, and there was no reason to stay. He could do nothing for Rhiann; he seemed only to cause her more pain. He must leave her to her women and their songs.

'Prince.'

It was Linnet at the door to Dórn's stall. Eremon stood by the stallion's flank, tightening the buckles holding his sword to his saddle. The shadows inside were a cool respite from the blazing day, and the headache that pounded on his temples. Silently, Eremon wrenched at the saddle straps with sweaty fingers, until he fumbled and cursed, and had to rest his head against the horse's shoulder.

'You forget yourself,' Linnet prodded softly. 'She is not in her right mind. You must ignore what she says.'

Eremon cut her off with a raised hand and a jerk of his head. 'It is not what she said, but what she's done! All the while she said she loved me, and she was ridding her womb of my children!'

Standing in the drifting dust motes, Linnet stared at his creased face for some time without moving. 'Forgive me,' she murmured then, 'but you react too strongly. Do not allow an old wound of your own to make you foolish.'

He flinched, for she struck too keenly, this priestess. 'Rhiann may be your charge,' he bit out, conscious of keeping some rein on his temper. 'I, however, am not, and so I would ask you to stay out of my mind and heart.'

Later, when he had calmed down, Eremon would admire Linnet's forbearance at that moment, and how she did not answer his insult with anger of her own. Instead, sympathy darkened her eyes.

'Rhiann is not like other women, Eremon. She questions her life more deeply than others do – for good or ill. And that, I believe, is also what you love in her, even though the fire, strength and stubbornness

273

can descend into such darkness.' She strode into the shadows to grip his shoulder, and that gesture revealed more of her distress than even her face. 'Yet she loves you as she has never loved anyone, not even me. You must trust that.'

'You heard her,' Eremon muttered, his breath catching in his throat. 'She doesn't love me; she hates all I represent as a warrior. I can only bring her more pain.'

'Her grief has taken her into a place of rage,' Linnet argued. 'It is not you she hates, but life. She does not know of what she speaks. You must believe that.'

'I can't,' Eremon said flatly. 'I just . . . can't. She lied to me, and she severed the thing that could join us for ever – all the last long dark, when I thought we were so happy!' A fist tightened around his heart. 'Manannán save me, but you don't understand either!' He twisted to face her, one hand tangled in the bridle. 'I lost my *kin*, lady, my *home*, my place in the world! A family could return this to me – Rhiann could give me that, and I could do the same for her, if she'd let me.'

Linnet hesitated, and her dark eyes flickered. 'I do not understand her choice in the matter of a child. Yet you are reacting out of old pain that has nothing to do with Rhiann, and this is a mistake . . .'

'Nothing to *do* with her? She won't let my child take root in her. She rejects the greatest bond we could forge, a bond of blood. She therefore rejects me, in the deepest way.'

Linnet's mouth trembled with pain. 'You are being too cruel,' she whispered.

'Perhaps I am!' Eremon suddenly cried. 'But there, I will be strong no longer, nor wise, nor steeped in the control you so value!'

Linnet's eyes dropped and she turned away. 'All of this will pass, prince, remember that. The shock has broken, the tears have come, and even they must dry eventually. Just give her, and yourself, some time.' She glanced back. 'She needs women around her now more than men. Let her come to some healing, and she will see things more clearly. Remember the love. It is real.'

Eremon wanted so much to believe her, and yet . . . he just couldn't blot the image from his mind, of Rhiann drinking her tea, bare hours after sharing the inner places of her body with him.

And with that memory the hurt suddenly bloomed anew, with exquisite, surprising force. He knew then that his uncle's betrayal had never healed at all.

Chapter 43

Despite the spectacle taking place outside the camp gate, Samana's heart was as heavy as the dark clouds marching over the sky from the western mountains.

An army of 5,000 men arrayed for battle was a new sight to her, for in all the time she'd known Agricola his units had either not been at full strength in Alba, or dispersed over the territory. Now many of the elite soldiers and auxiliary regiments of the Twentieth Valeria Victrix legion had been gathered in force from Viroconium in Britannia's west, and marshalled here on the gravel plain by the Forth for their journey north.

It should have stirred Samana, excited her, yet the proud eagle emblem on its tasselled pole, the bronze discs of the *signum* standards, the ranks of iron helmets and shining, segmented plate armour across chest and shoulders left her unmoved. For she was drowning in a soup of bitterness, indignation and, would she admit it, fear.

There was a burst of cheering and cacophony of trumpets from the remaining garrison, as a mounted Agricola passed under the gatetower to lead his men, flanked by his tribunes in their parade armour and the legionary legate, that humourless fool Lucius. And of course, Agricola did not even pause to look up at Samana on the bank, or throw her one crumb of farewell. His dark eyes remained narrow and keen beneath his polished helmet, its red feathered crest rippling in the harsh wind that blew from the clouded west.

Samana cursed him under her breath. Of course, he had not been so cold two nights before, when she took him in her mouth and made him cry out to all his gods twice over! Hypocrite! And what had she won with such artistry, but careless rejection? All that begging and pleading to let her accompany him and his legion on this northern expedition, and where had it got her?

I have an important meeting with my legate and centurions, Samana. Leave me now.

Samana had merely smiled, pulling up Agricola's tunic once more and touching her tongue to his thigh. Yet to her horror he had actually thrust her away, and his words were still reverberating through her skull.

This is a huge gamble.

Those savages could pour down on us from the mountains at any moment.

You don't belong with an army on the march, or with me. I can afford no distractions.

With an effort, Samana could overlook such words, for Agricola was beset by worries. Yet the worst thing of all was that he was slipping out of her hands again for some moons. And so soon!

Her smug assumption about the settled peace of Britannia had proven premature. Another rebellion had sprung up in the far south-west, just as her Alban countrymen launched their own uprising in the north, forcing Agricola to split his command. He was only accompanying the Twentieth northwards for one week, to assess the situation on the Caledonii plain, and would then meet a ship at the Tay to take him south to Londinium with his Ninth Hispana legion, leaving units from the other two legions to guard the province.

Yet if Samana could not stay by Agricola's side, how could she cling to the control over his body? Grinding her teeth, she abruptly turned her back on the lines of soldiers as they flowed away in a rustling, rippling flood towards the north. However, though her eyes no longer looked, she could not block her ears to the sounds: the grate of thousands of soldiers' boots on the gravel road; the neighs of horses and lowing of oxen; the rumble of cart wheels; and the murmur of men's voices.

Samana clamped her lips together, her muscles quivering with the effort of holding her temper. Below her, at the base of the great bank which formed one side of the camp, ten of her own Votadini warriors lounged. They seemed to have accepted their surrender to the Romans easily – in fact, though they had only recently arrived from Samana's dun, they had already become a shade too enamoured of Roman dicing games for her liking.

Samana strode down to them, drawing level with her leading warrior, captain of the little band. He straightened from his dice roll most swiftly.

'In two days, we will follow them,' she murmured to him, pressing her knuckles into one palm, her eyes restlessly scanning the barracks and tents spread out before her, and the dome of the tiny bath-house.

The man was silent, but she felt him staring at her. 'Will that be safe, my queen?' he at last ventured. 'The mountains are near, and we do not have the markings of the northern tribes on our faces.'

'I know!' she hissed, furious that he, of all people, had to speak aloud her own persistent fears. She skewered the man with her black eyes, twisting the rings on her fingers with agitation. 'In two days,' she repeated, 'we will follow that army. You organize the men and supplies. Tell the Roman quartermaster that we are returning home, and need food for the journey.'

The man's mouth set beneath his sweeping brown moustache, his eyes flicking up to the bank and the palisade. 'As you wish, my queen.'

'I do wish. Now leave me and do something useful with yourselves.'

When the warriors had collected up their dice and disappeared towards the stables, Samana climbed the bank again and stared out at the ranks of disappearing spears, the glistening of the mud churned by the passing of thousands. Just where the encroaching hills loomed, a veil of rain was sweeping down from the high ground, swallowing the marching army in its dark folds.

The thought of leaving the safety of the frontier to trail along behind that army into enemy territory terrified Samana. But, she reminded herself fiercely, it was nothing to the deeper terror of doing nothing – and thereby losing her precarious hold over Agricola. If that happened, she was truly lost.

She raised her chin to the first spatters of rain, clenching her hands. This was the better way, no matter how dangerous. It would give her more time with Agricola, to soothe his muscles, satisfy his desires, show him he needed her wherever he went. Then he might take her south on his ship, and keep her by him through sunseason.

After all, she chided herself, at last drawing her wool hood up against the rain, how much safer could one be but *behind* a Roman army? Yes, she was foolish to entertain such fears. She would put them resolutely aside, and plan what she would say to turn Agricola's wrath when she at last came upon him.

As the nights passed, Rhiann's will gradually grew weaker.

At first, the desperate numbness she clung to had carried her through not only her days, filled with the few repetitive tasks that she could manage, but also her nights. Even the news of Eremon's sudden departure had fallen into her empty soul with barely a ripple, sinking to the dark depths inside. And though the dark monsters of her dreams were lurking there whenever she slipped into unconsciousness, she warded them away with sheer will.

The monsters soon grew fiercer and more wily, however, lunging at her when her dream focus faltered, snapping at her heels relentlessly, as she ran from them through a colourless landscape of empty, frozen plains and dried-up rivers. And like any pack, they eventually began to wear her down.

When Rhiann realized that her will was faltering – that snatches of violent memory were beginning to intrude on her dreams – she tried to stop herself sleeping. Yet even then she had to lie and listen to the stifled weeping of those who grieved with her, and worst of all, the murmurs of comfort that the Sisters offered each other, but which she could not accept.

So she drifted for endless days between dream state and waking, searching for a haven that did not exist.

Linnet hovered there on the edges with Caitlin and Fola, but Rhiann found the pity in their eyes the worst pain of all. For it conjured up the faces of the others who were lost for ever, and the bitter guilt would rise and sear Rhiann's throat, and she had to turn away from them.

Eventually, Rhiann had no choice but to fall into exhaustion. And as soon as she did the pack was on her, and after so many nights she had no strength left to fight. She saw and felt it all: *the sword that split Nerida in two; blood spattering the Stones; Didius's face, sliced into ribbons; Maelchon's burning eyes; the wrenching of his hand between her thighs.*

. . . I did it to them I killed them it was me he came for it was my fault my fault . . .

Rhiann screamed, and suddenly hands were on her shoulders, shaking her, and she opened her eyes to see Linnet's face hovering over her in the lamplight.

'Child, it is only a dream!' Linnet's face was streaked with tears from her own weeping, her hair wild and unbound. Behind her, Fola's cheeks were creased with sleep, her eyes haunted by wherever she had been called from by Rhiann's scream.

Fola dropped to her knees, taking Rhiann's trembling hands in her own. 'It is gone, Rhiann,' she whispered fiercely. 'We are here with you.'

Linnet sank onto a stool, balancing the lamp on one knee as she brushed her damp hair back with unsteady fingers. Judging by her face, she had been crying for some time. The dead ones had been in the house this night, and not for Rhiann alone.

Shaking violently, Rhiann curled her legs up, pressing Fola's hand into the covers. But it was Linnet's eyes she sought. 'I have to know,' she forced out. 'I have to find a way to know why.'

Linnet swallowed. 'Know why?'

Rhiann swung her head to Fola, trying to calm her shivering. 'The elder sisters knew, didn't they? The way they were speaking, the way the Ban Crés gathered their secrets, the way they sent us away. They knew.'

Slowly, Fola nodded, and Rhiann stared again at Linnet. 'Then why did they let it happen? What did they hope to gain?' Her voice broke, harshening with desperation. 'Don't you see, I have to understand!'

Slowly, Linnet reached out and set the lamp on the table by the bed. The flame trembled and shook, then steadied, and Linnet stared into it so unmoving, for so long, that Rhiann began to hear the quiet noises of the house: the whimpers and murmurs of the girls; Fola's harsh, uneven breathing; the tiny hiccups of Gabran in the other bed. Caitlin was so tired out by his crying that she had not even woken.

'Why, aunt?' Rhiann at last burst out. '*They sacrificed themselves, and I have to understand why!*' Rhiann groped for her fingers. 'I . . . don't think I can go on unless I know . . . help me to find a reason, or all will fall into darkness!'

Linnet drew a deep, shaking breath. 'If as you say, they knew,' she said heavily, 'then perhaps there is a reason, though we may not be able to find it, child. It may be a reason beyond Thisworld, indeed, beyond this time.'

'No.' Rhiann's eyes fixed unseeing on the lamp flame. 'It is for now. They said they would give their strength to aid our people.'

Wearily, Linnet shook her head. 'Surely there can be no good in this,' she murmured, touching her fingers to the tracks of tears on her face. 'It is acceptance we must find . . .'

'*No!*' A blaze of anger burned Rhiann's chest, and she hauled herself up on her elbows. 'I will not accept,' she whispered furiously. 'I can accept anything but this!'

Fola's cheeks were flushed with high colour. 'My sister . . .' she began, as Rhiann turned on her, breathing hard.

'There is but one thing we need that we have not gained.' Rhiann kept her voice low, yet it came out in an impassioned rush. 'An alliance of all the tribes. I hoped that if the Ban Crés believed in it, they could help to forge it – but perhaps that was not how it was going to be.'

As some realization dawned in Fola's eyes, Rhiann sat upright. 'Perhaps there was only one thing that could convince the tribes to join: an outrage so complete, so painful, that the actions of the Romans could no longer be ignored!'

The implications of Rhiann's own words unfurled in her mind. *If I can find a reason, then I will be able to go on without them.*

'Rhiann—' Linnet implored.

Yet surprisingly, it was Fola who spoke. 'She's right,' Fola whispered, her dark gaze turned inwards. 'The words hold truth.' Her eyes sharpened. 'All tribes share the Sisterhood; women from all tribes are trained on the Sacred Isle; all tribes celebrate the Mother's gifts; all sing to Her at Beltaine. This raid strikes at the very heart of Alba, and if the warriors did not know it before they will now. For is it not only when the heart is wounded that it is truly felt?'

'Daughters,' Linnet's brow creased with pain as she looked from one to the other, 'we are all grieving. We must not grasp at what may not be there.'

Rhiann's fingers closed over Linnet's. 'Tell me one thing,' she demanded quietly. 'Put aside the mother and be the priestess. Do you think I am right? Could this be the turning point we were searching for?'

The strength of her gaze, hardened by desperation, bored into Linnet. For a long moment Linnet's jaw tightened, then her lids sank closed, breaking the link. 'Yes,' she said, in a quiet voice heavy with sadness, 'I think something has happened to sweep us forward to a new future. But I don't want to think it; I don't want to know—'

'It doesn't matter what we want.' For a moment Rhiann squeezed Linnet's hand, before sinking back and staring up at the thatch, ridged by the lamp-flame and shadows, her thoughts taking flight. The violence of the dream-monsters was fast subsiding, and she felt empty again, and therefore clean. 'It doesn't matter what any of us want. We can only deal with what must be.'

The further Eremon rode from Dunadd, the more his anger faded, and the deeper his shame began to bite. He tried to stoke the rage by reminding himself what Rhiann had done, but day by day the ashes grew colder.

What his mind relived instead was the expression of pain in Rhiann's eyes at his childish words, a pain that overlaid the terrible marks of grief and fear already scoring her face. *How could he?*

As his horse ate up the leagues, Eremon's head sunk lower onto his shoulders, weighed down by shame. The scouts who led him seemed disinclined to break such a brooding silence, and kept to their own fire at night, as he kept to his.

And every day the pain found some way to intrude. One day they surprised a doe and her fawn who leaped across the path before them and into the forest. As the two were caught in a shaft of sun, and the doe's sides lit up to the exact colour of Rhiann's hair, Eremon found the breath knocked out of him, as if he had fallen to the ground. When they passed the isolated steadings, and people came out to gape at their weapons and armour, a pair of blue eyes would always spear him in his saddle, whether they bore a resemblance to hers or not.

So he drove the party relentlessly, exhausting himself so that sleep came quickly, before the despair could bite too deep.

Eremon was greatly relieved when they met the first of Calgacus's scouts, and were led deep into the northern mountains to the camp of the warriors. There, he could take up his mantle of war leader again. There, he could lose himself in talk of battle and raiding and strategy.

Calgacus's camp was hidden near the head of a broad glen that split the Mountains of the Sea, which ran down the eastern spine of Alba. The valley was leagues long, and gave good access to the interior of the mountains. At its inner, western end it branched into smaller side valleys, like a river delta, and in one of these the camp lay, a collection of hides and tents strung between the overhanging trees and rock outcrops. It could function as a long-term abode if needed, yet also be abandoned at the first cry of a scout. All that the Albans needed to wage war on the Romans they carried on their bodies: long swords; a brace of spears; a quiver of arrows. And, most valuable of all, the knowledge of the land.

This was brought forcefully home to Eremon as the scouts led him by paths that he could not see, over what seemed impassable ridges, until he came upon the valley so suddenly he didn't even know it was there. As he picked his way down the steep, precarious path between the rocks and bracken, this realization of the advantage they possessed gave Eremon the first pang of pleasure he'd felt for two weeks.

For despite the Romans using scouts from conquered tribes, bought knowledge could never match the innate lore of a man born and bred to this particular glen, and the hills that surrounded it. Such a man knew all the paths in and out: which could be blocked, or were impassable in certain weathers; which gave access to ridge paths that could carry one far. He knew where the boggy ground was, the hard ground, and where the bracken hid broken rocks that could snap a man's leg. He understood all the different clouds and how they moved over the mountains, when they presaged storms and snow, and when only light rain; how long a certain kind of mist would linger.

At Eremon's request the scouts led him to Conaire's shelter, six deer-hides roughly cobbled together with rawhide, stretched from the ground to a central sapling pole to a large rock that formed the back wall. More muddy hides covered the ground beneath the bed rolls, for the mountains were always damp, running with water from the high peaks. In the centre a hollow had been scooped out for a fire, over which was strung a skin bag of simmering broth.

Conaire grinned and slapped Eremon on the back as he dumped his pack and armour, and then took one look at his brother's carefully masked face and grasped both shoulders in an iron grip. 'By the Boar, brother, is it worse than you thought? Is Rhiann . . . ?' Conaire bit off his words, but his blue eyes widened with sudden fear, white against his sunburned cheeks.

Faced with the warmth of Conaire's hands on his shoulders, all of Eremon's intentions to bury what had happened crumbled. He bent back to look up at Conaire, exhaustion sweeping over him. 'Caitlin is well, as is your son. Rhiann is alive and unhurt, though much grieved.' Eremon broke away and turned his back, blurting, 'And I acted like a complete fool and hurt her even more!'

Conaire remained silent, until Eremon wearily rubbed the stubble on his face with both hands, and told him all of what happened at Dunadd. When Conaire had digested it he moved to stand before Eremon, pity in his eyes. 'I have never known Rhiann to do anything without good reason,' he offered carefully.

'Well, I never stayed to find out the reason.'

'Yet love so hard to win cannot be easily undone, brother, or put aside.' Conaire paused. 'And there is nothing that cannot be forgiven, after all.'

Eremon stared bleakly past his foster-brother to the sky outside, heavy and grey, as rain began to spatter the hides above his head. And he remembered lying in the honey-moon hut with Rhiann's hair trailing between his fingers, thinking that what they had was unassailable. He was a warrior – he should have known that nothing was unassailable.

He blew out his breath and cocked one eye at Conaire. 'Anyway, don't you wish to know of your boy? He crawls so fast Caitlin can hardly keep up.'

'He crawls!' Conaire's face couldn't help but light up with pride, and Eremon knew then there was no earthly way for him to avoid the pain such love brought him. He would just have to bear it: there it was.

'But tell me of what has happened here.' Eremon gritted his teeth and bent to search his pack, tossing a leather flask to Conaire. 'And by the way, Eithne has made a new batch of blackberry ale. Caitlin pressed it upon me, for you and I to toast the longest day together.'

Still eyeing Eremon with concern, Conaire stored the flask on a shelf in the rock, balancing it alongside a few tallow candle-stubs, two grooved sharpened stones, some travel bread wrapped in leaves, and flint and tinder. 'We have done little since you left, brother. Yet Calgacus himself has been busy – he asked the Vacomagi and Taexali kings to withdraw their people into the hills. He has also evacuated his own dun.'

'Ah.'

Conaire leaned against the tent pole, arms folded. 'The young people were in the hills with the cattle anyway, and all who can move have done so. The duns are empty, and Calgacus seems sure the Romans will leave the crops.'

Eremon nodded, watching the strengthening rain kick up splatters of mud on the path outside. This is what he wanted, to bury himself in this. 'No, they won't burn the crops – they need the supplies for their own men. They will target the duns, where they believe the warriors are.'

'Well, they won't find anyone at all.'

'And that will draw them on northwards.' Eremon chewed his lip, a faint and familiar excitement stirring his gut. 'Yes, I see what Calgacus is thinking.'

'Then you can explain it to me.' Conaire squatted at the fire and poked at the floating lumps of deer meat in the skin bag. 'If Calgacus wants to keep the Romans away from his dun, then why draw them north? We have been tracking the whole army for two weeks, and not once has he ordered an attack.'

Eremon smiled and stretched the saddle soreness from his back, feeling a purer, cleaner energy flow into his limbs. This was what he did best. 'The less resistance we offer for now, the further on the Romans are drawn, their guard going down. By the time we do attack, they will be far from their frontier, far from their reinforcements.' He laughed. 'Agricola has gambled much on this; he must be getting desperate.'

'Brother, save your gloating.' Conaire jerked his thumb over his shoulder. 'When Calgacus got news of your approach, he called a meeting of all the leaders. We'll need your cool head now to douse Lorn's fire – perhaps you can calm him down before Calgacus does so with his fists!'

As they left the tent, Eremon's mind turned over Nectan's words: *if a man's heart is full of rage, he should take it to battle.*

It must not be long before he drew his sword again – in fact, he intended to lead the first charge himself. Perhaps then he could blot out the sight of Rhiann's anguished eyes, and forget all the harsh words they had spoken.

The wreaths of hawthorn and meadowsweet floated in pale rings on the copper sea, the largest ones – for Nerida and Setana – already disappearing into the flaming heart of the sinking sun. The glow was so bright Rhiann could not look at it, standing on the shore of the Isle of Deer, singing the Sisters' souls into the west.

All through the rite on this warm, still eve, Rhiann had held back the anger and pain, forcing the chants of farewell and blessing out of her rigid throat. She felt she must not give in to the memories of love, for they were twined with the grief, and her fragile control would shatter again. Then she would be unable to give the Sisters the honour they were due. So she swallowed it back down, praying that they would see from the Otherworld what burned in her heart.

Yet as Rhiann turned away from the sun, her eyes fell on Linnet and Fola, still staring out across the shining, flat sea. Both of their faces were masks, every line of humour and softness sagging as if their features had melted, and Rhiann knew that after all these weeks her own must look the same. She jerked her eyes away.

Caitlin was standing back, for she was no priestess, but tears ran down her cheeks. She, who did not even know the Sisters, wept for them all the tears Rhiann could not shed. Rhiann found she was biting down hard on the inside of her cheek, and she closed her eyes to the soft, purple sky above the island hills, and the glide of a curlew over the bay, and tasted blood in her mouth instead.

And so it was the blood that undid her. Blood, drawn by Maelchon's hand. Blood, wet on Nerida's skin.

Suddenly, the swell of the curlew's cry and the far murmur of the sea faded from Rhiann's ears, as the memory of Nerida's last words arced like an arrow into her mind. *In you lies our hope.*

Her gaze settled on the girls, who had turned from the water and were now stumbling along the darkening beach towards the boats in a ragged group, the dignity and grace trained into their bodies crumbling under the weight of grief. The strong, calm light of common purpose that had always held them was gone, leaving them all floundering. Their souls had vibrated as one song; now each one's spirit trembled alone.

And what came to Rhiann then was simple: *I must lead them. It is surely what Nerida and Setana charged me with.* With the expression of that thought, so came the first warmth Rhiann had felt in weeks, settling over her in a blanket of relief.

She would turn this outrage into triumph, the pain into action, for the Sisters, so their sacrifice was not in vain; for these girls, to help them assuage their grief; and for her people, to give them the aid the Sisters had promised. Slowly, she began to breathe out, her shoulders widening, her fists unclenching as she searched herself for the strength she would need, a strength she had thought irrevocably broken.

Rhiann's glance strayed then to the north, and the highland mountains. *This too I must do for Eremon. So we stand in my dream side by side again. So I make him proud of me. So he can forgive me.*

On the way home, Rhiann peeled away from the others, for she had one more offering to make. On a natural slab of rock on a hillside above Dunadd, the ancestors had made carvings for the souls of the greatest heroes. Here, over the centuries, spirals were drawn to remember the bravest of warriors, and here Rhiann had sent a carver a day ago to add a spiral for Didius.

Now, alone beneath the deepening sky, Rhiann knelt on the cold rock and traced the new design with oil and ochre and rowan ash, remembering what he had done for her. 'The spiral is to show you the way home, Didius,' she whispered, as the shadows gathered around her from the oak woods beyond. 'Your soul comes from the Mother, and now it returns to the Mother, because there is no end or beginning.'

After filling the curving lines with mead, infused with sacred meadowsweet, Rhiann wrapped her cloak closed against the cooling night and shut her eyes. Then she sang a prayer, her voice carrying far on the clear, still dusk: that after resting in the Mother's womb Didius would follow the path of his spiral back out to breathe again of Alba's air.

For he had loved her land so.

★

The next day Linnet wished to return to her home, and Rhiann insisted that she, Caitlin and Fola accompany her. Caitlin kept her eyes fixed on the back of Rhiann's head for the entire ride, concerned at this sudden burst of energy after the slow, unspoken grief of the previous day.

They ate fresh baked salmon in the shade of Linnet's oak, played with Gabran and talked of small things, and all the while Caitlin could see Rhiann bursting with something. And when they had finished eating, Rhiann could wait no longer, rising and pressing her hands together. Then she announced that she had an idea, at last, of what to do about the Sisterhood.

Cross-legged on a deer-hide, Caitlin stayed silent as she listened, one hand on Gabran's back while he rocked on his hands and knees. Yet as Rhiann continued to speak, Caitlin's heart sank.

Rhiann explained how she originally considered establishing a new seat of the Sisterhood at Dunadd, but had immediately realized that without the elder Sisters that kind of power had been lost. 'So then I thought that perhaps something different was being demanded of the Sisters now.'

Rhiann began pacing. She had wound her auburn hair in tight braids about her skull, and her cheekbones and jaw were all stark angles, her eyes hollowed. Caitlin knew she had hardly eaten for weeks, despite her and Eithne's best efforts to tempt Rhiann's palate. The softness of the extra weight her sister had put on this last year was already being stripped away. 'I thought that we must harness the grief of this attack. As the news passes across Alba, and the Ban Crés do not return, the people will surely cry out for vengeance.'

'Vengeance is not the way of the Sisters, daughter,' Linnet interrupted quietly.

Rhiann came to a halt. 'No, aunt, I speak of bringing the tribes together in defence!'

Caitlin read Rhiann's desperation and grief, and longed to go to her. She sighed under her breath. Yet perhaps she could do nothing; perhaps the only thing to reach Rhiann would come from the Sisters.

Rhiann explained that thirty of the young Sisters were initiated, and knew the songs, rites and chants, the healing knowledge and the lore. So she proposed embarking on a journey north around Alba, visiting the kings who had not yet joined Eremon and invoking their people's outrage, leaving a priestess at each royal dun to replace those who had been lost.

Caitlin immediately sat up straighter, alarmed at this suggestion, yet Rhiann was staring at Fola. Her friend was sitting forward on her knees, her dark eyes eager. 'It is the rallying call,' Fola murmured, her voice trembling with excitement.

'Exactly! For the tribes will find it difficult to ignore this outrage when the Sisterhood itself – what is left of it – arrives on their doorstep!' Rhiann's eyes burned, though her mouth remained pained. 'These girls will show that no sacrilege is beyond the invaders! They will be a reminder for all those kings, when their resolve to defend their land falters.'

Fola sank back and linked her arms around her knees. 'It is daring, courageous – a good idea. A fine idea!'

In Fola's eyes, Caitlin saw an echo of Rhiann's own strange glitter. She could stay silent no longer. 'But . . . but surely when all of you are so grieved, it would be better to stay here and rest, and help each other?'

Rhiann stared down at Caitlin as if she'd just seen her. 'What good is it to give in and surrender, sister? Then the Romans and Maelchon will have won!'

Lost for words, Caitlin drew a squirming Gabran into her lap, appealing to Linnet. 'But they're only young. Surely you cannot have them traipsing all over the mountains, not when their hearts are so sore.' *And yours*, Caitlin thought desperately, looking up into Rhiann's closed face. *What about your heart?*

'The girls cannot be ordered in this; you will have to ask them,' said Linnet with a resigned sigh. 'The youngest can return to their families, yet the older initiates gave their service to the Goddess with their vow. If only we could be sure this is what the Mother asks.'

'*I* feel sure,' Fola declared, scrambling to her feet. 'Rhiann told me that the elder Sisters said in the future *all* priestesses had to live among the people, be part of their lives.'

'Yes, they did,' Rhiann said, surprised.

'And I cannot believe they meant this to be the end,' Fola added passionately. 'They must have meant for something good to come out of this – there *must* be something good!'

Suddenly Caitlin found herself on her feet, hauling Gabran into her arms. He jerked in surprise and broke into choked whimpers. 'You are not strong enough to do this, Rhiann!' Caitlin burst out, raising her chin as Rhiann's eyes flashed. 'You should be here, with those who . . . who love you.' Trembling, she kissed her son's head, trying to soothe his hiccupping cries.

'Caitlin,' Rhiann said, 'don't you understand? I have to do something.'

'But you need time to grieve, to sleep—'

'*This is my time!*' Rhiann cried, and for a moment her fierce mask faltered. 'Doing something so that their deaths are not in vain – can't you see what this means to me?'

'And I will be by Rhiann's side,' Fola interjected.

Moving Gabran to her hip, Caitlin's head bowed. 'It isn't right,' she repeated stubbornly. 'But it isn't my decision.'

'There is more to this than even you know, sister,' Rhiann whispered, and when Caitlin raised her head she saw that Rhiann was staring into Linnet's eyes. 'There is a greater pattern here, something I am being driven to, and this is part of it, I see that now.'

Linnet had gone completely still, the pallor of her face tinted green by the overhanging oak leaves. Yet Caitlin saw the faint understanding that passed between them.

'So,' Rhiann said, with a swift turn of her skirts, 'it is decided then: I will ask, and the girls will decide. Let us go now, for I can waste no more time.' Fola swiftly rose, and together she and Rhiann made their way towards the horses tied against the house.

Caitlin's hand, however, fastened on Linnet's arm and pulled her back. 'How can you let them do this!' she hissed, fright and distress loosening her tongue. 'You sat there and said nothing!'

Linnet's eyes finally met Caitlin's glare, and all at once Caitlin saw there what Linnet had been keeping hidden.

'My child,' Linnet murmured, the pain pulling down the edges of her mouth, 'I know you worry for her, but Fola loves and knows her well. Do not be wounded by the anger – the tide of fury can carry one far, but eventually it washes up on some shore, and then ebbs away.'

'Yet that shore will be far from us,' Caitlin whispered in anguish. 'And you did nothing to keep her here, where we can help.'

Linnet's eyes closed for a moment as the leaves stirred in the breeze, and then her trembling hand reached out to cup Caitlin's cheek. 'I have been shown I can do nothing to hold her back; nothing to change her future, for it is already written.' Every year of Linnet's age seemed to descend over her face at once, stopping Caitlin's protests in her throat. 'She must find her own way, or she will not find it at all. Believe me.' She dropped her hand and looked around her yard, winding her arms around her chest. 'And when I am here alone,' she murmured, 'that is what I will cling to.'

Swept with pity, Caitlin took Linnet's hand as Gabran paused in his whimpering to stare up at his grandmother, blue eyes swimming with tears. 'You will not be alone, mother,' Caitlin whispered. 'I may not be a priestess, but Gabran and I can bring our own healing.'

As they moved into the sunlight spilling over the hut's roof, Linnet took the child in her arms and held him close. The horses were already untied, and Rhiann was in the saddle, impatient for home.

Chapter 44

The reaction of the young initiates to Rhiann's plan was instant and unanimous, and many faces that had been drawn by grief and bewilderment seemed to strengthen with a new resolve and boldness. No one showed any fear, and Rhiann felt great pride as she looked around at them on the hearth-benches of the King's Hall. The Sisterhood was still strong, she told herself. The spirit of the elders lived in them all.

Nectan and his men had not yet returned north to his home, held at Dunadd by shared grief and his concern for the remaining Sisters. He immediately volunteered the services of his warriors, and Rhiann and her party had their escort.

The next day Linnet and Rhiann made one of the yearly offerings to the old spirits at the stone circle in the ancestor valley, laying meat and mead in a hollow at the base of the stones. At the same time they sang another chant to invoke the Source in that sacred place, to bless the Sisters for their journey.

'Where do you intend to go?' Linnet asked Rhiann as they packed their baskets and left, stepping carefully over the peat on piles of pebbles.

Rhiann moved her basket to her other hip and glanced back at Linnet. 'We will go to the Creones land first.' She remembered well how scornful the Creones king had been at Calgacus's last council. 'Once his chieftains are banging on his door, baying for blood, perhaps he won't be so quick to dismiss the war leader of the Epidii again.'

When they reached the horses on the solid ground beside a stream, Rhiann began to strap her basket behind her saddle. 'Aunt,' she said then, for she had something most difficult to broach. Linnet paused from untying her stallion and Rhiann took a deep breath and ploughed on. 'You have never said anything of what I revealed to Eremon that awful day. About babies . . . my decision.' Rhiann fixed her eyes on her fumbling fingers, tying the leather thongs too tight.

Linnet said nothing at first, then she stepped forward and raised Rhiann's chin with a gentle hand. Her eyes were paler in the direct light of the dawn sun, but the colour shifted with some strong emotion. 'I sent Caitlin away for my own reasons,' she whispered, 'then nearly lost her for ever. I have tasted the bitter cup of guilt as priestess and mother both. Who am I to judge you?'

Rhiann swallowed the lump in her throat. 'But Eremon,' she said. 'I never wanted to hurt anyone like that . . . as I have been hurt.'

Linnet's hand dropped. 'A large part of Eremon's hurt was done to him long ago, and not by you. That is why his sense deserted him. He will find himself again, child, in time.'

Yet Linnet's words did little to assuage Rhiann's gnawing guilt on the ride back to Dunadd. And she pondered on time, and how much of it she and Eremon would be granted together. Perhaps when Eremon's hurt had dulled, when she had a triumph to lay at his feet, then she could go to him and look him in the eye once more.

Samana and her escort, hugging the eastern coast, were only two days behind the Roman army now, judging by the vast, abandoned marching camps they came across on their way north. As nervous as she was, Samana could not help but marvel at the speed and efficiency of the Roman military machine, the vast ditches the army delved and high earth walls that were raised to camp for one night.

Yet even though her party was on horseback, Roman soldiers were trained to march twenty miles a day with a heavy pack, and so Samana pushed her own warriors hard, rousing them early and driving them late, barely stopping for food and drink. She had to get to Agricola's side before he turned back south.

At last, though, the captain of her Votadini guard said the men must take a proper night's sleep, if they were to be any good to her.

Samana chafed at the decision even as she accepted its wisdom, and grudgingly called a halt in a clearing by the Isla river, its banks wooded with scrubby alder and willow, the higher ground behind thick with spreading oaks.

'Do not fret, lady,' her captain said as he helped her to dismount beneath a tall elm tree, the shadows already cooling with approaching night. The man was irritatingly cheerful now he was closer to a full belly around a fire. 'There's been no hint of any trouble, none at all. The highlanders won't come down so close to the Roman forts anyway.'

Samana whipped around. 'Fool! They raided and burned some of those forts to the ground! And how? With magic?'

The warrior's face fell as he sought for some other platitude, yet Samana only hissed impatiently and turned her back, stalking off to the gravel banks of the river. Far to the west the mountains reared, dark banks of cloud shrouding their peaks. The surface of the swift river at her feet was dark and opaque in the valley, breathing a mist that curled over her skin.

Agricola had always spoken of keeping to the coast, and Samana wanted nothing more than to stay as far from those mountains as possible. But she couldn't. The swiftest route was along this broad valley, which funnelled them between the mountains and a range of heavily wooded hills closer to the sea. She didn't like it, but the ease of the ground meant she would be out of danger and in Agricola's arms all the sooner.

No one would attack me, she blustered to herself. *Why would they?* The highlanders sought only Roman blood.

Samana had been repeating the same litany in her head for the past three days, though it did not shake the dread that kept sending cold tendrils up her spine. And she'd put herself in this situation for a man who had tossed her aside like some common whore. Well, when she gained his side once more she would not let go, and he could take her south with him, or . . . or . . . she would think up some threat significant enough to make him agree.

Anger was better than fear, and so strong was her ability to ignore what troubled her that when Samana was woken in the night by a scuffle outside her tent she did not at first register what it might be. Then her mind, scrambling for awareness, at last recognized the sounds: the grunts of men being stabbed by blades; the gasps of the dying.

By the time the flap of her tent was wrenched back and a brand thrust inside, Samana was crouching against the far wall, her meat-dagger clutched in her hand. As she held a fur across her shift, one thought sparked in her mind, appalling her: few women possessed her sensual beauty, she always gloated few could catch a man's eye like she could . . . Samana's mouth went so dry her tongue stuck to its roof, but she faced down the four men who pushed their way into the tent, stinking of sweat and blood and Goddess knew what else. Their hair was straggling, their tunics filthy, but they were armoured, too, with helmets and hardened leather breastplates, and all bore swords.

Now the one with the brand held it higher, and that was when she saw the blue tattoos curling fiercely over their cheeks; some depicting bears and stags and wolves, but all bearing on one side the sharp outline of the great eagle.

The eagle. *Calgacus.*

For the first time in her life, Samana knew visceral, gut-loosening fear.

'This is her,' one of the men said, and spat onto the fine furs of otter, wolf and seal tumbled across her bed roll.

'You know who I am?' She tried to sound imperious, but sweat was trickling down under her breasts, and her palms were slippery on the knife.

The man who held the torch was studying her with appraising eyes that held little pity. 'No,' he replied curtly. 'But we've been tracking you for days. And what would a beautiful Alban maid like you be doing marching in the wake of a Roman army?' He stepped closer, then wrenched the fur cover away from her and dropped it. 'Why would you show no fear of them? Why would you hurry to catch them?'

Samana backed up against the wall of the tent, the slope of the taut leather pressing down on her head. 'I . . . I was a prisoner. I am of the Venicones, and the Romans took me because I am high born. He,' she bit her lip, 'they were sending me south, to be a slave in their camps.' She forced a tremulous smile, reached out to him. 'And thank the Goddess you saved me! My people will be grateful.'

The man shook away her touch as if he'd been scalded. 'Prisoner? Do you think my lord gives fools his command?' he demanded. 'If you were a prisoner, you would be travelling under Roman escort, not your own. And you are going north, my lady.' At last he smiled. 'My *lowland* lady.'

One of the other men spoke up now, and his eyes were indeed roving over the curves of Samana's body. 'What do we do with her, then? I've got an itch here I haven't scratched for weeks. Shall we throw dice for who's first?'

Samana could not repress the cry of horror that burst from her, yet the leader's flinty eyes darted warningly to his men. 'No. She is a friend of the invaders, so we'll take her back north. Our lord and the other chiefs can retrieve all the information she undoubtedly carries.' A cruel smile curved his mouth. 'She'll be more use that way.'

'But Gerat, she can buck under me as well as talk!'

'I said no.' The leader's gaze met Samana's own, and in it she saw contempt, not lust. 'She's high born all right; she told the truth there. Our lord would not allow it, as well you know. Now get back outside: take all their weapons, their food. Hurry!'

After letting her dress, Samana's captors dragged her outside into the cold night air, and she stumbled, averting her eyes from the twisted bodies scattered around the campfire.

Beyond, the river ran black and swift under a shining half-moon, indifferent to her plight. Yet it was only after Samana was thrown into the saddle of her mare, her hands tied, that her dazed brain could begin to comprehend what had happened.

Our lord and the other chiefs, the leader said. And who were they? Who were Calgacus's allies? She was taken with a shudder of shock, and had to hunch her shoulders so her cloak did not fall.

Agricola hadn't known for sure, but the recent fort attacks bore all the marks of the Erin prince, and snippets of other information had hinted that Calgacus and Eremon had grown close. Had that closeness now turned into true allegiance? It felt true ... it must be true.

So that was where they were taking her.

To see Eremon again.

A font of hysteria bubbled up, and Samana began to snort with laughter, to shriek with a terrible, wild mirth that she could not contain. Then the leader turned his horse back and slapped her across the face with a hard hand, and she slumped into stunned silence and did not laugh again.

BOOK FOUR
SUNSEASON, AD 82

Chapter 45

The waiting time was over at last.

Eremon's plans had been carefully laid with Calgacus; now they walked through the encampment on the night before those plans would be set in motion. Together, the king and the prince wended their way from campfire to campfire in the valley, speaking to their men, sharing ale and jests, giving reassurance and information as needed.

Yet Eremon had another subject to broach with his Caledonii ally, and had only been waiting for an opportunity to speak alone, which came rarely in a camp of 1,700 men. Perhaps, too, he had waited to gain some measure of control over his rage. In that, he feared he had failed.

He and Calgacus were making their way down a gully beside a swift, stone-tumbled stream bed, caught in the dark reaches between two campfires, when Eremon found himself blurting out what he had wished to raise calmly. 'You have not yet given me your answer about the Orcadian king.'

Calgacus halted, and in the half-dark Eremon could sense the tension that tightened his shoulders as he sighed. 'I think perhaps I was avoiding the discussion, in truth,' the king replied. 'For you won't like what I have to say.'

Eremon's held breath was expelled in a soft hiss, and Calgacus's head reared in dark outline against the bloom of fire below.

'You know I wish to exact revenge on him as much as you, prince – my mother was a priestess, after all. But we have an entire legion of Romans down there on the plain; *they* are our priority, and you know it. We don't know how badly wounded Maelchon is, or how well fortified his dun, or how many men he has. No one has ever known. If you take your warriors and leave, you weaken us. Revenge is not worth that.' The king's stiff posture softened. 'Rage can be a man's undoing, Eremon. It can make him foolhardy, but I cannot afford one moment of foolhardiness. You are not my vassal, and can do as you wish. But I cannot give you men to aid you against Maelchon. I would counsel you to leave him alone. For now.'

Eremon's blood pounded on his temples. He had known, somewhere, what the verdict would be, for he himself knew that the king's reasoning was sound. 'Yet Maelchon remains a danger at our rear,' he argued gruffly.

'I fear so. But the Decantae have allowed me to station scouts in their lands with their own, to watch for any movement from the Orcades.' Calgacus's hand squeezed his shoulder. 'Let this thought comfort you, prince. Maelchon has shown where his true allegiance lies. I do not think another year will pass before you meet him on the end of your sword. Then you can have your revenge, and it will be all the sweeter for waiting.'

When Eremon rejoined his own men at a fire outside his shelter, Conaire glanced up at him, eyebrows arched in enquiry. Eremon replied with a tiny shake of his head, but as he seated himself on his folded cloak, Rori, oblivious, displayed far less tact.

'My lord,' he blurted eagerly, laying his bow across his knees, 'when are we setting sail to challenge the Orcades traitor?'

At the expression on Eremon's face, Colum winced and looked down at the sword he was sharpening and began to whistle, applying the stone with vigour. As the strained silence stretched out, Rori realized he had said something wrong, and shrank back, his eyes darting from Eremon's face to Conaire's set mouth.

'We must leave King Maelchon for the time being.' Eremon's voice was admirably calm. Yet he didn't feel it; by Hawen's breath and balls, he didn't feel it. 'We cannot spare the warriors at this delicate stage. But the time will come, soon.'

Fergus muttered a curse, dipping the base of a spear-point into the fire-pot of birch tar. But after a warning glance from Conaire the youth sat back with a silent scowl, setting the sticky tang of the point into its pale ash shaft.

Thank the gods that Lorn preferred a fire with his own men on the other side of camp, Eremon thought sourly, for if *he* was here they would never hear the end of it. Irritated by the lengthening silence, he took a more normal breath and glanced around at his men with a raised eyebrow. 'Speaking of this delicate stage, are we all clear about what we have to do? Do you have your supplies ready?' Immediately, Colum and Fergus nodded.

Eremon, in large part to assuage the potent brew of guilt, hurt and rage that was fermenting in his gut, was leading the first attack on the Roman army. For the oncoming column had now reached the narrowest neck of land, the point where the eastern hills came closest to the sea – a place not too far from their hidden glen.

'Rori?' Eremon's eye now fixed on his youngest warrior, as she recognized the embarrassment still painted on Rori's freckled cheeks.

Rori held up an arrow. 'I am going with the Caereni archers tonight, my lord.' His smile was tentative. 'I have food and water packed.'

'Good.' Eremon grinned at him. 'That is quite enough glory for now, eh? Remember that you get to strike the first blow, Rori, before we get anywhere near!'

It had been Conaire's suggestion, carefully thought out, to give this first attack to the archers, not the swordsmen. Eremon would follow with his troop of warriors, but they would remain in reserve, as Nectan's men cut the horses out from under the Roman cavalry and officers. The Albans hoped this would not only make retreat harder, but also instill panic into the rest of the Roman ranks, for fear was a potent weapon that worked outside the range of a blade.

Suddenly, Conaire's eyes flickered upwards, and Eremon turned to see one of the Caereni archers standing on the edge of the pool of firelight. 'My lord.' The little man went down on one knee, his head bent in the usual deference these strange, half-wild people showed Eremon.

'Yes?' Eremon's mind scrambled for a name; the Caereni men all looked similar with sloe eyes and raven-black hair. Yet then he remembered it was Nectan's brother, left in command in his absence. 'Yes, Domech?'

'Our people will sacrifice to the Goddess, the Great Mother, this night. As Her consort, the King Stag, you must come and eat of the deer's heart and be marked with his blood. Then She can protect you in the forest.'

Eremon sensed his men's bemused reactions, although Rori and Fergus stiffened at the implicit demand in the man's words.

Smiling to himself, Eremon agreed immediately, and rose to gather his weapons. He straddled two worlds now, as he was sometimes reminded, and suddenly a snatch of the sweet wildness he had felt that night in the stone circle floated up inside him: the fire and the leaping shadows; the antlers heavy on his brow. Perhaps this sacrifice would help him to focus once more, to be clean.

'When the moon rests on that peak there, I will return,' he told his men, pointing with a spear. 'Be ready for me then.'

Lucius Antonius Saturninus, the legate of the Twentieth Valeria Victrix legion, watched the sun creeping over the low wooded rise that lay between his army and the northern sea.

Behind him there was a series of twangs and slaps as his slaves unpegged his leather tent and dropped it to the ground to begin folding and rolling. Around him in the half-dark, narrow vale in which they'd camped, the legionaries and auxiliaries quickened their preparations for departure. Hundreds of fires winked out one by one, extinguished by sand; cookpots clanked as they were packed on to bed rolls; buckles chinked as armour was donned and weapons fastened. The mass mutters and movement of nearly 5,000 men sounded like a high wind over the trees of a vast forest.

Sniffing the damp, salt-tanged air, Lucius climbed the few steps to the top of the wooded rise, pushing through the tangled screen of gorse to see the sea. It seemed calm today. Lucius sighed and edged his way around the knoll to face back towards the mountains. He only wished he was so calm.

He should have been. He commanded the largest army sent into northern Alba so far, a mixed force drawn from his own Twentieth legion, consisting of a detachment of elite legionary foot soldiers, supplemented by auxiliary infantry and cavalry drawn from the conquered peoples of the Empire. Yet it had been ten days since the army left the safety of the Venicones lands between Forth and Tay, and still they'd seen no sign of the people who were said to cluster on these fertile east-coast plains. They had come across smaller duns, and sacked and torched them, yet they had been deserted of defenders.

His *primus pilus*, the leading centurion, was uneasy, and that made Lucius uneasy. Yet Agricola's orders, before he boarded the ship to take him south, had been explicit. The army was to keep advancing until it reached the point where the north-east plain opened out to its fullest extent. It was then to seek out the main tribal duns and subdue them with artillery, specifically, the Caledonii king's seat of power. Or, if faced in the open by a significant force, it was to give battle.

It sounded simple, and yet there was a problem. The populace had fled. There was no one to fight, which, among these fierce barbarians, was unheard of.

So Lucius had gone on, but with increasing unease. And as they went north, the hills and the broken glens that spread from them gradually drew closer to the east coast, forcing the army into a narrow marching order that left it strung out for a league. The auxiliary cavalry was in the front, the baggage and artillery next, then the elite legionaries on foot and finally more auxiliary infantry guarding the rear. Lucius was anxious about marching in such a narrow column – he preferred open country when he could use the cavalry to guard the flanks properly – but there was no choice.

And it wasn't just practicalities that pricked at him, it was the land itself.

The line of mountains to their left, with their dark flanks and roiling cloud-crowns, the unnatural silence of the valleys, the absence of cooking fires, and, worst of all, the utter lack of any resistance were conspiring to make him afraid.

And though the soldiers tried to laugh at the aged skulls hung in clusters from the oak groves, and strange symbols scrawled in blood on house walls, and lines of raw, staked-out skins, the Alban druids had done their work well. Lucius heard the increasing mutters of the young tribunes around him, as well as the experienced centurions, and saw the swift, fearful glances sent over hunched shoulders. These damned barbarians were attacking their resolve and courage without dealing a single blow!

What Lucius wanted, with increasing desperation, was to come across a great force of savages spread out on the plain before them, shrieking their war cries. Lucius would understand what to do then, knew the attack formations and strategies that would ensure victory. But this desertion was worse than resistance, for there was no way on the gods' earth that the barbarians had given up. Lucius just couldn't believe that, not after those vicious fort raids.

Eventually, Lucius came down the slope to commence armouring, standing still with his arms out as a slave tightened the straps of his cuirass and knelt to fasten his greaves around his calves. Another slave then led his horse to him. As Lucius swung into the saddle, he fixed his eyes on the eagle emblem of the legion, borne proudly by the standard bearer standing to his left. Its bronze wings spread fiercely, gleaming in the sun's first rays, as did the discs on the standards of the *maniple* regiments, held up by each unit's signifer officer so the men could fall into rank behind.

Yet far above the flowing stream of bold crimson shields, iron helmets and lance tips, Lucius could also glimpse the Alban hills that lay between the army and the higher mountains. The native colours were subdued compared to the red tiles and blue sky of Roman lands. This Alban sunrise was flaming, but the wind-scoured trees and open heaths were all dull greens and purples and umbers, the hollows still steeped in cold shadow. Between the open tracts of heath were dark wedges of close-clustered trees, huddled along the banks of the many small streams that cut the plain into ribbons.

Lucius had put the remnants of his faith in that open land, and his scouts. There was no chance that a rebel army could creep up on them unawares. His men had been watching that land constantly, and the hills above.

The sun was high enough now to stretch the combined shadow of Lucius and his horse on the ground, its tip trembling as his helmet plume waved in the cool breeze. The shadow was that of a giant, a beast with long legs and a huge head, and Lucius smiled at it to bolster his spirits.

With their superior weapons and tactics his men surely *were* giants compared to the savages of this land. He must remember that.

The men had at last formed up, and Lucius raised his gloved hand as a trumpet cleaved the air with the order to depart. With his other officers, surrounded by their own personal guard, Lucius moved out behind the auxiliary cavalry, casting a glance back at his men.

As they streamed out of the vale, the strengthening dawn glittered over the army as if it were a great, many-legged insect; armoured with hard, polished iron plates, bristling with the teeth of javelins, rumbling with the tread of heavy feet. Each part moved together, each man could react to his officer's orders as if he were part of one beast. His fears dampened by a surge of pride, Lucius turned his attention forward.

They were at the narrowest part of the plain now, the scouts said. Not far to the north the line of the mountains angled back the other way, and the great north-east plain would spread out before them. Then they would no longer be hemmed in so close to the coast.

That thought lent an eagerness to the angle of Lucius's seat, and his horse responded by quickening its step.

It was still morning when they came to the river crossing Lucius had decided to avoid the previous night. The shallow pool at the ford was already churned by the passage of many hooves when his own horse picked its way down into the swirling water.

Lucius was leaning down, closely watching his stallion's step across the slippery river cobbles when his reverie was shattered by a whinny. Clutching the reins, Lucius jerked his head up, his eyes locked with disbelief on a horse that lurched its way up the bank and collapsed on its forequarters, its rider flung to the muddy ground.

Then chaos erupted all around him, with piteous cries and horses stumbling and falling. On the solid ground behind, the baggage and artillery carts rumbled to a halt, and there were shouts and whip cracks as the drivers tried to make their beasts retreat. Dazed, Lucius barely registered the whining all around him, like angry bees, until his prefect cursed and crowded his horse close, nudging Lucius through the water and up the bank.

'Archers!' the prefect cried. 'From the woods!'

'How . . . ?' Lucius began, before his own horse suddenly reared up, nearly unseating him, and he felt the impact shudder through his own body when an arrow found the stallion's chest.

Then Lucius had no time to listen to the screams of horses or terrorized men, as his body hit the ground with a blow that took his breath away. His cheek pressed into the mud, Lucius could only stare as one of his tribunes was crushed by his falling horse, his face twisting into a rictus of agony, as death rained from the skies above.

★

Eremon watched from a knoll that rose above a stream fringed by alders and willows. His heart pounded relentlessly, from fear and excitement, and with sheer admiration for Nectan's archers. All of them, including his men, had gone without sleep and food for three days now, as they crawled in stages out over the plain. They'd travelled only by night, keeping to the patches of trees where they could, the fierce hatred of the Caereni for those who attacked the Sacred Isle immuring them to cold, hunger and damp.

After three days the little men lay safely hidden, spread out in mires and woods and gullies on a narrow front, and the Romans did not even know they were there. With their clothing and their way of moving as if one with the trees and swamps, the Caereni were invisible to the Roman scouts.

This will be the last time we have the element of total surprise, Eremon realized. He tried to keep himself perfectly still, though he and his own men lay further back than the line of attack. Yet the midges were biting fiercely in the damp dawn shadows, and he worked a hand up now to scratch his nostril. His whole face itched terribly, from the dried stag blood with which the Caereni had marked him, and from the cracking river mud that smeared their naked torsos from head to trousers, to make them blend in with the land. Unfortunately, Eremon had missed his earlobes, and it was to these fleshy parts that the midges were applying themselves with vigour.

Beside him, Conaire's eyes were glowing white in his mud-smeared face, but he didn't speak. Instead, they both listened to the shrieks of horses and angry yells of men, interrupted by the sound of confused splashing. For a moment, Eremon allowed himself some sorrow for the horses, but men on horseback could chase foot warriors and ride them down. There was no choice.

Then he caught a slight movement in the trees, and in a moment three archers trotted out to the base of the knoll. Jerking his head at Conaire, Eremon scrambled down the steep slopes to join Fergus and Colum, who waited there on guard.

One of the archers paused as they came up, grinning and wiping sweat from his brow, and only then did Eremon notice that this one was taller and ganglier than the others. He hadn't recognized Rori, for the youth's flaming hair had been completely caked with mud to hide its colour.

'We shot around six horses each,' Rori murmured, his eyes fierce but sad.

Eremon swiftly calculated that for one hundred archers, and smiled at them all. However a sudden crashing in the undergrowth put paid to any verbal compliments, as they all turned.

'They are in disarray,' one of the Caereni men whispered, 'yet those nearest to us began to regroup. In rage, a few have followed us into the woods, though their commanders called them back.'

'How many?'

The man glanced at his other tribesman for confirmation. 'We think nine. They stumble close together, but we have not the room to shoot between the trees.'

Eremon caught Conaire's eye, and both of their hands went to their swords. 'Hasten to our meeting place,' he said to the archers, pausing to grip Rori's shoulder with a proud squeeze that brought a shine to the boy's eyes. 'We will join you there soon.'

Eremon smiled grimly at Conaire, Colum and Fergus as the others hurried off, the pounding of his heart now a singing. This was what he wanted: blood. *This* would silence the hurt and the burning that would not ease. The strange, fierce power that had flooded him when the Caereni sung their stag chant still lingered in his limbs, surging along with his blood, but much hotter and purer and wilder.

'So, brother.' Conaire's eyes creased as he smiled, the side with the old scar pulling down the top of one cheek. 'Two each among us four. Then you and I must fight each other for the ninth.'

Eremon drew his sword, light on his feet as the rising sun at last penetrated the woods, gilding the leaves that shivered in the wind. Some things were unchanged in this suddenly unstable world of his: there was always a place for what he did best.

He grinned at Fergus, who was no longer scowling, and then glanced at Colum's determined face. Finally he raised his sword-tip to rest against Conaire's own. 'Then may Hawen give me the victory over you, brother!' Eremon turned to face the woods.

Chapter 46

The priestesses and their Caereni escort enjoyed fine hospitality on their way through the northern Epidii lands, and this more than made up for the difficulty in travel.

And even though Rhiann drove them relentlessly up the winding, narrow glens to the high passes, and back along muddy mountain paths, Fola watched her friend closely and understood why, even as her own back ached in the saddle.

It was as if a whip was being cracked over Rhiann's shoulder. Fola saw it in the way she sometimes paused and looked back at the darkening clouds being blown in on the western winds. And at night, Fola knew that the same things that chased Rhiann in the day were there in her dreams, for Rhiann whimpered and tossed and only became still when Fola went to her on silent feet and placed her hand on her forehead.

Fola was relieved that the early courage shown by the young priestesses had been borne out. For no one complained. Rhiann led them with a bright fever that somehow communicated itself to all: encouraging them, exhorting them and, above all, setting an example of single-mindedness to which they all held.

It will burn out eventually, Fola thought one day, her eyes on the back of Rhiann's rain-soaked hood as she rode ahead. *And for me, too.*

Fola herself could not have kept going without her private prayers each night, clutching the figure of Rhiannon the great goddess to her breast. In Rhiannon's compassionate, sweet face Fola saw a rope thrown to a drowning woman, the only thread that could stop her from falling beneath the waves of her own grief. Rhiannon whispered to Fola's spirit that what they did was right, and that they were loved.

On leaving Dunadd, Fola had seen Rhiann pick up her own figurines from the hearth, and then put them all down bar one, which she packed away somewhat furtively. It took seven days before Fola discovered which goddess Rhiann had taken for guidance, when she noticed that her sleeping friend's fingers were clutching something. Fola had gently prised Rhiann's palm open, and then she saw it was the war goddess Andraste, with her terrible face of righteous anger.

We may be right, Fola thought sadly, *yet there is a cost.* And she closed Rhiann's fingers again to veil those empty stone eyes, demanding vengeance for the sins of men.

By the time the priestesses crossed into Creones territory, sunseason had bloomed again with vigour, and the rain cleared away as if a curtain had been flung back.

Rhiann had taken Nectan's advice, which was to head for the most isolated Creones dun first. To reach it they had to cross a wall of high, bare mountains, and after the recent rains the glens and passes were even tougher to traverse, treacherous with boggy ground, and filled with streams in full spate. They were forced to lead the horses, and underfoot the mosses and sedges squelched into puddles of peat-stained water, spilling over their boots. Nothing stirred on the high mountainsides except for clouds snagging on the peaks, and the shadows of a few lone eagles, gliding high in the blue.

By the time they came over the mountain shield to a long loch on the other side, glittering under a bright sun, they were exhausted and unnaturally subdued. Yet the loch side was different from the high ground, hazed by the smoke of many houses clustering among the sprouting field-strips, the loch itself speckled with dugout canoes and *curraghs*. The sun glistened on piles of new thatch as people clambered to repair their roofs before more storms came.

As the priestesses picked their way down from the pass, the eerie silence of the bare slopes was dispelled by the hails of those working the fields, and shouts and children's cries echoed over the loch. From farther along, the low of a horn floated up from the chieftain's dun.

The dun was a crannog, a settlement built on a man-made island in the loch, connected to the shore by a narrow bridge that could be easily defended. Alder pilings supported a large platform on which sat two roundhouses encircled by a palisade of hazel saplings. The roundhouses were the chieftain's hall and guestlodge, for the bulk of the people lived on the loch banks and would only retreat to the crannog in times of danger.

The chief and his warriors were out hunting, Rhiann was informed by his timid wife, but the Sisters were given beds in the guestlodge and asked to wait for his return.

Rhiann's hair was a tangled mess of damp knots, so while the other girls took turns bathing behind a screen, Rhiann laid out her jewels and clothes and gave herself over to Fola's ministrations. As Fola tugged the antler comb gently through her hair, Rhiann stared at her pale face in her mirror. 'It is wet,' she observed of her tresses, unnecessarily. 'If you coil it and bind it up, no one will notice.'

'No.' Fola spoke around the pins in her mouth, working on a particularly stubborn knot. 'Let us leave the back unbound, Rhiann, and dry it by the fire. It is your greatest glory, better than jewels, I think.'

Rhiann smiled, casting an eye over the fine dresses spread over the bed. 'It seems a priestess of the island knows more of politics than she admits to.'

Fola was silent, as the tugging continued. 'I understand, yes, that you will need the power of your royal blood as much as the power of the Sisterhood, to win over these warriors and chiefs. That appearances do matter.' A sigh came from over Rhiann's head. 'Yet you do drive yourself hard, Sister. Perhaps we should rest here for a night first.'

'*No!*' Rhiann's belly tightened, and she clenched her hand over it. 'There is no time for rest,' she said fiercely. 'We must use this season, for the Romans will certainly be using it to their own advantage. Even now . . .' Eremon came into her mind then, unbidden.

Fola's hands stopped moving when she heard Rhiann's voice roughen, and it was only then, in the sudden silence and stillness, that Rhiann realized how truly afraid she herself was.

The fear had been growing the whole time they crossed that lonely moor, and as the plateau and its waters flowed around and away from her to the distant hills, indifferent to human suffering, she had felt unimaginably small, cold and alone. Insignificant.

How could *she* ever persuade these hard-hearted men, her tribal enemies, to do anything? She had not spoken of her lack of a specific plan to either Fola or Nectan, so desperate had she been to get away from Dunadd. Yet now she was here, and being groomed for shrewd warrior eyes like a mare for trade, her fear was fast sharpening into panic.

Abruptly, she stood up. 'Then while my hair dries by the fire, let us speak of what we will do here. Call the Sisters in, and Nectan, too. We have to find a way to turn their minds, and we must start as we mean to go on. Here, we must strike the first, and most decisive blow.'

The Creones chieftain took his wife's news about their strange visitors with a burst of irritation. He was by no means young, and after his hunt he was uncomfortably hot and stinking of sweat and hounds, as well as hungry and tired.

A bath had resolved the smell and sore muscles, and a platter of smoked trout the worst of his hunger, but what he really wanted was to lounge in his hall this night, drink ale with his men, and bed his new, young wife with as little effort as possible.

Now he glanced up at his wife, who hurried over and poured him more ale, and then at the young people crowding his firelit hall, lounging on rugs, cushions and benches around the stone hearth. The chieftain was the only old one, unfortunately. He had young sons, a young wife, young kin, all of them rude with vigour and colour and noise.

'I saw the Epidii princess, husband,' his wife offered. 'She is very young, but very gracious. I am sure she will not keep you long.'

The chieftain patted her ample bottom. 'I hope not. The sooner they retire, the sooner *we* retire, wife.' He leered at her, and she blushed and giggled, batting away his groping hands.

From outside came the sudden boom of a drum.

The chieftain had been in many battles, but this was not a battle drum, and his head reared up in surprise, staring at his hall door as the drum bellowed again. By now, the rest of his warriors and their women had heard it, too, and their chatter and laughter, the chiming of bronze and copper cups, and the discordant sound of the bard tuning his harp, all died away.

Aside from the hearth-fire, the hall was lit with pitch torches fastened to the roof-posts, and it was this light that glimmered on the first thing the chief saw coming through his oak doors – the black, shining eyes of a strange man.

The man was short, with jet- and silver-threaded hair, wearing a strange tunic and trousers that seemed the colours of woodland, heath, sea and rocks combined. He bore a fine beaded quiver across his back, as did the other men who followed him, a score in all. They bowed and lined up in two columns, one on each side of the doorway.

Despite their size, these men held themselves with compelling dignity, and it was only that which silenced the chief's impulse to demand what they were doing. The escort of the women, his wife whispered. Caereni archers guarding an Epidii princess. How curious. He did like curious things.

Now the drumbeat began again, solemn, and the lines of archers stared hard at the empty doorway, until the chieftain himself was leaning forward, peering at it expectantly.

Then suddenly a woman took shape from the darkness outside. She paused in the half-light, drawing out the moment, and all the chieftain could glimpse was a stray glimmer of gold on her body. His wife's breath fluttered in his ear, tickling him.

The woman glided forward into the light, and when she came to a stop all the people in the hall gasped. The chieftain lived on the edge of tribal lands, yet had travelled widely. He knew beauty and refinement when he saw it.

A blue cloak fell from the Epidii princess's shoulders, pinned back by the most extraordinary brooch of two rearing horses set with amber. Underneath the cloak was a saffron-dyed dress, its edges glinting with gold thread. On her feet were pale kidskin boots; around her arms, bracelets of bronze, snake-coiled, deer-headed. But as his eyes travelled higher up her body, the chief realized that these trinkets were nothing compared to the twisted torc at her neck, the ends two mares' heads. The torc framed a beautiful face, with a wide, full mouth and blue eyes that were tilted up at the edges, giving them an alluring cast. And though she wore a gold circlet on her brow, the woman's hair was her true crown. It was a rare hue, amber and fire and copper threaded together, and swirled loose about her shoulders, finer than a silk veil.

The chieftain was on his feet before he knew it, extending his hands to introduce himself with every extravagant word his memory could dredge up. The Epidii princess accepted his greeting calmly, and in her face he saw nothing of the imperious pride he'd been expecting. She was young and sweet, just as his wife had described. He ushered her to a bench beside his own, covered with his finest rug, and his wife approached with a jug of mead and a cup, visibly awed.

The Lady Rhiann accepted the cup with a gracious nod, yet the chieftain's wife still trembled as she poured and then retreated behind her husband's bench. The chieftain then signalled to his bard to play while they spoke, but the Epidii princess raised her hand. 'No, my lord. If you do not mind, I have a headache from our journey, and find that music makes it worse.'

The chieftain waved his disappointed bard away. 'Then, my lady, food will be brought soon, yet perhaps you could tell me how I can help you?' This wasn't strictly polite – he should feed her before asking her business. But he was old and tired, and here in the more remote lands manners became a little more fluid. He glanced up at the Caereni men, still standing stiffly by the door. 'And do you wish your escort to join us? There is plenty of ale and meat.'

The lady shook her head, and the torchlight glittered on her gold circlet. 'I thank you, but no.' She signalled to the warriors, and they turned and departed, leaving four of their number behind.

The chieftain stared at her, wondering at this dazzling young woman and her strange customs. He twirled his ale cup uncomfortably.

'My lord.' The lady suddenly fixed him with her blue cat-eyes. 'I bear news of what happened on the Sacred Isle at Beltaine.'

The chieftain blinked. 'The raid? A terrible business, terrible!' For a moment, his heart darkened with sorrow over the old Ban Cré, his king's sister and his own cousin. 'But I have already heard this news, lady. It travelled fast among the tribes.'

That direct gaze hardened imperceptibly. 'And were you told also that Maelchon of the Orcades led this raid?'

'By Manannán, no!' He started back, shocked. 'I received the news from my king, but no mention was made of Maelchon. King Maelchon led it? Are you sure?'

For a moment, that innocent girl's mouth was twisted by bitterness. 'Quite sure. I was there, you see.'

'I am so sorry, lady, it must have been dreadful for you,' he babbled, his heart going out to her when he saw the grief in her eyes. By Lugh, he had a daughter just this age! 'I am sorry,' he repeated, only just held back from taking her hand by the glitter of her finery. She was royal, after all.

'Then, my lord,' her voice softened, 'since the news has already reached all the corners of the land, have you heard also what your king plans to do about it?'

'*Do* about it?' he echoed. 'Are the Sisters' houses being rebuilt, lady? Do the Sisters need food, shelter? I am sure my king would be glad to help.'

The sweet mouth tightened. 'No, my lord. All that is left of the Sisterhood travels with me. There will be no rebuilding, not of the kind you mean.'

Behind the chieftain, his tender-hearted wife gasped. He'd not known or understood the extent of the loss, and a renewed surge of pity overtook him for this girl and her wards. It was a sorry business, a sorry business indeed. He would feed them as well as he could before seeing them on their way.

Yet suddenly the Epidii princess leaned forward, reaching into his vitals with those eyes and gripping him so he couldn't look away. Vaguely, he noticed that the four Caereni men had taken up position by the fire and the roof-posts.

'Do you realize,' the woman continued coldly, 'that apart from myself, all the Ban Crés were slaughtered among the sacred Stones – the blood kin of kings? Do you realize that the cauldron of wisdom guarded by the Sisters was extinguished that day – the healing knowledge, and the songs and rites that keep the Otherworld and Thisworld balanced, your crops thriving, your cattle swelling with calves?'

The chieftain found his mouth dropping open again, as abruptly, the Lady Rhiann stood. 'Then permit me to enlighten you,' she said, and raised her hand. The Caereni men took packets from their tunics and threw their powdered contents on to the hearth-fire and up over the torches, and the hall was instantly plunged into near darkness, the smoke tinged with a sharp smell.

The people cried out in surprise and dismay, but the Epidii princess's voice came again, carrying over the mutters of men stumbling to their feet. 'Fear not.'

The chieftain sank back on his bench, his old heart thundering, as his wife's small hand came out to grasp his shoulder.

The drumming began again outside, but this time it was a compelling beat that seemed to reach into the chieftain's chest and shake it. There was a rustling at the door, and a single voice broke into a high chant that made the hairs rise on the back of his neck. In the dim light of the coals, something pale entered and circled around the edges of the room.

The clear, piping voice continued to rise and fall in the wordless song, and in the chieftain's mind he was soaring over the mountains like an eagle, and then out to sea and back again. Another sound at the door, and then a second voice joined the first, then a third, and more and more, until the room shimmered with a veil of sweet, shifting notes, as pale wraiths glided around in the shadows.

He had rarely been so frightened or excited. Who knew what priestesses could do? His wife's hand grew tighter on his shoulder, as the sound swelled until it echoed off every beam of the roof, the pillars, the shields on the walls, even the cooking pots and cauldrons. And just as his heart could pound no harder, nor his wife grip any tighter, the sound abruptly ceased.

Before the chieftain could react, a circle of flame flickered into life around them. Peering at the edges of the room, the chieftain saw girls, dressed all in white, and behind every second girl, a Caereni warrior holding a burning brand.

The Lady Rhiann stepped forward into the cleared space before the door, and turned to face her audience. Immediately, most of the girls sat down in a circle around her, their fingertips touching, while several remained standing. The seated girls began another song, but this was a low, breathy chanting that wound soothingly among his people, and the chieftain felt some of the tension leave him in a rush, as he slumped back.

Now the Lady Rhiann was raising her hands, and her rings and bracelets sparkled in the flames as her cloak fell back from her arms. Higher and higher came her hands, her sleeves spreading out to either side like wings, and all the while the chanting continued.

'My lords!' The Lady Rhiann's voice was no longer soft, but strong and fierce. 'We have a tale to tell you, to sing you, to show you. Listen well, for the Sisters do not need your food or shelter, but your vengeance!' She flung out her hand to one of the white-robed girls, and the maiden drew closer. 'Here are the innocents whose lives were bloodied that day by the red invader. The others cannot sing to you, for they are dead, but let our song and tale speak for those who have no voices! Listen well, for they beseech you from the grave!'

And when the maiden came forward into the pool of torchlight, and began to speak of what she had seen, the chieftain was stirred by a terrible pity and horror.

One after the other, the standing girls spoke, and each seemed to him to have a sweeter face than the last, and eyes that swam with tears, and words that plucked at his heart. But when the Lady Rhiann at last took the floor herself and described, with the grace of a born storyteller, what *she* had seen, well, by then his wife was openly sobbing into his shoulder, as were all his women, and even he could not breathe past a choked throat.

At long last the priestesses fell silent, and all the chieftain could hear was the snap of a dying coal in the hearth. Those monsters, these Romans, had killed women like *this*, defenceless, peaceful women who made beautiful sounds and spoke beautiful words. Something had to be done about it.

The chieftain's reverie was shattered by his eldest son, who, with an oath, leaped to his feet, nearly knocking his own wife to the ground. 'This is not to be borne!' he cried, his face alight with fury. 'If it's vengeance you wish, lady, then vengeance you will have!'

The chieftain opened his mouth to protest, for he knew his hot-headed progeny well, but the Epidii princess was already smiling at his son. 'Last year your king refused an offer of alliance with the Epidii and the Caledonii,' she cried. 'But if the tribes had united then, this outrage would not have happened, and your priestesses – *your* birthright – would still be alive. I come here today to urge you to petition your king, to beg him night and day to join the alliance! Together, we can defeat the Romans, but only together!' She spread her arms, the gesture taking in all the girls arrayed at her feet, and standing by her side. 'Protect our land so that innocents like these, like your own children, can prosper in peace. Join with us!'

She held out one elegant hand to his son, the light glittering on her rings, and every other young warrior in the hall leaped to his feet, shouting curses at the Romans, and oaths to join the fight. Their women chattered excitedly and the hounds, disturbed by the noise, began to howl.

'Wait!' the chieftain roared, for he knew his king well, and that he had been fixedly against this alliance for the last two years. 'Heed me!'

Yet his son was before him, sword unsheathed, joy in his face. 'Father! Let us set out for our king's dun tomorrow, at first light! Let us lead the fight against the Romans – us, the foremost clan among the Creones!'

And the chieftain knew then he had lost, and sat down heavily on his bench as his wife threw her arms around his neck and kissed him soundly. With a rueful smile he pinched her under the chin and then sighed, feeling every one of his old, aching bones, as the hall erupted around him with a youthful clamour that could not be denied.

The Epidii princess was smiling broadly now, and though it was not a cruel smile, there was no sign of the sweet and innocent, either.

High in the mountains, the sun could be fierce in this season when it blazed free of the clouds, and Eremon had taken refuge from its midday heat under his tent canopy.

He'd informed his men before that he would not be hunting this day. Bewildered, they had left him in a whirlwind of shouting, whistling and clattering spears, and it was only as peace fell that Eremon realized his true motive for forgoing the outing: to shave, and therefore to think.

As he scraped the dagger blade over his skin, peering into the untarnished side of a bronze pot, Eremon's thoughts could range far and undisturbed.

Despite the rough conditions of the camp, he undertook this ritual with soaproot and dagger every few days. It was not for vanity, or even because he found beards itchy and breeding grounds for lice. Unshaven cheeks were a custom of Erin, and for some perverse reason he wanted to hold to his traditions, even in the midst of an Alban battle camp. Or perhaps that's exactly *why* he did it – he was war leader of an Alban tribe, married to an Alban princess, a close ally with the most powerful Alban king. He had to be stamped with something of Erin, and it would be his face, which he showed to the world. And when he agreed to be tattooed on the Sacred Isle he had insisted that the tattoos not include his face, for in Erin a king must be unblemished.

So he told himself then, but now? After three years away from his homeland, Erin had gone from being his reason for living to a background desire that no longer seemed to have much to do with day-to-day concerns. Abruptly, Eremon paused, the blade dripping water into the wooden bowl balanced on his crossed legs. Now that was a strange thought, for he remembered as if it were yesterday the fire that had driven him to take the boat from Erin, to keep his men alive. All he had wanted was to gain support for himself in Alba, and then return home to claim his Hall.

Yet somewhere along the way, without his realizing it, that fire had merged into another: to save the people of Alba from the Romans. When had the change occurred? He stretched his chin up to tighten the skin, spattering himself with water.

In these past years, he had sent no messengers to Erin. At first he'd been afraid to alert his uncle to his whereabouts, but now Eremon was powerful and secure. He need not fear his uncle any more – Donn might even be dead. So what held him back?

The blade hovered. Conaire would say it was his methodical nature, for he hated leaving things undone and had not yet reached the end of his Alban road. It would not be over for him until he drove Agricola out of Alba, or died trying.

And yet . . . for a moment, Eremon's heart ached with a longing for his own valleys, greener than any in Alba. He wiped bristles and soap on his trouser leg, closing his eyes as the breeze gusted the tent edge back, spilling sun over him. Perhaps when he was back at Dunadd he would at last send someone to see what had befallen his homeland. For he felt in his bones that this struggle between Agricola and Alba could not go on for more than another year. Perhaps it was time to give some thought to what should happen afterwards. After, when there was peace . . . peace to . . .

No! He would not think of home and hearth! That meant Rhiann, and memories of her were continually slipping under his defences, however carefully he guarded his heart against it.

At least the hurt had cooled after the lightning raid on the plain, when those few Roman soldiers came crashing through the undergrowth after them. It had been both easy and satisfying to fly at them from the damp shadows, striking down and then running, dodging trunks and leaping fallen logs until he and his men thought their lungs would burst. And then, the exultation of flinging themselves into the icy waters of a mountain stream, which seemed to carry away the shame along with blood and dried mud. Eremon had thought then that he had mastered his pain, pushing Rhiann into a more contained place in his soul.

That was until he received her news, two days ago.

Eremon had listened to Nectan's man with the silence of utter disbelief. Rhiann was not at Dunadd, but travelling through the mountains with the priestesses. She was winning over the chieftains, they were falling to her words like a scythe through grain, the messenger reported happily. Eremon had dismissed him at last, the shock seeping through him. And beneath that was fear for her – pride in her, yes – but hurt, too, all over again. It was not only that she had undertaken this mission alone, without his consent, counsel or help. If she was in the north, too, then why had she not come to him, to show him that she still loved him?

And why would she? his conscience taunted now, as it had been doing ceaselessly since he received this news. *You acted as an angry child, not a man . . .*

Irritated with this turn of thought, Eremon's hand jerked too quickly and the blade nicked his jaw. 'Hawen's balls!' He clapped his palm to his bleeding face, just as he heard a discreet cough behind him. It was one of Calgacus's men.

'Prince,' he said deferentially, 'Gerat's band has returned from the southern mountains. They have a captive with them who demands an audience with you.'

'Demands?' His finger still pressed to the cut, Eremon fished a rag from under his knee and wiped the last stubble from his chin. 'Has your lord Calgacus been informed yet?'

'My king has met the captive and determined that you are the best man to deal with the situation.' The man jiggled back and forth on his heels.

Eremon rose. 'When you say captive, do you mean this man is a Roman? A soldier from the army? That would be a catch indeed.'

The man pursed his lips, his eyes on the leather roof. 'Oh, it's a catch all right, sir.'

'Well, where is he?'

'At Gerat's campfire. Shall I have the captive brought here, sir?'

'No.' Eremon dabbed ineffectually at the cut, which was still smearing his fingers with blood. 'I need to clean up first. I'll go there myself. Thank you.'

After staunching the blood with a scrap of fleece, Eremon made his way through the camp, which tumbled down the steep valley. After the attack, he and Calgacus were waiting to see what the Romans might do, so the Albans were not preparing for battle, but snatching some much-needed rest. Some were lounging by their cook-fires in the shade, mending harness or polishing weapons. Others were practice duelling on the flatter banks of the stream that carved the valley, or washing off their stink in its deeper pools.

Eremon had to ask twice where Gerat camped, but eventually was directed to a small knot of men standing in the middle of a crescent of hide and brush shelters. As Eremon approached he heard a shout of laughter. He quickened his step, hoping that the captive had not been beaten in such a way as to render him incapable of giving information.

He was only a few steps away when one of the warriors saw him and muttered to the others, and they all peeled back from the object of their scrutiny.

Eremon's steps faltered and stopped, his curious smile fading as he saw what manner of captive had been brought to him.

Samana.

By all the gods . . . his breath slammed against a wall in his chest, and his hand came out to grasp something, to steady himself, but there was nothing to lean on. The last time he saw her, hatred had coursed through his veins, as hot as his lust had once been for her body. And despite the passage of more than two years, those feelings spiralled up even now, twisted together into an indistinguishable tangle.

At sight of him, Samana raised her chin. Her wrists were tied by a scrap of crowberry rope, her once fine green dress caked with mud and what smelled like horse sweat, yet still she stood for all the world as if she were a queen expecting homage from these men. From him.

'My lord.' The man called Gerat stepped forward, his own pleased grin freezing when he saw the shock in Eremon's face. 'This . . . lady . . . was travelling close behind the Romans. She said you would know her, that we must ask for you.'

Yet his question trailed away unanswered. For Eremon had not acknowledged him, and was staring at Samana as if no one else was there.

Chapter 47

Samana had only remained silent because she could not gain her breath; it fluttered and leaped wildly along with her pulse, making her dizzy. She'd been certain she was ready to see Eremon, after seven nights with these rough men, stopping her ears with her fingers to block out their crude jests. All that time she had thought only of the Erin prince, and what she would say to him. And now, she found she could say nothing.

The magic she wove to draw him into her bed two years ago had somehow ensnared her as well as him, yet nevertheless it should have worn off long ago. And yet, he looked more beautiful to her than ever: older and harder; his cheekbones burnished by the sun; his green eyes standing out against his tanned skin. Beneath his sleeveless tunic the faint hairs on his arms were tawny, and his legs were lean in their muddy trousers. Even his dark hair curled just the same over his temples.

Just like the morning he came from my bed, Samana found herself thinking, and was appalled at her weakness. Yet how could she help it? He stood there dusty and sweaty and sunburned, blood beading on a cut on his jaw, yet still he managed to shoot a barb through her formidable defences, a finely tuned bolt of exquisite lust that sang along her veins.

She could not make out his expression clearly. After his first shock, he looked as if she were a loathsome insect that had just crawled out from under a rock. But there had been a flash of something else there too, far back in his cool eyes. Something she could work with.

'Come.' Eremon seemed to collect himself, stepping forward and grasping her elbow with a bruising grip. 'We will speak in my tent.' He turned to the man Gerat and his men, who were all staring with intense curiosity at the little scene. 'You have done well, and King Calgacus and I both owe you our thanks. For this woman is the whore of Agricola himself.' Samana saw the slight curl of Eremon's lip. 'You could have captured no higher informant. I will see you gain an extra ration of ale for this.'

'Thank you, sir,' Gerat replied, his eyes flicking back and forth between them.

Eremon firmly turned his back then and half-dragged Samana all the way up a winding path, between clusters of tents, men, horses and bundled weapons. As soon as they were out of earshot, she hissed, 'You're hurting me!'

Yet he only glanced down at her with bright, hard eyes, and said nothing.

Then Samana was out of the harsh sun, and into the coolness of a tent. Immediately Eremon flung her from him as if she burned. Samana stumbled in the sudden gloom, tripping over a bed roll before sinking on to its hide cover.

When she looked up, Eremon was leaning against the pole that held the shelter, his hands folded tightly over his chest. 'Is this a trick? A joke?'

Samana twisted her sore wrists, breathing hard. 'Do you think I would allow my men to be slaughtered, my own person to be hauled through the mountains for a week by soldiers, like a sack of grain, without decent food or a bath or bed, for a trick?'

'Nothing you do would surprise me, Samana.'

'I was captured! And my hands are hurting. Could you at least get rid of this?' She held up her bound hands, and after a pause Eremon unsheathed the dagger at his waist and cut the rope with one swipe, making sure he did not touch her. Samana rubbed the indents on her skin, and then her pounding temples, muttering a curse under her breath. It was Agricola who had put her in this position, damn him!

Eremon's ears were keener than she'd realized, for he uncrossed his arms and took a step forward. 'Agricola?'

Samana smirked. 'Save your gloating – he's well out of your reach now.' Yet she could have bitten off her tongue when Eremon abruptly straightened.

'*Agricola does not lead this army?*'

Samana clamped her lips together, as he stored that snippet away with some pleasure. Curse him! She was used to being the interrogator, not the interrogated. It was the tiredness, that was all.

Eremon squatted down a handspan from her face. 'And how *could* your enamoured suitor bear to be parted from you, Samana? Leaving you without a single Roman guard?'

She'd thought of many ways to approach this, but she had first to see how he reacted to her.

'Could it be,' Eremon continued, 'that Agricola grows tired of your diversions? Could it be you are no use to him any more?'

'I have been of great use to him in recent moons, as it happens!' She so wished to tell him who was really behind the raid on the Sacred Isle, who had planted the whole delicious idea, but drew in a shaking breath to squash her fury. Before Eremon could draw further away she suddenly cupped his chin, her thumb stroking his mouth. 'Perhaps,' she murmured, 'I actually came looking for you.'

Eremon's hand shot up to grasp Samana's wrist in a bruising grip, his face leaning out of her reach. But yes . . . just for a moment, she'd seen his pupils flicker with something, and his lips had parted of their own accord. Stiffly, he released her and rose, putting a distance between them. 'I am no fool, Samana, so do not treat me like one. As you said, it was not your choice to become our guest, so you were hardly looking for me.'

Samana sighed, and then, despite her aching legs, she dragged herself to her feet. Honesty was occasionally a wise tactic to use, for it always surprised people. 'Perhaps not,' she admitted, 'but I have nevertheless longed for some way to see you again.' She softened her eyes. Across the narrow, dim space between them, her energy reached for him, her flesh yearning for his.

Eremon must have sensed her rapid breathing, for a wary stillness now came over him.

'Aren't you at least going to feed me?' Samana managed to ask, feeling surer now that he looked so unsure. He didn't know what to do with her, that was plain, but at her words something in him uncoiled, and he went to the edge of the canopy and called out an order to a nearby warrior to bring meat and ale.

Eremon said nothing while they waited, his features blurred by the shifting shadows of the canopy as the edge of the hide flapped in the wind. Samana was just as happy to be silent, for as he stared at the rock, she could feast her eyes on him, watching the rise and fall of his chest, the pulse at the hollow of his throat. She kissed that soft hollow once, long ago, and now he stood there like a stranger. Inside, she sighed.

Agricola still had a soldier's body, but he was ageing. His power and danger excited her, yet Eremon was a different proposition altogether, and not just because of his beauty. Perhaps it was that with Agricola she enjoyed the game, the careful artistry, yet with Eremon she sensed she could lose herself, because he matched her in fire as well as strength. And this tantalizing promise of capitulation and loss of control – her first and last surrender – was what trapped her as nothing else could.

Suddenly Samana heard the sound of returning footsteps, heavier this time, and her eyes jerked to one side as a loud oath was uttered. Goddess, it was that big blond oaf! Infuriatingly, he had always been quite immune to her.

'By the Boar!' The oaf now turned to Eremon, huge and loud and rudely vigorous in the sun, his size and bounding energy annoying Samana further. 'I heard the rumours of her on my return just now, brother. But I had to see for myself!' His bright blue eyes flicked Samana up and down, and when she glared at him, he grinned. He stank of sweat, and there were dark patches under the arms of his tunic. 'Still as haughty, I see, my lady. Perhaps you'll be less so after eating this.' He was holding out a chunk of half-charred flesh of indeterminate origin on a curl of birch bark, and a battered leather ale flask.

When Samana tilted her chin up, looking away, he chuckled and dumped both on the floor in the middle of the tent. 'Brother, I can stay and keep you company if you wish it.' The amusement was thick in his voice.

Eremon was silent for a moment. 'No,' he said thoughtfully. 'I can handle this alone.'

'Then I'll be cleaning my boar spears in the next tent; call if you need me.'

The oaf left, and Eremon stared down at the scorned food then back up at Samana. 'Not what you're used to,' he remarked. 'But then, the price of Roman luxury was too high for me.'

Samana felt herself colour. 'You are a man, and have a sword to protect you,' she shot back. 'What did I have?'

'Quite enough, obviously.'

Samana bit back a retort and, ignoring the food, swept across the space between them in two strides. 'Ah, Eremon, why do we quarrel?' She caught his arm, pressed it to her breast as she leaned into him. 'We talked pleasantly before, why can we not do so again?'

He carefully removed her hand. 'Why indeed? After all, you nearly got me killed, tried to make me turn traitor, then did so yourself. Why should we not talk like old friends?' He laughed and pushed her away. 'I thought you were hungry.'

Samana breathed to calm herself, her hands balled by her sides. 'You know why I made the choice I did—'

'Yet I still don't understand it!' Suddenly, Eremon looked very tired. 'I'm not going to debate such things with you, Samana. We are each set on our own paths.'

Our own paths. Samana stared at Eremon, and all of Agricola's harsh words of rejection came rushing back to her, consumed as he was with his war. 'Yes,' she answered at last, surrender in her voice. 'But my path is not immovable, and neither is yours, perhaps.'

Eremon snorted. 'So you'll help us, then? My men will be pleased.'

'Eremon.' Samana fixed him with her dark eyes and took one step forward. She had long thought she would never get another throw of the dice with him. And here it was, but one throw only. She took another step, slowly this time, drawing him with every fibre of her body. 'Eremon,' she whispered again, and suddenly she was up against him. 'It is you I wish to help. Let me join with you, as I offered to do before.' She licked her lips with her small tongue and yes, his eyes were staring at them, held there. 'You and I were meant to be together, *cariad.*'

It was at the endearment that Eremon flinched; she saw the pain flare in his eyes. And that was when she first sensed the chink in his armour. Her magic had always been sexual in nature, for her senses were attuned to such things. So she suddenly knew, by the ripple of tension in Eremon's arm, his harsh breathing, the flush across his cheekbones, that his body was suffering. A happily bedded man would not react this way. *Something is amiss with Rhiann.*

Samana pressed closer, moulding her body to his so softly that he would hardly notice until it was done, reaching up on her toes so that her warm breath was on his face. 'I would give you everything that is in me,' she whispered. 'For what we shared was rare, my love, so rare I have never forgotten it: how you buried yourself in me, how you suckled at my breasts, how you rode me until I wept for mercy.'

His breath was coming faster now, his eyes glinting with pain.

'All this and more will I give you,' she continued in the same murmur. 'Many halls to rule, many jewels to lay at your feet, many nights of pleasure in my bed.' She parted her lips, her eyes sliding to his mouth. 'And sons to rule after you, Eremon, strong sons.'

At these last words, Eremon froze. Then suddenly Samana's arms were encased in a brutal grip, and she gasped. The skin around Eremon's eyes was taut, his mouth a grim line. The moment drew out, a moment where she saw him waver, something writhing in his heart she did not understand.

Then, at last, he slowly and deliberately put her away from him. And when Samana was at arm's length he gave her a shove, making her stumble backwards. She regained her balance and clasped her arms about herself, open-mouthed.

'You are a prisoner, madam.' Eremon's voice was ice; there was no trace of that moment of weakness now. 'So are you going to tell me what you know of the Roman movements, and Agricola's plans?'

Samana rounded on him like a cornered cat, her shock transmuting into spitting rage. 'No, the Otherworld take me! Why would I help *you* – a stupid, blind, gelded stallion? Never!'

Eremon smiled, all warrior-lord once more. 'I didn't think so.'

'So what will you do with me, then?' Samana's chest heaved. 'Torture me? Or don't you have the *balls* to do that!'

Yet her fury washed over Eremon, as he stared above her head at the rock. 'No, I will not soil my hands that way. And I feel that it is not for me to judge you. Not me.'

'You will send me away?' Sudden fear extinguished Samana's rage, for if she was not with him or Agricola there would be little chance for her. And where would he send her? Her hand crept to the leaping pulse at her throat. She had been so sure she could bend his will by mastering his body. Yet he had surprised her once more.

Eremon strode to the edge of the tent and called the blond oaf's name. In a moment the man appeared, his grin still intact.

The prince gestured at Samana. 'Bind her hands again for all to see, take her back to Gerat's men, and send Gerat here to me to receive his orders. Oh, and send me Nectan's last messenger.'

Conaire cocked one fair eyebrow, his grin widening. 'Gladly, brother.'

Before Samana could even cry out, he swept her legs out from under her and tossed her over his shoulder like a sack. But it was as Eremon turned away from her with no glance, and no last words, putting her from his mind as if she meant nothing, that Samana snapped. With a screech, a stream of foul curses burst from her mouth, raining down on Eremon even as his brother shook with laughter and strode away from his tent.

Shaking, Eremon sank down to his bed roll, and rested his pounding head in his hands.

Hawen, but that was not what he had expected, none of it. Neither the rage that sprang up when he first saw Samana, though it was two years cold, nor the shocking pang of lust. He pushed his forehead into his hands until his eyeballs hurt, feeling ashamed.

His body had betrayed him, just for that one moment. His mind had stayed firm, of course, for he would never entertain terms with a traitor such as Samana. But for a single, drawn-out breath, his body had wanted to give in to the kiss, to be possessed by Samana in a frenzy that would drown out all hurts and memories just as the fighting had done.

For that moment, he'd yearned for the feel of a body *wanting* his, kissing him and murmuring soft words and stroking his flesh . . . and then the burning climax, followed by cool relief. Of course, there was nothing to stop him, nothing but the dictates of his own heart. For it was mention of sons that undid Samana in the end, the searing realization that it was Rhiann he needed to bury himself in, despite the hurt. Rhiann he wanted to bear his sons.

Eremon's chest clenched, and he took a deep breath. Rhiann would know he had betrayed her, and he could not hurt her again, or risk driving her further away. Slowly he let his breath out and raised his face, calmer. He had done the right thing; Rhiann would know he had done so.

He picked at the chunk of deer meat on the platter, wondering about his decision over Samana's fate. Should he actually try to extract information from her? He could threaten her with pain, but she was right: warriors did not torture women. And after that little show of theirs, he couldn't pretend an interest in her body just to deceive her. Ah, and he didn't have the energy for such games, anyway. The time for such things was long past, and that was why, he suspected, Agricola's attentions to Samana might be waning. Agricola must know, as Eremon did, that it was about war now. If she didn't know already, Samana would no doubt soon realize that her wiles had little place in such a situation.

He sighed and tore off another chunk of flesh, thinking about what Rhiann would say when she saw the gift he was sending her. For as he had stared over Samana's head, the impulse had come to him as a bolt of clarity. Samana had to be returned to the Sisters. It was for her fellow priestesses to judge her, woman to woman.

Eremon prayed that Rhiann would see it the same way.

Chapter 48

Rhiann's blood sang with a clear, hard strength this day, despite the sudden rainstorm that swept down the glen they were climbing, forcing them to put up their hoods and huddle over their horses. The progress north and west through Creones territory had been winding and difficult, but as the same scene from the crannog was repeated, and the calls for vengeance rang out in hall after hall, so the spirits of the young Sisters had soared. Rhiann's instincts had been right. When the chieftains saw the priestesses' faces and heard their tales, they had been stirred first to pity, and then to action.

At first, though, Rhiann had deliberately avoided the Creones' royal dun, the seat of its king. She knew that the news of their journey would travel faster than they themselves could. So the day she received an invitation from him to celebrate the longest day would remain scared in her memory for ever. From the moment of their arrival, the king regarded Rhiann with thinly veiled anger, despite the fact that his tribe's dead Ban Cré had been his own sister. Rhiann nevertheless understood him, reasoning that he was a man woven of the same cloth as Maelchon: a woman-hater, jealous of sharing power. But a king ruled only as long as his people wanted him to. He did their will, not his own.

And so he feasted the Sisters lavishly, and when they led the longest day celebrations with the most dramatic retelling of their story so far, Rhiann sensed in the mood of the people that the king would receive no rest until he agreed to join them. Through some careful questioning of the king's aunts and sisters, she discovered that most of the Creones chieftains were now demanding retribution; that his people, young and old, clamoured for revenge; and that his own wife pecked at him night and day, urging him to do something.

Of course, no mention was made of allegiance in any of the meticulously polite conversations Rhiann exchanged with him, but in the resentful cast of his eyes when he helped her to Liath's back Rhiann sensed triumph. She bid him farewell, unable to contain the pride that glowed inside her, and which carried her forward for many days thereafter.

We can do this for you, she said to Nerida, as her horse lurched its way over a high, windy pass.

She'd made gifts of half the girls now, distributing them among the Creones, and they'd all gone eagerly to their new positions. Now the smaller party was wending its way further north to Decantae lands.

'One of my scouts had news of the Decantae, lady,' Nectan informed her, urging his stocky pony along the slope of the hill beside her. The horse was hock deep in heather, the glowing leaf-fall purple of the blossoms dulled by the rain and heavy cloud shrouding the sky. 'They offered some warriors to Calgacus's warband, and allowed him to station his scouts on their coast.'

Rhiann turned to look at him. 'That means they are already well-disposed towards the alliance. It will be easier to sway them, perhaps, than the Creones.'

'It would not matter how difficult they were to win,' Nectan declared. 'You would still triumph!'

He grinned, blinking rain from his black eyelashes. He wore a speckled seal-fur cloak but had scorned a head covering, and his hair was plastered to his forehead like tendrils of dark seaweed.

Rhiann smiled to acknowledge the compliment. 'It is the girls who have triumphed, and you and your men have played no small part in that, my friend.'

Yet Rhiann's voice faded, as Nectan suddenly tensed, peering over her shoulder back down the glen. 'We are being followed,' he announced, and pulled up his horse. While he sent two men to identify their pursuer, Nectan urged the remaining Sisters off the high trail and down the pine-clad slope to the stream that raced along the narrow bottom of the glen. There they waited beneath the spreading canopy of pine trees, the rain pattering down through the branches to the carpet of needles below.

After a while they heard a high, swelling whistle, and Nectan and his men lowered their nocked bows. 'It is safe,' he told a relieved Rhiann.

Yet her relief quickly turned to puzzlement when the man following them caught up, delivering to her Eremon's message. Her husband was well, and so far had enjoyed great victories with their raiding, he reported. He had also sent her a strange gift, which was following with a band of warriors half a day behind.

'And he says I will know best what to do with this gift?' Rhiann repeated.

The scout nodded, unslinging his bow from his shoulder. 'He said that he hoped you would understand, lady, and not be angry.'

'Angry!' Rhiann's brows drew together. 'Do you yourself know its nature?'

'It is a woman.'

'A *woman*?' The pulse in Rhiann's throat skipped. 'Why would he send me a woman?'

The man shrugged. 'I do not know, lady. She was captured by the men that bring her. That is all I know.'

A terrible suspicion was worming its way into Rhiann's mind. Surely not . . .

'Rhiann?' It was Fola at her elbow. 'Are you well? You've gone so pale.'

Rhiann straightened and caught her breath. 'Yes, Sister, I am well.' She addressed the messenger again. 'They are half a day behind, you say?'

'Yes, lady. Once I'd found you, I was to go back and lead them here.'

It was afternoon already, and although the evenings were long this time of year, they'd been hoping to reach the next dun quickly, to escape the rain. 'Then we must wait, I suppose.'

They were carrying waterproof hides on the horses for sleeping outdoors, and Nectan and his men now strung these up in the pine branches to give some rudimentary shelter. For the rest of the afternoon they huddled there, the damp seeping up from the ground. Rhiann sat just under the edge of the hide, on a rock slick with moss and spray from the rushing stream, while the others shivered and sang to pass the time. Nectan miraculously managed to light a fire to dry them out, and proceeded to roast some hares his men had caught the day before.

Towards dusk they heard the whistle once more. Rhiann stood and tried calmly to face the men who came sliding down the slope from the path above, their boots skidding on the wet pine needles. There was no sign of their captive. 'Lady.' The leader of the men nodded awkwardly. 'I bring you greetings from your lord.'

'Thank you, and you are welcome among us. Yet where is your charge?'

The man's face contorted with amusement and resignation. 'She won't come down here. She waits on the path.'

Anger burned Rhiann's throat. 'And who is she who *waits* on us?'

'I still don't know her name,' the man admitted, stifling a smile. 'But your lord called her Agricola's whore.' His eyes darted to the young female faces behind Rhiann. 'Begging your pardons.'

Though her darkest fears had prepared her, still Rhiann flinched. Samana, here! Her traitorous cousin, who brazenly seduced Eremon just after he and Rhiann were wed. Rhiann hadn't loved Eremon then, or he her, but it still hurt . . . Goddess, did it hurt.

'Go now,' Rhiann ground out, tucking her wet, cold hands into her sleeves, 'and take hold of her and bring her to me here, slung over your shoulder if need be!'

The leader of the men grinned, and bowed his head. 'Yes, lady.'

And that was how Samana arrived, screaming curses and batting the shoulders of the warrior who carried her, until he flung her on the damp ground right at Rhiann's feet.

Despite her anger, Rhiann was shocked at the change in Samana. Always so perfectly bathed and oiled and groomed, her black hair had long ago escaped its braids and lay wild and tangled about her shoulders. Her dress was so encrusted with mud that the original colour had been obscured, and her bare ankles and wrists were scratched and bruised. She'd stopped cursing as the wind was knocked out of her by the fall, yet now she looked up at Rhiann from all fours, her dark eyes alight with fury. 'You!' she spat. 'You cannot treat me this way! I am a queen—'

'You are a Roman slave,' Rhiann cut in, straightening her spine, 'and when you betrayed your own people you gave up any nobility that we would recognize here.'

Samana merely hissed in rage and frustration and said no more, pulling herself into a crouch. Rhiann stared down, a distant part of her appalled at Samana's appearance and this uncharacteristic loss of composure. The way Samana's eyes drooped at the edges, her snub nose and dusky skin all combined, as Rhiann knew well, into an alluring and languid beauty. Yet that sensual potency had been muddied by the desperation Rhiann saw in her face now.

At another time, perhaps this knowledge would have drawn forth pity in Rhiann, for she also had known desperation and great fear. But no longer. She had no room for such feelings even in herself now, for her heart was too scarred to admit them.

'I would advise you to get up,' she told Samana. 'We will not carry you.'

Samana flung up her chin with ill-disguised hate. 'Then leave me here, cousin. I will be more trouble to you than I'm worth, I promise. Your husband could not get any information from me, and neither will you!'

At mention of Eremon, Rhiann's skin went completely cold, and the fingers folded in her sleeves tightened. Samana had supreme powers of seduction. She had been with Eremon, probably alone with him. He was no doubt still hurt by Rhiann's revelation. Had Samana enticed him again? Did he touch her?

Stop it!

With an effort, Rhiann gained control over herself and slowly uncurled her arms, standing tall. She would not give Samana power over her. But what was she supposed to do? Eremon said Rhiann would know, but she didn't. What she wanted was to be as far from Samana as possible. The revulsion was so strong it was tangible.

Perhaps she should send Samana with these warriors back to Dunadd, to be held prisoner there. Or better yet, with some of Nectan's men, for Rhiann was sure *they* would never succumb to her wiles. And yet, it was a long journey. Eremon had given Samana into Rhiann's safe keeping, and she could not risk her escaping. Nor did she wish to lose the protection of any of Nectan's men.

Eremon! Rhiann allowed herself a brief flash of anger at the position in which he had put her. But there was no time for that now.

'So, cousin,' Samana taunted, her eyes flashing. 'How inconvenient for us both. Your prince must be playing a joke on you.'

'Be silent!' Rhiann raised her palm before Samana's face, and to her relief, it was steady. 'I will deal with you later, Samana. For now, we must seek shelter.' The rain was showing no signs of lightening, and it would soon be dark. Rhiann glanced calmly at Nectan. 'Let us push on to the next dun.' Then she gazed down at Samana. 'It seems you will be our guest for a short time, until I decide what to do with you. You can make that painful for yourself, or relatively pleasant. It's up to you.'

Yet Samana was either speechless with rage, or she'd decided to regain her dignity, for she said nothing more and gave no more trouble, walking along behind the horses with her guards as they made for the head of the pass.

The bout of rain was just as cold and uncomfortable on the other side of Alba, yet Calgacus and Eremon agreed that it was fortuitous, providing cover and opportunity for another rapid strike attack. For after the culling of the horses and oxen, the Romans had not turned back, but kept to their northwards line of march.

As Eremon sat sharpening his sword, he wondered to Calgacus if this foolhardiness stemmed from the fact this army was not led by Agricola. 'Perhaps this new commander seeks to prove himself,' he pondered, looking out from his shelter at the raindrops, pounding the path into mud. He tossed the whetstone in his hand, brushing the surface of the smooth granite with his thumb. 'Perhaps he fears to be seen as cowardly.'

Calgacus agreed, warming one hand around a bronze cup of hot mead. 'It is time to split our forces once more, then. If we begin a barrage of harassment – short raids from the glens – we may not kill many, but we will instill greater fear.'

'And fear,' Eremon added, resting his blade across his crossed legs, 'may make our new commander do something foolish.'

They leaned in together over a crude map drawn on smoothed bark with charcoal.

The Romans, moving more slowly now with fewer beasts to draw their baggage wagons, had crossed the Dee river and were now following the course of the Don. And here, the Albans gained the advantage of terrain once more. For the mountains descended into lower hills on the plain, their courses broken and unpredictable. To keep far from the hills, the Romans would have to detour to the east, away from their more direct northern path. This, Eremon surmised, they were unlikely to do. To keep to their chosen, faster route, they would have to come within reach of the high ground once more – and the Alban camp.

'I think they still hope we will face them in open battle,' Calgacus remarked, picking up a chewn hawthorn twig and resuming the cleaning of his teeth.

Eremon nodded, grating the stone down his blade edge with short, practised strokes. 'And they may keep hoping. Yet I agree that we must show ourselves more now. Numbers of Roman dead are not important – the aim is to goad this commander and his men into making an error.'

They looked at each other, and then out of the tent at the rain, which was now being blown slantwise. The surfaces of all the little puddles were puckered with heavy drops and slews of wind. 'Mud,' Eremon said thoughtfully. 'Rain and mud are no friends of the Romans.'

Even though the Decantae seemed supportive of the alliance, it was the first night in a new tribal territory, and Rhiann knew they must all do well at convincing the chieftain of their cause. So with a heavy heart, she took extra time with her appearance, dabbing the *ruam* dye automatically on her lips and cheeks, settling the cold, heavy torc around her neck, the bracelets on her arms.

Rhiann had decided to question Samana afterwards, and as she emerged from behind the bedscreen in her jewellery and fine dress, she was glad, as her eyes fell on her cousin, that she had thought to wait. Rhiann's finery, and the power that always rose in her with each retelling of their tale, would make her more able to deal with this strange situation.

Since their arrival, Samana had sat unmoving by the fire in the guest lodge under the watchful gaze of two of Nectan's men, for Gerat and his warriors had returned to Eremon and Calgacus. Yet as Rhiann passed behind Samana now, she detected a faint trembling across her cousin's shoulders, and unconsciously Rhiann took a step to the side and quietly turned to go.

As she neared the door, however, she heard a rustle, and Samana suddenly rose to her feet in her mud-stiffened skirts. 'Whatever you're trying to do with these visits, it won't help,' she hissed.

Abruptly, Rhiann halted and turned. And that was when she

understood the quivering of Samana's shoulders, for her cousin's eyes were pits of hatred, lit with a rage that burned like live coals. 'The Romans are too strong, and always were,' spat the Votadini queen. 'You picked the wrong side, cousin. You and that prancing boy of yours.'

'It seems you were once unsure of that, Samana.' Rhiann struggled to keep her voice even. 'I recall you tried, unsuccessfully, to make Eremon join you. So you've had second thoughts since you turned traitor, and will do so again, no doubt.' She paused. 'Once a traitor, always a traitor. I wonder if that has occurred to Agricola yet?'

Samana's eyes burned brighter, and her mouth twisted into some kind of smile. 'You speak of second thoughts, Rhiann, and perhaps that's why I left your own lord's bed so warm. Could it be Eremon has had his own second thoughts – about you?'

The blow was physical, and Rhiann could not hide its force. 'That's not true.' She endeavoured to contain the sick hurt that turned in her belly. 'You're a liar.'

Samana's smile curved with a feverish triumph, and she took a step closer to Rhiann, clenching her hands by her sides. 'I saw it in his eyes, Rhiann, how you've let him down. You failed him, didn't you? *His body told me when it joined with mine.*'

The gasp escaped Rhiann's tight throat, and she clamped her lips harder, striving for calm. She knew it wasn't true, it couldn't be.

But couldn't it? something deep in her whispered. *You wounded him . . . he has been away from your bed for many moons.* She hated herself for even thinking such thoughts, but Samana was wielding a potent weapon of which even she was unaware. Memory.

Two years before, when Eremon followed Samana to the Roman camp, Rhiann took the rye spores to observe what he did. Her spirit saw him and Samana together then, their bodies thrusting in urgency. And once seen, such things could never be forgotten.

Rhiann hadn't loved him then, but she did now. No matter how, in her dazed grief, she'd denied them to herself, her feelings for Eremon had retreated, but not gone away. They'd merely contracted to a glowing coal beneath her numbness, and though she surrounded it with ice to keep the hurt at bay, she could not extinguish that warmth. It pulsed at times, catching her unawares, and now, faced with Samana's threats, it was strengthening, yet bringing with it a rising panic.

Samana took another step closer, her wide smile fuelled by the anguish Rhiann could not hide. 'Yes, Rhiann, he kissed me like a starving man. He suckled me. He buried his face between my legs—'

The crack of Rhiann's palm across Samana's face shocked them both, as well as the guards, who took a step forward, their hands on their daggers.

Samana gasped and held her reddening cheek. 'So you do love him,' she said, and laughed.

Rhiann's chest was heaving, and her eyes stung. Not only for Eremon, but also for the burning sickness that had arisen with Samana's words; how her images drew the dark spectre of Maelchon into Rhiann's throat and mouth, the memory of his touch on her breasts. It was all mixed up together again. Eremon. Maelchon. Her own desires. Her body. *Hers.*

'Your life,' she murmured, 'is under my control. And you will show me respect, as well as my husband, for he will cut your Romans into pieces.'

Her cousin only stared at her with that maddening smile.

With trembling legs, Rhiann barked at the two guards. 'Do not let her leave this room. Do not talk to her or listen to her, or let her out of your sight, even to pass water. Do you understand?' Rhiann saw them nod, but would not meet their eyes, for she was ashamed at her loss of control. Drawing the fine clothes around her, she swept out of the door without looking back.

Yet as she sat in the chieftain's hall that night, the sweet voices washing over her, she could not blot out the conversation.

Eremon hated Samana. He would never touch her. He would never do that to Rhiann. Her logical mind knew it, but . . .

Wouldn't he? that voice whispered again, in the pained shadows of her heart. And she remembered the deep hurt she had seen in his eyes. *Wouldn't he?*

Chapter 49

As they continued north Nectan took charge of Samana himself, ensuring that she was kept well away from Rhiann, even when they stopped at night.

Yet he couldn't blot out the sound of her imperious demands, as she sat straight in her saddle with her chin high, glaring around at them all. She grew louder and more disruptive the more she was ignored, until Nectan at last lost patience and gagged her mouth. Where before their party had been lively, with the girls singing and chattering, now an uncomfortable silence settled over them all, unrelieved by the return of the sunshine.

At the end of another hard day in the saddle, Rhiann was hunched lower over Liath's neck, angry with herself. Samana's lies should not have affected her so much. She had wielded the most potent of weapons, yes, but Rhiann had faced many things these past years. Look at what she was facing now! She shouldn't let her personal feelings get in the way of her task, yet they were.

And Rhiann realized that some of her strength and fierce drive must therefore be faltering, and it frightened her. For she still did not want to face what lay on the other side.

The northern hills and sky had been washed clean by the recent rains, the heather glittering with drops of moisture, the winding paths cut by rivulets that ran down from the bare rock peaks. As they passed a small, dark loch lying in a deserted valley, Rhiann watched an osprey arrow into the water after fish, barely conscious of Fola nudging her horse up beside her.

'Sister,' Fola whispered. 'We can't go on like this. What will you do with her?'

'I don't know.' Rhiann sighed and glanced ruefully at Fola. 'She had a . . . connection . . . to Eremon. She uses that to hurt me.'

'But this connection must be long severed.' Fola said it as a statement, not a question, and when Rhiann did not answer, she added hotly, 'How can you listen to her poison?'

'It is more complicated than that . . . but . . . I'm being a coward, aren't I?'

Fola shook her head. 'You? Never. Yet it is clear something must be done.'

Rhiann straightened her shoulders. 'I will try to get some information from her – Goddess knows that's the only reason Eremon could have sent her! Perhaps this time, with you nearby, our joint presence will get me further than before.'

Fola nodded thoughtfully. 'Perhaps you can convince her that her loyalties lie with her people.'

Yet Rhiann's only answer was the bitter curve of her mouth.

The dun they came to that night was on the western borders of Decantae territory, near to Calgacus's own fort. The chieftain already supported the alliance, and had sent some of his own men to join the Caledonii king.

'Word of your approach has gone before you, lady,' the chieftain said, on greeting her in the yard before his hall. 'You should rest, bathe and eat.'

Rhiann thanked him and accepted the offer of rest for the others, but that was not what she had in mind for herself. While the Sisters went into the hall to eat, Rhiann asked Nectan to bring Samana into the guest lodge, empty of everyone except she and Fola, who waited behind a bedscreen.

Samana was still gagged, but strove to look defiant as Nectan gestured her towards one of the hearth-benches. She resisted, until Nectan was forced to push her to her knees on the earth floor, none too gently.

'She will listen to no one,' he grumbled to Rhiann. 'By the Mother, let me imprison her on the most barren of the rock islands, out in the sea. There the wind can carry her voice away altogether!'

At his words, Rhiann noted the flash of Samana's dark eyes. She feared imprisonment, then, and that was useful information. Rhiann nodded at Nectan to remove the gag, bracing herself for Samana's rage.

It was not long in coming. Samana practically spat the gag out, her eyes sparking. 'How dare you treat a tribal queen like a common thief – me, a sworn priestess, a king's niece! *How dare you!*'

Rhiann regarded Samana calmly from a hearth-bench on the other side of the fire, as Nectan retreated to stand with his back to the door. 'As I said, you forfeited all right to those titles through your treachery, Samana.'

Samana narrowed her black eyes. 'You, my cousin, love to clothe all your words in ideals such as *honour* and *treachery*, when you're nothing but a jealous chit who can't satisfy her man, and objects when someone does it for her!'

Rhiann absorbed the blow without flinching, prepared this time. 'I'm not interested in your lies, Samana. That rock in the sea beckons you . . . ah, yes, I see how you fear it. So tell me what I want to know, and we may be able to come to terms.'

'*I* come to terms with *you*?'

Rhiann breathed out through her nose in the priestess way. 'Under pain of banishment, I expect you to tell me what you know of Agricola's forces, his plans, and the disposition of his men. Then, we may allow you to be kept in the manner to which you are accustomed, in a secure but adequate dun.'

Samana barked a laugh. 'Then I add stupidity to your sins, cousin. Do you seriously think I would tell you anything?'

'Have you forgotten who is in control of your fate here?' Rhiann snapped, then cursed herself for losing her temper.

Samana's thin, elegant brows arched high. 'Your prince never got any information from me, either, Rhiann. And he tried more persuasive means.' The small, pointed tip of her tongue slid out of her upper lip.

Rhiann dug her fingers into her palms, out of sight in her lap. 'If you repent of your treachery, we will keep you alive and safe until this war is resolved one way or the other. If you won't, I have no choice but to send you far away.' She leaned forward. 'Far from jewels and furs and warmth and ease, far from news and tales and music and every diversion you prize so much.'

'You have no right!' Samana struggled to her feet, her hands still bound behind. 'I am a queen of a powerful tribe. You break every kin law there is. My people will seek vengeance—'

'Really? Will your people seek vengeance from us when they know who betrayed their own king? When they discover how you really sold them to the Romans? When they realize that their queen became a Roman whore?'

Samana's mouth twisted with bitterness, marring her beauty. 'This was always about you and me, Rhiann, no matter what you say! You were always jealous of me, even on the Sacred Isle, and now you hate that Eremon wants *me* in his bed and by his side, and not you! You want to banish me, not because of your ideals but because you're *jealous*, because I'm more queen and priestess and wife than you'll ever be!'

That last barb pierced Rhiann to her core, because the dark part of her believed it herself. And Samana's priestess senses were not dulled beyond all recall; she saw the angry flinch, sprang after it like a hound on the hunt.

'That's right, isn't it, Rhiann?' She stumbled forward a step, and out of the corner of her eye Rhiann glimpsed Nectan moving closer.

'You're only half a woman, Rhiann, a broken half! A man like Eremon needs a real woman, and this you'll never be!'

The shame that rose in Rhiann at these words turned instantly to rage – rage at herself, and at Samana, who taunted her with a twisted tangle of everything she did and did not want to be. Samana's body exuded all that was lush, womanly, sexual, fertile. She had no memories of a dark king to douse her fire, or dull her passion. Yet the corruption that lay inside Samana made a mockery of all that her body promised, and even Rhiann's growing fury did not cloud that sudden understanding.

'And what are you, Samana?' she cried at last. 'A woman who uses sex as power? A woman who uses sex to abuse people and break them and make them betray themselves and others? Is *this* a real woman?' She flicked her fingers at Samana's torn and muddy dress, her wild hair.

'A real woman,' Samana spat, 'loves her man with passion, but you have no passion! are nothing but *dry, barren* and *used up.*'

Each word was a lash, laying open Rhiann's heart, and she forgot who looked on, flooded by all the fury and grief she had so carefully suppressed for moons. 'Dry I may be, but I love Eremon in a way you never could, because you are consumed, Samana, with your own lust for power and selfish desires! Where is the space for love in that? How could *you* – a woman who does not know the meaning of respect, or honour, or truth – love anyone? You cannot *give*, Samana, you only take, take and take until there's nothing left, and,' Rhiann's voice broke, 'Eremon deserves more than you could begin to give. I may not be complete, but I *am* real. I have a heart, and I have given it to him!'

Somewhere Rhiann was appalled at her loss of control, but the words sprang from a true place, and they found their target in Samana. The Votadini queen reared back as if she had been physically struck, and then screamed with frustration, her bound arms shaking as if to wrench themselves free. 'A weakling like you is no match for such a man! Power *is* all there is, power is everything, and if you can't see that, you little fool, then you're stupid as well!' Samana stamped her foot, her eyes feverish with madness. '*I* lead Agricola around by his balls – the leader of all Britannia, the commander of forty thousand men! – and he does *anything* I want him to! *I* control the men and so *I* am the power in this land! Who *else* could have thought of raiding the Isle? Who *else* had the power to make Agricola do it, besides me!' She was screaming now. 'I control him! He listens to me, and me only!'

. . . raiding the Isle . . .

'You?' Rhiann stammered. '*You?*'

A shadow fell over the walls, and Rhiann turned to see Fola walking slowly forwards, dazed, her eyes wide and fixed on Samana. The horror in her soft face was so raw it made Rhiann flinch. Yet it was Nectan who reacted, taking two strides to Samana's side and striking her full across the face. Samana crumpled to the ground, pressing her jaw into her shoulder, as Nectan – calm, steady Nectan – stood there trembling violently, tears glittering on his cheeks.

For a moment all of them were frozen. Rhiann's mind reeled; she could not absorb what Samana had just confessed. Yet as the moment drew out, it was Samana who spoke first, panting as she smiled up at Rhiann. 'Yes!' she hissed. 'I ordered the Romans to spill the blood of the Sisters, it was all *me*! So kill me for it, Rhiann, and be done with it! I no longer wish to look on your face.'

Nectan raised his hand again, but Rhiann stepped forward and caught his wrist. 'Peace,' she stammered, her voice shaking. Tension quivered in Nectan's arm, until he dropped it and turned away to the door, hiding his face.

Samana was backed up against the hearth now, and she levered herself to her feet once more. 'So what will it be, cousin? The sword? The dagger? I welcome both of them, if they will send me to the gods, to live among heroes who possess real courage, power and might.'

Still Rhiann could only stare at Samana as if she had never seen her like before, as if she were some vile, unnatural animal that had been banished from the world in ages past.

She killed the Sisters. She, a sworn priestess.

Rhiann could not comprehend such a betrayal. Samana had broken sacred bread with the priestesses. She had sworn her undying oath to them as the Stones looked on. But more than that, they had given her love and understanding and refuge.

Rhiann's eyes closed, and behind her eyelids she saw the bright sun glittering on Roman spears, the descending sword, Nerida's face. *Samana killed them. She killed them.* And those words, repeated over and over with the bloody pictures, at last penetrated Rhiann's shock. Dark rage began to beat on her temples – all the rage of all the moons past. All the rage of years. The need to strike out reared in her; the need to hurt as she had been hurt. Her eyes jerked open.

Samana saw her clenched fingers, and smiled. 'Yes, Rhiann, give in to it and strike me down! Do it! I don't care!'

Rhiann stared at that wild cloud of dark hair, the honey skin, the sloe eyes that showed nothing but twisted triumph. If she had a blade in her hand, would she stab it into Samana's breast, as Samana had pierced her own with grief? She thought she would, as the red fog clouded her mind. She *knew* she would.

Yet her training was strong, and instead she struggled to breathe first, to calm herself, because Nerida and Setana had taught her that. *Breathe,* she thought, as the room tilted around her. Goddess, breathe. The elder sisters were always calm, always gentle and wise. They would never strike or kill anyone. She had to be strong for them.

It was then that the voice came, slipping softly into Rhiann's heart.

Sister . . . Daughter . . . The voice was no more than a stirring of the currents in Rhiann's soul. Yet with its sudden, haunting cry, so the fog of her rage was arrested.

Daughter. Goddess daughter.

'No . . .' Rhiann moaned. *I hurt, I hurt and I must do something to release it . . .*

Abruptly, a wave of warmth swept Rhiann, smoothing the jagged edges of her anger. It surged and ebbed and surged again, growing greater each time, wrapping Rhiann's body in a cocoon of vibration too low to be heard. Over her shoulder she heard Fola gasp, but it was not a gasp of pain or shock, and then Rhiann knew that Fola felt it, too.

Suddenly dizzy, Rhiann closed her eyes, groping for the edge of the bench. And that was when the scene came back to her with true clarity, which her grief had veiled. Nerida stepping towards the soldier, her hands outstretched, smiling, as the blade rose above her. And Rhiann heard the words Nerida had spoken, even though she had not been close enough to hear that day. *Come, I forgive you.*

'Come,' Rhiann found herself whispering, as it caught in her throat. 'I forgive you. I forgive you . . .' And with the words came the feeling that Rhiann knew, right then, had flooded Nerida's heart when she gazed upon that soldier's sword, a sweet release, that was like nothing in Thisworld at all.

Slowly, Rhiann groped for Fola's arm and drew her forward to stand by her side. Fola's face was transfigured, shining beneath the tears, and for an endless moment they stood wreathed together in that light.

At long last, Rhiann blinked as if waking, the air warm and hazy around her, not knowing how much time had passed. Yet when she looked at Samana, and saw the glittering smile of triumph there, she knew it had been no real time at all.

'Sister,' she said – and Samana's smile faltered for the first time.

Yet Rhiann's soul had cleared, as if a veil of heavy clouds were drawn back by a breeze, and in that grace she pitied her cousin rather than hated her, for Samana had abused power, and for that she would never have love.

'We will not give you death,' Rhiann told Samana softly, simply. 'It is for you to make peace with the Mother when you meet her in the Otherworld. As for us . . .' She drew a deep breath. 'We forgive you, Sister.'

Samana screeched in wordless fury as Rhiann held up her palm. 'Yet there must be consequences from the choices you have made. First, you are hereby banished from the Sisterhood, and stripped of your status as one of the Goddess Daughters. Second, you are hereby named an outcast among the free tribes of Alba. The word will be sent out of your banishment from society.'

'You cannot do this!' Samana screamed, shaking her tangled hair. 'You have no right to do this!'

Fola put her hand in Rhiann's other palm. 'We are what is left of the Sisterhood. Rhiann is the last Ban Cré. We have spoken.'

'But . . . but . . .' Samana spluttered, 'you cannot make me outcast, you have no right!'

Rhiann raised one finger, reciting the lore. 'A person can be declared outcast by the elders of a tribe, a council of chieftains, a conclave of the druid brethren, or a conclave of the priestess sisters.' She pointed at Nectan, standing expressionless by the door. 'We are the Sisters, and we have here also a chieftain of the Caereni, who stands witness, and a chieftain of the Decantae to endorse the same. You will find no refuge the length of Alba, Samana, not even among your own people, when our message reaches them. Every person will turn their face from you, from the smallest child to the oldest servant. You have remained powerful here only because your own people do not know the full extent of your betrayal, yet they will now. You will be nothing in your own people's eyes from this moment on, and for as long as your life lasts. We have spoken.'

No one moved, except Samana, whose whole body was trembling, her black eyes wide and stricken. To be made outcast was a fate far worse than death. It meant the loss not only of status and recognition and power, but of home, food and shelter. It meant that no one would even recognize her as a *human*. She would be a wraith, even when she stood before those who had formerly hailed her as queen. Ignored, uncounted, unsung.

'You cannot . . .' she whispered again, yet Rhiann merely nodded at Nectan, and he cut Samana's bonds with his dagger, and then all three of them turned their backs and left the lodge without another glance.

For some time there was the sound of things crashing to the floor, as Samana vented her rage on the benches and stools in the guest lodge. But eventually, as the long, sunseason twilight descended, Samana was forced to emerge.

The news had travelled through the entire dun already, and the yard outside the lodge was crowded with men, women and children. The Sisters were there too, standing together. Yet when Samana appeared, walking tall as if to salvage some dignity, with a rustling of clothes and feet, every single person there turned their backs on her.

Her heart pounding, Rhiann stared into the shadows gathering between the houses, and listened to Samana's soft steps pausing behind her. 'He will still die; this I promise you,' came the hiss, and Samana spat on the ground at Rhiann's feet.

Then she walked out of the open gates into the northern wilderness, far from her home, far from the Roman lines. No one marked her passing or which way she went, for she was as invisible to Alba now as if she had never lived.

For a long time Rhiann stood without moving, like a slim, fair statue, as the people gradually dispersed back to their homes. Fola was the only one who remained, beckoning to the few Sisters left to shepherd their younger charges into the other guest lodge.

'Burn oil to sweeten the air,' Fola said softly, 'and make an offering to Ceridwen, goddess of birth and death. Then sing for the souls of our elder Sisters, for they have come close to us this night.'

She turned back to Rhiann, who still had not moved, gazing out of the gate where the mists of dusk were rising from the line of hazels and oaks that ran down into the valley. Yet when the damp evening wind blew up the path, Fola saw one long shiver run the length of Rhiann's spine, as if she was waking, and it was then that she took Rhiann's arm and silently led her back into the empty guest lodge.

The hearth was surrounded by the destruction of Samana's wrath – overturned benches, scattered ashes, spilled mead cups. But it was there that Fola led Rhiann, and when she turned to face her, Fola saw that to let the forgiveness come, all Rhiann's barriers had indeed melted.

For Rhiann was alive in her eyes as she had not been for moons. 'Hold me,' her friend said simply, and the grace of tears was the last given that day.

Chapter 50

Lucius shook the rain from his cloak, unheeding of the close confines of his tent.

As he handed it to his slave, he deliberately avoided the implacable eyes of his *primus pilus*, the highest-ranking centurion, who was standing with the tribunes and the camp prefect. They nearly filled the leather tent, pushing Lucius's camp bed and tables and brazier to the edges of the woollen rug, ducking to avoid the hanging brass oil lamps.

'Between you and me, Lucius,' the *primus pilus* said grimly, 'Agricola's orders were given before we knew what we were facing. Over the last month these new raids have demoralized the men – we've lost five hundred already, and not one in a pitched battle. I hear soldiers talking: they speak of devils that change from trees to men, that fly at them in the night, spiriting men away in their sleep in order to feast on their flesh.' He stepped before Lucius. 'Something is eating their *souls*, not their flesh! We must get away from these hills, and now.'

Lucius wiped rain from his cheeks with his palm, then ran his fingers through his dark, clipped hair. 'Our goal is the fort of this Caledonii chief.'

'Our *goal* was to engage the enemy, raid the duns, weaken the tribes,' said the soldier wearily. 'Yet we have done none of these things. They are not in sight to *be* engaged; the duns are deserted. I strongly advise that we turn back now, and return our men to base in one piece.'

One of the tribunes, a young aristocrat with little battle experience, snorted and started forward. 'We have already gone further north than any others of our kind! The commander charged us to seek for glory, to show these savages that we will not be cowed, that we will conquer!'

'All we are showing them is that we seek death!' the *primus pilus* burst out. His face was shadowed by the uncertain light of the swinging lamps, but Lucius read his frustration plainly.

This was no unfamiliar situation on campaign. The camp prefect and *primus pilus* had worked their way up from the common ranks. Yet legates – like Lucius – and tribunes were from the old families. They knew the mind of Agricola better, and must think of many things beyond this one campaign: namely, how Agricola's movements were perceived in Rome. Lucius's career depended on it, no less than his commander's.

'Sir,' the *primus pilus* urged, 'we must turn back, I beg you. They will not give us battle; they melt away like spring snows. It is madness to continue—'

'*All right!*' Lucius put up his hand. 'All right.'

In his secret heart, Lucius himself wanted nothing more than to turn back. Honour and glory – all that he needed to win wealth and influence – were to be found in battle. They were *not* found by having his men picked off by mud-covered savages.

The mules and oxen were gone, and they'd had to abandon many of their supply carts, so food was growing scarce. The foraging parties, forced further from camp, were easy prey for men who could move as part of the very land itself. And the unseasonable rain would not clear, leaving them imprisoned in a world of grey skies, clammy mud and ceaseless winds.

After much debate, and in the face of heated protests from his tribunes, Lucius at last gave the order to his exhausted men that they were to retreat. Spirits rose instantly that night and, despite the lack of horses and stores, the pace back along the coast the next day was faster than their advance had been.

All of them had become sensitized to the disturbing emptiness of the land, which made the news that Lucius received from his scouts four days later even more difficult to believe. 'Are you sure?' Lucius asked the excited messenger, who knelt before him in his tent.

The man nodded eagerly. 'There are a thousand barbarian warriors drawn up for battle, in the open. Waiting for us.'

Lucius took one of the few horses left and rode to see for himself, but two hours later he confirmed it with his own eyes, peering down from a heavily wooded rise through sheets of rain, which swept out of a wide valley breaching the mountains. The barbarians had picked the ground where the valley opened on to the coastal plain, and were arrayed there in silent, unmoving rows, many squatting in clumped groups. Yet Lucius could see immediately that their numbers were no match for his. Perhaps they thought this sudden turnaround meant that his army's will had been broken, that they at last had a chance. Well, they would soon discover their error.

Rising high in his saddle, knees braced, Lucius stretched his back with a grim excitement. For nigh on three months his men had been harassed and goaded until there wasn't a single soldier not strung out on tension and lack of sleep, fear and frustration. Now all that turmoil could be assuaged as it should be – in blood.

After a double-pace march from camp, the Roman army scrambled into battle formation a few hours later on the plain outside the valley mouth. The trumpeters blasted out the officers' commands as the centurions barked orders, and the legionaries drew swords and clanked up against each other's armour, rectangular shields overlapping. The auxiliary cohorts were moved to the front with their mailshirts and long spears, with the legionaries behind. In the empty space between the enemy and auxiliary lines, the tribunes and remaining mounted cavalry officers trotted the surviving horses up and down, exhorting their men to stand firm.

From his command post on a knoll beneath a dripping ash tree, Lucius could see the barbarian commanders moving among their own men, ordering them up and whipping them into some vague order. Their cursing and screaming rose as a roar through the rain, and the thrashing of their swords on their shields echoed the steady drum of the drops as they beat the earth.

Yet Lucius had no intention of letting these savages indulge in the usual battle posturing for long. His men, tired and wet and worn, were like hounds held tightly on a leash. He had only to release them, and this he finally did, the horns blaring out his order to advance and engage.

Out moved the auxiliary infantry, pausing to throw their first barrage of spears. The cloud of barbs flew up in an arc and disappeared into the sheets of rain, and though Lucius had little hope they would find their targets, such a barrage always demoralized the enemy.

Lucius cupped his hand to protect his eyes from the rain, straining to see how many had been downed by the spears, but the auxiliary infantry were now advancing as a single wall, and he found his eyes were locked instead on those rigid ranks, closing in on the shrieking enemy, who were still pounding their swords on their shields.

Even through the muffling drizzle Lucius heard the dull clash as the two armies met, and sections of his own lines wavered, the bright, tangled weave of barbarian clothes and weapons bleeding into the uniform ranks of Roman red, yellow and polished iron.

There was a momentary struggle, the flanks of both armies heaving in a confused ebb and flow of men, and then suddenly something changed. The barbarians were giving ground already, seeping back up the slope.

Lucius shifted in his saddle, uneasy. It was too soon for such a retreat – the barbarians had displayed little of their usual reckless ferocity. Then he glimpsed the prefect and the *primus pilus* racing over to him from different directions, and just then, the enemy line suddenly broke altogether and galloped up the rise, disappearing into the mouth of the valley.

An entire flank of his own auxiliary infantry, encouraged by this act of cowardice and the scent of an easy victory, took the opportunity to pursue. The prefect's shout carried faintly to Lucius beneath the ash tree, but the tribune in charge of the pursuing men could not stop the red tide, their soldiers goaded by weeks of fear and exhaustion into leaping for revenge. As the first lines pounded away over the churned mud, so more soldiers followed.

Lucius spurred his horse from the knoll across the wide space around the army's flank, the tribunes endeavouring to follow, but cut off from him by the surging tide of men. Lucius soon lost their cries behind as he galloped onwards, the rain and wind gusting into his face, his horse's steps stumbling dangerously at times on the boggy ground. And as he was the only horseman behind the attacking infantry, so Lucius alone saw what happened.

Just inside the valley mouth another tiny glen sliced up into the mountain wall, and into this cleft the retreating Albans were streaming, shouting Roman soldiers on their heels. Lucius kicked his horse harder, screaming desperate commands that were lost in the rain, for he remembered with dread Agricola's stern command never to follow the wild men into the hills. But it was too late.

Lucius's throat was stopped with horror as the sides of the narrow glen suddenly erupted in a volley of arrows, and from the bracken slopes above poured hundreds of fresh barbarian warriors, their swords driving downwards into the confused ranks of Roman soldiers. His men scrambled to retreat, but only stumbled over themselves and the rocks, and were pushed into disarray by those pressing from behind.

By the time reinforcements raced to the glen's mouth, it was over. The barbarians had not paused to ensure total victory, but merely killed and maimed as many as possible in the first downward rush and then melted away over the cliffs into the rocks and ferns.

Lucius lowered his sword, his voice spent in shouting. In the rain, he didn't notice the tears of rage running down his cheeks.

Every muscle in Eremon's body ached: his legs from running; his arms and shoulders from swinging a sword. And now, wedged here in a rock overhang in a high valley, it was his back giving him pain, awkwardly hunched on the damp earth. Yet he hardly noticed.

He barely registered the drip of rain from the cave wall, trickling down the back of his mailshirt; the angry rumble of his belly; or the jarring cold seeping up from the ground. The throb in his wrist, where he had caught a sword blow on his shield, took up most of his bodily awareness. Yet even that was only a reminder of the inner glow which consumed him and provided all the warmth he needed. It was the fire of triumph, victory, relief.

In the deepening dusk, Conaire's eyes glittered with excitement, and Rori's teeth flashed in the darkness of the shallow cave. Eremon grinned back. They felt it, too.

The night would be long, until tomorrow they moved out to regroup far from here. But for now, despite the lack of food or fire, they had all they needed.

So Eremon ignored the stink of drying blood and sweat, sank deeper into his filthy cloak, and let sleep claim him.

Chapter 51

Rhiann woke with a start inside the thick, dark walls of a northern dun. A storm was raging outside, the wind streaming over the grim peaks of the encircling mountains and down the valley to the little fort. Despite the hut's wooden door and thick door-hide, the gusts were so strong that they forced their way under the thatch roof and between the tiny chinks in the wattle walls.

Shivering, Rhiann burrowed deeper into the furs on the guest bed. It wasn't the storm that had woken her, though, but a dream, the first clear vision of Eremon she had received in moons. Yet it was a strange sending.

She was in the valley of light, holding the cauldron of Ceridwen in her hands. But its glow was dulled, and she could not feel its warmth in her fingers. In panic, she searched for Eremon, unable to see him. The eagles screeched their challenge into the clear air above, and around her she heard the frightened murmurs of her people. 'Fear not,' she said to them, yet she herself burned with fear.

Then there was a stirring among the people, and a light gleamed from far away, and she ran towards it until the hill slopes rose narrow and steep above her head. 'I could not find you,' she said to Eremon, looking up to him on his horse, tears in her eyes. 'I searched but could not find you.'

Eremon smiled as he slid to the ground, and took her in his arms. 'But I was waiting for *you!*'

They both laughed with relief, and when Rhiann pulled away from his embrace, the cauldron was a glowing bowl of heat in her hands. Alive again.

Blinking sleep from her eyes, Rhiann stared into the thick darkness, knowing that the dream had been triggered by the message she received that day. Eremon and Calgacus had won a great victory, and the Roman army had at last gone into retreat, weakened by the constant Alban harassment of the past few moons. And what should Rhiann's path be now?

Feeling heavy and dull from lack of sleep, she asked Nectan about their journey as they broke their fast the next morning, before a blazing hearth-fire. She had done her best with the Creones and the Decantae, and was satisfied at the murmurs of rebellion that were growing louder the further north they travelled. Now they were deep in the territory of the Boresti, a small, scattered tribe living high on Alba's mountain spine.

'We are nearly at the Smertae border,' Nectan confirmed, scooping up soft cheese with a crumbling piece of barley bannock. 'Yet I advise not going further into those territories. The Smertae and the Lugi are all that stand between us and Maelchon's lands, and they are, as far as we can tell, friendly with the Orcadian king.'

Something cold crawled under the surface of Rhiann's skin. 'No, I wish to stay clear of the far north,' she replied evenly. 'Do those tribes command many warriors?'

Nectan shrugged. 'Not large enough to warrant the risk.' He swallowed and glanced at her carefully. 'By the Mother, your husband would be my friend no longer if I took you closer to the Orcades. Very soon, lady, we will reach the limits of our journey.'

Rhiann's heart soared at those words, for it meant they would soon be home, and she could lay down the mantle of control and fierceness she had donned moons ago. Now, after Samana, she wanted only to turn away from that hardness, and find and nurture something soft in her again.

Later, as the party climbed a long valley, she remained at the rear, musing on her dream. It wasn't difficult to decipher – she needed to be back by Eremon's side. Their individual power was at its most potent when they were joined.

With a surge of excitement Rhiann raised her face to the sun, which was struggling free from the shredded clouds above. Soon, her self-appointed mission would be complete, and she could not just tell Eremon she loved him, but make him believe it with her body. For Samana had been right in the midst of her twisted hatred. Rhiann *had* been incomplete, the passionate part of her imprisoned by the past.

Now, it was as if something had been awakened, for Rhiann's body hungered just to feel Eremon's bare skin against her own. And it was with her body that she would anoint them both, with the Mother's light that shone through death and grief.

And betrayal.

Yes, surely where there was love, even betrayal, there was a place from which one could return.

★

On his return to his camp by the Forth, Agricola had not paused to bathe the dried salt spray from his face, or the grimy sweat from his body. Taking the *haruspex*, the priest he had brought from Eboracum, he made his way directly to the small temple he had caused to be built earlier in the season.

It was a square timber building with an open courtyard in the centre, and a room that held the sandstone shrines to the deities, with alcoves for the eagle emblems of the legions. The double timber gates had been left open all summer, to allow the god Janus to join his men on the field of war, and would not be closed now until all his units were back from their campaigns.

This day was one of double celebration for Agricola, though he had as yet heard no news from Lucius in the north. Perhaps it would be a triple triumph!

In the patch of sky framed by the temple courtyard, dark clouds milled restlessly, driven by the same keen wind which had slapped the waves against Agricola's ship all the way north. Yet he barely felt the cool air on his bare arms, watching instead the ox blood run down the sacrificer's knife with a secret smile. Agricola himself then dedicated the fallen beast to Mars, Jupiter and Venus Victoria, for his great triumph over the south-western British tribes whose rebellion he had just this summer quelled.

It had been an easy triumph, and the sight of those crushed bodies beneath his hooves as he inspected the battlefield afterwards had gone a long way to restoring the confidence that had been torn from him by last year's Alban defeats. That, of course, and the holy island raid before he left, which had likewise been thoroughly successful.

Agricola savoured these things, as the priest touched the warm blood to his forehead. Yet as he bowed his head then, his prayers turned to something far more personal. For on his return to Eboracum he received the news that his wife was to bear him another child. And the conception at the time of a full moon, a diet of imported Thracian figs, sweet chestnuts and almond milk, and the shape of her already swelling belly guaranteed a son. At last!

Agricola smiled, as the smoke of the burnt flesh on its brazier curled up into the sky. He was in control again, as confident as he had been when he first set out to attack the Novantae. Since then, he'd allowed himself to fall into the sin of fear far too often. He would endeavour to rid himself of such a weakness from now on.

Slowly, he left the gates of the temple, unlacing his leather breastplate and handing it to a slave. It was time for the bath-house now, followed by food.

The air held the barest hint of crispness, for the cold season came earlier every year here in the north. Still, if the victories kept coming now, he would be bathed in the sun of his own land perhaps sooner than he originally hoped.

With a spring in his step Agricola nodded at his door guard and entered the outer chamber of his quarters. There he stopped to sniff the rich scent of beef stew and malted ale, letting his eyes adjust to a darkness relieved only by two lamps and the single window set high in the wall, covered with thin, oiled hide.

It was only as Agricola's sight cleared that he realized he wasn't alone. A man was seated in one of his rush chairs, with his head in his hands. A suspicious dread breathed over Agricola, with a chill greater than the Alban air outside.

Then the man raised his face and Agricola had to stop himself from stepping back, with an instinct to ward away what was coming.

It was Lucius.

The *optio* in command of the small ridge fort tilted the gate to shield himself from the cold wind. On either side of him, six legionaries stood with their swords drawn, and above on the rampart more soldiers had their spears trained on the intruder, though the person was not only alone, but also a woman.

She stood, a shivering, dark shadow against the vivid bracken and birches lining the slope behind her. Their leaves were already beginning to turn, yet the *optio* knew, after three seasons in Alba, that the flame of autumn colour licking over the land was a trick for foreigners such as he, for it heralded the most bitter cold. He hated the wind in particular, which was why being drawn away from his warm brazier and his dice to deal with this sudden arrival had put him in a brutal mood.

The *optio* peered at the woman. Beneath her shapeless, brown tunic, dirt-streaked cheeks and lank, black hair, he could now glimpse a hint of beauty, and he wondered, with a stab of warmth, whether her body matched the fineness of her eyes, vacant as they were.

'I must see your commander, Agricola,' she repeated, as she had for his scouts, and then for the men on watch. The woman's words and demeanour had only added to the enigma she presented. She spoke faultless Latin, yet though her words were authoritative, her voice was colourless, and she hunched into her tattered cloak and would not meet his eyes.

'And what might you be wanting with him, sweetheart?' the *optio* mocked, peevish with cold. The soldier beside him laughed and, boldened, the commander stepped closer to the woman. She reeked of unwashed flesh and damp wool.

'That is for him to decide.'

Her head was down now, her cheek turned away, and on impulse the *optio* took hold of her jaw and turned her face up to his. Even in the

346

shadow of the fort palisade, the combined beauty of the woman's skin and exotic features was unmistakable. 'You're a pretty one to be wandering these border lands all alone, without the protection of men.'

The woman shrugged, her large, dark eyes drifting past him to gaze at the sky. They were most unusual, those eyes – almond-shaped, the edges slanted – and something about their languid cast made the warmth pulse in the *optio*'s groin. 'I am the queen of the Votadini,' the woman murmured, 'and I am under Agricola's protection. I need no more.'

At this ludicrous claim, the guards on the rampart above the gate guffawed, resting on their spears to gain a better view.

'Queen, eh?' the *optio* jeered, tilting her chin higher. The cold sun glinted on the fine, downy hairs on her smooth skin. He dropped his voice to a whisper. 'You might need to peel off those rags and show me how much of a queen you really are, pretty maid. Dance under me with some royal flair and I might believe you.'

No flicker of emotion passed across those black eyes, only the reflection of the clouds. 'Will it make you take me to Agricola quicker?'

The *optio* was confused, his desire rapidly cooling. Alban women were known for their fight – that's what made them so alluring – but the dullness of this one's voice only made the hairs on his neck rise.

'If you please me,' he muttered, releasing her jaw. With a breath he pushed his disquiet away, for he was a practical man at heart. Mars knew when he'd have the opportunity to bed anything female, let alone some flesh as fine as this.

The woman shrugged again, uncaring, and pulled the ragged edges of her woollen cloak over her breasts, her hands trembling with cold.

'Come, I will question you in my quarters,' he announced loudly, for the benefit of his men, and made to lead her towards one of the two long timber barracks. She did not even try to avoid the mud puddles in the rutted track, but plodded along behind him listlessly. 'You'd best tell me everything you know, and quickly,' he ordered, swallowing down his unease.

A week later, Agricola had been able to hold to his self-made promise about resisting fear.

It was easy, of course, in the face of the rage that overwhelmed him as he heard Lucius's tale of woe, a rage that was given a final, painful twist with Lucius's stuttering recitation of the numbers of Roman dead.

Another 1,500 men. Agricola was still struggling to believe it.

And then suddenly Samana had returned, scratched, thin and dirty; alive only because she gained food from those people who had not yet learned of her banishment. Amid his anger, Agricola had marvelled with a kind of disbelieving horror how these Albans, so obsessed with royal blood, could turn on a noble so resolutely that the order would be followed by every man, woman and child in the land.

Of course, his fury had little to do with empathy for Samana herself. What truly burned in his gut was the arrogance of the Erin prince, snatching a party of Agricola's allies under the nose of a legion, and the careless swagger with which he had dealt with Samana, blatantly defying both the threat of the Roman forces and Agricola's personal wrath.

Samana had assured Agricola that the raid on the sacred island would destroy much of the tribes' resistance, but resist they still did.

Agricola glanced at Samana now, curled in his bed asleep, shivering despite the glow of the brazier that brought sweat to his own brow. Anyone observing his utter stillness, as he sat on a stool, chin resting on fingertips, would think he had reached some place of cold acceptance. Yet they would be wrong. The more he commanded his muscles to immobility, so the anger only roared brighter.

In another week, the Ninth Legion units he had taken south with him would return on foot. So far, Agricola's wrathful eye had fallen on the north-east of Alba. There lay the richest lands, the flat plains his men could easily reach while being protected on one side by the sea. Most of Alba's population also lived there, and if they'd only stayed to fight perhaps all this would have already ended, and he would be in possession of the entire nation.

Yet the promised enemy had melted away into those hellish mountains, and all Agricola's men got for their pains were cowardly raids that came out of the night, the rain and the woods. He could not afford to lose any more soldiers on such a fool's chase, and the fort of the Caledonii king seemed, unfortunately, too far to reach after all. But there was another option, and it had been slowly taking shape all through these hours of darkness.

Now there was a rustle and stirring among the bedclothes. Agricola brought his gaze back from the shadowed roof-beams to meet the black emptiness of Samana's eyes. He had never seen her as she had been this last week; lifeless, the dark fire of her doused. Yet now she was at least fully awake, and in the glassy stare with which she fixed him he saw a spark of life, and knew somehow that she had sensed the drift of his thoughts. He'd always found it uncanny, that ability of hers.

'You must strike at the den of the wolf himself,' Samana whispered, her eyes suddenly hungry. 'Take your revenge and mine, for the season of sun is fading. You have not far to go.'

Mesmerized, Agricola stared at her, his chest stirring with a sudden, unnamed yearning.

'Not far,' she whispered again, and raised a finger to point west, white and crooked against her tangle of black hair. 'Just over the mountains. Dunadd.'

Chapter 52
LEAF-FALL, AD 82

Far in the north, the season turned early. At a sacred pool in a remote glen, birch leaves torn free by early storms swirled across the surface of the water, as an evening wind crept up the back of Rhiann's neck. The rowan boughs dipped and shivered, their scarlet berries bright splashes of colour in the dusk shadows. From a nearby valley over the hills floated the creaking boom of a stag in rut, and drifting from farther west, another.

Their thoughts on the south and the harvest being undertaken even now at Dunadd, Fola and Rhiann watched the bronze finger-ring shimmer to the bottom of the stream-fed pool at which they knelt. After a silent moment they came to their feet and, as Rhiann pinned her cloak around her shoulders, she glimpsed Fola's face in the last rays of the sinking sun, and saw how pale it was; as white as the birch trunks behind her.

On the path, Rhiann slung her arm around her friend's shoulders. 'I have a surprise for you. We are turning back this very day. Nectan and I agreed this afternoon.'

She glanced at Fola, and was pleased to see her tired mouth lift a little. 'On the island, I dreamed sometimes of the life you led, Rhiann. I thought it exciting then . . . but now . . . I yearn only to be by the fire in Nerida's house . . .'

Rhiann heard how she bit off her words, and so she stopped and took Fola by both shoulders. There was pain in her friend's face, yet Rhiann wasn't afraid of it any more. She hadn't been able to let it in for fear she herself would falter. Now she could give back to Fola what she had received. 'And you will soon be by *my* fire. At least I can give you that.'

Fola forced a smile, laying her fingers over Rhiann's hand. 'As you will soon be by *his* side.'

She turned to hop over the stream on the mossy stepping stones, and Rhiann followed, hugging to her the knowledge that her own reunion with Eremon would come sooner than even Fola knew. For Rhiann had already made up her mind what she would do – send the others to Dunadd while she sought out Eremon in the east.

A day later, Rhiann's band was wending its way back down among the mountains to the west of Calgacus's dun, when Nectan's last scout found them. And with him was someone Rhiann knew immediately, for his hair flamed in the sun as he galloped towards them along the loch shore.

'Rori!' Rhiann exclaimed, as the Erin youth drew rein before her horse. Her legs tightened unconsciously on Liath's back. 'Is he hurt?' she blurted, heedless of anything but the sudden, overwhelming panic that gripped her.

Panting, Rori shook his head. 'No, lady, no, my lord is well.' His freckles were veiled by ingrained dirt, his hair lank with grease, his clothes unrecognizable from those in which he had so proudly ridden from Dunadd moons before.

Rhiann's heart threw itself against her ribs. *He lives. He is safe.* Yet Rori had not finished, and it took another moment for his words to penetrate Rhiann's ears.

'I have both fortunate and ill news, nevertheless, lady,' he continued, and wiped sweat from his upper lip, tawny with unshaven fuzz. 'It is a tale I must tell you from the start,' he added significantly.

Despite her renewed dread, Rhiann at last remembered her manners. 'Come, you will be hungry and tired. We have some cold hare from last night; some ale.'

In moments they unpacked the horses, and Rhiann, Rori, Fola and Nectan settled themselves in the sun on a tumble of grey boulders on the loch shore, cloaks pulled around their knees against the keen wind. Rori gulped a few mouthfuls of meat and drank deeply from a flask that Nectan handed him, took a breath, and straightened his shoulders. 'My prince had a visitor a week past. A man came in to camp after being taken by the southern scouts. He was travel-weary, for he had come a very long way – he is of the Damnonii people.'

Rhiann frowned with confusion. All the Damnonii leaders had been killed, she thought; the people scattered.

'This man was among the warriors who fought beside my prince two years ago. Somehow he escaped Agricola's revenge, then a year ago he was taken to be a Roman scout, for he knows the lands that border your own.'

'Go on.' Rhiann drew up her knees and leaned forward on them.

Rori took another breath, his hand tight around the ale flask. 'He has deserted the Romans, lady, because he found out something that made him remember us and how my lord helped his people. The Romans forced him to become a scout by virtually holding his wife prisoner, but then she died in childbirth, and their hold over him was broken.'

'So why did he seek out Eremon?'

Rori shook his head in agitation. 'He found out what they were planning, that's why, and he couldn't let what happened to his own people happen again.'

'Slow down, lad,' Nectan interrupted, his hand on Rori's shoulder. 'What did this man come to tell the prince of Erin?'

Rori glanced at Rhiann, his blue eyes tight with anxiety. 'Another army is massing at the Roman camp on the Forth. Yet this man says he knows their target is due west, this time, not north.

Rhiann's heart plunged. 'West?' There was nothing west of the Forth; no great duns, no tribal centres, only mountains, and on the other side . . .

'Dunadd,' Nectan announced, the gruffness of his voice betraying his emotion. 'They seek Dunadd.'

Rhiann's belly dropped to her toes. 'But what if this man is a spy? What if he is wrong?' The dying sun on the water glittered harshly in her eyes, and she blinked to clear them.

Rori was unhappily shaking his head, peeling wind-blown hair from his face. 'My lord and the lord Conaire and King Calgacus and King Lorn spoke to this man all night. He is broken by his wife's death and what he's done, and greatly shamed. They all believe him, and my prince says it is a sign of the gods' favour that he came to us in time.'

Rhiann barely realized she was on her feet, balancing precariously on the rock, the wind whipping her cloak back. 'Where is Eremon? I must go to him now.'

'Lady.' Rori propped the flask beside him and rose, not meeting her eyes. 'He is gone south already, with most of the warband. He says the scouts must learn the truth of this immediately, and if it is true he aims to reach the pass to Dunadd before the Romans do.' Rori bit his lip, at last glancing up at her from under his pale lashes. 'And he wants you to stay in the north. That's why he sent me, so you would know how seriously he asks you, nay, begs you, to heed him.'

'Hide away?' Rhiann's fear made her voice rise. 'Caitlin, Gabran, Linnet and Eithne are in Dunadd! Does he think I will abandon them?'

Rori now appealed to Nectan with his eyes, and Rhiann turned her indignation on the Caereni chieftain. 'You know I must go straight back to Dunadd. No one is ordered to come with me, but no one can stop me, either.' She stared Nectan down, folding her arms.

Fola was also on her feet. 'I will come with you, Sister,' she offered. 'I promised to stay by you, and I will.'

At that Nectan sighed and spread his hands. 'As did I, lady,' he conceded. 'Though, if I aid you in this, it may be the end of my friendship with your prince.'

He sounded so mournful that Rhiann was suddenly flooded with a fierce, energetic resolve. 'If Dunadd is threatened, rest assured I will save my people and then abandon it. I am not mad, whatever you may think of me!'

Rori's wide eyes darted from Rhiann to Nectan. 'But . . . my lord charged me with this task!' he sputtered. 'I cannot fail him, I cannot!'

Biting her lip, Rhiann considered him with pity, wondering how to handle his pride. 'Rori, you swore to your lord, and I am your lord's mistress,' she said slowly. 'I am also the highest-ranking member of the Epidii present, your adopted tribe. In the absence of both Lorn and Eremon, I assume I am in command.'

Rori frowned, searching for an argument that did not exist.

Rhiann smiled. 'And if I am in command, then I am very lucky to have such loyal friends by my side.'

Rori blinked at her, and his shoulders finally lowered. 'I am here to serve,' he said stiffly, his hand leaving his sword hilt.

Nectan jerked his head to the west, where the sun had already been swallowed by the hills. The vale in which they stood was now steeped in purple shadows, and the deep waters of the loch were nearly black, the surface faintly silver with the last light. 'The coast is only two days away, in Caereni lands,' he said. 'I can easily find us a boat to take us south. That will be the quickest route. Now, let us make camp higher, away from the water.'

Despite her thwarting him, Rori leaped forward to help Rhiann mount, cupping his hand for her foot. 'Lady,' he murmured, 'there was another message from my lord, but he told me to deliver it to you in private.'

Rhiann settled in the saddle and took the reins from him, noticing that the youth's ears had flushed the same colour as his hair. 'What was it?'

Rori ducked so his fringe fell over his eyes. 'Ah . . . that he sends his . . . love.'

Silence fell between them.

'That's all,' Rori added awkwardly, patting Liath's neck, and when he at last looked up into Rhiann's face he immediately dropped his hand and hurried to his own horse.

Eremon blinked rain from his eyes and fixed them on his boots, caked in mud, scraped raw by rocks, the leather cracking around the toes. Those boots reflected what had been done to his body these last moons, but now he needed to ignore how tired they made him feel, and focus on keeping them moving, to the exclusion of all else.

He was utterly exhausted, they all were, but he would let nothing slow the rhythm of those feet, eating up the leagues of boggy ground between him and the pass to Dunadd.

And because he forced his iron will to shore up his muscles, every single man in his warband kept up the same pace, through the rain, sleet and fierce winds that drove down the mountain sides. No one flagged, not when their war leader drove them on as he had never driven them before.

Beside Eremon, Conaire loped with long, fluid strides, and in the rare moments that Eremon's screaming muscles and clenched chest threatened to betray him, one look at Conaire drove all physical pain from his mind. For Conaire's wife and son were at Dunadd.

His brother had sent an urgent message by horse warning Caitlin to take to the hills, but they could not guarantee her safety. And even if they could, neither Conaire nor Eremon had any intention of allowing the Romans to destroy those others who remained behind and who had, after three years, become their people.

Eremon cast a glance back over his shoulder. Calgacus and the other kings had returned north to defend against sudden Roman counter-moves, but despite their season's losses, Eremon still led nearly a thousand men, strung out behind him down a long glen. Mud splattered up with every step and men slipped and stumbled, pulling themselves up before they fell behind.

Eremon leaped around a jutting rock almost blocking the path, and beside him Dórn lurched over it, the warrior on his back gripping the stallion's neck tightly. Under Eremon's orders, the foot soldiers were all taking turns at riding the stock of 200 horses. Using such a system of rotation, Eremon hoped to keep them all going longer and faster.

Just behind him, Lorn led his horse with a grim determination, his pale hair stuck to his forehead under the leather hood, the coldness in his eyes that of single-minded will. He glanced up now and met Eremon's gaze, and though no emotion softened his features, some mutual strength was passed between them, one to the other. They could not, *would not* let Agricola get ahead of them to Dunadd, for they had both sworn to protect it before the eyes of the gods.

Yet it was an immense gamble. The Romans only had a three-day march across from east to west coasts, whereas Eremon must bring his men diagonally down a rougher, more mountainous route – some four or five days. But the Damnonii scout said the Romans were taking their time to prepare. It was no small task to provision such an army late in the season, especially as the Romans themselves had rid the lands they would cross of food-producing farmers.

Eremon was also relying heavily on the lie of the land, the Mother Goddess. Because of the broken western coastline, carved out by lochs, and the spine of high mountains, it was extraordinarily difficult to bring a large army to Dunadd from the east. There was only one main pass – a steep and winding pass – and if that was ignored, an army must travel far north before being able to cross the mountains anywhere else.

Eremon grasped at this, repeated it as a prayer to power his steps. If they could just get there ahead of the Romans, and somehow hold or block that pass, they had a chance. And if that chance was lost, then all would fail – for the Damnonii scout had also reported that Agricola was massing a force of 4,000 men. Eremon looked back again, at the steaming horses running with mingled sweat and rain, at the white faces of his frozen, exhausted men, visible beneath their hoods.

One thousand worn-out men, against a fresh army four times the size.

'Hawen,' Eremon muttered under his breath, nearly stumbling over another up-thrust rock, 'give us this victory so we know you walk by our sides. Your people need you as they never have before.'

Then he gritted his teeth and kept running.

Agricola had provisioned his army as quickly as possible, though the preparations and march had not been as swift as he would have liked, due to the depletion of the land so late in the season.

And this first night, as the wind tore at the flap of his tent, setting the poles shuddering, the towering will driving this whole expedition was already faltering. Here, marooned somewhere on the dark, windy Clutha plain between the east and west coasts, Agricola's morbid thoughts wrenched themselves free and leaped about like the shadows thrown from the oil lamps. He had sought no company tonight, for he was waging a war with himself, and he must win it in isolation.

The task facing him was daunting. The intelligence amassed about Dunadd made one thing abundantly clear: it was difficult to advance on it by foot, for the land itself was a fortress that could rebuff them. And he had seen all this mirrored in the eyes of his officers, damn them. They thought him foolhardy to send men this way so late in the campaigning season, though they endeavoured to hide their disapproval. But he had fewer choices than even they realized, and this lightning strike was, in reality, his most desperate throw of the dice.

The odds were slim. He couldn't use his fleet for support, since it was now in the east, and would have to sail north around the entire hostile coastline of Alba in uncertain seas, and he had heard nothing from the Orcadian king, Maelchon for moons. Nor could he bring his entire land force with him, out of the necessity of protecting his eastern and northern flanks. And the leaves were already turning, the mists seeping out of the ground as the cold air crept south, heralding the coming of snow.

Yet could I really have done nothing? Agricola asked himself again, pacing his tent. Should he have retreated to winter quarters, left the field to the wolves? No, and *no!*

For he knew now that he had underestimated the Erin exile. Eremon mac Ferdiad wielded a much wider influence than Agricola had ever suspected. Now the prince was caught far in the north, according to Samana, and this gave Agricola a unique chance that may never come again. With the bulk of the unsuspecting Alban forces still far away, he could strike at their undefended flank and cut the prince off from his power base, decimating his source of provisions, felling him at his knees.

This was the reasoning Agricola had used when his officers protested.

Of course, they didn't really know the rest: that the attacks on Lucius's legion were more crushing than the loss of men; that the emperor always kept one beady eye on his provincial leaders.

And what the last year had shown Agricola, all too clearly, was that to take all of Alba from coast to coast, he would need to muster an enormous army. If the news of his recent defeats were not followed by a significant success, the emperor might think again about those men he had recalled. Then the conquest would surely falter, along with Agricola's standing, which he had worked for twenty years to gain, in extremes of heat and cold, in the face of constant danger.

Abruptly, Agricola breathed out, flattening his palms on his thighs as he stared into the flickering lamp-flame. He must rediscover the rage at the Erin prince which had consumed him only weeks ago, when Lucius returned. Samana always helped with this, for her sexual fire drew out other, baser emotions in him. Yet Samana's fire had also been quenched, and she was not here.

Agricola threw himself to his camp bed and sat with head in hands. Jupiter! He had to find the cold fury again, the sharp edge of it. For that was the only way to ignore the deeper parts of him, the dark sea inside that heaved and roiled with fear – a greater enemy than even the Erin prince. He must not let it get the better of him.

He could not – for that way lay defeat.

Chapter 53

Closing her eyes, Rhiann sank lower in the wooden tub beside her own bed, letting the scented water lap her chin.

In the three moons she had been away from Dunadd she had enjoyed fine hospitality, yet all that time the burden of responsibility had sat heavy on her shoulders. The first thing she had done on her return was walk into Caitlin's arms, and hold her sister in silence for an age. In the tightening of her embrace, Rhiann asked for forgiveness, and it was given freely, without Caitlin needing to speak. And despite the threat that now lay over them, the second thing Rhiann had done was draw a bath.

For until she let go of all that tension, and the confusion of her rushed journey home, she knew she wouldn't be able to think clearly about what to do next.

Caitlin, of course, had been unable to leave Rhiann alone even for the length of that bath, and she stood behind the tub now, lathering Rhiann's wet hair with soaproot, as Gabran pulled himself up, standing on the bedscreen. Rhiann reached out one wet hand to stroke his soft head, the blond hair spiralling into curls at his nape. He jerked and looked up at her with Conaire's eyes, big and blue above Caitlin's little, pointed chin.

'I had many messages from Conaire, Rhiann,' Caitlin was gabbling. 'Many hundreds of Romans were killed in that last attack; perhaps a thousand! A great victory!'

Rhiann closed her eyes again as soap dribbled down her forehead. 'And is that all his last message said?' she asked, as Caitlin's fingers stilled in her hair.

'No . . . he also told me to leave Dunadd.' Caitlin's voice dropped for a moment. 'But I couldn't go, Rhiann, not without you. I knew you must return before the snows. I was going to wait at least until the storms came.'

Rhiann tilted her head back on the tub to peer at her sister through the steam. She was very glad to see that Caitlin's health had returned in full – she was brown as a nut, her nose sprinkled with freckles, lean and robust from being outdoors. In fact, she looked as if she'd been living in her buckskins and sleeveless tunic, putting aside her dresses while they were away. 'You should have looked to your own safety first,' Rhiann reminded her. 'For Gabran.'

Caitlin's cheeks flushed, and she bit her lip. 'Our scouts would tell us as soon as the Romans crossed the mountains, and then I would have gone.'

'Yet many others have already left. I would have been happier if you had been among them.'

'Rhiann!' Caitlin pushed Rhiann's head upright and vigorously rubbed her hair. 'The Romans will never set foot here, and you know it!'

Rhiann wiped drips of water from her eyelids. Her sister's chatter had a brittle edge, and despite her ruddy health her eyes, usually open and guileless, were veiled. It came to Rhiann then that of course her sister's fear ran as deep as her own, and Rhiann reached one hand behind to grip Caitlin's wrist.

'They will come back to us,' Rhiann whispered. 'And I am home now to hold you as you held me.'

For a moment the tendons of Caitlin's wrist were hard beneath Rhiann's fingers, until Gabran broke the moment, falling over with a loud thud and a squawk.

Caitlin bent and retrieved her son, swinging him up into the air and over her shoulder, pretending to bite his rump, as he squealed and kicked, his tears forgotten. 'He's nearly walking, Rhiann, did you see?'

'I saw.' Rhiann smiled up at them both, as Caitlin balanced Gabran on the side of the wooden tub. His mother had sewn him little boots that laced up his calf, and a set of buckskins like those she wore. 'I also see he'll soon be too big for you to lift! He takes after his father, in truth.' Rhiann reached up to touch Gabran's cheek, but three moons in a baby's life are an immense span of time, and the little boy shrunk back and buried his face in Caitlin's shoulder.

'He will get used to you again,' Caitlin reassured her briskly, seeing the hurt in Rhiann's face.

Rhiann slid back down into the steaming bath. 'If we were at peace, I never would have been away from him.' She swirled the water with her fingers. 'Yet I must tell myself it was worth it. All those cold, rainy days, those aches and pains, surely they were worth it, even if the help has not yet come.'

When Caitlin did not answer, Rhiann glanced up, and this time her sister's face betrayed a tense excitement. 'I wanted to wait until you were warm and fed,' Caitlin whispered, hardly daring to speak aloud. 'But I am terrible with secrets.' She hoisted Gabran on her hip. '*Two* messengers were just yesterday lodged in the King's Hall. They are waiting for Eremon.'

Rhiann stared up at her, frowning in confusion. 'But who are they?'

'They are from the Creones and Boresti, sister.'

Rhiann sat bolt upright, water streaming from her bare shoulders, and Caitlin's hand covered Rhiann's fingers with a fierce grip. 'They have come to swear allegiance to the Epidii war leader and to Calgacus. They are going to join our men, Rhiann, because of you!'

Eremon stared down at the Pass of the Winds in the mountains to Dunadd's east.

'See there,' Conaire pointed out now, his hoarse voice betraying his own tiredness.

Eremon squinted up and down the valley, his eyes burning from exhaustion. He had traversed this very pass many times before, always in small parties. Yet now, looking through the eyes of desperation and survival, he could see much more.

A narrow, winding path came from the south, doubling back on itself over and over to climb the heights of the pass. On one side of this trail rose steep slopes of loose scree and hanging boulders. The other side fell away to a river that rushed in white, foaming turmoil along the valley floor.

Eremon scratched at his jaw with a dirty nail. 'We cannot be sure they will come this way.'

'But, brother, they don't know we have arrived before them, and all the Epidii scouts agree – if they want to get to Dunadd quickly, it must be this way.'

Pursing his lips, Eremon dug the butt of his spear into the earth at his feet. As he did, he dislodged a large clod of mud and gravel, and several stones rolled free and came to rest against his toes. He stared at them, deep in thought, and then his eyes roved further, over the valley slopes. The days of rain had cleared, yet every surface ran with water, and small rocks and slides of mud had already peeled away from the slopes higher up. The river below was in full spate, foaming over its dark rocks. Then his gaze locked with Conaire's, and something leaped between them.

'How much time do the scouts think we have?' Eremon smiled, the dried sweat and mud around his mouth cracking.

Conaire was also beginning to grin, his blue eyes blazing. 'Their best estimate is two or three days. The men could manage four hours of sleep, and then be back up here felling trees – and there might be some logs in the stream bed.'

'So the land itself will aid us, making it that much harder for our friend Agricola to come calling.'

'They will be packed into this valley like butter in a mould, brother,' Conaire replied.

Two days later the sun was directly above Agricola, the glare blinding him as he stopped his horse and peered up the length of the valley that crossed the mountains. Ahead, a thin, white trail snaked up the steep glen, disappearing behind the looming shoulder of one of the close-crowding hills.

Agricola hated Alban mountains. The careless contempt with which they seemed to watch over the humans below aggravated him, and the valleys were just as hostile, with slopes that rose directly from barely visible sheep paths winding about their bases. And everywhere, always, there was water: mud, sleet, snow, streams, rain, drizzle, fog and mist.

'Stop babbling!' he snapped now. 'Summarize my options, and be concise!'

'Yes, sir.' The Alban scout standing before him gestured with his yew bow, slurring his way through the Latin words. 'Halfway up this glen, another valley breaks off to the west. But it ends at a sea loch, and you must then turn north to reach the same place you would by going directly over the pass. Or you could go back to the loch of the beacon and continue north, but then it is a long way before you can safely turn west again.' He watched Agricola warily. 'Your third choice is climbing, but the mountains are treacherous in every way, shrouded by mists.'

Agricola smoothed his horse's warm, gleaming neck, his thoughts racing. He had told his officers never to chance the narrow valleys and high hills of Alba, but there was no way to avoid them now. If he wanted Dunadd, they were the obstacles he must negotiate. Yet the scout had reported something else – a rockfall blocking the path up this valley, their best route. Such landslides were common here, apparently.

Agricola swallowed the temptation to rail at his own gods, and instead contented himself with cursing every Alban god he could recollect. There was little choice but to clear the path and press on. After all, he had committed himself this far, and the closer he came to Dunadd the more the memories of the Erin prince taunted him, beckoning him over these last few miles.

His force this time was mixed, drawn from the Ninth Legion units he had not taken south with him, and the Second Adiutrix Legion, which had also remained in Alba and was therefore fresher. Now they began to advance in a shining red snake up the narrow path, strung out with baggage trains, foot soldiers and some auxiliary cavalry in front and rear.

What awaited them at the top was nothing that the scout had anticipated.

With a loud curse, Agricola yanked his horse back as the first arrows skittered off the rocks above his advance guard. Ordering his mounted officers to pull up just beyond firing range, Agricola surveyed the rockfall before them.

An enormous pile of broken scree and mud had been brought down from the loose slopes above, and the agents of that dislodgement – logs and brush and branches – were all mixed in with the rock, spilling over the path and into the chasm of the stream on the other side. It formed a barrier like the rampart of a fort – a defendable rampart. On top of the blockade and high on the slopes behind it, archers were now visible, and other figures moved along the edge of the bank.

Because the path was so narrow, Agricola saw immediately that he could not get enough men together to walk abreast in any defensive formation, to protect themselves from barbarian missiles. Cursing to himself, he withdrew his officers to a safer distance to confer. 'How many men do you judge to be defending?' he asked one *primus pilus*.

'There is no way to tell, sir,' the man replied, his hand moving restlessly over his sword hilt. 'Only around a hundred are visible, but they could have a thousand waiting for us over the other side, for all we know.'

'And they have the advantage of the terrain.' Agricola's pulse was pounding with irregular, frustrated beats, and he sought for the Alban scout. 'Can we enter that side valley without getting within range of those archers?'

The Alban immediately nodded, hawking and spitting on the ground. 'You must go back some way to cross the river. Then you'll be on the other side, from where the second glen opens up.'

'Good.' Agricola turned to his officers. To his horror his hands were trembling, and he laid them flat on his mount's neck, taking a deep breath. It was against all his better judgement, yet there was no other way. 'We will split our forces. Half the men can come with me. We will take this side valley and come at the barbarian defenders from the other side of the blockade. The other column can advance from this side. If we both attack at the same time, trapping them, we can clear the path and join our men again.'

The eldest tribune was frowning beneath his crested helmet, his horse side-stepping nervously. 'We don't know how many men are over that barrier, though. I suggest that we shouldn't weaken our forces by dividing them.'

'And what would you suggest?' Agricola barked. *We can't go back, not now we are so close. Not now I have committed them. I cannot lose this . . .*

It might be his last, and only, chance to strike such a blow with the Erin prince's warband so far away. And all that Agricola could gain was yanking on that noose of rage and fear that had been tightening for moons. His only chance, and it could all be over.

'Not a single one of you has come up with a better plan.' A trickle of sweat ran from under Agricola's helmet and down his cheek. 'There can be only a few scattered defenders, for we know, to Lucius's cost, that their larger force remains in the north, and I have sent some mounted units by ship to keep *them* distracted. They do not even know we are here! Yet tell me another way to get us to this Dunadd and I will listen.'

No one spoke, or met his eyes.

'Then we will leave now.' Agricola wiped the sweat away with a gloved hand, and pushed his wet hair from his eyes. It was infernally hot in this direct sun. 'I want to be at the shores of this western loch come nightfall, and then we will advance on them tomorrow.' His eyes sought out the legate of the Ninth Legion. 'Take your men back down to that spur of flat land against this loch of the beacon. There you can camp for the night. With the water at your back, it is defendable, although these lands are deserted from what we can see. Tomorrow, come back up here and wait for our signal to attack.'

The officers were dismissed and, with trumpets and cries from the centurions, the soldiers and cavalry were rearranged and turned around. The huge force gradually broke in two as the first column started back down the valley, seeking for the river crossing.

Agricola rode near its head, focused on the safety of his horse's footing over the slippery rocks and gravel, endeavouring with all his will to quiet the conflicting voices that seethed within.

Eremon would allow no fires, but that dusk, in a narrow, high valley to the north-east, he judged it safe enough to light a single torch stuck into a low crevice in the rock wall. Crouched around this feeble flame, his troop leaders stared up at the returning Epidii scout with mounting disbelief.

'They've split their forces?' Eremon repeated hoarsely. 'Are you absolutely sure?'

The man nodded and leaned on his spear with both hands, his eyes shining in the glow of the sputtering flame. 'My lord, we tracked them far enough to know they've committed to this division. Half their men will be nearing the Loch of the Salmon as we speak.'

'And the other half?' Lorn asked, the edge in his voice betraying profound excitement.

The scout's teeth gleamed in the half-dark. 'They've retreated to the Loch of the Beacon, and set up camp on its shores.'

Eremon gazed at the rock shelf above Lorn's head, its crevices black with shadow. His heart had leaped into life, pounding with insistence against his chest as if demanding his attention. 'They have left us a force of two thousand men by the loch; *two thousand*, to our thousand.'

'Much better odds,' Colum murmured, to his left.

'Then, by the Mare, we can take them!' Lorn laughed, slapping his thigh. 'What do you say, prince? Shall we storm them at dawn?'

Eremon fought to think clearly through the tide of elation that swept his breast. They'd listened, his gods. They favoured him once more! He slowly rose, placing his palm against the cold rock to centre himself. The evening wind that came over the peaks above caught at his face, and the sudden chill focused his mind.

'No,' he said at last, addressing the crescent of faces lit up in the torch's glow. 'We will attack tonight, when they are sleeping. There will be enough moonlight, once the wind clears these few clouds. The Caereni archers can go in first, to shoot the sentries. This will buy us a little time. Then we cross the palisade and run down their tents.'

Lorn sprang to his feet, one fist clenched. 'Then I will be first to bury my sword in a Roman neck!'

There were murmurs of approval from the other Epidii warriors, and the atmosphere was instantly charged with a fierce exultation.

Across the leaping of the torch-flame in the wind, Eremon fixed Lorn with a calm gaze. 'I honour your courage, son of Urben, yet we can't allow any wild rush in the dark. It's too dangerous, once the Romans all awaken.'

Lorn's pale eyes narrowed dangerously, but Eremon stilled him with a raised hand. 'This is the time to act as one beast, as they do, with control. I want to use the formation we have practised: over the bank; kill as many as possible in their tents; then undertake a controlled retreat at an appointed time. If we break apart as a group, they will soon wake and organize a counter-attack.' He held Lorn's gaze. 'We cannot risk leaving Dunadd at their mercy.'

Lorn's mouth worked with frustration. 'The gods have put this chance in our hands! We must meet it as Albans, shouting the war cries so the gods know we fight for them!'

'This we have done already, for moons.' Eremon's voice betrayed his own irritation. He and Lorn would never see eye to eye on the question of Roman versus Alban tactics. 'But now we have a chance to attack a Roman camp on open ground – *this*, at last, is where our practice can bear fruit! We can't let our forces fragment, and that's my final word.'

Lorn looked as if he dearly wished to argue further, but then he seemed to remember his vow of allegiance, as he always did, and at last his eyes slid away. 'Well,' he added, with a familiar toss of that silver head, 'when a Roman throat meets my sword, I won't care how it got there.'

As the troop leaders dispersed to rouse their drowsing men from the heather, Eremon called Fergus to fetch him a Caereni messenger. 'Go to Conaire at the rockfall and tell him what has happened,' Eremon ordered the messenger. 'I want him ready to withdraw as soon as he gets news of our progress. He's not to be there when Agricola comes back up that valley from the other side, understand?'

The messenger nodded and trotted away, and after Fergus had gone to clean his weapons Eremon leaned his forehead on his arm, staring down at the guttering torch. He could not believe his luck – first the desertion of the Damnonii scout, and now this. Rhiann's dream had to be true, then. The Albans were meant to triumph over the Romans. The gods decreed it.

He smiled to himself and rubbed his sprouting, itching beard with his shoulder.

The arrow that took the Roman sentry in the chest just missed his heart, and so allowed him enough time to watch a dark tide of men flow over the silvered plain before him. Down the ditch they poured, and up the bank to where he lay, sprawled between two of the wooden stakes that had been stabbed into the ground just that day to form the camp palisade.

Then the haze around the sentry's sight thickened, and he sensed the heavy tread of boots all around, the brush of fur on his face and stink of sheep wool, before a cold blade caught the moonlight above him. Then he knew no more.

Deep in sleep, one of the eight soldiers in the tent nearest the gate was woken by a horse's whinny, and as he blinked and yawned, struggling to adjust his eyes in the dark, the whinnies were joined by faint cries of alarm.

But he only got as far as freeing his hand from his bed roll to grasp for a weapon, when the tent flap was torn asunder by a sword thrust. Immediately, the sloping leather walls were rent by a flurry of whirling blades and stamping feet, and he only had one moment to wonder if it was the gods come to earth in one slicing, many-legged beast of fury, before he, too, fell into darkness.

Eremon kept his shield close to Colum on his left side, giving him protection while keeping his own right hand free to wield his blade in a stabbing motion, different from the sweeping slashes they were used to. Fergus to his right did the same, and so on down the line. It was a rough approximation of the Roman fighting fashion, even though their longer swords were not as suited to it as the short Roman *gladius*. Yet it ensured that his men stayed together in one block.

Eremon risked a glance back at the lines behind him and to either side. All of the Epidii warriors were tightly bound, rolling over the

Roman camp, rending and stamping down the tents, and stabbing the men within. Some knots of fighting had broken out away to his right, as the Roman soldiers on watch and those who'd reached their weapons scrambled to put up a defence. But there Eremon glimpsed Lorn's hair, as the Epidii king rallied the Albans and laid into the defending men with his own formidable sword.

Eremon dodged a fire pit outside a tent, scattering coals with his sword, and knocked a stand that held the standard and weapons of the men inside clattering to the ground with a contemptuous thrust. Then he shouted to draw his own line onwards, to where fresh ranks of tents beckoned. These were already a mass of movement as panic-stricken Roman soldiers stumbled out into their own fires, greeting the oncoming Albans with cries of terror.

Eremon drove in with his shield edge and slashed and stabbed with his sword, barely noticing the hot blood that spattered on his hands and face, the screams and sudden clouds of choking smoke as his men set the tents alight.

He worked methodically, Colum on one side, Fergus on the other, and when at last he realized that the surviving Romans had managed to group into formation at the edge of the camp, trapped against the loch shore, Eremon shouted the order to retreat. At least a third of the enemy were dead or wounded, and he had no intention of becoming locked into an even fight with the rest. Down the lines, the retreat order was repeated, and the Alban force began to fall back.

As they streamed from the camp, over the torn remnants of the brushwood gate, Eremon stood off to one side near a stand of alders, barking orders and peering through the billowing smoke. Fergus and Colum had led the nearest warriors free, yet by the clash of swords over on his right Eremon realized that some of the men were still engaged in hand-to-hand fighting. He roared at them until he was hoarse, and at last they appeared through the smoky gloom, fighting as they retreated.

As they reached him, Eremon took a step forward, judging it time to abandon his own post. Just then, he caught a whirl of movement from the corner of his eye, and instinct took over. He swept his sword around in an upwards arc as something struck him with force in his flank and, with a cry of anger and fear, he stumbled, slashing at the wild Roman eyes that swam before him.

The tip of Eremon's sword caught the man's neck, snagging in his tunic, and Eremon wrenched his shoulders around to grasp the hilt with both hands and drive it deep into the flesh beneath. With a grunt the man fell, and Eremon tripped over the body and sprawled on his face, his helmet rolling free on the ground.

Immediately, someone yanked his hair and then his shoulder. 'By all the gods!' Lorn thundered, as the remnants of his men raced around him for the gate. 'Your own orders were to be away, brother, so why dally here?'

Stumbling to his feet, Eremon was unable to answer, for the blow under the edge of his mailshirt had taken the wind out of him. But when he swayed, Lorn cursed and caught him around the waist. 'Lugh's balls,' he muttered, and held him away, staring into Eremon's face with puzzlement. Then Lorn slowly pulled one hand away from Eremon's left side, and Eremon saw, as if from far away, that his palm was running with something that shone black in the moonlight.

'You there!' Lorn cried. 'Grab that horse, and you two, help me with the prince and his weapons! We must be away from here, *now!*'

Chapter 54

In the morning light, the peaks of the mountains threw sharp, jagged shadows over their lower flanks, and the river was a silver thread in the dark cleft of the valley. Agricola balanced unsteadily on top of the now-abandoned rockfall, looking down the eastern path on the other side, his hand shading his face from the low sun.

He knew now why the trail was empty and silent, for a few moments ago a courageous, desperate messenger had arrived from his camp by the loch, to bring Agricola the news of his Ninth Legion.

Agricola did not shade his eyes this way to better observe his eastern forces, for they were recovering and regrouping – and burning the dead. He did it so he did not have to look into the faces of his officers; so he could grind his teeth methodically, and stare into space with burning eyes; so no one asked him questions or ventured opinions or tried to make him feel better.

Seven hundred men had died in one night, because of his decision.

He should somehow have sensed the significant Alban force lurking in the mountains. Despite his own scouts scouring the land ahead of them, they had remained invisible. Yet the men who attacked his camp were no rabble of peasants with scythes, or even a desperate band of local warriors. The messenger described a highly organized warband, attacking the camp with an Alban rush, but then switching to Roman tactics, with deadly effect.

It was stamped with the mark of the Erin prince, Agricola had to admit. Somehow – the gods knew how – he had flown here from the north ahead of the Roman force. For a crazy moment, Agricola actually wondered if the prince was magical somehow: a sorcerer, or a demi-god like Hercules or Achilles. At the least, he was well blessed by his own gods. How in Jupiter's name had he known they were coming?

From the west, a cold breeze blew up the back of Agricola's neck, finding its way underneath the guard of his helmet. But he did not turn to face it. He would not turn to face the west.

He only had a little more than 3,000 men left, and the odds had now tipped. It was far too risky to go on, with a force of 1,000 Albans under the Erin exile's control lurking somewhere near, and Agricola's own army in unfamiliar terrain. It could easily turn into another cat-and-mouse game, just like two years before, and this was not what Agricola had been expecting. His men would become trapped in these barren hills until the snows and storms found them – and after all the defeats of the last few months, he could not afford to lose even a few hundred more.

With a great force of will, Agricola breathed out, dropping his shoulders beneath the fine, red cloak that covered his bright breastplate. The prince had won this round, damn him to Hades. Perhaps a war such as this could never be won this way.

Slowly he turned, his eyes looking through his officers arrayed behind him. He was silent for so long that some of them began to stir, leaning on their sword-hilts, sweeping off their helmets.

Yet Agricola was remembering his own words to Samana, given in a firelit tent two years ago: *I will goad them, and taunt them, until I bring them all to bay in a place of my own choosing, and then I will crush them.*

Fresh to Alba, Agricola had known then what to do. Yet since then he had allowed himself to be seduced into this pointless game with Eremon of Erin and the Caledonii king. Now it was time to return to his earlier, and mercifully clearer plan. This season was all but over, and he would have to admit defeat and send his men back to their winter quarters in the south. But next season . . .

I must corner them in one place, like hounds with a stag. The stag was fiery, yes, formidable and strong and wild. But the hounds always won, for they listened to their master and worked as a pack, and so the stag was brought down and its throat torn out.

Agricola dropped his hand and turned to his officers, a kernel of renewed determination cooling the pain and shame in his breast. 'We will return to base, and there lay plans to avenge our comrades, and in the name of our emperor scour these barbarians from this land!'

Relief flowed over his officers' faces, as they saluted him. 'In the name of the emperor!'

The news of the great victory resounded among the Alban mountains with the force of an eagle's cry.

This time, Rhiann wanted the people of Dunadd to outdo themselves in their welcome, to receive their warriors with the biggest home-coming they had ever seen.

A muddy, road-weary rider came in, informing her of the expected arrival of the warband in three days, and she then lost no time in sending out a request for people to don their best cloaks and dresses, and all their jewellery. Many nobles had left for the remote duns when they first heard of the Roman advance, but with the news of victory they came streaming home.

Hardly able to sit still, Rhiann nevertheless took great pains with her own appearance, and she and Caitlin bathed in scented water while Eithne and Fola combed and braided their hair. Rhiann considered her dresses carefully, and then chose that which she wore at her binding ceremony, with a new scarlet cloak and the amber necklace that Eremon had given her as a wedding gift. Caitlin wore her own bridal dress, soft blue with golden flowers, and when at last they were ready they looked at each other and burst into nervous laughter.

Then Caitlin sobered, leaning into Rhiann and whispering, 'All this effort, sister, yet I fear our men will waste no time looking at our finery, but only waiting to take it all off!'

Rhiann blushed. Her smile had hardly left her face these past days, and she felt as light-hearted as a girl, especially after such a long season of barrenness and pain. 'Perhaps, sister, but they will love us all the more for looking pretty for them.'

'And making their arrival such an occasion!' Caitlin beamed, as they pinned on their cloaks and made ready to leave the house. Finan had announced that the warband had at last been sighted on the southern road.

Outside, a blue haze of cook-fires hung over the village, rich with the scents of roasting pig, deer and beef from the baking pits, fresh bread and honey porridge – all the ingredients of the great feast that would follow that night. Baskets of shining salmon had been gutted and spitted on sticks propped over fragrant pinewood fires.

In their bright, patterned clothes, the crowd spilling out of the great gates and lining the walls looked like drifts of new-sprung flowers, their petals edged in gold and bronze. The warriors guarding the dun had polished their helmets, scabbards and spear-tips, even the bronze bosses on their leather shields, and Finan had lined them up along the timber palisade. Beside them, drummers and pipers clustered, ready to announce the army's arrival with suitable fanfare.

Rhiann and Caitlin positioned themselves directly in front of the village gate, with Aedan to one side, ready to commit the occasion to song, and Gabran in Eithne's arms to the other. Rori was beside Eithne, unable to take his eyes off her dark beauty, displayed to good effect in a new crimson dress. Behind them, Fola waited in her blue priestess cloak, making secret faces at Gabran to keep him amused.

Now there was a shout from a warrior on the gatetower, and Rhiann raised herself on tiptoe, desperate for the first glimpse of Eremon's boar helmet coming over the rise, out of the cover of the trees and blue hills. She was trying so hard to be dignified, but within her sleeves her fingers were twisting themselves into knots, and beneath her cloak her feet jiggled on the muddy path. All she yearned for was the freedom to race across the bridge, her heels kicking up, and throw herself into Eremon's warm arms.

A boar-head trumpet blasted out from above as the first men appeared on the track from the south, marching in muddy ranks. As they came into view, Gabran let out a garbled shout, breaking the tension among those closest to Rhiann. They all laughed, and Caitlin took him from Eithne. 'Yes, love, that's your daddy come home now! Home to us!'

The people all around them broke into peals of excited shouting, jumping and stamping, and over Rhiann's head the warriors lined along the palisade beat their swords on their shields, joined in the din by the pipers and trumpeters, trying to hold a tune over the tumult. The timbers of the gatetower above shivered with the pounding of their feet.

Rhiann's heart swelled along with the music, and soon the warriors had marched close enough for her to tell them apart. At the front of the columns were the mounted ranks. There rippled the banner of the White Mare, led by Lorn on his stallion, and under the Boar of Dalriada Rhiann glimpsed the flash of Conaire's blond hair.

She frowned, unable to recognize Eremon's helmet. For a few breathless moments she studied every man on horseback, sure she would make him out from all the others. But she couldn't see him. Rhiann's breath faded away to nothing. She would have run forward, darting among the riders until she found him, but her feet seemed to have melted into the churned ground beneath her. The cheering people were focused on their own loved ones, and the thrill of the occasion, and sensed nothing amiss. Even Caitlin's face was still shining, her eyes full of her own love as she bounced Gabran, pointing at Conaire.

The front ranks were over the bridge now, and that was when something seemed to communicate itself to the crowd, for the men who came along the road were not cheering back, or waving their spears and shields. They seemed oddly subdued, their shoulders drooping with exhaustion, their heads low. They were dirty and unkempt and bloody, as would be expected, yet it was also obvious many had been wounded, for some limped, and some were held up by their comrades. And so some vivacity seeped away from the crowd in return.

'Where is Eremon?' Caitlin asked innocently, but when she looked at Rhiann's face her own smile withered in shock.

Rhiann was only vaguely conscious that the crowd's cheering had died away into uncertain mutters and confused murmurs, that the eager music from above was trailing into odd, discordant notes. And then the group on horseback that led the first column parted.

Behind them, a litter appeared, carried by six warriors, and on it lay the man for whom Rhiann had been searching. Further back she glimpsed more litters and more still bodies, but her eyes could see only one.

Lorn's hand raised now, and all the marching warriors came to a ragged stop, as the litter bearers rested their burdens on the ground. Then Rhiann's feet at last came to life and she broke into a stumbling run, her vision narrowed to the utterly still figure on the first pallet.

As Rhiann reached the litter, Conaire slid from his horse and caught her, stopping her from throwing herself across Eremon. Rhiann stared up at Conaire wildly, her fingers digging into his forearms, yet his face was barely recognizable with its taut, lined cheeks and hollow eyes.

'I couldn't,' he was saying to her, his voice breaking. 'I couldn't send you a message. I had to spare you, give you these last days.'

'He's dead?' she whispered, wondering who was speaking, for the sound came from far away.

Yet Conaire shook his head, and then Rhiann wrenched free of his arms and threw herself to her knees by the litter. There was a thudding as Rori raced up behind her, stifling a curse, held back by Lorn's arm.

Eremon was unconscious, his hair matted, his face pale under the dirt and blood. And Rhiann realized with a shock that this was the drawn face she had seen in her strange vision moons ago, when Eremon first took his leave to join Calgacus. His shield had been laid over his torso; his helmet resting between his hands. Rhiann tore them both away and let out a guttural sob. Low on Eremon's left side, just above his hip, the tunic was rent by a long slash. The wool all around it was stuck to him and the rough bandage underneath with a dark, dried stain. In the middle, the bindings were streaked with pale yellow.

Rhiann took Eremon's burning hand and pressed her face into it, oblivious of the men standing around her. Rori's breath rasped loudly in the silence, as if he had been running for hours. Conaire knelt by Rhiann now, and in a sudden flare of rage she glared up at him. 'How could you not send for me?' she cried. 'I could have been with him!'

Conaire shrugged helplessly, his eyes red-rimmed. 'I just knew that I needed to get him home. He needed to come home.'

Lorn spoke over her head gently. 'It would have taken the same time to send for you as to bring him, Rhiann.'

Rhiann stifled a moan and pressed the heel of her palm into her eyes, trying to contain the panic. She had to find the healer in her, the control. She was dimly aware of Caitlin's soft steps as she came to stand behind Conaire, and Finan and Aedan arriving, gathering by Colum's side. After a few gasping breaths, Rhiann managed to look down at Eremon again, touching his forehead. It was taut and dry with heat.

'How long since the blow?'

'Four days,' Conaire whispered. 'The wound bled a lot, but at first he talked to us and it didn't seem so bad.' His mouth twisted, and he dropped his head as Caitlin silently stroked his hair.

Colum cleared his throat. 'But the bleeding continued, no matter how much we staunched it, and then he got the fever, and slipped away. He hasn't woken since the night before last.'

Rhiann peered more closely at the wound itself now. She couldn't see beneath the dirt-encrusted bandages, but when she touched her hand lightly to the area it was hot, and her nose caught a tell-tale whiff of sick sweetness.

'It's turning bad,' she heard herself say, and now it was Conaire who muffled a sob. Slowly, Rhiann got to her feet, blessed numbness flooding her as her mind reasserted itself. 'I need to get him to a bed. Take him to my house.'

Chapter 55

The days that followed held no natural rhythm for Rhiann, no sunlight or darkness. The only changes were the peaks and troughs of Eremon's fever, the periods of chills and shaking, despite the warmth of his skin, followed by the restless tossing off of sheets as he burned.

The fever was agonizing, but Rhiann applied herself to the wound first, laying water-lily leaves over it to draw out infection, and bathing it with yarrow brews and tonics of daisy. Linnet, who came as soon as Caitlin sent for her, moved with Rhiann through her trance, binding on the ivy and groundsel poultices with gentle fingers, and dribbling potions into Eremon's mouth when Rhiann could be persuaded to rest.

The others hovered close by: Eithne preparing fever brews of golden rod and sorrel; Caitlin mashing and straining meat into nourishing broths. Conaire, who had no practical role, merely sat staring at Eremon as if will alone would bring him back. It was left to Fola to hold the sacred space, chanting the prayers and offering milk and mead to the figure of Sirona, the healer goddess.

To Rhiann, however, her loved ones were merely wraiths. She barely noticed their hands as they passed things to her, or their voices, faintly penetrating her haze. She saw only the minute changes in Eremon's face – its colour, heat and dampness – and his wound – how crusted with pus, how taut the skin around the ragged rent, whether the dreadful red lines of poison were spreading up towards his heart.

In the awful blank spaces between poultices and potions, Rhiann sponged Eremon endlessly with cool river water and wrapped his burning body in sheets soaked in the Add. Then, her fingers would linger on each white scar that graced his muscles, and she would tell herself that he had survived this wound there, this cut there, and still lived, that he could do it again. Even though she knew he had never received a wound like this one.

After three nights of his delirium, Linnet was the only one to voice the thoughts Rhiann had been avoiding. 'I have never seen anyone endure such a fever for so long,' her aunt murmured. 'The prince truly fights like the warrior he is.'

Rhiann stared down at Eremon then, smoothing one gaunt cheekbone with her finger. 'Yes,' she whispered. 'But . . .' She swallowed her words, for they were too painful to say aloud.

But it must break soon or he will die.

One day later, as despair pressed ever more heavily, Rhiann's prayers were heard.

She had just collapsed into an exhausted sleep when Caitlin roused her from the bed. 'Come,' Caitlin breathed in her ear, her fingers tight on Rhiann's shoulder. 'The fever has broken.'

Rhiann rushed to his bed in her shift, her hair tumbling about her face. There Linnet greeted her with a tired smile, a cool cloth in her hand. Eremon was lying quietly for the first time in days, and the sheets underneath him were soaked with sweat, his hair stuck to his forehead in dark tendrils.

'Praise be to the Goddess,' Fola whispered from the end of the bed, yet Rhiann could do no more than sink to her knees and hold his hand, her burning eyes pressed into the damp bedclothes.

By the end of that day the drawing poultices did their work, and the wound burst with a foul trickle of pus and clear liquid that stank, making those in the room not used to such things gag. Yet Rhiann and Linnet's eyes met, for they knew what it meant, and Rhiann would have gladly endured the smell every day for the rest of her life if he would only live.

Now they could clean the wound properly, and pack it with honey, and as Eremon's temperature continued to fall, Rhiann's preparations changed from fever brews to potions for strengthening the blood and heart and wasted muscles. She forced herself to spend even more time by his bed, even though she frequently fell asleep over his arm or hand, and woke stiff across her back. For soon, surely, he would wake.

Yet two more days slid by, and it became clear that something was not right.

The wound, though drained, remained an angry red, and the sides would not close no matter how tightly bound. And though Eremon's sweating abated, he still did not return to a normal temperature, and his skin remained too warm to the touch. Rhiann watched hungrily for a flickering eyelash, a jerk of his arm, any tiny movement of Eremon's blistered lips. But they never came.

He no longer tossed and turned and murmured – he no longer

moved at all. He lay as still as a man on his funeral pyre, and only his rapid, shallow breaths showed her that he still lived.

When Eremon's condition had remained unchanged for another two days, the watchers around her, by necessity, began to resume normal lives. Clothing must be made, and food stored, for the warm season had now faded, and brown leaves shivered on the trees. As Rhiann sat motionless by Eremon's bed, Fola and Eithne and Caitlin willingly took over her harvest duties: Fola blessed the grain pits and cattle slaughter; Caitlin supervised the salting and brining; and Eithne replenished their stores of herbs, berries and hazelnuts.

As for Conaire, Caitlin grew so alarmed at his unabating despair that she finally took drastic measures. One day she deposited Gabran in his lap without a word and disappeared, forcing Conaire to remove himself to the King's Hall with his son in order to leave Rhiann in peace. There, as Caitlin had reasoned, the other men sought to keep his mind busy.

So the house fell into silence and stillness, broken only by Linnet's soft steps and gentle voice. And that was when Rhiann's torture truly began. For there was nothing physical to be done, and she could no longer take refuge in her healer mind, in duty.

This day she sat as usual on the stool drawn up to the bed, Eremon's right hand clasped in both of her own, her forehead resting on the cradle they made. His sword was laid across his feet, as if somehow it might draw his warrior's strength back to him.

Rhiann heard the clink of the chain as Linnet lowered the cauldron closer to the fire, yet suddenly an abrupt silence fell and Linnet was standing behind Rhiann. 'It has been more than a week, *cariad*. You cannot go on like this, you will sicken yourself.'

For a moment, Rhiann did not answer, her eyes closed. 'Aunt,' she then whispered. 'Tell me the lore about such people, who sleep and do not wake.'

'Do not do this, daughter.'

'Tell me!'

At Linnet's silence, Rhiann raised her face. Her eyes fixed on Eremon's gaunt cheeks, the faint fluttering of his chest. 'When all has been done for the patient,' she recited, 'and the patient has not succumbed to the wound or illness, yet will not rise to wakefulness, it is because the soul has become lost in its wanderings, far from the body.' She gripped Eremon's hand tighter. 'And why do souls not return, aunt?'

'Rhiann,' Linnet sat down on the bed beside Eremon's feet, her face stricken, 'I beg you—'

Yet Rhiann only pressed her forehead into Eremon's fingers, until his nails stung her skin.

'The soul,' she whispered, 'will be drawn back to a healing body only if it is anchored by something: love, or desire for life, or belonging, or deeds undone, or words unsaid. So you see, it is my fault indeed that his soul can't find its way back — *he doesn't have a reason to return.* He doesn't believe I love him, and how could he? I tried to come back to tell him, but I was too late.'

Linnet leaned over to grip Rhiann's knee. 'Daughter, he knows you love him.'

Rhiann flinched from the touch. 'No,' she choked. 'I should have given myself to him with all my heart when I had the chance, and given him a child. And I should never have let him ride away so hurt.'

From within the circle of Linnet's arms she stared with dry eyes at nothing, for the regret burned too fiercely for tears.

With dismay, Linnet saw the way Rhiann slid into an ever-deepening desolation, a faltering of her will that was more disturbing than any weeping. Alarmed, she called in Caitlin, who managed to persuade Rhiann to take some broth by the hearth one dim afternoon, when the winds shrieked over the thatch outside, and bucked the door-hide on its thongs. After she watched Rhiann eat a few bites, Caitlin rested a sleepy Gabran in her sister's lap and curled up on the bench next to her.

For a long time Rhiann watched Gabran in a dazed, exhausted silence: the glow of the flames on his pearlescent skin; his sweet, round mouth; and chubby fingers plucking at the ends of her braids. And when she glanced up, it was to see Caitlin staring at her with thinly veiled eagerness. Rhiann smiled bleakly, just to soften the fear in her sister's eyes. 'A child is indeed a great tonic.'

'And I have you to thank for him, sister.' Caitlin regarded her son sombrely. 'Without you, he would have died in my womb. Remember how you made me fight, how you gave me the strength to go on? When all was lost, when all was hopeless, you brought me home.' She grasped for Rhiann's hand. 'I know you can do the same for Eremon, Rhiann. Your love for me saved me, and it will save him. You'll see.'

She said this with such simple confidence that tears flooded Rhiann's eyes, and she dropped her head until her lips were resting in Gabran's soft hair. 'I never gave him a child,' she whispered, staring at the fire. 'He went to war thinking I did not love him, and he may die thinking that.'

'No, Rhiann!' Caitlin's hand tightened. 'He knew, more than any man could. Did you not walk up to the gates of a Roman fort in a blizzard, alone, for him? Did you not throw yourself before a knife once, to save him? Did you not call the stags for him? And travel the length and breadth of Alba, to gain him allies? He knows, Rhiann. He knows.'

Rhiann blinked, and the tears slid down her cheeks. Gabran gazed at her, then reached out a finger to touch one.

'Rhiann,' Caitlin whispered, 'you give us all the greatest of love, in the things that you do. Do not speak of yourself this way – I won't have it!' She raised her chin, her lip trembling. 'You put yourself in danger for us, and have done so many times. When we were trapped here by Urben, and thought Gabran might die, it was you who saved him! You found a way, because you always do . . .'

Gabran sensed his mother's distress and began to wail, holding out his arms.

Yet as Rhiann watched Caitlin soothe her son, she found herself not only moved by these words, but caught in the net they cast. Instantly stilled, she stared at the back of Gabran's head. Nerida had told her to judge herself by what she did, not by what she thought. What she *did* . . .

Suddenly, Rhiann's pulse was racing, her palms clammy. She was afraid, but Caitlin was right. She had always been able to put aside her fears if someone she loved was in danger.

When Linnet returned, Rhiann was alone by the fire. She'd stirred herself to brew a blackberry tea, which she could see pleased her aunt, and when she asked if she might spend this night alone with Eremon, Linnet surprisingly agreed.

'Only if,' she added, one finger raised, 'you allow me to feed him at dawn. I don't want you up all night again.'

When Linnet had gathered up her few possessions to take to the King's Hall, Rhiann stopped her at the door. 'I hope you know I love you. You made me who I am, and for that I will always be grateful.'

Linnet's eyes shone with tears, and she nodded, and tenderly touched Rhiann's cheek before leaving.

For a drawn-out time Rhiann sat by Eremon's bed, the rush lamp set close on a stool. Outside, she was aware of the moon slowly rising, for she caught a glimpse of its light creeping beneath the door-hide. 'I am afraid,' she confessed to Eremon at last. 'But Caitlin is right. Have I done so much for others, only to quail at doing so for you? You are worth that to me, and more, so I must find the courage.' She kissed his hand. 'You once called me courageous, but I don't feel it now. I need to find that spark. Help me to find it.'

There was no answer, of course, only the slight wheeze of Eremon's breathing. From outside came the rattle of the night wind on a metal plough, and the answering bark of a dog.

'If I come to you,' Rhiann whispered, 'will you see me? Is it truly that you are lost – or do you wish to leave?' She rested her forehead on his hand. The longer she delayed, the greater the risk that Linnet would return and stop her from carrying out her plan. So at last she straightened, and wiped the nervous sweat from her face. Eremon's soul wandered, yet was still attached to its body by a thread, because he breathed. So, quite simply, she would have to retrieve him. There was no other choice.

With those words repeating firmly in her mind, she lit another lamp and took it to her workbench. There, she stretched up to the top shelf that curved around the wall, rifling among the pottery jars and rolled packets of bark and oiled linen, until between the last two jars her fingers found the round, nubbled packet tied with three knots in a line.

After resting a pan of water in the coals to boil, she unwrapped the bark on her workbench, curl by curl, until the mound of black, pod-shaped spores was laid bare. They looked so harmless, yet not only would this powder release her spirit from her body, it was a poison that could cause an agonizing death. She had used it twice in her life now, more than most druids ever did. Would she be permitted a third time?

Her blood thumping in her throat, Rhiann stared at the spores. If she used too little, perhaps she would not travel far enough, and Linnet would find her retching uncontrollably on the floor. Too much, and she might travel too far, and never come back. She and Eremon would both die.

In the end Rhiann closed her eyes and prayed to the Goddess as she pinched off a tiny piece into her pestle. She ground it into a fine powder, all the while intoning the ritual words to prepare her soul, trying not to think of Linnet and Caitlin, Fola and Eithne. They had their lives, and they would have to live them. But Eremon had entered Rhiann's deepest and most secret heart, a place where no one else had ventured.

Taking a deep breath, Rhiann washed her face and hands and combed out her hair, then lined the goddess figurines up along the hearth-stone.

Once when she did this before, she had fancied she saw disapproval in Ceridwen's stone face. Now all the goddesses struck her as impassive, and she had the strong sense that it was up to her to change this fate.

The last time Rhiann used the spores was in desperation and urgency, and she had not prepared herself properly. This time, she knew she could put no foot wrong. Before swallowing the brew she sat cross-legged on the floor, breathing in the priestess way down to her feet and out of her crown, striving to still her trembling and focus on the glow of her heart.

Only when she could sense the cord of silver light running the length of her body did she take the liquid. Then she lay on the bed next to

Eremon, taking him in her arms. She had imbibed such a large dose that she did not have to wait long for it to sweep her away.

First her awareness contracted from the edges of her body, growing smaller as the dark walls around her loomed larger, swaying and moving like reeds in the wind. Gradually, her toes and fingers went numb, and there was a terrible burning on her tongue – the mark of the spores. As her tiny spirit began to rush down the glittering, swirling tunnel of light, she pictured the cord as her will, knowing that her conscious strength was the only thing that would guide her back.

Struggling to hold her sense of self, she fixed an image of Eremon in her mind, the way his true smile spread over his face. And suddenly the tunnel opened out into a night of flaming stars, and Rhiann's spirit flew free and became one of them, spiralling through the sparkling dust of ages, forgetting at once who she was . . .

When was the time, and where the place?

After an age of spinning and soaring, free in the ecstasy of the void, Rhiann's soul was called by something behind the wild, sweet music of the Otherworld voices. It plucked at her, and when she ignored it, captured by the song of a passing swirl of colour and light, it began to tug at her more insistently.

And Rhiann remembered, fleetingly. There was a silver cord, and she must breathe into it. For that moment out of time, the impulse was compelling, and the shimmering voices around her faded. She saw the cord behind her, and breathed, recognizing herself. Its light grew stronger, pulsing with power and, amid the gas and glittering dust around her, something grew solid.

It was ground, and still, thick air above, soft with a diffuse light that came from everywhere at once and nowhere at all. She remembered only to breathe; that she had a will to breathe. And so the call drew her on to the end of a path, beyond the clamouring voices, which sought to pull her back.

Suddenly, she was at a waveless shore, and there she took flight once more, not into the void but out over an endless, dark sea.

For a flame was trapped at the heart of the sea, and to that flame she was drawn. It was a soul-flame twin to her own, yet unlike her steady light, it dipped, like a guttering candle in a storm. When she came to it, she knew that she must envelop the flickering flame with her own light, so it would not sink beneath the dark water.

She tried to curve around the light, but she found she could not move; her wings of flame were attached, bound to her by fear. And then she knew, in the way that instant understanding came in this place, that to shelter him, she could not be contained, by anything.

She must let go of the last boundaries of her heart.

Chapter 56

hiann's eyelids were stuck together, the edges heavy. There was,
too, a leaden stiffness in her limbs, and from these sensations,
Rhiann's mind grasped that she had been lying like this for some
time.

It took an immense effort to move her throat enough to swallow, to
coax some moistness from her dry mouth and tongue. And then, the
lashes trembling, she tried to open her eyes. Yet just as the merest thread
of light parted the darkness behind them, she was struck by the awful
thought that she might wake alone.

Her eyelids clamped full shut again, but her breaths had grown
harsher, and she felt the ache of unused muscles expanding across her
chest as she tried to contain them. She didn't know where Eremon was,
but if he wasn't here, she did not want to open her eyes. That was it.
She would slide away again, back into that strange dream world where
people sang with silvery voices, pulling her back from her endless
search.

Lying perfectly still, Rhiann closed off those memories and tried to
send her senses outwards, delaying the inevitable moment when she
would have to face the world, whatever world it was.

She sensed soft furs brushing her chin.

The snap of a fire.

The whuffling squeak of what, she could swear, was a hound lost in
sleep.

And someone's warm breath, so close it stirred the fine hair at her
temples.

Immediately, Rhiann's eyes flew open and looked straight into
Eremon's face, and for a long moment, that was all she could see. The
orbits of his eyes were bruised with shadow, yet beyond the red-veined
signs of fatigue the irises were a deep hazel in the rosy light of the fire,

keen and fully aware. Regarding her, in fact, as someone looked at a new baby when they held it, as if she might break at any moment.

Rhiann found she could say nothing, and was dimly surprised when a tear suddenly welled up and trickled down one cheek. Eremon reached out a finger and scooped up the salty drop, his eyes clouded with profound relief.

Blinking, Rhiann's gaze ranged lower. One of her arms, as white as the linen sleeve that encased it, lay along the fur covers of her own sickbed. At the end of the arm, Cù's dark eyes now regarded her, the tip of his tail waving uncertainly over his head, and as she watched, his pink tongue came out and touched her hand. Then Eremon muttered a firm command she didn't catch, and Cù's snout and tail subsided out of view.

Rhiann's eyes returned to her husband. He was lying alongside her, propped up on pillows. His other arm, she saw now, was in a sling to stop it moving. He wore a tunic, loose and untucked, and under it was the lumpy suggestion of the other bindings around his torso. Rhiann struggled to focus on his face. Yes, it was fuller and rosy, and her groggy mind clutched at the realization that some time must have passed since she took the spores that desperate night.

The relief that she was home, and Eremon by her side, was a tide sufficient to exhaust her meagre energy, and already she felt her eyes grow inexorably heavy with fatigue.

As darkness closed around her, she sensed the warm, moist imprint of Eremon's lips on her brow. 'Sleep, a stór,' he whispered. 'I will watch over you now.' And in a voice suffused with gladness, 'Lady Linnet?'

The next time Rhiann swam slowly upwards towards the light, Eremon was sitting on the stool by the bed, his chin on one hand, the other holding her outstretched fingers. His cheeks were clean-shaven, and the lines of sickness that had marred his face had now unwound. His dark hair was brushed and braided back from his temples, and there was a look of thorough wholeness about him that Rhiann could almost scent.

At the rapid, gasping rise of her breathing, Eremon leaned close and brushed her cheek. 'Do not fear, love,' he murmured. 'We are together now, and the dark time is past.'

Rhiann swallowed the thickening in her throat. 'I sat by this bed for days, just as you do now,' she wheezed. 'I was afraid you would not return.'

Eremon bowed his head over her fingers and kissed them. 'I . . . don't think I knew how, but then you came for me.' He glanced up at her suddenly, and she saw the dazed awe lingering in his eyes, as he sought to grasp what was beyond understanding.

Rhiann's fingers tightened on his, unable to speak, and Eremon's eyes shifted to the wall behind her, glazed with memory. 'I remember only darkness and loneliness and cold, and feeling trapped, and then . . .' He looked at her, wondering. 'And then I thought I heard you. I heard you calling me. And there was a warmth, a . . . a . . . *taste* or sense of your eyes and smile holding me, just a feeling, no touch, just . . . you.'

'Eremon.' Rhiann rolled her head to one side, incoherent words pouring from her lips. 'I had to let it go, and I did . . . I breathed fear out and . . . the flame, the fire, it spilled over . . . I'm sorry—'

'Sorry?' Eremon cupped her face. 'You brought me back.'

'No.' Rhiann shook her head to clear it. 'I am so sorry I did not before; that I let you slip away.' Desperately, she gripped his hand on her face. 'So today, now, it is in *Thisworld* that I truly pledge myself to you, and in Thisworld you will know my love, I swear it.'

The old, crooked smile spread over Eremon's face, yet his eyes glowed with an intensity that did not match its wryness. 'I already know it,' he said quietly, and then there was no more need for words, for as Rhiann stared into his eyes it was as if they stood naked before each other in the void all over again.

After a long moment Eremon sat back on the stool, stroking her hand. 'Just get well for me now, *a stór*, that is all I ask.'

'And I,' came another voice, from the opposite side of the bedscreen. Linnet was standing over Eremon's shoulder, a bowl in her hands, wreathed with curls of steam. 'Come, child, it is time you took in some more earthly nourishment.'

With an effort, Eremon levered himself stiffly to his feet. He smiled gently down at Rhiann. 'I will only be gone a short time, love – I'll be back before you've missed me.'

Rhiann's eyes remained glued to his back until it disappeared, and then her gaze shifted apprehensively to Linnet, who had drawn the stool closer to the bed, settling herself on it.

'Eat this now,' her aunt ordered brusquely, a spoon of hot broth held to Rhiann's mouth.

Rhiann dutifully swallowed, all the while absorbing the lines of despair engraved on Linnet's face, the film of shock over her eyes. Rhiann's own heart grew hot with guilt. 'I had no choice,' she whispered. 'As you would reach out for me, so I had to reach out for him. You must understand.'

The length of Linnet's spine stiffened with suppressed emotion, as her eyes rose to Rhiann's face. 'I should be furious with you,' she murmured. 'But all my fury has been long burned away, daughter, in the nights I sat by you, absorbing every breath because I was sure it was going to be your last.'

Rhiann winced. 'How many nights?'

'It is five days since Eremon woke to us.' Linnet sighed heavily. 'It was a fight to bring him to the health you see there before you, for he would barely move nor eat as you lay near death. I have never seen such grief assail anyone.' Her eyes darkened as she stared up at the wall hanging over Rhiann's head. Then a ghost of a smile touched her mouth. 'In the end, I asked him how he'd feel if you woke after all your pains only to see him dead of starvation and exhaustion. *Then* he listened, by the Goddess he did, and with sheer effort made himself well.'

'Aunt, I'm so sorry.' Rhiann's voice was low. 'You brought me back from that place, didn't you?'

After a hesitation Linnet nodded, her cheek tilted away. Then, abruptly, she rose and turned to the chest at the foot of the bed, groping for the bronze water jug.

'I do know what I put you through.' Rhiann strained to see Linnet's face. 'Yet I couldn't let him go. There's been too much letting go.'

After a time, Linnet began to speak, her back turned. 'When you were small, you drove me mad with your stubbornness – Goddess, the battles of will we waged! And yet, if you could have heard the pride with which I spoke of you, laughing to the women about how strong you were, how wilful. I nurtured this in you, child, sure it would make you a great Ban Cré, a leader. So how can I rail at this, when I loved you for it so deeply?' Linnet paused, then swept back to the stool. '*However*, I have *never* heard of the spores being used in such a way before, with no support, no preparation!' Her nostrils flared as she raised the cup to Rhiann's lips. 'You must promise me never to do it again, daughter. *Promise me!*'

'I promise.' Rhiann coughed, splattering water down the front of her shift. Her head fell back against the pillow. 'I do not think, aunt, that I will be permitted to return from such a journey again.'

Chapter 57
LONG DARK, AD 82

'Ouch!'

Rhiann's fingers paused over Eremon's raised, red scar. 'The skin has knitted well; it can't possibly hurt that much.' She cocked an eyebrow at him. 'Shall I stop, great warrior?'

Eremon grinned. 'Your fingers are cold, wife, that is all.'

Rhiann wiped the offending digits on a rag and put the pot on the stump table. 'Well, the comfrey is doing its job, so don't complain.' After a last peer at the healing wound, Rhiann wound another bandage around Eremon's torso, ducking his kisses, both of them chuckling.

'Brother!' There was a thump on the wall outside the door, announcing Conaire's arrival. He swept in with Caitlin, Gabran in her arms, and an icy wind that blew in under the door-hide. Rhiann's recovery was proving even slower than Eremon's, and during their illness the cold season had arrived.

'Why don't you come in?' Eremon asked wryly, pressing Rhiann to the bed and drawing a fur around her legs. Though she had no wound, the spores and the depletion of her spirit had taken a toll, leaving her with strange headaches and a debilitating exhaustion.

With a smile, Caitlin gave Gabran to Rhiann's outstretched arms, brushing raindrops from his blond curls and drawing off her own wet cloak. Conaire remained standing, his eyes searching Eremon's face as if still unable to believe in his brother's recovery. 'The scouts have returned from the east,' he reported, giving Eremon's shoulder a squeeze before drawing up a stool.

'And?' Eremon perched on the bed beside Rhiann, as Caitlin dropped onto the other side.

Conaire folded his arms with a tired smile. 'And the Romans have already retreated to their long dark quarters.' Rhiann glanced at him over Gabran's head. The shadow that had slipped from her and Eremon's shoulders was still lurking in Conaire's gaze, and all the boyishness in his face had bled away these last weeks. 'There will be no more attempts made on Dunadd this season.'

Rhiann, helping Gabran to roll his wooden lion over the covers, heard the outrush of Eremon's breath in her ear.

'Thank you, brother.' Eremon shifted to ease his side. 'Though I would still give my left leg to get another message to the Creones and Boresti.' He had been fretting over this ever since Conaire told him the two riders had returned to their duns before the snows. 'I need them to know I have evaded a more permanent visit to the Otherworld!'

'I told them that, brother, do not fear. They will come back with the thaw, as I asked them to.'

Conaire held Eremon's eye with an intensity that was new to him, and Rhiann realized that she and Eremon were not the only ones who had been changed by the chance blow of a sword.

'Well, I can only hope that the tales of our success are being told around fires this very night.' Eremon sighed. 'Perhaps the Alban alliance we have so yearned for may finally be within our grasp.'

Those words should have been a joy to Rhiann. After all, for what else had she traipsed the length and breadth of Alba? Yet instead, a chill curled into the pit of her belly. She had been too near death, too recently, to draw it closer. 'Do you think an alliance will be needed any more?' Her voice sounded too faint, and she cleared her throat.

Caitlin broke in. 'Perhaps Agricola will take his men and leave Alba now, knowing he can never win. It has been three victories for us, after all.'

Eremon grew perfectly still, and Rhiann saw the fleeting look he gave Conaire. 'Perhaps,' he said.

When Rhiann took her first steps outside in the freezing wind, supported by Caitlin, she could discern that the sun was much lower in the sky, its feeble glow nearly obscured by snow-swollen clouds. In the weeks of her illness the world had been transformed, from the blazing flame of leaf-fall into a stark landscape of thin, cracked snow and frosted roofs, bare branches, and grey shadows creeping over the humps and dips on the marsh. Outside each doorway and on the paths the pale slush had been pounded back into bare mud, and all the house beams and posts, the unhitched carts and water barrels, were dark and slick with moisture, black against the frost.

Rhiann's women friends were bursting with some secret, exchanging smiles over Rhiann's head, which they thought she missed. And then Caitlin looked up from winding wool one day to announce that it was time at last for Rhiann and Eremon to visit the men in the Hall. To boost their morale, she said.

Ever since Rhiann's awakening, her door-hide had been continually lifting and flapping back into place, as Rori appeared with armfuls of wood, working out his distress by stoking the room to a blazing heat, and the rest of Eremon's men drifted in to mend harness and polish weapons on the floor. They only gathered in Rhiann's little house to be close to their lord, and he in turn to Rhiann, yet despite the nature of the heart-warming scene, Eithne had eventually reached her limit and herded them all back to the King's Hall.

From her rush chair by the fire, Rhiann now peered over Gabran's head at Caitlin. 'Morale, is it, sister?' Eithne was stirring the cauldron of barley porridge a little too vigorously, and there was a distinct twist to Fola's smile as she pounded herbs at the bench. 'Well, whatever prank you plan to play on me, I will be grateful to be free of my bondage, at least, and eat something more solid than porridge and broth.'

'*Duh!*' Gabran demanded, wriggling for more of his horse game, and Rhiann smiled down at him and gripped his hands, bucking him on her outstretched leg.

Caitlin deftly tied off the skein of wool around its wooden peg. 'I see your tongue has *quite* recovered then, so we will expect you tomorrow night. Eithne's going to help you dress.'

Rhiann's suspicions were washed away by her bath the next night, the warm water infused with Linnet's last packet of imported lavender. As Eithne laid out her clothes, chattering away, Rhiann found herself growing excited by the simple prospect of leaving the house. Despite her lingering tiredness, and the soporific effect of the bath, she practically leaped from the water and sat bouncing up and down on the bed as Eithne dried her hair with a towel, and helped her into a fresh undershift.

Just then Eremon appeared, for he had dressed in the King's Hall. Eithne, falling silent, swiftly collected up the damp towels and excused herself, as Rhiann turned and looked up at her husband. She could not help but catch her breath.

His arm was still bound in a length of snowy linen, to immobilize his left side, but he had also donned his betrothal tunic, which was the exact colour of his eyes, embroidered around the hem with gold thread that drew the light into his braided hair. He wore a scarlet cloak, and blue and green check trousers, laced up the calf by ochre-dyed boots. Apart from his neck torc, the boar tusk gleamed among the folds of his right sleeve, while around the other arm was Rhiann's stag. And for the first time in many moons, he wore the green jewel of his father's, bound on the brow by a gold circlet.

Rhiann feasted her eyes on him until a faint blush stole across his cheeks. Then her gaze fell on his empty sword belt.

'I thought it well,' he said, 'for us to have one night that is not darkened by the shadow of the Romans. We have many more moons to think of fighting.' As if to make his point, he looped the thong of the boar stone over his neck and laid it on the stump table.

Her vision blurring, Rhiann rose and laid the back of her hand along Eremon's cheek. 'The waves were blessed, prince of Erin, that brought you to me. Without you, I would be living in a place far more barren than that in which I found you.'

'And I.' Eremon's thumb caressed her ear, brushing her hair back from her temples.

Rhiann sighed, and in that moment something shifted imperceptibly between them. In their convalescence they had shared only brief kisses, both conscious of avoiding bodily hurt. And perhaps also an irrational fear lingered, that something had been lost, not gained; that something had changed in them.

Yet now, falling into Eremon's charged gaze, Rhiann was aware that her chest was tightening from something other than shock. With no will of her own she swayed towards him, their bodies touching along their lengths. And while her heart hammered out its own song, Eremon bent his head and kissed her.

His lips were warm, his breath as sweet as she remembered. Yet he only pressed his mouth to hers once, brushing her lips as lightly as a moth, and it was she who groaned and pulled him closer, grasping him around his hips. Eremon responded eagerly, but not with lust. Instead, he cupped her face once more, holding her so he could explore her mouth with his tongue, swirling and lingering, and it was silk and honey melting through her, until she lost all sense of where she was.

At last they broke apart, breathless and trembling. 'My love,' Eremon said in a thickened voice, 'we must go, before I kiss you like that until dawn comes.'

Rhiann stared at his swollen mouth, surprised at the strength of her desire. 'And what of it?' she murmured, brushing his lower lip with her thumb.

With difficulty, Eremon clasped her hand and pressed it safely to his chest, smiling shakily. 'Indeed, but I fear there will be some disappointed people if we do not go, and they have worried for you so much.'

'So they *have* been planning something!' Rhiann stepped away, her hand still linked with his. 'I knew it!'

Eremon laughed, and ran his fingers through to the ends of her hair. 'So they have, but act surprised, won't you? And leave your hair unbound, so that I can feast my eyes on you, if not my lips.'

Rhiann grinned up at him, the exhaustion of weeks suddenly falling from her heart. 'Are you sure you would not rather have been a bard, prince? You've missed your calling, I fear.'

'Perhaps I would have been happier for it, my princess.' For a moment, a shaft of bleakness dimmed the joy in Eremon's eyes. 'But now I will escort you, and we will speak no more of dark things. Only promise you'll kiss me like that later, and I will be content.'

The King's Hall fell strangely silent as Rhiann entered on Eremon's arm, but at their appearance it erupted into cheers and foot-stamping, and she saw that it was packed with people, not only the nobles living on the crag, but a great many villagers as well.

Rhiann smelled the decorations before her eye travelled upwards to the carved posts supporting the roof, and the beams laid along the underside of the thatch. Each was festooned with boughs and garlands of sharp-scented pine and yew, and wound about with tendrils of ivy. 'The longest night!' In shock, Rhiann glanced at Eremon and then sought for Caitlin, who was beaming alongside Conaire and Eithne. More moons had passed in illness and recovery than she had realized.

That night, Rhiann's lingering weakness meant that she was forced to let the tide of music and laughter wash about her, while she remained quiet. And so it was that perhaps she alone, floating somehow outside the night, was able to sense something lurking behind the wild abandon of the drink and jests and music. A sourness ran beneath the pungent smells of roasting meat, honeyed fish and pine resin, and in her stillness Rhiann could scent it. Fear.

Despite Eremon's words and Caitlin's efforts, the shadow of the Romans could not be banished now, not even for one night.

This was the first winter Agricola had ever spent in Alba. Every other year, all his men except the fort garrisons had returned to their legionary headquarters in the south.

He turned his head, making out Samana's black hair against his pillow. The coals in the brazier still threw a bloody light over her skin. Yet the rest of his bed chamber was in darkness, the shadows swelling and creaking with cold, as the wind scraped the thatch roof above.

He was warm within the nest of heaped furs, but he could see that the damp on the roof beams had frozen to frost, and his nostrils burned with cold at every clouded breath. These mud and timber barracks were no match for an Alban winter, he was quickly discovering. So, he wondered for the tenth time, why had he stayed?

He could find no escape from Alba, from its undefeated challenge – that's what it was. He must have it, he would have it, and, as autumn darkened into winter, the desire for it had mixed with unassuaged rage and frustration until the feelings seared his veins like a fever. It simply wasn't possible for him to leave here again, to retreat to his warm, bright home in Eboracum. For beneath his rage he had sensed, with a twist of superstition, that if he left he somehow gave up the right to possess this land. If he left, he was branding himself as unworthy.

The sacrifices at the mid-winter feast of Saturnalia had been favourable, at least. Though it was a dour, cold affair, and not at all like the noisy, well-fed revels he was used to in Rome, the *haruspex* had read only good fortune in the steaming entrails of the white hare. And that was the crux of the matter. For if his own gods were to stake a claim to this land, Agricola, their envoy, must stay, too.

The *haruspex*, trembling with cold as he poked at the bloody offal on the snow, had in the end only confirmed what Agricola himself felt in his own bones. This was the year when all would be resolved in the matter of Alba.

Samana murmured now and rolled over, her naked breast bulging against Agricola's chest. His senses were immediately alive to the skin melting into his own, and the musk perfume drifting up from between her legs. Agricola sighed with a strange resignation.

On his return from the west, the defeat that he had put behind him only reignited Samana's old anger, drawing her from her listless despair. Yet surprisingly, she never made the connection that had come immediately to Agricola when she told him of her banishment: if she was outcast, she was no use to him at all. Contact between her and her tribe had ceased, and with it, all news of native Alba.

At first, this turn of events amused Agricola, perhaps because of its absurdity. Yet once the bulk of his men rode away to winter quarters, leaving a modest garrison, Samana's demeanour had begun to grate on him instead. Agricola chafed at his confinement, forced inside by howling, sleet-driven winds, and had little to do but eat, think and pick over the bones of his recent failures. His unrelenting rage at the Erin prince could find no external ease, either, for Samana talked of him incessantly, her hatred a fire that she nursed with great zeal.

So the pressure grew, the air in Agricola's quarters taut with repressed tension, until the day came when Samana's mutterings sent him over the edge, and he struck her. One hand to the red mark on her cheek, Samana glared up at him not with anger, but with a flare of lust. And so Agricola was lost. Before he knew it, they were rutting like dogs across his bed, on the floor, and against the cold walls, and the climax eased his rage. For a time.

Soon, he was seeking that same escape between her legs, over and over, and the storms battered the roof while they thrust at each other. For a while some cold part of him did stand outside himself, thinking of his wife sheltering his son in her body. But eventually, the resignation had descended. He could not leave Alba, and if he sent Samana away he would go mad – from fury that could find no release, and frustration at the obstructive snowstorms that delayed his revenge. So Agricola's world narrowed to the soft, wet place that Samana opened for him, praying that if he had to pay for this abandonment to lust, the debt would become due only after victory.

Half-asleep, Samana now crooked her leg over Agricola's hips, and he rose instant and hard against her. '*Nemo liber est qui corpori servit,*' he muttered to himself. *No one is free who is a slave to his body.*

Then his sigh was swallowed by Samana's writhing tongue, and the desire, as always, easily drowned both logic and the fears that stalked him.

At Dunadd, though the feast would continue until late, Rhiann and Eremon needed no urging from a concerned Linnet to seek their bed in Rhiann's house.

In silence, Rhiann unpinned her brooches, slid off her rings and torc, and folded her cloak and dress over them on the chest. Gradually, Eremon's jewellery joined hers in an untidy pile, as she slipped beneath the furs in her shift, shivering.

In the faint chinks of firelight, Rhiann could see the dark outline of Eremon's back as he bent to pull down his trousers, and the black sweep of hair against the linen bandage around his torso. Her heart began to fling itself against her ribs so violently he surely must hear it, and her fingers were pressed to her lips as if to taste the kiss that still lay there between them.

Rhiann couldn't see Eremon's eyes when he slipped naked into bed beside her, but was struck speechless when he leaned over and gently kissed her on her forehead. 'Sleep well, my love,' he murmured, and yawned, then sank down on his back, his face turned away from her towards the bedscreen.

For a moment, hurt and confusion bloomed in Rhiann's chest. All night, she had breathed in his male scent, and watched his lips moving and smiling for others, as his eyes slid over her throat, her curves, their heat drawing her gaze again and again. And now . . . this?

Stabbed with indignance, Rhiann reached out to Eremon's shoulder. But before her fingers could clasp him, she sensed the quiver that ran through his muscles. With an outraged snort she pulled him over as gently as her anger would allow. 'Eremon!' she cried, and he uncurled and was suddenly holding her, the dim firelight showing his grin.

Rhiann batted at his chest. 'You mean fox! How can you tease me like this!'

'Tease, my lady?' Eremon frowned. 'I was only sleeping. Why, what else do you want me to do?' He shook his head, and his unbound hair fell into her eyes.

Rhiann pushed it back with both hands and tucked it around his ears. 'You know very well, rogue!'

'What?' Eremon had become very still. 'Tell me what you want me to do.' She heard the new note in his voice, and knew that, as before, he needed her to ask, no, demand it of him.

Because Maelchon now lay between them, dark and cold.

Because Eremon was still unsure of the depths he moved in her.

So Rhiann drew Eremon's head down to her, and this time it was her tongue that parted his lips, until his breath came in gasps. 'I need,' she whispered, 'to take you within, and make you mine again.'

He groaned, and buried his mouth in the curve of her neck, where her shift gave way to soft, scented skin. Arching her back, she closed her eyes as his lips lit their way along her throat, from below her ear to her collarbone. Then she gasped and buried her fingers in his hair, as he spread the fine linen shift against her chest and closed his mouth over one nipple and then the other, blowing on the wet cloth to make them burn with cold.

Then Eremon's fingers were at her waist, drawing the shift up, and she tensed as his lips whispered over the delicate skin between her thighs. The slightest flick of his tongue caught her by surprise and she cried out, but before she could murmur anything sensible, the heat of his tongue was bathing her, swirling as he had drunk from her mouth, and she could only dig her fingers into his arm, emitting high, sharp gasps.

When he groaned again, at first she thought she had hurt him with her fingers, but then he stilled, and she pulled back the covers to free his face. 'Your wound!' she exclaimed. 'Goddess, you shouldn't be doing this.'

Breathing heavily, Eremon edged onto his right side and then his back, a spasm of pain on his face. 'Should be,' he managed.

Rhiann placed her palm over the bandage, relieved to feel that it was dry. Catching her breath, she smiled and trailed her fingers higher, over his chest. 'So,' she murmured, 'I have an invalid at my mercy.' She leaned over and kissed the soft place beneath his right armpit, breathing in his scent. 'And such a beautiful invalid, too. What *am* I to do with him?' With small kisses, she edged her way around his ribs, gliding upwards to suckle his nipples.

'You may wish . . . to reconsider those kisses,' Eremon whispered, gasping with every flick of her tongue. 'For I *will* take you, though we both bathe in my blood.'

Rhiann raised herself over him, her hair falling about them in a tent of roan and amber. 'Or,' she said, '*I* could take *you*.'

Fixing her gaze on Eremon's eyes, Rhiann sat up and slowly drew her shift from her shoulders, so that it fell around her waist in a cloud of white. And the feeling that took her as she did it was the same she had felt in the Otherworld: as if she was revealed in all her power and love; that which made her.

Eremon groaned, his head rising as he was drawn to her, but she pushed him back down. 'Careful,' she said sternly, and slowly bent over his face, until her nipple was against his mouth.

With every flick of his tongue on her breasts then, the sparking between Rhiann's legs grew brighter. At last she broke free from his mouth and leaned behind her, stroking the lean belly below the bandage, gliding down his upper thighs. His muscles were rigid under her fingers, and she kneaded them as her palm slid around to his inner thighs. Eremon's breath froze in his chest. 'Speaking of teasing . . . ' he forced out.

Yet he only gasped when her searching fingers found him, so curiously hard yet sheathed with silk. And suddenly Rhiann knew that all her fear of this power he wielded was gone from her, for as she glided her fingers up the length of him she felt her own self opening, pulsing, and when she slid onto him they both groaned.

The sweetness rose first as trembling waves of heat, as the soft parts of her melded with him, and she threw back her head and gripped his arms. Then the heat flared, and Eremon cried, 'No! Look at me!'

So Rhiann did, holding his cheek with one hand, her thumb under his eye, so she shared the explosion in its depths even as the flame burned her body away.

In the days that followed, Rhiann was aware of no one but Eremon: the tilt of his head when he spoke; the dark shine of his hair against the snow; the breadth of his shoulder when he shrugged off his cloak; the movement of tendons in his wrist when he patted Cù.

Rhiann was nearly sick with the wanting of him. And in the darkness of their bed they soon made up for all the moons they had been sundered. Yet despite the opening of their bodies that they could not, and did not want to control, Rhiann was still keeping a secret from Eremon.

For that first night together, as the ecstasy consumed them, she had seen with her spirit-eye the flame of Eremon's soul spiralling up from his body. But there had also been another light, a cloud of shifting hues that surrounded them both, yet which came from neither.

Now, looking down at her flat belly as she sewed by the fire, Rhiann resisted the urge to touch it. For she was not ready to think about what the light might mean. Not ready at all.

BOOK FIVE
LEAF-BUD, AD 83

Chapter 58

U nder a dark sky, the small barge rocked precariously in the
tumbling, storm-fed waters of the stream that split the Roman
camp by the Forth. From the broad, wind-whipped expanse of
estuary, the oarsmen had struggled upstream, obviously determined to
deliver their cargo however violent the weather.

Agricola was returning from the bath-house, a heavy sheepskin cloak
wrapped around his head and shoulders. When he saw the barge
through the obscuring sleet, though, he slid to a halt on the icy path. No
vessels were expected up the Forth until full spring, and the first month
of it was only dawning now. It was too early in the season to be
chancing the seas, surely! Only a madman would do so . . . or one with
urgent news. Agricola's pulse, heavy and slow from the heat of the bath-
house, suddenly pounded harder in his neck.

Samana, her head down as she sought refuge in her own fur wrap, ran
right into his back, her feet slipping on the frosted stones. 'Why do you
halt?' she cried, shuddering with cold. 'Come, before we are frozen
through!'

Her imperious tone slid from Agricola like the drops of melting sleet,
for he was too absorbed in the sight of that barge approaching the plank
pier on the shingle bank below. What news could be so urgent that a
crew would risk their lives to bring it to him by sea? Without a word to
Samana, Agricola turned and hastened to his own command quarters.
Whatever it was, he would rather receive it at ease in his own chair by
the brazier, with a cup of fine wine in hand.

By the time the messenger made his way to the door, both Agricola
and Samana had shaken the sleet from their hair, discarded their soaking
boots, and were wrapped in dry, fur-lined robes in the outer chamber.
Three well-stoked braziers gave ample warmth, and lamps blazed on the
map table, the wall shelf and the side tables beside the chairs.

The messenger took in the golden lamp-glow and warming air with visible relief, as rain dripped mournfully from his black hair and the hem of his thick cloak into a puddle around his feet. His face was pale, and one hand hovered over his belly.

With a distinct lurch in his own nether regions, Agricola saw at once that this man was from Rome itself. For Agricola knew him – he was in the pay of the household of Tacitus, Agricola's son-in-law. Tacitus had spent only one season here on the frontier, but ever since had been Agricola's most vocal advocate with the emperor.

'Sir.' The servant tried to salute in the military way, but was shaken by a terrible sneeze, trailing off into a series of shudders that made his teeth chatter beneath his long tunic and cloak.

'Warm yourself, man.' Agricola indicated the brazier and, as the man shuffled to it and spread his hands with a sigh of relief, Samana moved to the map table, with a glance at Agricola of desperate curiosity.

Almost immediately, the servant's shivering began to calm, and his sneezes faded into occasional sniffles, which he wiped on his sleeve, all Roman fastidiousness gone. 'Forgive me,' he managed at last, turning to Agricola and going down on one knee. As he did, he pulled a tube of ivory capped with gold from the belt of his tunic, and from this withdrew a parchment scroll rolled in oiled leather.

Agricola took the scroll, noting with a stab of excitement the wax seal of his son-in-law. In silence he broke it and unrolled the message, unusually informal and hastily scribed.

Greetings to my esteemed father-in-law,

Forgive me for dispensing with our social niceties, but you will understand when you hear what I have to report, after a frustrating wait of two years. The emperor has enjoyed a major triumph in Germany and, with the resulting consolidation of his forces, I have been able, at last, to prevail upon him the urgency of returning all your forces to you. It has been a difficult road altogether, entailing many tedious visits to his various villas, innumerable boring dinners, and far too much time spent in the company of that odious man. But he has heeded me at last (now that it suits him, of course – I make no claim to have changed his mind) and has become freshly enamoured of the complete conquest of the island of Britain, including Alba. To that end, your men of the Ninth and other legions are being returned, and after a particularly successful deer hunt I even secured four cohorts of Batavian cavalry and two of Tungrians for you, plus the ships they arrive on. The men will be setting out on the Kalends of April, barring bad weather, and I hope you will have them by early May.

Your official notification will follow, of course, but I decided to send you word early enough for you to make whatever added preparations are necessary. Poor Marcus, I don't know what state he has arrived with you, but a trip at this time of year was beyond the call of duty and I hope you will treat him well before sending him home.

With the proper resources, at last, I anticipate a great increase in the glory of your name,

Your respectful son-in-law,

Publius Cornelius Tacitus

Agricola read the letter through once more, and again, then crumpled it on his knee, staring into the brazier.

When it became apparent that he was overcome with some emotion, and was not going to speak, the messenger, 'poor Marcus' of Tacitus's letter, rose to his feet. Drawing his wet cloak from his shoulders, trying to stand straight, he said, 'Sir, I have another message for you, for our ship put in at Eboracum. I understand you are awaiting some news from there.'

Agricola's head immediately jerked up, and he fixed the man with sharp, eager eyes. 'Yes?' he barked.

Marcus swept his head down gracefully, using the movement to surreptitiously wipe his nose once more on his sleeve. 'I have the pleasure of informing you that early in the winter your wife was delivered of a son. I am to convey to you that she and he are in good health.'

Instantly, Agricola was on his feet, the scroll falling unheeded to the ground. Samana shot him a black look, but he cared nothing for that. It was as if the coals of the brazier were filling his own breast with enervating warmth, and suddenly he knew that the darkness of the long winter was behind him.

This year.

The gods had smiled on him, at last, setting their glorious hands over his head, blessing him with luck and joy. They had shown him the fates, they had given him the signs. Five thousand men returned to him, after such a wait. And a healthy son, born of his house, after so many years of stillbirths.

Now, this year, Agricola knew he would find resolution. And the Albans would find death.

None of the women close to Rhiann took notice that, in the first weeks after the longest night, she did not unpack any of the bundles of dried moss from the storage chest on her shelf.

Caitlin's moon bleeding had not yet returned, as she was still feeding Gabran, and Linnet's came no more. Eithne and Rhiann's cycles had once waxed and waned together, yet with Rhiann's absence over sunseason this pattern had been disrupted. Fola, too, followed her own rhythm.

If anyone thought of it, Rhiann knew that they would assume it was the aftermath of the illness, along with the sudden tiredness which forced her to bed every afternoon. Indeed, Linnet began to peer at her sharply once more, feeling her head, and, to Rhiann's mortification, even went so far as to send some stern healer's words Eremon's way, for their eager nights abruptly slowed into bouts of more tender affection.

Indeed, Rhiann mused if a good sleep was all she needed. Yet somehow, she knew it was more than that, especially when she remembered the other light dancing around her, in the explosive fire of the longest night.

Though the festival of Imbolc was nearly upon them, the weather was still too unpredictable for long gathering expeditions, and Rhiann had little chance for time alone. Yet every now and then, a few bright hours seeped between the clouds which swept across the crag. Then, Rhiann would take Liath and plough through the snow sludge and bare, black woods to the eastern spring above Dunadd, and kneel there on a deer-hide by the frozen fringes of the water.

What she asked then was not something of the Goddess, but something of herself.

Why, she wondered, with Eremon's seed being spent inside her every night, had she refrained from brewing the womb herbs? It could have been from simple fear of Eremon's reaction, but after what they shared in the Otherworld, she didn't think she feared that severing any more.

Sitting there by the spring in the feeble sunlight, among the frosted branches of rowan, Rhiann touched her belly with awe, unable to name even to herself why she had let this be. The apprehension about how it might affect her position had not changed, nor the questionable wisdom of bringing forth a child at this unstable time.

And yet . . . Rhiann had travelled far to reach Eremon, and she found she could not rid herself of a part of him that had taken root in her. It would be a denial of all they had shared, the value of his pain and hers. It would be sacrilege, not because of the Goddess, or Linnet or Caitlin, or even Eremon, but because of Rhiann herself and the promise she had made, to love him in Thisworld and keep no part of her heart back.

Rhiann now spread her hands fully over her belly, each finger glowing in the weak sunlight. The air was still so cold it felt like a burning on her skin. 'Hello,' she whispered, hardly daring to breathe it aloud. And under her fingers, something trembled and was woken, and she knew it was not the child, for it was too early for that. No, it was something in her that had woken, something that quivered with new life, as tiny and fresh as the child itself.

Mother. Me.

A part of her that had only been sleeping, perhaps; sleeping like the soul of the child had slept in the Otherworld, waiting for her call.

★

Despite the late thaw, Imbolc dawned clear. The stream of mare's milk fell straight into the river; a column of polished crystal, gleaming in the sunlight.

This was Rhiann's first official duty since her illness, for Linnet had led the longest night rites to call back the sun with drum and voice. Now as Rhiann leaned out over the water, tilting the fluted bronze jug, she had the uncomfortable sensation that all the keen eyes of the women were fixed on her belly under the wool dress. With her free hand, Rhiann clutched the folds of her sheepskin cloak closer around her, telling herself she was imagining the sharp edge to their collective gaze.

No one knew. No one could know, so early. Yet she was glad when the river rite was over, and the women all trooped to Aldera's house for hot mead and gossip.

Aldera had prepared them a special treat this day, slaughtering an old ewe that had been kept alive on dried grass all through the long dark. The meat was roasting over her fire-spit as they all took their places on the benches and chairs, the scent of fat and flesh a thick, greasy mist above the hearth.

It was as the women chatted about their concerns – who was breeding, who was ill, who was lying with men other than their husbands – that Rhiann began to notice the prickling at the base of her spine. She shifted in her seat, narrowing her eyes at the embroidery in her lap. She was embellishing a tunic for Gabran, as he was growing at an increasing pace, and she was just finishing the intricate curls of the hound chasing a boar around the hem.

Then Aldera stood to baste the ewe with fat from the drippings tray, and a rich surge of meat scent flooded Rhiann's nostrils. She realized she was breaking out in a fine sweat across her forehead and, frowning, she closed her eyes and lowered her face so her hair swung forward to cover it. Yet the prickle in her spine soon swelled into robust life, curling tentacles around into her belly, and she bit down on her lip and swallowed, her tongue thick and slimy in her mouth.

She glanced up to see Linnet looking at her appraisingly, and Rhiann smiled and sat straighter, struggling to contain the turning of her stomach. Yet it was so hot and close, the air heavy with the smells of flesh and sweat and someone's cloying, imported perfume.

'Excuse me.' Abruptly, Rhiann stood, her throat moving. 'Aldera, I left a brew simmering that I must check.'

That was all she could get out, and ignoring Fola's sharp glance of concern, she bolted for the door. Outside, the glitter of sun on the icy cobbles was a welcome distraction, as Rhiann ducked around the back of Aldera's house, past the pig pen, and bent over. Yet her buttocks against the mud wall and the blast of cold air steadied her almost immediately, sweeping away the heavy richness of the fatty meat, and her nausea ebbed.

Thankful that she'd escaped vomiting before every noblewoman in the dun, Rhiann straightened. Yet as she did, her eye fell on the remains of the drain Didius had constructed for Bran so long ago, now filled in with the season's mud and animal bones. And at the thought of him, and his people, Rhiann's hand crept across her belly. What was she thinking, to bring a child into the world at this time? It was wrong, it was all wrong.

'The air *was* stifling, was it not?' Linnet's hands were folded into her blue cloak, her deep-set eyes floating around the yard with apparent interest, despite the fact it held only a scattering of rusting, half-finished cart wheels and ploughs, all protruding from the snow.

Rhiann blew out her breath. 'Yes, I find I am not as recovered as I'd like to think.' She squinted down at her boots, the soles wet with melting frost.

'Well.' Gently, Linnet took her arm. 'These things take time, as we both know.' With a soft pressure, she urged Rhiann up the main path through the village, as Rhiann tried to think of some better excuse for her abrupt departure. And another part of her was wondering, as she did, why she shied away from telling Linnet her suspicions then and there.

Yet at the door of Rhiann's house, Linnet took her by both arms and looked deep into her eyes. 'In fact, child, take all the time you need. There is no rush, after all.'

Rhiann watched Linnet glide away, realizing that her aunt was giving her the time to come to some understanding of her own feelings. And so inside her house, Rhiann stood unmoving before her fire, her gaze lost in its flickering glow, wondering just when these feelings would become clear to her.

Traders were not expected so early in the year, but just before the moon turned again, two visitors did find their way to Dunadd out of the frosted reaches of the northern mountains.

Rhiann was standing beneath the gatehouse, peering dolefully out at sheets of rain which were marching grimly down from the valley of the ancestors. She stared at the two warriors as they dismounted in the shelter of the gatetower, struggling out from under long skin riding capes that covered them from head to toe, and realized with a shock that she knew them. One was the Creones messenger she had greeted the preceding leaf-fall on her return to Dunadd, when Eremon was in the east. He had proven to be a more amiable warrior than his king, and now he nodded respectfully as he recognized Rhiann.

'Lady,' he said by way of greeting, brushing drips from his moustache and shaking his hair so the rain ran from the ends of his braids.

It was common courtesy to warm and feed such arrivals before seeking their news, but Rhiann could not stay silent, not when she had watched Eremon being eaten away by frustration these past moons. She cleared her throat. 'It takes courage to come so far in such a season.'

The other man, the Boresti, paid Rhiann little attention, his dark eyes darting to the Epidii warriors who warmed their hands before a fire under the eaves of a nearby storehouse. But the Creones warrior turned to Rhiann with a grin, and she saw then he was much younger than she'd first thought. He leaned close to her, with a swift glance over his shoulder. 'My lord king has enjoyed no peace this long dark, for the fire that you lit, lady, shows no signs of dying. When I returned with news of your war leader's victory, defying the Romans before your very gates, the frenzy of our swords and shields was deafening – like a storm breaking over the mountains!'

Another frustrated bard, Rhiann noted. 'Yet when you left, my lord was gravely ill,' she replied. The words brought an echo of panic, even now, and a sudden suspicion: that the Creones king might be seeking to confirm a weakness among the Epidii. 'So I am gratified to see such support still burning among the Creones,' she added carefully.

'I understand.' The messenger spoke just as carefully. 'Yet that is why we have come. If he is still your war leader, then we still wish to give him our allegiance.'

Rhiann blinked, her mittened hands over her mouth. She waited for the rush of joy . . . *this was what she had worked for . . . travelled all that way for* . . . but it was not forthcoming. All she felt was a recurring lurch of sickness. Abruptly she clasped her belly as if she could keep the contents of her stomach down there by will alone.

'Lady?' The warrior ducked his head, peering at her in the dim shadows of the gatetower, and Rhiann forced a shaky smile, raising her face.

'Then your journey was not wasted,' she informed him clearly, 'for if you come with me, my lord will greet you himself in the King's Hall.'

At these words, the sleek, wet head of the Boresti messenger also swung around, and Rhiann led the way up the path through the rain, the two men behind her. Yet she found her steps were heavy in the mud, a weight echoed strangely in her heart.

That night, Eremon gave an intimate feast to seal the new bond between the tribes. Determined to be the gracious hostess, Rhiann nevertheless found her stomach turned yet again, this time by the copious stench of male sweat and ale fumes. Poor Aedan only got halfway through a new lay he had composed, when his song was swept aside by a shout from an increasingly drunk crowd around a *fidchell* game, and he put away his harp and went off to sulk somewhere else. Taking her cue from him, Rhiann caught Caitlin's eye, and they took Gabran to join Fola and Eithne at Rhiann's house.

Soon, Rhiann found herself aching for bed, so tired, in fact, that she was almost glad that she had it to herself, for she was sure Eremon would stay with his men in the Hall.

Yet deep in the night he crept in beside her, his nose chilled from the night air, his hands warm as they roused her from sleep into desire. Without pausing to undress, he slid on top of her, the legs of his trousers rough against her thighs, his ale-soaked murmurs drawing forth not tenderness, but an urgency that was just as sweet. Blinking sleep away, Rhiann clung to him as he entered her, her nose buried in his smoky tunic.

Later, as Eremon fell down into a solid sleep, Rhiann lay under his weight, stroking his thick hair back from his temples in the dark. She knew what these messengers meant to him, and yet her own feelings were mixed. If the other tribes joined Eremon, war was a surety. And if they did not, the Romans would roll over them like a stormcloud. Was there another way? An alliance was what Eremon wanted, but perhaps the whisper of the child had lent Rhiann a new acuteness of sense, for the sickness in her belly, the dread, told her that an alliance would also take them to a place from which there would be no return.

A place where this man of hers, whose heart now beat in her own breast, would face the greatest danger of his life.

It was a terrible time to be breeding, as she had always known it would be.

Chapter 59

'**G**oddess Mother of All!' Caitlin's frustration released itself in a barrage of white-fletched arrows that sang through empty air, spurning the dead oak tree for which she was aiming.

'Look!' she squeaked, brandishing her bow angrily at Rhiann and Linnet, who were seated on hides on the slopes of the ancestor valley, where the low morning sun warmed the turf to a brilliant green. 'I am useless now,' Caitlin grumbled. 'Worse than useless, in fact! Like a child with its first bow.' She disappeared behind the tree and began plucking wayward arrows from the undergrowth, muttering to herself.

'Such impatience,' Linnet murmured, cutting another slice of cheese with her herb-knife. 'I think she shares that with you.'

'I can hardly defend myself on that point,' Rhiann agreed.

By careful study of stars and sun, the druids marked the leaf-bud solstice – when day and night were of equal length – by burning offerings in the stone circle at the end of the ancestor valley. Declan and his brothers had concluded their rites to the sky gods at dawn, and now Linnet and Rhiann would shortly make another offering to the ancestor priestesses at the base of the stones. Since Gelert's departure, the dealings between druid and priestess were proceeding with a lot more ease and respect, at least.

Linnet had also asked Caitlin to come this day without Gabran, and now she seemed in no hurry to begin the rite, taking a leisurely meal on the flat ground outside the lichen-stained stones. At the top of the slope the hazels and oaks reared wet and nearly bare, though the hazel catkins misted the copse with a veil of green.

Another curse floated from behind the stump, and an arrow sailed across the clearing into the shadows of a hawthorn thicket beyond, its branches clouded with the first blossom.

Momentarily distracted, Rhiann took the cheese and bannock from Linnet and bit into it, watching her aunt out of the corner of her eye.

Ever since arriving at the circle, Linnet had been speaking in a most uncharacteristic way, a brittle chatter that set Rhiann's teeth on edge. Now Linnet was staring down at the deer-hide, one fingernail tapping the hardened leather of a small mead flask.

Rhiann swallowed, the cheese and bread a hard lump in her throat. She only had one thing to say, yet the words kept sticking there, for somehow speaking them aloud made them real. A part of her still felt that the babe was a dream, she supposed. Voicing her news meant that a door would close behind her: a time when it was her secret alone. Hers and the child's.

Furtively, Rhiann leaned back on one hand and peered down at her flat belly. The babe itself was still a vague concept to her. She stared harder, half-expecting the child to sit up and make itself known. Something was in there, she told herself again. No, *someone*. At that thought, a thrill of mingled terror and wonder shot up Rhiann's spine. A person was in there, not an idea, a person closer to Rhiann than anyone had ever been. And she was giving that person life.

The oak tree let out a satisfied clunk. A sigh of pleasure followed.

Raising her gaze, Rhiann saw that Linnet's eyes were now fixed on her, expectant. 'Never have a priestess for an aunt.' Rhiann forced a smile, but Linnet's mouth was pained, uncertain, and Rhiann's attempt at flippancy trailed away.

It was then that Rhiann understood that this babe was not just hers after all. This child was for her kin, as much as for Eremon, and would be loved by them all. It was all the more precious because of those they had lost – Rhiann's mother and father, her foster-family, the Sisters.

Linnet, who had lived with so much loss, was waiting for the gift Rhiann could give her.

'Aunt,' she said, the words unfurling naturally after all, drawn by Linnet's shadowed eyes, 'I think I am with child.'

For a long moment, Linnet did not move nor speak, then she, always the most elegant and constrained of women, buried her face in her hands. 'Oh!' Her voice was muffled, queerly breathless. 'I knew, but I couldn't be sure.' She dropped her hands, her face now a hot rose from cheek to cheek. 'It is three moons now, child, is it not?'

Rhiann smiled shakily. 'Nearly. I should have known I could not keep it from you.'

'I thought perhaps it was the illness but . . .' Linnet shook her head, as a smile of relief broke through. 'But I have had dreams of a child, a coming child.'

'I have had no dreams,' Rhiann replied, suddenly realizing that it was true. No dreams at all.

Linnet's delighted smile faded. 'Are you not pleased, daughter? I understand the difficulties you had before, and I never judged you for them, you must know that.'

Rhiann's eye fell on Caitlin, who was bent over once more scrabbling for arrows, the weak sun bright on her fair hair. 'When Caitlin first had Gabran, she chafed at being left behind, at not being able to ride by Conaire's side. She could not travel, or even practise, as you see. She could only be a mother.' Rhiann stared down at her spread hands. 'I was terrified of the same thing, and that's why I took the brew. My dream has carried Eremon and I across Alba – what if I could not be Ban Cré and mother both?'

Linnet's reply was low. 'A Ban Cré is often a mother, my love. It is fitting.'

'I know!' Rhiann replied with some desperation. 'But no Ban Cré has ever faced what we face now, aunt. I feared becoming useless to Eremon, to my people. You must think what I did terrible, but I . . .' She broke off, for the taste of the glory and the power of the dream was sharp on her tongue, and she knew, suddenly, that wanting it was an indelible part of her. She needed it to be complete.

Linnet took Rhiann's hand and turned it upwards, tracing the lines on her palm. 'You walk a path like no other. It is not for me to say what you should do, only love you for all you do.'

Rhiann bit her lip, her eyes stinging. 'I never told you this, but two years ago, on the Sacred Isle, Nerida and Setana told me to root myself in this world, by being wife and mother as well as priestess. They asked me again, just before they died. And aunt, as skilled and clever as you may think me, it has taken me these years to find that, with Eremon.' Rhiann looked up into Linnet's calm eyes. 'In that Otherworld place, I pledged myself to him by surrendering all, and after that could no more stop our child growing in me as leave him altogether.'

Rhiann's pulse was beating erratically now, fluttering within her as if it did not know which way to fly, and Linnet folded her fingers around her hand. 'Then let me ask you this, daughter. *Now* it is done, how do you really feel?'

Rhiann stared at her aunt, as tears welled up with every thump of her breast, laying bare all that confused her. 'That's just it,' she whispered. 'I feel so happy and I don't know *why!*'

Linnet smiled her broadest, and pulled an unresisting Rhiann into her arms.

'What's wrong?' Caitlin was standing there now, nervously twisting the stone guard on her bow wrist.

As Rhiann struggled to speak, Linnet answered for her. 'Rhiann is to have a baby.'

And following those simple words, a cry of joy rang out over the green, sunlit slopes, echoing off the ancient, grey stones and up into the sky.

If Rhiann had felt coddled when she was ill, it was nothing to what was lavished upon her by Caitlin, Fola and Eithne on their return from the valley. Against all protests, Rhiann was tucked up in her chair by the fire, a blanket wrapped around her despite the fairness of the day. Eithne disappeared to appropriate eggs and milk for a pudding, while Fola repaired to Rhiann's workbench and began opening and sniffing every jar she could reach on the shelves. As if to affirm the whole business, Caitlin plucked a sleepy Gabran from the bed and swung him into Rhiann's lap. Gazing down at his slow-blinking eyes, Rhiann allowed herself to imagine, for the first time, what the weight of her own child would feel like in her arms. The sharp tug under her ribs caught her by surprise.

'*Muh*,' Gabran grunted, his hand grasping for her hair.

In passing, Linnet's touch rested on Rhiann's shoulder. 'These tears will not be the last,' her aunt murmured, 'for the changes that come with the babe make one's heart . . .' She flicked her fingers, casting about for words, but it was Caitlin who answered as she bounded back with another blanket.

'They make you leak like an old, rusty pot, Rhiann!' Caitlin smiled indulgently. 'But they are the best kind of tears, I promise.'

Rhiann returned her smile uneasily, holding up her hands to prevent a near-drowning in bed coverings. 'You all have to stop doing this, much as I love you for it. You see, I have not told Eremon yet.'

'Oh!' Caitlin's brow furrowed. 'Well, go and tell him, then.'

'He's watching the training,' Rhiann observed dryly, 'and I really don't wish all those hairy men to know the inner workings of my body.'

'Rhiann.' Fola grinned over a basin of ground roots, rubbing a smear of dark powder over her cheek with the back of her hand. 'I think you'd better tell him soon. You cannot expect us to keep such a secret from him for long!'

Rhiann glanced around at each glowing face in turn. 'No,' she agreed, with a smile. 'I don't suppose so.'

In theory, it should have been a simple matter to get Eremon to herself over the next few days, and yet it proved difficult. The two messengers had lit such a fire in him that although Rhiann had forbidden him from wielding his weapons, he soon threw off any lingering exhaustion from his illness and began scorning not only bed rest, but indoor activity of any kind. With ill grace he had delegated the training to Conaire, yet still managed to spend all of his time knee-deep in frozen mud, shouting at the Epidii warriors over the shriek of the sleet winds.

Rhiann was finding it increasingly difficult to stomach the heat and stench of the King's Hall, and eventually had to stop taking her meals there. And as Eremon laid plans with Conaire and Lorn late into each night, she was invariably asleep when he did come to bed.

Another fine day drove back the wet winds, and Rhiann, finding herself irrationally short of temper, decided to seek some sea air. Wrapping up well in wool underclothes and sheepskin tunic and riding breeches, she crossed the causeway on Liath, glancing at the men drilling on the river meadow. Peering hard, she could not discern Eremon among them, and she shrugged and glanced up at the clear sky, nudging Liath towards the Trade Path. She had strapped baskets to both sides of her saddle to collect the seaweed thrown up by the leaf-bud storms, for it made a fine red-purple dye.

At the Bay of the Otters, Rhiann wandered over the dark weedy rocks in peace, enjoying the sun and salt-tanged air, however cold. Then she wedged her second basket in a crevice and stepped down onto a sliver of sand, pausing to watch a curlew glide in low over the muddy shore. Its lonely, plaintive cry always took Rhiann's soul with it up into the sky, and she was still shading her eyes to follow it when a voice boomed out from the screen of gorse bushes behind her. 'Ah, what is this? A pretty seal maid come ashore?'

Jolted out of her sun-warmed reverie, Rhiann smiled up at Eremon as he leaped from rock to rock towards her. Yet when he reached the shingle he gave her no chance to greet him, only swept her up boisterously and then, with great efficiency, tripped her in order to tumble her to the sand.

'Eremon!' Gasping, Rhiann fell awkwardly, instinct taking over as she twisted to protect her belly and at the same time lashed out with one foot. Her heel gained contact with Eremon's groin, yet although he grunted, his hands immediately grasped her wrists, his eyes laughing down at her. 'Feisty,' he murmured, trying to kiss her. 'Just as I like it.'

Rhiann hardly heard him, for she was terrified that her fall had hurt the child. 'Get off me!' she croaked, wriggling and tugging on her hands.

Eremon's grin faltered. 'Well, that's not a warm welcome, is it?'

'No!' Rhiann struggled harder, fear surging into sudden fury. 'I said, get off me, you oaf!'

Eremon sat up and released her, brushing sand from his hands. The edge of his mouth turned down. 'It's been so long; I thought you missed me.'

Rhiann raised herself gingerly to her haunches. 'So you had to attack me to get me alone?' She was breathless, desperately focusing inwards to see if she could feel anything amiss, confused at the anger. This was not how it was supposed to be.

'As it happens, yes,' Eremon retorted. His eyes were green slits, his cheekbones flushing dusky red. 'Though it seems to me I could have saved myself the trouble.' He sat back on his knees. 'Obviously my attentions aren't welcome.'

'Goddess!' Rhiann pressed her fingers to her eyes with frustration. 'Don't be silly.'

'And don't speak to me like a child.'

'Don't act like one then!'

Eremon's head dipped, the tips of his ears reddening as he stared at his bent legs. 'Every night you leave the Hall early, and then when I do come you curl yourself away from me in sleep.'

'Yes, well.' Even angrier, because they were arguing, Rhiann levered herself upright and wrapped her arms around her chest. 'There is a reason for that, as it happens.'

Eremon rose too, his eyes deliberately cool. 'Then perhaps you'll share that with me.'

Suddenly, a wave of disappointment swept over Rhiann, and she blinked back tears. *Curse that stupid, leaky pot!* Struggling to contain them, her face screwed up into what must have been an alarming expression, for Eremon took her by the shoulders, his concern naked. '*A stór?*' He peered down at her. 'Are you really hurt?'

'No!' Rhiann snorted wetly, sniffed once, then looked him full in the face. And when she saw him chewing his lip, for all the world like a guilty boy, her anger dissolved. 'Nothing is wrong,' she whispered at last. 'I was scared, that is all. Because . . . because you pushed me onto my belly, and I feared . . . that it would come to harm . . .'

'*It?*' Eremon repeated blankly.

Rhiann merely nodded. She'd said it now; let him make the connection.

And so he did. She watched it dawning over him, like the sky as the sun nears the horizon. 'A babe?' Eremon murmured, searching her eyes with disbelief.

Rhiann nodded again, and so the sun broke free in Eremon's face, and he swept her up in an embrace that was both fierce and tender. 'A child . . . ha!' He lifted her high in his arms and spun in the sand, whooping with such delight that she laughed, the tears spilling now onto his upturned cheeks.

'When?' was all he said as he put her down, clasping her close.

She smiled. 'The longest night, *cariad.*'

Slowly, the memory of that joining flooded Eremon's eyes. 'I knew that I could never forget that night, and now I will never forget, ever!' He laughed exultantly, with a glance at the sky. 'Praise be to Hawen and Manannán both, for they have blessed me more than I could ever ask!'

'Perhaps the Mother had something to do with it as well,' Rhiann observed, her sense of humour restored by her relief.

Eremon laughed again, and kissed her forehead. 'The Mother, too. All the gods, for they have blessed our love now with the greatest of gifts.'

Rhiann brushed sand from his cheek with the back of her hand. 'This always meant so much to you, didn't it?'

'More than you will ever know, wife.' Eremon's eyes glowed. 'Now I have a family, a real family of my own. A belonging no one can ever take from me.'

Rhiann's breath caught somewhere in her breast. That was why he had felt so betrayed by her, after all. 'And I,' she whispered, half to herself. She held his face with both hands. 'But I never understood. Nerida and Setana knew, they tried to tell me.' She leaned up and kissed his lips, then his cheeks, his chin, anywhere that came within reach. 'I am sorry for what I did before, so sorry.'

'Rhiann.' Eremon stopped her words and frantic kisses with his fingers, salty against her mouth. 'None of that matters now. So long as you love me, that is all I care about.'

Rhiann nodded, her breath catching somewhere between a sob and a laugh. 'Loving you is the easiest of promises, I have found, for I have no choice in it!'

'There is always choice.' Eremon was suddenly serious. 'I know well how little you have wanted to be in Thisworld at times. Yet in the end you did choose me, as I chose you.' He rested his hand gently on her belly. Rhiann had to close her eyes at the sudden sweetness of it. 'And perhaps,' he said, 'this little one has chosen us, too, because he knows what wonderful parents we will be.'

Rhiann grinned. 'I'm sure *she* does know that, indeed.'

In the late afternoon, Eremon galloped his horse along the riverbank to where Conaire was training a group of young, new-blooded warriors recently come from the mountain duns. Leaping to the ground and flinging Dòrn's reins over an alder branch, Eremon approached Conaire from behind, trying to walk with some dignity.

'That's not a line!' Conaire was roaring, pointing with his practice sword. 'Crus, get your legs in close to Urven and raise your shield the way I showed you, man!' The youths shuffled closer, elbowing each other with their sword arms and shoving with their shields, laughing, until Conaire's glower wiped the smiles from their faces.

'Brother,' Eremon murmured, stepping close by Conaire's side.

'What?' Conaire threw him a distracted glance. 'Oh . . . Crus! Urven! *Do it now or I will crack your heads together!*'

'Rhiann is to have a child,' Eremon blurted, rocking on his heels, a smile breaking over his face. 'I am . . . to have a child.'

Conaire's head snapped around. 'Hawen's balls!' With a delighted grin, he threw his arms around Eremon, nearly lifting him off his feet. 'That is fine news!'

Eremon gasped with pain as Conaire crushed his injured side, and his foster-brother immediately set him down, contenting himself with a hand on Eremon's shoulder. 'Our sons will grow together now, brother, as we did!' Conaire's face was bright. 'While we sit and drool into our ale, eh!'

Eremon grinned, his chest feeling as though it could burst with pride. 'While we thrash them at sword-fights, you mean! I have no intention of drooling.'

Yet now Conaire was staring thoughtfully through the trees, over the gleaming, brown rush of the sunlit river, his hands on his hips. 'It is the finest of things, Eremon, as you will discover,' he added, more sombrely. 'Someone to carry your name.' He swung back, rubbing the stubble on his jaw. 'Someone to fight for, aye? It changes things. It makes you more . . .'

As he cast about for words, the young warriors resumed their shoving and elbowing in earnest, and suddenly, with a yell, the loosely knitted formation broke apart into a series of muddy scuffles.

Eremon never got to hear the rest, as Conaire shouted a curse and waded into the fray, applying the broad palm of his hand to restore order.

Rhiann, perhaps naively, expected that all would return to normal, yet she had not reckoned on Eremon. He urged a cloak on her whenever she stepped outside the house, despite the strengthening sun and lighter winds. He watched over every bite that passed her lips, which made for uncomfortable digestion, and interrupted almost every activity that kept her busy, from sewing to weaving to grinding roots, entreating her to sit by the fire or rest on the bed.

In this mission, he was aided by Eithne and Fola and even Caitlin, though she had fought against such attentions just the same when she was breeding.

Eremon's concern was real, yet Rhiann knew that his over-attention stemmed from boredom, for he still could wield no weapon, and must remain an onlooker as Conaire supervised the men's training.

Occasionally, Rhiann managed to evade his notice, and one day was trudging happily through the boggy marsh, her calves black with mud, her herb-knife on guard for early stands of creamy meadowsweet. Suddenly, away to her right there was a snuffling, and the tips of the head-high grasses swayed and trembled as something bore down towards her. A moment later, Cù burst out into the open and bounded up to her, pausing only to emit a triumphant howl that was no doubt intended for the larger object thrashing through the marsh behind him.

Rhiann turned to face the intruder. 'You *tracked* me?' she all but yelped, when Eremon broke through to the path, breathing heavily. 'With a dog? Like a . . . a *pig*?'

He had the grace to blush, looking down at his feet.

'Eremon, by the Mother, I am not ailing!'

His head snapped up, indignant. 'I just want you to be careful!'

Rhiann waved her knife, gritting her teeth. '*Cariad*, I feel wonderful. Even the sickness has gone. But if you coddle me like this, you will *make* me ill, I swear it!'

They glared at each other, Cù glancing from one to the other, his feathery tail waving uncertainly.

Suddenly Rhiann dropped her hands with frustration. 'Aargh!'

At that, the edge of Eremon's mouth twitched, and Rhiann pursed her own lips, squashing the grin that threatened to break out. 'Now,' she said more calmly, 'if you let me be, as your healer, I'll allow you to begin proper training again – *gently* – in two more weeks.'

'Two weeks!' he protested, stretching his arms above his head and waving them in wild sweeps. 'Hawen's balls, I've been exercising it. I'm ready now!'

She raised one eyebrow, striding forward to draw up the edge of his tunic and touch the soft skin at his waist. The wound had left a jagged scar that would be with him for life, and though the line was still dark red, the comfrey had done its job and knitted the skin well. Rhiann prodded the muscles underneath with deliberate pressure, watching Eremon's face. There was a distinct flinch in his eyes.

'Two weeks,' she pronounced, 'and go gently then. If I see you whirling that blade of yours around your head, I'll give you another reason to suffer, I promise you.'

Eremon grinned. 'No one told me how comforting a scolding wife can be.'

'Yes, well, you made the mistake of choosing a healer and a priestess for a wife.' Rhiann cocked her head at him, squinting in the sun. 'Perhaps you would have been happier with a quiet, plump little cattle-lord's daughter?'

Eremon's only answer was a snort, yet he cupped her belly with both hands, softly rubbing the skin through the wool of her dress. In the week since Rhiann told him her news, he had scarcely kept his hands off her belly, for it was just starting to swell between her hip bones.

Now Rhiann closed her eyes with a little sigh, enjoying the warmth of the sun on her eyelids and the heat of his hands over her stomach. The lack of sight made all the sounds around her leap forward: Eremon's faint breath; Cù whuffling somewhere in the reeds; the buzz of the myriad, awakening insects. She was suddenly very conscious that they were alone. With a queer flutter Rhiann opened her eyes, dazzled by the light, moving towards Eremon's hazy outline, searching for his kiss first with her fingers and then her lips.

Pressed up against him, Rhiann felt the answering hardness against her thigh, and heard the slight catch in Eremon's throat. Under her fingers, his pulse beat in his neck as rapidly as her own, and eagerly her mouth opened to him. They were alone, and it was warm out of the wind if they retraced their steps to the firmer ground among the grasses . . .

Yet suddenly Eremon's hands were on her arms, putting her firmly but gently away from him, and he turned his face to whistle for Cù. Rhiann was too surprised to respond as Eremon dropped a tender kiss on top of her head. 'You are right,' he said, his voice faintly husky. 'I promise I will harass you no more.' He grinned down at her, though a dark flush still stained his cheekbones. 'I will see you in the Hall, aye?'

Speechless, Rhiann watched him thread his way along the path, her herb-knife still clutched in her fingers. Then she looked down, cupping her belly in an echo of Eremon's touch.

That night, Rhiann lay sleepless by Eremon's side after another chaste kiss that effectively turned aside her hands, which had been sliding their way across his back. With dawning dismay, Rhiann realized that Eremon was unable or unwilling to rouse himself to the fire that she still felt burning in her own blood.

But why? What did this mean? Rhiann turned over on her side, blocking her ears to the soft, contented wheeze of his infernal breath. Could it be that her fears were coming true after all? For if her own husband was treating her differently, this was surely just the beginning. Soon, all the dun would know of her condition.

In the nights that followed, fed by the lingering darkness, an irrational dread began to take form in Rhiann's gut. The people would see her as no more than a dumb, breeding woman. Perhaps they would no longer seek her healing, preferring Fola instead, for she was unadulterated by worldly concerns. Perhaps the men would no longer pay heed to Rhiann's thoughts, even though she had accompanied Eremon on many of his adventures and had travelled Alba to gain warriors to his side.

On the heels of this dread, a greater terror began to worm its way into Rhiann's mind. For ever since the long dark, not once had she received so much as a hint of her dream, or any stray glimpse of what was to come. How could this be? Had something changed in her? The warm season was wheeling closer, the campaigning time drawing near. How could the meagre remains of her sight fail her now?

It seemed to Rhiann that something in her had turned away from the outer world and was contracting inwards, curling around the life that grew inside her. *That's* all she could feel.

That's all she dreamed.

There, in that dark, the sounds of the world came only faintly, as a dull hum. People's feelings were no more than the buffeting of a distant storm, a powerless tempest that did little but stir the swirling warmth in which they floated, the child and her.

In her sleep, Rhiann saw and felt as it did. She was surrounded by her own steady heartbeat; floated on a dreamy stillness; gazed with sleepy wonderment at the lights that flickered around them. She couldn't talk to the child, for as yet it had no thoughts, and the rhythm of its life was so slow as to be pure sense only. She merely drifted with it . . . and *nearness* was all they shared.

Yet it was this very nearness, this feeling that Rhiann was unable to describe even to herself, which was the source of the joy that pierced her along with the terror. For a part of her had always felt alone, and as much as she loved Eremon, they were separate beings. But *this* being was inside her, fused with her, *made* of her.

And so, the joy.

The joy was a primal thing, which had no time for Rhiann's terror. It just existed, as the babe existed, untouched by the outer world, drifting and turning in the timeless, sheltered womb in which she held it. The joy was not under her conscious control. The joy was the light beneath and behind all others, and it held Rhiann as she held the child, curling around them both.

Chapter 60

Rhiann released Liath's bridle as one of the stable-boys led the mare into the first empty stall. It was a fine day, and most of the pens were empty, their residents either training by the river or being exercised by masters who were just as eager to escape the stifling confines of the dun.

Rhiann had just returned from Lorn's own dun, there presiding over the blessing of the new-sown barley fields.

Linnet could have gone, but despite her promise to Eremon, Rhiann's aunt still found it difficult to look upon Urben's face. Rhiann had managed to ignore him, even though she felt his pig eyes bore into her back as she sprinkled the blood of his first lamb into the turned earth. It had, in fact, taken the whole ride home for Rhiann to realize what had stopped her from throwing the contents of the mead cup in Urben's face: his son had saved Eremon's life.

Satisfied at her show of restraint, Rhiann paused to set down the basket of chickweed and burdock leaves she had collected on the way home, then reached up to stretch her back. Her shoulders had spent too much of that day somewhere around her ears.

Suddenly, she jumped at a loud clunk in the last stall, at the opposite end of the stable. It was the unmistakable sound of a sharp edge on wood, followed by a swish and a scrabbling of reeds underfoot, followed by another clunk.

With narrowed eyes, Rhiann crept towards the last stall. The front of each partition was fenced, with wide spaces between the horizontal palings. And from ten paces away Rhiann now glimpsed the gleam of dim light on polished iron, and a man-shadow forcefully swinging a blade around his head in great swoops.

Silently, Rhiann edged closer, her head low, until she was right at the junction of the last two stalls. Then, abruptly, she straightened. '*What are you doing with that sword?*'

There was a foul curse as Eremon jerked, the downward sweep going wide, his knuckles cracking on the far wall. 'Hawen's balls!' Whirling, he dropped the sword and immediately stuck his grazed fingers in his mouth, which somewhat diluted the effect of his glare.

Rhiann advanced, leaning both arms on the stall gate. The light, hazy with the motes of chaff and horse dust, shone on the thin film of sweat that coated Eremon's bare torso, and his chest was heaving up and down with exertion. The lines of tattoos across his belly were blurred by the flush of his skin, but the jagged scar that cleaved his left side had only grown more vivid with suffused blood. Even in the half-shadow it was an angry score, reminding Rhiann too well how it had looked when infected.

'By all the gods, woman!' Eremon removed his bloody fingers from his mouth. 'Never, ever creep up on me again when I have a blade in my hand!'

Rhiann's own mouth dropped open as Eremon stooped to retrieve his sword. 'And why are you whirling that thing around when I distinctly told you it was too soon?' she snapped. 'You could hurt yourself!' She was suddenly shaking with anger, and hardly knew why.

Eremon shrugged one shoulder, brushing straw from his blade and peering at it. 'I've got to exercise these muscles, and I didn't want anyone to see, not until I can do it without wincing.'

'*Wincing?*' Eremon's head jerked up at Rhiann's tone. 'Conaire is doing an able job of training the men,' she stormed, 'as I just saw! They don't need you yet.'

Eremon was at the gate in two strides, a muscle jumping in his jaw. 'Of course they need me! And I won't waste any more time acting the invalid for you!' Breathing hard, he rested the blade along the top of the fence, eyes bright with reined-in frustration. 'We are running out of time.'

Rhiann gasped as if he had hit her, and Eremon frowned and ducked under the gate to take her arms. 'I will not be crossed in this, *a stór*,' he said quietly.

Rhiann turned her face to the shadows. Suddenly she could not rid her mind of the scene she had witnessed on the river meadow moments ago. It was the pattern that had drawn her attention: swordsmen in rigid formation, spearmen and distinct lines of archers. Mounted warriors had been galloping up and down in thunderous charges, but in perfect time, the horses turning on their hind legs as one. One beast . . . she had heard Eremon speak of the Romans moving as one beast.

'Eremon,' she forced out, 'you are drilling all the men together as one again. As an army.'

The heat of Eremon's indignation faded away, and his brows drew together as he paused to choose his words. 'Rhiann.' His hold on her arms softened. 'I thought you understood. Agricola has only two choices now. I see them before me as if they were my own. He can give up, or,' he took a deep breath, 'he must find a way to engage us with all his forces, in one battle that will decide all. The time for raids and ambushes is over.'

Fear roared in a bright flood along Rhiann's veins. 'For two years you have triumphed over him, Eremon! Two years where you used what we have to win: our valleys, mountains—'

'That was because I did not have the men for anything else! But now, if the gods will it, we may be joined by others. And then we have a chance, a real chance!' Eremon's eyes flared. 'Remember that the vision Declan once had was of *all Alba* rising behind me. And all of Alba we will have, at last.'

Rhiann swallowed the lump in her throat. 'You cannot face the Romans in open battle, Eremon, you cannot. Not when you have found a better way: to hide, and strike. To run, and fight another day. This is how we won before!'

'And is that what you want for our child, Rhiann? Always to be running, always hiding, always fearful? For if we do not defeat these Romans once and for all, that is the only world our babe will know.' Rhiann turned her head away again, as if to stop his words, but Eremon grasped her face, resolute, and gently pulled it back to look at him. 'Do you want him to hear Roman boots thudding across his own land? Do you want him to cower, waiting for the sword in the night, or the ships with their bolts of fire?'

Rhiann's jaw clenched within his fingers. 'Not open battle,' she begged, her eyes swimming with tears. 'Not when defeat leaves you nowhere to run.'

'Rhiann.' Eremon shook his head, and sweat-soaked tendrils of hair fell across his brow. 'You gave me your dream, of the eagles crying, the cauldron and sword. You have shared it with me now for three years. In it, there is a great battle, you told me yourself.'

'Not any more!' The words exploded from her. 'Eremon, I do not dream this any more, I have not for three moons, ever since the baby . . .' She blinked stinging eyes. '*I cannot see what will happen any more.*'

Yet Eremon only regarded her calmly, prying her hands free and clasping them to his chest, cradled in his palms. 'It does not matter, *a stór*, for the dream has come enough now. We know the outcome.'

'No, we don't! You don't understand, Eremon, I can't *see* anything at all, I can't feel it, I can't sense it. The dream was all I had and without it I am blind.'

Eremon pressed Rhiann's wet cheeks into his shoulder. His skin was salty on her lips. 'You have already done all you could, my love, more than I would ever ask of you. It is because of you we even have the chance of this alliance.' He groped for her hand, pressing it to his wounded side. Under Rhiann's finger pads, the knitting skin was nubbled, already forming a hard ridge of scar tissue. 'It is only because of you the Epidii even have a war leader. You have done your part, Rhiann, and now it is up to me to do mine.'

Yet his words did nothing to calm Rhiann. 'And what good is a dead father to this child?' she blurted, pulling away from him.

Eremon released her suddenly, and the momentum made Rhiann stumble before she righted herself. His eyes were cold now, the lines of his face carven as if from stone. 'Our people must live free or die; it is how we are made.' He paused. 'Even you, Rhiann.' Then suddenly his brow creased with confusion. 'You have ever been my staunchest support in this. Why has your heart changed? Why?'

Rhiann's hand went to her belly. 'Because I have a family now, as well as a people. It . . .' She swallowed, her voice hoarse. 'It has changed me, as I knew it would. For the child's sake, I don't want to fight. How many battles do you think you can survive?' She shook her head, tears flinging out from her eyelashes. 'I don't know. *I don't know!*'

Eremon had gone very still. 'It is because of this child that I want to fight, Rhiann. To make this land free, for him, for her, for all that will come.' For a moment, his mouth softened. 'The decision is made,' he said simply, neither angry nor apologetic. 'We must fight the Romans openly for this to be resolved. All I wait for is the men.'

Unable to look on him any longer, Rhiann turned and left, striding blindly, the sunlight fractured by the tears in her eyes.

That night she avoided the King's Hall, and instead took to her bed early, thinking over what Eremon had said. Now that her anger had cooled into a dull knot of dread, she could acknowledge that one of his points was right: the dream *had* hinted at a great battle to come. Yet something else had been wrong, and Rhiann frowned as she sought for it, tried to pin down the unease in her belly that was nothing to do with the child.

You have already done all you could, Eremon said.

Rhiann examined her memories of the dream, holding them up one by one, and then she knew that was Eremon's mistake. For she had not yet done what the dream had asked of her: to gather the Source and, in that, save her people. The destiny that had called her for more than three years had not been fulfilled. All she had done, the travels in inner and outer worlds, had been a prelude to the real exercising of her power.

And that was what struck Rhiann with such fear, lying there in the warm darkness. For if she had not discharged her duty, then she was not in fact meant to slip away into the slow season of motherhood. She would be called on, in a way she could not foresee.

Much later, Rhiann opened her eyes to the dancing shadows cast by a single lamp. Eremon was lying with his arms behind his head. '*Alea iacta est*,' he said.

Groggily, Rhiann blinked. 'What?'

Without looking at her, Eremon gathered Rhiann close with one arm, as if they had not quarrelled at all. 'I've never told you much about my home, have I?' he said, his voice rising and falling in a dreamy cadence. 'We were on a busy trade route, despite being in the far north of Erin. We had traders come direct from Gaul, and even as far as Hispania!' The hollow of Eremon's throat moved as he smiled. He smelled of damp night air and woodsmoke. 'Some would think Dalriada a backwater, but we received a fair amount of news and goods from the empire of Rome. You could even get scraps of copied texts – if you knew who to ask, and if you paid well.'

Rhiann murmured, 'And you were interested in such?'

'Yes!' Eremon chuckled. 'My father would not have understood, but my druid teacher did. He was so proud I could read a little bit of Greek – the druids always respected the Greeks, he said. That is how I found out about the Greek historian Polybius, and what he wrote about the Roman army.' His chest moved in a sigh beneath her cheek. 'All young warriors are interested in fighting, but I was fascinated by the thought of fighting in far away lands, fighting with armies.' He hesitated. 'Little did I know I would call upon that knowledge after all.' Then he gave a faint shrug. 'I also found out about Julius Caesar, the Roman general. Once, he crossed a great river with his army, invading his own country and breaking its law to seize power. After they crossed, he said, "*Alea iacta est*". It means "the die is cast".'

Rhiann rolled off Eremon's chest so she could see his face, resting her chin in her hands. 'But what does it *mean*?' she asked.

The edge of Eremon's mouth lifted wryly, his eyes on the roof. 'It means, sometimes there is no going back.' Both of them lay entirely still. 'I think, *a stór*,' Eremon added quietly, 'that we reached that place some time ago, though I never marked its passing.'

Rhiann swallowed hard, her fingers folding the edge of the linen sheet, remembering her dream. If neither of them had fulfilled their destiny, there was no running away. 'Yes,' she whispered, knowing now that she must surrender such thoughts. 'I think so, too.'

They were both silent, and when Rhiann saw how Eremon's gaze still moved dreamily over the firelit roof, she suddenly said, 'Is it very beautiful?'

'What? Erin?' Eremon smiled, his eyes lighting up. 'As beautiful as the dawn. So green . . . a green never seen in this land, *a stór*, so bright, so pure. The grass is sweet and fresh, the winds are mild, the cattle are fat!' He laughed like a boy. 'The rivers run with gold, the plains are flat and endless, and you can race your horse for leagues and leagues, as fast as the wind!'

Rhiann watched Eremon's hand move gracefully through the air, drawing pictures. *I would like to have seen him then*, she thought suddenly, warmed by the curve of his smile, soft with memory. *Unburdened, before the hardening.*

Suddenly Eremon's eyes came back to her, and he reached out to tuck Rhiann's hair behind one ear. 'I would love to take you there and show you, *a stór*. Show you my home.'

His tender fingers drifted to the soft skin behind Rhiann's ear, and suddenly a column of heat swept through her, tingling along her thighs. She gazed down at him, frozen, her breath so shallow that he could not fail to sense it. And indeed, by the faint stirring of the sheet between his legs, she knew he was quite aware.

Yet Eremon didn't meet Rhiann's eyes, and when her fingers played over his mouth he did not suckle them, but pressed his lips together into one of those annoying, firm kisses that he kept dropping on her head. Rhiann reared back as if stung, pounded her pillow and flung herself down onto it, her face turned away so he would not see her trying to stop her tears. Curse these breeding emotions! And curse him for making her feel so close to him, making her forget her anger.

'*A stór?*' Eremon leaned over her, awkwardly patting her shoulder. 'Do not cry, love. I've said I will keep you safe.'

With a splutter, Rhiann rolled over and glared up at Eremon, her brows drawing together as if that might firm her trembling lips. 'You've changed,' she suddenly blurted. 'You don't want me any more. I don't know why but ever since the baby.' She blinked suddenly, defiant with hurt. 'Is it that you find me ugly?'

Eremon was as surprised as if she'd slapped him. 'Ugly? Don't be . . . I only thought . . . the baby would be hurt.'

Rhiann frowned, swallowing hard. 'Eremon, I am not sick. I need your comfort, I need your life, to know we are alive.' Tears welled in her eyes, and she didn't force them away. 'But you won't touch me and you leave me feeling so alone.'

With one sweep, Eremon caught her to his chest. 'Hawen's balls,' he muttered, and then laughed, an explosive sound in Rhiann's ear.

Enraged, Rhiann pushed at his chest, her mouth muffled in his shoulder. 'Don't you dare laugh at me now, Eremon of Erin! If you find me so repellent, there are other women no doubt waiting for the attentions you are determined to deny me!'

Eremon drew back and looked down at Rhiann, his eyes sparkling for the first time in days. 'Hmm.' He put one finger to his chin, tapping it in consideration. 'Well, you are enough, at times, to drive any man away.'

Rhiann gasped and furiously tried to wriggle free, but Eremon only smiled and held her there, his hands firm on her shoulders. 'That's enough misunderstanding for one week. I thought breeding women did not want . . . oh, never mind.' And his mouth came down on hers, hard and bruising, as his hand cupped one swelling, tender breast.

So among the shadows of their bed Eremon set about showing Rhiann, with demanding hands, that his reluctance had nothing at all to do with waning attraction. And he took her gasps from her with his open mouth, as she rode above him, his hands cradling her buttocks as he had cradled her belly.

Rhiann slept, her breaths deeper and more even than they had been before, every now and then punctuated with a little sigh. In the last flickering of the stone lamp, Eremon touched his finger to the tears still wet on her cheeks.

This wife of his had often been able to lead him where he did not wish to go, and now she wielded a weapon more potent than any she had possessed before. For while it was true he had avoided her for the baby's sake, if he was brutally honest, there was more to it than that.

Eremon lay back now, one arm behind his head, the other curving around her, their thighs touching. The truth was that in his own dreams something was calling him. It would, he knew, draw him to a battlefield, where a great hill reared behind him, and an army larger than any he could imagine spread before him.

Eremon turned his head slightly, his gaze sliding over the line of Rhiann's throat, the amber hair framing her shoulders, the pale tips of her outflung fingers. Below, he could just make out the swell of her belly beneath the sheets. He sighed, a drawn, pained sound.

He had avoided her, because in their joining he lost the separateness of himself. And he feared now the twining of that uncontainable bond with a baby, for in that summons to the battlefield he had also sensed a severing.

So he had tried, like a fool, to carve a tiny gulf between them, a way to make the severing less painful, if that was what the gods decreed. Yet Rhiann, with her honey scent and the fire in her lips, and her emotions flickering from dark to light, had pulled Eremon back. She had tempted him once more to surrender his heart, and he had gone and done it, and so lost himself in her again.

Now, tonight, Eremon knew he was doomed. For as he abandoned the edges of himself, and gave it all to her, he had heard the song of the child around them both, the three heartbeats wound together. Now he understood that there was no drawing back from that marriage of souls, that unending vow.

Alea iacta est.

Chapter 61

At Beltaine, Rhiann's visions began, more vivid and more disturbing than anything she had felt before.

As she stood on the tomb mound, the night was so calm she could clearly hear the crackling of the two great bonfires beneath her, and beyond, further down the ancestor valley, the faint lowing of the cattle that would soon be driven between them for blessing. The stars were faint, outshone by a great bronze moon that had risen over the eastern hills. It hung above the dark slopes, spilling light over the oak woods and leaching the bright colours from the people's robes, jewels and crowns of hawthorn blossoms.

As Rhiann stood with her arms out, willing herself to open to the Source, the breath of the crowd spread out below seemed to her like the soft lapping of a wave on a shore. She used its ebb and flow to anchor herself, to seek for and find a thread of the Source, running as a vibration beneath her feet.

As she did when she searched for Eremon, Rhiann closed her eyes, feeling the love she had for her people, the strength of her need to protect them. And in answer to her summons, a golden glow surged up from the ground, brighter than the moon, and sparkling light streamed up from each person's heart to meet it. It was their own love, for their land and for each other, made visible to her by the *saor*.

The people did not yet know of Eremon's acceptance of the inevitable Roman return. They knew only that their war lords had brought them great victories, and beaten back the shadows, just as, day by day, the sun beat back the cold of the long dark. They knew only that soon they would lie with each other in the darkness of the valley, and so honour the gods many times in the long nights to come. The fields were sprouting, the boats hauling in silver fish, and the woods fruiting with good eating.

Eventually, Rhiann was able to give herself up to the song that swirled from her mouth, bestowing the Mother's promise of a season of soft air on bare skin, the tart taste of strawberries, and long twilights that melted into warm, starlit nights.

It was as Rhiann stood entranced, enveloped by the wings of the people's joy, that it happened. The world around her abruptly darkened.

And she was in a wind-whipped, shadowed place with the salt of a wild sea stinging her face, her arms still outstretched, the insistent tug of wind on her sleeves. The golden wave of light was now made of night and freezing water, rearing above her in white-capped, whirling fury, an ocean wave higher than a cliff, which would bring death in moments.

Someone called her name, a name to which she once had answered, though no longer. The voice was urgent, yet also sought to imbue her with calm, so that her growing despair did not claim her. And Rhiann knew the voice as she knew her name, and the strange, familiar shadow of the woman's headdress outlined against the lightning. Her robes, pulled against her body by the screaming wind, were of a curious, shimmering cloth, the jewels on her rings unlike anything she had seen, and yet she knew them.

The imperious voice came again. 'Hold this in your soul!' it cried. 'Do not forget!'

And then Rhiann was tumbling, her mouth and nose filling with salt water. Desperate to clear her lungs she cried out, and suddenly found herself returned to the Beltaine rite, stumbling to the bench on the mound. She sank on to it, gripping the edges of the seat, head forced down to her knees. Immediately, Linnet was there.

'Did you see it?' Rhiann gasped, her hands fluttering over her chest, for she couldn't breathe.

Linnet squatted beside her, her anxious eyes swimming in and out of Rhiann's wavering sight. 'See what? What ails you?'

Rhiann sucked desperately at the air, clung to every wisp of it. Abruptly, the dizziness that had risen up ebbed away, and the night leaped into focus: firelight flickering on Linnet's face; the ragged music of pipe, flute and drum; the raucous cries of the people. Even the cloying scent of the roast boar was welcome to Rhiann, for it meant fire and warmth, that the sucking, freezing sea had been no more than a vision.

Rhiann shook her head as she coughed, the hawthorn crown on her brow scattering its pale blossoms. Then she forced herself straight. 'I am well, aunt. A moment of dizziness, that is all. The *saor* . . .'

Linnet turned to take a cup of mead from Eithne, and pressed it into Rhiann's cold hands. 'Drink this,' she ordered. 'It will draw you back to your body.'

Rhiann sipped, the warmed mead trailing down her throat.

'What is wrong?' Eremon's solid presence was behind her now.

Rhiann took another deep breath, clutching the pottery cup in both hands. 'I am well,' she said, steadying her voice. 'The Source was strong this night, that is all.' She closed her eyes, concentrating on the glow of warmth between her fingers. 'Please do not worry.'

Eremon's hand stroked the hair back from Rhiann's temples. 'A fine sentiment, but quite beyond me.' He addressed Linnet now. 'I will take her back to the dun. She shouldn't be doing this when she carries the child.'

'Eremon!' Rhiann struggled to rise, her hands on her belly, which was still only a subtle swelling beneath her robes. 'I am the Ban Cré, and it is my duty to hold the Mother's light for the people. The *saor* does no harm to the child; we are both well.' She said it emphatically, holding Linnet's eyes now. This Beltaine might be their last together. She must be with her people, all of them. 'I will sit a while, and warm myself, and watch the dancing.' She turned to Eremon. 'I *won't* miss this Beltaine.'

Eremon nodded slowly, with resignation, but kept close to her for the remainder of the night, fetching her moon cakes and mead, and seating her between his legs on the valley slopes, so he could wrap his cloak around them both.

In contrast to the wild antics of the Epidii, Conaire and Caitlin and the rest of Eremon's men were subdued. They knew why Eremon had instructed Conaire to push the warriors so hard all through the long dark, why he quizzed the Epidii scouts every night, and scratched out endless new versions of his charcoal maps, poring over the lay of Alba's land.

'What do you think the Romans will do, my lord?' Rori asked later, in a low voice, tossing a dagger restlessly in his hands as he watched Eithne by the fires.

'Agricola will try to force us to face him,' Eremon answered. Rhiann was conscious of his heartbeat against her ear, the stirring of his muscles when he picked up his mead cup, the rumble of his voice. 'He knows, as I do, that neither side can ultimately win through these raids and counter raids.'

There was a long pause before Aedan said, 'How will he force us?'

From the corner of her eye, Rhiann saw the swift glance that Conaire sent Eremon.

'We don't know,' was Eremon's simple reply.

Rhiann was only half-listening, for her heart had not resumed its normal beat.

The vision she had received bore no relation to anything she had experienced before: neither the seeings on the Sacred Isle when she was younger, nor the deep connection to the Mother and the Source that she yearned for; neither the haziness of *saor*, nor the journeys to the Otherworld.

It was as if she had been *there*. Was it some aberration, someone else's stray memory that had darted between Thisworld and the Otherworld? She dismissed that. It had felt, in truth, like *her* memory, of another, lost life. And why would she receive her dream of the eagles no longer, yet suddenly receive this? If it was a message, she could see no meaning in it. If it meant she was regaining some power, she did not know why, for she had not yet fulfilled her task. In fact, only two things had changed in recent moons. One was her surrender in the Otherworld; the other was the child.

And as if in answer, Rhiann suddenly felt a delicate, queer feeling in her womb, a fluttering, like butterfly wings beating against her insides. She gasped, all her racing thoughts forgotten, and her hand cupped the swelling under her cloak.

The gasp was so faint that Eremon and Conaire remained oblivious. Only Caitlin heard, her small face rosy in the firelight, peeping out from the circle of Conaire's arms. And when Caitlin met Rhiann's gaze, her eyes were shining.

Eremon waited only long enough for the worst effects of the Beltaine mead to wear off, before he dragged all the warriors back to the training field the day after the festival.

Yet as Rhiann returned from the riverbank that afternoon, a damp bag of lily tubers and comfrey leaves looped across her chest, she glanced up to the inner palisade in case he was there. Eremon had resumed his own training, and command of the warriors with Conaire and Lorn, but he often broke away to climb the crag, and there observe the war games from above.

Coming through the Moon Gate, Rhiann carefully climbed the stairs to the staked wall built on the rock. '*Cariad*.' Nestling up behind Eremon, she rubbed the back of his neck, and reached around to kiss his jaw. 'I see you thinking much, but resting little.'

Eremon kept his eyes fixed on the men below. 'There will be little rest from now on. *I* cannot afford it, at least.' The day was overcast, with a threatening dark bank of clouds rolling in from the sea, which is what had driven Rhiann back inside. The cold, gusting wind was now drying the sweat on Eremon's sleeveless tunic and bare arms. He had obviously been training hard, making up for lost time.

'You cannot afford to become ill, either, from pushing yourself too much.' Rhiann followed Eremon's gaze, because he didn't seem to be listening to her. Across the river meadow, Conaire and Lorn were now gesturing angrily at each other, Lorn from his chariot, Conaire on foot.

Yet while in the past Conaire would have probably put an end to the argument with his fists – and laughed while he did it – now he reacted as only Eremon would, folding his arms and planting his feet, calm authority written into the line of his shoulders. At last Lorn threw up his hands, spun the chariot with an expert flick of the reins, and tore back up the field to rejoin his men, mud flying grandly from his wheels. Without another glance, Conaire turned back to his foot warriors, directing them in another tight, wheeling formation.

Rhiann sighed and leaned her arms on the palisade, stretching her aching back. 'I don't understand why Lorn still acts this way, after all that has happened.'

'Do you not? He has his eye on the aftermath of this war, wife, that is all. He gave me his oath, but he must be seen to challenge me as well, or be thought weak by those he rules.'

Rhiann threw her hands up. 'Men! I cannot see women getting themselves into such a muddle.'

Yet Eremon did not respond to her teasing, and there was a frown between his brows now, as his agitated fingers tapped the oak stakes. Rhiann placed a gentle hand on his shoulder. 'Tell me,' she said.

'You have enough to carry,' Eremon replied grimly.

Rhiann shifted the bag across her, and patted the swelling. 'We are your family, babe and I. All fears must be faced together now.'

Eremon kissed her fingers, his eyes still veiled. 'You know them well. Agricola will come, he must come, this season. I feel it. We will, the gods willing, have an army to match his. All I need to know, and decide, is how the pieces will be moved across the board.'

'Yet there is still something else,' Rhiann said quietly.

Eremon sighed, his eyelids flickering shut for a moment. 'Where is the quiet, plump little cow-herder's daughter when I need her?'

'You mean the one who never asks you anything? The one who bores you silly?'

'Aye, that one.' Amusement warmed Eremon's eyes.

Rhiann smiled sweetly. 'This is not very informative, Eremon.'

Eremon grunted in exasperation, and gripped the palisade. 'Saying it aloud seems some kind of defeat . . .'

'What is it?' Rhiann demanded, her patience wearing thin, the wind cold on her drying dress.

Eremon raised his chin; Rhiann saw the resignation clearly in his eyes. 'I think we must abandon Dunadd.' As Rhiann drew in her breath, he added hastily, 'Only for this season, not for ever. I know Agricola will take a stand, but not where. If our fighting force was mobile, we could react much quicker.'

Closing her eyes, Rhiann saw a flash of Dunadd as she had once seen it in a vision: an empty, grass-smooth mound. Her throat suddenly ached.

'Dunadd is a target,' Eremon continued. 'Our men would move more freely and fight more whole-heartedly if they knew their loved ones were safe, and it means we will not have to leave warriors to guard it, either.' At last he glanced sidelong at Rhiann, plainly apprehensive.

She took a deep breath. 'I agree.'

'You do?'

'Yes. Agricola has struck at Dunadd twice now, and you cannot afford to be concerned for us when you are so far away.' She looked directly at Eremon, his relieved smile going some way to easing the barb lodged in her chest. 'It makes sense, Eremon. Calgacus's people took to the mountains last year. We can, too.'

He was watching her closely now. 'Can we?'

Rhiann clasped his hand, for her own fingers felt so cold. 'Yes. We can survive in the warm season; survive and be safe. After all, you say this war will not be fought in the hills, but in the open.' Rhiann bit her lip, her eyes fixed on the village below, its pall of cooking smoke blown into long streamers by the wind. 'It is just . . . as my dream comes no more, there is no guidance there from the Mother.' She shivered, and leaned into his side. 'I will follow what you say.'

Eremon drew back to look down at her, squeezing her fingers. 'Rhiann. The abandonment of Dunadd I must leave to you.'

Samana's mutterings were shattered by a violent oath, as the bone needle missed the edge of her hem and stabbed her finger. She cursed again, and sucked at the bead of blood that appeared. '*Whore-son* . . .' She glared down at the needle, gleaming quite innocently now among the folds of her dress.

Sewing! Samana had never done her own sewing, but as the supply of servants and bolts of cloth had abruptly dried up since her banishment, there was no other way to keep her two dresses in some kind of repair. As if called forth by her curses, the dark, greasy head of Agricola's body-slave appeared around the doorway of the bed chamber. 'Lady,' he murmured, his fat, sleek body following the head.

'What?' Samana cocked one sharp eye at him from the bed. She and the slave had at last formed an uneasy alliance, after some years of profound hatred on his part, and condescension on hers. Yet now, after this winter, the little fool had seen for himself the depth of control Samana wielded over his master. It was bizarre that at the very moment Samana lost her own tribal power, the slave decided to court her favour.

'The soldiers are massing on the parade ground for inspection. The others have arrived. All of them.'

Samana's finger popped from her mouth with a small, sucking noise. 'All?'

The Britannia legions had arrived back from winter quarters days ago, and Agricola's missing men from the east were also expected from Eboracum by sea. So, they must have arrived. Trust Agricola not to think of informing Samana of a group inspection. Well, she wasn't missing that. She had sacrificed much to bring this about.

Samana threw down her torn dress, and groped for her cloak, hanging on a peg near the bed. 'Perhaps,' she took a breath, 'perhaps you would escort me.' She tried not to make it a question, but an assumption, verging on a command. Luckily, the slave grinned, his plump cheeks bunching up like a squirrel's. He would not be able to go to the parade ground alone, and neither would she.

With a peek outside, Samana saw that though it was a cool, windy day, the sun was bright in a clear sky. Pausing at a chest of her own belongings, she extracted her parasol, the Greek fancy Agricola had given her years ago. When he gifted her with things. When she had information to give him.

Crushing that line of thought, Samana flicked the parasol open and took to the path outside, the slave trotting in her wake. The parade ground was on the flat land to the south of the camp, and while they passed few soldiers on the pathway, when they reached the meadow Samana realized why. Instantly she was frozen to the spot under the gate, barely able to breathe.

For never in her life had Samana seen anything to match the spectacle of a Roman army, 20,000 strong. She had seen the detachments of the legions numbering a few thousand, even a whole legion of 5,000, but not this.

The sun spilled down with abandon, its eager rays glittering on thousands of lance-blades, helmets and segmented breastplates; leaping from sword-tip to shield-boss, the brass disks of the *signum* poles, the bronze eagle standards standing proud above their massed legions. The coats of the Iberian horses gleamed among the cavalry, the mail shirts of the barbarian auxiliaries rippled as if alive, and the banners of fur that crested their helmets and lances ruffled in the breeze.

All had come, just as that snivelling brat Tacitus said they would. Samana still hated him, but she could not hate what he had wrought. She could do little but gaze, feasting her eyes on the streaming scarlet cloaks, the feather crests and bronze-tipped parade armour that the officers wore, high on their shining horses.

The light of the reflected iron was the glitter of conquest, and conquest was Samana's passage out of this cold, backward land. These weapons were the doorway to her new life. So she gulped down the sweet saliva that surged in her mouth, drawing deep lungfuls of the scents of churned mud, male sweat, oiled leather and horses. Her heartbeats shook her whole body, and there was a warmth between her legs, a loosening, as she thought, not of the fervour with which Agricola was sure to take her this night, but of cool Roman halls, perfumed baths and delicate foods fed to her by slaves. It was all waiting for her to pluck, like some ripe, exotic fruit. And pluck it she would, and devour it, then lick the juice from her chin.

Now Samana glimpsed Agricola himself, stepping down the lines on his horse, the feathered crest on his gilt parade helmet rippling. He wore a blinding white tunic edged in purple, and over that a polished breastplate and fringed leather apron, with a scarlet cloak pinned on one shoulder.

In this last year, Samana had seen Agricola furious, excited and lustful. Yet now, in the set of his shoulders, the quick movement of his hands on the reins, she saw more than he could ever reveal in his eyes. And why would he *not* look as though the sun itself had risen in his face? Who would not think himself a god, at the head of this army?

As Agricola drew nearer, to her surprise and satisfaction he turned his head, catching her eye. And even though the curving plates of his helmet masked his true expression, Samana felt the stab of lust that pierced her where she stood. She drew back a little, her legs trembling. He was well within her control again. She knew it, with all the certainty of her sex magic. This man, holding this power in his hands, had been hard to win, but she had done it.

And this magnificent army, arrayed before her as if *she* were its queen, would crush the Alban rebels who had dared to scorn her. All the land would be won for her, and all those who had opposed or ignored her would be given painful deaths, or sold into slavery. And then, when it was done, and the land cleansed of her kin by fire and sword – why, then she would leave it behind for ever, to take up her life of luxury in Rome.

It was so close now, for Agricola had his men. And she had him.

Samana suddenly felt the stickiness of blood still oozing from her stabbed finger. She put it in her mouth and sucked it, savouring the taste.

Rhiann squatted awkwardly by the pit. Carefully, she scooped some of the barley grains out with a bone spoon and rubbed them between her fingers. By some mysterious process, stored grain in clay pits did not grow mouldy, and she was relieved to see the same success repeated in this pit. The grains were clean and smelled earthy, with a touch of malt.

Rhiann rose, looking at the women gathered around her. 'Thank the Mother; this is whole as well. We will be needing all of it, so if you run out of baskets, Aldera is supervising the collection of pots of various kinds in the storehouse by the pier. We need to empty these other two pits in three days.'

As the women clustered around the hole in the ground, stooping to their task, Rhiann turned away, with Eithne trotting at her heel.

It was a difficult season in which to evacuate large numbers of people.

The crops were growing, but far from ripe, which meant they would need to abandon their fields, depending on how long the threat lasted. Luckily, there were many pits with grain tithed from the past five years of harvest.

Rhiann tried not to think what the lack of crops and cattle might mean to surviving the next long dark. One thing at a time, she reminded herself. 'Have you been to the dairy sheds today?' she asked Eithne.

Eithne nodded and shifted the basket of greens in her arms, a mix of nettle, elder buds, sorrel, bracken, borage and chickweed. These could not be preserved, and Rhiann had instructed the women to gather as much as possible to feed their children before they left the dun. 'Milk is starting to flow in from the other duns, lady. Caitlin and Fola said the girls are coming along very well with the cheeses; Bran's sons and the carpenter's whole family are putting together the frames.'

'Good.'

They entered the storehouses now, the cool dimness redolent with the scents of salt and herbs and smoked flesh. Despite the humped barrels of pickled meat, and the salted sides of beef that swayed against the rafters in the breeze, this storehouse was nearly depleted after the long dark. Those taking refuge in the farther duns and homesteads could access meat from the herds on the hoof. Yet the warband would need provisioning as well.

Rhiann tapped a nail on her teeth. 'We need meat cakes for the men, to take into the field. Which means smoking more sides of beef, and rendering more pig fat. Berries we can do little about. We will have to take every woman's dry stores.' She turned in a slow circle, as if the stores might just magically appear if she wished hard enough. 'Perhaps honey would replace the berries.'

'I'll give the orders, lady,' Eithne said. 'Cattle and pigs for slaughter, then preserving. Honey and berry stores. Baking of meat cakes.' She smiled. 'I know how.'

Rhiann gazed at her in surprise. Now approaching sixteen, Eithne had grown physically this past year, but that was not the change Rhiann saw now. It was more in the set of her head on its slender neck, the way she no longer hunched, or peeked out from behind her black hair. Then Rhiann remembered all Eithne had gone through, and recognized the new steadiness in her eyes, the firmer chin, for what it was.

'I am small,' Eithne admitted, blushing only slightly beneath Rhiann's scrutiny. 'But the women heed my orders, as do the men.'

'Do they?' Rhiann raised both eyebrows. 'And why is that?'

The flush along Eithne's cheekbones deepened, and she fingered the new strand of blue-glass beads at her neck, a gift from Rori. 'I've learned how to speak to them from listening to you.'

Rhiann hid a smile, suddenly amused at the thought of her own commanding tone issuing from Eithne's slight body. Then her smile faded, and she placed her hand softly on the girl's shoulder. 'I have the utmost faith in you, Eithne.' She nudged her out into the sun. 'And when is Rori going to capture this prize for himself? Perhaps it is he I need to be hurrying!'

'Oh, no, lady!' Eithne's arms tightened around the basket, her dark brows drawn together. 'He wishes to discharge his duty to his prince, he said, before he'd take a wife. We are still young, after all.'

Yet Rhiann's attention had been caught now by Lorn, racing bareback on one of his black chariot ponies across the causeway and up to the gates of Dunadd. He and Conaire had been busy training on the field; Conaire with the foot warriors; Lorn with the chariot teams.

Then she saw Eremon, who had been briefing the guards in the gatetower and was now taking the stairs to the ground two at a time, on his way to meet Lorn. Without a word, Rhiann handed her own basket to Eithne, and crossed the yard as fast as she could with her new awkward gait, arriving at Eremon's side just as Lorn thundered up, the pony snorting and rearing.

'What is it?' Eremon's voice was admirably calm, but Rhiann could sense the tension in his stance and jaw.

'A rider has just come down the northern road from Calgacus,' Lorn informed Eremon, his grey eyes dancing with a fierce joy, his pony shaking its head so the enamelled bridle rang. '*All* of the tribes, bar the Lugi, sent messengers to him as soon as the weather broke.'

Eremon seemed to freeze.

'They have sworn to the alliance, at last.' Lorn grinned and rose in his saddle, holding his spear aloft, clenched hard in his hand. The fox-tail on its sheath streamed out in the wind. 'Sword brother, we have our army!'

BOOK SIX
SUNSEASON, AD 83

Chapter 62

The altar before the kneeling form of Agricola was crusted with the blood of many sacrifices. Before him, set into niches of the mud wall, stood the statues of Mars, god of war, and king of all the gods, Jupiter. Agricola's hands, spread before his bowed head, were also sticky with the blood of the ram that he insisted on sacrificing every day to ensure good victories and ward away the evils that had befallen him these past two years. The fragrant smoke of the burning incense wreathed his face, as the *haruspex*, who had been joined by another this spring, stood chanting in the shadows.

Yet the peace Agricola was enjoying in the temple was already being disturbed by the shouts of men outside, the rumble of carts and whinnies of horses. With calmer weather, a constant stream of supplies and messengers had been coming and going from the civilian towns and legionary headquarters further south. The subdued, settled part of the province was slowly coming alive again, and though Agricola preferred to spend his days as a soldier, not a glorified tax collector, the rest of Britannia, unfortunately, still needed his attention.

As he emerged from the temple precinct now, one man, who had been throwing dice in the shadow of the walls, detached himself from the other soldiers by leaping to his feet. This claimed Agricola's attention, as did the nervous agitation of the man's hands.

'Sir,' the soldier said, saluting him, his crested helmet under his arm, 'I bear a message from your home in Eboracum.'

Agricola stood still, arrested by the man's choice of words: *your home.* His tongue worked on a stray drop of ram's blood that spattered his lips during the sacrifice. He felt strangely unwilling to meet the soldier's eyes. 'Accompany me to my quarters,' he ordered at last, ignoring the curious gazes of the other soldiers lounging by the temple gates.

Within the safety of his room, Agricola turned to face the messenger.

'Well?' he barked. 'Give me the scroll then! Or is it a tablet you have? Quickly now!' He held out his hand.

The messenger gulped, sliding an unobtrusive finger up to wipe sweat from his upper lip. 'It is no scroll,' he offered, his voice quavering slightly. Then he cleared his throat and stood straighter, his heels together.

Agricola received the news of the death of his son without even a flicker of an eyelash.

The soldier passed on the brief words with which he had been charged, and waited to be dismissed, but the dismissal was not forthcoming. His commander did not move. Carefully, in the now eerie silence of the room, the soldier saluted, stammered his condolences and slipped away.

Slowly, Agricola turned and looked down at the vellum map spread before him – a crude arrangement of lines that sketched out Alba's eastern coastline, its south-west and south-east reaches, and a vague indication of its central mountains. His hands gripped the edge of the table. That land had taken his strength, his peace of mind, the very heat of his blood. That land – its cold, damp breath – *had taken his only son.*

As the table crashed to the floor, maps and pens and inkwells flying, Agricola heard a movement at the door to his bed chamber. He spun on his heel, the blood shrieking in his ears, and his eyes focused slowly on Samana, who was lounging against the doorframe. Her face was heavy with sleep, the lids swollen, her eyes blinking languorously. Agricola's gaze ranged lower, seeing, as if for the first time, the perverse lushness of Samana's body, the curves and hollows and swellings that laid before his outraged eyes, an obscene parody of Alba itself.

In the gleam of saliva on her parted lips, he saw the countless streams that wound over this land, entwining and trapping his soldiers. In the soft rising of her chest, he sensed Alba's foul mists and fogs, smelled the rotting stench of its marshes. Samana's breasts and hips and the cleft of her sex beckoned him, drawing him to lose himself just as his men had lost their way in Alba's treacherous valleys and twisting glens.

Agricola's fists gradually clenched at his sides. Despite his will, he had allowed this abomination to seduce him. He had fallen into her exotic folds, lolled in greedy debauchery while his son sickened and died. With some part of himself, Agricola had known he would have to pay for that winter where he lost himself in lust, and now he knew the price. The gods had exacted their revenge.

Alba had made him weak, drawn from him false fears and false bravado. It had tantalized him into the sins of doubt and, on occasion, pride. Worst of all, it had led him to forget that he was Agricola. It, Alba – *she, this harlot* – had made him forget, in a cascade of sight and scent and touch, that he was Roman.

'My lord?' Samana's voice was low; it slid into a man's loins like a serpent's tongue. 'What ails you? What has happened?'

When Agricola didn't answer, struck with an overwhelming horror at the foulness he had let into his body, his bed, his very self, she came forward and tried to take his arm, to press against him as she had so many times before. 'No!' Agricola spat the word with disgust, with loathing, and the blow of his fist that came with it sent Samana reeling to the floor.

There she lay and looked up at him, white with shock, a hand to her bloody mouth. But in the fall her skirt had been dragged up, and her honeyed legs were gleaming against the earthen floor, the black patch of hair between them still taunting him with its moistness.

Enraged, Agricola stood astride her and yanked her clothing down, covering what disgusted him so, and when she tried to speak, to rise, he only struck her again across the ear, and again, until she lay still with terrified eyes, and said nothing.

By nightfall, the entire camp knew of what had befallen Agricola's heir. The commander himself took refuge in the temple once more, and did not emerge for two days.

No one could discern any sound from within, and the only movements from outside were the ten rams and two oxen that were led through the gates as sacrifices for the boy's soul.

Samana stood with the growing crowd of soldiers who, on breaks from their duties, began to cluster about the temple gates. They kept themselves busy by debating what would happen, what was happening, yet by the end of the first day the only visible sign was the thick pall of blue smoke that rose above the temple, tainting the air with the sweet scent of roasting flesh, and the acrid stench of entrails.

Swathed in a veil to hide her bruises, Samana kept to a safe place in the cold shadows of the wall, trying to let the soldiers' rough talk flow over her like water over a rock. Trying not to think what Agricola's outburst meant for her.

At last, at sunset on the second day, the two sacrificers emerged, their white robes untouched by blood, their faces stern. When Agricola himself appeared behind them, Samana understood, with a plunging horror, just why those priests were so clean. In the dying light of the sunset, Agricola's face, throat, bare arms and feet were drenched with blood, his robe stiff and dried with gore. Within that encrustation, the whites of his eyes shone out.

Around Samana, the soldiers fell into a deathly hush, those by the gate drawing away to let their commander pass onto the open road. He moved slowly, as if dazed, and seemed to see no one. Yet when he spoke, his voice rang out over the throng with as much authority as it had ever held. The rage was gone from it now, and yet Samana was more afraid of this calm than any blows from his hand.

'Command my legates and tribunes to attend me,' Agricola directed his secretary, hovering by his elbow. 'Summon also the *primus pilus* of each legion. I want them in my quarters in one hour.'

'Do you not wish to bathe first, sir?' the secretary suggested, trying not to eye his commander's filth-encrusted robe.

Agricola turned slowly to stare at him and, although Samana could not see the look, the officious secretary froze. 'Call them to me,' Agricola said again, his voice like winter. 'They will all attend me by nightfall.'

Samana shrank back against the temple wall as Agricola passed, shivering uncontrollably, though the sunlit days had warmed the mud brick. She did not understand what had happened, but her belly roiled with a sick fear. As the other soldiers drifted away, she stood and pondered what to do. She did not wish to be near Agricola, and the only other men with whom she had enjoyed discreet liaisons were being called to attend their commander. Biting her lip, at last she came to a decision, and moved off down the path. One of the tribunes was very young and greedy, and cared enough about his position to remain silent on the subject of her occasional visits, when she sought the company of a firmer body.

She would hide there in his room until he returned, at which time she would draw from him, with her lips and hands, what had transpired in the command meeting.

Deep into the night, Agricola's quarters were still a hive of activity, bustling with men arriving and leaving, their orders in hand, noisy with calls for wine and food, and the raised voices of his officers as they pored over the maps, debating and weighing plans.

The edge of the sun was just rising over the eastern ground between the camp and the flat waters of the estuary when Agricola was at last done, and at last alone. He stood in his outer doorway, watching the feeble rays creep over the camp palisade, outlining the tile roofs of the new barracks, gilding the apex of each of the thousands of tents, gleaming wet with dew, and the pale dome of the bath-house. Far away, the mist rising from the Forth obscured any glimpse of the northern shore. As the sun warmed Agricola's clothes, the blood stench reawakened and, although it turned his belly, he forced himself to breathe in.

It would be a reminder, this day, of how close he had come to losing himself completely, and how deep his penance must run for the deaths of all his soldiers, and the loss of his son. It would remind him of his child's heart, beating no longer, of the outrages committed against

Roman citizens by these savages, of the vengeance that Agricola was now bound to extract from this land, with its whore of a Goddess and her lying promises.

For Agricola had been bound to this new course not only by the will of his own gods, but by the illumination that had come to him in the temple. As he slashed the artery of one great ox, and tasted hot blood running down his chin, as he drew the incense smoke deep into his lungs, searing them, all the lascivious desires that had consumed him for months had been utterly burned away. And so too, he realized then, this land Alba must burn.

A shuffle came from behind him, and he turned to see his body-slave clearing up the platters of half-eaten fowl and drained cups of wine. 'I wish you to find the Votadini whore, and bring her to me tonight,' Agricola said quietly.

The slave's eyes darted to one side.

'I do not care who she is with,' Agricola added wearily. 'It matters no more. Find her and tell the prefect Marcus to hold her in the bath-house until dusk. Then someone is to bring her here. And heat me water; I will wash now.'

Biting his lip, the slave bowed and scuttled away towards the tribunes' quarters, and Agricola turned back to the sunlit east, where Rome lay.

He had been kind and just, but like a primitive beast, Alba continued to bite the hand of friendship and peace that his empire extended. Finally, it was time for it to pay, in blood and burning, razed crops, dead women and children.

All the children of Alba, in payment for his own.

At first, Samana had raged at her confinement in the bath-house, stamping up and down, and working herself into a state of fury.

Yet after some hours, she realized she could not afford to give vent to such emotion. The only hold she had on Agricola was sexual, and it had proven a strong one so far. All this overwrought storming was making her red-cheeked and dishevelled. When she came before him, this was not what he would want to see. He valued her self-possession, her calm intelligence and her startling beauty, and these she must give him. She needed to dredge up an air of complete assurance that she was by his side, bonded to him for ever. She had to find those parts of herself despite her thudding, erratic pulse, which gave her no peace and made her feel sick.

So in the time left to her, Samana bathed her face and body in the cold pool, straightened her clothing, combed her hair, and racked her brains for any scrap of useful tactical information that she had left to offer. There was nothing. She bit her lip, wondering what lie she could fashion that would hold him. And then she remembered the burning eyes of the blood-drenched man, and she put aside thought altogether.

Eventually, two soldiers came inside for her, and Samana emerged from the bath-house into deepening dusk. As they walked with her up the path she had trod so many times before, she turned at the highest point and looked out over the basin of the Forth. The breeze was growing colder off the sea, and it lifted Samana's unbound hair, drying the dampness at the nape of her neck. She filled her lungs with it, attuning herself only to surface things.

The camp sat as a dark, rectangular scar amid the wilds of Alba, with its creeping tangles of encroaching woods and looming hills. Samana ignored what her land was telling her, and focused instead on the straight lines of tents and barracks and walls within the rigid confines of what was Roman: the smell of campfires; the whinnies of horses; the shouts of men gaming with dice.

She did not venture deeper into herself, for there her priestess senses were alert to other things, dangers and threats she did not wish to face. These prescient glimpses stirred within her, but she would not give in and examine them closely. They would make her weak and fearful, and she could not afford to be weak before him.

The room Samana entered in Agricola's quarters was more familiar than her own home. She had shivered through one winter here, on a hill exposed to the north winds, and endured the stench of men and horses through more than one summer. She could barely remember now the noises of her own dun, for the myriad sounds of Roman life had formed the background of each day for two years now.

Agricola sat at ease in one of his chairs beside the lit brazier, a bronze goblet held loosely in one hand. Lamps filled the room with warm, soft light, and beside him was a three-legged table set with a dish of oysters and a silver spoon. Samana glanced at him cautiously, and saw that he was now bathed and dressed in a simple white tunic belted with gilded leather. All trace of the bloodied madman was gone. In fact, he looked much more as she had first seen him: alert but relaxed, his hooded glance revealing nothing.

Relief trickled into Samana's heart, and her shoulders lowered. 'You sent for me, my lord?' She pitched her voice the way he liked it, rich and throaty, and was pleased to see Agricola's mouth lift at one edge.

'Come,' he said, indicating the chair next to him. 'Enjoy a cup of our finest wine; the civilized nectar you covet so much.'

Gingerly, Samana sat in the chair, a little discomfited at the formality of Agricola's manner. Then, as she drank the proffered wine, Agricola reached out and took her other hand, turning it over to stare at the glittering rings that adorned it, all gifts from him. She could read nothing in his lowered eyes as he traced fingers over the soft skin of her wrist. There, the blood beat swift and shallow; a sign of fear she could not hide.

'What do you want with me tonight?' she murmured, taking back her hand. 'How can I please you?'

Agricola smiled, eyes still lowered. 'Yes, I do want something *from* you. Something that will please me very much.'

Samana saw her chance. Resting the cup on a table by her side, she slid to her knees on the rug before him. Her hands spread themselves over his chest, and then she realized she did not recognize the tunic he wore. It was of fine linen, so fine that she could glimpse the grey hairs of his chest through its folds.

'I will do anything to please you, lord.' Samana took Agricola's hand and cupped it around her breast. 'Anything.'

Agricola's eyes met hers then, and there *was* a fire there, though unlike any she had seen in his gaze before. 'You are a woman of rare appetites, are you not?' he murmured now, drawing his hand back to his lap. 'I have discovered there is little in the bed furs that you will not do.'

Despite his throaty tone, Samana's skin pebbled with a sudden chill. 'Everything I do is to please you, my lord.' She tried to smile, though her lips stung from his earlier blows.

Yet Agricola only clicked his fingers, his eyes sliding away. 'Ay-met, come.' It was only then that Samana sensed another person in the room; someone who had been waiting in Agricola's bed chamber all along.

The huge figure blocking the doorway walked forward into the lamplight: a strange man, foreign. He was tall and almost obscenely broad, his torso naked, his loins clad only in a short, pleated linen skirt. His face was dark-skinned, his eyes black but impassive, and he kept his gaze on the wall over Agricola's head. His hulking muscles were oiled, and his arms were clasped by gold bands of a serpent design. His skirt was held with a belt of chased leather, buckled in gold, and from it hung an unsheathed dagger with a jewelled hilt.

'He is an Egyptian,' Agricola offered, dangling his cup in his fingers. 'Tacitus sent him on a ship two days ago, as a gift for me. He thought he would make an amusing body-guard.'

As Samana continued to stare at the man, mouth agape, Agricola let out a dry chuckle that did nothing to reassure her. 'Of course, I do not think these people really go around dressed like that any more; perhaps it is a jest on my son-in-law's part.'

Samana's tongue had gone dry, and there was a warning buzz in her ears. She groped for her wine cup on the table and drank deeply. 'Perhaps,' she responded woodenly, her eyes fixed on her feet.

Abruptly, Agricola leaned forward in his chair, one hand clenched in the folds of his tunic. Now she knew it was Egyptian linen – she had heard of its fineness. 'Ah, but perhaps there is something else you do not know, lady. These Egyptian soldiers are bred for height and strength, and with that comes a . . . shall we say . . . *corresponding* length and breadth of the sexual organs.'

Samana started, her cheeks flushing. 'Indeed.'

'Unless one is a eunuch; they have those, you know. Are you a eunuch, Ay-met?'

The subject in question must have shaken his head, though he was no longer within Samana's field of vision.

'Wonderful!' Agricola sat back, taking up an oyster with the silver spoon. Samana's eyes darted cautiously to his face, watching his throat as he gulped the meat. 'Then I wish to watch while this man takes his pleasure with you, Samana. That is what will light the fire in me.'

Samana's cup jerked, spilling red wine down her hand. She stared at Agricola as she quickly licked it, trying to force the sudden fear away from her face.

'You have been such an entertaining bed partner, that I find myself growing tired of our usual diversions.' Agricola shrugged one shoulder. 'I need something different.'

Samana clasped the cup firmly between her shaking fingers. *He wishes to reassert his power over me, that is all*, she thought fiercely. *He wishes to put me in my place.*

She glanced from under her lashes at the burly, silent Egyptian, his strong, corded thigh muscles gleaming with scented oil, his smooth chest rising slowly up and down with each breath. And Samana realized, with the slightest stir of perversion, that in other circumstances she would find it no burden to lie with this man, while being watched by a hundred Roman officers. But not now, for Agricola's manner was unnerving her, with its whiff of scorn underlying every word.

Trapped, Samana struggled to breathe calmly through her nose, staring hard at the rings that glittered with such mockery on her fingers. One of them was the head of Mercury, the trickster god. The other was Bacchus. Agricola had shown some private amusement when he gave her that one, though it had taken some time to wheedle the reason from the slave; that Bacchus was a god of hedonism, wine and debauchery. This was the Roman world which called to her, then, the world for which she lusted. She could hardly quail now, at its first test.

'Very well, my lord.' Abruptly, Samana stood up before she could change her mind, resting the cup back on the table. 'If it will please you.' She was a fine actress, after all.

She stood before the Egyptian, waiting until his eyes at last travelled down from the wall to rest on her. Then, holding his dark gaze, she unclasped the two brooches that held her dress, letting the soft folds of wool fall to the ground around her feet. The man's eyes roved over her nakedness almost hungrily, pausing at each breast and dropping to the cleft between her legs. He only broke this scrutiny to glance once at Agricola's face, over her shoulder.

Whatever he saw there must have encouraged him, for at last the linen of his skirt stirred as he grew hard. Samana thought about going on her knees to take him in her mouth, but knew, with a sinking feeling, that she could not. Somewhere, deep and buried in her now, she was still a queen. He must worship her – yes, that was it. He must worship her beauty.

Tossing her hair back boldly, Samana began to caress herself, her hands cupping her breasts, rubbing the nipples until they rose against her fingertips. Then she slid her palms over the curve of her hips, moving her feet slightly apart.

The Egyptian's eyes followed her hands, until she saw that his skirt was standing out from his thighs like a tent. Beneath their feet a thick rug lay, muddy from the passage of many boots, but nevertheless the only soft thing on that hard floor. To this Samana now drew the dark man, folding down to lie on her back, trying to keep her breath even as he lowered himself over her. For a moment the Egyptian paused, his weight held on his thick forearms, the sinews standing out with effort. Yet it was not her face from which he sought permission, but Agricola's. So Samana did the same, and it was Agricola's eyes she met as the first thrust came, a painful, dry entry because of the man's size, and her own fear.

At the second and third thrusts, Agricola's face remained immobile, his gaze inscrutable. He looked neither excited nor affronted, and when Samana gasped – a gasp of pain she disguised as pleasure – a mere flicker passed over his eyes.

The Egyptian was grinding faster, arching himself over so that he could reach her nipples with his mouth. He sucked on them painfully, but it only merged with the pain between her thighs, and Samana gritted her teeth against both, desperate not to cry out. The man's grunting grew deeper, and he grasped the leg of the chair for purchase, so he could drive into her harder.

Then suddenly Samana came to herself, realizing that she must excite Agricola, please him, or he would be angry. So she forced herself to moan, and clasp her legs about the thighs of the Egyptian, arching herself up to him so that his thrusts battered painfully at the gate to her womb. Gasping, she closed her eyes, seeking for some shred of desire that would ease the passage . . .

One face came to her then, a man who had stoked in her the hottest of flames. A man she hated, but whose memory could still melt her body. So Samana clung to it then, the memory of Eremon of Erin, his dark hair falling about her face, his broad back tensing beneath her hands. And mercifully she felt her cheeks flush, and the softening begin inside. Her breath, which was being pushed out of her by each thrust of the Egyptian's body, now quickened of its own accord, fluttering high in her throat.

Eremon, she repeated to herself. *Cariad* . . .

A hiss broke through Samana's trance, and her eyes flew open to see Agricola standing right above her head, his eyes glowing in the light of the lamps. 'So the whore of Alba is laid open once more, as she will always be.'

Ice suddenly flooded Samana's veins, the cold of premonition, and she clawed at the shoulders of the man impaling her. Yet he pressed down harder, his face a dark mask of determination, and when she felt the hot spurting begin within, she could only wrench her head back and glare at Agricola with fury, her throat long and exposed. 'Bastard!'

Agricola only smiled. 'Fitting isn't it, my whore?'

Then his eyes flickered over her head to gaze into the face of her attacker, and Samana gasped and pushed upwards with all her strength, as the man's oily mouth came down upon her split lip and bruised cheek. From far away, it seemed, she heard Agricola speak once more.

'Did it never occur to you, queen of traitors, that in the end you would be one risk too many?'

Samana tried to scream, choked by the writhing tongue in her throat, but it was too late. With the last of her priestess senses, long scorned, she clearly felt the dagger enter her throat, before the eternal darkness took her.

Chapter 63

The trills of the thrushes and robins rippled through the sunlit woods, along with the trickling of water into Linnet's pool. Rhiann was completely still, the cacophony of bird calls and wind in the leaves and creaking branches the only external senses penetrating her trance.

For inside, her blood was running to another tide, as the circle formed by Caitlin, Fola, Linnet and herself pulsed with warmth. The heat flowed from Caitlin's hand on her left, and out through her right hand to Fola. In between, Rhiann's whole body vibrated like one of Aedan's harp strings.

In a low voice that echoed from the rock bowl of the spring and the ridge above it, Linnet called on the Mother to bless the warriors and protect Dunadd while it lay empty.

For a long time after Linnet fell silent, Rhiann was loath to break the circle, for the warmth and sense of bonding soothed her as much as the sun, spilling over her hair from the clearing in the trees. Yet at last they all stirred and broke apart, blinking and smiling at each other. Linnet had set a stone jug of mead to cool in the water, and now she filled five ash cups, and poured one out as an offering to the spring.

Rhiann took her cup and sat on the lip of the pool. 'Aunt?' she ventured, brushing fallen birch leaves to spiral across the still water. 'Have you decided where you yourself will go while the men are away?'

'Go?' Linnet turned, her brows drawing together. The sunlight struck sparks of copper in her hair. 'I intend to go nowhere, child. If our people are safe in the high duns then I will certainly be safe here on this mountain.' She sipped her mead, her eyes sharp over the lip of the cup. 'In fact, you all could come and stay with me.'

Rhiann's gaze lifted to Caitlin's, who was biting her lip, her mead untouched. Meeting Rhiann's eye, Caitlin, rather unhelpfully, did nothing but screw up her face.

Rhiann sighed and twirled her cup in her hands, mustering a smile for Linnet. 'Actually, aunt, Caitlin and I have decided to follow the men.' Just as she had as a child, Rhiann fixed her eyes intently on her feet, waiting for the explosion.

Yet Linnet herself was silent.

'*What?*' Fola erupted, her cup falling to the mossy ground and spilling its contents. Ignoring the splashes on her skirt, she looked wildly from Rhiann to Linnet, just as Caitlin chose the moment to leap in.

'Mother,' Caitlin said, stepping forward to Linnet, 'I have come to ask you if you will take Gabran for me.' She smiled weakly. 'He is weaned now, he takes after his father in his love of solid food.' She squared her shoulders. 'Though my heart aches to leave him, we must be practical. Aside from my own concerns as a mother, he may be the next king – we cannot risk him.'

'Yet you will risk yourselves!' Fola glared down at Rhiann, trembling. 'I cannot understand – you are safest here!'

'Peace, daughter,' Linnet murmured, laying a hand on Fola's arm. 'It is love that drives them, and it overrides such matters as safety.'

Relief flooded Rhiann, and she rested her cup on the spring's lip. 'I confess we thought you would fight us, aunt, though our minds are set. We have talked about it at length, together.'

'And what do your husbands think of this?' Fola demanded, her hands clenched by her sides. 'I cannot believe they will support such folly.'

Rhiann and Caitlin exchanged rueful glances. 'They do not know yet,' Caitlin confessed, raising her chin. 'But we think that their way lies dark before them, and they will need the light we can give – at the end.'

Fola's own chin jutted out, her calm face set with a hardness Rhiann had never seen before, and she drew her priestess cloak closer as if seeking its strength. 'And what about your child, Rhiann? How can you go riding about the land at six moons along – into war! It is ridiculous!'

Rhiann appealed to Linnet with her eyes now, and to her surprise her aunt seemed to rouse herself from some deep thought. 'The early days are more dangerous,' Linnet pronounced. 'If she takes care, she will be well.'

Fola gasped at Linnet's response, obviously confused. Then she snapped her mouth shut and crossed her arms. 'Then I am going, too. She needs my help.'

'Old friend.' Rhiann rose and took Fola by her elbows. 'You must stay here with my aunt. If anything were to happen to us, I want my people to have the benefit of your skills and wisdom. There is little left of the Sisterhood; we must keep it safe.'

'If you are so concerned about preserving all that, then you would do best to save yourself, Rhiann! Your people need *you*!'

'That may be true,' Rhiann countered gently, 'but I have risked much for Eremon. Nerida and Setana told me to open to his love, and now that I have unleashed that power, I cannot turn my back on it.' Fola's whole body was trembling, and her dark eyes welled with hurt. When Rhiann saw what lay there, she simply stepped forward and wrapped her arms around her friend, foreheads touching, nose to nose. 'Bramble I used to call you once – blackberry eyes. Do you remember?'

'I remember,' Fola whispered. 'And I called you Little Seal because you loved the sea.'

'And then we lost each other,' Rhiann murmured, 'in the darkness that fell over me. Through Eremon I have found that light again, and I cannot let it go.' She pulled back and held Fola at arm's length. 'I feel that if I follow it, if I hold to that love, then I *will* find safety. I share this with you, as one priestess to another, and ask you to accept it.'

Fola's eyes shone with a film of tears. 'Let me come,' she whispered.

'No.' Linnet now drew herself straight, her eyes commanding as they rested on Fola. 'I have seen some of what will come, and child, you are not there.'

'Seen it?' Rhiann immediately turned to Linnet. 'When?'

Linnet breathed in deeply, and let it out, her shoulders lowering. 'At your birth I saw it.'

'My *birth*?' Rhiann strode to her, excited. 'What are you talking about? Why did you say nothing?'

Linnet's eyes flickered with something that resembled guilt. 'I could not be sure it would come to pass.'

Rhiann was suddenly breathing hard. 'That is why you won't argue with us, isn't it, aunt? You know we must be there.'

Linnet's throat bobbed as she swallowed, and at last she nodded. 'I saw you, Rhiann, on a great battlefield. Not Caitlin, not then, for of course I thought her lost to me. But you, I saw clearly.'

Instantly, Caitlin was on her feet, her fair braids flinging out as she grasped Linnet's arm. 'And our men, mother? What did you see of Conaire?'

'Yes!' Rhiann echoed. 'What of Eremon?'

Yet Linnet's palms came up to hold them at bay, and abruptly she turned to look out over the wind-rippled surface of the pool, her face hidden by the shadows. 'Of the men I saw nothing,' she said. 'I am sorry.'

Although the people were grieved to abandon their homes at Dunadd, they did it without question. For days Rhiann and Fola laid offerings in pits before doorways, burying the household gods, closing the houses and sprinkling the lintels with sacred water.

Aldera and Bran's house was the last. With a blessing, Rhiann laid a joint of pig meat, some loom weights and one of Bran's finer arm-rings in the pit before the door. She then recited the ritual words slowly, her hand gripping the spade, for the strange lurching visions were coming more and more now since Beltaine, slipping in almost between each thought.

A few days ago while baking bannocks, it was as if the house around Rhiann shifted subtly, and she was suddenly *somewhere else*, clad in furs, cracking mussels over a fire – she actually tasted the salty meat on her tongue. And just now a brief flicker had come of a red wool tent that bucked in a searing wind, unlike anything in Alba.

'Lady?' Rhiann had been unmoving for so long that Aldera was obviously concerned.

'I am . . . well.' Flushing, Rhiann took Aldera's arm to straighten, pushing that odd, dizzy feeling and the roaring away. 'The offering will keep the house safe for your return,' Rhiann murmured, smiling at Aldera with sympathy.

'So it will,' Aldera agreed, sighing. 'Hush,' she ordered, when her youngest began to wail in her arms, and then, 'I hope your own birth goes easy, Rhiann.'

Rhiann did not miss the lack of her formal address, and it warmed her, for Aldera had known her since she was born. 'Thank you. I pray so, too.'

Aldera's eyes were suspiciously moist as she reached for the hand of her next eldest child, a boy lingering against a broken plough-share in the yard. 'Come, laddie,' she murmured, and set her chin resolutely towards the gate, where her kin waited with their carts. She did not look back.

Chilled despite the bright sun, Rhiann stood for a moment in the yard behind the open village gate. Most of the roundhouses were already deserted, as people moved away from Dunadd in family groups, going north, east and south, following the winds.

The paths between the houses and workshops had fallen silent, devoid of all the sounds that had cradled Rhiann since she was young: dogs barking and children wailing; cook pots clanking; the thunk of axes and hammers; men arguing; women scolding. Only the chanting of the druids floated down from the shrine, for Declan and his brethren would ritually close the King's Hall, supervise the battle offerings and bless the warband on departure.

Yet departure for where? Eremon had not decided yet.

A pang of grief welled up from deep inside Rhiann, and she wrapped her arms about her chest, allowing it to pool in her heart, for once not forcing it back down. There was no one to see her, after all, and her grief was the proper way to honour Dunadd, she realized suddenly, her tears a blessing for all who had lived here.

Yet she was given little peace for such musings. The watch horn suddenly blasted out from the walkway above, startling her, and Rhiann wiped her cheeks with both hands and composed herself, walking a few steps to peer under the tower. Eremon was coming over the causeway on Dòrn. He had been gone for four days, visiting the scouts on the eastern borders, and Rhiann strode forward eagerly to greet him.

Eremon's boots and trousers were splashed with the mud of hard riding, as were those of Conaire, Rori and the five other horsemen who had accompanied him. Yet what Rhiann saw in Eremon's face as he dismounted seemed to darken the bright sun. She glanced at Rori, his freckles standing out like drops of blood on his white cheeks. Conaire's features, too, were closed in and set.

With no word, Eremon threw Dòrn's reins at Rori, then his fingers closed hard around Rhiann's elbow as he immediately steered her up the stairs to the top of the palisade. There he released her, gripping the pointed oak stakes instead of her arm, looking out over the river meadow.

'What is it?' Rhiann said at last, for Eremon seemed reluctant to speak, or even look at her. His knuckles were pale ridges beneath his tightened skin.

'The scouts were reporting people fleeing over the mountains from the east and south,' Eremon said at last, something held in check in his voice. 'They are Damnonii tribesmen – and Venicones.'

'Venicones!' Rhiann had only ever heard this tribe mentioned along with curses, for they had been among the first to ally with Rome four years ago. 'Why would they come west?'

'They were driven.' Eremon spoke so softly Rhiann had to crane to hear him. Suddenly, he turned to face her, white-lipped with fury, his eyes dark with anguish. 'Let me tell you all at once,' he forced out. 'For then I cannot speak it again.'

Sheltering her throat with her hand, Rhiann nodded dumbly. And so, in a slightly trembling voice Eremon told her, the terrible words flowing straight from his fathomless gaze into hers.

The entire Roman army from all Britannia had been gathered, and was on the move – yet this time burning every league of ground, razing every homestead, byre, hut and hill-fort. No one, not even allies, were being spared, from the Votadini lands north. And no mercy was being given. After crushing the desperate warriors, the Romans were skewering children, even babes in the womb, with lances. Old ones were cut down by sword or arrow as they stumbled away. Women were being ravished, their throats cut.

The Romans were leaving nothing to be salvaged once the army passed.

They had left nothing for Alba.

When Eremon had finished, Rhiann's fingers were pressing into her throat so hard she coughed, the spasm turning into a gag of nausea that she swallowed down. It stung her, as tears welled and slid from under her closed eyelids, down her cheek and over the back of her hand. Yet even with eyes closed, Rhiann couldn't shut out the visions Eremon had conjured.

'What does this mean?' she whispered eventually.

'It is Agricola's way to force us into open battle,' Eremon said slowly. 'If we do not stand up to him, he is making it clear there will be nothing left and no quarter given, even to the innocent. He will not rest until it is done, and by all reports he has gathered an army more than double the size of anything unleashed on us before.'

Rhiann had begun to tremble. 'And you now have your own army.' *Because of me. Because of the Sisters. I brought Eremon to this.*

Without an army of his own, Eremon could not possibly have chosen to fight such a force. They would have fled, whether he hated to do so or not. They could have gone into hiding. Yet that would never happen now, because the Sisters sacrificed themselves, and because Rhiann had taken their story into every dun across the land.

Rhiann rubbed her eyes with balled fists, as Eremon took her arm. 'Rhiann, we will need more than just our own warriors. We must gather every man that can hold a spear, any weapon at all. Even the farmers, the herders, the fishermen must come with us.'

'Where will you go?'

'The Roman force is in Venicones lands, directly east,' Eremon's voice was bleak. 'They cannot cross the mountains, so they are heading north, as they did before, yet more slowly because of the destruction they are wreaking. We need to gather our forces at Calgacus's dun, then come down from the north and meet them.' His hands moved up Rhiann's arms, gently pulling her fists from her eyes. A kiss touched her forehead. 'Our parting has come sooner than I wished for,' he whispered brokenly.

Rhiann gulped a deep breath and opened her eyes, groping for his hands. 'No, *cariad*. There is no need for partings.'

'What do you mean?' Eremon's frown descended over his face like a thundercloud.

Rhiann brought his hands to her lips. 'I am coming with you.'

The cloud in Eremon's face abruptly cut off all remaining light, and he reared back as if she had slapped him. '*No!* You and the child must be safe—'

'You have just been telling me that nowhere is safe!'

'Yet I will not invite that danger by flinging you in the path of a Roman army!'

Rhiann cupped Eremon's cheeks with her hands. His jaw was like iron; his eyes even harder. 'The safest place for me is with you, Eremon.

Caitlin and I are coming with you and Conaire to Calgacus. Aldera and Bran and the druids will lead the women.' Eremon swore, his teeth grinding as he tried to pull his face away, yet Rhiann summoned every shred of strength to hold him still. 'I'm not letting you leave me behind.'

'*You* seek to order *me*?' Eremon gripped her hands and tore them from his skin. 'I will remind you of who leads this warband.'

'It is not a matter of leading, or authority!'

'No? What is it, then?' he cried. 'Foolishness? Mule-headed female stubbornness?'

'Eremon.' Rhiann raised her chin with dignity, curling her palms about her elbows. 'It is a matter of love,' she said quietly. 'We must face what will come, together. Triumph together, or die together. You know in your heart this is right.'

A muscle leaped in Eremon's neck; his eyes narrowed with anguish. 'Gods, Rhiann, of course I do not want to be parted from you! But how could I forgive myself if you were harmed?'

'It will most likely come down to one battle; you told me so yourself. We will wait out of sight. If you are defeated, then there is no safe place for us in Alba anyway.'

'That is not true!' Eremon burst out. 'You could run far into the mountains. Gods, what if you fell into Agricola's hands?'

'I've already told you, I won't run!' Rhiann held his hot, angry gaze with her own, unflinching. 'No one has the right to tell another how to face their own death. And have you forgotten I am Ban Cré? Have you forgotten my dream, and how we lead the people *together*? Have you forgotten my duty to *them*?'

That hit home; Eremon's eyes darted wildly around as if seeking some way out. Then to Rhiann's surprise he gave a loud yelp of frustration and violently kicked the palisade with one muddy boot. From the force of the kick, everything he had heard that day had gone into it. The timbers shivered, and the guards further down the walkway glanced up, startled. Yet Eremon ignored them, turning his back on Rhiann and gripping the stakes again.

She gave him a few moments, until his ragged breathing slowed, and the blood rushed back into the white bones of his hands. Then Rhiann slipped her arms about his waist, curving into him as much as the baby would allow, her thighs against his. She could feel the trembling running through his body. 'The time for being ruled by our heads is fast receding, *cariad*,' she whispered. 'The Goddess is love, and if we cling to love, She will help us to our path.'

Leaning up on her toes to peer over Eremon's shoulder, Rhiann saw his eyes close, and another oath pass over his lips, silent this time. For a moment the battle in him surged along every nerve in her arms. Then at last quiet fell. Slowly he turned, his arms coming out to hold her, tucking her head under his chin. He smelled of horse sweat and drying mud.

'Then I will cling to love,' he muttered into her hair, 'and perhaps your Goddess will look well on me when at last we meet.'

Rhiann craned back to look up at him, the tears drying across her cheeks. The sun sheened his eyes, so they appeared as clear as sea water. 'When that time comes, *cariad*, we will take that path together, whatever it may be.'

Chapter 64

Rhiann fixed her eyes on the valley between Liath's pale, twitching ears. The dip was deepened by the shadow of the gatetower above, which fell across half of the mare's head, and half of Rhiann's body. One of Rhiann's arms was in sunshine; the other cold in the shadows. Perhaps it was easier this way, if she only saw what was around her as blocks of light and shadow, and did not allow them to form pictures. Then she wouldn't really know she was leaving Dunadd until she was far away.

Yet she could sense the silence which had crept over the dun as houses were abandoned. Now that silence lurked by the gate, waiting for its possession to become complete.

Outside, though, everything was a bustle of jingling harness, snorting horses and shouted orders. Beyond the hundreds of milling riders, the plain was covered with the ranks of foot soldiers, and the sounds of their voices and impatient stamping and adjusting of armour and weapons was a faint roar.

And below all that ran something else that Rhiann could hear with her heart, and so less easily ignore: the soft murmur of women and children releasing their men and fathers to war, their hands reaching up to horses, the stumbled words that tried to gather years of love into one farewell, yet could never manage it.

Rhiann shifted uncomfortably in her padded saddle, glad that the sight she could bear least was being conducted in utter silence. For off to her right, Caitlin stood by Conaire's knee as he bounced Gabran on his horse. The little boy was holding the reins in silence, bewildered, perhaps picking up from his parents that all was not well. Rhiann's hand crept to the amber necklace at her throat. She was lucky that she was following her love, yet she too was leaving behind those with a claim on her heart.

'Rhiann.' Fola was breathless, pushing her way through the people to stand at Liath's head. Some way behind her, Eithne was lingering with Rori in the shadow of the walls, their heads bent close even though Eithne had to strain to hold back Cù on his rope. 'I have looked everywhere,' Fola gasped out, 'but I cannot find her. She was here to say goodbye to Caitlin . . .' She spread her hands helplessly, and Rhiann swallowed hard, a knot of disappointment tightening in her belly. 'I am sure she will come . . . perhaps she will try and see you alone.'

Rhiann nodded, knowing that Linnet hated to farewell Rhiann in public. She reached out to flick Fola's braid from her shoulder. 'I will return, you know. This is not the end.'

'I know.' Fola looked up at her, and her dark eyes were now calm. Over the past few days she had remained silent, but no longer seemed angry.

'You do?'

'Yes.' Fola's mouth lifted wryly, in the old way. 'I never had the skill with seeing that you do, but three nights of fasting and little sleep gave me something in Declan's pool, at last.'

'You fasted for three nights, just to get a glimpse of my fate?'

'You are not the only one who loves, Rhiann,' Fola said softly.

'That is true.' Rhiann leaned forward to still Fola's fingers on the bridle, for they were not as calm as the owner's eyes. 'But what did you see?'

Fola sighed, folding her arms in the sleeves of her dress. 'I saw you and I together again, with stars above our heads, and sand beneath our feet. That is all. So much hunger, for so little!' She grinned. 'Yet I am content with that, and will hold true while you are gone. I am sorry for being angry.'

'I am sorry for making you so.' Rhiann tried to continue, but was distracted by Caitlin's sudden appearance. Her sister ducked under Liath's neck, Gabran in her arms, as from somewhere in front of the mass of horses, a horn blew.

'Here,' Caitlin said, thrusting the squirming child at Fola, who sagged under his weight, mouth open. To Rhiann's astonishment Caitlin then ducked away again, the side of her averted cheek bright red.

Fola raised her eyebrows, stroking the soft hair on the crown of Gabran's head as the boy began to wail, wriggling to get down.

'Here, my beautiful boy.' Beckoning, Rhiann got Fola to hold Gabran up so she could kiss his sticky cheek, which did little to allay his distress. 'May the Goddess watch over all of you,' Rhiann murmured, giving Fola a hurried priestess kiss as Gabran broke into loud, hiccupping sobs. The restless throng of horses were all starting to flow in the same direction, and so Rhiann gave Liath her head at last and moved off.

She was nearly at the bridge over the river when there was a ripple in the ranks, and over her shoulder Rhiann glimpsed Caitlin's golden head darting through the milling horses to sweep Gabran up and rain kisses down on his screwed-up face. Rhiann considered waiting for her, but soon spotted Conaire leading both their mounts back against the onwards stream of men and horses, and so she let her sister be.

By the time the leading ranks of the warband entered the lower reaches of the valley of ancestors, it streamed out far behind, with 500 cavalry arrayed in front, sides and rear of 2,000 foot warriors. In front of Rhiann rode Eremon, with Rori holding the Boar standard until Conaire caught up again, and next to him Lorn under the White Mare. Behind the foot soldiers the chariots of Lorn's troop were being transported in the care of his clansmen.

It was as Rhiann passed the cluster of ancient stone uprights that marked the end of the tomb mounds, that she at last saw Linnet. 'I must go to her,' Rhiann said to Eremon, kicking Liath up beside him. His eyes shadowed by his boar helmet, Eremon glanced back to the long, wavering lines of men streaming in a haphazard order that bore little resemblance to Roman marches, despite his best efforts. It would take some time for them to clear the valley.

'Catch up with us when you can,' he said, briefly touching his fingers to Rhiann's lips in a private kiss.

Rhiann urged Liath away from the men, splashing across a shallow stream to reach the turf around the stones. The monoliths were set in pairs, leaving an avenue that ran between them, and after Rhiann slid carefully onto a low stump nearby, Linnet drew her around the tallest upright, out of sight.

'I said my farewells to Caitlin this morning . . . but had to speak to you alone,' Linnet gasped out, holding her side as if she had been running. In the shadow of the stone, carved in ancient times with spirals and hollows, Linnet's face seemed to glow with some Otherworldly light.

'We have said all but farewell,' Rhiann answered, her voice faltering.

Linnet laid her hand along her cheek. 'Many times have I watched you leave, daughter. I even saw that you would be changed by your last journey to Calgacus.'

'And you were right.' Rhiann smiled shakily, laying her hand over Linnet's. 'Let us pray this journey is as fruitful.'

Yet Linnet's eyes were looking past her, down the avenue of stones, staring at something beyond. 'It is not only you who will be changed this time, child − the world will change.'

A chill crept up Rhiann's arms beneath her sleeves. 'Have you seen who will triumph?'

'I have seen . . . burning and swords. Many will die.' Linnet's voice was faint, and then she focused on Rhiann's face again, as if memorizing her bones. 'And there are words for you, that came in a dream.'

A sudden gust of wind soughed across the empty grasses, and it was as if Rhiann and Linnet stood in a world of their own. Rhiann barely heard the tramp of feet from the path behind. 'Tell me,' she whispered.

Linnet closed her eyes, opening her chest so that her words were carried on the wings of the priestess voice, vibrating with the wind. 'On the mountain, it is acceptance you must find above all other things. As the journey is made clear, so let your heart fly free of what you wish to see, what you have seen, what you are seeing.'

Rhiann was silent for a moment. 'I do not understand.'

'Nor do I. Nevertheless, that is all I can give you, except something from my own heart.' Suddenly, almost fiercely, Linnet took Rhiann's face in both hands. 'That I do not think this is our final parting, child of my heart.'

'No.' Rhiann fought back tears. 'I do not think so, either.' She glanced over her shoulder to the front ranks of men, who had long since disappeared into the higher reaches of the valley. 'I must go now.' Rhiann pulled Linnet to her in an embrace, and remounted.

Yet as she neared the stream, Rhiann wheeled the mare. 'Aunt, I will call up a vision of that next meeting of ours, in Thisworld and no other, for the time being.'

Linnet smiled. 'For the time being.' She rested her palm flat on the sunlit shoulder of the largest stone, as if listening. Her priestess ring gleamed once and then was still.

Chapter 65

They met the first farmers six days out from Calgacus's dun.

A small, ragged group of them came sliding down a wet scree slope, clad in rough tunics and trousers, with an assortment of shaggy sheepskin cloaks and furs tied around the packs hefted on their shoulders. They wore no armour of any kind, and only carried rough spears of sharpened ash and a mixed collection of farm implements, such as mattocks and picks.

As the Epidii warband continued along the shores of the great loch which ran north to Calgacus's coastal fort, more men appeared, trickling down the slopes of the hills from every high pass and remote valley, emptying all the isolated homesteads. They fell in with Eremon's men, swelling their ranks until the gathering streamed away along the entire length of the loch.

'That's where our army is coming from, then,' Conaire remarked one day to Eremon, as they sat waiting for Lorn to bring his chariots over a shallow river ford. He frowned. 'Though what good these farm boys will be in battle, I do not know.'

Eremon shot a swift glance at him, patting Dòrn's shoulder with a murmur. The stallion had shied, as Lorn, ankle-deep in rushing water, shouted a curse at a chariot stuck in the muddy riverbank. 'We have done more with far fewer.'

Conaire's gaze strayed over his shoulder towards Caitlin and Rhiann, who had now disappeared among the hazel woods that ran east from the river. 'When we had fewer,' he murmured gruffly, his frown a deep valley between his brows, 'we won because those we had were all warriors. But this . . .' Conaire gestured at the herdsmen and farmers splashing through the icy water, dodging Lorn as he stormed around the bogged chariot wheel.

'My brother,' Eremon said, calming Dòrn again, 'if we are lucky, we will outnumber the Romans three to one – there is no other way I would face them. The force of our charge must carry the day.'

Conaire snorted, and to Eremon's surprise his normally open, amused expression had hardened into belligerence. 'Eremon, if you thought it only about numbers we never would have trained the Epidii so carefully these last years. I'm no idiot, man!'

As Eremon stared at him, speechless, Conaire flushed and fixed his gaze on the twitching ears of his stallion. 'Brother,' he said more softly, 'it is me you're talking to, remember? Don't treat me like the others.'

'I . . . ah . . .' Eremon's eyebrows shot up. 'I suppose I have become used to it.' He scratched the back of his sweaty neck, under the edge of the helmet guard. 'Certain platitudes have become habit.'

'Well, spare me, please.' Conaire eyed Eremon with grudging forgiveness. 'So? Speak truly, and it goes no further. Ever since we joined this Great Glen you've had something stuck in your gullet.'

Eremon tilted his head to stretch his neck, letting the stifling mantle of fear settle over him. He stared forward between Dòrn's ears, gathering his reins in tight hands. 'Somewhere down deep, I'm so scared my bowels ache with it. We have trained the Epidii and some of the Caledonii, but that is, what, three thousand men? And what about the rest? Few warriors face a Roman army and win, no matter how fierce the charge.' He sought for Conaire's blue eyes, held on for dear life. 'You see, brother, I cannot be sure that even with triple their number, we can win.'

The chariot came free with a loud sucking noise and rattle of wheels. Muddy to the knee, Lorn stalked back to his horse. With yips and the snap of reins, the creaking phalanx of chariots closed around Eremon and Conaire, sweeping them along the path through the trees.

'Mars release me.'

Agricola heard the muttered oath from Lucius, but he was far too pleased with the view in front of him to reprimand his legate. He squinted back out across the bay at the white sails of his fleet, all twenty ships at anchor.

'I have been looking forward to this sight,' Agricola remarked to his officers. 'And the requisition has also gone out for every available trading ship from Londinium north, although they won't be as pretty.'

They were standing on one of the oak piers of the makeshift port established two years before on the south bank of the Tay inlet, on the eastern edge of hostile lands. Behind on the shore lay a cluster of barracks and storehouses, home to the garrison of 300 that guarded the port.

The Venicones lands had proven a rich source of stores for Agricola's invasion force. Of course, he amended to himself, those lands that spread west and south from here were no longer a larder, but ashes. It was a good thing that after this year, he would have all Alba from which to feed.

Briskly, Agricola rubbed his hands together. Apart from Lucius, the other officers were bright-faced, showing little strain from the marching, the camping or the cleansing of the land with fire and sword that had brought them to this northern shore. Yet Lucius himself was pale and red-eyed.

The eyes could be accounted for by the pall of smoke through which they had been riding for weeks; their clothes and hair stank with it. Yet the pallor was something else. It could not be cowardice, could it? Agricola wondered. Surely not. No legate of his would have such a weak stomach for witnessing the punishment that had been inflicted on Alba. Then he remembered that Lucius had already taken this northern road once, and not far from here was where disaster first struck. There would be no such disaster this time, Agricola promised himself and his gods.

There was a suitably respectful silence, before Lucius spoke up wearily. 'How can we be sure the devils won't just run as they did before?'

'They won't run.' Agricola looked out to sea, shading his eyes from the harsh glitter off the waves. The surface of the bay was ruffled into white-caps by a rising wind, and his sleek, beautiful ships strained on their anchor ropes. 'The bait has been set, and they will take it.'

'And the trap close around them,' the young tribune Marcus joked, the others joining in with grim laughter.

Agricola allowed himself a thin smile, breathing deeply of the sharp air, letting it fill his chest as wind filled a sail.

Stretching the nagging ache in her back, Rhiann took a moment to realize Caitlin had drawn up her horse in shock. 'Mother of all!' Caitlin squeaked. Blinking away her exhaustion, Rhiann straightened.

They had previously come to Calgacus's Dun of the Waves on the banks of the Ness river for a council of war. They had seen the river plain before its gates clustered with men, thick with the smoke of campfires. Yet to see that same effect multiplied ten times was more than arresting.

Every handspan of ground was sprouting with tents, lean-tos, banners and racks of spears. The grass was nearly obscured by ruddy leather, hides and standards of all colours, and of course, men — men clothed in every hue of cloth, fur and skins, the whole tangled mass of them glittering with helmets and swords, the farmers with their picks. Yet the hum of voices was less thick than the dense wave of smell that assailed

Rhiann's nostrils: of sweat, horse, birch tar, lanolin, mutton-fat and greasy meat.

'I imagined it, that many men,' Caitlin was saying, 'but thinking, and then seeing . . .' She shook her head. 'Goddess, Rhiann, do those banners not stir your heart? Look!'

Rhiann slid a hand up the back of her neck and rubbed it, seeking for the knots that ached so much. She felt as if every part of her had been trampled by horses, and though her mind could marvel at the sight before her, her feelings kept sliding into fuzzy exhaustion.

As they pulled up before Calgacus's main gate, Caitlin slipped nimbly from her saddle and patted Rhiann's knee. 'I'll give you a deeper massage this night,' she whispered. 'They have helped, have they not?'

Rhiann eyed Caitlin's bright eyes with envy. Though her old riding buckskins were stained with the dirt of travel, and her hair was half-bound tangles, Caitlin at least was bursting with health. The sun had sprinkled her cheekbones with freckles, and she had regained the ease in the saddle that she once enjoyed. She had found an eagle feather and tucked it into her braids, and it stuck up jauntily over the top of her head, echoing the arrows in her quiver. 'They have helped greatly,' Rhiann conceded, 'yet I doubt I will ever feel in one piece again. Fola was right; riding while pregnant is not to be recommended.'

Caitlin clucked in sympathy, unable to hide the excited bounce in her heels. After a few days she seemed to have pushed her grief for Gabran into a place she only visited at night, or when she lapsed into thought.

Calgacus had been alerted to their arrival and was waiting for them before his gate, the kings and war leaders of the other tribes clustered about him. Rhiann shook off her exhaustion long enough to feel a flush of pride at this honour accorded to Eremon, which was furthered when Calgacus embraced him as warmly as he would a son, before all those nobles. Rhiann's pride deepened to satisfaction when her eyes fell on the glowering Creones king. He had brought the men he promised, though he looked far from happy about it.

Eremon helped Rhiann dismount, and she was glad he was holding her tenderly by the arm when she reached the ground, for her legs were so cramped she nearly fell over. Her fingers dug into his skin as she cursed under her breath, and Eremon shot her a look of concern mingled with amusement at her choice words. Slowly Rhiann straightened, suddenly conscious of her exposed belly before all these men and wishing that she had ridden inside the gate out of sight.

Yet Calgacus dispelled her embarrassment. As the other kings dipped their heads to her, he greeted her with a deep bow, taking her arm to turn her away. 'You must be very tired from your journey, lady. There are still some women here to attend you – they have a bath waiting.'

A bath. Rhiann's whole body ached with yearning. For a moment she hesitated, until Eremon leaned close to her ear and gave her braid a tweak. 'Don't worry about missing anything,' he whispered. 'I'll tell you all later.'

'I'll hold you to that,' she returned sweetly, and let a serving woman lead her away.

As dusk fell, the kings returned to their guestlodges to bathe before the night meal. Calgacus invited Eremon to his private alcove on the second floor of his hall, screened from the rest of the bed gallery by a long wool hanging depicting a hunting scene of stags and boar. The brazier squatted on its three legs, cold and unlit, for heat floated up from the great fire below.

'Many of the Venicones escaped north and were taken by Taexali scouts,' Calgacus informed Eremon. 'The traitors at last know, to their cost, the value of a Roman vow.'

'I heard this news.' Eremon sighed, staring into the shadows of the curving wall. 'You know of course that Agricola took this road once before – in the western lands of Britannia, the lands of my grandmother's people. He laid waste to them, conquered them utterly.'

The words hung in the air between them, as a draft of warm air lifted the edge of the hanging, making the shadows tremble. 'This is destruction that cannot be ignored, prince,' Calgacus said heavily, sinking into his carved chair. For the first time that day, the Caledonii king allowed all his feelings to show. 'It is meant to drive us to war.'

Eremon reached for his ale cup. 'That it is. What else do you know?'

Calgacus leaned back. 'Our scouts estimate a Roman army of ten thousand. They are moving slowly, so thoroughly are they scouring the countryside of any sign of life.' His mobile mouth turned down with brief pain.

'We will have almost three times that,' Eremon remarked.

Calgacus nodded. 'So it appears.'

Eremon took a deep breath and met Calgacus's gaze. 'So. Where are they, where are they heading and what are we going to do about it?'

That at least brought a smile to the king's face, and he sat forward, his forearms resting on his chair. 'Aye, my young friend, you do bring a fresh breeze of energy into this Hall. The truth is I am waiting on the latest reports to come in, hopefully in the next few days. Then we can make a plan with the other kings.'

'Then let us speak plain now.' Abruptly, Eremon also leaned forward towards the bark map spread on the bench, its edges weighted with daggers. 'I believe the Romans are making for this dun specifically. They wish to finish what they started last year.'

Calgacus nodded, tenting his fingers under his chin. 'I feel this, too.'

'Your lands are the gateway to the interior of all Alba,' Eremon continued. 'From here, the glens spread north, south and west, allowing easy access to the high ground. If the Romans take the Caledonii lands, the mountains are laid open to them. There will be nowhere left to hide, for any of us. We cannot let them get this far north.'

'Indeed we cannot,' Calgacus agreed, his eyes beginning to glow with the fire that Eremon could always stir in him. 'And I have thought of a place to make our stand.' He stabbed at the bark with one finger. 'Here. It is a lone ridge that rears from a wide plain. From it, one can see far. It is a strong place, called the Hill of a Thousand Spears by some. I do not know why. Perhaps a battle was fought there, long ago.'

Eremon nodded. 'Soon it may have a new name, then. Yet let it not be where the hope of Alba was lost.'

Calgacus turned those keen, gold-flecked eyes on Eremon, and gripped his shoulder. 'Hope will never be lost while we can raise a sword.'

For a moment, Eremon let himself be held by that male strength, relieved that it was not only his to muster for others. Then he smiled and reached for his cup, holding it up to the king's hand. 'Let us drink to that, my friend.'

Yet the chink of their bronze cups was a cold sound within the pool of warm lamplight.

Chapter 66

It was the strangest, most frustrated turning of Rhiann's life.

For as the bustle of the war camp swirled around her in an escalating blur of noise, smell and urgent movement, she became ever more still, drawn away unwillingly to another world unfolding inside her.

Her body was growing more heavy and slow, and for those few days at Calgacus's dun Rhiann sat on a bench on the sun-warmed walls, her hands spread over her belly, as from below came the roar of the men in training, the clash of swords and shields, the thunder of horses. Yet it was not only Rhiann's increasing weight and tiredness holding her there. For though her energy had played a large part in creating this – 30,000 men in a frenzy of excitement and preparation – she sat silent in their midst now, her thoughts and heart turned entirely inwards, with no part to play.

Suspended in this void of activity, so Rhiann's inner life sprang into full being. The tangled visions had now formed themselves into some kind of parallel world, running alongside and within her own. They were frustratingly inconsequential: women weaving and nursing; birthing babes and tending cauldrons; singing and stamping their feet around a fire. Sometimes there were even glimpses of priestesses, robed and white-masked, singing to the Stones. Yet Rhiann didn't recognize either the women or their clothes, or even their songs, though the meaning tugged at something buried in her subconscious.

As Rhiann looked out at the plain before the dun, covered with tents and hazed with smoke, she could still sense these inner sights and sounds as a murmur all about her, and if she closed her eyes and sought one vibration, like Aedan tuning his strings, that picture became more clear than the rest, before subsiding back into the whispering stream once more.

And though the visions themselves were not violent, as the days passed Rhiann grew ever more fearful. For the first time she was completely at a loss, spiralling down into a world she did not understand. She knew she had not fulfilled her dream, yet why then did she not receive it? It was as if the single, fierce guiding light she had followed so fervently for three years had suddenly been extinguished, to be replaced by all *this*: visions so clear they lived and breathed, yet seemingly useless to her all the same. They weren't about battles, or warriors, or even kings. They were just . . . life.

And what of the babe? The visions began with the child and, at first, as every one came, it would kick. Now, with the visions like a continuous stream, the child never seemed to sleep, turning and rolling and kicking until an anxious Rhiann would hold her belly and sing to soothe it.

Rhiann didn't want to scare Caitlin, yet she did ask, hesitantly, if Caitlin had experienced anything like it during her pregnancy. Was it something that came to all mothers, she wondered, an opening caused by the baby that allowed stray memories of other lives to flood in? But no, Caitlin frowned in confusion when Rhiann tried to explain, so she let the matter drop, and her fear increased. It wasn't normal, then.

Every night, Rhiann lined up her goddesses by the side of her bed, and prayed with desperation to receive the dream of power just once more. The alliance was based on one woman's dream, and one man's vision. *What if she and Eremon were wrong?*

Every night, though, her prayers went unanswered.

Only the child flew with Rhiann in sleep, its soul-flame a tiny bloom of fire next to her own. Holding hands, she and the babe skimmed the mountains, cold among the stars, and out over glittering, moonlit seas. The child showed her Alba, spread out below, but its thoughts were formless, the feelings vague.

Love of the land.

Grim beauty . . .

Turning slowly in the starry sky, Rhiann's anxious mind groped to understand what the child was trying to tell her. That all would be well, and Alba remain hers?

Or that she was meant to say farewell?

It was the eve of the longest day, and Eremon paused for a moment, imagining all the things he would rather be doing. Instead, here he was, squatting in the shadows of a stifling, smoky hall, with sweaty warriors shouting boasts and laughing far too loudly.

The atmosphere among the nobles now was that familiar battle mixture of excitement and aggressive bravado, driven by buried fear. Everyone was getting drunk, and trying to outdo each other in war stories, singing and even wrestling. Yet the tension didn't make

Eremon's blood sing as it had every time before, and so he had retreated behind one of the oak pillars that held up the roof, where the thatch sloped low to the eaves.

Conaire still managed to find him. 'Here.' He handed Eremon an empty cup and squatted against the curving wall, his long thighs jutting out. 'I had to lop off a few heads to get this.' He waved something before Eremon's nose that sloshed invitingly, then poured a stream of ale into his cup. 'So why are you hiding over here?'

Eremon glanced sidewise at Conaire as he drank, considering that familiar rise of cheek and eyebrow. He realized that though Conaire had always read his mind, lately Eremon had found himself speaking aloud almost everything that ran through his head. It was odd, but relieving.

'I was just thinking,' Eremon murmured, his head swinging back into shadow, 'about the times we stood here at this hearth, fighting for an alliance. I thought then that when the time came I would feel different. Exultant.' He shrugged uneasily.

Conaire swigged the ale. 'And how do you feel, then?'

'That this hall stinks of old blood, from weapons and men and animals, and yet . . . that is nothing to the blood that will run in a battle with the Romans, and much of it Alban.' He turned, seeking for the calm of Conaire's eyes. 'And I brought them here. Without me, perhaps they would keep running, hiding—'

'And their lands would be stolen.'

Eremon shook his head. 'Perhaps so, but still they would live.' He gulped the ale.

Conaire's silence echoed the sympathy in his face. His broad hand came down on his brother's shoulder, a weight Eremon knew as well as that of his sword. 'You are tired, brother, that is all.' Conaire ground Eremon's shoulder bones in what passed for a brotherly squeeze. 'You only gave them a chance. It was their choice to seize it.'

Eremon digested that, but could not shake off the sick dread that had settled in his belly. All those lives in his hands.

'So! At last we move out tomorrow, and I am glad to hear it!' Lorn's voice shocked them, booming out of the shadows to their left. He raised his own flask, shaking the contents. 'I appropriated this earlier. Can I take a seat, my friends?'

With a sigh, Eremon shifted along on his haunches and then sat down with his back against the wall, his legs stretched out. Lorn curled up cross-legged, placing the flask before him.

Calgacus had called this feast to announce the latest information from the scouts tracking the Roman army. If the Albans moved out tomorrow they would be at the Hill of a Thousand Spears in four days. The Romans, coming up from the south in one block, could not reach the same point for at least six days, giving the Albans time to choose the ground. All that remained tonight was to go over their battle dispositions once again.

Eremon tried to shrug off the nagging doubts he had, drawing confidence from the ale, its warmth seeping into his belly and uncoiling the worst of the fear. The Albans outnumbered the Romans three to one. The Albans were defending their homes, a thought which gave a man's sword arm great strength.

In common with the Britons and those of Erin, the Albans did not make a formal battle plan, or recognize separate units. Each man fought on foot or horse as he wished, relying on courage and weight of numbers to carry the day. Eremon's wings of infantry, under Conaire, cavalry under himself, and chariots under Lorn had therefore excited a great deal of attention, and not a little scorn. Yet in the week they had been here, drilling their men on the plain, warriors had been joining their units in droves, boosting the cavalry to 2,000, and the chariots to 1,000. Conaire had 2,000 specially trained foot soldiers under his command, drawn from the Epidii and the best of the Caledonii. The rest of the warriors and commoners would fight on foot under their own kings and chiefs, with Calgacus as overall war leader.

'Calgacus has received the final tally,' Lorn said. 'I was nearby when his druids came.' He drank, and wiped his chin. 'You were right, Eremon – with his infantry and all our units, that makes about twenty-eight thousand, with more coming every day. Can you believe it?'

Eremon smiled wearily. 'Since the Romans have, by all reports, ten thousand, I would have to believe it, or despair.'

'Do not despair!' Lorn exclaimed. 'At the very least, we will die a glorious death, and the bards will sing of our names for ever, while we feast in the Blessed Isles. I can live with that.' He chuckled.

Eremon thought suddenly of Rhiann's hair in the sun, the tumbled threads of flame and copper, amber and roan.

No, he thought. *It is not only a name I wish to leave. There is more to me than that.*

Much later in the night, Eremon escaped the noise and heat to walk alone on the long walls of the dun, letting the cold moonlight and sea-wind cleanse him of ale fumes and smoke. The revelry in the hall and camp showed no signs of letting up, and Eremon grimaced as he thought of all the sore heads on the ride south tomorrow. He couldn't begrudge them this time, though.

On the other side of the river rose a dark smudge of low hills. Rhiann had said she was going up into those woods to conduct the rites for the longest day, and although Eremon warned them to stay hidden, he had sent Rori and Fergus to guard Rhiann and Caitlin from afar.

Eremon only sensed the soft step behind him when it was already too close to do anything about it. Nevertheless he tensed, whirling, hand halfway to his sword-hilt.

'Prince, I greet you.'

Eremon's breath rushed out of him as he recognized Nectan's voice, floating from the shadow of the gatetower. 'I should have known it was you; the only man to walk on feet of air.' He grinned, beckoning Nectan forward into the moonlight. 'How are you, old friend? When did you arrive?'

'Just this dusk,' Nectan replied. The Caereni chieftain was arrayed in his finest, with beaded quiver, shell necklets and wrist guard. His face tattoos appeared darker in the pale grey light, drawn over with dye or ash. 'And I have brought a gift, prince – all who can wield bow or spear among the Caereni and Carnonacae; some three thousand men. They came for the King Stag, to give him their strength.'

Eremon's breath hissed out from his teeth in surprise. So many!

'It is no more than we vowed to you,' Nectan added softly.

'Even so, I thank you. You are a staunch ally, and great friend.'

Nectan's head bowed in solemn acknowledgement, as the wind stirred the feathers at the ends of his braids. 'Prince, apart from greetings, I searched you out to speak of Maelchon of the Orcades.'

Eremon had straightened before he knew it. 'I have not forgotten him, if that is what concerns you. Calgacus will despatch a small guard for our rear, yet there is only so much shoreline we can watch.'

'I know this.' Nectan's teeth bared in a grin. 'That is why I have left a chain of scouts across the land to the north. They will fall back to this dun when we have left.'

Eremon muttered another oath, shaking his head. 'I wonder what we would do without your foresight, friend. I know that Maelchon has been far too quiet for too long. Yet I had not forgotten him: after all, the tribes have only come together here because of the Sacred Isle raid. Be assured that his presence still writhes in my gut, but though I long to hunt him down, there are more pressing matters at hand.'

'True, yet while he lives, my service to the Mother will remain incomplete.' Briefly, Nectan touched a new tattoo on his brow: a crescent moon. The moon was the face of the Goddess for these people, Eremon remembered Rhiann telling him. 'Like you, prince, I do not feel we have seen the last of the Orcadian king,' Nectan murmured. 'Well do I hope it is my shaft in his neck that brings him down.'

Eremon shook his head. 'No, friend, it is my blade that must end his life. You seek vengeance for your goddess; I seek it for my wife.'

Chapter 67

The druids had offered a prince's ransom in weapons to the Ness, the banners of the eagle had been taken down from their gold-tipped poles and, with solemn ceremony, the great gates of the Dun of the Waves had been ritually closed.

Now the greatest army ever assembled in Alba lumbered its way around the edge of the northern mountains, crossing coastal lowlands only now coming into their full sunseason glory. The air was heavy with the scents of flowers and ripening hay; the fields spilled over with green barley.

Amidst all the richness, Calgacus rode at the head of this enormous, restless beast of war, Eremon and Conaire at his shoulders. Watching the Caledonii king from the corner of her eye, Rhiann saw that he stared straight ahead, sparing no glance for the wealth of his land, which would, left untended, leach away after its brief flowering. Or worse, be burned into a blackened ruin by Roman soldiers.

Rhiann herself was living with the same threat of darkness that she saw reflected in the king's eyes, running beneath the warmth of the sun and hum of bees. For as they left the dun, the domestic thread of her visions shifted; the sense of them shot through with looming destruction and danger, though nothing came clearly.

At dusk on the second day, the army only halted when there was barely enough light left to unpack and make camp. Rhiann was already on the ground when she noticed that Caitlin still sat on her horse, unmoving and staring into the last glow of the sun over the western hills.

In the long, shallow valley in which they would camp, mist was beginning to curl up from the damp ground, and Rhiann shivered, then blinked her vision away from her inner world to this one. 'Caitlin?' She reached out tentatively to touch her sister's knee.

A shudder flowed over Caitlin's skin, and she turned to Rhiann as slowly as if she were awakening. After leaving Calgacus's dun she too had grown quiet, her excitement seeping away the further they rode east. 'I was just thinking how Gabran loves warm weather,' she whispered. 'He hates wearing clothes.'

Rhiann squeezed her knee. 'He will be a little brown hazelnut when you see him again.'

The last light had almost faded now, a copper smear low on the horizon, as campfires flared into life all around them. 'Will I, Rhiann?' Caitlin asked, so quietly Rhiann had to strain to hear her. 'Will I see him again? And will he forgive me if I do not?'

Rhiann looked up into her stricken face. 'I saw him as a king on the day he was born. And so you will be with him again, for he needs you to guide him to this kingship.'

Caitlin's sweet mouth twisted. 'He needs his father for that.' Then her chin dropped, her jaw tight with shame. 'Oh, Rhiann, I suffer from such dread—'

'Sister,' Rhiann clasped Caitlin's cold hands on the reins, 'you have always been so brave. Do not fail Conaire now, when he needs you most.'

Caitlin's eyes closed as she swallowed, and when they opened again some measure of strength had been forced into them. 'You are right. I must be proud of him, and send him to war with an open heart. I *must*.'

Rhiann released her, drawing the edge of her cloak closed with a sad smile. 'I do not think the Goddess can ask that of us.' She held her belly as she reached up to her saddlepack and fumbled with the buckles. Perhaps if she could quiet the child, she would then be able to quiet her thoughts, and be calm for when Eremon returned from his war council this night. He needed her here, in Thisworld, however strong that strange call of the Otherworld was proving to be.

Rhiann was already asleep when Eremon came to her bed at the edge of camp, in a little hollow screened from the other men by hawthorn bushes. Slipping under the pile of furs and hides on their bed roll, Eremon clasped Rhiann's curved back into his belly, his face and hands cold from the damp night air.

'I have spoken to Calgacus about our battle site,' he murmured, in answer to Rhiann's sleepy enquiry. The sounds of horses and male shouts were faint, muted by the shoulder of the small ridge. 'The Hill of a Thousand Spears runs down to a plain, and to the west of that is a wooded rise – high enough for you to see our progress, but far enough away to allow an easy retreat, should you require it.' The stilted words were at odds with the trembling force with which Eremon pressed Rhiann's back into his chest.

'Caitlin and I will be safe there,' Rhiann murmured, reaching up to stroke the back of his neck. 'We will.'

All of Eremon's breath rushed out of him then, and Rhiann sensed the control he had been exerting with the men slide away. She hesitated about sharing her fears with him when he had so much on his mind, but she could keep them inside no longer. What if there was some message for him, for the men, that she was somehow missing?

So Rhiann told him all that had come to her, and what did not, and he lay still and said nothing for a long time. 'I am so confused,' she whispered at last, 'so scared of letting you down. But Eremon, try as I might, I cannot pierce these mists and tell you anything clear.' Her voice lowered. 'It is like watching thousands of lives, but I cannot see the meaning in them, the pattern, the message. I am sorry I cannot be more—'

'Shhh.' Eremon's arms tightened around her. 'I do not understand the priestess sight,' he began slowly, 'though I have always listened to you, *a stór*, and respected what you told me. And if there was a message for me, you know I would hear it. Yet I think . . . I think you are just meant to hold the baby now, Rhiann.' His breath was warm in her ear. 'And if that is what is calling you, then heed it. Curl around our babe and shelter it with your thoughts as well as your body. If you do no more, you have already done enough.'

Tears stung Rhiann's eyes, drawn both by his tender words and by frustration. For he would go to war, and she could not fight by his side, nor aid him at all, it seemed.

'Perhaps . . . perhaps we should not . . .'

'No.' Eremon cut off that thought with one soft word. Then his lips were pressing behind her ear. 'We have come too far for that, *mo chroi*. We are set on this course now; we must face it with courage.'

At dawn Eremon was wakened by a touch on his shoulder. In the cold, grey light Rhiann recognized the white gull feathers dangling from the ends of Nectan's dark braids. His feet were before her face, the boots dark with dew. The air was chill and silent, broken only by the dancing call of a thrush from a dripping rowan tree on the ridge-top.

'It has happened,' the Caereni chieftain announced, his face an expressionless, pale blur in the dawn. 'The Orcades king has come.'

Rhiann choked back an exclamation, as Eremon sat up, the hides falling about his waist. 'Tell me,' he barked to Nectan, extracting the ends of his twisted tunic from between their bodies, straightening it over his chest.

'Maelchon has forged an alliance with the Lugi,' Nectan said. 'Luckily for us, two Lugi scouts deserted him, and nearly killed themselves reaching my men.'

Her heart pounding, Rhiann remembered the raven sail of the Lugi king from her first sunseason visit to the Sacred Isle, and Setana standing on the shore as the ship slid away past the Stones.

'So where is he?' Eremon demanded, running fingers swiftly through his unbound hair.

Nectan fingered the dagger at his waist, its hilt inlaid with pearl shell. 'He landed on the coast to the north-east, yesterday. The plan appears to have been for him to remain in hiding, then come upon our rear in battle.'

'How many men are with him?'

'Two thousand, all on foot.'

Eremon paused for a moment. 'Go and inform Calgacus. We must leave at once if we are to head him off. I will take five hundred on horse, plus as many of your own men as you require.'

Rhiann only waited until Nectan trotted away before struggling free of the bedclothes. 'Eremon, you cannot go after him with so few!'

He was already pulling up his wool trousers and lacing them at the waist. 'I will make it enough.' He reached for his mailshirt. 'I cannot take any more and reach him in time – I must be back at the battle site a day before the Romans come.'

He quickly eased the mailshirt over his head and tied it with deft fingers, glancing at Rhiann when it was done. She was standing frozen, her knuckles at her mouth. The fierce light in his eyes softened. 'Don't forget, we will have the element of surprise, *a stór*.'

'Eremon.' *Not so soon . . . I am not ready . . .* 'Let Maelchon come and be dealt with by the whole army. Do not face him with so few, *please—*'

Something absolute settled over Eremon's features. 'I must make him pay for what he did to you, and I must do it with my own hand. Nor can we afford to deal with him at our backs when we have the Romans to face.' He turned away, groping for his sword-belt, and swung around with it laid across his palms. 'Do you not understand, Rhiann? You, of all people?'

Rhiann's love for him twisted inside her. *No!* she almost screamed. Looking at Eremon now, she could hardly remember the fierce hatred that drove her to stab Maelchon in the eye. She could find no echo of the fury that burned in her, making her strong and hard. All she could see was the softness of Eremon's vulnerable throat, the place she had kissed so many times.

Then her own words to Caitlin came back to her. *Do not fail him.*

With shaking fingers, Rhiann took a step forward and grasped the heavy sword, sinking awkwardly to her knees in the dewy grass. Eremon looked down at her in surprise. Reaching around his waist, she reverently buckled on the sword-belt, settling the chain and scabbard over his right thigh. Then he helped her to her feet, and she gently took his hand from her arm and stood straight before him, pale and composed. 'May you avenge my honour, husband,' she said quietly. 'My love will be the wings that carry you; my fury the strength in your blade.'

Eremon's hands came out slowly, and he took her cold cheeks within them. His eyes were shining. 'Rhiann, it begins today.' He took a deep breath, struggling to find the words. 'You have seen me fight but once, yet you know what I have to find inside me to do it.'

Rhiann swallowed and nodded, holding his eyes. 'I know.'

'The man you held in your arms last night, you will not see him again, not until this is all over. You understand?'

At their feet, the tumble of hides and blankets was already cooling from the heat of their bodies. 'Yes,' Rhiann whispered.

Eremon pressed his lips to her forehead. 'Then forgive me, and love me all the same.'

Rhiann choked back the tears that lodged in her throat. 'The Goddess go with you,' she said, and Eremon drew her to his chest. Then he swooped down for his boar helmet, spears and cloak.

'Wait for me on the wooded rise at dawn in two days. There I will come to you and our child.' He held her eyes. 'I swear it.'

Chapter 68

Eremon stood on the crest of a ridge, peering into the lightening gloom of the narrow glen as if he could pierce it with the intensity of his gaze. Across the dark chasm he could just see the glitter of the rising sun on the swift-flowing river in its cleft. It was the second dawn after leaving the army camp, and Rhiann.

'How can we be sure they will come this way?' he asked one of the Lugi deserters, a thin, weasel-faced man with a squint.

'There are bogs and hills to be avoided, lord.' Crouched at Eremon's feet, the man pointed. 'This river valley is the fastest route, and King Maelchon pressed upon us the need to move fast.'

'Yet they may have changed their plans when they realized you were gone,' Conaire remarked, picking dirt from his nails with a dagger.

The other Lugi scout now turned to gaze at Eremon from where he squatted under an oak. He was almost all hair; his head covered with a wild black mane, his face by a beard, his ears tufted. Buried in all that hair, his eyes gleamed like berries in a hedge. 'Many of the scouts felt as we did,' he said. 'We have given allegiance to the Orcades king in many matters of the north, but not in order to kill our own kind, not for the sake of the red invaders. They will keep our flight secret. So long as you do not harm our king.'

Eremon absorbed that. 'Do you know if others in Maelchon's army feel the same?'

The weasel man broke in, eager to please. 'We were all too feared of *him* to speak of it openly. He has many spies among us, too.'

Uncertain, Eremon studied the ground below, gnawing the scar on his lip. The broken, confusing shadows of dawn still stippled the lower parts of the glen, even as the higher slopes were touched with gold. Yet he could make out the dark humps of boulders, the gleam of dew on the deep beds of bracken, and the white foam of the river as it hurled itself against its rocks. He swung around to Nectan, waiting silently in the shadows behind Conaire. 'What do you think?'

Nectan's keen glance rested briefly on each scout in turn, then rose to the ridge on the other side of the valley. 'My men and I can go to the north there, and watch for his approach – on the coastal flats he cannot hide two thousand men. If he appears to commit to this path, we can get back here before him.'

'And what if he chooses another path?' Conaire wondered, uncrossing his long legs. 'He takes a chance this way, and he will know it.'

The weasel scout grinned his gap-toothed smile, startling within the grime on his face. 'You are all on horses, Erin lord. There will be other places to confront him if needed.'

'Yet here we have the advantage,' muttered Eremon, 'and I cannot risk him getting closer to our forces.'

'He will come, lord,' said the second scout. 'It is said that he knows no fear, and that is his greatest weakness.'

'My king.'

The sibilant voice slid into Maelchon's ear. Uncanny how they could do that, these withered, stinking druid priests.

'What?' Maelchon did not take his good eye from the marshy ground beneath his feet. The last thing he needed was to twist his ankle, and he was slowly – grudgingly – growing used to the extra care he had to take now his vision had been compromised. Yet to one side he saw the ranks of his heavily armoured guards draw back from the pale, dirty robe of the druid as he glided forward. The stench that emanated from the old man's skin and breath was greater than Maelchon could bear, and the king drew away by stepping around the edge of a sodden hollow of sedge and reeds. The path inland from the northern coast had changed from sand to boggy lowlands, crossed by many rivers and streams.

'I do not like those hills ahead, my lord. My senses are sharpened by them.'

Maelchon spared the old man a swift glance, though he avoided looking at him as a rule. Yet those Otherworldly eyes, like the unblinking stare of an owl, were not fixed on him but on the sweeping, wooded ridges ahead. *Firm ground*, Maelchon thought sourly. *At last!* 'The scouts have reported no sign of the enemy.' He slapped at a midge biting his earlobe. 'Their entire force is at least two days away to the south-west – I know their exact position.'

Choked by a sudden, fine cloud of insects, Maelchon swatted at his neck. Damn lowlands! He was rarely so bothered on his own cold, windy islands. He spared a thought for the irony of this, since it was lust for these very lowlands that had driven him for so long, though he never would have led such a warband himself had Agricola's message not made it plain that continued Roman support relied on him proving his loyalty in person.

'Lord,' the druid whined again, as irritating as the midges, 'we should be cautious. I tell you the path is perilous.'

Maelchon halted, breathing hard at the effort of maintaining pace. Some way behind him, the Lugi king and his men struggled in the same way, though Maelchon wondered, and not for the first time, if their lack of speed was indicative of wavering resolve. He wiped sweat from his brow and flexed his shoulders to adjust his mailshirt. 'The river valley is the swiftest south-west route.' He rolled his good eye at Gelert. 'There are treacherous bogs around these foothills, and to the west the land gets too high. You know that speed is of the essence.'

As the druid frowned, Maelchon sighed. The priest had been useful in the matter of the Sacred Isle, but that was the business of the gods – and this was war. He simply could not afford a slower march, and risk getting caught in the open, cut off from his Roman allies. Agricola had said to meet his men on the coast at a very particular time. He had clearly communicated his displeasure should Maelchon be late.

The king hawked and spat on the ground, hitching his sword-belt up around his ample belly. 'Your fear weakens you, druid. The Lugi scouts report a safe traverse of these hills. Go back to your mutterings. You may speak to me when you have more than foolish fancies to report.'

Silent at last, the druid bowed, and Maelchon swept beyond him. He didn't particularly care what the man did now; the time was past for dealing with such Otherworld matters. Now it had come down to warriors: his men; Calgacus's rabble; and the blight on his heart that was Eremon of Erin. And, of course, the prince's red-haired whore. She who had scarred him.

At that thought the ruined eye stabbed him with pain, as it often did, and Maelchon schooled his face into calmness. It hurt when he was angry, and therefore he would only become angry now when he needed to, when the prince of Erin faced him across his blade.

Savouring such thoughts, Maelchon did not take note of the druid melting away, to where the lines of baggage ponies brought up the rear.

Eremon sharpened his sword blade in a hollow among the bracken, more to pass the time than anything else, for he always kept it obsessively honed.

He found, to his surprise, that he was more excited than nervous. For the first time since his arrival in Alba, he was to lead a confrontation between tribesmen, not against Romans. And among these people, as among his own, there were certain rules of war. The concepts of honour and glory were strictly defined, and would, he hoped, deliver him his victory.

Eremon's eye now fell on Aedan, crouched alone in the wet bracken lower down the valley. He had taken himself away from the rest of Eremon's men, who huddled in the damp, blowing on their sword hands and flexing them to keep them warm. The bard was wrapped in his embroidered cloak, yet studying his averted head, Eremon did not think he was terror-struck. Alba had been a forge for them all, and not the least Aedan.

The bard now turned his head, a silent song moving on his lips. His grey eyes were glassy with the bardic trance and his cheeks were flushed, but he seemed to be cradling some inner core of calm, and Eremon bent back to his sharpening, satisfied.

Conaire's feet padded up through the damp undergrowth behind him, and his foster-brother squatted down. 'Nectan has them sighted, brother.' Conaire grinned, folding his arms around his knees like an excited boy. 'Lugh blessed us with his light, for it was the sun on their spears that gave them away.'

The Epidii spear-tips had been wrapped in scraps of hide and cloth, and each man had shielded his horse's eyes with leather, and muffled the snouts. No sound of horse or sight of man had been allowed to escape their hiding place.

'I think we will need the blessing of every god we can muster,' Eremon remarked, laying his sharpening stone on his knee.

'Oh, I don't know.' Conaire's eyes glittered. 'It is the weakness – and strength – of men we are relying on.'

'I would drink to that if we had one, brother.'

'Later,' Conaire said, slapping him soundly on the back. 'At Dunadd, when all this is over. Then I will drink an entire keg of Rhiann's mead with you, and gladly suffer for it.'

Maelchon's men shied like horses as the first of Nectan's arrows flew out of the dark trees clothing the upper slopes. His warband was halfway along the bracken-filled glen, strung out in a long line by the banks of the rushing stream.

It took a moment of shock for the Orcadian king to register that the missiles had not been loosed to kill, for they thudded into the ground a short distance before the leading scouts in a neat arc, their shafts vibrating from the impact.

With surprised oaths, Maelchon's guards fell back around him, as the Lugi warriors edged into a similar ring around their king. Yet those curses were mild compared to the growl that now tore itself from Maelchon's barrel chest as a lean, dark-haired warrior rose to his feet a good way up the hillside, unfurling his limbs from the bracken around him. He was naked to the waist, his gleaming torso crossed only by the jewelled strap of a magnificent sword that hung across his back. On his head was a helmet of polished iron with a bristling boar-crest of bronze.

'Well met, Orcades king,' the young man said pleasantly.

At the sound of that familiar voice, the day around Maelchon darkened into a night of rage.

Aedan now brushed past Eremon, his head high, his cloak drawn back over his shoulder to unveil his polished harp. The instrument was his badge of office, the sign that made him sacred, untouchable. Only for this reason would Eremon bring him anywhere near a battle.

'Take care,' Eremon muttered to Aedan, as the bard strode down towards the seething column of warriors. Now that their leaders had halted, the men were milling along the side of the stream and part way up the slope near the eastern valley entrance, their agitated murmurs growing louder than the rushing water.

Maelchon's eyes were obscured by the shadow of his helmet, yet he had remained still and silent since Eremon appeared from the bracken. The men behind the king surged in confusion, the edges of the crowd disintegrating as some flowed further up the near slope to gain a better view. Others were hemmed in by the river on one side, and the rest of the warriors pressed in from the rear. Their ranks of spears dipped and swayed as they jostled each other, cursing and snarling.

Aedan halted some way up the slope, his long fingers drawing themselves across his harp strings with one flourish. As the high, piercing chord echoed off the peaks all around, the men below grew quieter, for it was appearing less likely by the moment that they would be subjected to attack.

'Honourable fighters, fierce warriors!' Aedan's bardic voice rang out clearly over the hushed crowd of men and the sound of the river. 'We salute the fire of your eyes, the strength of your arms, the heat of your hearts. So hear me, and honour my own lord, Eremon mac Ferdiad, war leader of the Epidii, consort of the Ban Cré, King Stag of the westlands, rightful king of Dalriada in Erin.'

At the announcement of Eremon's identity, a ripple of mutters ran over the warriors below, and the edge of Eremon's mouth quivered with a certain satisfaction. So not even Maelchon could stem the tide of rumour; it flowed everywhere at will.

The Orcadian king obviously thought he'd try, though, for he suddenly came to life, shouting 'Silence!' at the top of his voice, and raising his clenched fist. His whole arm shook with visible fury. 'Spit out your words, harper, and quickly! After we deal with your rabble we have a battle to join.'

Aedan ignored him and kept his head high. The rising breeze blew his dark curls back from his high forehead, and streamed his blue cloak out behind him. 'I bring a challenge out of the old tales; a challenge for only the most valiant, noble and skilled of men.'

So baited, Maelchon lurched forward one menacing step, opening his mouth to cut Aedan off. Yet before he could speak, there was a stir among the other warriors, as a man of Calgacus's age pressed free of the men who guarded him. Like Maelchon he was of dark, northern blood, yet slight compared to Maelchon's bulk. Eremon could see little of his face beyond the beard that fell to his chest, yet his thick gold torc and profusion of gleaming armbands confirmed that this was the Lugi king.

'What is this challenge, bard?' the king demanded, his posture wary rather than hostile.

'Our forces are hidden all around in the trees,' Aedan answered. 'Two thousand horses, two thousand spears, two thousand swords. We do not have to let you leave this valley alive. Yet my lord offers you mercy – a battle to be decided in the old way of the tribes. By a duel of champions.'

The Lugi king made some exclamation of surprise, as the murmurings of the warband swelled restlessly.

Aedan held up his hand for attention, raising his voice. 'Further, my lord, the greatest swordsman in Erin will act as his own champion – and he calls out the Orcades king to meet this challenge and take the field himself.'

Eremon expected the shock, and on the edge of his vision he saw the impact of the words vibrate along the wedge of men like a hammer striking iron. Yet Eremon's eyes were fixed on Maelchon, and though the planes of the king's florid cheeks were broken up by his writhing blue tattoos, still Eremon saw from afar the slight curve of his smile.

Maelchon could only react in two ways, and Eremon wasn't sure yet which he'd take. Accepting the challenge would be quick and clean – and satisfying for them both. But there was something greater that Eremon hoped for, upon which he had gambled.

And Maelchon chose much as Eremon expected. The Orcadian king threw back his head and laughed, a rasping sound with a sharp edge that sought to cut deep with its scorn. '*I*, fight *him*? I will not soil my own sword, my honour, by crossing blades with a homeless exile, a *gael*, a man with no kin or lands! Well may I fight with any peasant from the fields! Be gone, harper, and bring on your men, for I'd wager you lie about their numbers.'

Aedan said nothing in reply, but merely shrugged, turned and walked back up the slope, stepping onto a rock that had fallen from the cliffs and now lay half-covered with bracken. There, he flung out one arm towards the gathered men, none of whom could fail to see him clearly, outlined in the morning sun.

'Hear me then, men of Alba!' he cried now, with all the force his trained voice could muster. 'So the craven coward is revealed among you at last! He, your king, would sooner shed your blood than his own! Follow him and he will lead you to death – your names will be as mud and ashes to your people, and your lives fall into dark forgetfulness, because of your shame!'

With a roar, Maelchon drew his sword with a ringing sweep, rage twisting his face.

'Aye, shame!' Aedan continued, spreading his cloak out like wings. 'Shame for betraying your land, your Mother, out of greed and lust and lack of courage to stand your ground against the traitor in your midst!' He pointed with dreadful finality at Maelchon. 'This traitor, who has betrayed you, and led you to your own betrayal!'

Maelchon was now alone in the empty space before his men, shaking his head like an enraged bear. 'After me!' he screamed, the cords in his neck standing out in the sun that spilled down the valley walls. 'After me, to pound this rabble into dust!' His own guard, some two hundred men, rushed forward to surround him, howling their war cries as they swung their swords over their heads.

Yet the rest did not act as Maelchon demanded. The Lugi king had flushed a deep red, his mouth twisting in dismay, for to be so accused by a bard could be the ruin of his kingship. Suddenly he seemed to come to some decision, crying out, 'Back! Back! The bard speaks true: let the challenge be decided!'

Hardly believing his eyes, Eremon watched the movement gain ground as all the other men – Lugi and fur-clad Orcadian warriors both – began to melt away from Maelchon and his guards, drawing back from the front ranks like an ebbing wave, the mutters and murmurs now open cries of anger and shame. Many turned tail and fled altogether, shoving for all they were worth on the men gathered behind.

As all order disintegrated, a thrill of relief shot up Eremon's spine. Aedan's words, and Maelchon's refusal to take the field as champion, had undone what years of fear and intimidation had wrought, melting the weak bonds of loyalty like leaf-bud snows. *Fear is a foolish way to control people.*

And so Maelchon's own realization of this hit him, that his allies and even his own tribesmen had deserted, and would not fight. The king's scream then became a terrible roar of rage, issuing from his open throat, just as Eremon raised his hand. From the trees on his side of the glen his horsemen burst out, their swords pointing down as their mounts charged the valley floor. And from the lower ground, hidden among the boulders, Rori and Nectan's archers let loose another volley of arrows, this time set to kill.

Trailing Dòrn, Conaire reared to a halt beside Eremon, with Colum,

Finan and Fergus behind. Eremon was already in the saddle as he reached back over his shoulder for his sword.

The men around Maelchon were fine fighters; they tightened into a circle with their shields facing out, deflecting the arrows, and the first volley of their spears took down a few leading Epidii horsemen. But when the mounted charge hit the shield wall, it crumbled, and then all order was lost in a mass of rearing, screaming horses, slashing blades and war cries being hurled in all directions.

As he ducked and dodged the first violent sword-swings, Eremon's blood pounded with a wild, unleashed fury – the desperate need not to kill all the men, but one man only.

This single flame of rage powered Eremon's blade almost of its own accord, and he stabbed with desperation, pushing closer to the protective circle around the Orcadian king. Conaire was close by his shoulder, and when Eremon was bodily hauled from the saddle and set upon by hordes of heavy northmen, Conaire yelled and flung himself from horseback, quickly joined by Fergus and Colum. Together they fought to regain their footing, and formed themselves instinctively into a tight wedge to pierce the inner circle around Maelchon.

The last shreds of coolness in Eremon's head were shattered when the back of Maelchon's helmet came into view, his huge shoulders bunching and heaving as he swung his great sword. With an unearthly howl, Eremon launched himself forward, slicing through the net of arms that sought to hold him back. On both sides his own men parried swords with the other warriors, freeing Eremon to dart through when a breach opened before him.

The edge of his blade caught Maelchon's helmet just as the king himself whirled to face this new onslaught, and as the helmet clattered to the ground Eremon was arrested for a moment by the ruin of Maelchon's face. The whole of his right eye was a pulpy mass of scar tissue that sealed the lid shut. From the socket, a crimson scar sliced down in a cruel curve, scoring the cheek like the tracks of bloody tears.

Rhiann.

At the thought of what Maelchon had done to release such terror in her, rage burned Eremon's chest, and his sword was flinging itself at Maelchon's unprotected neck. The king parried the blade, and then suddenly cut under Eremon's left side with the edge of his shield. The shock ran up Eremon's arm, and with a grunt he dropped his own shield, his fingers momentarily nerveless.

Yet the smile that then curved the Orcadian king's face, drawing the scar down, was fuel to Eremon's fire and, pushing himself past the pain, he grasped his hilt with both hands and began to rain blows down on Maelchon's sword just as he had trained to do with the equally large Conaire – hard and fast and unrelenting.

Eremon had a fleeting impression of space around them both, as Maelchon's guards were either cut down, or fled. The sun was high enough now to flood the valley with light, yet all brightness was sucked into the void that was the Orcadian king's remaining eye, framed by the greasy hanks of his hair and beard. The hatred that lay there seemed to reach grasping hands around Eremon's throat, throttling the life from him.

Yet slowly, agonizingly, youth and vigour began to outweigh size and weight. Eremon sensed Maelchon weakening, in the rasping sound of his breath, and the slight slowing of his reflexes. It was then, when he was tiring, that Eremon decided to target the king's right side, for he surmised that the damaged eye would affect Maelchon's depth perception.

Without warning, Eremon suddenly leaped far into the king's right-hand field of vision, twisting as he went. The matted black head shot around, but Eremon had already drawn his blade across Maelchon's flank, under the edge of his mailshirt.

The cut was deep enough to take Maelchon's breath from him, and the king stumbled, bellowing. Recovering his balance, Eremon brought his foot around in a circle and kicked Maelchon's feet out from under him. The king went down, and Eremon jumped on to both wrists, pinning the sword arm while the tip of his own blade pressed into the hollow of Maelchon's throat. Abruptly, all sound of the fighting around them receded.

Maelchon hissed, attempting to speak, but Eremon flicked the tip of his sword, nicking Maelchon's throat. A line of blood beaded the furred hollow, and the Orcadian king made a swallowed gargle of fury far back in his throat. Swiftly, Eremon's blade moved lower, slicing the thongs that bound the mailshirt and tunic beneath. Then, panting, Eremon stopped and stared down at the naked bloated belly and chest. This beast had done this to *her*, for she had once told Eremon, and wept as she spoke of it.

Eremon rested the edge of his blade on that heaving mound of fat and muscle. 'No mercy did you show her, and no mercy will you be given,' Eremon forced out, turning his head only to spit blood from a cut lip.

'Whelp . . .' Maelchon tried to wrench his arms free, and without hesitation Eremon flicked up the blade and pressed it home with all his weight, skewering Maelchon to the ground above his collarbone. This was not the killing blow either; the king gasped and writhed, his eye flaming in agony.

Yet Eremon did not wish to look upon his face; instead he raised his head to meet Conaire's gaze. His brother was panting, his helmet under one arm, his blond hair stuck down with sweat, dirt and blood. But in his eyes was understanding, and from that look Eremon took the strength he needed.

Tilting his head, Eremon deliberately met the hatred in Maelchon's face. 'I will allow you to speak once more,' he ground out, pulling the sword free. 'To beg me for a swift death. Yet know that whatever comes out of your mouth is your last farewell.'

Chapter 69

Agricola took a deep, satisfied breath of the northern air; the scent of sun-warmed bracken and heather mingled with damp earth churned to mud by hooves. The sky was hazy with moisture and heat, but his own mind could not be clearer. The Albans appeared to have taken his bait.

His army had moved slowly these last weeks, to give them time to gather, and to ensure the destruction of everything that would shelter them afterwards. He wanted these savages to know there was nothing waiting, no safety or succour, so they would throw their all into this fight. He wanted them to succumb to the usual folly of barbarian tribes: a single charge of mindless ferocity. Their wave would rise up, then break harmlessly over the rock of his own disciplined troops.

For two weeks Agricola had known they were massing somewhere in the north, though not exactly where or when they would make a stand. Yet two days ago his scouts had finally returned. Now he knew their numbers, and the alliances that this implied.

Since then, Agricola had brought his army swiftly to the southern edge of the tribes' chosen ground: a plain of rolling country, rippled with rises and dips, scattered with hazel and oak woods. On one side it was backed by the higher ground leading into the central mountains, and on the other, by the coast.

'Sir,' Lucius said now, turning in his saddle, 'they have already mustered on the other side of *that*.' Agricola followed Lucius's outstretched hand to gaze northwards at the enormous forested ridge that reared from the plain, its peaks crowned by bare granite outcrops. He had good eyesight, and could just make out movement along its crest.

From the far side of the hill, a haze of smoke drifted in an acrid fog, smearing the blue sky. There were campfires, many of them, out of sight to the north.

'I want to swing around to the north-east and camp there, so we are facing them. We cannot chance them outflanking us, or getting between us and the sea.'

'Yet they have already taken the advantageous ground on the slope,' the tribune Marcus remarked.

For a long moment, Agricola squinted eastwards into the sun. Then he turned back to the columns of soldiers still feeding into the far end of the long, broad valley behind them, and said in a flat voice, 'It will not save them.'

Night had fallen over the sprawling Alban camp, the last night before battle. Sleepless but exhausted, her whole body trembling with frustration and fear, Rhiann paced the crest of a low hillock crowned with oak trees, a short way from the nearest bed rolls.

The leaves whispered all around her, as restless as the child in her belly, and she stopped her nervous steps. Staring out over the camp, she paused with her hand flat against a gnarled trunk, as if to draw some peace from its solidity.

It was late, yet the campfires scattered all over the dark plain still flickered with the shadows of men, thousands of men, and the sounds of drunken singing and shouted laughter floated up to her. The warriors were working themselves into the battle frenzy already: challenging each other to wrestling and sword duels; showing off their weapons; boasting of their prowess before the fires.

They were excited, eager, straining. And yet the outcome of what they yearned for had woken Rhiann in a cold sweat. For from the sea of Otherworld dreams two terrible visions had arisen, more vivid than the rest, and she had been *in* them.

First there were women and men in white druid robes, whirling around a string of bonfires on a beach, hurling curses across a stretch of dark, gleaming water. And bloodied by the firelight, huge armoured men with Roman helmets swam horses towards the shore . . .

Then a woman was fleeing in blind panic, a boy held to her chest as bolts of fire and iron rained down around her, setting fire to thatch roofs, spearing the men who rushed past to defend the walls. And the woman had no breath left to scream, but threw the child down beneath an overturned cart, covering him with her body . . .

Still shuddering from these nightmares, her skin chilled by dried sweat, Rhiann's fingers now clenched on the rough bark of the tree. As she stared up at the dark Hill of a Thousand Spears, which loomed above them, blotting out the stars, she knew somewhere that the visions were actually memories – memories involving Romans. And this is what had dragged her fear for Eremon up into her heart and throat.

Where was he? Was he even alive? Had the destruction of her visions also swept over him?

Rhiann had heard from Calgacus himself that the Romans had been sighted making their way around to the north and east, delving a camp on the far side of a stream and wooded ridge. She didn't understand why Calgacus would stand back and let them do this, and not attack as the columns were on the move. Yet Calgacus had explained to her that he had already taken the higher ground on the slope of the hill, the strongest position, and to retain that advantage he would let the Romans camp where they would.

'We came here to challenge them in open battle, lady,' Calgacus had reminded her gravely. 'This is exactly what we planned, your prince and I.'

Rhiann now buried her face in her shaking hands. Perhaps she was just going mad after all. She felt as if she were overflowing, her body straining to contain her love and fear for the baby, her terror for Eremon and the constant whispering of this other world.

Soon, she gave up all pretence of sleep. For the remainder of that endless night she held a wakeful Caitlin and sang under her breath to the baby, using her voice and her sense of the child to anchor her in Thisworld, to keep her fear for Eremon at bay. At the first hint of dawn, she and Caitlin said their farewells to Calgacus and were led by two of his warriors to the hill on the western side of the battleground, where they found a place to gaze out on the sea of pearl-grey mist below.

Rearing from it to the south was the Hill of a Thousand Spears. In reality it was not one hill, but a long ridge with many peaks that ran east-west, the eastern peak a pointed outcrop surrounded by an old hill fort. Rhiann stared hard at the ridge, searching for some kinship, yet its granite tors remained impassive.

'Sister.' Caitlin was by her side, holding out a wooden cup of steaming broth. 'This will warm you.'

In the centre of the summit of their hill was a cleared space beneath a leaning rock, and there the two guards had made a small fire, propping over it a skin bag of water, barley and beef bone.

'It will be hot today,' Caitlin observed, looking likewise to the north for Eremon and Conaire.

Rhiann nodded, and sighed. Heat was tiring; it tormented with thirst, drew sweat into eyes, made sword-grips slippery. Still, no day was a good day for battle. Not to a woman.

One of her sister's cheeks was smudged with dirt, and she had donned the old battered helmet she had been wearing the first day Rhiann saw her. That helmet and the quiver of arrows across her back had helped Caitlin to throw off her outer mantle of fear, yet the tight lines of her mouth and shadowed eyes could not be so easily hidden. Rhiann instinctively searched her mind for some comforting words, and realized all of them had been said.

Yet suddenly a change came over Caitlin. Following her sister's gaze, Rhiann narrowed her eyes into the rising sun. It seemed that something glittered once on the far edge of the plain.

With a yelp, Caitlin threw her arms around Rhiann and kissed her soundly on the head. 'There are horses, and men on their backs with many spears.'

Rhiann's blood drained from her face, then rushed back in a wave. Disentangling her limbs, she pulled herself awkwardly up the rock to balance there.

'I am going!' Caitlin called over her shoulder, already leaping from boulder to boulder towards the tethered horses. 'But I will come back soon!'

Breathless, her fingers twisting into knots, Rhiann watched her sister disappear. Then she swung back to the plain, craning to see more without overbalancing. Among the stirring masses of men revealed by the lifting mist, she could discern nothing clearly, and eventually she gave up, and carefully levered herself back down on the rock. She must wait for him to come to her.

The sun was falling full on the rocks below when Eremon at last arrived, Dòrn picking his way up the steep path. Rhiann wondered why he did not look up to her, and then suddenly her heart was chilled with an odd sensation; that somehow she did not know this man who approached her.

When the horse lurched up the last rise, Rhiann rose to her feet, and only then could she see what the shadows had hidden before. Eremon was naked from the waist up, and though he seemed to have made some token effort to wash, his skin was still smeared with dirt in places, and the tint of blood, dulling his blue tattoos. Streaks had spattered his fine helmet, and there were cracked remnants of dried blood in the creases of his knuckles where they rested across his reins. Yet it was on looking into his eyes that Rhiann finally understood what Eremon had meant, that last morning in camp, about what he would need to call forth, and how it would take him over until its job was done.

Dòrn came to a stop a few paces from Rhiann, shaking his head and pawing the earth. Without a word, Eremon freed a bag that was tied to his saddle, a rough pouch of hide, soaked through with blood as if it had been dipped in a pool of it. Then he threw that bag at Rhiann's feet.

When he spoke at last, he didn't seem to want to meet her gaze. 'In my eyes,' he whispered, 'a man could as soon take your honour as take the moon from the sky. But I do not understand how women reckon these things.' He pointed his chin at the bag. 'There, I bring the man parts of him, in exchange for what was taken from you. Burn them, or bury them as you will.'

Rhiann stared down at the bag in dawning horror, the full realization arriving as a blow to her belly. Then she glanced back at Eremon, and it was the hard light in those familiar eyes, burning in a pale face, that finally brought home to her that war had reached them. It wasn't the sight of tens of thousands of men, or the sun rising on a battlefield, or the trumpets, or flashing weapons. It was the look of a man she loved, who had gone somewhere she could never follow.

Something of this must have been revealed in Rhiann's expression, for without another word Eremon turned Dòrn and started back down the hill. 'Eremon!' His name sprang to Rhiann's lips as only a faint cry, yet abruptly the horse halted. For a moment they were both still, until with a sharp yank of the reins Eremon urged the stallion back up the hill.

Rhiann rushed forward then when he drew rein, and pressed her lips desperately to his hand, heedless of the taste of dried blood. She squeezed her eyes shut, determined not to weep.

At first Eremon's touch on her hair was uncertain, awkward, but then his fingers grew more sure, more tender, as he traced the line of her jaw, her cheek. Finally he lifted her chin, and now Rhiann couldn't see the savagery, only the straight line of his shoulders, the tilt of his head and the calm strength in his eyes.

Words fell from her lips then as they had from Linnet, unbidden, unthought. '*Do not forget the east,*' she said. '*Yet know also when to turn away.*'

Eremon did not question her, but merely drew a deep, shaking breath. 'I will remember.' He leaned down from his fighting saddle, and there in the early sun of that new day, kissed her softly. 'Remember me also.'

He was a little way down the hill when he reined in again and turned in his saddle. 'Rhiann, there is something you should know. You took Maelchon's sight, and by that I was able to defeat him.' He held her eyes. 'It was you therefore who truly dealt the killing blow, and should claim the honour of it.'

Slowly, Rhiann nodded, unable to speak past the choking lump in her throat. She stood and watched him pick his way back down to the plain, until he was swallowed by the edges of the war camp.

Then, Rhiann burned the bloody bag on the campfire, and sent the smoke as an offering to her Goddess.

The blood of the yearling calf soaked into the torn-up earth before the Roman camp gate, as the *haruspex*, arms raised to the sky, exhorted Mars, Venus Victoria and Fortuna to grant victory this day.

The mist from the stream that ran between the camp and the hill was still clearing, yet from horseback Agricola could see his armoured warriors drawn up perfectly in battle formation: the auxiliary infantry-men in the centre; the cavalry on the flanks; and the legions at the rear, directly in front of the defensive turf banks, delved the day before.

At the head of each maniple of 160 men stood standard bearers, with their wolfskin head-dresses and, at the head of each legion, the *aquilifers* holding aloft the bronze eagles. Beside the officers' horses were the trumpeters, ready to transmit the order to march once Agricola had given his address to the troops.

The marshalling ground was quiet, each man staring straight ahead in his line, the only movement their breathing and the occasional stamp of a hoof or shake of harness. It was so silent that, from a league to the south, Agricola could hear a faint murmur of weapons and voices. Chaos, waiting for them.

He drew breath for his speech, pausing for a moment to let his eyes travel up once more to the outline of the great ridge, mottled with heather along its bare spine. So many aspects of Alba drifted in the realms of mist and dreams – the weather, the people, the boundaries of tribe and alliance. Agricola had found nothing that was solid, except one thing: the uncompromising bones of the land. They were strong, unyielding, unchanging.

This clarity now appealed to him. Since Samana's death, nothing foreign had entered his sight or psyche. All emotion had receded, leaving in its wake nothing more, nor less, than the clean, focused mind with which he had first entered Alba.

Annihilation, as a goal, left pleasingly little room for uncertainty.

Chapter 70

A sudden gust of wind blew the smoke of the burning flesh straight into Eremon's face, and he coughed, leaning back on his knees. When the acrid stench cleared, he blinked his watering eyes. It would be easy, now, to let the smoke of this offering blind him, to buckle his sword on and go mindlessly back down the Hill of a Thousand Spears to join the army. Yet he could not.

Thirty thousand men were risking their lives because of his decisions, his efforts, and though he could not look on all their faces, he would damn well look into the eyes of his own men – those whom he had dragged across the sea from Erin, and now, perhaps, condemned. He owed them that, for all the others who would fall this day.

On the other side of the fire, Aedan's solemn face swam into view, his eyes fixed on the flames licking at the base of the haunch of boar meat, which rested on a small pyre made of rocks, bracken and ash twigs. Eremon did not know what the bard saw there in the smoke they were sending to their Erin god Hawen. Nor did he need to know – there was no going back now. Last night the Romans had made camp to the north-east, and were even now forming up in ranks outside its hastily erected bank, for Eremon could see them from this ridge-top. Yet the horns would let Eremon know when Calgacus needed them back.

His gaze shifted to Rori now. The youth's face was streaked with dirt, his lips pressed together as he watched the smoke drift up into the sky. Eremon was put in mind of the storm that brought their boat to Alba, and how Rori's lip had quivered then in fear. Eremon had not seen that kind of terror unman Rori for many moons.

He glanced then at Colum, chewing the end of a stick, and Finan, his sword brother of long ago. They rarely showed fear, for it had been ground out of them in the same way they honed their swords, over many years. They simply followed where their prince led, and this realization flared as another sick lurch in Eremon's gut. Good men, they were, who trusted him without question.

So was Fergus, his fierce, eager young face bringing back to Eremon so clearly the memory of his close friend Angus, dead these two years after rescuing Eremon from his own folly. *He was where he wanted to be*, Caitlin had said then. Eremon wondered now if that would indeed be enough for them all, when he called in the debt of their sworn oaths.

A fresh waft of smoke caught at the back of Eremon's throat, but he closed his nose and let it bathe him. This offering was going to Hawen; perhaps it would take Eremon's fierce hopes with it if it touched his skin. And the Caereni archers had painted over Eremon's tattoos with woad and blood, drying and stiff now across his naked chest and belly, so something of the Stag might be taken in the smoke, too.

Eremon's fingers went to his bare upper arm, stroking the ridged surface of the boar tusk that was tied there on its leather thong. As he did, his eyes met Conaire's, and he saw the same idea dawning there. Swiftly, Eremon picked at the thong as Conaire began to untie the matching tusk from his own arm and gave it to Eremon with a smile. The two tusks chinked faintly in his palm as his fingers closed over them.

Eremon rose then, and stood before the small pit they had delved next to the pyre. 'My lord,' he murmured, raising his arms, his two fists together, 'let your weapons be restored to you in exchange for giving Your strength to our own. Bring us victory this day, so that we may return to Erin and pay our respects on Your own soil.'

Eremon pressed his lips to the tusks and laid them in the hole, beckoning to Rori with a flick of his hand. The other men rose from their knees, and with a few words each, deposited their offerings in the pit: an arrow from Rori; an engraved spear-point from Fergus; and an arm-ring from Colum, won in a game of *fidchell*. From Finan came the dagger he kept at his waist. Eremon gazed at it with surprise – it was not jewelled, but the leather sheath was scarred and stained from years of use, and even the blade had been nicked in an ill-advised fight years before. Unable to speak, Eremon reached out blindly to clasp Finan on the shoulder.

'Nay, lad,' Finan murmured as he turned to go, his weathered face creasing for a moment into a smile. 'Don't spend such on me or Colum – we've lived a good and long time. What can be better for an old warrior than that his last fight is the greatest yet?'

In silence Eremon watched them leave the hill crest one by one, filing down the path towards the northern slope, where the Alban army was assembling.

'I have no gift to offer yet,' Aedan said then, laying his harp over his hands as Eremon often did with his sword. 'Yet I once told you I would be here to sing your glory, and that will be my offering.' His grey eyes shone. 'I will craft a song of your deeds this day, lord, that will reach Hawen himself on the wind, telling him of the bravery of one of his favourite sons.'

'That is a fine gift,' Eremon said, taking Aedan by his slight shoulders. 'Yet put something in it of your own bravery in the face of the Orcadian king, and I will be happy.' Without a hint of a blush, Aedan bowed formally, shouldered his harp and strode away, his cloak flapping in the rising sea breeze.

'It looks as though it will be hot,' Conaire remarked, reaching for his mailshirt.

Suddenly, Eremon's strength deserted him, and he collapsed onto the nearest boulder, his bloody tunic crushed in his hands, as all the tension of the rite finally made itself known. Slowly, he drew in one breath and then another, taking the pieces of himself that had broken apart as he looked at his men, and pushing them back together. He needed to be whole this day, of all days.

'All I have done has been to bring me here.' His own words sounded far away to his ears, as he strove to capture the parts of him still floating above this scene. Yet it still seemed unreal. Below to the north he'd glimpsed the sunlight glittering on Roman spears: 10,000 spears, and all no doubt held in perfect alignment. In contrast, from the hillside on which the Albans were assembling came a muted, confused roar of voices, weapons, horses, pipes and drums.

'No,' Conaire contradicted quietly, buckling on his sword. 'All you did has prepared you for this, but this is not why you came to Alba, brother. And this is not all you are. Remember that.'

'Then what am I?' Wearily, Eremon stood and drew his stinking tunic over his head, then reached for his mailshirt and began tying the thongs under his arms. From far away, Roman trumpets blew, and the sense of unreality grew as his blood began to beat loudly in his ears.

Conaire stood before him, grave beneath his polished helmet. 'You are the best of friends, a fine husband and, soon, a father.'

Eremon snorted, and picked up his sword from the fire. 'And I don't do any of those things well enough!' Briefly, he raised his face to the sun. He wanted to take that in, that one small sensation, before all the soft senses were overrun by the noise and the blood and heat.

'Eremon.' He opened his eyes to see Conaire staring at him with creased brows, his golden hair already sticking to his forehead with sweat. 'I tell you this, because I want you to remember what you have to live for. You are war leader, but do not sacrifice yourself to that.' Conaire's fingers closed around his sword-hilt, and his gaze, so unusually intense, devoid of his old lightness, pinned Eremon to the spot. 'You did not bring them here; you do not have to stay if all is lost.'

491

Eremon's smile faded as he looped his sword-belt around his waist, then clasped Conaire by the shoulder. 'I could say the same to you, brother, for you are all those things and more.'

'I never forget what I have to live for,' Conaire answered, looking north to the low hill where Caitlin waited.

Chapter 71

Noise was to be Alba's first weapon, as her warriors waited in the strengthening sun of that new day to see whether the Romans would take up the challenge. And when the distant lines of the enemy appeared on the edge of the cleared plain, the Alban army, arrayed all over the north-facing slopes of the ridge, set free a tumult to shake the Romans where they stood.

First the strident calls of the boar-head trumpets cleaved the air, joined by the clashing horns and screaming bone pipes, all of it echoing off the clefts of the rocks until it multiplied on itself, spiralling upwards into a cacophony of rage and growing blood-lust.

Then the battle songs began, rising and falling on the discordant din of instruments, the bards standing on the yokes of the chariots to sing and chant, each tribe and clan striving to outdo the other. There were oaths being shouted, too, and curses and prayers for victory, and the men were whipped into an increasing frenzy by the druids, who stalked the lines with arms raised, their robes sweeping out like the wings of war crows.

In between the lifted ranks of glittering bronze trumpets, the banners of wolf and bear and stag streamed out in the wind, their poles shaken in frenzied hands, stabbed into the earth and raised again to make the standards soar and dip, and the sun glanced off gleaming leather and iron weapons in a confusion of piercing light and shadow, as the warriors leaped and danced, shouted and screamed, and brandished their spears and swords in the air.

In the midst of all this chaos, Eremon sat astride Dòrn, close to Calgacus in his gilded chariot. The Caledonii king was splendidly arrayed, with a war helmet of eagle shape, its bronze nose-guard a sharp beak, its winged crown sheathed in gold. He wore a leather breastplate, tooled and gilded, and over that a fringed cloak woven with many colours. His chariot horses were black, and they stamped and snorted within coral and enamel-studded harnesses, their eyes rolling white beneath horned war masks.

'The sun is still in our eyes!' Calgacus now cried over the tumult. 'I assumed they would take longer to assemble.'

Eremon tore his gaze away from the Romans, marching ever closer, and squinted up at the sky. 'When they are in position, the sun will be higher.'

'Your sight is better, prince,' Calgacus remarked, leaning in. 'Tell me what you see.'

Eremon was silent for a time, struggling to bring his galloping pulse under stern rein. The best outlet for fear was the battle frenzy, but he must stay under control for a good while yet. 'The centre is on foot,' he shouted at last. *They are just men*, he told himself. 'The armour of the centre is different from the rest: these must be the auxiliaries. Behind them, I can see the eagle emblems of the legions, held in reserve.' Silently, Eremon's lip curled. Agricola was doing his best to avoid shedding pure Roman blood, then, and used his auxiliary units from other conquered peoples of the Empire for the front lines. 'On the right and left flanks, there are auxiliary cavalry.' *And each man is armoured in iron, we have only leather and farmboys with picks.*

'Then our plan holds?'

Eremon sucked air in to calm his racing thoughts, and looked up at the Caledonii king, high in his chariot. His helmet felt heavy on his neck, prickling with sweat along his scalp. 'Our plan holds, lord.'

At that, Calgacus smiled and reached down to take Eremon by the shoulder. 'No place for titles now, my friend.'

Around them, the noise was surging, as the Romans drew closer.

'Our trail has brought us by twisting turns to this place,' Eremon said. 'I pray it also takes us from it, riding side by side.'

The king grinned, all the hardness in his face, and the years spent guarding his throne given over to the fierce anger of a young warrior protecting his home. 'You once boasted that you fought as well as you spoke, prince of Erin. Now, to my great pleasure, I can see if your boast holds true! May Lugh guide your steps, and Manannán your arm!'

Eremon tightened his grip on the king's wrist before dropping his hand. 'And may Hawen bless all the days of your life.'

Calgacus held up his sword and saluted Eremon. 'To Alba! She thanks you for her deliverance.' Those fierce golden eyes looked deep into Eremon, as they had done so on the first day they met. 'Go well, my son.'

'And you.' Straightening in the saddle, Eremon settled his helmet lower on his brow to shield the sun, turning Dòrn away down the hill. Rori fell into close step on his roan stallion, holding aloft the scarlet and white standard of the Boar of Dalriada.

494

As they picked their way down the slope between the heaving, screaming ranks of Albans, Eremon tore his gaze away from the steadily encroaching tide of Romans far across the plain to search out his own men, clustered under the White Mare banner in ranks on the flat. He was looking for one man in particular.

I will meet you in the middle, Conaire had said, his grin lighting up his face. Yet Eremon had been unable to find any words of farewell, because they had always fought side by side.

So long as you leave some Romans for me, Eremon had managed to croak at last, and then all was as it had always been with them before battle; the banter blotting out the fear.

Despite the keenness of his gaze, Eremon could not see Conaire now because of the rippling banners of the Alban warriors. Yet he knew the time for engagement was near, for around him the songs had settled into one great war chant, surging and ebbing like a storm sea, swords beating on shields in an ever-increasing drumbeat, growing more urgent and primal, until it became part of the pulse of blood through the veins, through the heart.

Alba! Alba! Alba!

Below, the great war machine of the Romans came to a rumbling halt only a league away.

From his horse on a ridge to the north-east, Agricola watched the advance of his men with an impassive face.

'Savage fools!' one of his tribunes muttered, as a wave of barbarian charioteers, set free by the blare of a trumpet, flung themselves down the hill-slope to crash on to the plain. 'We haven't used chariots like that for centuries! Backward barbarians!'

The chariots had wheeled as one body, careening wildly up and down the bare alley of land between the two armies, horse-tails flying from the tips of the drivers' spears. Their screams carried clearly to the mounted Roman officers, yet before that aural onslaught Agricola's auxiliary infantry stood silent and firm, their oval shields interlocked into a formidable wall. At the end of each pass, each chariot whirled and tilted at a crazy angle, one wheel spinning in mid-air.

Someone snorted behind Agricola. 'Insanity! Bloody insanity!'

'They will only tire out their horses,' Agricola remarked.

'I doubt that anything could tire that one out,' Lucius commented, pointing at one screeching savage with silver hair flying behind his helmet, his face writhing with blue tattoos. The man was naked but for his bright cloak and a gold torc, and those tattoos curled all over his chest, arms and legs, all the way to his bare feet, braced on the wicker platform.

'Still, one can't help but admire such recklessness, however fool-hardy.'

'My dear Lucius,' Agricola laughed, 'admire as you will.' He leaned back in his saddle. 'They will still die.'

The rush of wind into Lorn's open mouth tore his war shout from his throat. His heart was soaring, unfettered, and as the chariot clattered over the stony plain, swaying from side to side, he leaned out towards the Roman lines, steadying himself with the reins.

'Fear us, red invader!' he screamed again. 'Our swords are thirsty for your blood, our arrows for your throats! Fear the sons of Alba! Fear the sons of Arawn and Taranis and Lugh the mighty!'

Though the chariot troop was a screeching onslaught of noise and colour, with the painted wicker, the decorated, flying horses, and the thunder of their iron wheels, Lorn kept them all just beyond javelin range. Yet the Romans made no move to come forward and challenge him, the cowards.

Another turn, and Lorn's heart delighted as he heard the hundreds of chariots behind following his lead. He slapped the reins across his stallions' backs, and the beasts stretched out their necks and raced faster. Letting loose another yip of glee, Lorn raised one hand. At the signal a host of small, dark men sprang up from their hiding places at the feet of the charioteers, and their bows curved high, unleashing a rain of death on the Romans.

Those long, foreign shields were raised in sudden, startled defence, and at last Roman curses flew up to join Lorn's own, as many of the barbs found their mark, and the first of the invaders fell beneath the feet of their fellows.

As the chariots spun once more out of javelin range, Nectan easily kept his feet beside Lorn, his arm a blur as he took arrow to string and released, over and over. Glancing behind, Lorn gazed up at the black hordes of his own countrymen massed on the slopes, cheering him on, cheering for Alba, and at that moment Lorn did not care what would come to him that day. There was only the wind, the thundering wheels and the perfect tension of his muscles as he swayed in his chariot. There was only the noise of the war chant above, lifting him up, making him more than he was.

Alba! Alba! Alba!

It swelled and roared, and bore him up to the rarer air, making of him a god.

Leaning back in his saddle, Rori held his reins in one hand, his fingers clenched around the scrap of blue cloth tied to them, which he'd torn from the hem of Eithne's dress. If he held it streaming through his fingers and thought of her, then the fear seemed to loosen its stranglehold on his chest, and he could breathe.

Suddenly Eremon glanced back over his shoulder, his prince, whom he had followed over sea and mountain both, and in Eremon's wide grin Rori forgot even the terror that thundered in his ears.

'By Hawen, so it begins!' Eremon called to him. 'Yet now he comes off the field, I must speak to Lorn. Come!'

He dug his heels into Dòrn's black flanks, and Rori followed, until they were both charging down the hill-slope side by side. In his other hand Rori gripped the banner of the Boar, and it streamed above his head, the ends snapping and cracking in the wind. These were all he lived for, what he held in his hands: the Boar for his prince; the blue for Eithne. They carried him beyond fear, beyond the dread that clawed at his guts, propelling him towards the cold, silent mass of alien men, who stood waiting on the plain below, watching the whirling chariots with empty eyes.

From the corner of his eye, Conaire saw the Boar banner racing down the slope, and Dòrn bearing Eremon to the left of battle to join his cavalry.

Yet Conaire could then spare no further glance for his brother, for directly in front of him, across the stretch of scored turf and torn-up bushes, the Roman trumpets had called, and the lines of foot soldiers had braced their javelins into attack position. In contrast to the Albans they were silent, their faces impassive at this distance, battle-hardened. It was time.

Conaire raised his sword, gazing around fiercely at the Epidii and Caledonii elite who had formed their battle wedge and were awaiting his order. *His order*, and his only. Alongside the bright surge of blood-lust, pride crested warm in Conaire's chest. If his son could only see . . .

He glanced again over the tight ranks of his foot warriors, their shields drawn up into a wall to echo that of the foreigners they faced. Here, now, all the days of training in snow and sleet and wind would carry. Here with his 2,000 – the first to engage – whose job it was to thrust into the Romans as one blade, breaching the solid defences of the infantry pack that awaited them. To each side of the point of the wedge, other men formed protective wings, like the hilt of a sword point.

For a brief moment, Conaire allowed himself to wish for Eremon – not because he was scared, but because they had always fought side by side, since their first battle as boys. When their war shouts echoed together, even the fiercest of fights seemed to grow lighter, and Conaire could easily believe that they were invincible, beloved of the gods. He risked one last glance, yet Eremon had his own job to do, his own troop to lead, and he was already on the move. And though he wasn't here, he was relying on Conaire as he never had before.

A Roman trumpet screeched, and Conaire's sword came down, and Roman javelins met flying Alban spears mid-air, with a terrible whine and clash. Then his men were charging forward in formation all around him, screaming for the Mare and the Boar both.

Screaming for their lives.

Chapter 72

At the thunderous impact of the two armies, Caitlin's arms tightened around Rhiann's shoulders. On the sidelines, there was no comfort to be had from speaking, and they found that all they craved was the warmth of touch. Like two frightened cubs, they burrowed into each other, Caitlin standing on a rock behind Rhiann, arms clasped about her; Rhiann holding her hands.

Conaire held the centre, they both knew that. And Rhiann also knew that Eremon led the cavalry, and therefore had not yet joined the battle. Her cold fingers crept up to brace Caitlin's hands. 'They have trained for this, *cariad*,' she whispered. 'I know Conaire will triumph, I know he will.'

Rhiann could feel Caitlin's heart thudding against her back, her chest rising and falling swiftly. Yet Caitlin's reply was cut off by a sudden crackling that came from somewhere in the undergrowth around the hill.

Instantly alert, Caitlin's arms slackened. 'Go and see what that is,' she instructed the two Caledonii warriors, who were standing behind, watching the battle with ill-concealed frustration. As they unsheathed their swords and crept away, Caitlin released Rhiann and unslung her bow from her back.

'Look!' Rhiann's attention had been claimed by a black horse racing beneath a scarlet and white banner. Eremon had finished with Lorn and was crossing the hill again to the other side, behind Conaire's lines, leaving Lorn and his chariots drawn up out of range to the left.

Yet Caitlin was not following the progress of the black stallion. 'It is Conaire!' she suddenly yelped. 'Look, Rhiann, he has broken the Roman line!'

From the hill to the right of battle, Eremon gazed down with tense pride, as the wedge of the Epidii infantry pierced the Roman ranks, like a sharp prow through water. Then the centre block of Roman foot soldiers was disintegrating, confused at this show of discipline from their barbarian enemies, unable to charge the hill because of the wings that spread out neatly behind the wedge, in a bulwark of men.

The seething mass of Calgacus's warriors on the hillside erupted into frenzied cheering, shaking their spears and swords, only held in check by Calgacus on his chariot, hair and arms and horses a great blaze of gold.

However, there was no time for Eremon to pause and watch, for Conaire would need aid very soon. Below, to the east of the hill, Eremon's own cavalry troop of 2,000 horsemen waited for him. On the western side of battle, Lorn's chariots had cleared javelin range and spun to re-form in lines. As yet, the Roman cavalry had received no order to advance, and all eyes of both sides were on the centre, milling with infantry.

'Hold your men,' Eremon muttered as he galloped down the hill to his horsemen, his eyes darting sidewise to the Epidii wedge. 'Hold them, brother!'

Dòrn came to a halt in a flurry of scattered stones, before Finan's bay stallion. Behind, Rori reined in under his banner, breathing hard.

Finan turned to Eremon with a grin that split his lined face, his eyes alight with excitement. 'He broke them, lad, he did it! They cannot advance!'

Struggling within the dense mass of screaming, grunting men, Conaire ducked another javelin and caught it on his shield. As he wrenched it free, a Roman sword stabbed out from the interlocked shields before him, seeking his belly, and he remembered, in a vivid flash, how Eremon's roll and upthrust once killed a man in this situation.

So Conaire dived, his sword pivoting beneath him, and the Roman went down with a scream, tearing a hole in the shield wall. With a cacophony of screeches the men to each side of Conaire poured into it, slashing away with their longer swords, wrenching the rent wider.

Rolling to his feet, Conaire struggled to beat back the red fog of rage and forced himself to cling to cool wits. He had a responsibility to Eremon, to his men, not to lose himself in the battle lust.

Conaire yelled an order now, urging the men to hold their tight formation, darting back and forth in an attempt to be everywhere in their sight and hearing at once. Through sheer force of will and by his own example, he would not allow any warriors to descend into their own wild abandon, and so splinter the wedge they had carefully constructed.

The Roman lines had struggled to re-form around the breach, and now the Albans were fighting on three sides. Yet no matter how they hurled themselves against the Epidii warriors, the Romans could find no weakness, no way in beneath the tight shields, or between the men fighting side to side with their designated partners.

Instead of a disorganized rabble that could easily be separated and cut down, the Romans faced men fighting much as they did, and as no quarter was given, so none could be won. The fighting became more brutal, as desperation took hold, as men were coaxed out from behind their shields, and swords hacked at ankles and knees and elbows.

'Hold your line!' Conaire screamed at his men, swiftly wiping sweat from his sword hand down his tunic. 'Hold, damn you, or Manannán's wrath will be upon you!' He couldn't see whether he was making any difference, whether the Romans had broken through elsewhere. All he could see was the sun, splintered into a thousand shards of light, and the world of darkness beneath, a world narrowed to screams and grunts and cries, hot blood, and the sweat running down into his eyes.

Then, far away, as if in a dream, Conaire sensed the thundering of hooves, and he knew without looking that Eremon's horsemen were on the move. With a wild yell, he took his sword in both hands and ploughed into the breach that had opened before him.

'They are faltering, Mars take them!' Agricola's emotions at last made themselves felt, as the first hint of doubt chilled his belly. His 3,000 auxiliaries should have been a match for this rabble, however great their numbers.

But their forward troops were not acting as they had any time before, in his sight at any rate. They held together as a group, wheeled and thrust as one weapon. His own men were trained to deal with reckless charges, yet now they milled and fell back in confusion, before pushing forwards again, exhorted on by their captains. Agricola could read their doubts from afar, in the surge and ebb of their bodies.

'Send the cavalry in,' he ordered, and breathed through his nose, pinching the bridge, as the order was passed on down the line, with shouts and then trumpet calls. From behind the massed ranks of legionaries held in reserve before the camp walls, the auxiliary horsemen edged forward, taking up a stance at each flank of the fighting infantry.

'Look, their own cavalry is massing,' Lucius observed, pointing towards the chariots on one side, and the large troop of horsemen that had detached themselves from the greater sea of screeching Albans on the other.

Agricola jerked his reins, as his mount tossed and shook its head. The shadow of his helmet plume waved and quivered on the turf beneath its feet. 'We've seen all the chariots can do,' he sneered. 'As for the other wing . . .' He smiled. 'Why, it is their surprise we hold.'

The red-clothed Roman cavalry flowed out from both sides of the auxiliary ranks. At the sight, Eremon at last gave the order to release his own men. As Dòrn charged down the hill towards them, he leaned back in the saddle to break his descent, sparing two glances only.

One was for Conaire's infantry. Though beset on three sides, it was successfully pinning the auxiliary troops on the flat. His other glance was for Lorn. Far away over the mass of struggling foot warriors, the charioteers had lined up as Eremon taught them to. Lorn, now re-dressed in tunic and armour, had freed his sword for his own charge.

Good man! Eremon thought with satisfaction, marvelling that after all his truculence, Lorn had obeyed at the last, when it mattered. Yet now Eremon's attention was drawn down the length of his own sword, and bracing himself in the saddle he let loose the war cry of Dalriada. 'The Boar! The Boar!'

Instantly it was taken up by the remnants of his men around him, and the Epidii chant and the Caledonii cry rang out, as the tide of horsemen rushed across the plain. There, to the eastern side of battle, his men met the first wing of Roman cavalry in a turbulent crash of sword and shield that shook the very rocks from the peaks above.

Nearly choking on stinging bile, Rori hacked about him and endeavoured to keep his head as his lord kept his. He must stay by Eremon's side, as Conaire had asked him to do.

Terror leaped and plunged in his heart with each thrust, and he was sure that every screaming Roman that came under his blade must surely be his last. Some of his blows went wide, and he had to twist and duck under the counter blow, relying on his fine horsemanship to swing him out of harm's way. Some strokes met with a sickening crunch of splintered bone, the give of flesh when he cleaved it. Blood gushed hot down his hands, spattered in his eyes, yet somehow he lived.

Suddenly there was a terrible ring of iron, and Rori clawed the blood from his eyes to see that Eremon had blocked a blow meant for him. With a wink that damped down the fire in his face, Eremon spun Dòrn again into the fray, whooping and whirling his sword above his head, and bringing it down in twisting blows that Rori had never seen a man make, or thought possible. Before Rori's eyes, his prince was transformed into a glorious, blood-soaked, laughing god, corded arms brown under the sun, blade a blurred shaft of light in his hands. A hero from the old tales. A man to fight for.

With a hoarse yell that barely made it past his cracked throat, Rori spurred his horse forward into the breach Eremon had torn, desperate to follow that god wherever he may lead. *Son of the sun*, the Epidii had once called Eremon. But it was not until this day that he had earned the name.

In a far corner of his mind, Rori resolved to tell Aedan this as soon as he was able, to make a song fitting for his lord this day. A song to last a thousand years.

Tearing her gaze away from the slaughter unfolding below, Caitlin rose from her crouch on the rock and glanced nervously over her shoulder, brushing her braids from her sweaty neck.

'The guards have not returned,' she said.

Yet Rhiann barely heard her, for her own eyes were fixed on that horse charge, even though from this distance she could not discern any one man from the others. But she could *feel* Eremon's heart clamouring in his chest, as her own echoed it, could sense the rasping breath, the sharp grunts behind each stab. It was almost as if she were there with him.

'Rhiann!' Caitlin barked, grasping her shoulders. 'Where are those guards?'

Rhiann blinked up at Caitlin as if waking, breathing hard. 'They have most likely taken up position lower down, sister. Perhaps it is a better way to protect the hilltop. Do not worry.'

'No.' Caitlin frowned and shook her head. 'I just don't like the feel of it.' She busied herself tightening the quiver across her back, leaving one white-fletched arrow lying at her feet. 'I must go and see; that is what Conaire would want of me. It would be Eremon's order.'

Rhiann was suddenly chilled. 'Then I will come with you.'

Caitlin darted a meaningful look at Rhiann's belly. 'No. You will be safer here, not stumbling about on this uneven ground.' She picked up her bow and the arrow, and wet her fingers to run them down the fletching. Then she nocked the arrow on the string and pointed upslope with her chin. 'Go and stand among those hazel trees, right at the edge. At least there you are better hidden.'

As Caitlin crept away, Rhiann pushed down the sudden prickling of fear at the base of her spine, and clambered back up the rocks to take refuge under the young trees as directed. Panting from the heat, she watched Caitlin until she merged with the hawthorn scrub further along, and then a great shout wrenched Rhiann's attention back to the battlefield, so she was once more oblivious to her immediate surroundings.

The Roman cavalry was wavering around him; Eremon could feel it. Hemmed in by his charge, their horsemen stumbled back into the mass of their own infantry, who were being pushed into their rear by Conaire's wedge. The Roman horses reacted instinctively, lashing out with rearing legs, crushing many infantry warriors under their hooves.

With a rush of exultation, Eremon sensed the order of Roman infantry and cavalry start to crumble around him, and he rallied his men with another war cry, torn from a throat hoarse with thirst. From the other side of the river of Roman auxiliaries, a Dalriada war cry answered him, and Eremon knew it came from Conaire.

This was it: this was when the tide began to turn. Eremon could sense it in the minute slackening of the Roman charge, a subtle easing of the ferocity with which the horsemen had first plunged their way into Eremon's carefully formed lines. He cried out for joy, for pride, because it had worked: melding the Alban fire of the sword arm with Roman order and discipline. *He* had done it. He, Eremon, had dared to take what was strong in both peoples, and hurl the combined force as one. And there it was again; he was sure now. The Romans *were* pulling back.

'Hold!' Eremon screamed, desperate for his men not to break their formation at this first sign of retreat. The heat was infernal, thick with the stink of horse and blood.

To his surprise, the Romans nearest to him were rearing back, twisting in their saddles to turn their faces from Eremon's men. Turning to the east. And Eremon realized dimly that he had heard a far blare of trumpets, and it was to this sound that the Romans were drawn, all their heads lifting as one.

Do not forget the east, Rhiann had said. *Do not forget the east.*

But he had. And with a knowledge like darkness dawning, Eremon turned also. On a long ridge that formed the horizon towards the sea, a fresh wave of Romans was pouring down on to the battlefield.

They were horsemen, thousands of horsemen. And with them came an endless red tide of foot soldiers racing beneath proud eagle emblems, which spread dark wings against the hot sun.

The horror hit Rhiann like a felling blow, and she stumbled back from the edge of the rocks.

Eremon's charge had drawn her out of the shadow of the trees into the sun, yet she couldn't feel any warmth, only something icy and dark that slithered over her skin. Instinctively, she curled her arms around her belly, but when a twig snapped in the undergrowth behind her she whirled, blinded by the harsh sun and her own tears.

'Caitlin!' she cried. 'There are *reserves*! Agricola had reserves!'

Yet Caitlin did not answer her.

Beneath the rustling trees on the crest of the hill, a shadow detached itself from the others and stepped forward into the sunlight, moving slowly but with implacable will.

'Yes,' Gelert whispered. 'They have come. And so have I.'

Chapter 73

With a speed belying his age, Gelert darted forward and made a grab for Rhiann's wrist. She threw herself back, the instinct to get away clogging all rational pathways in her mind, then she felt the ground give beneath her feet. Before she could grasp anything, her arms were flailing. Crying out, Rhiann plunged over the hill to where the slope fell away to an old landslide of tumbled rock and dark earth pierced by tree roots. As she fell she twisted, trying desperately to cushion her slide down the slope on her haunches, yet the angle was steep, the scree loose and her heavy, awkward body increased the momentum of her rush. In terror she felt herself begin to tumble over, her arms flung out wildly, fingers scrabbling in the gravel and damp earth. Yet there was no stopping herself, not now, and just as she was tossed over on to her front she came up hard against a jutting rock, and was caught there, the impact tearing deep into her belly.

Her cry became a scream of pain, and Rhiann curled herself around into a ball, her belly pierced with fiery stabs of agony. Around the edges of her sight the sunlight darkened, and there was a terrible shrieking in her ears. *Was it the baby crying?* She must not lose consciousness, she must not. Rhiann bit down hard on her lip, tasting blood, and the world stopped spinning long enough to open her eyes, her scraped cheek pressed into the soil.

From one eye, she watched Gelert crawling his way down to her sidewise, like an old, bleached crab on a rock. Desperately sucking in air, Rhiann dug her fingers into the soil, and managed to lever herself up against a large rock, one palm curling around a sharp, pointed stone.

Gelert stopped a few paces from her and squatted down, and though Rhiann's sight wavered with the pain, she followed his yellow eyes as they travelled eagerly over her scratched and bleeding legs, before coming to rest with fascination on her belly.

An unearthly light seemed to gleam in the druid's pupils, and he smiled, his thin lips parting to reveal stained teeth. His once-white robe was torn, mud-brown and blood-spattered, and over it he had slung a fresh wolf-skin, the stench making her gag. His straggling beard covered his chest, and the bare remnants of his hair sprouted in weedy tufts to each side of his mottled scalp.

'All this way,' he muttered under his breath, his voice a perverse singsong. 'All this way, all these leagues, all the patience . . . yes, patience. And then you get what you want, if you have been true.'

Rhiann struggled to breathe through the agony in her belly, which was spreading now in cramping waves, encircling her whole torso and lower back in bands of tightening iron. She could not move, for her legs were numb and weak, and all her strength was seeping away into her pain.

'Where . . . have you been?' she gasped, hoping desperately, if she kept him talking, that Caitlin might find her. *Caitlin may already be dead,* she thought then with sickening fear.

Gelert smiled, cocking his head as if listening to some voice, his bony knees sticking out to either side, his long fingers kneading restlessly at the earth in front of him. '*She* dares to ask me questions. *She,* the daughter of a whore, and . . . ah!' One eye lit up, the white brow arching. 'My gods tell me that another daughter comes. Another daughter of the Great Whore, another daughter to darken the world of men.' Gelert shook his head. 'Not to be borne. Not to be *born* . . . ha!'

Rhiann's fingers tightened over her pulsing abdomen. Her insides felt as if they were being stabbed. And then the pain crested, there was a tightening and a rush of warmth from between Rhiann's legs. She bit her lip again to stop herself from crying out, though she knew immediately that her waters had broken. *But he must not know, he cannot know. Oh, my child, do not come now, not so early, not now.*

Painfully, Rhiann shifted her buttocks so that the dress between her legs would not darken with the rush of fluid. Yet despite the strength of her will, tears of agony and grief welled in her half-closed eyes.

Seeing them, Gelert smiled again. 'Always so proud,' he murmured, 'so scornful. Yet I knew that all would be taken from you and that mewling prince of yours. I knew if I found patience that you would weep before me, one day.'

'You gain nothing from harming me,' Rhiann managed. 'Caitlin is here, and she is looking for me.' She tensed, her breath freezing in her throat as a pain ripped through her again. 'She will kill you.'

'Ah, yes, the other one,' Gelert mused. 'But why do you think she is not here? The powers of my gods are greater than that. It is a little thing, see, to set the traps of vision, of strange sounds that draw her away. She hears you crying, yes? She hears the clash of swords, like the men did. But she goes the wrong way; they all do, for the forest is my realm, and there my magic holds sway.' He laughed, a wheezing, wet sound. 'You think she will find her way through my mists and dreams back to you? Ha! You always thought too much of the Sisterhood. Women's hearts are as weak as their bodies.' He smiled again and shook his head. 'Nay, pretty, there is only me and you and the little new one – a fine sacrifice to my lord gods, indeed!'

Icy fear drenched Rhiann's pain. 'No gods demand such blood,' she gasped out. 'You are a travesty of the Brotherhood! Your gods will turn their faces from you after death, if you commit such a deed!'

Yet the words fell as droplets of rain on parched earth, and drifted away into dust. For from beneath the wolf-skin, Gelert produced an unsheathed dagger, and started over the ground towards her.

Eremon had only one option: to force away the knowledge that Agricola had held back thousands of men, perhaps as many as 10,000 – doubling his initial forces. To give the Albans false confidence; to make them believe they could win; to draw them here to battle.

To draw me. I did it. It was my decision.

No! Eremon would not give in to these thoughts yet, not now! He must wheel his flagging men instead, rally those who had frozen in terror, and meet the challenge coming at him head on. He tore the Boar standard from Rori's numb grasp, and clenching his knees, rose up in his saddle and waved the banner in great, sweeping arcs. 'To me!' he cried. 'The Boar, the Boar!'

His men did not hesitate.

Wheeling their horses on the spot, they screeched their war cries and hefted their blades with as much vigour as when they were fresh. Eremon flung the standard back at Rori, and leaned down to pluck a spear from a dead horse's belly, before digging his heels into Dòrn. The rest of his horsemen streamed away after him, merging swiftly back into formation as they ate up the ground that separated them from the onrushing Roman reserves.

Behind them, the Roman cavalry who had now been released from Eremon's onslaught saw their chance. Pouring through the breach that opened between Eremon's men and Conaire's infantry, they charged up the slope at the greater mass of Albans who had been holding back under Calgacus.

And finally, answered by a howl that shook the entire hillside, the golden king slashed down his sword and gave the Albans leave to attack, and the whole flank of the hill seemed to slide down on to the plain.

Save them, Eremon thought desperately, as his horsemen and the Roman reserves crashed into each other like storm-tossed waves. *Save us all.*

★

Rhiann's palm grew still around the stone, hidden under a fold of her dress.

Then, as Gelert raised the knife higher, his fingers trembling, she flung scattered dirt at him with one hand and stabbed upwards with the other. The sharp rock caught Gelert in the soft flesh under his arm, and with a screech he dropped the blade and fell onto one knee, teetering off balance.

Ignoring the tearing pain in her belly, Rhiann kicked out with a flailing foot and managed to connect with Gelert's other shin, sending him tumbling down the slope. He was old, and his leg caught in an arching tree root and twisted. There was a loud snap of bone and a terrible scream.

Blinking the tears and dust from her eyes, Rhiann desperately tried to haul herself up the rock to her feet. Yet the pain felled her with one blow, wrenching open her vitals, and her legs buckled again, her sight laced with stabs of flame. Sobbing, Rhiann began to crawl instead, dragging herself over the stony earth, up the path between the rocks, anywhere, so long as it was away from him. Her legs and hands scrabbled for purchase, her overwhelming fear for the child her only strength.

'Don't come now,' she whispered to it. 'Stay inside, stay safe and warm, and I will hold you. I will hold you . . .'

The pain had resolved itself into waves now, each one bearing her up to a bright place of agony that verged on unconsciousness, followed by a trough of darkness that promised another kind of oblivion. And each time, Rhiann fought the urge to let herself go into that shadowed place, to escape from the pain. For if she did let herself sink into it she was lost, and so was her child.

Her daughter.

From behind came an inhuman moaning, and after a moment of silence a rhythmic scrabble and rasping slide, punctuated by harsh grunts of effort.

Lorn's chariot had immediately become hemmed about with Roman horsemen, and a cool part of him realized, even as he hacked about him, that a chariot could not stand up to such an attack. One horse was manoeuverable, where a chariot was not.

With careless grace he danced along the yoke, cut the harnesses with two swipes, and slapped one stallion away from the fighting while he leaped on to the other's bare back. Behind him, the chariot stumbled and rolled, and was lost among the ranks of trampling hooves. His men began to do the same, and many of the Romans fell as their own horses ran into the careering, tipping chariots.

Then, in the midst of the desperate fighting, Lorn sensed a slackening of the onslaught, and realized that a troop of Roman cavalry had managed to form up on the Alban side of his men and were racing up the slope to barrel into the waiting warriors under Calgacus.

Lorn wondered how these Romans had got past Conaire's walls, and it was then that he heard the Roman trumpets and the wild cheers of their infantry. Desperate to see, Lorn shouted to his men and wheeled his stallion, fighting his way back up the slope with a thrusting spear, unable to swing his sword bareback without a saddle.

Pressed by the Romans on all sides, Lorn was relieved when he heard the sudden hiss of arrows overhead, and looked up to see Nectan and his archers covering their retreat, calmly despatching all the Romans who surged at their rear. In response to curt commands, the foreign horsemen and foot soldiers immediately gave up, returning their attentions to the Epidii infantry.

Lorn halted his horse before Nectan, clutching at the cut remains of his chariot harness as his reins. 'A thousand thanks,' he gasped out, pulling off his crested helmet to wipe sweat from his brow. The sun beat down as the swords had beat on the shields, and Lorn's dry throat was sticky with thirst.

Nectan did not take his eyes off the Roman lines below as he continued shooting in a measured rhythm, a forest of arrows stuck into the ground at his feet. 'Look there,' he said evenly, 'where the prince took the eastern flank.'

Lorn blinked sweat from his eyes and peered in the direction Nectan indicated. His breath caught. Thousands of new reinforcements had flooded down the rise to the east into Eremon's ranks. The cavalry originally engaged by Eremon now had a clear opening to plough into the waiting mass of Albans.

Just then, released by the Caledonii king's great sword, the Albans crashed over the Roman lines, and all order disintegrated before Lorn's eyes. Conaire's wedge was immediately lost in a surge of whirling swords, spears and screeches, and all demarcations between the two armies vanished.

Then, as more trumpets blew, the waiting legions at last began their march forward in one deadly wall of men.

'All the gods above,' Lorn could only say, his dry throat closing over. 'There must be above twenty thousand now,' he croaked. 'Eremon never knew there would be so many.'

'There,' Nectan said, and this time he paused to catch Lorn's eye, pointing with his chin. Then Lorn saw that the little man was not as unmoved as he'd first thought. His dark eyes glinted with a sorrow that was not masked. 'The banner of the Boar has gone down.'

Another surge, and Rhiann's whole body was caught in one towering font of agony.

For a moment, it ebbed just enough for her to pull herself over another handspan of earth, her eyes running with sweat and tears. Now there was more fluid soaking the soil between her legs, and from the sharp, copper scent she knew it was blood.

'I come,' Gelert's voice rasped, and now there was no humanity in it. 'And I take you with me, in fire and blood, and your whelp as well.'

Rhiann tried to shut out the evil words, and instead forced every fibre of strength into her raw fingers and the muscles of her arms, screaming with cramp as she would like to scream if she had the breath. Vaguely, she felt the amber necklace snag on a stone and snap, and heard the clatter of beads rolling away.

And there, in the cold shadow of a great, bulbous rock, Gelert's hand at last closed over her ankle.

The white face of the Roman foot soldier swam before Eremon's vision as he ran him down, hacking into the man's neck.

Dark eyes lifted in terror, a snarl on the bloodied lips, but Eremon didn't see the broken javelin clasped in the man's hands. He only felt the lurch in Dòrn's stride as the stallion's desperate scream rose above the other cries that swirled in his ears. And then the world tilted, and Eremon's only thought as his mount fell beneath him was to wrench himself away from the dead weight.

He nearly succeeded.

Jerking up his knee and pushing against Dòrn's back flung Eremon wide, as the impact with the ground jarred all breath from his body, his sword falling from his grasp, his helmet rolling free. But the dying horse writhed and bucked in agony, and though Eremon clawed desperately in the soft earth to drag himself away, Dòrn gave one last roll and trapped Eremon's ankle beneath his heaving flank, before collapsing into stillness.

The pain was not great, nothing like the terror that flooded Eremon's veins as he realized his helplessness. His fingers groped for his sword, lying a handspan away now, as a dark forest of legs trampled the ground all around him. In the chaos of ringing swords and grunts, screams of horses and thud of falling bodies, Eremon could see and hear nothing clearly. He glimpsed a flash of Rori's hair, and Finan's grey head, but they were pressed by enemy soldiers, and Eremon's throat was so dry from the heat and screaming that when he tried to shout to his men nothing came out but a feeble croak.

Then a wild yell suddenly sounded above Eremon, and the sun was darkened by a looming shadow that leaped up onto the stallion's curved belly, laying about him with a sword that flashed dusty sunlight from its bloody blade. All around the shadow leaped other men, and squinting up at his attacker Eremon scrabbled at his waist for his dagger, tensing to stab at any flesh that presented itself.

Suddenly there was a cleared space around him, as what he now recognized as Alban warriors pushed back the encroaching wall of Romans, guarding him from harm.

'Away with the knife, man!' Conaire rasped from above, his voice gravelly with exhaustion. 'I nearly lost my balls to a boar already!'

Going limp with relief, Eremon sank on to his back once more. 'My ankle,' he whispered, all traces of his voice broken.

Conaire's grin gleamed through the bloody grime on his face, and he sprang lightly to the ground on either side of Eremon's head. Bending over, he began to push at Dòrn's slack weight with one arm, while tugging at Eremon's ankle with the other.

'And what are you doing all the way over here?' Eremon muttered. 'You, of all people, breaking ranks on me?' His pulse had resumed now, though it was still erratic, and to take the sting from his words he clasped Conaire's thick arm, wrist to wrist, as his brother released his foot and bent over him upside down.

'I decided,' Conaire said firmly, 'that I belonged by your side, Polybius or no.'

Eremon was still holding him, their arms pressed together along their lengths, when there was a great Roman shout, and the Alban line close by suddenly collapsed on top of them, a tide of Romans surging past the fallen Albans. Conaire half-turned, but before Eremon could free his hand he felt a sickening thud, which jolted through Conaire's arm and travelled in an instant of knowing to Eremon's heart.

Conaire's eyes widened in surprise, and only then did Eremon see over his brother's shoulder the maddened face of a Roman soldier, both hands grasped around his short sword, all his weight behind the thrust.

Eremon sensed the tight springs of his brother's great muscles falling slack as the sword entered his upper back just above the mailshirt. Then Conaire slowly collapsed over to one side, the light in his blue eyes already starting to fade.

Eremon did not feel his own voiceless scream, for all noise and pain and even light was extinguished in the shock, as he desperately grasped the moment and held it still, unwilling for time to continue. He only vaguely noticed Rori and Fergus leap screaming onto the Roman, bearing him down beneath their shields, and the other Albans rally with hoarse yells, desperately forcing the Romans back once more.

Then Eremon's attention narrowed down to one tiny detail: the blood pooling at the edge of Conaire's mouth. He rolled Conaire to his back, his shaking fingers pressing his brother's mouth closed. *If the blood cannot come he can't leave . . . can't leave me . . .* 'Don't,' Eremon found himself whispering. 'I won't allow it.' He tried to lift Conaire upright, but his weight was too great and Conaire's head only fell back, his helmet tumbling off to spill golden, bloodied hair over Eremon's arm.

There was a choking gurgle, then a soft rasp of escaping air, and Conaire's eyes flickered open, glassy with fear. 'I can't . . . I can't feel my legs . . .'

Barely conscious of what he did, Eremon dropped Conaire to the ground and straddled his chest, gripping the neck of his tunic with both hands as he screamed into his face with a torn voice. '*No!* I order you to stay here, *I order you*! I won't allow this.' Eremon's shoulders slumped, and in a whispered sob he repeated, 'I won't . . .'

Yet Conaire was already looking beyond Eremon, the racing clouds reflected in the blue veil of his eyes. And the light that was him at last darkened, and there was nothing left then but empty pupils staring up from a bloodied face.

Eremon blinked once and gazed down at the old scar below his eye that Conaire gained in a fight on Erin long ago. The lines of battle hardness seemed to have melted away, leaving only the bewildered, soft face of a boy he had once known.

Without a word, Eremon curled his body around Conaire's head and waited, calm and eager, for the same killing blow in his own back.

Gelert hauled with surprising strength on Rhiann's ankle, and though she dug in her broken nails, still he pulled her closer, scraping her belly against the pebbles and gravel beneath. With a choked sob she braced herself for the cold blade, the pain that at least would release the rest of her body. All along her limbs her skin tightened, the muscles quivering as if desperate to be free.

Yet suddenly there was a curious thud, and Gelert's hand tensed into a claw on her ankle and then fell slack. Rhiann rolled to one side, wrenching her skin away from those clammy fingers, before peering back at the druid through her tears.

He lay with arm outstretched, pinned to the ground by a white-fletched arrow that swayed and fluttered in the middle of his back. His eyes were flickering and, as Rhiann watched, they guttered out, leaving only an old man. His wrinkled face collapsed into deep folds, his lips still drawn back in the same rictus of rage, slick with spittle. And from the rock above, Caitlin came leaping, her face grim beneath the smeared dirt and pale tracks of weeping.

Without a word she laid down her bow, gathering Rhiann's head on her chest. 'I walked in dark dreams,' Caitlin whispered, 'yet came as soon as I woke. I am sorry, my sister, that I was no swifter.'

Rhiann's shoulders shuddered, and for a moment she forgot her agony in the relief of being held somewhere safe, and rocked.

'Hush,' Caitlin murmured, her tears falling on to Rhiann's upturned face. 'For all is well now. All is well.'

Chapter 74

Lorn identified Eremon and his men not by the trampled Boar banner, but by Rori's hair, bright among the dark ranks of Roman fighters.

Rallying his own warriors with the Epidii war cry, Lorn found himself urging them into the formations he had learned on the plain before his own dun, enabling them to swiftly hack their way through to the remnant of Erin and Epidii men defending Eremon from attack.

Rori snarled like a maddened wolf when Lorn at last made it to his side, ducking the boy's wild sword slash and grasping him by the shoulders. 'Where is the prince?' Lorn screamed, shaking him until a flicker of sense came back into the boy's eyes. Rori tried to speak, but only managed to squeeze out a cracked, exhausted sob, and then Lorn followed the direction of his pained gaze.

Fergus was straddling Dòrn's body, leaping at anyone who came near, and on the ground beneath him Eremon was curled around Conaire, the big man's ankles falling slack on either side. Around them was a cleared space, the cut and thrust and screams of war and death held at bay by the boundaries of its stillness.

Lorn paused on his way to Eremon to step carefully over Colum's body, his belly sliced open by more than one manic slash. Half-trapped beneath him was old Finan, lying where he had fallen defending his prince, his grizzled head nearly severed from its neck.

Bending down, Lorn saw immediately that Eremon still breathed, and though he was drenched in blood none of it seemed to be his. 'Prince.' He pulled on Eremon's shoulder. 'Come away now.'

Eremon did not respond, however, and Lorn yanked at his arm until at last he tore the prince's hands away from where they were folded on his brother's face. Underneath his palm, Lorn saw the pooled blood and empty eyes, and closed his own lids for the briefest of moments. *Fare thee well, son of Lugaid.*

'Eremon,' Lorn said aloud then, urgently. 'Calgacus and the others have been overcome . . . all of them . . .' His throat closed over for a moment. 'They are beginning to flee, and so we must, or die here.'

Yet Eremon only stared up at Lorn dumbly, blinking as if he could not understand the words. His fine helmet was gone, his hair plastered to his forehead with drying blood that had run down his face, encasing it in an unrecognizable mask.

'Calgacus is lost,' Lorn repeated hoarsely. 'The battle is lost. They were too many for us . . .' There was no reaction from Eremon, and it was then, as he looked into the empty void of the war leader's eyes, that Lorn knew he himself must take charge.

He straightened and drew a deep breath, trying to marshal his spinning thoughts into some sort of order. 'You there!' he barked to the remnants of Eremon's men. 'Get him to his feet now, or you will lose him. And bring his sword, and that of his brother!'

Leaving Fergus and Rori to carry out his order, Lorn urged the rest of the Epidii who were with him to form their version of the testudo, the Roman tortoise formation, their shields a protective circle around their war leader and king. Then with shouted encouragement, Lorn got the cluster of warriors moving, painstakingly fighting their way to the west of the field, driving forward in another wedge to break through the Roman cavalry lines. All around them was chaos, with desperate Albans having abandoned all order, throwing themselves into the knots of hard-faced Romans. Behind them, Conaire's body fell away from view, his golden hair soon merging with the shattered reflections of sun on broken weapons, and the armoured forms of the others tangled in death.

Lorn forced himself to ignore the mayhem around him, the screams of dying men and horses, the dirt beneath that was now a slick field of blood-soaked mud, the burning heat. The earlier, exultant fire in his soul had flickered out, and all that remained was an icy calm.

He had to concentrate on saving them, his people. There was only him left to do it now.

'The gold-haired sword king and his guard have fallen. The Caledonii and their allies are shattered.'

It was an Alban scout who spoke, in halting, guttural Latin, a Votadini man Agricola had kept by him to comment on the battle. They stood as they had for the past few hours, on the little rise to the west and rear of the new Roman camp, in a patch of cool shade thrown by an oak tree.

'And what of the Erin prince?' Agricola demanded, still on horseback. He swilled wine in his dry throat and spat it out on the ground in a stream of dark red.

The scout shrugged, and shifted his weight to lean on his spear. 'I cannot see, but all order is lost. There are no groups holding steady ground any more.'

Agricola grunted. *So*, he thought. *I catch up with them at last.*

'It worked then,' his youngest tribune Marcus remarked.

Agricola glanced at him. 'We needed a small enough land force to draw them into the open. The master stroke, though, was bringing the other ten thousand by sea. It taxed the horses – and the ships! – but it was worth it, eh? Remember that, Marcus; you may need it some day.' Marcus returned a tight smile, and Agricola's gaze swept back over the field.

Even he was surprised at the scene of utter desolation that stretched before him now. For the famed ferocity of the Alban warriors had been no exaggeration. So desperately did they throw themselves at his soldiers, so foolhardy were their charges, so reckless the men who waded into the fray single-handed, swinging swords around their heads, that they had done his soldiers' work for them.

Of the thousands of Albans who had been ground into the bloody dirt, mere hundreds of Romans appeared to have met the same fate. The barbarians had no chance, not against a machine as perfect as Agricola's army. *It should not have taken them so long to understand, but it doesn't matter. It doesn't matter now.*

'Scour the plain and the woods,' Agricola ordered, turning his horse away towards the camp. Even now, his tent was being assembled; the lamps lit, the wine poured. He would not gloat over the carnage he left behind him – the stink of blood and entrails, the weakening calls of the dying. Yes, he had wavered often in his assault on Alba, but in the end he had discharged his true duty with dignity.

For the rest of the day, his men would despatch the wounded and hunt down those who fled. And sometime, perhaps tonight, perhaps at dawn tomorrow, what was left of the Alban force would no doubt surrender. Then the emperor would have his victory.

Without another glance, Agricola rode away, looking forward to the best sleep he had enjoyed in four years.

The swirling dust thrown up by the battle covered the low sun, turning its light a dreary red. Then, well before true dark, it slipped behind the high mountains to the west, and the hilltop on which Caitlin and Rhiann waited was abruptly eclipsed by shadow.

Yet they barely noticed the darkening of the light, for they were engaged in their own battle.

Caitlin recognized now, with desperate eyes, the destruction wrought on the plain below; realized from the rent banners and methodical movements of the Roman troops that the day was indeed lost. Yet Rhiann's moans soon brought her back from the edge of the rocks on which she stood, and her sister's twisted face pierced Caitlin's heart with fear.

Tenderly, Caitlin wiped Rhiann's sweat-soaked brow with the edge of her tunic, wet with ale from her flask. 'Sister, we must move from here. It is not safe.' Caitlin tried to keep her voice from trembling, to blot out what she had seen on the plain below. Yet Rhiann only moaned again and shook her head, her hands clenching on Caitlin's arm.

Because of the fall, and the rock, the child was coming – they both knew it.

Swallowing her tears, Caitlin studied the hilltop above, her eyes alighting on the copse of hazel trees to which she had directed Rhiann before. Behind it, a skirt of tangled hawthorn branches swept almost to the ground. 'There,' she said, pointing. 'We must get to those trees, to the scrub behind them. We can hide there.'

Her voice sounded certain, but inside Caitlin was reeling. *Where is he?* her heart screamed. *Where have they gone?*

Rhiann arched her back now, her belly rigid, her breaths squeezing out in pained gasps. Caitlin bore the fingers clawing her arm for as long as the pang lasted, holding Rhiann's head to her breast. Then as her sister fell back in her arms she tried again. 'We must get you up there,' she coaxed. 'We may die if we don't. The baby will die.'

Immediately, Rhiann's eyes flickered open, the lids red and drawn, the pupils glazed. 'I did it before,' she whispered. 'I can do it again.'

'Good girl.' Caitlin looped Rhiann's arm around her neck and managed to haul her to her feet, half-carrying her to the screen of thorns. They crawled their way beneath the bushes, the thorns tearing their hands and faces, but in the centre they broke free into a space carpeted with soft grasses, the branches meeting just above Caitlin's head where she squatted over Rhiann.

There it was dark, but the wind stirred the leaves, whispering some comfort that Caitlin could not quite grasp.

Rhiann did not notice day fading into night, for the pains splintered into searing lights behind her eyes, pushing closer together until there was no break, and she existed in one long scream of agony, a wave that bore her up and swept her away. She panted and writhed, almost insensible, rearing up in Caitlin's arms again and again to push. Her own groans floated to her as if from afar, and she wondered in her daze what wild animal bellowed in such distress.

She barely felt the child crowning, lost as the sensation was amidst the bands of iron squeezing her, the knife contractions tearing her. And so, in the end, the baby slid out from between her numbed legs in a rush of fluid, almost unnoticed by her.

The tearing pain then abruptly stopped, however, and in relief

Rhiann almost slipped away to the darkness within. But something prevented her, urging her to stay awake. She dragged her eyes open, Caitlin still busy with the child between her legs, and all she could see above was the patch of grey sky that filtered through the hawthorn leaves.

There, the last remains of dusk light still lingered – it had not been long after all.

There was no sound from the child, and she squeezed her eyes shut, a wave of desolation greater than the pain cresting over her.

'It is a girl,' said Caitlin then, and despite the thickening of tears her voice sounded a strange note. The grasses rustled as Caitlin turned back to Rhiann's head, and then she was pressing something into Rhiann's arms, a tiny, wet, slippery thing, slick with blood and stirring feebly, as she had stirred all those moons in Rhiann's belly.

Caitlin hunkered down close to Rhiann's ear. 'She's alive!' she whispered, her tired gladness the only light in that dark, dreary dusk. 'Rhiann, she's alive!'

Chapter 75

Two cheeks, held close together. A tiny breath in, shallow and fluttering; a tiny breath out, bird wings brushing Rhiann's cheek. The baby mews weakly, and curls up her fist, but her eyes do not open. In the gathering dark, Rhiann cannot see her skin; if it is healthy and pink, or blue and pale. She does not know how much time is left to them. She knows only that it is early, much too early to leave the womb. All the distant clashing sounds of the battlefield fade away, and Rhiann strains to listen to only one sound. The tiny breath in; a tiny breath out.

The baby is pressed close to Rhiann's cheek, close enough so that Rhiann can set her own lips to the side of her tiny mouth, pushing the air in and drawing it out. Giving her the life this rude expulsion from the womb will soon deny her.

Sometimes, Rhiann is vaguely aware of the marching of feet, twigs cracking, the underbrush rustling, and harsh male voices. At these times, Caitlin curves her slight body over Rhiann and the child, her hair, smelling of sweat and birth blood, falling into Rhiann's eyes. She has delivered the afterbirth and buried it to hide the scent, though few would pick that out among the blood of this day. Yet the baby herself makes no sound to give them away. She does not cry. She only struggles, writhing with her meagre strength. Fighting to live.

Live, baby, live! Rhiann cries inside. *Take my breath as you take your own. I will always bear you up; I will always hold you safe.*

Goddess, let her live.

Starlight now filters down amid the darkness, and from somewhere below rises the faint glow of fires.

'Why haven't they come?' Rhiann's voice is cracked, plaintive.

'They will come,' Caitlin murmurs, and places one cold hand against Rhiann's cheek. 'They will come.'

Eventually, the footsteps and fierce male voices and jingling of weapons fade away. The Romans retreat from the hill, leaving it still and quiet, and soon even the soldiers' fainter shouts are swallowed by silence.

Damp begins to creep up from the earth beneath, and Rhiann holds the baby against her skin, inside her tunic, her cloak wrapped around them both. There, she feels only the faintest fluttering of the child's heart, cradled against the steady beat of her own.

Caitlin is upright now, crouched by the edge of the thicket. After a time, she whispers reassurance to Rhiann and melts away into the shadows outside. The patch of sky between the leaves is now sprinkled with stars. Rhiann stares up at them, her eyes dry, her belly and the raw skin between her legs cramping with pain, weeping with fluid. Yet her soul is scrubbed clean of any human emotion, leaving her blessedly numb.

Suddenly, Caitlin is back. 'Can you walk, Rhiann?' she whispers urgently. 'Do you think you are bleeding?'

Rhiann turns her head to the side, and a thorn scratches her cheek. 'No.' Her voice is flat, empty. 'My body surrendered her so easily, in the end. I did not even fight to keep her.' And it was true; despite the cramps the baby was so small and early that the lacerations of Rhiann's birth canal were slight. The gate had shut behind the child already.

For a moment Caitlin says nothing. Then her lips are warm on Rhiann's cold forehead. 'I ask you this, sister, because more men are coming up the hill. But they creep slowly, silently, and my heart,' her breath rushes in, 'my heart speaks to me that these are our men, returned at last.'

Our men. Something about those words chips away at the ice around Rhiann's heart. *Eremon.* 'Where?'

Caitlin points with her chin, one hand cupped over the baby's crown. 'They come up the path on the other side, from the west. Perhaps they have lain hidden until dark; perhaps that's why they left us so long.' From outside their thicket, a long, wavering whistle rises and falls in the damp air, soft enough to be a last bird's call. Caitlin's hand tightens on Rhiann's shoulder. 'It is them.'

As Caitlin crawls out from beneath the bushes once more, Rhiann rouses herself. Holding the baby to her breast with one hand, she gingerly pulls herself up on to her knees. Then, sliding forwards, she manages to work her way to the edge of the concealing bushes, looking inwards towards the centre of the hill.

There is very little light now, the campfire having gone out after the guards were drawn away and . . . killed? Captured? Rhiann doesn't know; it all seems so long ago. But there is starlight, and across the silvered clearing the moon is rising, and dark shapes of men are stumbling. For the first time in hours, fear for Eremon stirs in Rhiann, a far, remembered pain, and she crouches in the shadows, her eyes straining against the light, which throws strange reflections on faces, the tree trunks, the rocks.

She is close enough to recognize Caitlin's lithe form as it slips across the clearing to the outcrop of rock, where the ashes of the fire are still smoking. She is close enough to see one shape detach itself from the rest. It is Eremon; Rhiann knows the tilt of his head, his walk, the width of his shoulders, even though he stumbles.

Caitlin, however, seeks for another. Rhiann recognizes the eagerness in her out-thrust chin; her outstretched hands. Yet there is only Eremon, catching Caitlin by the shoulders and holding her there, murmuring in her ear. There is only Eremon to sink with her as she sags in his arms.

Then they are alone on the ground in the moonlight, and in their mute grief Rhiann reads all.

Chapter 76

Lorn and Nectan had brought Eremon, accompanied only by Rori, Aedan and Fergus. Working together, the majority of the Epidii and Caereni had managed to escape the carnage, so Lorn explained to Rhiann in a dull, weary voice. Yet it had been too dangerous to remain in a large group, as the Romans had been scouring the copses and hollows and stream beds, killing where they found survivors. So the other men had been sent across the western hills, to make their way home as best they could.

It was imperative to move away from this hill, this very night. Now.

Since releasing Caitlin, Eremon had remained unmoving, swaying as if he would collapse. Rhiann had torn a scrap of her cloak to bind the baby against her skin, under her tunic, yet did not show Eremon the child. She had seen in his eyes that he was not capable of asking questions or understanding answers.

'Let us go from this place,' Rhiann heard herself say now, Caitlin trembling within her arms, skin icy with shock. It was a stranger who spoke, though, for Rhiann never wanted to take up such a mantle again. She did not want to be calm, and make decisions. She wanted to scream, and throw herself to the ground, and sob for her child, and for Conaire and Caitlin, and for Eremon's fractured heart, and for all the dreams of Alba that lay bloodied and trampled on the plain below. 'Let us go,' she whispered, and her arm about Caitlin, turned them all to the west.

Rhiann could never clearly recall the trek that ensued through the hours of darkness, as Nectan took them by paths that were soon lost to memory, among high, broken ground, and narrow rock walls that enclosed them in the night scents of moss and dripping damp. There was only Caitlin's stumbling steps, and the harsh breathing of someone behind her, and Nectan's dark head dipping and weaving before her. There was only Lorn's hand as he steadied Caitlin when they stumbled over scattered rocks, and cold, mountain wind lifting Rhiann's damp hair from her neck. The ache in her back and soreness between her legs she ignored, for they were as insubstantial as the wind itself.

The only thing Rhiann was fully aware of was the pressure of her cheek against her child's head, as she sent her senses within to memorize the beat of that tiny heart, the minute traces of breath, the birdlike weight in its bindings. The baby was the barest sensation across Rhiann's chest, yet present nevertheless – enough for Rhiann to know she was real.

At last the trail ended, in trembling exhaustion, rain that seeped down beneath a sheltering rock overhang and a dampness that crept into all their hearts. It ended with Caitlin, who at last sank into Rhiann's arms and wept, and there was no end to that weeping, not while the hours of dark lasted, until dawn came again.

Chapter 77

Nectan was the first to stir at dawn. Rhiann saw him crouched at the lip of the overhang, staring across the valley to the west. Around Rhiann the others slumbered on, taking refuge in sleep, curled in tight balls of misery. Even Caitlin had cried herself into so deep an exhaustion that grief could not keep her awake.

Rhiann glanced over at Eremon, lying as one dead, his eyes wide open, his face a mask of dried blood. Rori had laid Eremon's stained sword at his side, though he made no move to touch it. And when Rhiann tried to speak to him in the night there was no one there, though his body moved and walked. So she knew his soul was wandering, as it had before, and only when it came back could she give him comfort.

Rhiann had no energy to call to him, anyway. Her focus was elsewhere, and that was why she herself had not slept. For every shallow breath the baby took might be her last, and as Rhiann had expelled her, pushed her forth when she was not ready, so she would not abandon her to take her last breath alone.

Rhiann now watched the sun slowly creeping up the sides of the valley, outlining first Nectan's crouched leg, then his arm, bound about with a shell-embroidered thong, and then his hair, blue-black in the dawn light.

Her dazed exhaustion was so great that at first she did not register Nectan's sudden alertness. Then, when he rose slowly to his feet, Rhiann, fearing the worst, eased Caitlin down to her cloak and went to join him. Her legs were shaky and cramping, and the dress between was stuck to her skin with dried birth blood and discharge. She peeled it free and edged towards the light.

At the sound of her step, the Caereni chieftain's head swung around, his black eyes shining with wonder. 'Look!' he whispered fiercely, pointing down the valley to the west. The shadowed cleft was thick with woods of hazel, birch and alder, fringing a stream that tumbled in pale curls over dark, mossy rocks. The walls of the valley were steep, rising to heather slopes at the top. Rhiann stared up and down, seeing nothing, hitching the baby up so the dark fuzz on her tiny head came free of Rhiann's tunic.

'I saw it,' Nectan murmured, peering up at a high saddle ridge that curved around the head of the valley, the upper peaks glowing with the dawn light. 'I saw *Him*. He has come to guide us, to show us which path to take.'

'Who came?' Rhiann asked.

Nectan's voice was subdued with awe. 'The Forest Lord. The Dawn Stag. The light was on His antlers – such great, branching antlers, the like of which I have never seen! He has come to lead us, to show us the pass over the mountain shield.'

At the expression of this simple faith that someone still guided them, protected them, Rhiann tensed, then lowered her face, tears hot on her cheeks. 'But Nectan, all is lost. Alba is ours no longer. Our gods will walk this land no longer.' *And the Goddess has abandoned us*, was her deepest thought; a whisper in her soul.

Yet Nectan turned to look at Rhiann, and though his once fine clothes were torn and spattered with blood, his cheeks scratched, his braids torn loose, still his face was not twisted with grief. The dawn drew a fine, golden veil across his dark eyes, and he smiled. He reached out one gentle finger and touched the crown of the baby's head, the only one yet to acknowledge her. In response, the child stirred and mewed faintly.

'Where there is death, there is yet life. The Mother told us this, before time began. Alba cannot be taken, or won. It just is, and its gods will always speak to those who pause to listen.' Nectan pointed towards the western sea. 'I will see you safely to the shore, and then seek my own home. And if the Romans find me there, and I die, it will only be as a sleep, a rest in the garden of the Mother, until I come again. Why fear such things?'

Yet Rhiann's heart remained cold, for as Eremon could not hear any words at all, she felt as if she could not hear these, could not accept them. The baby mewed once more, and Rhiann heard her own grief in the weak sound. She broke away to bury her face in the tuft of soft hair on her crown.

'Come,' Nectan said gently, 'we must follow the Dawn Stag across the spine of the mountains, for He will bring us safely down to Dunadd, and home.'

Rhiann wondered if anywhere could be home again, because home meant safety and peace. And that perhaps was not to be their fate on the shores of Alba.

The crossing of the mountains was a nightmare from which none of them could wake. Moons later, when Rhiann was able to think on it, she realized that the leagues of Alba they crossed – this land for which they had fought so hard and loved with such intensity – did in the end pass them by, unseen and unappreciated, because of the grief that lay so heavy upon them.

They walked silently, hardly resting, driving themselves high up the passes and then down the long valleys. Rhiann did not raise her eyes to the sky, and only noticed what passed beneath her: rushing, icy water; rain-sodden peat; scree slopes beside dark lochs; heather clustered on dry paths. And always there was the fear of pursuit pushing them from behind, for Eremon, the glory of the Alban resistance, the shining warrior whom all would follow, was now its greatest fugitive.

Rhiann watched him whenever they stopped for the night, and saw the way he took himself apart, sitting alone as the dark drew in. She tried to offer him comfort, and even managed to sponge the blood from him, yet her words and touches merely sank into the cold, black pool of his grief and disappeared without a trace. Caitlin at least clung to Rhiann in her pain – inconsolable, yet undeniably alive.

The only light that pierced those dark days for Rhiann was the baby. For she struggled, that child – she shamed Rhiann with her struggle. By rights she should have died at birth, or hours after. She still could not nurse, though Rhiann tried, biting her lip against the pain of her swollen breasts. But the child was too small, too weak, and only the trickle of water Rhiann managed to dribble into the side of her mouth kept her alive.

For four days, the baby lived, her translucent eyelids shut, her breath hardly stirring the air, so insubstantial that it was hard to believe she existed at all. And step by step, Rhiann's world narrowed down to nothing but that child. During the day she listened for each breath, and at night, among the dark caves and woods, she held a tiny, shell ear to her mouth and in a low voice sang all the songs she would have sung over the cradle: of Rhiann's parents and grandparents; the kings and Ban Crés; the healers and warriors; Linnet and Caitlin and Gabran. And above all, Rhiann told the baby of her father: how he looked the day Rhiann met him, standing in the boat from Erin, shining in gold and green, and how he had whooped for joy to know of her coming.

It was then that Rhiann's heart faltered, and the shame claimed her with terrible heat. For this babe had no chance, and yet fought so fiercely for life, as fierce as any warrior-maid. Had Rhiann done as much for her? *No.*

Rhiann had warded her away with her brews, and when she did come, Rhiann's body had not fought to keep her in the womb, safe and warm until her time. So when the songs failed, and Rhiann's shame and anguish were a hot, red tide in her veins, she held the child and said nothing, but sought to give to her, at the end, the love she had not given so freely before.

After two days of solid rain, the fifth day since the battle dawned like a wild rose blooming. Rhiann lay out in the open on the damp grass beside a splashing stream, drowning in the beauty of the sky. It was a clear arc between the peaks of the hills, washed with soft purple and gold, and the air was already warm. There was no breeze; all was silent but for the far cry of a lone eagle. It was a rare day; a day of gentleness and grace.

And so Rhiann knew what this day would bring, and she rose as soon as it was light enough to see the trail. Taking no food or drink, she shook the beaded dew from her cloak and wrapped it around her, then went to Nectan, who was already sitting on a flat rock by the stream watching the sunrise. 'I must climb to the peak of that mountain,' Rhiann murmured, pointing to the ridge above as she cradled the baby with her other hand. 'I beg you, let no one come after me.'

Nectan nodded down at her from his rock, his dark, liquid eyes resting on the baby's head for a moment. 'I think we can stay here for one day,' he said softly. 'Be assured, lady, that you will have your peace.'

No one marked Rhiann's leaving, for all were lost in their own exhaustion. Yet as she left the valley, Rhiann's own deep tiredness suddenly began to fall from her. She raised her chin, and stepped more strongly. For she could do no less for this special child, but to match its strength with her own.

The path eventually petered out, giving way to great sweeps of heather slope, and then there was only sky, and Rhiann felt as if she was walking directly up into a land of clouds and blue air. Yet her feet were still affixed to Thisworld, and slowly, carefully, she edged her way along the ridge-top to a place that would be sheltered from the winds, looking west. There was Alba's heart, and far, far out across the waves, the Isles of the Blessed, the land of the ever young. Rhiann would not face her child east, not to Rome and the pain it had brought.

Rhiann sat on a rock there, the babe wrapped in her cloak. As the sun slowly rose, the stones around her warmed, the sky coming alive with nesting kites and, far off, a great eagle. The chill burned off, and the air began to stir with a breeze that ruffled Rhiann's skirt and her hair, which she had unbound to make a shelter for her child.

To Rhiann's people, the passing of a soul at dawn or dusk was fitting, for it was a subdued time when light and dark mingle, when the veils between the worlds were thin. Yet, as in all things, this child was different. When the sun was at its highest, beating bright and insistent on Rhiann's eyelids, and the wind had risen to an impatient, exuberant pitch that tugged on the edges of her cloak, so then the child opened her eyes for the first and last time.

Rhiann stared down as the transparent eyelids flickered, her priestess senses seeking to touch the baby's soul. But just as the light of it flared in those milky eyes, so it softened, and then faded, and the eyelids sank closed again. The tiny chest beneath Rhiann's palm gave a few flutterings, and then there was a sigh, and Rhiann's hand moved no more, no matter how she fixed her eyes on it.

She had waited for this – for days she had watched and waited for it – but such a thing could never be truly felt until the time was here.

A terrible, wrenching gasp took Rhiann by surprise, bursting from her own clenched throat, and suddenly she was on her feet, the wrapped bundle tumbling to the ground. And one of the baby's arms fell free of her cloak, the tiny hand unfurling like a pale, moonlit flower, and Rhiann's world went dark around her.

The darkness was a storm, but greater and blacker than any storm front she had seen, and the pressure of its coming beat on her temples.

The darkness was the wings of that storm, a wind wilder and stronger than any she had felt, scouring the flesh from her bones, until her heart lay exposed and shivering.

The darkness was fury.

Chapter 78

Rhiann came back to herself hunched over the child's body, and she realized she had been screaming, for her voice was cracked and empty. The stained folds of the cloak were clenched in both fists, her forehead resting on the babe's still chest, and she could only taste one word on her lips; the word that had formed there in the shadow of the storm, and that she thought would be carved there all her life: *Why?*

Her face jerked up to the bright, mocking sun that blinded her, and she thrust at it with the word, sending it outwards like a flailing fist. '*Why?*' She screamed it hoarsely, launching it at the sky as if she could shatter its pale, impassive beauty, make it answer her. 'Why have you done this, Mother? *Why have you forsaken me?*'

Rhiann struggled to her knees, her eyes clenched against the flood of light. 'What else could I have done?' she cried. 'I fought for you, toiled for you, endured for you . . . held people and healed them and wiped their tears and bore their anger. Yet more than anything, I *loved* for you!' Anguished, Rhiann struck at her chest as if she could prove what lay there. 'I did what you asked, loved him, loved them all, and you made me take them to defeat and then I opened to *her*, and you took her . . . you took her when I had done all you asked. *I loved her and you took her away!* Why? Why?'

With a strangled gasp, choked by the tears of that dark storm, Rhiann ground dirt into her cheeks as if it were ashes. 'I surrendered to love! I did it and I let her in, let him in. I loved them and I am worthy of them, don't you see? How can you not see what I am? *I love and I am worthy, I am!*'

I am. I am. I am.

I am worthy.

Those words, flung out at the world, echoed in the shining, upturned bowl of the sky, its smooth sides curving to the horizon. And back they came, as if Rhiann was answered at last, though she had screamed that answer herself.

I am worthy.

Like an arrow of light the words pierced her breast, and because it was time, soared easily through the layers encasing her – the cold and the numbness, the fear and the fury, the things that had hurt her and made her despair – straight to the core that had been entrapped for years, caged by what lay around it.

The glowing point cleaved the core like a red-hot knife through ice, and all the vibrancy and brightness, hoarded, sleeping, was suddenly released in one explosion of light. And Rhiann saw instantly all that had been, and some of what would be, and knew that what she had searched for was a place she had never left.

I am worthy, and I always was.

The voice was right there beside her. Her name, said like a song, the first syllable lifting and high, the second low and gentle.

Ree-ann.

Ree-ann.

Come, daughter, and see.

Rhiann looked up, dazed, and saw that the air itself was now made of light, and she could see nothing of mountain or sky or ground or rock. Yet the light near her was thicker somehow, stirring and shimmering with a real presence of spirit that was familiar to her.

The voice was Nerida's, and behind and through it chimed the chords of Setana and other more ancient whispers of woman and mother and sister. *The child is with us; feel her.*

'I can feel her,' Rhiann said, for there was no bitterness now to stop the soft touch of the child's spirit from reaching her heart. Rhiann felt it brush her cheek, and the small, glowing flame that fluttered around her was also familiar, for she had seen it on the night the child was conceived.

She chose to leave Thisworld now, for her time of full growth is not yet. She will return when the need is greater.

'Then why did she come to me at all?' Rhiann whispered, and if there was grief in those words it was a pure and clean pain, and there was now no shame in it.

Why indeed? the voice echoed, and the answer came as a memory. She saw again the night glade on the Sacred Isle; Nerida and Setana circling her, singing. *Through your body she had to pass, to take up what we gave you, to hold it in her soul.*

And then Rhiann finally understood the gift, which she had carried in her body along with the child.

'But . . . she is not the only one gone. There is . . . more.'

There is more. There was a smile in the ether around her; a flickering of the myriad, shifting hues. *Though you have already understood much, and that had to come before the rest. So, Goddess-daughter, seer of the Sisters, beloved aspect of the Many-in-All – speak to us first of the truth you have found, and then we will share with you the other.*

Taking a deep breath, Rhiann closed her eyes. Yet even behind the darkness of her lids, she felt as if a cup of light was again spilling into the top of her head and running down her body, and she was caught there between earth and spirit, the connection to both a flowing, free stream of the Source, just as it had always been. She began to speak aloud then; her voice at first only a cracked whisper, then growing in strength. 'I was never forsaken; only by myself. I faltered not because I was unworthy . . . but because I thought myself so.' Rhiann opened her eyes. *I thought myself so . . . but in the end I freed myself with rage, and won . . .*

The voice came again, many-layered no longer, but Nerida's alone. *You clouded your own light with shame, and turned your own face away, and so you lost what you loved so much. The surrender we spoke of so many times was not only for love of others, but for the greater love of yourself. Take up this love now, for grace is here surrounding you, to help you to accept.*

And an echo of Linnet's last words floated up from Rhiann's own memory: *On the mountain, it is acceptance you must find above all things.*

So Rhiann's last surrender came, like a sigh that settles the heart into rest, and the pulse of Nerida's joy shimmered in the air.

Then as you have opened your eyes to the light of your soul, so you can become a beacon for others. After all, this is what you were shown, long ago. Come, see what you have waited to know all your life.

And this time, Rhiann saw, at long last, the truth behind her dream, and how her thread on the Mother's loom was woven into the greater pattern of Alba for all time to come.

The last light of the sun was slipping behind the western hills when Rhiann came down from the mountain.

To Caitlin, raising her head from where it rested across Conaire's sword, the sky's glow seemed to have come to rest in Rhiann's face. Yet her cheeks ran with tears as well, and she looked all the more tranquil and beautiful for that.

Rhiann came straight to Caitlin, and gently lifted her to her feet, setting the sword aside. 'Sister,' she said softly, looking down with a calmness that somehow curled itself around Caitlin's shattered heart and cradled it, 'though you have doubted it, the veils between the worlds are thin, for this day I have touched the other side. Conaire is gone only as far as the other shore, across the great sea.'

Her words drew Caitlin's breath from her body, as tears stung her eyes. 'But I . . . I am here and I . . . cannot see him . . .'

Rhiann kissed the tears from her, one by one, then pressed her lips to Caitlin's forehead. 'Yet you share my blood, and so we can show you, Linnet and Fola and I, how to sense him, and speak to him.'

A wild hope fluttered in Caitlin's breast. 'Truly?' she whispered, searching Rhiann's face. 'I can reach him?'

'I swear it. For the love that bound you in Thisworld binds you still.' Gently, Rhiann placed a hand on Caitlin's chest. 'Feel it in your heart.'

As Rhiann held her, a warmth began to spread into Caitlin's breast, and though the pain of the severing sharpened, making her gasp, so the icy numbness that had slowly been invading her also melted. Instead, it was held at bay by the strength of Rhiann's love, and so the same strength flowed into Caitlin's weakened body, and for the first time in days she saw Gabran's beloved face in her mind.

Rhiann kissed her again, and even though her sister turned away, her lips left a warmth that spread itself down inside Caitlin's heart, so that when she wept again later in the dark something was there alongside the pain, holding her through the night.

Rhiann stepped to Eremon now, and held out her hand. 'Come, husband, for the babe has gone, and we must lay her to rest in a place of her own.'

Caitlin saw Eremon's face transfigure, its cold emptiness spasming for a moment into terrible pain, and she swallowed hard, hanging her head again in sorrow. Yet as Rhiann led an unresisting Eremon towards the mountain path, Caitlin sensed someone hovering near her, and she raised her puffy face, her mind hazy with grief. Lorn was holding out a bone cup of something that steamed. 'Here,' he said gently. 'You must be hungry.'

Caitlin wavered, unsure, her thoughts still groping for firm ground. Somewhere nearby Conaire waited for her, perhaps calling her onwards through the veils towards him. Yet Gabran too waited, there by the sea. For a single moment, Caitlin's heart turned its back on the thought of returning to life and pain, for perhaps if she hurried, if she just lay down and let the cold take her, Conaire would be there on the shore of light, holding out his arms to her.

Yet then Caitlin's eyelids clenched shut. For she also remembered how she fought for Gabran, and how Conaire himself had been fighting for him when he died. *We made something of our love in Thisworld.* So she owed Conaire more than memories, she owed him his son, full grown and master of his own Hall.

Caitlin took a deep, shuddering breath, and held out her hands for the cup.

Rhiann took up the wrapped bundle from where she had left it, on a rock at the first bend of the track. Eremon was silent, but she heard his footsteps following as she moved further around the hill horizontally this time, along a thin, winding sheep trail, out of the shadows that were creeping up the valley with the cold of approaching night.

Eventually, they came to a cluster of rocks that curved around a shallow ledge still lit with the last sun. Sheltered by the rocks, a tiny, gnarled rowan tree had grown, the thin, feathered leaves fluttering in the wind as the baby's breath had fluttered.

Rhiann stopped and pointed. 'I wanted her to face west. It doesn't need to be a large hole.'

In silence, Eremon fell to his knees, and with the hilt and tip of his fine, jewelled sword, began to scour out a shallow grave from the sun-warmed earth. Rhiann watched him with calm eyes, holding the bundle to her breast. Though she still floated with the light, she could also clearly feel the tide of Eremon's pain, running as deep as an underground river beneath icy stones. It was there, but he could not feel the dark tug of its current.

Rhiann wondered how to reach him, and then realized she must trust. Trust had flowed through her when she opened her heart to the Goddess, and as the Mother cradled Eremon's heart, too, She would know how to reach him.

'It's done.' They were the first words that Eremon had spoken since the battle, and his voice wheezed with strain. Rhiann joined him on his knees, placing her cloak on the ground and then slowly unwrapping what lay within. Then the baby was laid out there, sleeping, it seemed; the fading dusk soft and forgiving on her raw skin, outlining her perfect features in gold. Rhiann took one of Eremon's hands, the nails now grimed with earth, and placed it on the child's head. But Eremon drew back as if stung, and so Rhiann let him be, murmuring the ritual words of death over the small, still form.

It was only when she went to gather up the body from her cloak that Eremon's hand shot out, trembling. 'Don't put her naked in the soil.' His voice was so soft Rhiann hardly heard him, but suddenly he was stripping off his blood-stained tunic, and from a place under the left arm that was still vaguely blue he cut a long strip with his dagger. Then Eremon handed the cloth to Rhiann, and Rhiann gently wrapped the body in its new shroud, folding carefully as if it were a swaddling cloth. For a moment she sat looking down at her hands, remembering the feel of the child's feather wings on her cheek, the dancing fire that said there was no need for the grief of separation. Only for a time, perhaps.

Slowly, Rhiann twisted off her gold priestess ring, and drawing out the baby's hand from where it curled up under her chin, placed the ring in her tiny palm, and folded her fingers back over. 'This is for the love I bear you,' Rhiann murmured, 'and for what I am in my own soul – a Goddess-daughter like you.'

Through all this Eremon made no sound, or movement, even though

Rhiann could feel the trembling, fragile eggshell of control around his pain. Yet as she began to gather up the bundle once more, Eremon suddenly said, 'Wait,' and with a quick movement shrugged off the leather thong around his neck.

The dark boar stone gleamed in the soft light, the low sun picking out the engraving of Calgacus's eagle. 'She can have it,' Eremon whispered now. 'I don't need it; the stone and what it meant dies with her.' As he spoke those words, his voice darkened with something Rhiann recognized well – deep and unrelenting shame. 'I don't need it,' Eremon repeated again, his hands shaking, the stone swinging on its thong. But what Rhiann heard behind the words was *I don't deserve to wear it.*

She held the child out to him. 'Then put it on her, *cariad.*' The wind ruffled the tiny wisps of hair on the exposed curve of the baby's skull, and though Eremon's eyes widened, Rhiann gave him no chance to protest, but merely laid the child in his arms.

The small, limp body teetered, and instinct made Eremon curl his arms about his daughter for the first time. As she came to rest against his heart he let out a strangled whimper, and then his struggling breaths ceased for one, long moment. Rhiann reached for him as he crumpled over the baby, and the sounds that came from him then were those of a wounded animal. Rhiann rocked him, as he wept for the child and for Conaire and for Alba, as the light slowly died in the west.

Yet as Rhiann gazed down at her fingers buried in Eremon's dark curls, she suddenly realized he was not yet ready to hear what she had to tell him – of the dream, of the light beyond the pain.

First Eremon had to cry his pain free, and that Rhiann understood, for she had done it herself here this day, and only then received the grace. *We will stand in a place with stars above and sand beneath,* Fola had said. Perhaps if Rhiann could just get them all to that place Fola had seen, safe and alive, perhaps then Eremon's ears would be opened to receive her gift.

'Rhiann,' Eremon groped for her hand, his sobs shaking his shoulders, 'all is dark, and I cannot remember . . . I cannot see what the light once was.'

In answer, Rhiann pulled him closer to her breast, holding both her loves for the first and last time together. 'I hold the light,' she murmured, 'and I have it safe here for you. Come to me, love, and let me keep you warm.'

Rhiann's tears fell on the nape of Eremon's neck as his own fell on the child, but hers were soft and not bitter. So anointed, the baby was laid to rest for her long sleep, as the last light left the sky.

Chapter 79

For the long days that followed, it was Rhiann who walked at the head of the party, and neither Lorn nor Nectan tried to take her place, not after seeing her face when she came down from the mountain.

It was a silent trek, but not in Rhiann's mind. For as she passed every place in her land where the spirits dwelt and the Source drew close, so she said its name in her thoughts, to mark its passing from her life: *the Place of the Wind; the Pool of Willows; the Ford of the Boar; the Moor of Fire; Roe Deer Ridge; the Headland of Arrows; the Hill of Mist; Yew Tree Rock; the Playful Water.* So she released them with every step, with sorrow as well as acceptance.

The undamming of Eremon's own grief, however, did not mean the healing of it, and he still stumbled along like one in a dream. Rori and Fergus watched his steps as if they were their own, and Rhiann let them be, for she could see it eased their own hearts.

She herself turned back from the lead only when Caitlin needed her, and the warmth Rhiann could impart to her sister's heart when the pain became too much to bear. In this, Rhiann was aided by Aedan, who fought to draw Caitlin from her despair as he had once fought to draw her from birth pain. Though the songs he sang into the soft light of the long evenings were slow and full of grief, the tears that he wrung from all of them were pure, and eased them so that the next morning they could rise again and go on.

At long last they came around the bare shoulders of the sacred mount Cruachan, the rushing streams that cut the wide valleys on its flanks no more than shining threads amid an immensity of rearing peaks. Slowly they picked their way along the streams until they reached the tree line once more, and stood above the long, shining Loch of the Waters, stretching south-west for all the leagues to the ancestor valley, and their own lands.

They were cold and damp and hungry, their bones showing through their flesh, their skin grimed with dirt. Yet the loch lay like a path of silver, drawing them towards some hope, and they knew now that the bleak rocks, cold and mist of the highest mountains were behind them.

'Now we need only follow the loch to Dunadd,' Lorn said, leaning on his spear. The forested slopes on which they had halted were still steep, knee-deep in bracken and thorny brambles that had crept from the lower ground.

'We will not go to Dunadd,' Rhiann replied quietly, shading her eyes from the silver flare of the loch surface. 'If they have discovered that Eremon is alive, then he is the most wanted fugitive in the land. We cannot risk drawing the Romans to Dunadd.'

'The people are still living in the hills,' Lorn argued, all boldness stripped from his voice by grief. 'We can hide there until we know what the Romans intend.'

'No.' Rhiann turned and smiled at him to take any sting from her words. 'It is your realm now, Lorn, and for you to order as you wish. But an end must come for Eremon on the shores of Alba. If he is forced to keep running, and hide who he is, then his heart will truly be lost, and nothing at all will be salvaged from this battle.'

As Lorn stared at Rhiann in utter bewilderment, Nectan spoke up. 'Come north to my lands,' the Caereni chieftain offered.

Rhiann smiled again and placed her hand on his shoulder. 'No, friend. Those lands are a haven for you, but not for us.' Her face swung back to the long bank of shining water, merging with the misty haze in the west. 'It is to Erin we must go.'

The two men were silent, and this time no one argued with her.

Without waiting for an answer, she pointed with the staff of rowan Nectan had cut for her. 'My friends, make camp down there on the loch shore, in the shelter of those pines.' Then she turned and gazed higher up, to where the shoulders of Cruachan shook themselves bare of trees. 'There is a shrine somewhere not far, a little pool built long ago for travellers. I must go to it now, for I have a call to make.'

They came down towards the Bay of the Otters three days later, as the dusk was drawing in. From the last of the high hills they had seen the western horizon over the sea aflame from end to end, and all its calm waters pooling like molten gold around the dark peaks of islands.

Yet Rhiann did not let them stop there for the night, and drank in that view while her feet kept moving. The sky was clear, and there would be stars, and she knew that under starlight they would leave, for Fola had seen it.

By the time they reached the little hollow outside Eithne's old, deserted house, just north of Crinan, the shore was steeped in twilight, the flame in the sky cooled to dark blue embers. The slight breeze stirred the dried strips of seaweed on the sagging fence, and the hissing of the waves over the shingle drifted up from where the hollow opened out on the shore.

Beneath the first pinpricks of stars, Rhiann saw immediately that her call had been answered, as the weary travellers around her crunched their way onto the pale shell beach. Eithne's father's fishing *curragh* was already drawn up on the sands, and by it stood three dark figures, one holding a bundle that squirmed and fussed, and one a hound that raced up the beach towards them, yelping.

With a wounded cry, Caitlin dropped her pack to the ground and ran to Eithne to sweep Gabran up in her arms, and for a moment no one moved, as she buried her sobs in her son's hair. Gabran went quiet and still, and his soft whimper of 'Muh?' was the only human sound on that starlit beach beside the hiss of the restless waves.

Then Linnet and Fola were hastening to Rhiann's side, and Fola reached her first, enfolding Rhiann in her arms. 'I told you,' Fola whispered, her voice trembling. 'I told you I would see you here.'

Rhiann kissed her on the forehead. 'And so you have, dear friend. Yet it is not the last time so.' She smiled directly into Fola's dark eyes. 'Throw off your grief, because I need you more than ever.'

Fola stared wide eyed into Rhiann's face, and something in her own features relaxed, and her hand gripped Rhiann's fingers only once before she released her.

Around them, the others had come to life: Rori and Eithne falling into an embrace, the men dropping their weapons with a relieved sigh and soft exchange of conversation. All except Eremon, who stood like a pillar of ice, ignoring the leap of Cù at his legs until Rori pulled the dog away.

Now Rhiann reached for Linnet, waiting tall and silent behind Fola, her hood drawn up in sorrow. 'Your voice woke me and drew me to the pool,' Linnet whispered. 'I heard you, and saw you as clear in my vision as I do now. I am so sorry, so sorry . . . ' Her voice broke, and she held Rhiann at arm's length, her eyes straying to her distended belly, and the shudder of pain that passed through her vibrated within Rhiann's breast, too.

'No, aunt,' Rhiann murmured, easing back her hood. 'As you have seen within me before without words, so see now. For I have touched the soul of that child, and I have walked the mountain with Nerida, and I found the acceptance, and I saw what must be done. There is grief for all, but beyond it is light.'

Like Fola, Linnet met Rhiann's eyes in the starlight and searched them, and gradually a wonder dawned over her face, melting the lines of pain and fear into something that glowed as Rhiann herself glowed inside. 'So shall it be,' Linnet murmured at last, and bowed her head.

The others were silent, watching them: Eithne in the curve of Rori's arm; Caitlin tucked into Fola's side. Rhiann stepped into the centre of the sand. 'This then is what I dreamed,' she said, raising her voice to them all, 'for each of you has a part in it, if you wish.'

As her steps drew closer to him, Eremon's head swung around, his nostrils flaring with fear. And though Rhiann spoke to those around her, it was Eremon alone whom she held with her eyes, breathing a thread between them on the chill night air so that her words might travel along it and be heard, eventually, in his heart.

'A woman was in a valley of light,' Rhiann began, her voice filling the space around them, 'with all the people of Alba. And though danger swept the air above, the woman cupped the cauldron of the goddess Ceridwen, gathering the Source so that it drove back the shadows. And by her side there stood a man of Erin, a leader such as this land has never seen.'

At those words, Eremon slowly sank to his knees on the damp sand. As Aedan and Fergus started towards him, Rhiann raised a warning hand to stop them. She moved closer to Eremon again. 'This man held a sword that brought not death, but protection and truth. And he and she had come together again, as they had in many lives, to hold the Source against the darkness. But it was no battle this man had to fight, and it was not to wield power that this woman gathered it. For there is more than one way to save a people.'

Eremon gasped, his head sunk low on his breast, as Rhiann went down on her knees before him. 'Don't mock me,' he whispered fiercely, his face in his hands. 'I failed the dream. I drew them to war, and they died, and Alba is lost.'

Rhiann shook her head, and held Eremon by the shoulders. She could feel his trembling beneath her fingers. 'Alba is not lost,' she said gently, 'not while we hold the Source in our hearts. The war was part of the Mother's loom, and each man's thread is woven by him and Her alone: it was not your will and choice that took the warriors there, only their own. But that wasn't what the dream was about, Eremon!' Rhiann stroked the damp hair back from his temples, though he wouldn't raise his head. 'There are other ways to lead, other ways to protect, and I will tell you.'

Rhiann drew a breath which misted in the cooling air. 'Sometimes people must lose what they love in order to make them love it more; it is the heat of the fire which forges the strength of iron! And Alba's people will need their strength, for I saw glimpses of what will come: Alba will be fought over for generations. Yet just as the dream foretold, we are part of what saves it from one of its greatest enemies.' She gazed around at her friends. 'Believe and trust that the Source in my dream *can* be protected and guarded all through those dark times, for it is all of what makes Alba free and fine and beautiful: the music and stories,' she sought out Aedan's face, 'the lore of growing things and raising animals, and aye, the lore of men!' Her eyes rested for a moment on Lorn and Fergus and Rori. 'The chants and the ways of opening and closing, blessing and healing.' She smiled at Fola and Linnet, then at Caitlin. 'And the shepherding of the children, so that we may give the Source into their hands when we die, and they to their children, and so it is held safe until the time when war is passed for ever! Then will Alba still stand steady when the storm is passed, the hidden treasure beneath it only sleeping!'

Rhiann felt the shuddering of Eremon's arms in her grasp, and she took his face and gently but firmly turned it up to her. 'And to you, husband, I say this. Those who will guard the Source need a leader, a man to protect them with his righteousness. That was your role, that was what She asked of you all along, to help us all make a fertile place where children can grow, where the lore can be nurtured and passed on.'

'I can never raise a sword again!' Eremon suddenly burst out, his eyes tightening with anguish. 'For I chased war blindly, like a madman, and in the end it took him . . . and her, the child, *it took her, too!*'

Rhiann brushed the tears from his cheek with her thumb. 'It is not your skills of war we need, *cariad*. It is your wisdom, your soul sense, your gentleness, your strength, your eyes, your hands, your heart! It is not to challenge your kin that we go to Erin, but to find a place, a quiet place away from battle to nurture that which the darkness will seek to destroy. Is that not worthy of a life?'

Eremon stared up at her, and Rhiann saw the faintest flicker deep within their starlit depths, of an understanding that could grow. Yet the pain was so bitter. '*Is it?*' he said hoarsely. 'Is it enough?'

'My love.' Rhiann drew his face up to her and kissed his cold nose. 'You travelled in the Otherworld with me,' she whispered. 'You know it was real; that we lived there, you and I, though our bodies slept here. So you know this, too: that though those we love sleep in the ground, their soul-flames have already flown to a place of great bliss, and there they live in the light.' She pressed her lips to his eyelids, one by one. 'And they do not wish you to walk in darkness, *cariad*, they wish you to raise up your face and honour them with your joy.'

Eremon gazed up at Rhiann, his hope warring with his pain. Yet he had no chance to fumble for a reply, for there was a muffled sound from behind them now, and Rhiann turned. Linnet had been drawn forward by her words, and now she fell to her knees, raising her arms to the sky.

In her face, Rhiann recognized the trance of true prophecy, as she had seen it few times before.

'If your heart will be cleansed, prince of Erin, then hark to me, for the gods give you something that will be enough even for you!' Linnet's priestess voice was deep, her whole body trembling with the fire of her vision. Imperceptibly, all the men drew back, as she closed her eyes, the moonlight seeming to pool there in a silver glow around her. 'For a kingdom of Dalriada is born this day, and it will span the sea from Erin to Alba. It will spring from two lines – that of Eremon mac Ferdiad, and Conaire mac Lugaid – and in the years to come the lines will mingle, and from that mingled strand will come the greatest kings of Alba! Yet there is more.' Linnet paused, flinging out one hand towards Rhiann, her eyes opening, terrible and fierce in their joy. 'From your line will come she who brings nations together.' The other hand reached to Eremon. 'From your line will come he who rids Alba of the Romans for ever! Hark that Rhiann's vision was no vision alone, but truth. So shall it be.' Linnet's hands dropped in her lap, and she bowed her head, breathless.

Slowly, Rhiann stood from her crouch and walked towards her aunt, resting one hand on the back of Linnet's hair. Her head shook slightly beneath Rhiann's fingers, as Rhiann looked around at her friends and family, their faces expressing shock and sadness and bewilderment. 'My aunt speaks the words of the gods. We will take this boat now and sail to Erin, and all who wish to come with us are welcome.' Her eyes came to rest on Caitlin, and she read there the torn anguish. 'Yet remember what was said. Those of us in Erin will be joined with those in Alba, as one kingdom, our blood mixing so that we are one people. This is also how we will serve the Source, for the sea is not very wide, and the crossings will be many.'

Beneath Rhiann's hand Linnet at last stirred, and Rhiann stooped to help her to her feet, beckoning Fola to hold her aunt's arm. Yet it was Caitlin who moved next, coming directly to Rhiann with Gabran in her arms, her back straight, though her cheeks were marked with shining tears.

'Gabran is meant to be king at Dunadd,' she whispered, raising her chin, the night wind stirring the hair over her shoulders. 'So that must be my home, too. For once it is safe to emerge, he will need me to guide him to his Hall.' Her lips trembled, and she pressed them together. 'It is what I promised Conaire, there in the mountains.'

Rhiann smiled at her, though her heart clenched with one pang of pain. 'I knew this would be your choice, dear one, and it is fitting.' She held Caitlin and Gabran close, her mouth next to Caitlin's ear. 'And remember,' she whispered, 'it is not far for a swift boat across the waves.

You will greet us often in your Hall, and we will greet you often in ours, for our kins must become one.'

Caitlin nodded and stepped back, unable to speak, but Linnet came forward herself now, moving with her old grace, and put her arm around her blood daughter. 'I will stay with Caitlin,' she murmured, her eyes hidden by the shadow of the boat's single sail, snapping faintly in the breeze. 'Daughter of my heart, though it would grieve me to leave either of you, her need is the greater, and my place here.' Her hand came out to rest against Rhiann's cheek. 'And now we can speak in our souls and minds, so the waves sunder only our bodies, not our hearts. I will spend much time at my pool, and this time not be frustrated with what I cannot see.'

Rhiann laid her palm along Linnet's hand, and the three of them did not move for a long time.

'I, of course, will stay,' Lorn broke in at last, his eyes straying with sorrow to Eremon's bent head. He hesitated for a moment, and then approached Eremon and leaned in on one knee. 'Good sailing, sword brother,' he murmured, but at that last word Eremon flinched, and the hand he had been extending to Lorn dropped again to the sand in despair. Bracing himself, Lorn rose and bowed to Rhiann. 'Rest assured, lady, although I do not understand all of what that prophecy held, Caitlin and the child and your aunt will remain under my protection.' Then he drew from a belt across his back Conaire's sword, which he had carried all that way, and laid it across his palms. His pale eyes glinted with a deep grief, yet also a hard, grim strength, and Rhiann realized that the cocky youth was gone for ever.

Rhiann impulsively laid her hand over the unsheathed blade. 'You saved Eremon's life, not once, but twice, and for that I am grateful. Your oath has been discharged.' She dropped her voice to a whisper. 'And do not fear, for I have this to add: you will lead your people for many years, and hold your lands free against the Romans.' With a bowed head Lorn sheathed the sword, unbuckled it and handed it to Caitlin for Gabran.

Nectan came then, and sank to his knees before Eremon with his bow across his own palms. 'King Stag,' the Caereni chieftain intoned, 'you need someone to guide this boat over the waves to Erin. Let me perform this last service to you, for my people will always keep their oath, until the Goddess calls us home. You earned this, and you hold it still.'

Rhiann's breath froze, for Nectan sought to return to Eremon the respect he saw as destroyed. And for a long moment Eremon stared at Nectan with wide, pained eyes, his mouth twisting. Yet at last he stretched out his hand – trembling, hesitant – and as he placed it on

Nectan's bowed head, his eyes closed in some surrender. Rhiann let out her breath.

Only two other choices were to be made. Fola declared immediately that she would not leave Rhiann's side again, and that she was long overdue for an adventure of her own anyway. And when Rhiann turned to Eithne, the glow in her dark eyes as they rested on Rori told her clearly what the maid's choice would be: to become Rori's wife in Erin.

As the others said their final farewells, Rhiann approached Eremon, who had now risen on shaky legs. She could not read his eyes clearly, but the faint moonlight showed her the clean lines of his face as she had first seen him, when he stepped from a boat to Alba's shore. And though his jaw was tense, there was a softness there, too. 'Rhiann,' he whispered, his eyes raising slowly to meet hers, 'I told no one beyond Conaire, but at leaf-bud, a man came from Erin. He had searched for me for moons to tell me my uncle had died.' As Rhiann gasped, he gripped her fingers. 'They wanted me to return – as king.' He stared into her, willing her to understand.

'Yet you fought for us,' Rhiann said, wondering. 'You turned your back on the chance you had waited for . . .'

Eremon nodded painfully. 'And I still don't want it, not now. I don't ever want to see that Hall again.'

Rhiann's breath rushed out of her, and she smiled. 'Nor will you, *cariad*. We will find the quiet place instead, the safe place. It waits for us, too.' Slowly, she pressed her mouth to Eremon's cold lips, sensing the uncertain melting of him towards the comfort of her warmth. 'Come, husband. It is time to show me your green Erin. Show me your home.'

And at last Eremon's arms came slowly out to hold her close.

The sea lapped softly beneath the dipping bow, silent as the night above, and Rhiann stared back at the receding shore, the touch of Caitlin's lips still warm on her brow, the scent of Gabran's hair on her skin. She could no longer see the dark figures on the beach, and she gripped the sides of the boat with effort, cradling the keening grief inside her with the greater light of what she now knew.

As the *curragh* slipped between the dark islands and the white-crested rocks, the splash of the men at the oars was muted suddenly by the voice of Aedan's harp, its first notes soaring to the stars above. He sang for Rhiann the lament of the beautiful Deirdre of Erin, who had loved Alba well before she was drawn home against her will.

Farewell to fair Alba, high home of the sun
Farewell to mountain, the cliff, and the dun
Where roebucks run free, and dappled does roam
Where my true love did dwell, and the sun made his home

Farewell!
Farewell!

In the darkness, it was not long before the land fell away out of sight, and all they could see was the silvered glitter of the stars on the black water, leading them on to the west.

The Tale of Rhiann and Eremon

For years, Rhiann watched him, eyes bright as a hawk guarding its nest.

For she worried that the denial of Eremon's kingship would be a loss too great to bear after all that had been. And for a long time it was, as, broken and dispirited, they gathered those few supporters still loyal to him and built their own quiet homes far away from royal duns, in a soft, green valley that ran down to the sea.

Yet babes came, and they lived and thrived, and something was healed in them both the moment they held their firstborn son Conor in their arms, and he blinked milky eyes up at Eremon while he lay on his broad chest.

Leaf-buds came and wheeled to leaf-fall and wheeled again, and on the day that Eremon taught their second son Dáire to swim, Rhiann heard the high, tinkling laughter of boys, and saw the three of them – Eremon and their two sons – jumping off the rocks below the village and twirling through the water like seals, brown skin gleaming. And as Eremon's laughter rang out the loudest, Rhiann knew that what they had found would be enough for him.

As each babe came, Rhiann herself looked into their faces to discern their fates, and never once did the face of a king look back at her, as it had on the long ago birth day of Gabran. She thought Eremon would sorrow at that, too, but he never did, for though their sons' eyes did not blaze with kingship, they shone with laughter, kindness and strength, and their daughters' eyes with wisdom, loyalty and grace.

And perhaps it was better that way, for never would those sons ride off to war, and come back on a bier, rent and bloody. Instead they turned their hands to the earth, to growing grain and husbanding the swelling band of cattle. And those sons were beside Eremon all the days of his life, learning his sword skill, though they might never use it;

mending harness beside the fire on snowy nights; birthing lambs in coursing rain; breaking the muddy ground with the plough.

And the day that Conor at last grew taller than his father, Rhiann watched them both walking back from the marshes, late in a golden afternoon, geese draped over their spears. They both threw back their heads as they laughed, and the son slung his arm around his father's shoulder, and they were friends. And if, as the dying sun shimmered, the boy's hair seemed to light for a moment into pure blond, like ripe barley, who was she to ask why?

All Rhiann knew was that from her body and his had come soul friends as great as those who had been lost, and she knew also that in that moment, Eremon was at last truly content.

Time was a wheel ever turning, however; and ever closer now they came to the end of their path. Yet many good years had passed.

It was Eremon, hale and sound even in his later years, who was the first to grow weary of Thisworld. After a particularly bad fever, and in defiance of every tonic Rhiann could brew, his cough settled in his chest, and his eyes grew bright, his skin tight and burning over his bones. She fought to the last, but even she knew when to admit defeat.

She stayed by Eremon's bed for three nights, dry-eyed with a deep grief that cleaved her in two. Yet she merely nodded when he asked to be taken to the headland above the village, for he wanted his last sight to be the sea.

Rhiann walked beside the men as they carried him out to where the green turf fell away to the sea-rocks below, and there on the edge they laid him, propped in Rhiann's arms. At her request they left them then, alone. The evening wind gusted strong and fresh off the water, as sure as they had been in the leaf-bud of their youth. But leaf-bud was no more, or sunseason, and even the leaf-fall years were long over. The wheel turns, death follows life, and the womb of the long dark beckons once more.

Rhiann had been taught these cycles since before she could walk, and understood these truths to the depths of her being. Yet as she held Eremon's burning body in her arms, she was gripped with a pain that left her gasping. For all she cared about was that he would not be here with her.

Now Eremon felt her shaking, and reached up with one hand to lay it alongside her cheek. Rhiann looked down at his wasting arm, and she remembered how wide and strong it had always been, how it had held her safe and warm through years uncounted.

Yet glancing further to the little crescent of bay beyond, Rhiann could see the tide was on the ebb, and she knew the time of passing was near. So she stilled her sobs, and held Eremon closer, singing the songs she had breathed into his ear all the times he lay in fevers, the songs she had chanted atop the ancestor mounds, when she looked down at his face bright in the Beltaine fires, and the songs she murmured in the honey moon hut above Dunadd, as their bodies lay spent.

The sun was low in the west now, so low that Rhiann could look right into its flaming heart, and the whole of the sky had become a sheet of burnished bronze. '*A stór*,' she whispered, 'the sun is so golden, as golden as you appeared to me the first day I saw you, rising from the west into the morning light. Do you remember how you dazzled us, how clever you were?'

'I remember,' Eremon wheezed.

'Of course, I was not taken in.' Rhiann smiled, and Eremon's hand tightened on her own where it lay curled in her lap.

'Not then, anyway,' he croaked, but the brief spark of mischief died in a fit of coughing.

Rhiann's mind ranged then beyond the time of blood and Roman death, to days spent on this beach collecting shellfish, and the laughter of tottering baby steps, and mead and stories by the village fire. And she knew that though their sorrows had been great, their joys had been greater. Truly, she should not begrudge Eremon his place in the Blessed Isles, at the table of the gods. And yet, and yet . . .

'Rhiann,' Eremon whispered, and she leaned closer, 'in every act of love have we said all that we need to say.' He paused, wheezing, then gathered himself again. 'I have not the strength to speak much. All I want you to know, *a stór*, is that our love has made this a blessed life for me.'

Rhiann broke then, and the tears, dammed behind walls of honour and duty, flowed unchecked. 'Oh, Eremon, I cannot bear it, I cannot!'

Eremon reached up to cup the back of her head. 'Hush, love. You will be brave, as you always have been. And you will be strong, for when I leave this body I need you, only you, to see me safely to the next life.' His voice grew soft. 'For the first time, I am afraid.'

Rhiann hugged him to her fiercely. 'I will see you safely away,' she whispered. 'Do not worry, for you will not be lost in the space between worlds. The light will guide you on.'

And I – I will be left in darkness! Oh, Eremon!

The sun was down now, but its glow lingered on. And the purple sky soon spread above them like a great upturned shield, rimmed in silver. For one last time, Rhiann gathered Eremon close to breathe the scent of his skin, the youth and maleness that still lingered beneath the sickness. And through her fingers she ran the lengths of his hair, still full, though laced with silver, and he rested his head back and she kissed his lips, and they burned her own with fever. 'Eremon, Eremon!' she whispered fiercely, mouth pressed to mouth, suddenly desperate to breathe his last breaths with him, as if that way they could not be parted.

Yet Eremon reached out his arm, and cried into her, 'The ship comes! Now it comes!' And the last of his breath faded from her, and his hand fell lifeless into her lap.

It was hours before they came for him, for her children asked for her to have this time. As the crowd approached in respectful silence to do due honour to their lord, they could see their lady kneeling beside his prone body, her head bowed.

Rhiann had her back to them, but she heard their murmuring as they grew closer. In a moment they would be here – they would break the spell, and Eremon would be truly gone from her, his body returning to his tribe.

In that last moment Rhiann looked down and saw in the starlight that Eremon had become a prince once more. The lines had fled from his skin, the underlying bones spoke again of his strength and courage, and a great light of peace was in his face. She bent down to kiss his cheek. 'I will see you safely, my lord,' she whispered. 'But do not set sail across the Western Sea just yet. Wait, wait for me!'

Then Rhiann rose and turned to face the people, as they came to a stop and stood still and silent in an arc around her, heads bowed in sorrow. Rori the Red was there, with his wife, Eithne of Alba, and Fergus the Bold with his children, and Aedan the bard to sing his lord's lament from the cliffs out to sea.

Yet before anyone could speak, for she could not bear words, Rhiann drew herself up and walked slowly away from Eremon towards the village. Only her daughters' hands came out as she passed, and she paused as they kissed her fingers, and she stroked their faces for one moment before she continued walking. Her back was as straight as a girl's, her step as graceful as a young doe. Her man had always loved the way she walked, and for this she would not bow to grief, though her heart lay broken within her.

Rhiann reached the village, which was now deserted, as all had gone to the headland. The houses lay under a great silence, and even the beasts were still in their pens. In Rhiann's hut the embers of the fire were now cold, but she did not notice. In the dark she sat on their bed and looked around her, not needing light to see the symbols of their life together: the cradle Eremon carved for their children that first, bitter, long dark; Rhiann's loom, threaded with a tunic he would no longer need; Eremon's sword and shield, long idle yet lovingly burnished; and his farm tools up against the wall.

As if in a dream, Rhiann moved to the shelves lining the wall, her fingers seeking the birch-bark packet of herbs that she had hidden there against this day. And when she sank back on the bed, the bark crackling in her hand, that was when the guilt assailed her.

546

So she pictured her children's faces, holding each up to the light of her heart.

They were all grown now; all strong and fair. Her daughters' eyes shimmered in her mind, and Rhiann knew she had taught them well, and all the lore of the Source had been passed into their safety, as was foretold. They were young women now: Maeve was wise, just like Linnet; Nessa was compassionate, just like Fola; and Emer, the youngest, shared a full measure of Caitlin's fire. Would they begrudge their mother now, putting love before duty, at last? She did not think so, for their hearts had always beaten with her own in perfect time, as they had in the womb.

Yet there was one more to whom Rhiann must speak.

She lay back on the furs, and looked at the roof, the birch packet held to her breast. 'My Mother,' she whispered, 'only you have the right to take life as you give it. I wish to be released . . . I need to be released to his side. Will you let me go?'

And the answer came in vision, for it seemed to Rhiann that the roof was no more, and she looked out on an arch of stars, brilliant against the black heavens.

The priestess daughters sensed the change and hurried from the headland, the eldest through the door first, a torch held high against the growing darkness.

They all stood for a moment, seeing the shape of her flung across the bed furs, and the youngest Emer sprang forward with a cry. 'Mother, no!'

'Hush!' said Maeve, and they moved towards the bed, shoulder to shoulder for comfort.

The middle girl Nessa, she of tender heart, reached out to where a white hand lay, and she unfurled the fingers, and within was a fold of birch-bark, and they all knew from the sharp scent what it contained, for they had been taught well.

Yet the fold was unopened and unused.

And Rhiann was young again and running, though she seemed to fly, and there up ahead a familiar soul-flame burned, sailing on a sea of light, in a boat drawn by the god's horses.

'Wait for me!' she cried. 'My love, wait for me!'

The boat slowed and stilled, and turned back for the shore.

Historical Note

The Dalriada Trilogy is based on what archaeology and history tell us about the time and place in which it is set. However, while I have stuck to the facts if they are known and accepted, there is much that we don't know, or which is the subject of debate among scholars. In these cases, I have made suggestions based on Celtic evidence elsewhere, or common sense. At other times the story itself takes precedence.

Dalriada

Later Irish and Scottish annals speak of a people who came from a part of Ulster in northern Ireland called Dalriada, to colonize Argyll in western Scotland sometime in the sixth century AD. This colony of Gaels, as they were known, established their king's seat at the fort of Dunadd. However, most scholars agree that, because of their close coastlines, the northern Irish were probably in contact with western Scotland centuries before the accepted colonization. So the first blood mixing could easily have occurred in the first century, as Linnet proclaims. A note of interest: Gabran was a Dalriada king, though he lived later than Conaire's son.

Dunadd

Dunadd was the royal seat of the Dalriada kings from the fifth to tenth centuries AD. However, excavations have proven that people were living on, or at least visiting the site for thousands of years before that, including the time around the Roman invasions. Excavations have focused on the later stone walls, yet it is entirely possible that traces of earlier timber houses were destroyed by this later building. To my knowledge, the plain around the crag's feet has not been excavated.

People

The term 'Pict' was not used by Roman writers for the peoples of Scotland until the fourth century, and may come from a Roman term meaning 'painted people' – possibly because they tattooed themselves. However, although my Scottish characters obviously 'became' the Picts, we don't know what they called themselves, and so I've fallen back on an old name for Scotland – Alba – and called them Albans.

The Sacred Isle

I equate the Sacred Isle with the Isle of Lewis in the Outer Hebrides, because here, on a lonely headland facing the Atlantic Ocean, stands the greatest British stone circle after Stonehenge and Avebury: Callanish. The broch tower where Rhiann once lived is mostly still standing nearby; it is called Dun Carloway. Interestingly, the historian Plutarch relates the story of a traveller, Demetrius of Tarsus, who visited a 'holy island' probably in the Hebrides, during Agricola's campaigns.

Places

The fort of Dunadd in Argyll and the Sacred Isle exist as described, as do the tombs and stones in the 'ancestor valley' at Kilmartin. Calgacus's Dun of the Waves is an invention, sited near present-day Inverness. The spiral carvings that Rhiann visits to mourn Didius are the carvings at Achnabreck; the stone circle she visits with Linnet is Temple Wood; and the standing stones among which she says her farewell to Linnet before the last battle are the Nether Largie stones. All are in Kilmartin valley. The first loch the priestesses reach on their missionary journey is Loch Tay, which is well known for the remains of its 'crannogs' – man-made island forts. The sacred mountain of Argyll is Ben Cruachan, and it does lie at the head of Loch Awe, which means something like 'Loch of the Waters'. This loch leads from Cruachan to the Kilmartin valley, and Dunadd.

The Sisterhood

We have evidence of a Celtic priestly caste called druids, however I'm proposing that a female-centred religion of the Bronze Age peoples survived in Alba as a relic, involving an order of priestesses. There is no historical evidence for this.

Herb Use

With some simple research, anyone can discover the medicinal properties of British native plants. Untrained use of such preparations can be, of course, very dangerous, and I do not advocate that anyone try them. Many plants have psychoactive properties, and some people believe the druids used such plants in their rites. For safety reasons I didn't detail what *saor* might have contained, for many plants could have produced this 'out of body' effect. Likewise, the ancient people knew of both contraceptive herbs, and those which could produce abortions; I haven't named them. The Romans apparently over-used one contraceptive plant to the extent it was made extinct.

The Rye Fungus

The ergot fungus grows on rye plants under certain conditions. It contains psychoactive compounds that some scholars think may have caused the effects attributed to the action of witches during the Middle Ages – uncontrollable twitching and fitting, hallucinations and a burning sensation in the extremities and tongue. There have been occasional suggestions that it was ritually used by ancient peoples. It is *extremely* toxic, and ingestion is usual fatal. Its use in this book is purely fictional.

Tribes

The names of the tribes on the map are taken from a text by the Greek geographer Ptolemy, writing in the second century AD. Some people think the tribal names relate to animals, and could indicate totemic affinities. Thus the Epidii might be related to horses, and the Lugi to ravens (which is why the Lugi king has a raven sail). On Ptolemy's map, the Caledonii are shown as the Caledones. However, by the fourth century, when the last book in this trilogy is set, the name seems to have become 'Caledonii' to Roman writers, so for simplicity's sake I've used that.

Names and Gods

I don't follow one naming scheme, since we don't know what language the Albans spoke: was it closer to Welsh or Irish at this time? So some of my names are Irish, some Pictish, and some invented. We have a list of later Pictish kings and I've used names from this list for major male characters including Maelchon, Gelert and Nectan. We don't have records of female Pictish names, so these are mostly Irish or invented. Rhiann, though based on Welsh, is not a traditional name. All of Eremon's men have Irish names, although Eremon is a mythical name – the first Gaelic king of Ireland. Since we don't know what the Albans called their gods, I've used a mixture of Welsh gods (Arawn) and goddesses (Rhiannnon, Ceridwen), British goddesses (Andraste), and Irish gods (Lugh, Manannán). Taranis and Sirona are Gaulish.

Stones and Mounds

All of the standing stone arrangements and tomb mounds in the United Kingdom were built by Neolithic or Bronze Age peoples before 1500 BC, not by Iron Age peoples in the first century AD. However, Iron Age peoples probably venerated and possibly used older monuments for their own rites. Though there is evidence for this in other parts of Scotland, there is no evidence for it in the Kilmartin valley, or at Callanish.

Symbols

The Picts left behind extraordinary carved stones dating from the sixth or seventh century AD onwards, so I had the idea that the same symbols were used to decorate wood, walls and bodies much earlier. The symbols used for chapter headings are Pictish symbols, as seen on the later stones. The body tattoos are based on Pictish carvings of bears, boars, stags and eagles. At Dunadd there is a famous later Pictish carving of a boar, and as my Dalriadic line began with Eremon and Conaire, I gave them this boar as their totem.

Interesting Facts

Since stirrups were not invented until much later, ancient cavalry saddles probably had leather horns to grip the rider's leg, and enable him to brace and swing a sword.

Wheat and barely were stored in clay-lined pits, and the fermenting grains on the damp edges used up all the oxygen and produced carbon dioxide, which together kept it fresh.

Duels of champions such as that forced on Maelchon were a noted feature of Celtic warrior society, and involved strict codes of honour. Bards were feared for their abilities to shame even kings into changing their behaviour.

The historian Tacitus says the Celts at Mons Graupius did use chariots.

The glimpse Rhiann has the night before battle, of Romans swimming across a strait, refers to the sacking of the druid sanctuary of Anglesey off the coast of Wales in AD 60. The woman hiding with her child from falling iron bolts recalls the Roman destruction of the great hillfort of Maiden Castle in Dorset, soon after the Roman invasion of Britain in AD 43. Skeletons were found here with Roman ballista bolts embedded in their spines.

The snippet of song at the end is adapted from the Irish myth of Deirdre as she leaves Alba to return to Erin.

The Roman Campaigns

The basic information about Agricola's campaign in Scotland from AD 79 to 83 is taken from his biography, written by his famous historian son-in-law Tacitus. However, this account is sketchy in places, and I have made some small changes to fit my story.

AD 81: Domitian's succession as emperor was in September; I moved it to spring. Tacitus says that this year Agricola 'crossed [water] in the leading ship' and subdued unknown peoples, drawing up his troops facing Ireland. Gordon S. Maxwell notes that scholars have long debated what this section of Tacitus means. In *The Romans in Scotland* (1989) he suggests the translation could be re-interpreted thus: the Roman army did not cross water at this time but the 'trackless wastes' and moors of Galloway in south-west Scotland. I took this idea and on it based Eremon's first campaign among the Novantae. It should be noted that many scholars think this actually means Agricola crossed the Clyde and campaigned closer to Epidii lands.

AD 82: Tacitus says this year began with an uprising of the tribes north of the Forth, who did attack several forts. While the detail of Lucius's campaign up the east coast is my own, Agricola did split his forces, which encouraged a surprise night attack on the Ninth Legion by the enemy. A. R. Birley's translation of Tacitus's text *Agricola* uses the words: 'They cut down the sentries and burst into the sleeping camp, creating panic.' Tacitus states that Agricola came to the rescue just in time, but I made the Albans victorious instead. Tacitus was eulogizing his father-in-law, and it is quite possible that any Roman defeats were played down or omitted. This year, Agricola's wife did bear him a son.

AD 83: In the spring, Agricola's infant son died. Tacitus infers that his grief was buried in a renewed determination for conquest. The Roman army met the Scottish tribes at a place Tacitus called Mons Graupius, where the 'Albans' had drawn up a force of 30,000 men. We don't know exactly where Mons Graupius was, but the prominent hill of Bennachie near Aberdeen is one good contender, particularly as the large Roman matching camp at Logie Durno is close by. Tacitus reports the battle occurring at the end of the season (autumn) but I have moved it to summer. The leader of the Scottish forces was called Calgacus, which means something like 'the swordsman'. I followed Tacitus for the rough format of the battle – and Agricola did use cavalry reserves. Tacitus reports 10,000 of the enemy dying, in comparison to 360 Romans. The tribes did not surrender the next day, but fled into the hills, burning their homes as they went.